Alexander Thom and Co.

The sixty-first report of the commissioners of national education

in Ireland

For the year 1894

Alexander Thom and Co.

The sixty-first report of the commissioners of national education in Ireland
For the year 1894

ISBN/EAN: 9783742805553

Manufactured in Europe, USA, Canada, Australia, Japa

Cover: Foto ©Andreas Hilbeck / pixelio.de

Manufactured and distributed by brebook publishing software
(www.brebook.com)

Alexander Thom and Co.

The sixty-first report of the commissioners of national education

in Ireland

THE

SIXTY-FIRST REPORT

OF THE

COMMISSIONERS

OF

NATIONAL EDUCATION

IN IRELAND

(FOR THE YEAR 1894).

Presented to both Houses of Parliament by Command of Her Majesty.

DUBLIN:
PRINTED FOR HER MAJESTY'S STATIONERY OFFICE,
BY ALEXANDER THOM & CO. (LIMITED).

And to be purchased, either directly or through any Bookseller, from
Hodges, Figgis, and Co. (Limited), 104, Grafton-street, Dublin; or
Eyre and Spottiswoode, East Harding-street, Fleet-street, E.C.; or
John Menzies & Co., 12, Hanover-street, Edinburgh, and
90, West Nile-street, Glasgow.

1895.

[C.—7796.] *Price 3d.*

CONTENTS.

THE

SIXTY-FIRST REPORT

OF THE

COMMISSIONERS OF NATIONAL EDUCATION
IN IRELAND,

FOR THE YEAR 1894.

TO

HIS EXCELLENCY GEORGE HENRY EARL CADOGAN, K.G.

LORD LIEUTENANT-GENERAL AND GENERAL GOVERNOR OF IRELAND.

May it please your Excellency,

We, the Commissioners of National Education in Ireland, submit to Your Excellency this our Sixty-first Report. In this Report all the statistics connected with the number of schools, number of pupils on the rolls, and the average daily attendance, refer to the year ended 31st December, 1894, and all statements connected with the expenditure of the public grants refer to the year ended 31st March, 1895.

School-houses and Teachers' Residences.

1. On the 31st December, 1894, there were 8,965 schools on our Roll.

2. Of these, 3,500 were Vested Schools, classified as follows:— *Vested schools.*

(a) Vested in Trustees,	.	.	.	2,471
(b) Vested in our Board,	.	.	.	1,029
Total,	.	.	.	3,500

Our grant towards the erection of Vested Schools is two-thirds of the estimated cost.

3. There were also 5,465 Non-Vested Schools. *Non-Vested Schools.*

The Non-Vested Schools are erected from funds locally provided, or, in a few instances, from loans available under the Act of 1884, 47 & 48 Vic., cap. 22. The loans are repayable at 5 per cent. per annum (principal and interest included) in 35 years.

Number of Grants to new schools : (a.) Buildings. (b.) Salaries

4. The number of applications for grants to new schools considered in the year 1894 was 194. In 172 cases we gave the required assistance, either as grants for building new premises, or as grants in aid of the maintenance of Schools previously established but not in connexion with the Board. The remaining 22 applications were rejected. Of the 172 Schools added to our list during the year 1894, the number in each Province, and the nature of the Aid granted, were as follows:—

Provinces.	Grants for Building Vested Schools.		(b.) Grants in aid of Non-vested Schools.	Total Grants.
	Vested in Trustees.	Vested in Commissioners.		
Ulster, .	24	2	22	48
Munster, .	18	5	4	27
Leinster, .	37	–	16	53
Connaught, .	35	3	6	44
Total, .	114	10	48	172
	124			

Amount of Grants.

During the year a total sum of £48,840 7s. 4d. was granted by us towards the creation of Vested school-houses and the enclosing of their sites. The school-houses proposed to be erected by aid of these grants will afford adequate school accommodation for 22,235 children.

A total sum of £3,555 13s. 0d. was also granted during the year towards the improvement of existing Vested National Schools. Of this sum £1,509 6s. 8d. was granted for the purpose of providing additional accommodation, either by the enlargement of existing rooms, or by the addition of new class-rooms. The remainder, £1,956 7s. 1d., was granted for various purposes, such as new floors, furniture, &c.

Amount of Loans.

We also forwarded to the Board of Works applications for loans to the amount of £3,504 towards the creation of new Non-Vested school-houses, and £2,210 towards enlarging or otherwise improving existing Non-Vested school-houses.

Local aid towards building and repairing school-houses.

The amount subscribed in the year 1894 by local parties towards the erection of new buildings, additions to school premises, &c., was £29,385 7s. 8d., and similarly for repairs, improvements of house and furniture, and other local expenditure, the amount was £38,684 10s. 6d. Total, £68,060 17s. 8d.

Residences.

5. During the year we also approved in 48 cases of loans to provide Teachers' Residences, and in 1 case of a loan to improve an existing Residence. The total amount of the loans sanctioned was £11,745.

Since the year 1875, when the Residences Act came into force, 1,417 applications for loans, also 72 applications for grants, as dis-

tinct from loam, to provide Residences for Teachers, have been
approved by us.

The number of free residences for Teachers of National
Schools, as returned by the Managers, is 1,370. (This excludes
Convent, Monastery, Model, and Workhouse Schools).

6. As regards the Vested schools, especially those which are
Vested in our Board, and which are kept in repair by the Board
of Works, the adequacy and suitableness of their sites, their
sanitary arrangements, and their general fitting up for school
purposes, afford fair grounds for satisfaction.

The Non-Vested Schools are, in large proportion, held in
excellent houses, and on suitable sites, but many of those schoolhouses are of an unsatisfactory character. A large percentage of our
teachers also are as yet unprovided with suitable residences. The
Local Managers, however, are making due efforts to remedy these
deficiencies, and in view of the powers now available under the
Act of 1892, for the compulsory acquisition of sites for Schools
and Residences, we hope that improvement in both respects will
be perceptible in the near future.

The Acts of 1892 and 1893 unfortunately do not define the
extent of a site, and it would seem desirable that there should be
further amendment so as to enable one statute acre of land to be
provided for a garden in connexion with each School or Residence.
The teachers would then be in a position to give practical
instruction in the cultivation of small farms and gardens, a
desirable supplement to the merely theoretical teaching in the
subject given in most of our schools at present.

In 1894, 21 applications were made to us to authorise the compulsory purchase of sites for schools, and 11 applications for
authority to purchase sites for residences.

We gave the necessary authorisation under our Seal to the
Trustees to proceed with the purchase in 4 cases, in which the
parties failed to come to a voluntary agreement.

Since the Act of 1892, as amended, came into operation, we
have received 130 applications for power to acquire sites by compulsory purchase. We gave the required authorisation in 21 cases,
and we refused the authorisation in 1 case. In 44 cases sites were
subsequently obtained by voluntary arrangement, 65 cases were
not proceeded with, and 5 cases are undergoing investigation.

Schools in Operation, and Attendance.

7. On the 31st of December, 1894, we had 8,505 schools in
operation. During the year, 150 new schools were brought into
operation—viz, 90 Vested in the Commissioners or in Trustees
and 60 Non-Vested; while 104 schools were amalgamated with other
National Schools, or placed on the Suspended List, or removed
from the Roll of National Schools; thus giving a net increase
of 46 schools in operation for the year 1894.

In the schools in operation on the 31st December, 1894, the
accommodation afforded was sufficient for 821,236 pupils, allowing
eight square feet for each pupil.

Inoperative schools.

8. Four hundred and sixty schools on our roll were not in operation in 1894—201 were not completely built—158 were on the "Suspended List," chiefly owing to failure to maintain a sufficient attendance of pupils, and 11 Model School departments were amalgamated with adjoining departments.

Free schools.

9. From the returns we have received, it appears that 7,997 schools were absolutely free from school fees in 1894. In 466 schools "excess average fees," authorised under the Act of 1892, were charged to pupils over three and under fifteen years of age.

Average No. on rolls.

10. (*a.*) The average number of pupils on the rolls for the year ended 31st December, 1894, was 832,831, showing an increase, as compared with the previous year, of 276.

Attendance on last 14 days of Results year.

(*b.*) The number of pupils on rolls who made at least one attendance within the last fourteen days of the month immediately preceding the Results Examinations was 720,977, showing a decrease, as compared with the previous year, of 115.

Average daily attendance (all ages).

(*c.*) The average daily attendance of pupils for the year ended 31st December, 1894, was 525,547, of whom 256,821 were boys. This was a decrease of 1,518 in the total average daily attendance as compared with 1893, and must be attributed to the severe weather, and the prevalence of epidemic disease during the latter half of the year.

Proportion of attendance to No. on rolls.

(*d.*) The per-centage of the average daily attendance of pupils for the year to the average number on the rolls was 63·1; whilst the per-centage of the average daily attendance to the number of pupils on the rolls who attended on any of the last fourteen days of the month preceding the Results Examinations was 72·9. The corresponding per-centages in 1893 were, respectively, 63·3 and 73·1.

Average daily attendance (3 to 15) and (15 and above).

(*e.*) The number of pupils over three and under fifteen years of age (the limits of age defined in the Act of 1892, sec. 16, sub-sec. (5)) in average daily attendance in 1894 was 509,800; and the average attendance of those who were fifteen and above was 10,247.

Attendance for 75 days or over.

11. The number of pupils of 6 and under 15 years of age who made at least 75 attendances in June half-year was 379,134; and the corresponding number for December half-year was 326,830.

Literary Classification of pupils.

12. The following table shows the literary classification of 720,977 pupils who made an attendance within the last fourteen days of the month immediately preceding the Results Examinations in the year ended 31st December, 1894:—

—	Junior Classes.				Advanced Classes.				Total.
	Infants.	Class I.	Class II.	Class III.	Class IV.	Class V.	Class VI.	Class VII.	
	263,838	107,114	98,647	96,187	75,650	57,643	57,996	40,003	720,977
Per-centage,	37·2	14·9	13·7	13·4	10·4	8·0	8·0	5·4	—
Per-centage,	37·2		41·4			89·5			

13. The following Table exhibits for a series of years, to 31st December, 1894—(a) the number of National Schools in operation, (b) the average number of pupils on the rolls, (c) the average daily attendance, (d) the per-centage of the latter to the average number on the rolls, and (e) the number of pupils who made an attendance within the last 14 days of the Results Period :—

Year.	Number of Schools in operation. (a)	Average number of pupils on Rolls. (b)	Average daily Attendance. (c)	Percentage of Average Daily Attendance to Average Number on Rolls. (d)	Number of pupils who made an attendance in Last 14 days of the Results Period. (e)
1886	8,024	848,847	478,445	47·8	708,465
1887	8,113	853,081	513,088	48·6	715,748
1888	8,192	846,435	493,548	48·3	711,085
1889	8,351	878,608	507,948	49·5	718,480
1890	8,478	872,530	459,144	52·0	494,882
1891	8,546	834,718	506,336	61·4	708,570
1892	8,408	826,573	493,384	62·7	681,281
1893	8,439	821,445	497,950	47·8	711,281
1894	8,565	858,831	511,671	62·1	728,877

See Table A , pages 38 and 39.

14. The number of pupils who attended our schools within the year, counting those who made even a single attendance at any school, was 1,028,281. This number includes not only those in attendance throughout the year, but also those who commenced attendance late in the year or left early, and those also who died or removed to other schools within the period. *[Total pupils at any time on rolls.]*

The religious denominations of the 1,028,281 pupils who made even a single attendance within the year were as follows :— *[Religious denominations of pupils.]*

   776,221 or 75·5 per cent were Roman Catholics.
   120,893 or 11·7 ,,   of the Late Established Church.
   114,913 or 11·2 ,,   Presbyterians.
   11,105 or 1·1 ,,   Methodists.
   7,160 or 0·7 ,,   of other Denominations.

The pupils are classified according to their attendances as follows :—   *[Classification of pupils according to attendances.]*

Under 50 attendances,						220,643 = 21·4 per cent.
,, 50 ,,	but under 75,					101,681 = 9·9 ,,
,, 75 ,,	,,	100,				106,378 = 10·3 ,,
,, 100 ,,	,,	125,				146,465 = 13·7 ,,
,, 125 ,,	,,	150,				138,393 = 12·5 ,,
,, 150 ,,	,,	175,				130,196 = 12·7 ,,
,, 175 ,,	,,	200,				118,621 = 11·0 ,,
,, 200 ,,	and above,					67,137 = 6·5 ,,

                           1,028,281 = 100·0

Schools attended by Roman Catholics and Protestants.

15. The following tables show, according to provinces, the number of Roman Catholic and Protestant Pupils on rolls of 3,769 Schools, attended by both denominations, and the per-centage of each denomination:—

(a.) Schools under ROMAN CATHOLIC Teachers exclusively.

Provinces.	Number of Schools.	Number of Pupils.		Per-centage of each Denomination.	
		Roman Catholics	Protestants	Roman Catholics	Protestants
ULSTER, . .	940	77,388	9,1 3	89 4	14/6
MUNSTER, . .	940	88,752	2,395	97 1	2 9
LEINSTER, . .	945	71,043	2,991	96 9	3 2
CONNAUGHT, . .	393	66,785	2,923	95 1	3 9
TOTAL, .	3,859	304,531	10,598	94 6	5 4

(b.) Schools under PROTESTANT Teachers exclusively.

Provinces.	Number of Schools.	Number of Pupils.		Per-centage of each Denomination.	
		Roman Catholics	Protestants	Roman Catholics	Protestants
ULSTER, . . .	954	10,160	87,882	9 1	90 9
MUNSTER, . .	30	159	1,443	8 9	91 1
LEINSTER, . .	78	763	8,692	9 5	91 5
CONNAUGHT, . .	38	233	1,457	14 9	85 0
TOTAL, .	1,100	11,327	127,287	9 1	90 9

(c.) Schools under ROMAN CATHOLIC and PROTESTANT Teachers conjointly.

Provinces.	Number of Schools.	Number of Pupils.		Per-centage of each Denomination.	
		Roman Catholics	Protestants	Roman Catholics	Protestants
ULSTER, . . .	25	1,754	1,926	27 9	72 6
MUNSTER, . .	7	500	622	37 6	52 4
LEINSTER, . .	16	4,459	1,103	80 9	79 5
CONNAUGHT, . .	1	9	123	6 9	93 1
TOTAL, .	49	7,088	6,114	38 7	46 3

SUMMARY.

Number of Schools.	Number of Pupils.		Per-centage of each Denomination.	
	Roman Catholics	Protestants	Roman Catholics	Protestants
3,769	313,884	139,385	97 9	29 1

* See Table B, pages 50 and 51.

16. The following table shows, according to Provinces, the number of (A) Roman Catholic and (B) Protestant Pupils on the rolls of 4,689 schools attended *solely* by one denomination (A or B), and the percentage of each in such schools.

—	A.—Under Roman Catholic Teachers exclusively.		B.—Under Protestant Teachers exclusively.						Total pupils R.C. and Prot.	Per-Cent. age R.C	Per-Centage Pro-testant.
	Schools.	R.C. pupils	Schools.	R.C. pupils.	Pres. pupils.	Meth. pupils.	Others.	Total Protestant pupils.			
Ulster,	573	72,015	806	88,803	14,236	5,177	3,532	101,748	173,763	41·4	58·6
Munster,	1,293	159,185	104	5,219	849	360	103	6,234	165,431	96·2	3·8
Leinster,	809	119,258	200	10,931	993	471	160	12,147	131,843	90·6	9·3
Connaught,	902	109,764	48	2,020	264	107	87	2,428	112,162	97·6	2·2
Total,	3,631	460,293	1,158	94,963	55,844	6,315	2,837	122,559	583,191	78·9	21·1

See Table C., page 63.

17. The percentage of Schools exhibiting an attendance of Roman Catholic and Protestant pupils for each year from 1885 to 1894, was as follows:—

—	1885.	1886.	1887.	1888.	1889.	1890.	1891.	1892.	1893.	1894.
Ulster,	70·0	67·5	65·7	64·3	63·6	62·8	60·1	60·3	59·0	57·9
Munster,	36·3	36·3	35·8	34·1	31·3	32·9	32·8	33·0	33·5	33·6
Leinster,	46·9	44·6	45·9	45·7	44·4	43·2	43·9	42·3	41·8	42·5
Connaught,	36·4	39·2	38·4	37·0	36·6	36·4	35·1	33·4	35·9	35·4
Total,	51·2	50·2	49·4	48·4	47·3	46·7	45·7	45·6	45·0	44·3

18. The percentage of Schools exhibiting an attendance composed either *solely* of Roman Catholic pupils, or *solely* of Protestant pupils, for each year from 1885 to 1894, was as follows:—

—	1885.	1886.	1887.	1888.	1889.	1890.	1891.	1892.	1893.	1894.
Ulster,	30·0	39·5	34·3	35·5	36·4	37·2	39·6	39·5	40·1	49·1
Munster,	63·7	63·7	64·7	65·8	66·7	67·1	67·7	67·0	66·5	67·4
Leinster,	53·1	55·4	54·1	54·3	65·6	56·6	56·1	57·6	58·8	57·7
Connaught,	61·6	60·6	61·6	63·0	63·4	63·6	64·6	64·6	64·1	64·6
Total,	48·5	49·6	50·6	51·6	52·6	53·3	54·3	54·4	54·5	55·6

Of the total number of pupils on the Rolls, 43·2 per cent. were in schools attended by Roman Catholic and Protestant pupils, and 56·8 per cent. in schools attended by Roman Catholics solely, or by Protestants solely.

Compulsory
Attendance
19. In our last Report we referred very fully to the considerations of an embarrassing character which beset our action in regard to the compulsory provisions of the Act of 1892, especially the want of power in some municipalities to meet the expenses of enforcing the Act out of the rates, and the grave difficulties that were encountered in connexion with the composition of the School Attendance Committees.

The refusal of the local authorities in many instances to put the Act in force so long as certain classes of schools were excluded from a share of the grants for Primary Education, was another and a very serious obstacle to the working of the compulsory law.

We stated that an amending Bill had been introduced into Parliament to remedy the defects in the Act of 1892, but we regret that up to the present it has not been found possible to effect an amendment of the law.

The population of the 118 towns affected by the compulsory law, according to the Census of 1891, was 1,246,534.

The average daily attendance at National Schools in these towns in 1893, was 130,529, and in 1894 was 138,504. This was an increase of 7,975 in 1894 as compared with 1893.

The law was, however, *actively* enforced in only 48 of these towns, and the average daily attendance at National Schools in these 48 places in 1893 was 59,098, and in 1894 was 66,268. This was an increase in 1894 of 7,170 as compared with 1893, or 12·1 per cent.

Of course, until the Act is in full operation, we cannot form a satisfactory opinion as to its effectiveness, but it is gratifying to observe, that although the average attendance in the country generally somewhat diminished in 1894, yet in the 48 towns where the Act is enforced, there was a remarkable increase in the average attendance during the period.

20. The religious denominations of the Managers of the schools, distinguishing Clerical from Lay on 28th February, 1894, were as follows:— Religion of Managers of Schools.

Religious Denominations.	Clerical.		Lay.		Total.	
	No. of Managers.	No. of Schools.	No. of Managers.	No. of Schools.	No. of Managers.	No. of Schools.
Roman Catholic, . .	1,164	5,709	105	211	1,389	6,010
Late Established Church.	621	947	307	543	928	1,490
Presbyterian, .	368	673	169	213	537	696
Methodist, . . .	46	76	15	27	71	103
Other Denominations, .	15	30	35	48	50	78
Total, . .	2,224	7,525	691	1,042	2,015	8,567

Schools of a Special Character.

(a.) MODEL SCHOOLS.

21. The number of Model School Establishments in operation at the end of the year was 30, of which 4 (including the Central Model School) are Metropolitan, and the remaining 26 are District and Minor Model Schools. These contain in all 84 separate departments, each in operation with its own distinct staff and organization. Model Schools.

(a.) The average number of pupils on rolls for the year ended 31st December, 1894, was 10,480, showing an increase as compared with the previous year of 180.

(b.) The number of pupils on the rolls who made at least one attendance within the last fourteen days of the month immediately preceding the Results Examinations was 9,700, showing a slight increase of 86.

(c.) The average daily attendance at these schools for the year ended 31st December, 1894, was 7,757, of whom 4,581 were boys. This was a decrease of 7 in the total average daily attendance as compared with 1893.

(d.) The per-centage of the average daily attendance of pupils for the year to the average number on the rolls was 73·0, while the per-centage of the average daily attendance to the number of pupils on the rolls who attended on any of the last fourteen days of the month preceding the Results Examinations was 80·0. The corresponding per-centages in 1893 were, respectively, 78·3 and 78·3.

22. Of the number on the Rolls who made any attendance within the last fourteen days of the month immediately preceding the Results Examinations, 17·5 per cent. were Infants, 32·8 per cent. were in the Junior Classes (1st to 3rd), and 49·7 per cent. were in the advanced classes.

22. The following table shows the Religious Denominations of the Pupils of the several Model Schools who made any attendance within the year, the average number on Rolls, and the average Daily Attendance.

County.	Model School.	Religious Denominations of Pupils on Rolls who made any attendance within the year.						Average number on Rolls.	Average Daily Attendance.
		R.C.	E.C.	Pres.	Meth.	Others.	Total.		
Dublin, . .	Central . .	1,251	473	93	48	84	1,949	1,721	1,532
„ . .	West Dublin, .	242	68	7	1	1	359	632	282
„ . .	Inchicore, . .	577	378	5	8	–	844	624	527
„ . .	Glasnevin, . .	74	34	1	–	–	149	76	51
Kildare, . .	Athy, . . .	–	68	88	6	8	216	68	75
Cavan, . .	Ballieborough, .	1	77	48	7	–	128	100	79
Antrim, . .	Ballymena, .	1	65	383	26	47	600	351	300
Antrim, . .	Belfast, . .	54	900	946	161	118	1,813	1,672	1,562
Tipperary, .	Clonmel, . .	77	129	91	63	–	340	138	138
Londonderry, .	Coleraine, . .	18	85	297	14	14	346	344	273
Cork, . .	Cork, . . .	368	272	13	35	44	670	670	371
Cork, . .	Dunmanway, .	18	143	–	19	–	166	133	93
Wexford, . .	Enniscorthy, .	1	130	14	2	–	157	120	65
Fermanagh, .	Enniskillen, .	62	249	44	61	–	303	276	123
Galway, . .	Galway, . .	25	108	28	7	–	157	144	93
Kilkenny, .	Kilkenny, . .	4	85	13	9	–	130	81	45
Limerick, .	Limerick, . .	115	371	88	19	43	303	290	193
Londonderry,	Londonderry, .	2	136	393	44	13	613	434	300
Armagh, . .	Newry, . .	68	147	209	26	7	461	346	287
Down, . .	Newtownards, .	–	37	355	26	5	418	313	243
Sligo, . .	Sligo, . . .	10	595	68	36	78	954	675	300
Meath, . .	Trim, . . .	322	13	–	–	–	189	122	123
Waterford, .	Waterford, .	93	97	11	4	28	149	124	93
Antrim, . .	Ballymoney, .	3	48	390	1	9	448	323	287
Antrim, . .	Carrickfergus, .	8	123	376	54	48	598	273	232
Armagh, . .	Lurgan, . .	28	320	118	20	28	498	351	298
Monaghan, .	Monaghan, .	96	198	143	9	–	500	546	779
Tyrone, . .	N.-T.-Stewart, .	–	165	94	9	–	354	164	143
Tyrone, . .	Omagh, . .	8	498	341	60	7	503	420	373
King's, . .	Parsonstown, .	–	139	44	16	3	728	164	111
	Total, . .	4,599	4,623	4,063	773	479	14,743	10,493	1,337

24. The following Table shows (a) the *Total* expenditure on the Model Schools for the Year 1894, (b) the *Net* expenditure on the Model Schools out of the Education Vote, and (c) the total payments to the Teaching Staff from the National Education Vote and from Local Sources.

(Expenditure by Board of Works on repairs, &c., not included.)

(a)

Model School.	Expenditure from State Grant.		Expenditure from Local Sources.		Total Expenditure.
	General Expenditure (a Brass, Fire, Furniture, etc.)	Salaries and Allowances to Teaching Staff.	Part of School Fees to Teachers.	Union Rates to Teachers.	
Central				—	
West Dublin,				—	
Glasnevin,				—	
Inchicore,				—	
Athy,				—	
Ballieboro',				—	
Ballymena,				—	
Belfast,					
Clonmel,				—	
Coleraine,				—	
Cork,					
Dunmanway,				—	
Kanturk,				—	
Enniskillen,				—	
Galway,				—	
Kilkenny,				—	
Limerick,				—	
Londonderry,				—	
Newry,					
Newtownards,				—	
Sligo,				—	
Trim,					
Waterford,				—	
Ballymoney,				—	
Carrickfergus,				—	
Lurgan,				—	
Monaghan,				—	
Newtownstewart,					
Omagh,				—	
Parsonstown,				—	
Total					

(b)

Total Expenditure on Model Schools (see Table above), £41,807 7 1
Deduct £... School Fees appropriated in aid of Education Vote, £2,895 9 0
Deduct £... School Fees paid to Teachers,
Deduct £... Contributions from Local Rates, £... 9 5
Total Deductions, £5,832 12 8
Net Expenditure on Model Schools out of Education Vote, £35,983 14 11

(c)

Total Annual Payments to Teaching Staff—
From Education Vote, £30,485 16 4
School Fees, £251 10 0
Rates Contributions, £380 3 6
Total, £31,118 9 9

25. In order to facilitate Technical Instruction as much as possible, we have recently sanctioned, as a temporary arrangement, the use of a portion of the Galway Model School for Science, Art and Technical Classes, in connexion with the Galway Technical Institute.

(*h*.) CONVENT AND MONASTERY SCHOOLS.

Convent and Monastery Schools.

26. These schools are divided into two classes : (*a*) those whose teachers are paid according to the same scale of class salaries as teachers of ordinary National Schools; and (*b*) those in which the amount of salary awarded is regulated by the average number of children in daily attendance.

A Merit Capitation Grant of 12s. per pupil in average daily attendance is awarded to the Conductors of the schools paid on the principle of capitation, when the results of the Annual Examination are entirely satisfactory; and when such results are only fair or passable, a grant of 10s. is awarded. The numbers of the schools receiving the higher Merit Grant in 1894 were 250 Convent and 3 Monastery schools.

Convent and Monastery National Schools, whether paid on the principle of classification or of capitation, share with ordinary National Schools in Results fees, Gratuities for instructing Monitors, Customs and Excise Grant, and the "School Grant" provided by the Act of 1892.

27. (*a*) The average number of pupils on the rolls for the year ended 31st December, 1894, was 105,675, showing, as compared with 1893, an increase of 113.

(*b*) The number of pupils on rolls who made at least one attendance within the last 14 days of the month immediately preceding the Results Examinations was 91,593, showing an increase, as compared with 1893, of 1,170.

(*c*) The average daily attendance of pupils for the year ended 31st December, 1894, was 70,885, of whom 18,246 were boys. This was an increase of 869 in the total average daily attendance as compared with 1893.

(*d*) The per-centage of the average daily attendance of pupils for the year to the average number on the rolls was 67·1, whilst the per-centage of the average daily attendance to the number of pupils on the rolls who attended on any of the last 14 days of the month preceding the Results Examinations was 77·4. The corresponding per-centages in 1893 were respectively 66·4 and 75·5.

The numbers of these Schools, and the attendances, in 1894, were as follows:—

Class of School.	Paid by Capitation.		Paid by Classification.		Total.	
	No. of Schools.	Average Attendance.	No. of Schools.	Average Attendance.	No. of Schools.	Average Attendance.
Convent,	541	61,125	20	5,386	561	66,561
Monastery,	3	858	37	4,332	40	4,354
Total,	544	61,207	57	4,575	601	70,885

28. There are special industrial departments for girls in 50 of the Convent National Schools, in which, in rooms set apart for the purpose and furnished with the necessary appliances, instruction is given by skilled teachers in various branches of higher needlework, embroidery, lace-making, &c. The teachers of these departments are paid special salaries under the provisions of No. 52 of our Rules and Regulations.

(c.) Workhouse Schools.

29. The number of Workhouse Schools in connexion with us on the 31st December, 1894, was 153.

These schools were examined on the same system as the Ordinary Schools, and extracts from the reports of our Inspectors were communicated to the Local Government Board, for the information of the several Boards of Guardians. The salaries of the Teachers are determined by the Poor Law authorities, and paid from the Consolidated Fund; but the Poor Law Guardians have power, under the Act 38 & 39 Vict., cap. 96, to award to their Teachers, from the rates, the amount of results fees payable on the Inspectors' reports.

The total number of pupils appearing on the rolls of these Workhouse Schools during the year ending 31st December, 1894, was 8,411, and the average daily attendance was 4,725. The corresponding numbers for 1893 were 8,657 and 4,815.

(d.) Evening Schools.

30. Evening Schools are, as a rule, held on the same premises and taught by the same teachers as the Day Schools connected therewith. We regret to report that only 45 were in operation on the 31st December, 1894. The number of scholars in average attendance was 1,680.

Teaching Power.

31. The number of teachers in our service on 31st December, 1894, was as follows:—

Class.	Principals.		Assistants.		Paid.	Paper Assistants.	Workmis-tresses and Industrial Teachers.	Temporary Assistants.		Temporary Workmis-tresses.
	Males.	Females.	Males.	Females.				Males.	Females.	
1².	475	369	27	40	3,291	·	·	·	·	·
1².	793	489	73	89		·	·	·	·	·
2².	1,679	1,401	225	713	5,122	·	·	·	·	·
3².	800	340	154	100		·	·	·	·	·
3².	1,348	903	840	1,199	4,390	·	·	·	·	6 ·
3².	133	148	148	245		·	·	·	·	
Total.	4,737	3,538	985	2,528	11,703	22	859	17	85	7
	8,280		3,513					43		
Gross Total.					12,783					

The Conductors of 201 Convent and 8 Monastery Schools paid by capitation are not included in this return.

Mixed and Unmixed Schools. 82. Our returns for 8,463 schools show the respective numbers taught by masters and by mistresses exclusively, and by mixed Staffs; also the numbers attended by boys only, and by girls and infants only, and the numbers having a mixed attendance of boys and girls.

TEACHERS.	Schools for Boys only.	Schools for Girls (and Infants) only.	Schools for Mixed Attendance of Boys and Girls.
Masters only,	1,843	—	—
Masters only,	—	—	828
Mistresses only,	—	2,128	—
Mistresses only,	—	—	1,361
Master and Female Assistants,	—	—	888
Master and Workmistress,	—	—	187
Total,	1,843	2,128	4,404

New Teachers. 83. During the year 1894, there were 564 persons newly appointed as Principal or Assistant Teachers. Of these 209 had been trained and 355 were untrained. Of the latter 337 had been Monitors or Pupil Teachers; 11 had merely been pupils of National Schools admitted to Examination under special and exceptional circumstances; and 7 came from private schools or institutions.

ANTECEDENTS OF NEW PRINCIPAL AND ASSISTANT TEACHERS.

	Prin.	Asst.	Total.
Trained in "Marlborough-street" Training College,			
" "St. Patrick's"			
" "Our Lady of Mercy"			
" "Church of Ireland"			
" "De la Salle"			
Total,	74	135	209
Pupil Teachers, Paid Monitors, } In Model National Schools,			
Total,			
Paid Monitors, Pupils only, } In Ordinary National Schools,			
Total,	87	196	283
Paid Monitors, Pupils only, } In Convent National Schools,			
Total,			
From Private Schools, &c.,			7
Total New Teachers,	157	347	564

84. During the year 1894, 45 Teachers received retiring gratuities, on account of permanent incapacity through ill-health, before they attained the age for compulsory retirement on pension.

In accordance with the provisions of the Act these Teachers were awarded sums amounting to £4,607.

The number of Teachers who retired on pension was 93, and the number who died was 77, whilst 108 left the service, of whom 12 were dismissed.

36. The following Table shows the Number of National Teachers who in each year since the commencement of the Pensions Act (1st January, 1880), were in receipt of Pensions from the Fund; also the number of those to whom, on Retirement, Gratuities were awarded, with the Total Amounts each year.

	NUMBER OF TEACHERS.				Total Amounts of Pensions payable and Gratuities paid (under the Act) to retired Teachers.
	On Pension on 31st December of each Year.		Receiving Gratuities during Year.		
	Number.	Amount payable.	Number.	Amount paid.	
		£		£	£
1880,	157	5,633	81	8,330	9,056
1881,	724	8,473	67	6,540	14,013
1882,	588	10,988	78	8,189	19,688
1883,	671	15,718	71	7,184	23,672
1884,	830	24,176	61	8,044	34,219
1885,	480	17,883	65	6,804	24,387
1886,	671	20,843	61	4,873	25,733
1887,	653	23,728	67	8,852	30,381
1888,	738	24,960	66	8,431	32,391
1889,	826	20,818	67	6,688	38,183
1890,	878	30,872	73	7,388	33,380
1891,	848	38,083	76	7,168	45,398
1892,	887	33,338	61	3,880	37,648
1893,	1,018	35,818	63	6,238	38,848
1894,	1,088	37,133	65	1,607	41,738
Total,	—	—	—	—	488,953

BALANCE SHEET OF TEACHERS' PENSION FUND.

The Income and Expenditure of the Pension Fund during the year 1894, were as follows :—

	£ s. d.	£ s. d.
INCOME :—		
Two half-years' Interest on £1,300,000,	39,000 0 0	
Interest on Stock,	10,393 7 5	
Premiums paid by Teachers,	9,978 15 9	
		53,872 4 2
EXPENDITURE :—		
Pensions paid to Teachers,	35,957 14 9	
Gratuities,	4,607 13	
Premiums refunded,	1,593 4 4	
		42,157 12 1
Surplus of Income over Expenditure,		16,714 12 1
Amount realised by sale of £13,502 9s. 3d. Stock,		13,604 10 3
Cash Balance on 1st January, 1894,		555 7 3
		30,964 16 7
Sum Invested in purchase of £29,709 3s. Stock,		29,783 6 8
Cash Balance on 31st December, 1894,		1,175 11 11
		30,964 16 7

The Invested Capital of the Fund stood thus :—

1st January, 1894, Debt of the Irish Land Commission,			1,300,000 0 0
Stock in hand,	448,845 3 8		
Stock bought in 1894,	29,792 3 0		
	478,517 6 8		
Stock sold in 1894,	13,602 9 3		
In hand 31st December, 1894,	464,944 16 0	1,300,000 0 0	

36. Besides the regular Teaching Staffs we employ Pupil-Teachers in the Model Schools, and Monitors in both the Model and Ordinary National Schools. In some of the Model Schools male Pupil Teachers are boarded and lodged at the public expense.

There were 172 Pupil Teachers (108 Males and 64 Females) in our Model Schools on the 31st December, 1894.

Monitorships are practically scholarships open to the pupils of the schools in which they are educated. They are the rewards of efficiency on the part of the teachers, and of industry, ability, and good attendance on the part of the pupils and are much sought after.

The number of paid Monitors on the 31st December, 1894, was 1,780 Males, and 3,834 Females. Total, 5,614.

The following table gives the number of Monitors classified according to their year of service:—

Year of Service.	Male Monitors.	Female Monitors.	Total.
1st year	311	1,016	1,357
2nd "	451	832	1,283
3rd "	315	713	1,028
4th "	279	399	678
5th "	244	621	865
Total,	1,780	3,834	5,614

37. Annual Examinations are held by our own Officers in order to test (1) the fitness of Teachers for promotion; (2) the efficiency and attainments of Pupil Teachers and Monitors; (3) the qualifications of Candidates for admission to Training Colleges, and (4) the progress made by the Queen's Scholars in Training Colleges.

The number of Teachers examined in July, 1894, was 626; Monitors, 1,784; Pupil Teachers from Model Schools, 107; and of Queen's Scholars in the Training Colleges, 478; total, 3,250. There were 930 candidates for admission to the different Training Colleges examined on the same occasion. A considerable number of these, however, were also undergoing examination as Monitors or Pupil Teachers.

Advancement in Classification.

68. The advancement of the teaching staff in classification during the last ten years has been very marked, as may be observed from the following Table:—

Comparison of 1884 with 1894.

Teachers in the several Classes, Males and Females included.			Percentage to Total.	
Classes.	1884.	1894.	1884.	1894.
First Division of First (highest),	281	916	2·7	7·7
Second Division of First,	809	1,371	7·5	11·6
Second Class,	3,793	5,132	83·6	48·5
Third Class (lowest),	5,784	4,339	54·2	37·2

A synopsis of the Special Reports furnished by the Examiners on the character of the answering of the Teachers and Monitors at the Annual Examinations in the various subjects will be found in the Appendix to this Report.

Expenditure.*

Expenditure on Schools.

30. As far as we have been able to ascertain, the aggregate amount of Expenditure on the *Schools* from all sources, including Parliamentary Grant, Rates, School fees, and local subscriptions, during the year 1894, was £1,140,665 6s. 6d., as shown in the following table. This would give an average of £3 3s. 11¾d. for each child in average daily attendance during the year:—

(a) From Government Grants, 1894-5:—

	£ s. d.	£ s. d.
Paid out of Vote for Primary Education,	980,594 7 10	
Customs and Excise Grant,	78,000 0 0	
Do. (arising from previous years),	755 2 10	
		1,059,349 10 8

(b) From Local sources as under:—

	£ s. d.	£ s. d.
Subscriptions and Endowments, &c. (towards Incomes of Teachers),	22,465 0 2	
Subscriptions (towards Repairs, &c.),	33,894 10 3	
Rates from Contributory Unions (net),	5,857 15 5†	
School Pence paid by Pupils,	9,298 10 0	
		81,315 15 10

		£ s. d.
Total annual Income of Schools from all sources,	—	£1,140,665 6 6

		£ s. d.
Rate per Pupil from (a),		2 0 10¼
Rate per Pupil from (b),		0 3 1½
Rate per Pupil from all sources,		3 3 11¾

*NOTE.—Amount paid out of Vote for Board of Public Works for Buildings, Repairs, &c., of Vested Schools, is not included in this Section.
† The total amount of the contributions from the Rates was £23,172, but the sum of £17,304 was refunded to the Guardians out of the Customs and Excise Grant.

The Amounts paid by the State in the Financial Year 1894-5 to the *Teaching Staffs* of the principal classes of National Schools were as follows:—

(This does not include Rates, School Pence, and other Local Contributions.)

Class of Schools.	No. of Schools.	Average daily attendance year ended 31st Dec., 1894.	State Aid to Teaching Staff.	Average payment per pupil in average daily attendance.
			£ s. d.	£ s. d.
1. Ordinary Schools (including Schools with average 20 to 50).	7,767	455,810	890,116 13 10	2 0 10½
2. Model Schools	84	7,767	29,102 16 4	3 15 0½
3. Convent and Monastery Schools (Classification).	57	9,672	17,711 14 1	1 19 10½
4. Convent and Monastery Schools (Capitation).	264	62,507	106,969 2 5	1 14 1½
5. Modified Grant Schools (average under 20).	169	2,871	5,303 13 0	1 18 11½
Total of all Schools	8,341	513,625	1,051,303 5 5	2 0 9½

N.B.—Evening Schools, Poor Law Union, Lunatic Asylum, &c., Schools are excluded.

40. The *total income* of the *Teaching Staff* of all Schools, from the various sources, for the year ended 31st March, 1895, was as follows:— **Income of Teachers.**

	£ s. d.	
From Parliamentary Grant.	672,101 3 7, or 85½ per cent.	
„ Customs and Excise,	72,755 8 10, or 9½	„
„ Rates of Contributory Unions (Net),	5,267 15 2, or 0½	„
„ School Pence, Subscriptions, &c. (exclusive of Free Residences),	41,788 10 6, or 5½	„
Total,	£1,088,322 18 10	

41. The payments to the teachers out of the Funds placed at our disposal by Parliament are made under the following general heads:—(a) Salaries; (b) Results Fees; (c) Customs and Excise Grant; (d) Parliamentary School Grant; (e) Gratuities.

The (fixed) salaries of the National Teachers, as augmented under the Act of 1892, are as follows:— **(a). Salaries.**

PRINCIPAL MALE TEACHERS.

	Salary.	Increase 20 per cent.	Salary.
First Class—First Division,	£70	+ £14	= £84.
The old Second Division of First Class,	£60	+ £12	= £72.
The new Second Division,	£53	+ £10 12s.	= £63 12s.
The old First Division of Second Class,	£48	+ £9 12s.	= £57 12s.
Second Class, First and Second Divisions, New Scale,	£41	+ £9 16s.	= £49 16s.
Third Class,	£36	+ £7	= £43.

* (After refund to Guardians out of Customs and Excise Grant.)

PRINCIPAL FEMALE TEACHERS.

		Increase to per cent.	Salary.
First Class—First Division.	£55	+ £11 12s.	£99 12s.
The old Second Division of First Class,	£58	+ £10	£68.
The new Second Division,	£52	— £2 19s.	£54 19s.
The old First Division of Second Class,	£57	+ £7 8s.	£64 3s.
Second Class, First and Second Divisions, New Scale,	£54 10s. +	£6 11s.	£61 5d.
Third Class,	£47 10s. +	£6 10s.	£53.

ASSISTANT TEACHERS UNDER FIVE YEARS' SERVICE.

Males,	£35	+ £7	£42.
Females,	£37	+ £3 5s.	£39 5d.

ASSISTANT TEACHERS OF FIVE YEARS' STANDING AND OVER WHO ALSO RANK HIGHER THAN THE THIRD CLASS.

		Increase to per cent.	Bonus.	
Males,	£35	+ £7	+ £9	£51.
Females,	£37	+ £2 5s. +	£7 10s.	£39 14s

(?)
Results Fees.

42. The Results Fees paid from the Parliamentary Grant are determined upon the answering of the pupils at the Annual Results Inspection of the Schools.

The Teachers of Schools in Contributory Poor Law Unions receive the amount earned from the Parliamentary Grant, and one-half that amount, in addition, from the Rates, but paid through us. The number of Unions thus contributing in the year 1894–5 was 25; the number of schools situated within these Unions examined for Results was 1,464; and the total amount of Results Fees paid by us out of the Guardians' contributions was £23,171 13s. 8d. But of this amount £16,223 10s. 0d. was repaid to the Guardians at the close of the year under the Customs and Excise Act (1890), sec. 8, sub-sec. I. (s), (b).

(s)
Customs and Excise Grant.

43. As stated in our Report for 1891, it is provided that out of the Irish share of the Local Taxation (Customs and Excise) Grant a sum of £78,000 is to be annually paid over to us.

The sums accruing under this Grant are paid, in non-contributory Unions, to the teachers; and in Contributory Unions to the Guardians, as a reimbursement to the rates, partial or complete, of the contributions to the teachers. The balance, if any, unexpended, in any year is carried forward to the succeeding year.

In addition to providing for the claim of the Guardians of the Contributory Unions under the Customs and Excise Act, the amount paid by us to the Teachers of the Schools situated in Non-contributory Unions was £61,451 4s. 5d., distributed at the rate of 8s. per pupil in average attendance.

(t)
The Parliamentary School Grant (Irish Education Act, 1892).

44. The Parliamentary School Grant is a variable sum which provides (a) for increases to the salaries of Principal and Assistant Teachers, and increases to the Grants to schools already paid by Capitation; (b) for bonuses to Assistants of five years' standing, who rank higher than Third Class; (c) for Third Class salaries instead of Capitation to small schools with an average attendance of not less than 20 but under 30 scholars; and (d) as regards the residue,

a General Capitation Grant on the average daily attendance of pupils. This last amounted in 1894 to 4s. 1d. per pupil.

45. Gratuities were paid by us to Teachers during the year for the special instruction of their Monitors, in sums varying according to the year of the Monitorial service from £1 to £3, and amounting in the total to £8,983 15s. 8d.

46. By the Education Act of 1892, parents were wholly or in part relieved of the payment of school fees for their children. These fees were abolished from the 1st October, 1892, in schools where the average rate of fees received during the year 1891 had not exceeded six shillings a year for each child of the number of children in average daily attendance. In Schools where the average rate had exceeded that sum the fees to be charged were not to be such as to make the average rate higher for any year than the amount of the said excess.*

See Table D., page 48.

Training Colleges.

47. There are five Training Colleges receiving Grants, viz.:—
(1.) "Marlborough-street" (Dublin), for men and women, under our own Management;
(2.) "St. Patrick's" (Drumcondra, Dublin), for men;
(3.) "Our Lady of Mercy" (Baggot-street, Dublin), for women.
Both of these Colleges are under the management of His Grace the Most Rev. Dr. Walsh, Archbishop of Dublin;
(4.) "Church of Ireland" (Kildare-place, Dublin), for men and women, under the management of His Grace the Most Rev. and Right Hon. Lord Plunket, Archbishop of Dublin;
(5.) "De la Salle" (Waterford), for men, under the management of the Most Rev. Dr. Sheehan, Bishop of Waterford and Lismore.

Under the provisions of the scheme for the re-organization of the Training Colleges, promulgated in the letter of November, 1890, from the Right Hon. A. J. Balfour, then Chief Secretary for Ireland, the fixed grant payable for each Queen's Scholar in the Training Colleges, Marlborough-street included, is £50 for a male and £35 for a female Queen's Scholar, per annum.

In addition to these fixed grants, a bonus of £10 for each year of residence for every male Queen's Scholar, and £7 for each year of residence for every female Queen's Scholar, is granted on the award of the Training Diploma after a probationary service of two years in the actual work of teaching.

During the past College year, commencing in September, 1893, 688 Queen's Scholars, of whom 362 were men, and 326 women were *under instruction* in these Colleges.

397 *completed* their course of training. Of these 168 who had been previously employed as Teachers of National Schools, completed their course of one year's training, and 229 completed their two years' course of training.

Note.—Table showing the average incomes of Teachers will be found in Appendix.

48. QUEEN'S SCHOLARS in Training—Session, 1893-4.

Queen's
Scholars,
1893-4.

Name of College.	No. of Queen's Scholars admitted to Session 1893-4.	No. who remained until Close of Session.	Result of Examination (Christmas and July).			
			One-Year Students.		Final Year of Two-Year Students.	
			No. Examined.	No. Passed.	No. Examined.	No. Passed.
MEN.						
Marlborough-street, . . .						
St. Patrick's, . . .						
Church of Ireland, . . .						
De La Salle, . . .						
Total (Men), . .						
WOMEN.						
Marlborough-street, . .						
Our Lady of Mercy, . .						
Church of Ireland, . .						
Total (Women), .						

* Includes one Extern.　　　† Includes two Externs.

QUEEN'S SCHOLARS TRAINED at each of the Colleges during certain periods.

Number of
students
trained.

Name of College.	Period.	Numbers Trained.		
		Men.	Women.	Total.
Marlborough-street,‡ . .	1885 to 1894,			
St. Patrick's, . .	1883 to 1894,		—	
Our Lady of Mercy, . .	1889 to 1894,	—		
Church of Ireland, . .	1884 to 1894,			
De La Salle, . . .	1888 to 1894,		—	

RELIGIOUS DENOMINATIONS of the QUEEN'S SCHOLARS in MARLBOROUGH-STREET TRAINING COLLEGE who completed their Training Course in 1894.

—	R.C.	E.C.	Pres.	Meth.	Others.	Total.
Queen's Scholars in Residence, .	97	13	48	13	1	102

See Table E, page 44.

‡ 12,820 Teachers underwent courses of training in the Marlborough-street College from the commencement of the College in 1831 up to 31st August, 1883, when the College was brought under the same general academic regulations as the Denominational Colleges

49. The Inspectors in charge of the Training Colleges report in favourable terms as to the maintenance of the premises, and as to the efficiency of the system of instruction.

Their General Reports on the Colleges for the year ended 31st August, 1894, will be found in the Appendix to this Report.

The candidates for the position of teacher are in general well prepared; and selections are, as a rule, made by Managers with care and judgment. A large proportion of the recently appointed teachers have had the advantage of receiving a preliminary training as monitors.

The Teaching Body.

Results Examinations of Pupils.

50. In order to qualify for presentation at the Results Examination each pupil is required to make 100 attendances in day schools open for at least four hours a day for secular instruction, and 50 attendances in evening schools open for two hours each evening during the Results year.

Results Examination.

The total number of Schools examined for Results within the twelve months ended 31st December, 1894, by the Inspectors and for which we have been able to tabulate the particulars, was 8,485, viz.:—

No. of Ordinary Schools examined, . . . 8,207
" Model Schools (separate departments), . . 84
" P. L. Union Schools (Fees payable by the Guardians, at their discretion), . . . 155
" Evening Schools, ... 39

(a.) Number of pupils who attended once or oftener within the last fourteen days of Results year:—

Males, 854,683; Females 366,294; Total, 720,977.

(b.) Average daily attendance of pupils for the Results year:—

Males, 259,070; Females, 265,139; Total, 524,209.

(c.) Number of pupils qualified by attendance for presentation at examinations for Results:—

Males, 291,566; Females, 304,969; Total, 596,535.

(d.) Number of pupils who were present and examined on day of Inspection for Results:—

Males, 280,581; Females, 286,896; Total, 567,477.

51. The following results have been ascertained through individual examination of the pupils of National Schools by the Inspectors at the annual examinations:—

Classes.	Number Examined.	Number Passed.	Percentage Passed.	Percentage in each Class to Total Number Examined.
Infants, . . .	131,343	121,321	92·0	23·3
First Class, . .	85,843	73,709	85·1	15·1
Second Class, . .	85,234	70,774	83·0	15·0
Third Class, . . .	79,576	63,958	80·6	14·0
Fourth Class, . .	66,811	50,790	76·0	11·8
Fifth Class (1st stage), .	51,279	37,291	72·7	9·1
Fifth Class (2nd stage), .	34,778	25,032	72·0	6·1
Sixth Class, . . .	32,461	23,656	72·8	5·7
Total, .	567,477	466,557	82·2	100·0

52. The percentages of passes gained in Reading, Writing, Arithmetic, &c., in each of the last four years, are set forth in the following table:—

	1894.	1893.	1892.	1891.
Reading, . . .	94·6	94·3	94·1	94·4
Writing, . . .	96·1	95·7	96·5	95·7
Arithmetic, . . .	83·4	83·5	83·9	83·6
Spelling, . . .	82·7	82·6	82·2	82·7
Grammar, . . .	69·9	67·5	68·0	68·7
Geography, . . .	74·8	74·3	73·6	76·7
Agriculture, . . .	69·4	60·9	60·7	61·6
Book-keeping, . .	67·2	66·2	66·1	60·6
Needle-work, . . .	92·7	92·4	91·6	91·4

See Table F., page 45.

58. The following is a general Abstract of Results in Extra and Optional Subjects:—

—	Number of Schools	No. Examined	No. of Passes
Vocal Music, ...	7,150	66,578	57,900
Instrumental Music, ...	156	007	862
Drawing, ...	1,343	63,215	49,671
Kindergarten, ...	813	88,117	84,704
Girls' Reading Book and Domestic Economy, .	191	2,072	1,354
Sewing Machine and Dressmaking, . .	125	4,763	3,841
Cookery, ...	85	1,289	1,251
Management of Poultry, . . .	8	166	110
Dairy Management, ...	0	87	46
Handicraft, ...	14	220	190
Weaving, ...	8	107	98
Net Mending, ...	1	9	8
Typewriting and Shorthand, . .	2	20	6
Hygiene, ...	16	841	203
Geometry and Mensuration, . .	1,032	5,949	4,040
Algebra, ...	1,435	13,424	9,137
Trigonometry, ...	1	8	0
Mechanics, ...	3	8	3
Magnetism and Electricity, . .	8	96	73
Chemistry, ...	1	18	10
Light and Sound, ...	3	63	47
Physical Geography, . . .	823	8,697	2,410
Botany, ...	1	69	87
French, ...	94	923	730
Irish, ...	00	1,058	714
Latin, ...	90	194	187
Greek, ...	8	31	25

The money value of the passes gained in Vocal Music, Drawing, and Kindergarten, for the year was £16,540 9s.—See Table G, page 44.

The money value of the passes gained in other Extras was £6,423 3s. Of this sum £3,294 6s., represented the value in Geometry and Algebra; £619 10s. in Latin, Greek, French, and Irish; £803 5s. in Physical Geography, and £1,542 6s. in branches, exclusive of Needlework, for Females only. The remainder, £363 15s., was spread over the other subjects.

Vocal
Music

54. The reports of the Inspectors show that the teaching of vocal music is becoming more general in the schools, and as the number of trained teachers increases the subject is likely to be cultivated more extensively.

The suitability of the Tonic-Sol-Fa system for the purposes of school teaching is now fully recognized, and as it is almost exclusively adopted in the Training Colleges there is little doubt that its use will become in a short time universal in those schools where vocal music is taught. At the annual July examinations, however, a majority of the ordinary teachers and monitors still come forward for certificates in the system known as Hullah's. At present the teaching of singing is largely confined to girls' schools, there being comparatively little attempt to teach boys this subject. It is hoped that the Managers will recognise the importance of the subject in the education of boys as well as of girls, and that in future years we may be enabled to report that the number of boys enrolled in singing classes has largely increased.

The Training Colleges afford facilities also for learning instrumental music—chiefly the harmonium, which instrument is found very helpful to the teachers in connexion with the organization and instruction of singing classes in the schools.

Drawing

55. We do not consider that the circumstances of our schools at present would warrant us in making drawing a *compulsory* subject, as it is to a large extent in England, but we should be very glad to see it more extensively taught in the National Schools than at present, as it is that form of technical instruction which is most appropriate for elementary schools.

Industrial and Technical Instruction.

Needle
work.

56. The returns for the past year afford evidence that needlework is receiving careful attention in the schools; the specimens of plain sewing and knitting presented by pupils at the examinations for results were satisfactory, and the made-up articles produced by the pupils showed improvement both in quality and quantity.

In the case of female monitors, however, the Directress of Needlework reports that, with some exceptions, their sewing, knitting, darning, and cutting out, leave much to be desired.

During the year 167,732 pupils of girls' schools, or of schools in which female teachers are employed, were examined by the Inspectors, and 155,430 passed the required standard.

In the Training Colleges the amount of "good" and "excellent" sewing is reported as being on the whole less in 1894 than in 1893.

In the 52 Special Industrial Departments connected with schools where advanced needlework is taught to the senior girls, and to young women of the locality who are not pupils of the schools, the work done for the year was of a varied and useful character, and the proficiency was generally creditable. .

The number of pupils in average attendance in these Industrial Departments is 1,842.

Weaving classes, instructed by extern teachers, have been in *Weaving.*
operation in some of the larger Convent schools with success.
We grant special salaries to the teachers of Weaving. We *Net-mending.*
also have encouraged Net-mending, and have granted salary to
a teacher of the subject, in connexion with some island schools.
Domestic economy and the use of the Sewing Machine are taught
in a considerable number of the schools.

With the facilities now afforded through the Training Colleges *Cookery.*
for instruction in Cookery, it is expected that this useful branch
will find its way more and more into the larger schools, wherever
suitable appliances for giving the required practical teaching
are available.

Handicraft for boys has not been taken up to any material *Handicraft.*
extent throughout the country as a branch of school work,
though a good many teachers have now been certified as competent to teach it.

57. Instruction in Kindergarten is on the increase in large *Kinder-*
schools with regularly organized Infants' departments, while *garten.*
in infants' schools it is an almost invariable accessory. There
can be little doubt that through the influence of the Training
Colleges the system will gain year by year in popularity, as
its usefulness in the cultivation of the intelligence of the
children is better understood.

It is a matter of regret that the Managers, as a rule, have not
endeavoured to introduce the subject (even in a modified and
elementary form for the younger children) into the ordinary
schools. In the cases where the experiment has been tried it
has been found to exercise a beneficial effect on the training of
the junior pupils by awakening their interest in their instruction
and by stimulating their attendance.

58. With the object of preparing girls who have already passed *Industrial*
the Ordinary Programme of the higher division of the Fifth *Programme*
Class, for the practical duties of home life, or of qualifying *6th Class.*
them to pursue industrial employments suitable to women, the
Sixth Class Literary and Industrial Programme for Girls was
adopted in 1889; and in 1894 the Scheme was in operation in
1,405 National schools.

[TABLE.

The Results of this Alternative Scheme during the year 1894 in the 1,403 Schools were as follows :—

—	—	Number Examined	Number Passed	Percentage of Passed
	LITERARY PROGRAMME.			
	Reading (including Text Books on suitable Industrial Subjects and on Domestic Economy, with knowledge of the subject matter).	6,910	6,141	89·0
	English Composition (including Letter-writing on various subjects, which should embrace Geography, Grammar, &c.—skill in Penmanship taken into account).	6,838	6,278	91·7
	INDUSTRIAL PROGRAMME.			
Plain Needle-work.	Plain Needlework, including Shirtmaking.	6,610	6,120	92·6
Special Industries, Class A.	Dressmaking,	3,803	3,500	91·4
	Fine Underclothing,	2,160	2,181	91·0
	Knitting,	6,462	6,347	97·1
	Repairing,	83	71	85·9
	Clothwork,	87	87	100·5
	Flax, Treatment of,	9	9	100·0
Special Industries, Class A.	Lacemaking,	617	385	92·7
	Macramé Lace Work,	1,939	1,715	88·3
	Art Needlework,	666	583	89·0
	Gold and Silver Lace Work,	13	16	88·3
	Hosiery,	61	34	100·0
	Glovemaking,	83	41	78·8
	Artificial Flower Making,	8	8	100·0
	Other kinds of Cottage Industries,	18	18	100·0

Agriculture.

No. of pupils examined in theory of agriculture.

52. As set forth in Table F, at page 45, there were 82,596 pupils examined in the Agricultural Class Books by the District Inspectors in the Ordinary National Schools at their Results Examinations, of whom 51,531 passed. Instruction in the *theory* of Agriculture, for which ordinary Results Fees are payable, is compulsory in all rural schools for boys in the 4th, 5th, and 6th classes, and is optional in the case of girls.

School Farms.

The total number of School Farms in connexion with Ordinary National Schools on the 31st December, 1894, was 44, of which 30 were reported on. The boys in the advanced classes in schools with School Farms attached are examined in practice as well as theory of Agriculture, and Special Agricultural Fees are paid on the proficiency of the pupils and state of the farms. The names of the Schools and the extent of the farm attached to each will be found in the Appendix. The total number of pupils examined in Practical Agriculture, by the Agricultural Superintendant, within the results year, was 576, of whom 503 passed.

We had 30 schools with School Gardens attached. For the School management of these Gardens, and for the practical knowledge Gardens. displayed by the pupils, we also granted special agricultural fees, upon the reports of the District Inspectors. The number of pupils examined in these schools was 548, of whom 443 passed.

The Albert Agricultural Institution at Glasnevin has been Albert attended by the following classes during the year :— Institution.

Agricultural Students (Resident)	{ Paying,	16
	{ Free by Competitive Examination,	26
	Total,	42
Female Dairy Students (Resident)	{ First Session,	36
	{ Second Session,	34
	Total,	70
Queen's Scholars—From Marlboro'-street Training College, (Non-Resident at Albert Institution)		12
From "Church of Ireland" Training College, (Non-Resident) at Albert Institution)		12
	Total,	106

Considerable attention is given to instruction in the dairy, both male and female students being required to take part in the practical work therein.

The Queen's Scholars from the two Training Colleges above named attend at the Albert Institution regularly ; those from the Marlborough-street College twice, and from the " Church of Ireland " College once, each week.

The Munster Institution, Cork, continues to make good progress, Munster the attendances having been :— Institution.

Female Dairy Students, First Session,		84
" " Second Session,		80
" " Third Session,		84
Male Students,		71

The number of male agricultural students admitted to residence in this establishment continues to increase. The Dairy department for females at each Session had in attendance as many dairy pupils as the premises could accommodate.

In the Dairy School the results of the examinations were very satisfactory. At the competition for butter making the prizes offered by the Governors of the Institute were awarded upon a report of the Chief Butter Inspector of the Cork Butter Exchange, whose report shows that the pupils generally had acquired the art of making butter in a thoroughly satisfactory manner.

The Governors, co-operating with the Commissioners, continued their services in promoting the interests of this important School of Agriculture.

A Ladies Committee has done much for the school in promoting instruction therein in Cookery, Needlework, and Laundry.

The female Dairy Instructors appointed to visit centres Itinerant throughout the country for the purpose of giving instruction in Dairy improved methods of butter making, were, in 1894, engaged Instruction. principally in Cork and Kerry. The reports which we have received of the results of their teaching have demonstrated to us the advantage of the system of itinerant dairy instruction. Large numbers of persons of the agricultural classes attended at the lectures and practical demonstrations on butter making, and much interest in the subject appears to have been awakened.

The male Dairy Instructor has reported upon 100 creameries during the year. The reports show that whilst in some creameries the arrangements are excellent, yet in others considerable improvement is required. The suggestions of the Instructor are mainly designed to promote improved methods in respect of the structure and management of the creameries.'

Creamery Managers.

A special class for the instruction of Creamery Managers was held in last year at the Munster Agricultural and Dairy School, and was attended by 10 persons. These students are examined at the close of the session, and certificates of proficiency are awarded upon their completing six months of successful creamery management after the course of training at the dairy school.

We also decided to give a course of special dairy instruction to creamery managers at the Albert Institution; and in future, so long as it may be desirable to do so, a session for these managers will be held at the Institution in each year.

The course of their instruction embraces the science of Chemistry as applied to dairy practice, the keeping of accounts, the practice of butter and cream making, the testing of milk, and the feeding of farm animals.

Experiments on the Potato.

During 1894 experiments upon means for protecting the potato from disease by dressing the crop with a preparation of copper sulphate, were carried out at our Agricultural Establishments at Glasnevin and Cork, as well as at certain School farms in the country. The results of these experiments will be found stated in the Appendix to this report. The experiments on our farms with this antidote, extended over several years, tend to show that the copper sulphate remedy, if properly applied, is a powerful aid in the prevention of potato disease.

Agricultural experiments.

Other experiments of interest to agriculturists have been carried out at our Agricultural Establishments, reports upon which will be found in the Appendix to this report.

Industrial Classes.

In 24 Schools we made payments to the pupils of Industrial Classes for working on the small farms or gardens attached, under the direction of the teachers assisted by Agricultural Monitors. It is to be hoped that the number of these schools, with classes duly organized, will be largely increased.

The number of pupils who, on account of their regularity of attendance at the farm work, and proficiency at the examinations received payments was 236; and the number of Agricultural monitors who fulfilled the conditions prescribed in their case was 48.

We regret that the number of School Farms and School Gardens is still so small; but now that greater facilities exist, owing to the Education Acts of 1892 and 1893, for the acquisition of sites, Managers may possibly take steps to make practical Agriculture a branch of instruction in many more of their Schools.

With the consent of the Treasury we have increased the fees for the practical teaching of Agriculture, &c., and we hope that this will help to encourage a greater development of such instruction.

Books and Requisites.

60. During the year we received several applications from publishers and others to have books, &c., approved for use in schools. In the cases of such of these as we considered suitable we gave the necessary approval. Both teachers and pupils concerned have now a more varied and extensive collection of reading and other school books from which selection may be made.

In the cases of new schools, and where extensive structural improvements of existing schools have been carried out by private contributions, it has been our custom to make a free grant of books and requisites. We made 323 such grants during the year, the value of which was £1,032 16s. 11d. School Account Books, valued at £645 17s. 10d., were also supplied *gratis*. (These are charged against the vote for Her Majesty's Stationery Office.)

The number of orders for goods received from the schools during the year was 20,924. These orders were not only for books, but included school apparatus, and materials for drawing, music, kindergarten, needlework, and technical instruction. The number of reading books issued by us during the year was 1,368,263, and the number of copy books and drawing books was 2,746,004.

The books, requisites, &c., were sold at their cost price, and were sent, carriage free, to the schools or to the stations nearest to them.

The following Table shows the net cost of the Book Department during the year:—

RECEIPTS.	£	s.	d.	EXPENDITURE.	£	s.	d.	Cost of Book Department.
Cash received for Books, &c., sold,	31,525	13	10	Cost of Clerical Staff and Packers employed,	1,259	0	0	
Credit for Postage allowed to Teachers,	188	19	6	Carriage of Parcels and Purchase of Packing Materials,	8,250	1	0	
Credit allowed for Free Stocks issued,	1,932	16	11	Rail, Fuel, Light, Wear and Tear, &c.,	20	0	0	
BALANCE—Net Cost of Stores in the Sale,	4,745	6	13	Payment to Contractors for goods issued during the year,	31,146	0	0	
	£37,229	9	1		£27,230	9	1	

Private Contribution Funds.

61. The "Carlisle and Blake" Fund is at the disposal of this Board for the special recognition of distinguished merit of Teachers as school-keepers. The Premiums are awarded at the rate of £5 to one successful candidate in each school district in every fourth year.* The names of the Teachers who secured the Prizes for 1894 will be found in the Appendix.

The "Reid Bequest" Special Prizes, under the Will of the late R. T. Reid, Esq., LL.D., varying from £25 to £10 each, were awarded to twelve Male Monitors of National Schools in the County Kerry for superior answering in Competitive Examinations for the Prizes. The names, &c., will be found in the Appendix.

* Convent, Monastery, and Model Schools are excluded from the competition.

G 2

Under terms of this Will an Exhibition of £40 per annum to be held during his undergraduate course in Arts, has been granted by us to Mr. John Kennolly, an ex-Queen's Scholar of Marlborough-street Training College, from the County Kerry, who had matriculated in Trinity College, Dublin. A similar Exhibition was granted in 1894 to Mr. Patrick Buckley.

The School Accounts

62. The records kept by the teachers form the official materials of the history of the school and of the school life of the individual scholar, and it is therefore of paramount importance that such records should be complete and accurate. Changes in recent years have given increased value to the school accounts. The payments of the Customs and Excise Grant and the residue of the School Grant (under the Act of 1892) are made in proportion to the average daily attendance of pupils, and are thus directly dependent on *bonâ fide* and correct accounts of attendance. The Results Fees payable on the passes of the pupils examined are liable to be seriously affected by inaccuracies in the records kept by the teachers. The Irish Education Act of 1892 adds to the complexity of the school returns by drawing a distinction between pupils who are under and those who are over 15 years of age and determining payment of the residue of the School Grant in respect to pupils under 15 years.

During the past year many cases have occurred in which various inaccuracies in the school accounts caused lengthened correspondence and greatly increased the labours of Inspectors and of the Office Staff. The question of the practicability of improving the system of school accounts is under consideration.

63. Attached hereto are statistics as to the schools, the proficiency of the pupils &c., and our financial statement for the year ended 31st March last.

Commissioners.

64. On November 1, 1894, the Right Honorable Sir Patrick Keenan, K.C.M.G., C.B., Resident Commissioner, died; and at our meeting of the 6th November following, we expressed our deep regret at his loss in the following Resolution unanimously passed:—

"With feelings of profound regret we record in our Minutes of to-day the death of the Right Honourable Sir P. J. Keenan.

"His death is to each of us the loss of a personal friend, and to Ireland the loss of one of our ablest public servants. He was conversant with every detail of the System of National Education, which, as Resident Commissioner, he administered in conjunction with his colleagues for over twenty-three years, having previously served for about the same period as Professor, Head Inspector, and Chief of Inspection.

" But his public services were not confined to his native land.
" He was chosen by two Governments to deal with the whole
" subject of education in Trinidad and at Malta. The masterly
" way in which he discharged his new duties was fully appreciated
" by the Colonial Secretaries of the day, and by Her Gracious
" Majesty's conferring upon him the distinctions he bore.

" We desire specially to offer our condolence and deep sympathy
" to his bereaved children who were by a fatal accident, some
" eighteen months ago, suddenly deprived of their mother, and who
" are again plunged in affliction by the death of a loving father."

We also regret to have to record the deaths of two other valued
colleagues, Viscount Monck, G.C.M.G., and Right Hon. W. F. Cogan,
D.L. They had held seats on our Board for many years, and
brought to our deliberations the aid of their sound judgment and
great experience.

Warrants were received on February 14, 1895, from His
Excellency Lord Houghton, Lord Lieutenant, appointing to the
then existing vacancies on the Board:—

> The Most Rev. Archbishop William J. Walsh, D.D.
>
> The Most Rev. Archbishop William Conyngham Lord
> Plunket, D.D., and
>
> Stanley Harrington, Esq., J.P.

In addition to these changes, we have to record the recent
resignation of his seat on our Board by John E. Sheridan, Esq.,
whose services throughout his long official career were of the
highest importance to the cause of National Education in Ireland.
His place has been filled by the appointment, under Warrant of
His Excellency Lord Houghton (received 3rd April, 1893), of

> W. R. J. Molloy, Esq.

65. On November 19, 1894, we received His Excellency's letter
appointing the Right Honourable Christopher Talbot Redington,
D.L., Resident Commissioner, in succession to the late Sir Patrick
Keenan.

66. We submit this, as our Report for the past year, to Your
Excellency, and in testimony thereof have caused our Corporate
Seal to be hereunto affixed, this Sixteenth day of July,
One Thousand Eight Hundred and Ninety-five.

(Signed)

J. G. TAYLOR,   } *Secretaries.*
M. S. SEYMOUR,

TABLE A.—Showing the *total* number of Schools in each County; the
Roily; the Religious Denominations of these Pupils; the average

PROVINCES AND COUNTIES.	Total Number of Schools in each County.	Total Number of Schools from which Returns have been received.	Total Number of Pupils on Rolls within the Year 1891, who came at least once into Attendance.		
			Males.	Females.	Total.
ULSTER:					
Antrim, . . .	673	669	57,303	54,762	112,065
Armagh, . . .	273	272	16,597	15,893	32,420
Cavan, . . .	287	285	13,040	12,006	25,046
Donegal, . . .	423	416	21,045	19,306	40,341
Down, . . .	485	482	32,100	31,558	54,756
Fermanagh, . .	179	179	7,679	7,094	14,773
Londonderry, .	297	297	16,671	15,598	32,265
Monaghan, . .	190	189	9,207	8,877	18,084
Tyrone, . . .	375	371	17,580	16,808	34,628
Total,	3,189	3,161	192,542	182,017	374,559
MUNSTER:					
Clare, . . .	251	249	14,829	14,230	28,559
Cork, . . .	753	749	47,023	48,348	95,371
Kerry, . . .	358	358	22,494	22,806	45,300
Limerick, . .	261	260	16,204	17,087	33,091
Tipperary, . .	320	319	17,103	18,605	35,770
Waterford, . .	199	190	9,767	10,258	19,025
Total,	2,062	2,074	126,672	131,094	268,046
LEINSTER:					
Carlow, . . .	81	81	3,597	3,006	7,548
Dublin, . . .	315	314	85,912	39,913	75,125
Kildare, . . .	107	106	5,567	5,987	11,554
Kilkenny, . .	167	167	9,246	9,276	18,592
King's, . . .	124	123	6,648	8,466	13,114
Longford, . .	111	111	5,840	4,786	11,607
Louth, . . .	104	104	6,016	7,053	13,096
Meath, . . .	191	178	8,249	8,259	16,601
Queen's, . . .	126	124	6,397	5,983	12,380
Westmeath, . .	134	134	6,490	6,586	13,085
Wexford, . . .	163	164	8,508	9,820	18,418
Wicklow, . . .	124	124	6,006	5,590	11,596
Total,	1,757	1,748	108,107	114,597	222,034
CONNAUGHT:					
Galway, . . .	434	428	25,492	24,931	50,423
Leitrim, . . .	202	201	10,241	9,500	19,741
Mayo, . . .	408	407	26,584	26,200	52,774
Roscommon, . .	239	238	14,144	18,805	27,949
Sligo, . . .	211	210	11,136	10,999	22,185
Total,	1,494	1,479	87,587	85,485	173,022
ULSTER, . .	3,189	3,161	192,542	182,017	374,559
MUNSTER, . .	2,082	2,074	126,072	131,994	258,086
LEINSTER, . .	1,757	1,748	108,107	114,587	222,634
CONNAUGHT, . .	1,494	1,479	87,587	85,485	173,022
IRELAND, . .	8,505	8,463	514,258	514,028	1,028,291
Per-centage to total on rolls,	—	—	50·0	50·0	—

number from which Returns were received; the total number of Pupils on the
number on the Rolls; and the average Daily Attendance for the year 1804.

						Average Number on the Rolls for the Year 1891	Average Daily Attendance for the Year 1894.	PROVINCES AND COUNTIES.
R.C.	**E.C.**	**Pres.**	**Meth.**	**Others.**	**Total.**			
								ULSTER:
26,749	27,436	31,377	3,024	2,390	119,085	81,214	56,031	Antrim.
14,308	10,644	5,199	1,247	397	52,820	26,201	16,836	Armagh.
20,049	3,813	867	192	93	25,046	81,119	18,428	Cavan.
31,324	4,724	3,866	418	19	40,341	31,834	18,123	Donegal.
11,839	16,016	33,915	1,078	2,813	64,725	47,903	33,464	Down.
8,305	5,021	245	577	5	14,173	12,929	7,914	Fermanagh.
13,907	6,718	11,165	208	370	32,356	25,101	16,153	Londonderry.
18,949	2,359	2,509	65	4	18,064	15,291	6,905	Monaghan.
18,557	8,121	7,011	392	371	34,688	27,586	10,068	Tyrone.
161,282	86,054	112,007	9,282	5,654	374,559	290,802	186,470	Total.
								MUNSTER:
26,105	402	31	5	19	28,559	21,550	15,123	Clare.
48,864	5,117	310	536	240	93,871	60,784	31,464	Cork.
44,201	1,079	17	48	27	43,360	39,407	13,718	Kerry.
32,602	825	84	106	70	23,021	24,667	16,847	Limerick.
34,430	1,302	76	57	5	35,770	20,388	19,904	Tipperary.
18,483	479	31	43	10	19,024	15,368	10,142	Waterford.
216,989	9,354	549	780	304	239,066	219,371	144,357	Total.
								LEINSTER:
5,845	693	11	14		7,803	0,613	4,003	Carlow.
63,510	9,516	1,037	433	600	75,125	51,066	34,863	Dublin.
10,656	702	67	18	34	11,554	9,188	5,834	Kildare.
17,728	736	30	18	-	18,572	15,030	10,123	Kilkenny.
12,067	902	92	41	9	13,114	11,072	6,780	King's.
10,666	933	63	41	4	11,607	9,814	3,817	Longford.
12,066	725	238	31	10	13,009	10,904	6,802	Louth.
15,575	846	77	-	-	16,501	14,492	9,251	Meath.
10,737	1,390	60	69	14	12,280	10,346	6,319	Queen's.
12,362	651	30	37	5	13,155	11,209	7,092	Westmeath.
17,928	1,129	44	16	9	18,418	13,550	9,577	Wexford.
9,757	1,506	75	72	11	11,528	9,797	6,094	Wicklow.
190,177	20,096	1,843	818	703	222,634	177,132	112,187	Total.
								CONNAUGHT:
49,506	727	101	16	13	50,493	48,174	32,807	Galway.
17,872	1,509	31	125	7	18,711	16,867	9,786	Leitrim.
51,706	651	178	17	19	52,774	44,168	34,917	Mayo.
27,281	575	72	2	14	27,919	23,597	13,596	Roscommon.
20,348	1,523	132	72	60	22,135	18,719	10,714	Sligo.
166,775	4,889	514	280	117	173,072	145,525	82,533	Total.
161,282	86,054	112,007	9,282	5,654	374,559	290,802	186,470	ULSTER.
216,989	9,354	549	780	304	239,066	219,371	144,357	MUNSTER.
190,177	20,096	1,843	814	703	222,634	177,132	112,187	LEINSTER.
166,775	5,389	514	280	117	173,072	145,525	82,533	CONNAUGHT.
774,291	190,892	114,913	11,106	7,150	1,028,281	832,831	525,547	IRELAND.
75·3	11·7	11·2	1·1	0·7	-	-	-	Per-centage to total on rolls.

* E.C., denotes Roman Catholic; E.C., Late-Established Church; Pres., Presbyterian; Meth., Methodist; and Others, Other Denominations.

Table B.—Showing the Religious Denominations of the Pupils on the Rolls
Roman Catholic and

Provinces and Counties.	Total No. of Schools.	Under Roman Catholic Teachers.							Under	
		No. of Schools.	R.C.	E.C.	Pres.	Meth.	Others.	Total.	No. of Schools.	R.C.
Ulster.										
Antrim,	221	77	8,684	291	618	11	68	9,639	228	1,486
Armagh,	148	56	6,233	370	161	11	8	6,783	70	673
Cavan,	151	125	11,678	648	65	20	9	12,171	31	162
Donegal,	254	181	16,543	853	822	69	14	17,691	68	1,944
Down,	246	70	6,784	343	549	1	23	7,703	145	1,318
Fermanagh,	130	73	5,319	533	29	34	—	6,264	56	728
Londonderry,	307	63	5,769	291	443	4	16	4,710	137	1,834
Monaghan,	115	77	7,481	388	354	3	9	8,240	39	334
Tyrone,	376	128	10,083	1,139	643	60	12	11,683	186	1,193
Total,	1,839	840	77,869	5,317	5,838	164	100	86,643	964	10,180
Munster.										
Clare,	64	63	9,042	221	10	1	8	9,469	2	8
Cork,	244	244	33,419	796	15	28	12	34,341	15	83
Kerry,	135	131	17,581	431	4	8	5	18,224	4	22
Limerick,	70	74	9,780	244	15	13	21	10,026	2	23
Tipperary,	116	111	11,293	445	34	9	5	11,966	8	34
Waterford,	—	83	5,451	163	4	5	18	5,636	1	66
Total,	677	810	86,734	2,377	91	84	84	89,361	36	199
Leinster.										
Carlow,	38	38	8,630	131	6	8	—	8,767	2	22
Dublin,	105	38	15,420	369	21	—	4	19,814	68	253
Kildare,	47	46	5,057	131	17	1	13	5,289	1	7
Kilkenny,	66	62	5,160	224	9	—	—	5,709	4	173
King's,	38	34	6,383	224	8	11	—	6,550	3	11
Longford,	39	34	5,883	267	9	4	—	6,163	6	68
Louth,	44	39	5,905	111	7	—	—	5,991	5	19
Meath,	72	69	6,078	274	20	—	—	6,670	3	88
Queen's,	47	81	5,479	223	13	3	—	5,781	3	9
Westmeath,	43	82	5,347	186	5	—	—	6,148	3	10
Wexford,	51	73	8,561	289	9	1	8	5,673	8	62
Wicklow,	33	64	4,790	253	3	4	2	6,587	7	68
Total,	739	615	74,893	2,739	126	32	34	77,644	78	783
Connaught.										
Galway,	115	115	14,238	859	20	5	15	14,467	3	13
Leitrim,	108	86	10,117	510	15	2	9	10,678	8	63
Mayo,	167	162	15,380	337	55	9	12	15,766	5	46
Roscommon,	70	73	8,594	277	23	—	1	8,995	4	91
Sligo,	117	107	10,478	543	15	1	1	11,953	9	15
Total,	524	515	86,795	3,078	105	40	38	89,047	28	228
Grand Total,	3,769	2,620	356,611	12,531	5,927	250	286	312,505	1,106	11,357

of the 3,769 SCHOOLS from which Returns have been received, having both PROTESTANTS in attendance.

Protestant Teachers.					Under Roman Catholic and Protestant Teachers.							Provinces and Counties.
R.C.	Prm.	Meth.	Others.	Total.	No. of Schools	R.C.	E.C.	Prm.	Math.	Others.	Total.	
												ULSTER.
12,169	21,588	1,444	826	37,371	6	875	1,171	1,335	291	188	3,452	Antrim.
4,857	2,742	840	121	8,570	8	99	194	152	28	11	639	Armagh.
1,355	109	41	8	1,534		282	51	97	4	4	448	Cavan.
7,454	2,817	154	4	7,679								Donegal.
7,387	18,257	866	642	123,934		340	118	114	2	7	448	Down.
2,888	191	130		4,230		84	360	3	16		709	Fermanagh.
4,200	7,178	72	171	12,543	1	74	16	41			129	Londonderry.
1,164	1,164	82	2	7,618		79	120	120	9		253	Monaghan.
1,261	4,470	307	155	11,433	2	278	65	73			418	Tyrone.
40,073	51,033	3,454	2,140	100,550	23	1,234	1,354	2,080	272	185	5,343	**Total.**
												MUNSTER.
95	18			120		774	200	10			1,156	Clare.
691	24	91	3	813	4	774	260	10	56	51	1,156	Cork.
155				145		62	196	25	12	22	270	Kerry.
62				75	2	34	77	17	6		137	Limerick.
318	18			280	1							Tipperary.
47	7		6	97								Waterford.
1,388	54	110	8	1,582	7	930	498	53	56	65	1,579	**Total.**
												LEINSTER.
				148								Carlow.
3,784	291	179	330	4,534	16	4,855	854	90	51	60	5,865	Dublin.
94	21	8		86								Kildare.
158	8	8		300								Kilkenny.
111				112								King's.
162				200								Longford.
180	117	4		115		636					657	Louth.
127	13			181								Meath.
145	6	14		184								Queen's.
264	10	6		646								Westmeath.
251	172	10		940								Wexford.
												Wicklow.
5,202	624	256	872	7,430	16	4,433	910	90	51	60	5,554	**Total.**
												CONNAUGHT.
106	22	7		122								Galway.
360	6	22	8	480								Leitrim.
97	46	1		167								Mayo.
201	4	21	11	240								Roscommon.
428	84	26	25	505	1	8	67	22	24	8	181	Sligo.
1,222	182	58	68	1,632	1	8	67	22	24	8	181	**Total.**
48,007	52,833	4,462	2,548	116,774	48	7,388	3,554	2,179	468	314	18,376	**GRAND TOTAL.**

TABLE C.—The following table exhibits the religious denominations of pupils on rolls of 4,689 schools, attended *exclusively* by Roman Catholic or by Protestant children:—

PROVINCES AND COUNTIES.	Total Number of Schools.*	Under Roman Catholic Teachers.		Under Protestant Teachers.					
		Number of Schools.	No. of Pupils. R. C.	No. of Schools.	No. of Pupils—Protestants.				
					R. C.	Pres.	Meth.	Others.	Total.
ULSTER.									
Antrim,	247	89	18,494	279	18,806	28,228	2,562	1,410	44,728
Armagh,	132	48	7,758	84	5,325	9,388	630	199	6,057
Cavan,	184	65	8,392	45	2,151	613	127	10	2,791
Donegal,	145	125	12,562	39	1,590	833	234	—	2,417
Down,	234	44	8,730	192	7,567	18,318	1,212	1,619	28,723
Fermanagh,	49	73	2,291	26	1,626	62	162	1	1,646
Londonderry,	94	89	6,241	53	6,074	2,103	117	163	4,578
Monaghan,	70	43	5,114	27	939	372	13	—	1,824
Tyrone,	104	47	8,157	87	3,527	1,820	160	1,28	4,738
Total,	1,220	578	72,015	806	38,803	54,526	5,177	3,523	101,548
MUNSTER.									
Clare,	183	182	10,054	3	91	—	1	4	92
Cork,	495	430	54,590	64	3,648	250	335	44	4,340
Kerry,	288	221	24,341	12	418	13	40	23	453
Limerick,	182	176	23,063	6	359	42	75	17	533
Tipperary,	201	189	23,070	13	441	16	21	—	478
Waterford,	109	84	13,598	6	217	20	38	21	296
Total,	1,296	1,282	148,165	104	5,210	340	460	108	6,229
LEINSTER.									
Carlow,	43	28	8,234	14	680	4	10	—	694
Dublin,	206	161	43,707	87	4,497	327	202	97	5,323
Kildare,	89	44	5,679	13	624	48	14	17	701
Kilkenny,	171	112	12,155	5	346	—	3	—	355
King's,	84	51	5,673	14	510	84	12	6	680
Longford,	82	41	4,621	11	304	14	37	—	455
Louth,	89	62	6,139	8	375	115	13	17	520
Meath,	109	91	8,423	15	466	62	—	—	528
Queen's,	67	45	4,271	16	1,010	42	68	14	1,182
Westmeath,	79	73	6,405	7	323	32	22	2	396
Wexford,	80	76	8,616	16	453	25	4	—	484
Wicklow,	71	43	5,371	23	1,072	68	60	9	1,189
Total,	1,009	809	110,896	209	10,921	843	471	169	12,567
CONNAUGHT.									
Galway,	307	307	85,597	3	228	44	4	—	297
Leitrim,	95	77	7,692	15	302	3	68	—	335
Mayo,	240	293	52,353	12	420	87	14	7	488
Roscommon,	169	157	10,554	8	97	45	—	6	145
Sligo,	93	63	9,776	10	446	50	21	24	570
Total,	953	897	166,731	48	2,020	284	107	37	2,420
GRAND TOTAL,	*4,689	3,581	460,229	1,159	56,968	55,814	6,815	3,837	122,946

* There are five other schools, one in Donegal, one in Londonderry, one in Tyrone, one in Dublin, and one in Louth, with mixed attendance, which cannot be brought under any of the headings in this Table.

TABLE D.—The following table, compiled from returns furnished by the Managers of 8,300 schools, shows for each Province and County the amounts paid in school fees, the amount of Subscriptions, Donations, &c., the amount of local aid *on the average* for each school, and the amount of local aid *on the average* for each pupil.

NOTE.—In most of these schools no fees are charged, and in the remainder only the excess fees authorised under the Act of 1892.

Provinces and Counties.	Payments by Pupils.	Subscriptions, &c., &c.	Total.	No. of Schools.	Average Daily Attendance of Scholars.	Average per School.	Payments per pupil of average attendance.		
							School Fees.	Subscriptions, &c.	Total.
ULSTER:	£ s. d.	£ s. d.	£ s. d.		£ s. d.	£ s. d.	s. d.	s. d.	s. d.
Antrim,	1,775	1,143	2,919	681	57,890				
Armagh,	276	1,066	1,337	299	16,729				
Cavan,	32	575	608	291	19,963				
Donegal,	78	1,611	1,689	411	18,081				
Down,	891	1,615	2,507	478	33,796				
Fermanagh,	61	622	684	170	7,773				
Londonderry,	376	2,067	2,447	293	16,080				
Monaghan,	54	484	629	185	8,691				
Tyrone,	242	778	1,020	685	16,537				
Total,	**3,703**	**9,341**	**13,327**	**3,119**	**185,445**				
MUNSTER:									
Clare,	98	467	565	241	14,833				
Cork,	1,201	4,146	5,347	732	53,890				
Kerry,	295	1,347	1,643	340	25,387				
Limerick,	418	1,398	1,969	255	18,441				
Tipperary,	380	1,165	1,545	310	19,418				
Waterford,	268	874	1,112	136	10,664				
Total,	**2,471**	**9,369**	**12,061**	**1,925**	**141,784**				
LEINSTER:									
Carlow,	46	452	498	80	4,097				
Dublin,	1,080	3,519	4,599	80	68,641				
Kildare,	110	464	584	103	5,766				
Kilkenny,	68	702	768	110	9,045				
King's,	54	460	515	117	6,781				
Longford,	127	378	506	108	4,354				
Louth,	94	428	520	103	4,447				
Meath,	109	1,128	1,216	174	9,090				
Queen's,	42	873	931	133	4,703				
Westmeath,	98	380	471	131	4,421				
Wexford,	87	533	620	160	9,526				
Wicklow,	118	1,001	1,117	131	6,343				
Total,	**2,111**	**10,129**	**12,303**	**1,711**	**106,855**				
CONNAUGHT:									
Galway,	301	1,581	1,882	412	23,831				
Leitrim,	21	247	268	100	2,692				
Mayo,	138	774	933	404	24,366				
Roscommon,	211	578	789	221	18,668				
Sligo,	58	639	697						
Total,	**750**	**3,891**	**4,141**	**1,431**	**81,419**				
Grand Total,	**8,998**	**32,445**	**41,788**	**8,600**	**518,493**				

(a) This Total excludes £3,001 13s. received from the pupils, but appropriated under Treasury regulation in aid of the Parliamentary Vote for National Education.

(b) The Total excludes £7,948 9s. 1d., the value estimated by the managers of free residences for the teachers, but includes £1,970 1s. 5d., the estimated profits of free gardens or farms.

TABLE F.

The following Table shows the number of pupils examined for Results in the various subjects indicated, the number of passes, and the per-centages of passes to the number examined:—

Subjects and Classes.	No. of Pupils examined for Results Fees in subject.	No. of Passes assigned for advancing in subject.	Per-centage of Passes in the No. of Pupils examined.	Subjects and Classes.	No. of Pupils examined for Results Fees in subject.	No. of Passes assigned for advancing in subject.	Per-centage of Passes in the No. of Pupils examined.
READING.				**GRAMMAR.**			
Class I.,	82,643	81,241	94·9	Class III.,	79,876	66,221	75·2
„ II.,	83,284	79,287	87·2	„ IV.,	80,611	64,806	67·2
„ III.,	79,376	74,641	93·2	„ V.,	61,379	51,217	83·3
„ IV.,	66,011	60,745	83·2	„ VI.,	34,778	21,244	87·1
„ V.,	51,379	48,070	83·7	„ VI.,	32,461	31,977	87·7
„ VI.,	34,778	33,260	87·2				
„ VI.,	30,461	31,464	98·9	Total,	244,700	182,324	83·9
Total,	433,820	411,769	94·5	**GEOGRAPHY.**			
WRITING.				Class III.,	79,876	63,819	79·2
				„ IV.,	80,611	60,274	78·4
Class I.,	82,643	80,017	86·9	„ V.,	51,379	57,683	75·9
„ II.,	83,284	62,013	84·5	„ V.,	34,778	24,451	70·2
„ III.,	79,376	77,884	82·0	„ VI.,	32,461	31,552	67·7
„ IV.,	66,011	60,519	87·8	Total,	264,766	197,859	74·8
„ V.,	51,379	46,308	88·8				
„ VI.,	34,778	53,103	83·2	**AGRICULTURE.**			
„ VI.,	32,461	34,878	83·1	Class IV.,	22,722	16,428	67·4
Total,	433,632	413,740	86·1	„ V.,	22,611	14,151	62·9
ARITHMETIC.				„ V.,	13,254	16,342	67·6
Class I.,	82,643	76,714	88·9	„ VI.,	14,165	16,155	64·6
„ II.,	83,284	75,690	88·7	Total,	62,382	51,531	62·4
„ III.,	79,376	67,310	84·6	**BOOK-KEEPING.**			
„ IV.,	66,011	51,518	78·7	Class V.,	10,683	7,488	70·4
„ V.,	51,379	46,588	70·4	„ V.,	7,011	4,985	63·3
„ VI.,	34,778	25,827	74·5	„ VI.,	6,607	4,304	84·4
„ VI.,	32,461	24,248	74·7	Total,	24,581	14,964	67·7
Total,	416,632	363,816	82·4				
SPELLING.				**NEEDLEWORK.**			
Class I.,	82,643	79,619	87·5	Class II.,	46,850	36,768	88·6
„ II.,	83,284	71,465	85·9	„ III.,	39,276	34,621	86·1
„ III.,	79,376	59,743	75·8	„ IV.,	32,772	28,153	89·7
„ IV.,	66,011	48,126	73·3	„ V.,	23,844	23,180	91·8
„ V.,	61,379	41,972	68·1	„ V.,	17,220	16,313	94·9
„ VI.,	34,778	30,704	88·3	„ VI.,	14,818	13,744	89·0
„ VI.,	32,461	23,161	88·6	Total,	187,782	153,450	89·7
Total,	433,637	366,273	82·7				

TABLE G.

The following table shows the number of pupils examined in Music, Drawing, and Kindergarten, the number of passes, and the per-centages of passes to the number examined :—

		Number Examined.			Number of Passes.			Per-centage.		
		Boys.	Girls.	Total.	Boys.	Girls.	Total.	Boys.	Girls.	Total.
VOCAL MUSIC.										
Class II.		4,621	6,230	14,631	8,573	8,713	18,686	84.7	83.7	88.7
„ III.		6,152	10,716	15,574	4,448	8,176	13,948	80.1	88.4	87.7
„ IV.		4,132	6,283	13,734	3,707	8,133	11,808	83.7	87.3	88.3
„ V.		3,037	6,717	8,744	2,673	5,333	8,308	82.6	88.3	88.7
„ V.		1,805	6,710	8,703	1,713	4,231	5,845	88.1	88.7	88.8
„ V.		1,383	5,057	8,880	1,082	4,028	5,131	85.0	88.4	88.9
Total.		33,846	46,833	68,373	17,489	40,491	67,980	84.3	88.2	88.9
INSTRUMENTAL MUSIC.										
Class V.		1	918	813	2	810	813	1870	87.3	87.1
„ V.		—	238	238	—	8,17	817	—	83.1	83.4
„ VI.		—	467	467	—	433	433	—	83.6	83.0
Total.		1	885	907	8	850	883	1830	88.9	89.9
DRAWING.										
Class III.		7,732	8,378	77,135	6,237	7,438	13,685	88.7	77.3	78.9
„ IV.		7,387	8,307	18,541	4,873	8,618	13,388	83.1	77.3	77.1
„ V.		6,132	6,444	11,874	4,836	4,838	9,383	73.4	75.3	77.3
„ V.		3,747	4,631	8,388	3,480	8,883	4,343	83.9	80.3	83.1
„ VI.		8,633	6,887	9,089	3,385	4,883	7,434	81.7	83.8	83.3
Total.		37,684	34,633	68,618	23,830	37,371	49,071	83.1	78.8	78.3
KINDERGARTEN.										
Infants:		10,663	14,887	25,170	8,943	16,163	24,097	84.2	88.7	88.7
Class I.		3,843	4,683	7,948	3,847	4,873	7,383	88.3	87.3	87.1
„ II.		1,333	1,483	8,766	1,383	1,374	3,887	98.0	88.4	88.3
„ III.		160	89	341	143	88	230	88.4	83.9	88.1
Total.		14,973	31,344	68,117	14,830	33,434	84,704	88.0	88.9	88.1

STATEMENT OF ACCOUNT

FROM

1st APRIL, 1894, TO 31st MARCH, 1895,

SHOWING THE FUNDS AT THE DISPOSAL

OF

THE COMMISSIONERS

OF

NATIONAL EDUCATION, IRELAND,

AND HOW THESE FUNDS HAVE BEEN DISTRIBUTED.

The following STATEMENT of ACCOUNT will show the FUNDS at
the disposal of the COMMISSIONERS in 1894-95, and how they
have been distributed :—

	£	s.	d.
The balance on 1st April, 1894, ...	32,679	19	0
Parliamentary Grant for 1894-95, . . .	1,059,792	0	0
Model Schools:—			
School Fees received from Pupils attending Model Schools, a portion of which (£961 10s. 9d.) is included in the payments made by the Commissioners to the Teachers of these Schools, and the remainder (£2,001 18s. 0d.) is appropriated in aid of the Vote, ...	2,963	9	8
Agricultural Establishments :—			
Amount received by the Commissioners in Students' Fees and for Sales of the Produce of their Model Farms. These receipts are appropriated in aid of the Vote, viz.			
Albert Establishment (Glasnevin):			
Students' Fees, . £507 0 0			
Farm Produce, . £2,708 5 10			
———— £3,215 5 10			
Munster Establishment, Cork :			
Students' Fees, . £508 18 0			
Farm Produce, . £1,222 1 1			
———— £1,730 19 1	4,946	4	11
Book and School Apparatus Department :—			
Net Amount received for Books and other School Requisites sold to National Schools, appropriated in aid of the Vote, ...	31,835	18	10
Miscellaneous Receipts in aid of vote, . . .	268	13	9
Private Contribution Fund :—			
Dividends on Legacies and Donations (private contributions) invested in Government Securities, . .	362	19	3
Income Tax deductions, payable to Inland Revenue Department, ...	1,164	0	11
Sundry repayments of moneys due to the account of the vote of previous year (1893-94), ...	501	6	7
Local Taxation—Customs and Excise, . . .	78,000	0	0
Rates Contributions Account :—			
Contributions from Rates by the Guardians of Poor Law Unions in aid of Results Fees to Teachers of National Schools, ...	94,855	0	0
Stoppages from Quarterly Salaries of Teachers of one-fourth Premiums for Pensions, under Act 42 & 43 Vic., c. 74, 1879, ...	2,826	11	6
Premium of Insurance (North British and Mercantile Insurance Company), ...	1,077	18	3
Deposits by Students, ...	76	0	0
Carried forward, . .	1,287,279	15	11

The EXPENDITURE during the year was as follows:—

	£ s. d.	£ s. d.
OFFICE IN DUBLIN:		
Salaries and Wages,	25,770 6 11	
Travelling Expenses,	476 8 1	
Legal Expenses,	371 8 9	
Rent,	106 3 1	
Incidental Expenses,	175 5 2	27,299 11 5
INSPECTION:		
Salaries,	29,306 9 8	
Travelling and Personal Allowances,	12,114 4 6	41,420 7 2
TRAINING:		
Marlborough-street Training College,	8,410 7 10	
Training Colleges, under local management,	25,645 8 7	38,055 11 5
MODEL SCHOOLS:		
Central,	*4,193 5 11	
Metropolitan, District, and Minor,	*25,528 2 11	
Retiring Gratuities to Model School Teachers,	—	
Irish Education Act Grant (1892),	3,925 15 10	33,647 4 8
ORDINARY NATIONAL SCHOOLS:		
Principal and Assistant Teachers— Salaries, £458,289 12s. 8d., Results, £219,608 18s. 9d., Irish Education Act (1892), Grant, £205,391 13s. 11d.,	1876,422 3 1	
Workmistresses,	10,793 18 5	
Good Service Salaries,	872 17 5	
Monitors,	15,745 1 8	
Training Monitors, &c.,	8,862 15 8	
Retiring Gratuities,	38 11 8	
Incidental Expenditure,	56 8 9	
Free Grants of Books and School Requisites,	751 19 9	913,694 17 2
MISCELLANEOUS:		
July Examination Expenses,	718 14 6	
Organising Teachers,	486 0 7	
Commission to Local Postmasters,	165 5 1	1,370 0 2
Carried forward	—	1,055,487 19 0

* Including the portion of the School Fees (see page 13), appropriated towards payment of the Teachers
† Exclusive of £31,431 4s. 9d. from Local Taxation (Customs and Excise) Fund. See page 5.

Statement of Account—*continued.*

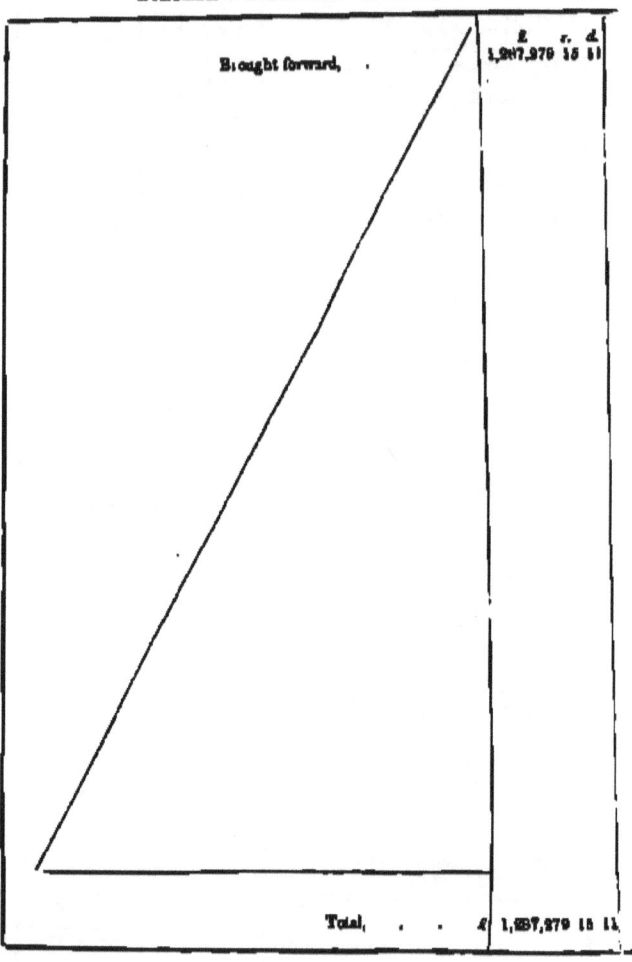

		£ s. d.
Brought forward,	.	1,287,279 15 11
Total,	. . £	1,287,279 15 11

EXPENDITURE during the year—*continued.*

	£	s.	d	£	s.	d.
Brought forward,	—			1,085,497	12	0
AGRICULTURAL ESTABLISHMENTS:						
General Superintendence and Inspection,	395	10	9			
Albert Agricultural Training Institution,	3,698	19	7			
„ Farms and Gardens,	2,915	3	3			
Munster Agricultural Training Institution,	1,008	3	4			
„ Farm,	1,765	0	9			
Agricultural Schools,	272	2	11			
„ Gardens,	85	19	6			
„ Classes,	208	4	4			
Experiments on the Potato,	8	5	4			
				9,839	19	9
BOOK AND SCHOOL APPARATUS DEPARTMENT:						
Purchase of Books and other requisites,	35,322	5	6			
Wages of Packers, &c., &c.,	676	0	0			
				35,998	5	6
Moieties of Rentcharge of Teachers' Residences repaid by Commissioners,	—			8,577	16	10
Private Contribution Fund, Payments to Schools from	—			390	0	0
LOCAL TAXATION (Customs and Excise):						
Paid to Teachers of N. Schools,	61,431	4	5			
„ Guardians of Poor Law Unions in aid of Poor Rates,	17,303	18	5			
				78,735	8	10
INCOME TAX:						
Payments to Inland Revenue Department of deductions for Income Tax,	—			1,271	10	1
Payment to Pensions Fund of annuals stopped from Quarterly Salaries of Teachers, under the Act 42 & 43 Vic., c. 74, 1879,	—			9,828	11	0
Insurance Premium paid over to North British and Mercantile Insurance Co.,	—			1,077	18	5
RATES CONTRIBUTIONS ACCOUNT:						
Paid to the Teachers,	—			29,171	12	0
Sundry debits to the Vote for 1893-4,	—			1	3	4
Deposits returned to Students,	—			92	0	0
Balance of Parliamentary Vote of 1893-94 surrendered,	—			2,421	0	4
Balance on 31st March, 1895,			£	35,779	1	6
Total,				£1,287,979	15	11

B.—Summary of Receipts and Expenditure at the Commissioners' Model Agricultural Establishments at Glasnevin and Cork.

Name of Farm.	Receipts.		Expenditure.		
	Farm Produce.	Fees of Pupils.	[illegible]	[illegible]	[illegible]
	£ s. d.	£ s. d.	£ s. d.	£ s. d.	£ s. d.
[illegible]	[illegible]	[illegible]	[illegible]	[illegible]	[illegible]
[illegible]	[illegible]	[illegible]	[illegible]	[illegible]	[illegible]
Total,	[illegible]	[illegible]	[illegible]	[illegible]	[illegible]
[illegible]	—	—	[illegible]	[illegible]	[illegible]
			[illegible]	[illegible]	[illegible]
			[illegible]	[illegible]	[illegible]

F. YOUNG,

Financial Assistant Secretary.

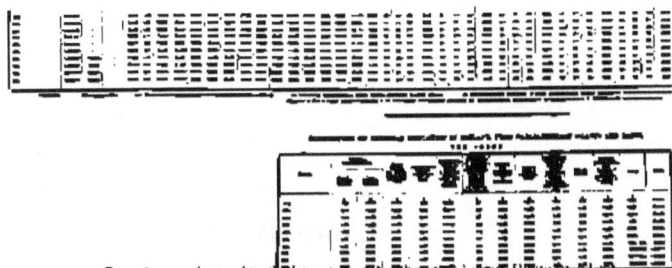

NAMES OF THE COMMISSIONERS

OF

NATIONAL EDUCATION IN IRELAND,

ACCORDING TO THE DATES OF THEIR RESPECTIVE APPOINTMENTS.

	Year of Appointment
Right Hon. Lord Morris,	1868
Edmund G. Dease, Esq., D.L.,	1880
Right Hon. Lord Justice FitzGibbon,	1884
Right Hon. C. T. Redington, D.L. (*Resident Commissioner*, 1894),	1880
W. H. Newell, Esq., LL.D., C.B., J.P.,	1880
J. Malcolm Inglis, Esq., J.P.,	1887
Sir Percy R. Grace, Bart., D.L.,	1888
James Morell, Esq.,	1888
George F. FitzGerald, Esq., F.T.C.D., F.R.S.,	1888
Rev. John W. Stubbs, D.D., S.F.T.C.D.,	1888
Sir Henry Bellingham, Bart., D.L.,	1890
Right Hon. Christopher Palles, Lord Chief Baron,	1890
Rev. Henry Evans, D.D.,	1890
Sir Rowland Blennerhassett, Bart., D.L.,	1891
His Honour Judge Shaw,	1891
Rev. Hamilton B. Wilson, D.D.,	1892
Most Rev. Archbishop Wm. J. Walsh, D.D.,	1895
Most Rev. Archbishop Wm. Conyngham Lord Plunket, D.D.,	1895
Stanley Harrington, Esq., J.P.,	1895
Wm. R. J. Molloy, Esq.,	1895

N.B.—The Appendix to this Report is in course of preparation.

DUBLIN CASTLE,

31st *July*, 1895.

GENTLEMEN,

I have to acknowledge the receipt of your letter of the 30th instant, forwarding, for submission to His Excellency the Lord Lieutenant, the Report of the Commissioners of National Education in Ireland for the year 1894.

I am, Gentlemen,
Your obedient Servant,

(Signed),   D. HARREL.

The Secretaries to the Commissioners
of National Education.

APPENDIX

SIXTY-FIRST REPORT

OF THE

COMMISSIONERS

OF

NATIONAL EDUCATION

IN IRELAND,

FOR THE YEAR 1894.

Presented to both Houses of Parliament by Command of Her Majesty.

PRINTED FOR HER MAJESTY'S STATIONERY OFFICE,
BY ALEXANDER THOM & CO. (LIMITED), ABBEY-STREET.

And to be purchased, either directly or through any Bookseller, from
HODGES, FIGGIS, & CO. (LIMITED), 104, GRAFTON-STREET, DUBLIN; or
EYRE & SPOTTISWOODE, EAST HARDING-STREET, FLEET-STREET, E.C.; or
JOHN MENZIES & CO., 12, HANOVER-STREET, EDINBURGH, and
90, WEST NILE-STREET, GLASGOW.

1895

[C.—7891.]　*Price 1s. 8d.*

CONTENTS.

APPENDICES

TO THE

SIXTY-FIRST REPORT OF THE COMMISSIONERS OF NATIONAL EDUCATION IN IRELAND (1894).

APPENDIX A.

INSPECTORS OF IRISH NATIONAL SCHOOLS.

NATIONAL SCHOOL DISTRICTS AND INSPECTORS IN CHARGE ON 1ST FEBRUARY, 1895.

HEAD INSPECTORS.

Name.	Centres.	District in Charge.	Districts in Charge as Head Inspector.
Newell, W. O'B., M.A.,	Cork,	50a	39, 48, 52, 54, 55, 56, 57, 58, 59, 60.
Considine, P.,	Dublin (42, Waterloo-road).	40a	39, 60, 43, 44, 45, 47, 49, 51, 53, and 2 Training Colleges.
Purser, A.,	Dub'lo (12 Palmerston-road).	37a	19, 23, 28, 70, 33, 30, 37, 41, 30, and 1 Training College.
Sullivan, M., LL.D.,	Galway,	34a	17, 30, 31, 32, 35, 27, 32, 54, 55, 42, 45.
Downing, R.,	Londonderry,	1a	1, 2, 3, 5, 6, 7, 12, 14, 15, 31.
Stronge, S. E., B.A.,	Belfast,	8a	4, 8, 8a, 9, 10, 11, 15, 17, 18, 22, 24.

DISTRICT INSPECTORS.

No. of District.	Official Centre.	Inspectors in Charge.	No. of District.	Official Centre.	Inspectors in Charge.
1	Letterkenny,	Kelly, P.J. (pro tem.)	10	Newtownards,	Beatty, H. M., LL.D.
2	Londonderry,	Alexander, T.J., B.A.	11	Largan,	Degan, C.W., M.A.
3	Coleraine,	M'Neill, J., B.A.	12	Sligo,	O'Connell, J.A., M.A.
4	Ballymena,	Cannon, J. S., B.A. (pro tem.)	13	Enniskillen,	Murphy, J. J.
5	Donegal,	M'Glade, P. (pro tem.)	14	Omagh,	Gee, Henry.
6	Strabane,	Brown, W.J., M.A.	15	Dungannon,	Dewar, R. P., M.A.
7 {	Magherafelt, Castlederrick, (pro tem.)	Warner, J. M'K., B.A.	16	Armagh,	Fitzpatrick, P. (pro tem.)
			17	Downpatrick,	Skeffington, J. D., LL.B.
8	Belfast, North,	Dalton, J. P., M.A.	18	Monaghan,	Worsley, H., B.A.
8a	Carrickfergus,	M'Elwaine, A.J.m.a.	19	Newry,	Ross, J., M.A.
9	Belfast, South,	Fallow, Wm., B.A.	20	Ballina,	Semple, J., B.A. (pro tem.)

B

Appendix A.

List of Inspectors of National Schools.

DISTRICT INSPECTORS—*continued.*

No. of District	Official Centre	Inspectors in Charge	No. of District	Official Centre	Inspectors in Charge
21	Ballaghaderreen,	O'Riordan J., B.A.	42	Gort,	M'Allister, J., B.A. (pro tem.)
22	Boyle,	Lehane, D., B.A.	43	Templemore,	Nicholls, W.
23	Cavan,	M'Clintock, W. J., M.A.	44	Athy,	M'Enery, D.T., B.A. (pro tem.)
24	Bailieborough,	Roycroft, J. O., B.A. (pro tem.)	45	Ennis,	Regan, J. P.
25	Dundalk,	Steele, J., LL.D.	46	Tipperary,	Craig, Jmes, B.A.
26	Westport,	Nowell, P.	47	Kilkenny,	Shannon, P.
27	Roscommon,	Codrington, A. J. (pro tem.)	48	Youghal,	Connolly, W. R., B.A.
28	Longford,	O'Connor, T. P., B.A. (pro tem.)	49	Waterford,	Morgan, A. P., B.A.
29	Trim,	Moran, John, LL.D.	50	Wexford,	MacMillan, W.
30	Dublin, North,	Hardley, P.	51	Limerick,	Dinneen, O., B.A.
31	Ballinasloe	Chambers, J., B.A.	52	Rathkeale,	Dukie, J., B.A.
32	Tuam,	O'Reilly, L.	53	Clonmel,	Smith, O.
33	Mullingar,	M'Mahon, J (pro tem.)	54	Tralee,	Coyne, J. A., B.A. (pro tem.)
34	Galway,	Welply, W. H., B.A. (pro tem.)	55	Millstreet,	Fitzgerald, P. J. (pro tem.)
35	Ballinasloe,	Keily, J., B.A. (pro tem.)	56	Mallow,	Byrne, J. J., B.A.
36	Parsonstown,	Aikman, S.	57	Killarney,	Cronin, E. S., B.A.
37	Dublin, No. 6,	Hanlon, W. P., B.A.	58	Bantry,	Hughes, R. W., B.A. (pro tem.)
38	Listowel,	Tobin, J. H., B.A. (pro tem.)	59	Dunmanway,	Daly, Louis, B.A. (pro tem.)
40	Dublin, South,	Reeves, John.	60	Cork,	Kennan, M., B.A.
41	Portarlington,	Brown, W. A., B.A.			

Inspectors to whom Districts are not yet assigned.	Inspectors' Assistants.	Stations.
Young, E., B.A.	Robertson, William	Derry.
Lyons, J. P. D., B.A.	Clements, William T.,	Belfast.
FitzGerald, D. P., B.A.	O'Sullivan, Michael,	Cork.
Macmillan, W., jun., B.A.	Bentley, William, B.A.,	Dublin.
Benson, E. T.	Bentley, Charles,	Clonmel.
Mahon, J. O.	Smith, John,	Galway.
	Martin, Thomas,	Tuam.
	Seaton, L. J.,	Kilkenny.
	Hanna, P. J.,	Belfast.
	Little, R. J.,	Tralee.

AGRICULTURAL SUPERINTENDENT,
Thomas Carroll, Esq., M.R.I.A.

APPENDIX B.

RETURN, showing the Population (Census 1891) and the Religious Profession of the Inhabitants of the 118 Boroughs, Towns, and Townships to which Compulsory Education Clauses of the Irish Education Act, 1892, apply.

Appendix B.

City, Town, &c.	Total Population	Roman Catholic	PROTESTANTS				
			Total Protestants	E.C.	Pres.	Meth.	Others
*†Antrim	1,285	171	1,114	488	567	53	48
Ardee	2,057	1,930	127	118	8	1	—
†Arklow	4,179	3,346	837	772	13	47	—
†Armagh	7,438	3,568	3,930	3,584	588	278	90
*†Athlone	6,743	5,530	1,211	1,520	148	147	71
Athy	4,530	4,145	391	321	44	62	14
*†Aughnacloy	1,119	457	662	338	143	81	8
†Bagnalstown	1,830	1,703	213	183	13	8	13
†Balbriggan	2,913	2,355	338	307	5	3	13
Ballina	4,846	4,333	533	308	138	87	10
†Ballinasloe	4,642	4,344	488	371	76	33	3
Ballybay	1,378	878	348	348	316	33	18
*†Ballymena	8,856	1,493	7,388	1,719	4,730	167	493
*(†Ballymoney	2,873	713	2,865	673	1,460	33	57
†Ballyshannon	2,473	1,933	484	388	104	67	1
†Banbridge	4,901	1,115	3,783	1,864	1,638	135	188
Bandon	3,488	3,620	848	673	48	143	57
*†Bangor	3,904	277	3,687	1,181	2,064	346	107
*†Belfast	255,350	67,378	188,673	73,853	97,534	18,747	13,509
*†Belturbet	1,873	1,448	512	338	42	88	1
*†Blackrock	8,448	4,388	8,014	4,887	188	369	844
†Boyle	3,434	3,124	388	377	88	17	17
†Bray	6,488	4,848	1,838	1,604	373	78	68
†Callan	3,373	1,888	85	84	—	—	1
Carlow	6,619	4,746	871	788	87	84	84
*†Carrickfergus	8,933	838	8,118	1,783	4,981	608	1,143
*†Carrickmacross	1,779	1,838	278	138	36	71	8
†Carrick-on-Suir	6,848	8,688	78	68	3	1	10
Cashel	3,818	3,388	138	133	8	8	1

* In the # cases marked thus (*) the School Attendance Committees are enforcing the Act.

† In the # cases marked thus (†) School Attendance Committees have been appointed.

Appendix B.   RETURN, showing the Population (Census 1891), &c.—continued.

Cıty, Town, &c.	Total Population.	Roman Catholics.	Total Protestants.	Protestants. E.C.	Pres.	Meth.	Others.
Castlebar,	3,558	3,231	327	228	27	14	1
*†Castleisland,	1,731	1,370	641	628	299	18	16
*†Cavan,	3,088	2,530	578	480	19	63	19
*†Clonakilty,	3,221	2,778	443	234	91	132	9
†Clones,	2,038	1,148	871	604	134	117	13
†Clonmel,	8,480	7,606	880	718	8	65	16
†Clontarf,	5,394	2,836	2,558	1,533	288	711	142
*†Coleraine,	6,815	1,290	5,560	3,531	1,635	196	333
*†Cookstown,	3,841	1,602	2,238	1,028	605	51	76
†Coothill,	1,553	1,171	452	281	62	46	16
Cork,	75,345	64,551	10,794	8,650	768	827	548
*†Dalkey,	2,197	1,234	963	758	83	63	36
*†Downpatrick,	3,153	1,343	1,530	880	480	90	132
Drogheda,	11,873	10,825	957	643	129	114	21
†Dromore,	2,330	630	1,050	635	603	187	534
†Dromconrath, Clonliffe, and Oldcastle,	7,634	3,113	5,111	1,488	189	567	143
†Dublin City,	245,001	201,013	63,583	35,126	5,463	1,708	2,559
Dundalk,	12,449	10,307	2,163	1,642	463	101	33
*†Dungannon,	3,518	1,668	1,834	1,118	614	102	63
Dungarvan,	4,888	4,311	183	83	3	33	1
*†Ennis,	6,082	3,187	283	204	63	8	6
†Enniscorthy,	5,843	4,133	853	420	48	80	8
*†Enniskillen,	6,870	3,846	3,873	2,044	188	263	63
Fermoy,	7,480	4,841	1,845	1,376	173	83	14
†Wexford,	1,807	1,830	78	78	1	—	—
†Galway,	13,880	18,374	1,488	983	303	115	42
*†Oxford,	1,578	648	737	464	370	33	3
†Gorey,	6,318	3,784	618	583	6	18	3
Granard,	1,804	1,780	181	183	1	—	—
*†Holywood,	3,248	828	5,834	1,148	3,362	184	373
†Brady,	1,430	880	430	313	803	1	8
†Kells,	2,877	3,713	811	179	33	1	3
Kilkenny,	11,048	9,838	1,162	1,033	63	46	33
Killarney,	5,510	4,938	323	188	11	13	8
*†Killiney and Ballybrack,	2,840	1,838	884	718	16	3	67
Kilrush,	4,083	3,871	194	163	4	33	1
†Kingstown,	17,353	11,743	5,843	4,833	873	135	388

RETURN, showing the Population (Census 1891), &c.—*continued.* Appendix B

City, Town, &c.	Total Population.	Roman Catholics.	Protestants.				
			Total Protestants.	E.C.	Pres.	Meth.	Others
†Kinsale, · · ·	4,695	3,603	1,122	639	61	108	108
*†Lurgan, · · ·	4,837	1,753	3,089	609	1,564	163	609
†Letterkenny, · ·	2,230	1,608	608	627	808	7	61
†Limavady, · · ·	2,700	863	1,811	673	861	60	70
Limerick, · · ·	37,155	32,664	4,361	3,364	315	351	321
*†Lisburn, · · ·	12,250	1,657	8,862	3,605	2,771	365	603
Lismore, · · ·	1,603	1,408	194	163	81	3	8
Listowel, · · ·	3,605	3,418	138	114	11	8	·
*†Londonderry, · ·	33,200	18,940	14,860	6,631	7,815	628	883
*†Longford, · · ·	2,823	2,153	685	603	67	67	6
†Loughrea, · · ·	2,814	2,762	77	67	—	5	—
*†Lurgan, · · ·	11,650	3,865	7,864	4,360	1,784	464	360
*†Mallow, · · ·	4,653	3,874	862	644	27	23	3
†Maryborough, · ·	3,803	2,377	426	366	13	66	5
Middleton, · ·	3,540	3,662	354	343	9	8	8
Monaghan, · ·	3,203	2,030	533	456	363	34	17
†Mountmellick, ·	3,863	3,140	463	663	63	65	68
Mullingar, · ·	4,523	4,433	360	773	65	63	8
†Naas, · · ·	3,726	3,265	460	364	61	6	31
*†Navan, · · ·	3,635	3,632	351	660	19	8	8
Nenagh, · · ·	4,722	4,433	363	363	17	5	8
†Newbridge, · ·	3,297	2,018	1,259	804	408	31	27
†New Kilmainham, ·	8,613	4,443	8,313	1,873	60	116	60
†New Ross, · · ·	6,347	4,656	353	363	6	63	63
†Newry, · · ·	12,530	6,915	4,146	3,144	1,653	364	316
*†Newtownards, ·	9,197	863	8,362	1,367	4,843	363	120
†Omagh, · · ·	4,603	2,306	1,603	363	561	163	60
†Portarlington, ·	4,613	3,466	767	680	70	60	13
†Pembroke Township,	24,360	14,616	9,734	7,473	1,233	603	463
*†Portadown, · ·	3,663	1,363	6,841	4,663	1,770	1,166	1.63
*†Portrush, · · ·	1,663	184	1,471	773	623	163	60
*†Queenstown, · ·	8,603	7,361	1,641	1,663	163	63	163
*†Rathkeale, · ·	2,672	2,697	116	85	19	13	1
†Rathmines and Rathgar,	27,760	13,681	14,913	12,763	1,665	561	3,873
†Roscommon, · ·	1,663	1,603	163	163	17	13	3
*†Rathkeale, · ·	6,563	3,766	674	363	17	173	19
Sligo, · · ·	10,574	3,663	1,363	1,633	273	313	137

RETURN, showing the Population (Census 1891), &c.—*continued.*

City, Town, &c.	Total Population	Roman Catholics	PROTESTANTS.				
			Total Protestants.	E.C.	Pres.	Meth.	Others.
Strabane, . . .	6,913	2,514	1,469	733	462	49	15
Tandragee, . . .	1,444	618	1,653	535	841	101	65
Templemore. . .	2,183	1,693	400	307	13	63	9
Thurles, . . .	4,911	4,500	119	100	1	8	1
Tipperary. . .	8,481	5,254	737	462	42	34	9
Tralee, . . .	9,518	8,508	930	794	42	112	28
Trim, . . .	1,571	1,494	107	82	6	14	8
Tuam, . . .	3,913	3,554	163	164	1	—	3
Tullamore, . . .	4,639	4,196	516	269	18	162	4
Warrenpoint, . . .	1,970	1,959	911	645	237	79	27
Waterford, . . .	20,393	18,390	3,013	2,402	135	188	393
Westport, . . .	4,078	3,793	285	279	43	38	14
Wexford, . . .	11,465	10,397	735	670	22	116	34
Wicklow, . . .	3,273	2,637	618	543	22	69	12
Youghal . . .	4,357	3,863	630	335	5	40	16
Totals, . . .	1,040,884	651,729	444,405	343,037	147,392	29,628	27,524

APPENDIX C.

RETURNS as to TRAINING COLLEGES. GENERAL REPORTS OF INSPECTORS, &c.

MARLBOROUGH-STREET TRAINING COLLEGE.

(For Male and Female Teachers).

Managers.—The Commissioners of National Education.

STAFF IN SESSION 1893–94.

Principal, Male Department,	J. Corbett, Esq., LL.D., F.G.S.
Principal, Female Department,	Thomas H. Teegan, Esq.
Vice-Principal, Male Department,	L. J. Ryan, Esq.
Vice-Principal, Female Department,	Miss Johnston.

PROFESSORS.

Geometry, Trigonometry, Geography, History, Science and Art of Education, Mechanics, Physics, Experimental Physics, and English Literature.	J. Corbett, Esq., LL.D., F.G.S. J. J. Doherty, Esq., LL.D., F.G.S.
Arithmetic, Algebra, Book-keeping, . .	T. H. Teegan, Esq.
Lesson Books, English Composition, English Grammar, Spelling, and Dictation.	G. Peyton, Esq., B.A.

SUPPLEMENTAL

Classics,	F. W. C. Robertson, Esq., M.A.
French,	J. W. Bacon, Esq., B.A.
Reading,	James Edgar, Esq., and Miss Mary O'Hea.
Drawing,	J. P. Moran, Esq., Miss Harpur.
Handicraft,	Mr. J. Johnston.
Needlework,	Mrs. Stoddart, Miss Kearney.
Domestic Economy and Hygiene,	Miss Felham.
Vocal Music,	Brendan Rogers, Esq., and Miss M'Kenna.
Instrumental Music—Piano and Harmonium,	Miss Gordon.
Practical Cookery,	Miss Devine.
Assistant to Vice-Principal,	Mr. E. Doyle.
Training Assistant, Male Department,	Mr. John Robinson.
Training Assistants, Female Department,	Misses Downey, Moore, and Mooney.
Matron, Male Department,	Mrs. Anderson.
Matron, Female Department,	Miss M'Carthy.
Assistant Matron, do.,	Miss Devine.
Medical Attendant,	T. Nedley, Esq., M.D.
Dentist,	A. J. Bradshaw, Esq.

St. Patrick's Training College, Drumcondra.
(For Male Teachers).

Manager.—His Grace The Most Rev. W. J. Walsh, D.D., Archbishop of Dublin.

Staff in Session, 1893-94.

Principal,	Very Rev. Peter Byrne, C.M.
Vice-Principal,	Rev. G. Campbell, C.M.
Chaplain,	Rev. W. O'Sullivan, C.M.

Professors.

English Language and Literature,	Henry Bedford, Esq., M.A., Cantab.
Mathematics, Mechanics,	Henry M'Weeney, Esq., B.A., and J.P. Browne, Esq.
Grammar, Geography, General History, Composition, Latin, Lesson Books,	Daniel Croly, Esq., M.A.
Methods of Teaching, School Organisation, History of Education, Arithmetic, Book-keeping, Mensuration,	Stephen FitzPatrick, Esq., First of First Class Teachers.

Supplemental.

Experimental Physics,	Very Rev. Gerald Canon Molloy, D.D., F.R.U.I.; Henry M'Weeney, Esq., B.A., Assistant Professor.
Hygiene,	John Campbell, Esq., A.B., M.B., T.C.D., F.R.U.I., M.R.I.A.
Agriculture,	Edward Carroll, Esq.
Music,	Joseph Seymour, Esq., and T. Logier, Esq.
French,	Mons. Cadic de la Champignonnerie.
Drawing,	R. Walsh, Esq.
Reading,	J. F. Taylor, Esq., Q.C.
Medical Attendant,	Charles Coppinger, Esq., M.D., F.R.C.S.I., M.R.C.P.I.

OUR LADY OF MERCY TRAINING COLLEGE, BAGGOT-STREET.
(For Female Teachers).

Manager.—His Grace The Most Rev. W. J. WALSH, D.D., Archbishop of Dublin.

STAFF IN SESSION, 1893–94.

Principal,	.	Mrs. M. L. Keenan.
Vice-Principal,	.	Mrs. M. G. Whelan.
Chaplain,	.	Clergyman from St. Andrew's, Westland Row.

PROFESSORS.

English Literature and Elocution, Hygiene, and Botany.	William Magennis, Esq., M.A., B.L.
Mathematics and Arithmetic,	John Healy, Esq., B.A.
Geography, Penmanship, Reading, General History.	Miss Mary Daly, Certificated First Class Teacher.
Methods of Teaching, School Organisation, History of Education, and Grammar.	Miss Anne Phelan, Certificated First of First Class Teacher.

SUPPLEMENTAL

Physics, .	Very Rev. Gerald Canon Molloy, D.D., F.R.U.I.; John Healy, Esq., M.A., *Locum tenens.*
Modern Languages. .	Mrs. Nolan, Convent National Schools, Baggot-street.
Instrumental Music, Organ and Harmonium.	Mrs. Mulhern, do.
Instrumental Music, .	Mrs. Brady, do.
Instrumental Music (Piano), and Tonic Sol-fa.	Mrs. M'Nevin, do.
Needlework, Sewing Machine, &c.,	Mrs. Nolan, do.
Drawing and Painting, .	Mrs. Kennedy, do.
Practical Cookery and Domestic Economy.	Miss M'Carthy, Certificated South Kensington.
Matron,	Mrs. Kavanagh.
Medical Attendant, .	Christopher J. Nixon, M.D., LL.D., F.R.Q.C.P.I., L.R.C.S.I.

CHURCH OF IRELAND TRAINING COLLEGE, KILDARE-PLACE.
(For Male and Female Teachers).

Manager.—His Grace The Right Hon. and Most Rev. Lord PLUNKET, Archbishop of Dublin.

STAFF IN SESSION, 1893–94.

Principal,	.	.	Rev. H. Kingsmill Moore, M.A., Ball. Coll. Oxon.
Vice-Principal,	.	.	Miss Williams.
Chaplain,	.	.	Rev. H. Kingsmill Moore, M.A., &c.
Assistant, Female Department,	.		Miss Smith.

PROFESSORS.

Mathematical and Physical Sciences,	James C. Rea, Esq., M.A., B.U.I., Math. Sch. Queen's Coll., Belfast.
Experimental Physics,	Rev. J. Smith, M.A., T.C.D.
English Language and Literature,	Laurence E. Steele, Esq., M.A., B.L.
General History, Geography, Grammar, Drawing, and Agriculture,	John Cooke, Esq., M.A., T.C.D.
Methods of Teaching, School Organization, History of Education,	Jeremiah Henley, Esq., First of First Class Teacher.

SUPPLEMENTAL.

Vocal Music,	Miss Smith.
Instrumental Music,	Charles Grandison, Esq., and Miss Grandison.
Needlework,	Miss R. Heron.
Practical Cookery,	Miss Todd, Certificated by Northern Union School of Cookery, England.
Matron, Male Department,	Mrs. Henly.
Matron, Female Department,	Miss Whiter.
Clerk and Accountant,	Mr. G. Earls.
Medical Attendant and Lecturer on Hygiene,	Henry T. Bewley, Esq., M.B., M.A., &c.
Drill Instructor,	Sergeant Ingram.

DE LA SALLE TRAINING COLLEGE, NEWTOWN HOUSE, WATERFORD.

(For Male Teachers).

Manager, The Most Reverend R. A. Sheehan, D.D., Bishop of Waterford and Lismore.

STAFF IN SESSION, 1893-94.

Principal,	Rev. Brother Thomas B. Kane, M.A., B.E., T.C.D.
Vice-Principal,	Rev. Brother Attall J. Gentil.
Chaplain,	Rev. Thomas Mockler.

PROFESSORS.

Method of Teaching, School Organization, History of Education.	Rev. Brother Thomas R. Kane.
English Literature, Lesson Books, Grammar.	Rev. Brother Potamian Michael P. O'Reilly.
Algebra, Geometry, Mensuration, and Trigonometry, and Natural Philosophy.	Rev. Brother Attall J. Gentil.

SUPPLEMENTAL.

Algebra, Arithmetic, and Drawing,	Rev. Brother Bart. J. Trubert.
Agriculture,	Rev. Brother Ananias J. O'Brien.
Method, Mechanics and Bookkeeping,	Hugh Kerr, Esq.
Music,	Edward Comerford.
Prefect of Discipline,	Rev. Brother Emlolan Moore.
Medical Attendant,	Thomas J. Tobin, Esq., M.D.

"ST. PATRICK'S" TRAINING COLLEGE.

	Passes.									
	First of First Class.		Second of First Class.		Second Class.		Third Class.		Total.	
Persons of Common answered										
Total										

Analysis of the Attainments at the July Examinations of 1893 and 1894—continued.

"OUR LADY OF MERCY" TRAINING COLLEGE.

	Papers									
	Holy of Christ Days		Account of First Class		Second Class		Third Class		Total	
	1893	1894	1893	1894	1893	1894	1893	1894	1893	1894
Number of Students examined,	.	.								
Attainments in per cent, or over,										
at least some 50 per cent,	.	.								
	.	.								
	.	.								
under 40 per cent,	.	.								
Total,	.	.								

Analysis of the Answering at the July Examinations of 1893 and 1894—continued.

"CHURCH OF IRELAND" TRAINING COLLEGE.

ANALYSIS of ATTENDANCE at the JULY EXAMINATIONS of 1893 and 1894—continued.

"DE LA SALLE" TRAINING COLLEGE.

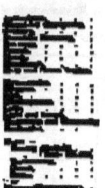

MARLBOROUGH-STREET TRAINING COLLEGE, DUBLIN.

Appendix C.
Reports on
Training
Colleges.

Mr. Peter
Connellan,
Head
Inspector.

Mr. CONNELLAN, Head Inspector.

Dublin, 15th June, 1895.

Classification
of
Queen's
Scholars.

GENTLEMEN,—I beg to submit the following report on the Marlborough-street Training College for the year ended 31st August, 1894.

As in all previous years, the Queen's Scholars consisted of those attending for a one year's course of training and those attending for a course of two years. For College purposes they are divided into First, Second, and Third Divisions. The First Division comprises teachers who rank as second class teachers before they come up to training, and who are candidates for first class. The Second Division are candidates for second class, and have completed their course of training, whether of one or two years. The Third Division are those students who have come up for a two years' course of training, and who have completed their first year. These are examined in July on papers set for candidates for third class.

Before Christmas every year there is a preliminary examination held by the Head and District Inspectors in charge of each College, with the view of ascertaining what candidates are eligible for promotion to first and second classes respectively. This examination was held by Mr. Browne, D.I. and me in last December.

The test examination in Practical Teaching—of which a written examination on Methods of Teaching, the Rules of the Commissioners, and School Accounts formed a part—was begun by us on 31st May, and continued without interruption until the 11th June. It was conducted precisely on the same lines as that of the previous year.

I commenced with the examination of the Female Queen's Scholars in Practical Cookery, and subjected them, besides, to a written examination on the text book dealing with the subject. The proficiency exhibited was excellent, and reflects great credit on their teacher, Miss Devine.

I then proceeded to examine the students of First and Second Divisions in Practical Teaching, and concluded by examining the students of Third Division in Reading and explanation of the matter and language of what they read.

The scholars in First Division, consisting of those teachers already highly classed who come up admittedly with the view of obtaining promotion in classification, enter the College with considerable practical experience, and, so far as the art of teaching is concerned, the main objects of the Professors in their regard must necessarily be to direct them in the use of the information and experience they have already acquired.

I am able to report favourably on the progress made in the art of teaching during the past year. This subject, which should form the principal feature of a training college, evidently received more attention during the past year than it did in 1893. In proof of this statement, I may mention that the average of marks which were assigned for teaching skill was slightly above the average marks obtained by the same students at the July examinations on their whole course. This is very satisfactory, as it shows that the college is becoming what every training college should be, namely, a place for training young persons to become useful teachers, and not a mere grinding school for securing promotion in classification. I believe every succeeding year will show an advancement in this direction.

In assigning marks at the "test examination" I took the following points into consideration :—(1) Skill in conveying instruction, (2) language employed, (3) power of maintaining discipline and of keeping up the pupils' attention, (4) the prepared notes of lessons, and the closeness with which they were followed, and (5) the criticisms which the students wrote on the lessons taught by their fellow students. I did not attach much value to these criticisms as they were nearly all of a stereotyped character.

It seems very desirable that skill in teaching should enter into the classification of the Queen's Scholars. The official value at present attaching to practical skill is that it constitutes one of the elements in determining, after probation, the claim of the Queen's Scholar to the training diploma. But no money value is attached to the diploma so far as the teacher is concerned, and hence the stimulus to practical efficiency in school management is so far defective in the existing arrangements.

A very interesting, and, I believe, a very useful part of our duties was the examination of the Third Division students in reading and explanation. The students acquitted themselves very fairly in this essential subject. I was surprised, however, to find that few of the students were accustomed to consult a dictionary, and none of those to whom I applied the test could show a class how to use it.

There was a great improvement in the prepared notes of lessons in one respect, namely, there was a much greater variety in the subjects selected, and they embraced subjects of a much more interesting character than in former years. The skill displayed in teaching the unprepared subjects was materially inferior to that shown in teaching the prepared lessons, but it was gratifying to see that the notes had been carefully prepared and were closely followed.

I feel it my duty to report that, in my opinion, the one great defect in this training college is the inferior character of some of the practising schools in which the students are supposed to see models for guidance and imitation.

No change took place in the professorial staff during the period covered by this report. Some changes have taken place since, which will be referred to in the report for 1894–5.

The residences in connection with the College are in a satisfactory state. The dormitories are well ventilated and suitably furnished.

I am satisfied that every attention is paid to the comforts of the students, and I am aware from inquiries in the country districts in which students previously trained have found employment, that this attention is gratefully appreciated by them.

C

Appendix C.
Reports on
Training
Colleges.

Mr. Peter
Connellan,
Head
Inspector.

As I have no authority to be present at any of the lectures given by the Professors, or at any of the model lessons given by the teachers of the different practising schools, I feel myself debarred from offering suggestions which I might consider useful. I have to acknowledge the personal courtesy of the Professors, who have frequently invited me to be present at some of their lectures, but under the circumstances I have not felt free to avail myself of their politeness.

The following is a classification of the students at the end of the session, according to religious denominations :—

—	R.C.	E.C.	Pres.	Meth.	Others.	Total.
Males, ...	34	11	39	19	1	98
Females, ...	57	14	57	13	1	142
Total, ...	61	25	29	12	2	167

I have the honour to be, Gentlemen,

Your obedient servant,

PETER CONNELLAN,

Head Inspector.

NOTE.—Owing to the long illness and retirement of my esteemed colleague, Mr. John Browne, District Inspector, this report has been too long delayed. His illness rendered it impossible to have communication or conversation with him on business matters. This will account for the absence of his signature. Before his illness we had agreed on the substance of the Report.

Mr. A. PURSER, Head Inspector, and Mr. W. P. HEADEN, B.A., District Inspector.

Mr. A.
Purser,
Head
Inspector.
Mr. W. P.
Headen,
District
Inspector.

Dublin, 23rd February, 1895.

GENTLEMEN,—We beg to furnish the annual report on the Training Colleges under our inspection. No important change or improvement has been made in the buildings or premises, which continue to be maintained in good order. In the case of the men's colleges a lavatory would be useful, and we believe it is in contemplation to devote to the purpose one or more rooms in St. Patrick's Training College, Drumcondra.

Health and
conduct of
students.

The health of the students in general was good, though a few had to be sent home owing to delicacy.

No complaints of misconduct on the part of the Queen's scholars have been made to us.

Effects
produced by
Colleges.

These colleges have now been in operation for more than ten years, and ought to be producing considerable influence on the system of National education. One effect they certainly have had, and that is, to increase the number of teachers in the higher classes or grades. But

It cannot be too often insisted upon that these colleges are not places for merely "grinding" the students in the courses prescribed for the several grades of teachers, so as to enable them to arrive easily and surely at promotion, especially as there can be no doubt a large proportion of the classed teachers enter the colleges mainly for this purpose. The aim of the college curriculum may be said to be summed up in the *diploma*—therefore the conditions on which the diploma is granted may be said to be the motive that determines the course of training. These conditions are that the teacher shall (1) pass successfully an examination on B Papers, i.e., on those prescribed for Second Class; (2) receive favourable reports from the Professors of his college; (3) teach two lessons satisfactorily in the presence of the Inspectors; and (4) conduct a school, or part of a school, efficiently for at least two years after leaving the college. The first of these is essential, and has for many reasons come to be looked upon as the most important; but plainly the students should come to the college to enable them to satisfy the *fourth condition*—to learn how to teach classes and conduct a school on the most approved method and principles, and the second and third conditions mentioned above are only tests to decide whether this has apparently been fulfilled or not, and the diploma grant fairly earned.

Our teaching-tests remain unaltered. The prepared lesson is taken first, the teacher's notes being before us while he is giving his lesson. The principal faults observable are in making the lessons mere lectures—omitting questions, explanation of difficulties, &c.; or else in taking up the subject in a disconnected, haphazard way, asking the class irrelevant questions, or such as could not be answered from the information imparted by the teacher. Both faults are still common, but the latter less so than formerly. The "notes" are, on the whole, much better used; but the lessons have an air of unreality about them, and the subjects are often not treated as they certainly would be in the school-room. The majority of the students acquit themselves sufficiently well to be passed, and it is only when there is a complete break-down and inability to teach a subject that the student is marked as failing. The unprepared lesson we find of advantage for confirming or correcting our judgment on the first lesson we hear from each Queen's scholar. We do not believe these tests are too severe, and we are conscious that the allowances made for the artificial nature of the lessons err if anything on the side of leniency. There is no doubt the students come up to the work with much more confidence than in the early years of the colleges; and though neglect and violation of common rules of method still occur, they are less frequent and glaring than they used to be. The subject may not be well treated, but as a rule the class is fairly attended to—taught first and questioned afterwards—and the blackboard is fairly utilised. There is still much tendency to begin with definitions and work out the subject from them by means of examples, instead of deducing rules and definitions from examples; and there is a further tendency to deduce rules from *single* examples. The criticisms are still a very weak point, partly, however, because they have to be hastily prepared while the teacher is still suffering from nervousness over the delivery of his own lesson.

The *special Method* papers are rather a matter of common sense than one requiring special study; we cannot say that as a rule they are as well worked as the paper of questions set from the manual.

These are the only tests we apply, and, as stated above, we had reason to be satisfied with the result in most cases.

In addition to these we make it a point to be present at one or more

(margin notes:)
Appendix C.
Reports on Training Colleges.
Mr. A. Purser, Head Inspector, Mr. W. P. Rowan, District Inspector.

Tests applied at examination of students.

Appendix C.
Reports on
Training
Colleges.

Mr. A.
Purser,
Head
Inspector.
Mr. W. P.
Fender,
District
Inspector.

Criticism
lessons.

Kinder-
garten.

Vocal
Music.

Drawing.

criticism lessons, and to visit the practising schools during the time the students are engaged teaching under the superintendence of the Professor of Method and of the permanent staff of these schools. This latter part of the colleges is carefully attended to; a further development of it with increase of time spent by the students in the schools would greatly add to the efficiency and usefulness of the colleges. This implies greater weight and importance being attached to the position of the Professor of Method. The criticism lessons are generally useful in themselves, and good points are frequently brought out and impressed on the Queen's scholars by the Professors. The students appear anxious to avoid unfavourable remarks on the work of their fellows, and hence their criticisms are generally vague and weak.

Kindergarten and Infant School training receive attention in the colleges for women, but not in case of the men. We quite agree with an English Inspector who writes:—" Whatever is true and wise in the Froebelian and Pestalozzian philosophy is in fact applicable to both classes of teachers [i.e. those for infant and senior schools] and to children of all ages. Attempts to treat Kindergarten as a separate institution, having aims and methods of its own, different from those which prevail in other schools, have often in America and Germany proved unsuccessful." These remarks are equally applicable to boys' and girls' schools. Viewed merely in the light of the requirements of the school programme how necessary is it that the teachers should be able to adequately instruct infant classes in ordinary schools. The programme requires infants to be examined "in a course of instruction suitable to their capacity with appropriate exercises: and as infant classes are common in schools under masters as well as under mistresses, male as well as female teachers should fit themselves to give these children suitable instruction.

The Queen's scholars show evidence of careful teaching in Vocal Music. The demand for teachers having a knowledge of music is so general as to render it almost impossible for a non-singer, especially if a woman, to get employment in a school. In the case of Drawing this indirect compulsion does not apply, and it seems unlikely that it ever will. Yet the subject is an important one owing to its great practical utility. We note with pleasure that increased attention is being given to Drawing by the students in all the colleges, but we cannot help feeling that much more is still needed in this direction. The importance of Drawing as a most efficient means of training hand and eye, and as the foundation of all technical education, commends it as a subject that should be taught in every elementary school. Certainly in every school in which a trained teacher is employed, Drawing should rank amongst the ordinary subjects of the school programme. Yet at the last July Examination only a small percentage of the Queen's scholars in their final year of training succeeded in obtaining a certificate of competency to teach Drawing. This is not encouraging. The subject is not taken up by all the students, and is not taken up with sufficient earnestness by any except in the rarest cases. We observe, too, in the matter of Freehand Drawing that many of the students have been allowed to contract what appears to us faulty and erroneous methods. Mechanical aids, such as dividing their pattern into sections which they copy seriatim, are freely used. In fact, the Drawing executed by many students in qualifying for their certificates is worked by plans which an Inspector would not allow the most elementary pupil to employ at a Result Examination. There is a species of drawing to which more attention might be devoted with great general advantage. "It is not the elaborate drawing" Mr. Fitch writes, "which will enable students to pass examinations or to produce finished pictures, but the power of rapidly illustrating, off-hand, with a few broad and effective touches, the structure of a leaf or an animal, the map of a country, the contour of a hill, or the main characteristics of a famous building." This acquirement is one which furnishes the teacher with a power of almost universal application. A rough outline of Ireland, or of their own locality, traced upon the blackboard in the presence of the class will interest the pupils far more, and teach them the features of the country with more permanent effect than the most highly finished map on the Board's list. The same power asserts itself in dealing with Geometry, in treating of any scientific subject, and in setting down clearly and intelligently matter of any kind upon a blackboard. All students might be reasonably expected to acquire a fair degree of facility in sketching off-hand on the blackboard a moderately accurate outline map of Ireland.

The Queen's scholars in the second year of training continue to take up a large number of "extras," and generally with very fair success. We need not further refer to them, as they do not materially differ from those mentioned in former years.

Of technical subjects, Handicraft is still successfully taught in the Church of Ireland College, and Agriculture receives due attention there and in St. Patrick's.

Cookery is taught to female students in training with satisfactory results, so far as we can judge. Considering the number of teachers competent to teach the subject, it is regrettable that Cookery should be taught in so few schools.

Needlework has shown great progress during the last few years. Sewing and knitting are, with few exceptions, very good; and "cutting out" is successfully taught. In each college there is a fine display of finished needlework before the close of the session.

Games, drill, calisthenics, and other useful exercises continue to be practised, and contribute to maintain sound health among the students.

Our intercourse with the College authorities continues on the same friendly footing, and we have to acknowledge the valuable aid and co-operation we always receive from them in the discharge of our duties.

We are, gentlemen,
Your obedient servants,

A. PURSER, Head Inspector.
W. P. HEADEN, District Inspector.

The Secretaries, &c

SPECIAL REPORTS.

"OUR LADY OF MERCY," Baggot-street, Dublin.

This college is in connexion with the Board since 1843, but was founded some years before for the purpose of training Roman Catholic female teachers. It is under the care of the Sisters of Mercy.

One hundred and forty-nine students were in residence, of whom 88 were in the first year and 61 in the second year. Two externs were allowed to attend the classes with the resident students. There is accommodation for 150 Queen's scholars.

Appendix C.

Reports on
Training
Colleges.

Mr. A.
Purser,
Head
Inspector,
Mr. W. P.
Headen,
District
Inspector.

The premises are in good order, but somewhat confined. The Sisters have a large country place at Blackrock, to which the students occasionally resort for recreation.

The large practising school attached to the college, with an average daily attendance of between 800 and 900 children, affords fair means of training the students in the art of teaching.

The Queen's scholars acquitted themselves very well in giving lessons in our presence to selected classes, and in this respect we are glad to be able to report considerable progress during the past year.

The July Examination of the students was fairly successful, though failures were slightly in excess of previous years.

"St. Patrick's," Drumcondra, Dublin.

The college is in connexion with the Board since 1883, but the present site of the college was not acquired until some years later, and the fine buildings now occupied were finished only last year. Besides the ordinary class and lecture rooms, and recreation hall, there is a good library for the use of the students; the Professors also have a well stocked library. It is proposed to fit up a laboratory in the near future. The recreation grounds are extensive. The college is under the care of the Vincentian Fathers.

There were 159 students in residence, of whom 89 were in their second year. The college is certified for 160 Queen's scholars.

The practising school has shown steady growth during the past few years, and will before long be fully adequate for training purposes. It is well conducted under a First Class teacher, and a full staff of suitable assistants.

The Queen's scholars acquitted themselves with moderate success in teaching their classes before us. Their answering at the July Examinations was highly creditable.

"Church of Ireland," Kildare-street, Dublin.

This college is in connexion with the Board since 1864. Considerable additions and improvements have been made almost every year, and the premises are in good order. The dormitories might be made more homelike and comfortable. The men's lecture-room and the library are elegant and artistic apartments fitted up in a very superior manner.

The college as at present constituted was founded to train, in separate apartments, male and female teachers belonging to the late Established Church of Ireland; but it had an earlier existence as the training college in connexion with the Church Education Society, and can claim to be the oldest existing college in the British Islands.

It affords accommodation for 54 men and 78 women. There were in residence 34 men and 66 women, of whom 24 men and 34 women were in their first year.

The practising schools are suitable and afford good models for the students in training. There are three departments—boys', girls', and infants'.

The Queen's scholars taught their lessons before us with much skill, and gave evidence of thoroughly efficient training. They also acquitted themselves well at the July Examination.

A. Purser, Head Inspector.

W. P. Headen, District Inspector.

DE LA SALLE TRAINING COLLEGE.

Appendix C.

Reports on Training Colleges.

Mr. Peter Connellan, Head Inspector. Mr. A. P. Morgan, District Inspector.

Mr. CONNELLAN, Head Inspector.
Mr. A. P. MORGAN, District Inspector.

Dublin, 25th May, 1895.

GENTLEMEN,—In compliance with your instructions we beg to submit our general report for the year ended August, 1894, on the above named Training College for Roman Catholic Male Students at Waterford.

On 16th July last the new college buildings were opened. They are tasteful in appearance, and can compare favourably with any similar institution in the United Kingdom. The situation of the college on the slope of a hill, which rises gradually from Waterford Park, is healthy and picturesque.

Ample accommodation is provided for the increased number of students (120). The large and lofty lecture halls, class rooms, and well ventilated dormitories leave nothing to be desired as regards utility or comfort.

Natural history museums, bathrooms, and a recreation room are included in the buildings, and the grounds have been recently extended by the acquisition of an adjoining field, which will be placed at the disposal of the students for exercise and amusement. No expense has been spared by the College authorities to have the furniture and appliances in every detail in accordance with modern requirements.

The members of the professional staff possess high and varied attainments. No change has taken place in their number during the period covered by this report; but the increase in the number of students will necessitate the employment of at least four additional professors.

The number of students on the College register at the close of the term was 78, of whom 19 had been summoned for one year's course of training, and 59 for a two year's course.

In July last 10 were examined in first class teachers' papers, 44 in second class teachers' papers, and 24 in third class teachers' papers. It is satisfactory to record that of the 78 examined only 2 failed to pass.

The test in practical teaching was conducted by us in the month of June last. It applied to all students undergoing one year's course of training, and to all students who were approaching the completion of their second year of training.

We find that the marks assigned by us on the occasion of this oral test average lower than those obtained by the same students on the papers set at the July examinations in methods of teaching. The discrepancy was greatest in the case of two years' students, many of whom had no experience in teaching previous to their admission to the college.

The Principal makes the strictest inquiry regarding the antecedents of candidates to the two years' course of training with a view to select, as far as possible, those who have shown, or are likely to show ability in teaching.

All students admitted for the two years' course of training were examined by us in reading and explanation. It gives us pleasure to record that the reading was tasteful and the explanation intelligent. The college authorities employ a capable Professor of Elocution, and attach great importance to the benefits derived from his instruction.

In this view they act with commendable discernment, as the students and teachers generally are apt to regard reading as a mechanical art for which they might be permitted to substitute a more ambitious study when they come to a training college.

No improvement has taken place with regard to the school buildings or surroundings of the practising schools. The new practising school which was to be built has not yet been commenced, as legal difficulties have arisen about the site.

The school continues to be efficiently conducted. Ample practice in teaching is afforded to the students by the arrangement that each in turn instructs a class two hours daily for a week at a time.

The farm recently acquired by the conductors is to be utilised for practical illustration of the lectures of the Professor of Agriculture. It is intended that the students shall visit the farm on Wednesdays and Saturdays in each week.

We are, Gentlemen, your obedient servants,

PETER CONNELLAN, Head Inspector,
ARTHUR P. MORGAN, District Inspector,

The Secretaries,
    Education Office.

Mr. P. CONNELLAN, Head Inspector.

Dublin, 23rd March, 1895

GENTLEMEN,—I beg to submit the following report on the group of districts of which I had supervision during the past year.

There has been no change in the boundaries since my last report for year 1893-94.

The following towns continue to be the respective centres of the districts which constitute my circuit:—Trim, Dublin, Templemore, Athy, Tipperary, Kilkenny, Waterford, Limerick, Clonmel.

There are two Inspectors' Assistants attached to this group, who have given valuable assistance during the year.

In addition to the districts mentioned, there is a special district of which I have sole charge, and in the inspection and supervision of which there is no District Inspector associated with me.

The important duties connected with the Training Colleges, Marlborough-street and De La Salle, Waterford, have occupied much of my time. As these duties are well known to the Commissioners, it is unnecessary to specify them, beyond stating that they consisted in examination of Queen's Scholars in the art of Teaching, in examination of the Practising Schools connected with the Colleges, and in frequent special visits.

As only one year has passed since my last report on this circuit was furnished to the Commissioners, there is little, if anything, to record now in the way of change. The districts, the Inspectors in charge of them, and practically the school attendance, are all unchanged. New schools have been taken into connection here and there, but the educational pace of the country remains the same.

The Compulsory Act of 1892 has not yet had any appreciable effect upon the state of education. Owing to causes to which it is unnecessary to make further reference, its application has been so restricted as to render a practical test of its value impossible. And yet, such is the influence of an expected change, although men's notions of it be hazy, that it interferes with even energetic men's work, and justifies idleness to the idle.

The teachers are human, and many of them regard the coming change as fraught with peril to their interests. They are all in favour of compulsory education, but they fear some of the changes that must accompany its application. While the minds of men are unsettled, earnest, calm, systematic work can hardly be expected from them.

The special district assigned to me continues in a very satisfactory state. The teachers are, without exception, intelligent and hard-working. I have never met a body of teachers more ready to adopt an Inspector's suggestions. Discipline is excellent, almost without exception. Efforts to cultivate the intelligence of the pupils characterise all the schools—of course, some to a greater extent than others.

The five Convent Schools in the district are models in every way, and some of them are not, by any means, favourably circumstanced. Townsend-street Convent School is in one of the poorest parts of the city of Dublin; and the space accommodation in Glasthule Convent School is painfully insufficient. Notwithstanding these drawbacks, the proficiency is very creditable in both schools.

As I have stated in previous reports, the classification of the teachers of this district is unusually high.

The following table shows the classification of principals and assistants at the end of the year :—

	MALES.		FEMALES.	
	Principals.	Assistants.	Principals.	Assistants.
Class I. . . .	7	—	7	—
„ I₂ . . .	—	—	3	3
„ II. . . .	5	1	5	3
„ II₂ . . .	—	2	1	—
„ III. . . .	1	1	3	9
„ III₂ . . .	—	3	—	1
	13	7	17	21

This table shows that 58 per cent. of the Principal teachers are in First Class.

Appendix C.

Reports on State of Schools.

Mr. P. Cremylins Head Inspector.

Dublin.

General observations on circuit.

Classification of teachers generally.

In this district there are only seven monitors, while there are fifty-two monitresses. The cause of this marked difference in the supply of monitors has been frequently referred to. It would appear that Dublin must continue to depend on the provinces for its supply of male teachers. In this limited district there were 3,493 pupils examined for Results' Fees during the year.

I now proceed to make a few general observations on the state of education in the different districts of my circuit.

There are seventy-seven Convent schools and seven Monastery schools in the circuit. Of these I have visited forty-three Convent schools and three Monastery schools.

Some of the Convent schools I examined fully, and the rest partly, but sufficiently to enable me to satisfy myself as to the quantity and quality of the work done in them.

Of the Monastery schools visited, I can speak of the discipline only, which was quite satisfactory.

Almost without exception I found the Convent schools in a highly efficient state.

I visited them prepared to judge them, and to criticize them impartially as I should schools taught by ordinary town teachers, and it is gratifying to be able to state that they were prepared for the strictest scrutiny. The conductors desired no lenient treatment. From me they get none. Experience confirms me in the opinion that the Convent schools are, on the whole, the best schools in Ireland.

The District Inspectors report improvement in the classification of teachers in the following districts:—Trim, Dublin South, Templemore (slight), Athy. The classification is practically stationary in the following districts:—Kilkenny, Tipperary, Waterford, Limerick, and Clonmel.

This progress can hardly be considered satisfactory.

It is very pleasing to be able to state that the District Inspectors of this group, almost without exception, report favourably of the improvement effected in the teachers by their course of training.

The following is a summary of their views on the point:—

Dr. Moran (Trim).—Effects beneficial.

Mr. Brown (Dublin South).—Excellent, both as to skill and attainments.

Mr. Nicholls (Templemore). —Not productive of such improvement as I should expect.

Mr. M'Enery (Athy).—Better able to communicate information; more ready to adopt suggestions; much better disciplinarians.

Mr. Craig (Tipperary).—Better disciplinarians, but not more skilled in imparting information.

Mr. Shannon (Kilkenny).—General improvement.

Mr. Morgan (Waterford).—On the whole beneficial; in a few cases refused to sign the certificate.

Dr. Bateman (Limerick).—Teachers lately trained are doing good work.

Mr. Smith (Clonmel).—Imparts a tone of refinement; increased literary proficiency not apparent.

I regard these opinions of able disinterested men, and all Inspectors of various degrees of experience, as strong testimony in favour of the practical utility of the Training Colleges.

The appointment, instruction, examination, and destination of monitors must always constitute one of the chief features in any national system of primary education. This statement, although now a truism, cannot be repeated too often. It is creditable to the teachers that the care bestowed by them on the instruction of their monitors is highly appreciated by all the Inspectors of this group of districts. It is gratifying to find that this care on the part of the teachers has had its reward in the success of the monitors at last July Examination. The proportion of failures was very inconsiderable. The returns I have received from two districts do not specify the numbers of passes and failures; but in both districts the results were satisfactory. In one there were "very few failures"; in the other the results were "much better than in 1893." In the other seven districts 193 monitors were examined, of whom 167 passed. These figures show unmistakable progress, and afford good grounds for hope that the teaching profession will every year more and more attract to its ranks the rising talent of the country.

In nothing is the advance of the cause of education more marked and encouraging than in the improvement of the school buildings, and the efforts of Managers to secure sites and State assistance to provide suitable accommodation for the pupils.

In this widely-extended school circuit there are only twenty-five schoolhouses unfit for school purposes, excluding those cases in which unsuitable houses are being superseded by houses in course of erection, or in which negotiations for building are approaching completion.

The necessity for school premises has not yet got sufficient hold of the public mind. The appreciation of that want implies a degree of civilization or culture not yet attained. Doubtless, a few years will effect much improvement in this respect. The Managers cannot do everything they may deem desirable. Money is hard to get in a poor country, and sites cannot be ordered at will.

The educational needs of the country are not a few. Perhaps none has attracted less attention than the pressing necessity for increased provision for the training of infants.

I know that in country districts the difficulties in the way of establishing Infants' Schools are almost insuperable. But even there "suitable exercises" should be more than nominal. It is not enough to have "suitable exercises" mentioned as part of the prescribed programme for infants, there should be a specified list of them, and their practice should be made compulsory, at least where a reasonable proportion of the pupils are classed as infants.

In towns—say, for a beginning, the 118 towns to which the Education Act of 1892 is applicable—either infants' schools or infants' departments of schools should be an absolute requirement. I do not think that this view requires any elaboration in support of it.

As I have often stated in my reports I regard good "discipline and order" as one of the chief marks of a well-conducted school. In fact, most of my efforts during the past year to improve the state of education in this circuit have been mainly directed to the following points:— Discipline, Letter-writing, and Explanation. Of course I could do little in the way of improvement without the hearty co-operation of the gentlemen associated with me. This co-operation was cheerfully given. I hope that another year's work on the same lines will have a good effect.

I believe the teachers are gradually, if slowly, becoming alive to the importance of the subject of Letter-writing. I regret to say, however, that the teaching of it is not yet skilful or systematic. I see no traces of Composition lessons. I am aware that the Training Colleges are doing something towards remedying this defect. For the purpose of securing mechanical correctness notepaper and envelopes should be used at Results Examinations. "Letter Writing" is certainly making progress; but Composition in the ordinary acceptation of the term has scarcely been attempted. I know a few schools in which "Letter Writing" is extremely good. In one of them I tried an experiment which was suggested to me by visits to some English schools.

At the beginning of last Results year I asked the teacher to make out a list of twenty or thirty subjects for Composition, and to submit them to me for approval. If I approved of them I promised to select some one of them for my Composition test at the next examination. I am so pleased with the result that I would venture to recommend the general adoption of the plan.

The reports of the District Inspectors are still unfavourable as regards "Explanation," only one speaks very encouragingly of the progress in this all important part of education. "Slight improvement" is the highest praise any of the others give. Of the teachers of my limited district I can repeat what I stated in my last report, viz., they are all doing their duty in this matter of Explanation.

I hope we shall not have much longer to wait before Explanation is made an essential part of the Reading pass, at least in all classes above third. Personally I think it could be safely and judiciously required in all classes above infants; and even infants can be made to take an interest in the objects of which their little words are names.

It is worthy of observation that all general reports of Inspectors for thirty years or so—since, in fact, reports began to be written—contain references to the very same defects as are pointed out by Inspectors at the present time. This is a fact that should not be lost sight of, and which proves the necessity for a radical change of programme, and a modification of educational aims and aspirations.

I shall not dwell further upon this point, as other opportunities may be afforded for expressing my views upon it. I mention it here as an introduction to the few observations I purpose making on the ordinary subjects of the school course.

In the part of Ireland to which my official duty is confined I have found the mechanical reading very fair. By mechanical reading I mean ready reading of words, tolerable observance of pauses, and fairly accurate pronunciation. If the reading test were to end with the mere reading exercise nearly all the "reading" in my circuit should be pronounced "fairly intelligent and intelligible."

I have already dealt, so far as I deem necessary, in this report with the subject of Explanation. I shall merely add that as "Reading" in its proper sense is by far the most important subject of the school course it should not be interfered with by the introduction of extras, which are very often, if not generally, introduced for the teachers' benefit rather than for that of the pupils. Every year we find new encroachments on the time set apart for "Reading." At the same rate of *progress* the subject will soon be relegated to that indefinite and undesirable part of school work called "Home Lessons."

To give sufficient time for all the subjects sometimes attempted to be taught in schools it would be necessary to lengthen not only the school hours but also the school life of the pupils.

Penmanship continues to be carefully taught. Where suitable slates and head-line examples are used for First Class, good writing is sure to be secured, if only tolerable supervision be exercised. It is very rarely, however, we meet with writing lessons, properly so called. The blackboard should be used for more than merely writing head lines on it for imitation. It should be used for correcting errors discovered in supervision.

There is nothing new to be reported under the head of Arithmetic. It continues to receive, at least, its due share of attention.

There is no change to be recorded under the head of Spelling. The want of care in marking the Dictation Exercises is still common. In no case have I seen adopted the simple plan of giving the same exercise day after day until the pupils can write it without any mistake. Very often the errors arise from carelessness on the part of the pupils, and, apart from spelling, to correct this carelessness is a valuable training.

Grammar is still the weak point in all our schools. Nearly all Inspectors are agreed that the time spent on the subject is practically time wasted. So much has been said, year after year on the subject, that nothing new can be said upon it. A system of primary education must be practical above all things. All that should be aimed at is to equip the pupils for the battle of life with means to express themselves in speaking and writing in simple grammatical language, and to avoid local solecisms ; their local accent is their own of which they have no reason to be ashamed.

That spelling is best learned through the eye by means of reading is maintained by many educated men (frequently bad spellers themselves, however). Whether this theory is true or false, most certainly the higher styles of composition can be acquired by no other means than by general reading, an advantage which can be enjoyed only after leaving the primary school.

Geography continues to be taught on the old uninteresting lines of pointing to a map and occasionally using a text-book ; but more, much more must be done before the subject can become what it should be—one of the most interesting that could be taught to children. Non-polemical facts might surely be introduced to give flesh and blood and life to the skeleton of names and positions of places.

I regret I cannot report any progress either in the theory or practice of Vocal Music. In the Convent Schools, which I have examined or visited incidentally, and in a few of the Dublin schools of my special district, the subject is cultivated with zeal and skill, and consequently with success. I shall not mention schools by name, as some schools are making great efforts to secure respectable proficiency.

There is one difficulty not easily overcome in schools with only one room. Teaching outside school hours becomes almost a necessity in such cases. If taught before school hours the children will not attend, and, for obvious reasons, after school hours is an unsuitable time.

I have nothing to add to my remarks of last year on the subject of Agriculture.

I have observed increased attention paid to Needlework under all the heads of the Programme. As I believe the "Alternative Scheme" is work-

undergoing revision, it is unnecessary to offer any remarks as to its working or its worth.

It is strange that Book-keeping is not a more popular subject in town schools than it appears to be. I believe that many teachers would rather cram a catechism of agriculture into the pupils than to teach them the simple principles of the first four acts in the Book-keeping Programme. I suppose the secret is that a catechism may be taught without explanation, whereas the simplest principles of Book-keeping require some mental exercise on the part of teachers and pupils.

Although I have no statistical returns before me, I think I can safely say that the teaching of the subject, where attempted, is improving.

As in the case of Agriculture, it is only specialists can write or suggest anything really worth considering on the subject of Drawing. I often meet with fairly executed exercises in Drawing from the Flat, very rarely with anything more ambitious.

There is no change to be recorded in the working of Model Schools since my last report.

> I am, Gentlemen,
> Your obedient servant,
>
> PETER CONNELLAN,
> Head Inspector.

Mr. A. PURSER, Head Inspector.

Dublin, February, 1895.

GENTLEMEN,—In accordance with your instructions I forward this general report on my circuit for 1894. The districts and the inspectors

in charge of them remain unaltered. The present Inspectors have been in charge for periods varying from one and a quarter to eight and a half years. Their work is performed with zeal and earnestness, by the junior no less than by the senior members of the staff. The present system of selecting candidates for the position appears to have been very successful in securing Inspectors, not only with high literary and scientific attainments, but also men imbued with a sense of the importance of their work, and with zeal and earnestness in carrying it out. Inspectors are so much thrown among all classes, among managers and teachers of such varied nature, that complaints would not but be frequent if there were any grounds for them; and the almost total absence of such complaints is the best proof of the Inspectors' practical success in dealing with those every-day difficulties which crop up in the performance of their duties. Their endeavour to advance education in their districts is undoubted, and the suggestions made by them are often of great value. In some cases the official minute on the annual examination is allowed to take the place of notes and suggestions in

the observation book. I cannot think this a wise course. The minute coupled with the marks on the examination roll is, no doubt, an excellent guide generally as to the weak and strong points of a school; but an Inspector's duty requires that he should endeavour to find the causes of defects, and suggest remedies for them. No doubt the great difficulty in the matter is, that an inspector has not time to look over and examine the written work of the pupils before leaving the school, and that he wishes to calmly consider all the circumstances of the case before making any remarks; and this is only reasonable. But I think this difficulty might be met by the introduction of a new form of observation book more like the British log-book.

The standard of examination is tolerably uniform—probably as nearly so as possible. In the case of the sixteen "check" examinations held by me during the year, my marks were sometimes better, sometimes worse, than those assigned by the district inspector, but in no case was the difference more than a few per cent., and in several cases there was only a decimal difference between our percentages. In nearly every case we compared the written work of the pupils and our marks, while the examination was fresh in our minds, and I hope arrival at a more uniform standard in the few cases where divergence appeared.

In Reading I find my marks generally a little lower than those of the district inspectors, from which I draw the conclusion that more word naming is accepted as reading in some cases. "Intelligent" reading is required by the programme, and this should include not only proper pronunciation of words, but proper grouping, intonation, and emphasis, so as to convey the meaning of the passage to the listeners as well as to the reader. As a rule, each pupil reads in a monotone, and not at all distinctly, and would be rather ashamed to read with some little display of taste. However, I am glad to state that I have lately met with several cases of greatly improved style of reading in schools formerly visited and examined by me, and I believe with earnest endeavour on the part of the teachers, and encouragement on the part of the inspectors, we may attain a satisfactory standard of reading and of repetition of poetry. Explanation, which is very defective at present, would be certain to share in this improvement, for the pupils seldom fail, except when the passage contains difficult and unknown words, to take up the meaning when a sentence is properly read for them.

Penmanship shows no material change. It is in general very fair so long as headline copies are written, but in the senior classes tends to degenerate, owing often to carelessness in the execution of written school and home exercises. Good writing is valuable, and at the same time easily acquired. Careful supervision of the written work will effect the desired result, but to judge from unmarked errors in spelling, in grammar, and in subject matter, I am afraid revision of exercises is much neglected by some teachers.

Spelling is generally fair in the junior classes; but not so good in case of the seniors, especially in fourth and fifth classes, in which too much reliance appears to be placed on dictation. I recently found spelling very well taught in a school to the senior classes:—the pupils were all required to write out the difficult words of their reading-lesson as a home task and to learn the spelling of them; every boy was heard his whole list (sometimes over thirty words) next morning, and required to go again over any errors, which were, however, surprisingly few.

In my last report I referred to some defects in Arithmetic observed during my visits to schools; this year's inspections have confirmed my observations. No part of the programme is well taught if it does not pay—i.e., carry a fee. Now, tables pay, for they come into the ordinary work, which cannot be done without a fair knowledge of the tables,

Appendix C.

Reports on State of Schools.

Mr. J. Purser, Head Inspector.

Dublin.

Uniformity of examinations.

Reading.

Writing.

Spelling.

Arithmetic.

Appendix C.

Reports on State of Schools.

Mr. A. Purser, Head Inspector. Dublin.

but Mental Arithmetic is unnecessary, because the "pass" is given on slate and paper work. Notation and Numeration do not pay—they are sub-heads. Most inspectors use "cards" for Arithmetic for second class and upwards, and some even for first class, so there is no need to be able to take down dictated sums; and even if an inspector does dictate sums, he has to correct the wrong notation before he can set the class to work. It would be an advantage if the sub-heads could in all subjects be included in the "pass." It appears to me that we expect too little in Arithmetic from our junior classes, and that higher results could easily be obtained. The third class pupils are supposed to have a knowledge of the simple rules, but the tests are not sufficiently extended to ensure a thorough knowledge. Hence, even in the senior classes inaccuracy of work is very common, though the more advanced rules are in general fairly known.

Grammar and Geography.

Grammar and Geography show no change of consequence. I think sentence-building would be more useful than analysing sentences as in parsing. Parsing is generally pretty fair, but how little it implies is shown by failure to grasp the meaning of the passage parsed. Local Geography is usually fairly well known. The examination should never be confined to questions on the text-book, but should always include maps. Recently I found a sixth class all passed by an inspector, and they well deserved it on their paper work, but they could not show me even the principal counties and bays on the maps of England and Scotland. For third class in country schools I still incline to requiring a knowledge of their locality—i.e., what they can see from the school, instead of, or along with, the outlines of the map of the World; if the locality were properly taught the "outlines" might be very limited. The map of the county in fourth class does not make up for this; it has the same defect as the map of Ireland, or the World for initiatory lessons, that it does not appeal to the pupils' observation; and furthermore, their own county is often less important than the neighbouring one to pupils—e.g., Kildare is less important than Dublin to Leixlip children.

Agriculture and Book-keeping.

Agriculture and Book-keeping continue to receive attention; and during the past year I have not met with so many cases of worthless catechisms being used in teaching the former subject.

Needle-work.

Needlework has made steady progress since the Commissioners have required that an hour a day shall be given to it in all schools having the services of a female teacher. A more specific programme and statement of requirements for each class would lead to further improvement. From causes mentioned elsewhere, the Alternative Industrial Scheme has not made progress or been popular. Very few of the "Industries" are taken up, and these could probably be grafted on the ordinary needlework programme. *Mending* is a branch of the subject that might with advantage receive more attention.

Singing and Drawing.

Singing and Drawing are not taught as often as they should be; perhaps they might be made compulsory subjects for schools under "first class" teachers, and for others holding certificates of competency to teach them.

Extra branches.

"Extras" are not common in this circuit. Algebra and Geometry are occasionally found in boys' schools; Physical Geography and sewing machine in girls' schools. I am glad to observe that shorthand and type writing are being taken up in some city schools.

Of the teachers I have to speak favourably as a rule. Most of them labour earnestly to discharge their duties faithfully; but it cannot be denied that some, owing to want of ability, and some, owing to infirmities of age, fail to do useful work. A few—happily the number is small—totally neglect their duties. To these last, after due warning, no mercy ought to be shown; and in every case where the school is inefficient, steps should be taken to bring about a more satisfactory state of things. Whether this should be done by depression in rank, or by dismissal, must depend on the circumstances of the case; and when an inefficient teacher divides his attention between his school and some other occupation, it would seem not unreasonable to require him to give up one or the other. It might be worthy of consideration whether teachers in training should not be limited to provisional promotion to *first* class—its confirmation depending on good service in their schools; and whether a revision of training diplomas after, say every five years, might not be desirable.

Falsification of accounts is still occasionally met with by inspectors. The object of this form of dishonesty is nearly always to maintain the official minimum of average attendance, or to qualify the school for the services of a senior or junior assistant. Falsification for "result fees" is very rare; teachers who might be guilty of this fault have learned that it is not worth the risk.

Individual examination of all pupils is probably the surest and best means of estimating the value of the literary work done in a school; but payment of fees on each individual "pass" is perhaps of doubtful expediency. The tone of a school, the discipline and order, the example of a painstaking teacher devoted to his work, all count for little or nothing. When first introduced the present system of payment for results was a great incentive to work. Teachers' class salaries were much lower than at present, and in many cases the result fees doubled their incomes. Now the result fees form but a relatively small proportion of their salaries, and the difference between the amounts earned by good and by middling teaching is very trifling as may easily be shown. Take the case of a school of forty boys under a second class teacher. The teacher receives a class salary of about £50, about £16 capitation fees, and about £14 result fees if he passes 50 per cent. of the pupils; about £11 10s. if he passes 70 per cent.; total in first case £80; in the second case £77 10s. The small difference bears no proportion to the difference of efficiency, and is an utterly inadequate reward for the more meritorious teacher.

The managers as a rule take great interest in their schools; and in many cases not a day passes without a visit from the manager or his deputy. They are slow to take the initiative when action becomes necessary with regard to making a change in the teaching staff, and are likely to be slower in future. Both they and the teachers are too often satisfied with an indifferent state of cleanliness, repair, and general suitability of school-house and premises; but an inspector, who takes up these matters earnestly and is supported by the Education Office, can generally effect considerable improvement within a few years.

In most schools the monitors are well taught and trained. The number of female monitors is much too large, as only a small proportion of them can ever hope to obtain situations as teachers.

D

Appendix C.

Reports on
State of
Schools.

Mr. A.
Purser,
Head
Inspector.

Dublin.

Model
Schools.

The Model schools in the circuit continue to be well conducted. The annexed table shows that the work done in them may in nearly every case be pronounced excellent, and it certainly is much above the general average.

School or Department.	Number of Pupils examined for "Results."	Percentage of those in Senior Classes.	Percentage of "Passes" at Examination.	
			Whole School.	Senior Classes.
Newry, Model (Male), . .	148	70	85	84
Do. (Female), . .	78	44	88	86
Do. (Infants), . .	78	—	100	..
West Dublin, Model (Male), .	121	64	80	91
Do. (Female), .	73	50	88	84
Do. (Infants), .	102	—	86	—
Parsonstown, Model (Male), .	48	27	73	84
Do. (Female)*.	74	23	80	80
Roscommon, Model (Male), .	28	73	74	70
Do. (Female)*.	79	46	81	88

* These schools are really girls' and infants' departments combined, hence the proportion of pupils in the senior classes appears relatively small.

A considerable increase in the average attendance has allowed of an addition to the senior staff in the Newry Infants', West Dublin Boys' and West Dublin Infants' Model Schools. In the latter the late principal teacher, Mrs. Hudson, after a lengthened period of useful service, retired on her well-earned pension.

In the Newry Model Infants' School a fair number of children have opened accounts in the Post Office Savings Bank. In the other schools nothing has been done in this direction beyond the few accounts which were opened before the Post Office afforded special facilities for School Savings Banks.

My own limited district continued without change during the year, but with the opening of the New Year the Ralph Macklin Schools ceased their connexion with the Board—the premises and endowments being employed for an Intermediate school with a commercial course. One of the teachers in the district, Mr. Doak, of St. Paul's (2) Boys' National School, was awarded a Carlisle and Blake Premium, and I know of no teacher who more thoroughly deserved it.

I am, your obedient servant,

A. Purser, Head Inspector.

The Secretaries, &c.

Appendix C.
Reports on
State of
Schools.

Mr. M.
Sullivan,
Head
Inspector.
Galway.

Mr. M. SULLIVAN, LL.B., Head Inspector.

Galway, 16th February, 1895.

GENTLEMEN,—In accordance with your instructions I beg to submit the following general report for 1894 on the circuit in my charge.

As in previous years, my circuit includes nearly the whole of Connaught, the greater part of Clare, and a very small portion of Westmeath.

During the year 1894 there were no educational events of marked importance in the circuit. Some new schoolhouses were built, some worn-out teachers resigned, and were replaced by younger persons; managers, on their own removal from one place to another, became connected with new sets of schools; but looking on the schools as a whole, their working went on quietly and steadily from day to day and from month to month.

The Compulsory Education Act, which came into force in January, 1894—more than a year ago—has hitherto produced very trifling effects. In most of the towns in this circuit affected by the Act, School Attendance Committees were duly appointed; but few of them took steps to put the Act in force. In some the existence of the Act seems now, practically, forgotten. It is not probable, however, that this state of things will long continue. No places stand more in need of a judicious but vigorous application of the Compulsory Act than small towns—(1,000 to 1,500). Of these there are many in this circuit; and any person who passes through one on a fine day, can know from the number of idle children in the streets how necessary is some form of compulsion. In rural districts the farmers, as a rule, send their children to school with fair regularity during the agricultural slack season, provided the school in the locality is a good one. If the school be not a good one the fact is soon known, and the attendance is sure to be more irregular and much lower than it otherwise would be. But many of the truant children in the towns have parents who are quite regardless of the character of the schools, and when dealing with such children and such parents compulsion seems indispensable.

In a previous report (1893) I pointed out the desirableness of an increase in the number of well managed *infants' schools.* Every town and every village, except the merest hamlet, should have a school specially devoted to infants—a school in which the infant children would be taught not only a little reading and spelling, as at present in ordinary schools, but singing, marching, and other suitable Kindergarten exercises. But to supply such schools will take time. Taking the schools as they are at present, one of the greatest hindrances to the efficiency of some of them is the unduly long time spent by pupils in the "Infants' Class." Most persons who look superficially at the results system probably think that it has the advantage of causing teachers to promote their pupils year by year. A boy who "passes" in 1st Class is at once placed in 2nd Class; a boy who "passes" in 2nd Class is at once placed in 3rd, and so on. If a boy in 1st Class passes in Reading and Writing, but fails in, say, Arithmetic and Spelling, the teacher may, and probably will, present this boy again in 1st Class; but on the boy's second presentation the teacher is paid only for passes in Arithmetic and Spelling. Hence, it is the teacher's direct interest to make each pupil in 1st, 2nd, 3rd, &c., Class pass in as many subjects as pos-

The
Circuit.
Work of
year.

Compulsory
Act.

Efficiency
and
inefficiency
of ordinary
schools—
Infants'
schools.

Class for
"Infants"
in ordinary
schools.

D 2

Appendix G.
Reports on
State of
Schools.

Mr. M.
Sullivan,
Head
Inspector.
Galway.

nible each year, and then to promote the pupil to the next higher class. So much is this the case, that weak teachers sometimes make injudicious promotions. If a 3rd Class pupil has failed in, say, Reading, Arithmetic, and Grammar, it would be much better for the pupil to remain another year in 3rd Class; but an injudicious teacher is quite at liberty to "promote" even such a pupil to the next Class (4th). Where a teacher regularly promotes pupils who fail, the school after a few years becomes a very bad one. I am not dealing with "injudicious promotions" at present; I only mention them to show that in 1st and higher Classes it is the teacher's interest not to keep the pupils unduly long in one class. But in the Infants' Class matters are quite different. In this circuit the number of infants' schools is so small that they may be disregarded, and the infants in ordinary schools learn the Reading and Spelling prescribed by the Programme, and nothing more. Now the Spelling and Reading prescribed for infants occupy only sixteen pages of the First Book, and a fairly intelligent and well-taught child of five or six years could learn the whole sixteen pages in less than a year. For children who begin school-life at three or four years, two years should be amply sufficient for these sixteen pages. The exercises in the sixteen pages commence with letters from the alphabet (a, o, i, n, s, &c.), and end with the not complicated sentence "The lark is on the wing." Many years ago I showed that it was possible for a child in regular attendance to spend six years in learning—or apparently learning—these sixteen pages, and to earn a fee and appear among the successful pupils each year. I only spoke of this as a possible case, but recently, in one of the schools in my circuit, I found an actual case which closely approached it. A boy, not wanting in intelligence, except as far as this was caused by neglect to develop his faculties, entered a certain school in May, 1889. The Results Examination takes place each April. Unfortunately the school register was not complete, so that I am unable to say whether the boy was examined in April, 1890, or not. Very probably he was, as he had eleven months in which to make 100 attendances. For the year ended March 31, 1891, the boy attended satisfactorily, and so in April, 1891, he "passed"; in April, 1892, he again passed; a third time he passed as an infant in 1893; and for the fourth, if not the fifth time, he "passed" in April, 1894. All these passes, for each of which the teacher was duly paid results fees, still left the boy in the class which is engaged with the first sixteen pages of First Book. I tested the boy in a more advanced portion of the First Book, but he could not read the sentence, "The owl sleeps all day." I examined him in writing, but he could not write the word "man," and in arithmetic he did not know what 6 and 7 or 5 and 9 make. I pointed out these facts to the principal teacher, and in explanation he said that the boy was rather slow, which certainly was not surprising, but that after another "pass" in the Infants' Class, that is after the April, 1895, examination, he expected to "promote" the boy to First Class. In April, 1895, the boy will be five years and eleven months in the "Infants' Class."

I am no advocate for the too rapid advancement of infants or of pupils of any age. In a well-managed infants' school, one especially in which kindergarten exercises are properly taught, a child may spend two, or even more, years with advantage in the "Infants' Class." But during each of these years the child makes progress—progress suitable to its years and its capacity. What I object to is, that a child should come to school day after day, week after week, and learn absolutely nothing. This is utter waste of the child's time, and in addition it

tends to make him dull and stupid.   Such an extreme case as the one
I have referred to does not often happen, but, after paying much attention to the subject, I am of opinion that a great many children spend
at least a year too long in the Infants' Class.   It must be disheartening
to parents, too, to see their young children going over the same sixteen
pages year after year, and if they once imagine that this is done merely
in order that the teacher, without any labour, may obtain results fees,
their dissatisfaction must be considerable.

The evils arising from keeping boys and girls too long in the
"Infants' Class" are much increased by the fact that the ages of children
are frequently under-estimated, and that pupils enrolled in the Infants'
Class are really not "infants" at all.   When a pupil first comes to school
he frequently has only a brother or sister with him, and neither the
new pupil nor his conductor knows the child's age accurately.
Even parents do not always know the ages of their children accurately.
The teacher has, therefore, no satisfactory means of knowing a child's age.
In more ways than one it is the teacher's interest not to overestimate a
pupil's age, and in guarding against this he is somewhat disposed to
underestimate the age.   Take the following actual case:—A boy, A. B.,
came to a certain school in May, 1893, was enrolled as six, and was
placed in the Infants' class.   The next results examination was held
in March, 1894, and the boy was presented as an infant aged six "on last
birth-day."   If this were accepted there was nothing to prevent the boy
from being presented as an infant aged seven in 1895, and as an infant
aged eight in 1896.   I took the trouble of ascertaining the boy's actual
age.   He was born on 13th January, 1886, and so at the examination
in 1894 was eight not six years.   If the error had not been corrected
this boy might have remained in the "Infants' Class," learning sixteen
pages of First Book but learning nothing else, neither writing nor simple
addition, until March, 1896, that is until he was ten years of age,
unless the parents, mortified at the boy's evident want of progress, withdrew him from school.

A little reflection will show that if a boy wastes a year in the Infant's
class he is a year older than he need be when he reaches each of the
other classes, 1st, 2nd, 3rd, 4th, V¹, V², 5th.   But as pupils cannot
remain indefinitely at school the result is that very many never reach 5th,
or V², or V¹ or even 4th.   Everyone knows how important it is that a
boy, or girl, should reach one of the senior classes (IV, V¹, V², VI)
before finally leaving school.   I am satisfied that the proportion of
pupils in the senior classes could easily be increased.   One of my
schools is a small Island school, practically every child on the Island
attends, the ages are correctly entered, and pupils are never kept unduly
long in one class.   Of these on Rolls

          23 per cent. are Infants.
          31   „   in Classes I., II., III.
          46   „   in Classes IV., V., VI.

Now, in one of the schools to which I have just referred, in connection
with infants, the corresponding proportions are—

          31 per cent. in Infants' Class.
          45   „   in Junior Classes (I., II., III.)
          24   „   in Senior Classes (IV., V., VI.)

For all Ireland (see Commissioners' Report for 1893, page 338) the
corresponding proportions, omitting decimals, are—

          38 per cent. in Infants' Class.
          43   „   in Junior Classes (I., II., III.)
          69   „   in Senior Classes (IV., V., VI.)

Appendix C.

Reports on
state of
Schools.

Mr. M.
Sullivan,
Head
Inspector.

Galway.

Ages of
pupils.

Appendix G.

Reports on
State of
Schools.

Mr. M.
Sullivan.
Head
Inspector.

Galway.

Not only were the children in the Island school much more highly classed than in the school in which the pupils are kept too long in the Infants' Class, but they answered much better in their classes. The pupils found worthy of promotion in the Island school were 90 per cent. of the whole, in the other school the corresponding per-centage was only 78.

Duly considering these and similar facts which have come under my notice, I beg to remark that, as far as the schools of this circuit are concerned, I am aware of no simple remedies which would tend more to improve their efficiency than—

1st. Correctly to ascertain the precise ages of the pupils.

2nd. To make arrangements by which pupils enrolled as "Infants" should show suitable progress each year.

3rd. To guard young pupils against being kept unduly long in the "Infants' Class."

Efficiency
of schools
depends
largely on
proper
"training."

Year by year the proportion of trained teachers in the Circuit is steadily increasing. Almost every young teacher now either goes to a Training College as soon as possible after his appointment, or merely defers going until he shall have obtained Second Division of Second Class. In future, therefore, the efficiency of the schools will be largely influenced by the character of the Colleges. These, no doubt, do not and will not forget that their primary object is to form good teachers—that is, to train teachers in the art of imparting knowledge and of developing faculties. Hitherto some teachers have been disposed to regard Training Colleges, to a great extent, as places in which assistance in preparing for Examinations—both for Class Promotion and for Certificates to teach Extra Subjects—is ably and successfully given. From various causes, some of which are self-evident, a teacher in charge of a school, or serving as assistant, rarely visits other schools in operation, so that many teachers are often wholly unaware of their own defects in the art of teaching. To such teachers a year or two in a Training College, having suitable "Practising Schools," must be of very great service. In all schools which are not efficient, and in which the teachers are young and untrained, I invariably advise them to go to a Training College as soon as possible. In cases in which the teachers are old and unskilful, it is useless to make any suggestions.

Model
Schools.

There are only two Model Schools in my Circuit (Sligo and Galway), and their influence on the general education of the province is small. In each the attendance is confined, with trifling exceptions, to non-Catholics, and as Sligo and Galway are inhabited chiefly by Catholics, the attendance at the Model Schools is small in proportion to the populations of the towns. To those who attend, these Model Schools give an excellent education at a very small cost to the pupils.

Monitorial
system.

Service as monitors is, practically, the only course open to persons in this Circuit who wish to become teachers, and as the office of teacher is one now eagerly desired, the supply of candidate monitors is practically unlimited. When a young person has completed his term as monitor he is "classed," and he then endeavours to procure an appointment as assistant or principal. Unfortunately the monitors who have obtained classification are far in excess of the number of vacant places in the staff of assistants and principals, so that year after year numbers of clever, well-conducted young people, who have creditably served an apprenticeship, find themselves in a very pitiable condition.

They have a "class," but they have no work. A few find temporary employment as substitutes for teachers in training; but the majority of the unemployed, after spending a year or two in "looking for a place,"

try to turn to other occupations. For the sake of these unemployed Appendix C.
young persons, and for the sake of the teaching profession generally, Reports on Mode of Schools.
which must suffer from having a number of young teachers who are
only too anxious to take any school on any terms, it is desirable that
the supply of monitors should not be largely in excess of the number Mr. N. Sullivan, Head Inspector. Galway.
of vacancies. This could easily be done by sanctioning the appointment
of monitors in thoroughly good schools only. The chief difficulty in
carrying out this policy would arise from the great desire of almost
every teacher to have one or more monitors. Managers, too, are
anxious that their schools should have as large a staff as possible. It
would not be easy to persuade either Managers or teachers that their
schools are not sufficiently good to be entrusted with the training of
monitors. Nor would a reluctant admission that his school was not
"thoroughly efficient" close a Manager's argument. I once got a
Manager who was pressing for the appointment of a monitor to admit
that his school was only middling, but he immediately added, "If we
had a monitor it would be much better; how can you expect one person,
unaided, to teach so many pupils?" There is, of course, something in
such an argument, and an Inspector requires some firmness to enable
him to recommend, unhesitatingly, that certain schools should and that
other schools should not be entrusted with the training of monitors;
but he would be much assisted by remembering that—in the interests
of the monitors as a class, of teachers as a class, and ultimately of the
schools—it is better that there should not be an excessive number of
monitors.

As a rule the monitors in the circuit are carefully prepared in the Female monitors.
subjects specified in their programme. Female monitors at their examinations generally answer better than male monitors, but this is easily
explained by the fact that the course for male monitors embraces
agriculture, book-keeping, geometry with mensuration, and algebra,
whereas the only subject which girls have and boys have not is needlework.

Plain dressmaking forms portion of the programme for sixth class
pupils, and consequently forms portion of the programme for female
monitors. As a rule female monitors spend several years in sixth
class, and in the years after the first their programme in needlework is
unchanged. It would, I think, be well to make a change in this respect,
and to require monitresses after their first examination in sixth class to
become acquainted with some recognised "system" of dressmaking.

Instruction in the art of teaching is not given as systematically as is Monitors. Art of teaching.
Instruction in the book subjects specified in the programme. In his
fourth year a monitor is expected to be able "to teach a fourth class,
from carefully prepared notes, lessons on any two subjects selected by
the teacher." The notes are frequently poor in quantity and quality,
and the teaching is wanting in animation and in thoroughness, and
often consists altogether of *questions*. I think that in his fourth or
fifth year a monitor should be able not only to teach a particular subject,
but also to manage a "division" of a large school, or the whole of a
small school to the extent, at least, of being able to make "changes"
properly, of taking the pupils to the playground, and of bringing them
from it back to the school.

A large proportion of the schools in this circuit consists of excellent Play-grounds. Play.
vested houses, each having a suitable playground. The playgrounds,
I regret to say, are not much used as places for play. Country boys
do not seem to know how to play. Even in cold weather the boys
during play-time lean listlessly against the walls, or stand idly in groups.
No doubt country boys generally have plenty of work at home, so that

Appendix C.
Reports on
State of
Schools.
Mr. M.
Sullivan,
Head
Inspector.
Galway.

physical exertion is not as necessary for them as it may be for city boys, but a few suitable games would quicken country boys, and would tend to keep them warm. In helping to introduce such games the teacher would find his monitor useful. Perhaps, too, the Training Colleges could assist by making young teachers acquainted with games suitable for various classes of schools. Drill also should be far more regularly practised than it is. Since I came to this circuit I have visited scores of schools during the play half-hour, and I have never seen either boys or girls playing any regular game, or engaged at drill.

Examina-
tion and
promotion
of teachers.

As regards the examination and promotion of teachers I have little to add to what I stated in my previous report. Promotion should depend, to a very great extent, on actual success in school work. The two most successful teachers in my "limited district" are only 3rd class. One of them obtained a Carlisle and Blake Premium, but as she is 44 years old and married, she cannot go to a Training College, and as she lives in a remote locality she could not easily obtain help in her studies for second class. On the other hand, a young teacher, male or female, may attain 1^2—a class within one step of the highest—at the age of 22, and without any reliable evidence of capacity for school management. This, he—or she—can do as follows:—Having served as monitor, he is, at 18, classed 3^2 and (say) appointed assistant in a school which has a good head master. In such a school the young assistant is morally certain to obtain 3^1 at 20 and 2^2 at 21. He then goes for nine months to a Training College and returns at 22 with 1^2. All the steps of this procedure do not invariably work out without delay, so that young teachers of 22 and classed 1^2 are not common, but teachers classed 1^2 and only 25, 26, or 27 are comparatively numerous.

Needle-
work.

When dealing with monitors I pointed out that a female monitor has a much easier programme than a male monitor. So, too, the programme for 3rd class teachers, for 2nd class, and 1st class, is much simpler for women than for men. I have no objection to this, but I think the programme

Promotion
of female
teachers.

in needlework for females should be more exacting than it is. Every candidate for classification should be acquainted with some recognised system of dressmaking, and the marks for this subject, as well as those for plain-needlework and shirt-making, should be included in the marks essential for classification. Candidates for promotion to 2nd or to 1st class should show proficiency in one or two additional subjects selected by them from the industrial programme.

Drawing.

In the schools of this circuit Drawing is seldom taught. As might be expected a teacher seldom succeeds in teaching a subject or art with which he is not, himself, soundly acquainted, so that little would be gained by forcing unwilling teachers to introduce Drawing into their schools. It might be well to allow marks for really good drawing to assist teachers in obtaining promotion at the July examinations. More teachers than at present might then take up this useful art, and they would gradually introduce it into their schools.

Managers.

The Managers continue to take an active interest in the schools. In a former report I drew attention to their zeal in school-building. No part of Ireland has made more progress in this respect during the past twenty years than Connaught, and the number of new schools just completed or now being built is considerable.

I remain, Gentlemen, your obedient servant,

M. SULLIVAN, Head Inspector.

The Secretaries,
Education Office, Dublin.

Appendix C.
Reports on State of Schools.
Mr. E. Downing, Head Inspector, Londonderry.
—
Accommodation:
—
Number and character of schools.
—
Efficiency of schools.
—
Absence of signs of growth.
—
Range of instruction.

Mr E. Downing, Head Inspector.

Londonderry, 1st February, 1895.

Gentlemen.—In compliance with your instructions, I beg to submit the following General Report for 1894, on the state of education in the north-west group of districts.

During the year considerable progress has been made towards providing increased and improved school accommodation. This is particularly the case in the city of Londonderry, where through the very laudable efforts of the managers of all religious denominations, it seems likely that, in the immediate future, every want will be supplied.

Through the circuit generally the number of schools is amply sufficient. I have not become aware of any locality where the children are at an unreasonable distance from a National School. Very generally too, the rooms afford sufficient space; but a good many are, in other respects, more or less unsuitable; and some are barely tolerated as better than none. We have still in use some cabins of the humblest type, with thatched roofs, low and unceiled, damp rugged earthen floors, and windows small and few, badly adapted for both light and ventilation. There are still in the circuit over one hundred schools that urgently need improved accommodation. A very large number of the schools are unprovided with a play-ground or garden.

The efficiency of the schools is slowly but steadily improving. When changes of teachers occur, as a very general rule, due care is taken by the managers in the selection of the successors. The recent appointments are, on the whole, satisfactory. I have also before me a good many instances of teachers who had not been giving satisfaction, and who have been influenced to reform. I inspected within the year over three hundred different schools from all parts of the circuit, and the impression left by this wide experience is one of decided improvement under the heads of punctuality, order, and discipline, energy, and fidelity of accounts.

Our schools are doing very fair work. Practically there are no local complaints of them. Nothing beyond the present curriculum is demanded. The local impression very generally is that the Commissioners, through their officers, are rather exacting.

This is certainly not my view; and, whilst anxious to do the schools and teachers justice, and to avoid under-rating the value of the good work that has been done, I feel that much more is reasonably possible in the future, and, consequently, I regret to be unable to record any new development, any enlargement of the scope of usefulness of the schools. No new subjects of instruction have been introduced: no improved plans have been devised: little or no advance has been made in industrial training: no increased attractiveness has appeared.

When applying myself to the annual duty of writing this report, I am always forcibly struck with the absence of signs of growth. From certain quarters blame seems to be attributed to the department for this dearth of development; but inquiry should satisfy any one that the cause must be sought for elsewhere.

Ample provision is made, in the form of results-fees for the encouragement of a wide range of subjects of instruction, such as kindergarten, practical agriculture, practical gardening, handicraft, and numerous forms of manual training for girls, as well as for the bases of all industrial

Appendix C.
Reports on state of Schools.
Mr. R. Downing, Head Inspector.
Londonderry.

Want of local interest.

Improvements possible.

instruction, namely, drawing and the natural sciences; but this provision is little availed of. Is it not the old story of leading to the fountain a horse unwilling to drink! One obvious cause of the absence of development is, unquestionably, the want of local interest, practically applied, to give impetus to an educational movement. As a very general rule, no one takes any practical interest in the school, and the teacher is left, in isolation, to his own resources and his own will, with no stimulus beyond what is afforded by the annual examination. The managers, as a rule, are satisfied with a very moderate standard of an old pattern.

Through this want of local interest, official interference is rendered the more necessary, and, at the same time, comparatively ineffective.

That the efforts, long and strenuously made, to promote the study of improved methods of husbandry have not proved more successful, is entirely due to the want of local interest. From the same cause the industrial instruction of girls is less useful than it might be. There is no one, as a rule, to lend any aid towards its promotion: the very materials are, almost invariably, and of necessity, provided by the teacher at her own expense.

Let but once a practical demand be made upon our schools, and they will be found equal to the occasion.

Other causes for this absence of development are to be found in the irregularity of attendance, the shortness of the daily school time, the difficulty of getting the children to attend early enough in the morning, the engrossing nature of the obligatory programme in schools with very limited staffs, and, finally, the want of local funds to supplement State aid.

Some important improvements might at once be effected, if the managers started the movement. The manner in which the infants are dealt with is very unsatisfactory, and a serious hindrance to future progress. The infants form an important proportion of the attendance, and future success depends largely on their judicious training. In three or four years they merely learn to read a few words of from two to four letters. I do not advocate much book work for these little ones: what I desire to see is a provision for their occupation, so that they may grow up bright and active instead of sluggish and indolent; an effort to cultivate their powers of observation and speech; and, in fine, the schools made attractive for them. There are, as I had occasion to report on former occasions, very many schools in this circuit in which the senior classes are so insignificant that the business should be conducted largely on infant school lines, by teachers trained for such work. In every school having a considerable infant element, the managers should insist on having at least one teacher well qualified to train infants. In such schools the suitable exercises prescribed in the programme for infants should embrace drill, a daily *conversational* lesson, kindergarten drawing, some of the kindergarten "occupations," and, if at all possible, singing by ear. For grants to a regular infant school or to a separate infant department, kindergarten should, in my opinion, be compulsory.

A large proportion of the time assigned, in the time-tables, to writing is wasted. The young children fill up their slates in about ten minutes, and remain idle for the remainder of the half-hour. There is, in poor districts, a difficulty in getting the pupils to provide themselves liberally with copy-books, and hence they write but one page a day. This, too, is finished in ten or fifteen minutes, and such pupils also idle for the remainder of the half-hour. During the time thus wasted drawing might be taught.

More important still is the training of the children in deportment, good manners, and neat and orderly habits, as well as the inculcation of sound principles. Very little is done in these directions. There is very little attempt at drill, and consequently, both boys and girls stand in clumsy attitudes and walk awkwardly. I regret to say I frequently see the pupils doing unseemly things without correction, as, for instance, spitting about the floor; and I hear, from time to time, complaints of the prevalence of this nasty practice in the different places of worship.

Every prevailing local bad habit should be counteracted in our schools, which will justly be held, in part, responsible for prevailing defects in the national character that are not at least undergoing modification.

I am glad to say that most of the pupils are enrolled in temperance societies; and I hope the influence of our schools will yet be felt in checking the premature and immoderate use of tobacco, and in cultivating self-restraint in many other ways.

How local interest in education is to be aroused, it is not for me to discuss. That is for the statesman. But I may, perhaps, be permitted to point out that to expect that some special industry will be started in a school with the vague hope that a market may spring up, and a local industry be developed, is not a practical view. The opposite is the natural and only practical course. The demand must come first. When it does come, our schools readily adapt themselves to the circumstances and give a good preliminary training, after which the necessary skill is soon acquired.

In every considerable industry there is much division of labour, so that the operation performed by each worker is a very simple affair. It is only those who direct or design that require anything deserving the name of technical training. Children under ten years of age assist, in their homes here, their mothers and older sisters at shirt-making, the prevailing industry. The cutting-out is done by men in the factory. In Carna, County Galway, girls under twelve years of age used to learn, in a few months, to knit the "combination" garment, and boys' fancy overalls. At Earnesmore, amongst the hills of Donegal, an agent appeared for hemstitching and embroidery, and the necessary instruction was at once given in the National Schools there: with detrimental results, I am sorry to add, to the school, for as soon as the girls had acquired sufficient skill, they stayed at home to earn money. In the Enniskillen district, again, as soon as a market offered for Inishmacsaint lace, the necessary instruction commenced in the Convent schools.

The introduction of industrial instruction for boys is attended with many and great difficulties. In every school are boys whose career in life will widely differ. No one kind of industrial training will well suit all. All the boys in a rural school will not follow agricultural pursuits.

My experience of National Schools, with farms attached for purposes of practical agricultural instruction, is not favourable to them. The efficient management of a school and the efficient management of a farm of any considerable extent by the same person seem to be incompatible. The possession of farms by teachers is one of the banes of education in part of this circuit. The most worthless teachers are either farmers, newspaper correspondents, or cycle agents.

The boys who intend to be farmers leave school at an early age, say, under twelve years. What can boys at that age be expected to have learned of farm management? Obviously only the simplest and leading principles, and such operations as sowing, weeding, thinning, transplanting, raking, and the like; all of which could be better learned in a school garden. No matter what career may be in store for a lad,

Appendix C.

Reports on State of Schools.

Mr. F. Downing, Head Inspector. Londonderry.

some practical knowledge of the management of a garden is desirable, whether for future use or pleasure. If, in connection with this, were taught the elements of chemistry and botany necessary for the elucidation of text-books on gardening, experimentally illustrated, there would be afforded a training of no mean value, at once practical and intellectual.

To make manual instruction widely useful and popular it should be based upon natural science. A simple course of natural science worked out experimentally and with apparatus made in the school, would afford a fascinating training for the hand and eye as well as for the mind.

Manual Instruction.

The construction of mechanical toys to illustrate the application of various forms of force to the production and modification of motion would be the proper occupation for boys, well within their capacity, greatly varied as to material and implements, highly attractive, and conducive to invention. This I feel confident will be the Irish floyd. Let not the mention of toys frighten the utilitarian. A toy was the germ of every one of our most wonderful inventions—of the steam-engine, the telegraph, the telephone. The ship builder begins with a toy—a *model* if you will. The kinetoscope is as yet but a toy although considered worthy of the greatest living inventor.

Besides the necessary expense for plant and material, there is another serious difficulty in the way of introducing manual instruction for boys, namely, in the finding time for it. With the present obligatory programme, and the present amount of school time the thing is impossible.

It seems, therefore, worthy of consideration whether some impetus might not be given to the introduction of manual instruction by allowing the option of substituting for grammar and geography of Sixth Class an adequate amount of hand and eye training.

Alternative scheme.

The Industrial Programme or "Alternative Scheme" for Sixth Class girls has been little adopted in this circuit, and is losing rather than gaining in favour. It was originally expected that within the two hours to be daily devoted to needlework the girls would not merely learn, but actually *do* some special kinds of work for the market, and receive remuneration.

This idea, which is certainly inconsistent with the spirit of the Factory and Compulsory Attendance Acts, has in no case been realized. No work is done in the schools here for which the children receive payment. Two hours a day are, therefore, not required for the purpose. One hour a day is amply sufficient for all the *instruction* given in any of the schools.

Too much prominence given to needlework.

The girls who remain to pass through Sixth Class are those who aim at the teachers' profession, or at some Civil Service or other appointment requiring the literary culture of the old programme. The girls who are to benefit by cottage industries leave school before attaining to Sixth Class, and must receive such training as is available in earlier grades.

Then again, this industrial profession gives too much prominence to needlework for a scheme of industrial school training, which, in order to be of greatest use to the largest numbers, should be that which would best fit a girl for the management of a humble household. With this in view, needlework, in this age of sewing machines, should take a secondary place. The devotion of so much time to needlework shuts out the possibility of introducing any other kind of industrial training. I accordingly am of opinion that the devotion of one hour and no more each day to needlework should be compulsorily required. Grammar and geography might be left optional in Sixth Class, so that the time otherwise required for them might be assigned to some useful kind of industrial training. A suitable course of arithmetic should be prescribed for all girls of Sixth Class; and the provisions for needlework in the old or literary programme of Sixth Class should be revised. The "plain patching" commenced in Fourth Class, and the darning begun in First stage of Fifth, may reasonably be expected to develop in Sixth Class into "good repairing of garments" and fine-drawing, that is to say, into the course prescribed in the industrial programme under head A 4. The girls who in Second Stage of Fifth are expected to be able to complete the knitting of a sock may well be taught, within the two succeeding years, to knit all the articles specified under head A 8 of the Industrial Programme. The pupils of Sixth Class, again, may reasonably be expected, within the two years of their course, and after the considerable preliminary training of the earlier grades, to measure, and cut out from the measurements, and put properly together the parts of any garment for a school-girl, including a plain working dress. All this could certainly be accomplished within one hour a day.

The work in our schools is, as a very general rule, limited far too much to merely preparing the children to earn results fees. Teachers frequently express astonishment, as at the revelation of a new idea, when I point out to them that as results fees form but a fraction of their incomes, so the grinding for the results examination is but a fraction of their duty in the discharge of which they should be influenced, not so much by the anticipation of the examination or the dread of Inspector, or even of the Commissioners, as by their conscientious obligations to the children entrusted to their care. I wish all the teachers could be got to realise the gravity of that trust: practically the education of the children of a nation. There is need for some means of infusing new ideas and arousing dormant energies. It is not reasonable to expect that a number of isolated men and women will carry on a great work with any degree of perfection without some collective advice and exhortation. When the teachers meet amongst themselves, the tendency is obviously to dwell upon real or imaginary grievances, to the exclusion of consideration for the public good. It seems, therefore, desirable they should be, from time to time, addressed by the Inspectors or other competent persons at convenient centres. Another expedient that should prove useful would be the issue to every manager and teacher in a district of a printed copy of the Inspector's General Report. These reports might then contain special references to schools of exceptional merit, and to important efforts towards progress, as well as, on the other hand, to irregularities, injudicious plans, and cases of intolerable inefficiency. Thus a great stimulus would be provided.

Formerly, in Galway, when preparing a general report, I used to require from every teacher a short report on what improvements of all kinds had been effected in his school within the previous three years. I found this useful, not merely for supplying me with "copy"; but further for getting the teachers to reconsider their lines of action, for directing their attention to expected progress, and for arousing and guiding energy. I think something of this kind should become general, and that a log-book should be kept in every school for records of all improvements and of efforts at improvement.

I may, perhaps, here be permitted to direct attention to the strange and fatal want of any system of conference amongst the Managers of National Schools as such, a defect in itself sufficient to account for our insufficiency of progress.

Appendix C.

Reports on
State of
Schools.

Mr. E.
Downing,
Head
Inspector.

London-
derry.
___

Neglect of
Infant class.

Reading.

I greatly regret not to be able to report any appreciable improvement in the teaching of English. The same helplessness as formerly at apprehending the meaning of an ordinary passage, the same prevalence of barbarisms and solecisms in the little letter required in Sixth Class continue. Surely children who learn but one language might be expected to make more progress at it than this. The imperfection of language-teaching is the most grievous defect of all in our schools, and should be grappled with once and for all. Because of its all-important seriousness I have never failed to direct attention to it, and, in former reports, I have fully discussed the cause of it. Here, therefore, it is necessary only to give a brief resumé.

The evil begins with the neglect of the infant class. An infant of seven years of age, if properly handled, might easily be taught to speak better English than many of our Sixth Class pupils can. With cultivated powers of observation comes the possession of language to adequately express the thoughts; and, when once a child can speak correctly, it is a comparatively easy task to teach him to *write* correctly. There is in our schools no systematic training of the observation, or of speech.

Then the practice of reading is quite insufficient. Much of the time spent at difficult arithmetic, parsing, and geography would be much more beneficially applied to reading aloud. For children who do not read at home, large practice should be provided in school; and, decidedly, some scheme should be devised for supplying the children with attractive reading at their homes. It is very questionable if the proper plan is to require the children of the more advanced classes to read over the same lessons again and again. A variety of books would, in my opinion, be preferable; and the text should be not in reading one particular book, but in reading any book of a prescribed degree of difficulty.

If at all transcription and dictation exercises, punctuation and division into paragraphs received strict attention, with an intelligent explanation from the teacher of the reasons for such divisions, a useful end would be served towards improvement in letter-writing. It would diminish the amount of disorderly rigmarole at present produced. The pupils should be, much more than at present, required to describe objects and occurrences from their own observation; and for orderly arrangement sake, some division of the subject should be required before the writing is commenced.

For the continued training of the observation in the senior classes, the teaching of the natural sciences *experimentally* should be further encouraged. Separate programmes of an advanced nature for light, sound, electricity, &c., as at present, are not conducive to the desired end. Children begin this study with a simple introductory general treatise; and, for the *primary* school, a course based on such a treatise is the proper one.

As I did not observe progress towards making the instruction given more systematic, I have, during the past year, given much consideration to devising some means of promoting this end. The best device capable of immediate application is to require in every school weekly *lesson-tables* to be prepared, prescribing fully for all the work for each day. These, after use, should be carefully preserved for the Inspector's criticism; and if once very carefully prepared, might suit, with slight modification, for year after year. At every inspection these should be examined with a view to see that a judicious amount of work is assigned to each day; that, in each subject, a proper sequence has been preserved; *Appendix C.* and, in fine, that due care has been bestowed on planning, in anticipa- *Reports on State of Schools.* tion, the coming week's work. The work of the day previous to the inspection, or of two or three previous days, should be tested in order to see if full and effective instruction had been given in accordance with *Mr. E. Downing, Head Inspector.* the prescribed arrangements. I think this suggestion will commend itself as of much practical utility, and, if so, I trust an immediate order *Londonderry.* will issue making it compulsory to have suspended in every school a carefully prepared lesson-table for the current week.

As some of my suggestions would, if adopted, impose an increase of duty on the District Inspectors whose hands are already quite full enough of work, it is proper I should also suggest how the requirements of efficient inspection may be met on the supposition that further assistance may not be available. It is, at all events, my duty to point out that the *inspection* of schools, as distinguished from examination, is not sufficient. This I assert emphatically.

The schools assume character and tone according to the nature of the inspections. So long as inspection shall remain, as at present, practically limited to the Results Examination and an incidental visit of five or ten minutes' duration, to check accounts, so long will the school work be limited to a mere grind for the examination, on the narrowest lines likely to secure success. A just estimate of the value of a school cannot be formed from the Examination Roll. Some most important portions of the teacher's duty are not included in the test. The estimate formed, on the day appointed for the annual examination, of order, discipline, organization, and moral training, by one who has not had other oppor- tunities of forming an opinion, is likely, as I am well aware, to be very fallacious. The tests themselves, at best, afford but rough measure- ments. Many of the branches of instruction are not adapted to this method of individual testing; such are kindergarten, geography, music, drawing, manual instruction of any kind. The waste of time in the present method of testing the proficiency in these branches is very obvious. Individual testing seems to me not at all in accordance with the spirit of kindergarten.

How much more valuable, after a brief *class examination*, would be the opinion of the Inspector who could report with precision on the mode in which the instruction in these branches had been carried on, and on the regularity and energy with which this instruction had been given, than the rude estimate formed from the present tedious individual examination!

The Results Examinations might, therefore, be simplified, and valuable time thereby saved for inspection proper.

I am of opinion that the extra branches might, with great advantage, *Grouping of extra branches.* be grouped. Thus, instead of separate examinations in geometry and algebra, there might be a suitable three years' course in elementary mathematics; and, instead of separate examinations in mechanics, hydro- statics, light, heat, electricity, &c., a suitable three years' course in natural science taught *experimentally*.

It is certainly of the gravest importance that the examinations should be simplified, and that the rewards bestowed on teachers should be made dependent, not merely on a partial discharge of their duties, but on the complete fulfilment of their obligations to the children entrusted to their care.

In connection with this, I hope I may be permitted to point out the importance of having all the accounts simplified as much as possible, so

Appendix C.
Reports on
State of
Schools.

Mr. E.
Downing,
Head
Inspector.
London-
derry.

that the attention of both teachers and Inspectors may be as little
as possible distracted from their primary duty of educating the people.
It is well to keep in mind that in every office there is a tendency
to attach undue importance to statistics, and at the same time to
remember that the elaboration of statistics will not educate our children.

Fees should not be allowed for the *mere theory* of any industrial
branch; and I have come to the opinion that agriculture should form
no exception to this rule. The theory of agriculture, as at present
taught, is not at all worth the money spent on it; and, therefore,
after due notice, no fees should be allowed for it, unless accompanied
with *practical* instruction in a school garden, or with chemical and
botanical demonstrations.

I am, Gentlemen,

Your obedient servant,

E. DOWNING,

Head Inspector.

The Secretaries,
    Office of National Education, Dublin.

Mr. S. E.
Strong,
Head
Inspector.
Belfast.

The circuit.

Mr. S. E. STRONG, M.A., Head Inspector.

Belfast, March, 1895.

GENTLEMEN,—As directed by your instructions of December, 1894,
I have the honour to submit the following general report upon the
state of education in this group of eleven districts. These eleven
school districts comprise almost the whole of the counties of Antrim,
Down, Armagh, Monaghan, and Cavan, and a few schools in Meath
and Tyrone. The number of schools within the circuit is 1,631.
These are of all classes, day and evening, urban and rural, Model and
Convent, Poor Law Union and half-time or mill schools, boys' and
girls' and infants' departments, or a mixed infant department, and a
mixed senior department. The last arrangement is the one usually
adopted in the city of Belfast.

Of this group of districts the city of Belfast is the centre. To
describe it as the most important town in the circuit as a centre of
education and commerce would be a mere platitude. If the population
of all the other towns in the circuit were combined, the total would fall
far short of the population of Belfast, and the same remark would apply
equally to the educational opportunities they afford and to their manufactures. While their growth is slow, that of Belfast is rapid—
perhaps as arithmetical progression is to geometrical progression.
Indeed it is to the rapid growth of Belfast itself that the slower
growth, and, in some cases, the decadence of the neighbouring towns—
especially where they have no staple manufacture of their own—is
owing. Similar instances of the rapid progress of one town at the
expense of others are of no infrequent occurrence in England. Even in
the villages in the most remote and isolated corners of the circuit the
influence of Belfast makes itself felt. All the best talent in education,
all the best skill in manufacture, and the most ambitious enterprise in
commerce naturally seek Belfast as the largest and best field for their

exercise. And thus very few of the schools in Belfast are taught by Appendix C.
second or third class teachers. A majority of the Principals have Reports on
attained to the highest classes under the Board. The larger number State of
again of these highly classed teachers were not born and trained in the Schools.
city, but have won their spurs in other towns or in rural schools, and Mr. S. K.
have then been attracted to Belfast as to a centre where there was a Strronge,
larger life to be lived and more valuable prizes to be won. This fact M. A. Head Inspector.
and the regularity with which the children in Belfast attend school— Belfast.
and did attend even when attendance was not enforced—are the causes
of the general excellence of the primary schools of the city.

As regards the regularity of the attendance both before and since the Regularity
Education Act of 1892 came into operation, a comparison of the of attend-
returns from the 231 schools within the municipal boundary for 1893— ance.
when the attendance was voluntary with those for 1894—the first year
of the enforcement of the Act—will show exactly the change that has
occurred.

1893.		1894.	
Number on Rolls, 31.12.'93 . . .	40,894	Number on Rolls, 31.12.'94 . . .	44,862
Average attendance for year ended 31.12.'93 . . .	31,667	Average attendance for year ended 31.12.'94 . . .	37,942

Thus while the percentage of attendance to the number upon roll in
1893 was a fraction less than sixty-eight, it was a little over seventy-five
in 1894, i.e., there has been a net gain in regularity of attendance of
between seven and eight per cent., or as the teachers put it in plain and
general terms, "we have not got many new pupils, but the Act has
steadied the attendance of those we have," or "those who used to attend
two or three days a week now attend four or five." The Act has thus
been of great benefit to the teachers in two ways. As it has made the
attendance more regular, the children will obtain more instruction, make
a better examination, and thus increase the teachers' results fees. Again,
the same regularity of attendance having raised the average attendance
per quarter, the residual grant, now paid in place of school fees, will also
be increased. Though the percentage of attendance to the number upon
roll is seventy-five, I think a stricter enforcement of the Act might
easily raise the percentage to eighty—a number below which it seldom
falls in Great Britain.

The Act, however, provides many loopholes of escape for the unwilling
or careless parent to take advantage of. The Attendance Committees
are very considerate and forbearing in their action towards the parents,
as if their object were to induce the parents to obey the law through
love of it rather than to coerce them into obedience through fear. Prosecutions have been very few, and the penalties upon conviction trifling.
I have heard of no complaint of harshness or hardship. Indeed I do
not think any could be made. In all the towns in the circuit in which
the Act has come into operation, the Attendance Committees have performed their duties in a business-like manner, and the percentage of
increase in regularity of attendance has varied from three per cent. to
eleven. I shall give one or two instances of the results of the operation Operation
of the Act. In Lisburn in 1893 the percentage of attendance to the of the Act
number on rolls was 68·6, in 1894 it was 74·4. In Newtownards in of 1893.
1893 it was 66·3 and in 1894, 75·2. In Larne the number on rolls
during 1894 increased by three per cent., and the average attendance by
eleven per cent—which is practically another way of stating that the
same increase has occurred there as in Lisburn and Newtownards. The

Appendix C.
Reports on State of Schools.

Mr. S. K. Strong, M.A. Head Inspector.
Belfast.

returns from the county of the town of Carrickfergus have an interest peculiar to themselves. The county of the town consists of twenty-six square miles. The whole of this area is considered as a township and is under the control of the Town Commissioners of Carrickfergus. Within this area there are in all twenty-three schools—eleven in the township proper and twelve in the country. In the town schools the percentage of attendance to number upon rolls in 1893 was 74·4, perhaps the highest attendance in Ireland before the Act of 1892 came into operation. There was not so great a margin left here for improvement and so in 1894 the attendance rose to 76·7 only. In the twelve rural schools the numbers on roll in 1893 were 881, and the average attendance 547·9 or a percentage of regularity of 62·1. In 1894 the numbers became 689 on roll and 607·5 in attendance, or a percentage of 70·6—an increase of almost eight per cent. upon the previous year. This is a valuable indication of the good effect which might attend the extension of the Act to rural as well as to urban schools.

Attendance in schools having an excess fee.

Upon the attendance at the Model schools and other schools in which a school fee—excess fee—is levied on all those who are able to pay, the Act has had no effect. The cause is not far to seek. The school fees in such schools varied according to the circumstances of the parents and were payable in advance. Parents who were wealthy enough to pay high school fees kept their children at school every day—never requiring to retain them at home to assist themselves. And thus before compulsion was introduced such schools showed a high percentage of regularity. The same classes of children still attend these schools and still pay what is termed an excess fee, and consequently the enforcement of the Act of 1893 has had no appreciable effect upon the regularity of the attendance at them. In Mill schools again, where half-time pupils attend upon alternate days, there has been no change, as these half-time pupils were and are most regular in attending their three days per week. The operation of the Act has not in any considerable degree benefited Infants' schools, as most of the children in this class of school do not, on account of their ages, come within the terms of the Act.

Work done in the schools.

With regard to the work done in the schools I have no hesitation in saying that more and harder work is now done than was ever done before. The teachers are as zealous and as earnest in the discharge of their duties as any body of workers could be. It is very rare, indeed, for an Inspector on calling in a school to find the teacher or his pupils doing nothing. I have often walked into the middle of the school-room or as far as the teacher's desk before I was seen by either teacher or pupils, so busily were all employed. The teacher is anxious that all should "pass" the Results Examination, and in order to attain this object or to approach it as nearly as possible, he will spare neither himself nor his pupils. Though I have heard it stated by some of my colleagues that it is in the hope of gain that induces and keeps up this high pressure, I am quite certain that in many cases it is not so. In teachers, as in others, there is a certain pride of profession, a certain belief in their own capacity to teach with success, and they will struggle and work hard—apart from all thoughts of gain—to maintain a position in their profession, and this position in their profession depends mainly upon the character of the Inspectors' annual reports. It might be urged that it does not matter what the stimulus is that drives the labourer on, that the more diligently he labours and the harder he works so much the better for the State which pays him, and that, as this is a question of plain common sense, there is nothing more to be said. There is, however, another side to this question of "getting full value for your money," and that is, that you think you are getting it but do not really get it. The Marking Sheet of the Results Examination of a school shows by figures 1, 2, 0 the values of the answering of the children in Reading, Writing, Arithmetic, Spelling, Grammar, Geography, Needlework, Music, and Drawing. Now it is to obtain the 1 in each subject, and failing that the 2, and to avoid the 0, that the teachers have been working all the year, and the Marking Sheet when filled in by the Inspector practically contains within itself the report upon the school. Yet this Marking Sheet will fall far short of showing the whole work done in a good school. Appendix C. Reports on State of Schools. Mr. A E Strange M.A. Head Inspector, Belfast.

The manner and address of the pupils, the discipline and, in one word, the training of the pupils will not appear upon the return. Yet the proper drill and training of the children under his care should be quite as much a teacher's aim as the explanation of discount or cube root, latitude and longitude, or the terms irregular and intransitive. When, however, I call the teacher's attention to the want of manner or bad address of his children, to their lounging in draft with hands in pockets and heads down, or to their rounded shoulders as they sit at desk work, the almost invariable explanation given is that "I have not time." Nor does this high pressure and hurry lead to the neglect of the pupils' training only; it affects also the teacher's school keeping, and, in a greater degree, the quality of the instruction imparted to the children. Work not fully shown by marking papers.

Though the time table, with suitable divisions of time and subject, is properly suspended, its arrangements are frequently more honoured in the breach than in the observance. The teacher thinks that his pupils are not making sufficiently rapid progress in one of the subjects of the programme and he violates his time table in order to devote extra time to it. When once a teacher begins to violate the provisions of his time table, he will resort again and again to this device and finally will abandon all system. A lax discipline and neglect of all training immediately follow, and nothing is left except Reading, Writing, and Arithmetic, and the quality of the instruction in these superficial and loose. The time table.

This necessity, too, of spending all his energy in cramming, causes the teacher also to be negligent as to the cleanliness of his school-room, except on the days of the Results Examination, and to devote little or no attention to keeping trim and tidy the plot of ground on which the school is built, not to speak of planting it with shrubs or flowers. The appearance of the exterior of many of the schools, as well as the appearance of the school yards or play ground is not such as is calculated to train the eyes of the children. What they are in the habit of seeing they will imitate. It is, therefore, of great importance in their education that both inside and outside the school-room their eyes should be trained by beholding tidiness rather than slovenliness, order rather than disorder, and carefulness rather than neglect. Neatness and cleanliness.

While, as I have already said, work in the schools excels in quantity, I have observed for some years back a great deterioration in quality and style. I have often—indeed in almost every school I have visited—called the attention of the teachers to the style of Reading, to the want of distinctness of articulation—so indistinct, indeed, as to be unintelligible to a mere listener—to false grouping of words, and the neglect of emphasising the proper words, to slurring, to omissions, and interpolations. I have often read sentences myself to show how the sense of passage should be conveyed. The teachers admit at once that good reading is taught only by imitating a good reader; that to teach Increase in quantity, deterioration of quality of work. Reading.

reading as I wished it taught would require two half-hour lessons at least for each class, and that they could not afford to give so much time to the subject. This mumbling loose style of reading has often reminded me of the quality and value of the knowledge of Latin and Greek acquired by candidates for Degrees in an Examining University. It would seem to be all the result of the students' unassisted labour without the guidance of the master to lay a sound basis, to guard against pit-falls, and to give life to the work. Now, Reading is the "pass" subject for which a fee is paid, but for the explanation or intelligent comprehension of the reading lesson, no fee is paid; and naturally enough, if the reading be bad the explanation will be worse. It is painful to recall the whole fifth classes of children, who, in the pictorial illustration at the head of the lesson on the Pyramids, thought that the Sphinx was the Pyramid, the numbers who denied that they had "European palates," that they had ever seen "hosiery," or an "ecclesiastical building." This report could be filled with examples of a similar kind. Nor is this want of soundness and thoroughness, this loose superficial instruction, confined to one subject. It appears in all, though less striking in some than in others. "Finger counting" and "lines of soldiers" in Arithmetic, carelessly written signatures in copy-books, names and not places pointed to on the maps, the rubbing out and measuring of lines and the moving round of the paper in Drawing, so as to avoid oblique and perpendicular lines, are to be met with every day. It appears to me to arise from an effort upon the part of the teacher to cover too much ground. Such an attempt is followed by the invariable result that part is always done badly and often the whole. The proverb, *festina lenis*, so quoted many years in regard to this very point by Mr. W. R. Molloy, is now still more applicable than it was then. "Do a little and do it well," applies to the work of the teacher more surely and more stringently than to any other kind of work. In the erection of an important building, time is always allowed at intervals, as the walls rise, for the "courses" to settle before another "course" is added. And so in education; each portion of a subject should be "marked, learned, and inwardly digested," before another portion is flung on the top. Education is a process and a growth. It is not the acquisition of fact upon fact only. If the inter-connection of the facts or the direction in which they, as a whole, point be not perceived, the time spent in storing them has been lost.

In order to remedy the defects here described, I am of opinion that considerable modifications of the present Results programme will be required. Under similar circumstances very great changes were introduced in England. It would, however, require much more than the limited space at my command here to even outline the changes which in my opinion ought to be made.

I have the honour to be, Gentlemen,
Your obedient servant,
S. E. STRONGE, Head Inspector.

The Secretaries,
Education Office, Dublin.

Appendix C.
Reports on
State of
Schools.

Mr. M'NEILL, B.A., District Inspector.

Mr. M'Neill,
B.A.,
District
Inspector,
Coleraine.

Coleraine, February 1st, 1895.

GENTLEMEN,—In accordance with your instructions I beg to submit the following General Report on the Coleraine district, of which I took charge on 1st April, 1893 :—

The district is well cultivated and prosperous ; the inhabitants are of *District.* more than ordinary energy and intelligence. Three fairly important towns—Coleraine, Ballymoney, and Portrush are included in its boundaries.

The number of schools at present in operation is 159, classified as *Schools.* follows :—

Ordinary	150
Model	6
Poor Law Union	2
Evening	1
	159

The district is well provided, in fact over provided, with schools. This is particularly the case in the northern part of County Antrim, where thirty schools could take the place of fifty with greater efficiency and economy. However, nothing except a very sweeping and concerted change would be of any use in remedying this. Very few of these fifty schools could be abolished without inflicting hardship on pupils of the locality. A group of three schools could very often be replaced by two properly situated, but there is no prospect of action like this.

The effect of this multiplication of small schools is disastrous. As the *Undue* average borders on the minimum there is the evident temptation to *multiplica-* falsification, there is the competition for pupils with neighbouring *tion of* schools in the same plight which prevents the insistence on thorough *schools.* discipline, and lowers the position of a teacher. Faults on the part of the pupils cannot be punished with proper severity, the failure of pupils to pass at examination is often concealed, and unwarranted promotion indulged in with the inevitable bad results.

The schoolhouses are, generally speaking, fairly suitable. Seven still *School-* remain which I regard as badly adapted for their present purpose, and *houses.* of them I have hopes that one or two will shortly be replaced by new vested schools. In one case the difficulty of obtaining a suitable site is the only obstacle.

I cannot give any considerable measure of praise to the manner in *Neatness of* which the schoolrooms are kept. On days of Results' Examination *school-* they of course look neat and tidy, but incidental visits reveal quite a *rooms.* different state of things. Slates and copy-books scattered about with an uncertainty on the part of everybody as to where they are or should be ; window sills used as convenient storehouses for all sorts of odds and ends ; a plentiful lack of dusting—these are defects not uncommonly met with. There is no reason why this should be so. I know several schoolrooms that at each and every visit are invariably models of neatness, order, and cleanliness. Too often attention has to be called to the state of the wall tablets, which bear evident traces of dust that has long lain undisturbed.

Appendix C.

Reports on
State of
Schools.

Mr. M'Neill,
B.A.,
District
Inspector.

Coleraine.

Teachers'
houses.

Order
and
manners.

Attendance.

Irish
Education
Act.

The teachers in this district are, as a rule, comfortably housed. The number of respectable dwelling-houses within easy radius of any school is nearly always considerable, and of these the teacher, as a rule, is in possession of one. In some cases distinct hardship still exists. The grant for building a teacher's residence has in several instances been availed of, and comfortable and commodious dwelling-houses have been erected. Difficulty of obtaining a suitable site again appears as an obstacle.

As a rule the teachers have their pupils well under control. This, too, although the northern character does not readily submit itself to strict discipline. I can also say that to the best of my belief order is maintained without recourse to punishments of undue severity.

In some directions there still remains considerable room for advance in this regard. The want of any attempt at drill is continually apparent. Such a simple order as to fall into the desks by fours or by fives will nearly always lead to considerable confusion. Movements are executed with unnecessary slowness, and valuable time is wasted over such details as giving out of pens, slates, &c.

I may here mention a fact which has often struck me. Northern boys and girls compare but badly with those from the south and west in the matter of manners and politeness. It is a prominent defect in the northern character that while the people are largely endowed with the valuable habits of energy, industry, thrift, and solid honesty, there should be associated with these a noticeable want of civility. This arises either from an unfortunate tendency to mistake rudeness for independence, or simply from not knowing any better. A reform in this matter might very well have its origin in our schools. The ordinary courtesies should be insisted on, pupils might be trained to simple acts of politeness, and shown that the best possible method of getting our own feelings respected is to respect those of others.

Except in spring when the crops are being sown and in autumn when they are being reaped the attendance of pupils is regular. As a rule parents are alive to the importance of sending their children to school, and securing for them at least the rudiments of an education. Nothing can be done to remedy irregularity during the months of April, May, September, and October. No perceptible effect has been caused by the remission of school fees. Apparently it has passed unnoticed. The effect of the Compulsory Attendance Act which applies to Coleraine, Ballymoney, and Portrush, calls for a more extended notice.

In each of these three towns, I am glad to say, a school attendance committee was constituted without any difficulty, salaries were fixed, and suitable officers appointed. The machinery of the Act has been put into motion, careless parents have been warned, directed to send their children to school, and as a last resource fined. At first it was thought advisable to deal leniently with offenders, but by degrees stricter methods will be adopted. In Coleraine and Ballymoney the Act has been successfully administered and bids fair to be of great advantage. In Portrush, owing to the employment of boys as 'caddies' on the golf links (in which capacity they earn good wages) no great improvement has been effected, but there is a prospect that better results will be achieved next year. The average attendance has, generally speaking, improved. Pupils who formerly were irregular in attendance now find it incumbent on them to attend with more steadiness. A good number have been compelled to attend who previously had not been receiving any schooling. These pupils are, as might naturally be expected, disorderly, mischievous, and inattentive, and

make great inroads on a teacher's time and patience. It is very
difficult to prevent the introduction of such pupils from lowering the
general tone of the school. However, these are precisely the children
who, unless reclaimed in some way, turn out idle and dissolute, and no
effort should be spared to give them an opportunity of setting themselves free from their bad associations.

And now it is necessary to take up the different school subjects in
order, and estimate the proficiency attained in each of them.

Reading. Broadly speaking, no subject on the programme is so unsatisfactory as this. I am becoming daily more and more convinced of
its paramount value. Compared with the importance of being able to
read intelligently and to understand correctly a passage of ordinary
prose, other branches fall into the background. It is on this that, after
school days are over, a man must rely largely for instruction, recreation,
and knowledge of what goes on in the world. It is deplorable then if
a pupil leaves school a heedless and inaccurate reader, with no definite
notion that the words which he mumbles over mean anything in
particular or are anything except unpleasant obstacles to be cleared at
a racing pace. Too little time is given to the subject for one thing, and
when, as always happens, another subject is going on at the same time,
reading goes to the wall, and is considered properly supervised by an
inattentive pupil or monitor. And pupils cannot speak out loudly and
distinctly lest other work should be interfered with. The result is that
a style of reading is acquired which often wants accuracy, and always
expression. Probably the easiest method of securing good reading in
any school would be to suspend all other work occasionally and let the
pupils in turn read aloud, it being insisted on that the passage read
should be distinctly heard by every one. I have noticed a wonderful
improvement in the reading of a school where the teacher and some of
the senior pupils had received a few lessons in elocution. Something in
this way might be done while the teachers are in training. I do not
mean the acquisition of elocutionary airs and gestures, but merely
correct and intelligent reading, than which there is no accomplishment
more uncommon. These remarks with reference to reading of coarse
apply equally to repetition of poetry. As a rule poetry is repeated in
such a fashion that it would be better left unlearnt and unsaid.

Writing affords a pleasing contrast to reading. It is very well taught
indeed. In a few schools owing to lax supervision of copy-books
scribbling obtains to some extent, but these schools are in a very small
minority. Most of our pupils leave school able to write a decent legible
hand. Incidentally during the year I came across a noteworthy point.
I found pupils who were able to write very well quite at sea when
called on to decipher any other person's handwriting, and even very
little at home with their own, supposing the matter had faded from
their memory. The custom which prevails in some schools of permitting
the pupils to correct each other's dictation exercises should remedy
this.

Letter-writing also comes under this head. The spelling displayed in
the letters written on examination days is by no means satisfactory.
One particular class of mistakes occurs with exasperating frequency—
the for *they, their* for *there,* and vice versa; next after this comes a
singular verb with a plural nominative—a fatal stumbling block. The
proper method of beginning and ending a letter is now generally known,
though even yet I sometimes find on inspection of the letters written
during the year, that they have been all addressed to one person—the

Appendix C

Reports on State of Schools.

Mr. M'Neill, # 3, District Inspector.

Caloulea.

teacher himself usually. Consequently when at examination the unfortunate pupil is directed to write to some other person trouble arises.
At examination leaves of an exercise book are distributed, and folded
in two so as to resemble an ordinary sheet of notepaper. This I
consider a better test than simply permitting the pupils to write a
letter on paper of ordinary foolscap size. These can be folded and the
address written on the outside. Very often these addresses take a
startling form, and show the necessity for attention to this point. As
to the composition of the body of the letter considerable improvement is
to be noted. The letters are now of fair length, the pupils no longer
hesitating to commit their views to paper. In some schools I have
found them able to write neat, compact and sensible letters such as
would pass muster anywhere. This is a subject to which I attach
particular importance, and I consider that there is no one more
valuable for improving the mental faculties of the children. At present
Fifth Class, Second Stage, are required at Results' Examination to
exhibit a certain number of letters written during the results period.
This regulation might be extended to Fifth Class, First Stage, and
Sixth Class. These letters should be kept in a separate exercise book;
and should show at once the progress made by the pupil during the
year.

Spelling.

The proficiency of the pupils in Spelling may be put down as
fairly satisfactory. Passages dictated to them from their lesson books
are written down with reasonable correctness, and the junior classes who
are taught the words arranged at the head of their lessons, almost
always spell them unfalteringly. I would be inclined to raise the
standard for spelling in Sixth Class. A passage for dictation might be
set to them not necessarily from their reading book—from a newspaper,
for instance. This should be of fair length, and, as taken down, should
be almost entirely free from mistakes. A pupil who has spent six or
seven years at school should be able to write any ordinary passage of
prose without mistake. The study of the Spelling Book Superseded
appears to have been largely given up as an aid to teaching pupils to
spell correctly. This is much to be regretted. The entire book could
not be prescribed, as it is much too lengthy, but there are valuable
sections in it which might be learnt with great advantage. Such for
instance as "The Rules for Spelling." A smaller book containing
perhaps about one-fourth of the matter in the present Spelling Book
Superseded would be found very useful in our schools.

The method of dictation is nearly always faulty. The passage is read
too slowly, sentences are repeated *ad nauseam*, and lagging pupils are
encouraged in their evil ways by knowing that they will be carefully
waited for. Sometimes I hear the passage read in a straightforward
and business-like manner and taken down similarly. This, however,
occurs but rarely.

Arithmetic.

Arithmetic is well taught. Long and complicated sums are solved
with ease. The work is generally speaking accurate, but I sometimes
notice a want of alertness and a disposition to plunge into figures without
properly ascertaining the conditions of the problem presented. Even a
clever boy will have little scruple in asserting by his answer that 40 sheep
cost less than 30. The latest set of arithmetical cards by making
increased demands on a pupil's intelligence in contra-distinction to his
power of working according to rules, will direct attention to this point.
Mental arithmetic is not by any means satisfactory. Simple sums such
as would be encountered in the purchase of any week's groceries are
often too much even for advanced pupils. This is unfortunate. The

faculty of making simple calculations speedily and accurately is one Appendix C.
that is being continually drawn upon in daily life. Reports on State of Schools

This subject may be classed with reading as unsatisfactory. It never
seems to lead to anything definite. Whether this arises from its inherent
unsuitability, or from defects in the method of teaching, I cannot Mr. M'Neill District Inspector.
determine. Most probably from the union of both causes. In any case
it is not unusual to find pupils who are able to parse long and compli- Calculation.
cated sentences quite unable to write a few ordinary sentences such as
would occur in a letter without some glaring grammatical errors. And Grammar.
yet if grammar is of any advantage whatever it is in this direction that
its usefulness should be apparent. I think that the study of grammar
should not be taken up early; it should be postponed until the pupils are
able to understand what the subject means, and are not driven to fall
back on memory. The definitions should be expressed in the plainest
and simplest language, and some of the present abstruse and complicated
efforts in this direction should be abolished. Analysis of easy sentences, on the other hand, might well find place in the programme.
A passage containing some obvious grammatical errors might be
assigned to the pupils for correction. A list of mistakes in grammar
which are most in evidence in the locality should be drawn up, and the
necessity of guarding against these mistakes insisted on. Otherwise
the fact that in the ordinary intercourse of life the pupils continually
hear these mistakes committed makes it impossible for them to avoid
them.

The subject of Geography does not call for any extended comment. Geography.
The proficiency of the pupils is generally very fair, and shows that the
text books on the subject are carefully studied. Third and Fourth Classes
answer very well, map painting presenting no difficulty. Blank maps are
not sufficiently availed of in teaching the senior classes, though this is of
course much the most valuable branch of map teaching. More attention
should be given to the necessity of imparting useful information or
interesting facts about the countries and places mentioned, so as to
prevent the lesson from becoming dry and uninteresting. There is a
good deal of emigration from this part of Ireland to America, principally
to the United States and Canada, and it is to be regretted that a more
minute knowledge of these countries is not enforced by the programme.

The answering from the text book on Agriculture is fairly satisfactory. Agriculture.
That the information obtained is of much practical value I can scarcely
assert. However, an excellent system of agriculture prevails in this
district, and in the case of pupils who are destined to an agricultural life
in a short period of practical work on a farm, will no doubt considerably
reinforce the lessons taught in the "Introduction to Practical Farming."

The "sets" of Book-keeping are written out neatly enough, but little Book-keeping.
real knowledge of the subject is found. Occasionally pupils are met
with who have thoroughly mastered it, but this is rarely the case.
I fear that the text book on the subject is somewhat out of date.

There is every reason to be satisfied with the proficiency in Needle- Needle-work.
work. Really bad needlework is very seldom met with, and the
requirements of the programme are almost always properly carried out.
The Alternative Scheme for Sixth Class girls has not been generally
adopted, and is not making headway. Fresh schools apply for
exemption, and practically the only important schools in which the
scheme is now taken up are the model schools. In these schools it is
taught with much success, and the work done by the pupils and
exhibited at Results' Examination is exceedingly creditable. This
work is afterwards found either useful or decorative in the children's

Appendix C.

Reports on State of Schools.

Mr. M'Neill, E.4. District Inspector. Coleraine.

Extra subjects.

homes. The favourite branches are A², knitting and crocheting of Jerseys, &c., D² Mountmellick work, and B¹ art needlework. It is a question whether the Industrial programme is particularly well suited to the circumstances of girls such as generally attend the model schools. In a town like Coleraine these girls as a rule belong to the well-to-do classes, and their parents would probably wish to see literary instruction forming a large portion of their work at school. Some modification of the industrial programme in the direction of concession to the literary element would be of advantage.

The extra and optional branches principally met with are Drawing, Music (both Hullah and Tonic Sol-fa), Kindergarten, Algebra, Geometry, and Physical Geography.

Drawing.

The results obtained in Drawing are as yet poor, though in all probability the recently increased fee will secure better results. No great amount of supervision appears to be given to this subject; copy books, pencils, and the harmful necessary indiarubber are distributed, and then the pupils, provided they remain quiet, are left to their own devices. About one-third of the time is devoted to drawing, the remainder to rubbing out what has been done. Instead of continual efforts in copy books, I should like to see an easy copy set on the black board, and, for the senior classes, sketching of ordinary objects of any shape should be introduced. A pupil is sure to take great delight in discovering his power of producing even a rough likeness of an actual chair or table. The favourite employment of pupils left to themselves seems to be the drawing of horses, ships, &c.

Vocal music.

Vocal Music is not taught so extensively as it might be. The revised programme is very definite, and it is easy to determine at once whether pupils are entitled to a pass or not. Hullah's system is the one generally adopted; Tonic-Solfa the more effective. In both cases the programme for Sixth Class covers a great amount of ground, and I do not often find the pupils of that class thoroughly prepared. In other classes the results are satisfactory. I am not content with the class of songs generally taught to the pupils. Sometimes both words and music are poor stuff, and the want of a recognised good selection of school songs is apparent.

Kindergarten.

There are five regularly organised Infants' Departments in this district, and in four of these Kindergarten is taught. Training in Kindergarten exercises I consider very valuable—it makes school time pass pleasantly for the children, and arouses their intellectual faculties to a marked extent. In all schools where there is an attendance of any considerable number of infants, provision should be made for their employment during part of the day at Kindergarten exercises, such as would not interfere with the other work of the school. This can be easily done, and the requisite materials can be procured at but a small cost.

Algebra and Geometry.

When Algebra and Geometry are attempted they are, as a rule, well taught. The time is gone past when a large number of pupils would be thrust forward in these branches in the hope that one or two of them would be lucky enough to avoid failure. Mensuration rather suffers in comparison with Geometry proper, and it is a pity that this useful subject should not get more attention.

School exercises.

The want of care in the selection and correction of school exercises forms an often recurring subject of complaint both at Results Examination and incidental inspection. The duty of attending to this point is so manifest that one would not expect to find its neglect so common. However, I am often vexed, though not surprised, to find exercises con-

taining grievous mistakes unnoticed and uncorrected. These identical
mistakes I find cropping up again with fatal effect at Results Examination. Letters are wrongly begun, wrongly finished, and badly
spelled, parsing exercises are quite unsuitable as regards difficulty, and
show no trace of supervision. Practically this amounts to an invitation
to the pupil to fail, and of this he usually avails himself. There is no
point of school keeping with regard to which there is more room for
improvement.

With regard to the teaching and training of monitors, I am glad to
say that I can report very satisfactorily. They are a useful help to the
principal teachers and attend well to their work. At the last July
examination all the monitors examined succeeded in passing, and
several of them made exceptionally good answering.

A general review of the working of the district leads me to believe
that a large amount of valuable educational work is done every year,
and that a conscientious attention to duty on the part of the teachers
prevails to a gratifying extent.

I am, Gentlemen, your obedient servant,

J. M'NEILL.

The Secretaries,
    Education Office.

Mr. J. M'K. WARNER, B.A., District Inspector.

Castledawson, 28th February, 1895.

GENTLEMEN,—I have the honour to submit the following report on
the schools of this district, of which I have been in charge since March,
1892.

The district consists of the Loughinsholin Barony of Derry, and the
southern portion of Coleraine Barony, together with a narrow strip of
the County Antrim, extending from Lough Beg to Rasharkin. It
contains about a dozen towns and villages, of which the largest has a
population little over two thousand. While the staple industry is
agriculture, a considerable number of the people are engaged in linen
weaving in their homes. In some places this affects the school attendance in the senior classes, the children being withdrawn from school to
assist in the weaving operations at the earliest possible age.

At the end of the year 1894 there were in operation one hundred
and fifty-two ordinary day schools, one evening school, one convent
school, and one P. L. U. school, the last having two departments.

The average attendance at the Magherafelt Convent School is nearly
one hundred. Of the ordinary schools about twelve attain an average
of seventy, most of these being in the towns and villages; upwards of
sixty range from forty to seventy, while about half are less than forty
in average, some twelve having less than thirty. The attendance at the
evening school was thirty-four. Some years ago there were several
schools of this class, mostly in the mountainous parts of the district,
but for the present they have ceased to be required.

Appendix C.
Reports on
State of
Schools.

Mr. J. M'E.
Farmer,
B.A.,
District
Inspector.
Cumberland.

Distribution
and multi-
plication of
schools.

Local
support.

School-
houses.

In some places the schools are excessively numerous. These localities would benefit educationally by the substitution of one or two large schools for the present small institutions, which cannot expect to command for any length of time the services of other than third-class teachers of but mediocre efficiency at best. This undue multiplication of schools can be understood where it arises from the desire of each religious denomination to have a school of its own. Four denominations are in this way represented in one village of less than four hundred and fifty inhabitants; but in one locality there are, within a radius of about a mile, five schools under similar management as concerns denomination.

Several schools, for the most part under the management of the London Companies, have hitherto retained the services of abler teachers than their attendance would command, in consequence of the substantial additions, from £15 to £30, made to the official incomes, together with residences and gardens in several instances.

The school-houses of this district are, as a rule, fairly satisfactory— many excellent. All but about twenty are fairly suitable buildings in themselves, and are also suited to the numbers in attendance. Some others of the older houses have rather low ceilings, but these have generally means of ventilation in the roof.

Of the minority of twenty, some three or four are much too small for the attendance. Two of these have been already enlarged, but the attendance continuing to increase, owing to the exceptional efficiency of the instruction, further additions to the buildings will be necessary. If the present conditions continue, I have no doubt the necessary changes will be made.

As a rule, I find that managers here perceive such defects as exist in the school buildings, and are anxious to remove them. One small and unhealthy building was almost entirely rebuilt last year, and is now a sanitary and cheerful house. Arrangements have been made by which, in a short time, four of the unsuitable buildings will be replaced by others, entirely new in two cases, almost so in the others. In four or five other cases, and those among the worst, efforts, which there is reason to expect will prove successful, are being made by managers to effect improvement, and in five other cases managers have promised to take action as soon as circumstances will permit. Taking the last two years, I could name five or six other schools in which enlargement or other extensive structural improvement has been effected.

There are about five schools of a very unsuitable character, as to which I fear managers are not yet convinced of the necessity for thorough change. In two further cases the managers are most anxious to improve, but have not as yet succeeded in persuading the residents in the localities concerned to give the necessary co-operation, the people considering the school-houses as good as their homes, and seeing no occasion for change. Managers under such circumstances have sometimes asked me to suggest to the Education Office that special letters on the subject should be addressed to them to assist them in their efforts with local parties.

The school-houses which I classify as unsuitable generally, as distinguished from being merely too small, are for the most part of one type. They have not been originally constructed for school purposes; the roof is very low, the floor is either of earth or of half-rotten boards resting directly on the soil, sometimes below the level of the ground outside, and without the necessary drainage; the windows are small and too low for light, and the lighting is still worse when the roof is of black unceiled thatch; ventilation is inadequate and unsatisfactory, as owing to the low level of the windows, the draft caused when these are opened, at or below the level of pupils' heads, creates a temptation to keep them always closed; there is no porch, no seemly provision for disposal of shawls, &c.; no suitable wall space for maps. The furniture is often in keeping with the rooms. As above stated there is, I think, a fair prospect that most school-houses of this class will soon have disappeared. In some cases improvements effected in non-vested schools have been no doubt in part made in order to render the school-houses better suited to general local purposes, but the result has been educationally advantageous at the same time.

Fifteen schools have each an assistant—one has two. Most of these are retained on the privileged average of 50, so the number of assistants may be expected to decrease. There are nearly 50 monitors.

Of the assistants about two-thirds are in third class. The classification of the principals is fairly high; about one-fifth are in first class, rather over the half are in second class. In another part of Ireland I was struck by the fact that a considerable proportion of the really good schools were under third-class principals, this is not so here; as a rule the classification of the principals is closely in proportion to their efficiency. With three or four exceptions, the first-class teachers are really doing excellent work, while, as a rule, the schools under third-class teachers are middling or bad. The exceptions in the latter case are mainly in the case of young teachers who may expect promotion soon. One excellent school is taught by a third-class teacher of middle age, who for special reasons has been unable to seek promotion. On the whole there has been, in the course of the year, an improvement in the *personnel* of the staff.

Speaking in general terms, I consider that of the 155 schools of all kinds about nine were excellent, upwards of eighty fair or good, over forty middling and about twenty absolutely bad. In six, however, of those classed as bad a change has taken place in the staff since the last examination, and improvement may be expected or hoped for. Some of the indifferently conducted schools are under young teachers. If these do not show signs of amendment there is a prospect of their eventual, and perhaps early, removal. It is different when such a school is in charge of a middle-aged or elderly teacher, who will not soon be entitled to pension. The manager, having allowed the teacher to remain so long, is loth to dismiss him now, especially if a family is depending on him. Sometimes, on a severe admonition from the Education Office, he makes an effort for a year, and does a tolerable amount of work, only to relapse into worthlessness next year. I fear there is no prospect of appreciable improvement while such a teacher is in charge; he is simply preventing the children of his locality from being taught. Some schools of this type exist almost wholly for infants, whose parents find this a convenient method of tending them for five hours. I fear even these children, who may attend school from three years of age, do not in the long run profit by having such an institution close to their doors; they are learning to dawdle.

In some cases where schools under well-disposed and really hard-working teachers are yet of only mediocre efficiency, owing to defective organisation and method, I have suggested to managers that they should request the assistance of one of the organisers; the suggestion has been readily assented to in some cases, but the experiments have not yet been made.

Appendix C.

Reports on State of Schools.

Mr. J. M'E. Warner, M.A. District Inspector.

Conclusion.

Infants.

The Infants' class forms a large proportion of the number in most schools. Sometimes indeed it is larger than proper, children being placed or kept in Infants' Classes whose years and opportunities would suggest First or Second Class at least as the enrolment to be expected. Something of the kind occurs in fair schools; in an inefficient one I found children, apparently in good health, to have been kept for six years in Infants' Class. This is a gross abuse of the Results System. The Convent School alone has an Infants' Department. I fear in most schools the provision for Infants' occupation is unsatisfactory; it is not uncommon to find them practically in absolute idleness through successive half-hours. The Time Table may state that they are copying figures or reading from tablets, but no one has set them a copy, or looks at any work they may do.

Reading.

Except in the best schools Reading seldom reaches the "fluency, correctness, and intelligence" of the programme. That the actual words of the books are pronounced is all that is commonly aimed at, and frequently this is not attained, even by pupils who have attended well. This is often, I believe, due to their being left too much to themselves at reading time, several drafts reading at the same time and the teacher attending only to one, and probably doing some other work at the same time. Independently of such defects of method or organisation indistinct articulation is very common in this part of the country, e.g., the *s* of the plural, or a final *y* is often scarcely sounded, and the last syllables of various words are constantly ignored or represented by one obscure sound. The efficient teacher checks this, the careless or unobservant either does not notice it or thinks it of no consequence. In the repetition of poetry absurd mistakes are made; it is often obvious that it has been left entirely to the pupils themselves.

Writing.

Writing is generally very fair in the junior classes. There are of course some teachers who do not really understand what is implied by imitation of a headline, and do not perceive defects in pupils' copies, I have sometimes, after pointing out the faults likely to occur in certain letters, subsequently observed that they were attended to. Few Managers care to go into details in such matters. Some, however, attend the examinations throughout, carefully follow the answering in all subjects, and I have reason to believe take practical steps towards removing defects. In Fourth Class I have often found the Programme neglected, pupils not writing small hand; in one school the pupils of Second Class write the No. 9 of Thom's series well. The requirement

Letter writing.

of something approaching Composition in Classes V. and VI. causes more variation in the proficiency from school to school. Except in the absolutely bad schools the subject is not neglected, but inspection of pupils' exercise books frequently shows very imperfect correction of errors.

Spelling.

Spelling is generally good in the junior classes, very fair in the higher; in the latter it is generally good in proportion to the handwriting.

Arithmetic.

In Arithmetic a good or fair proficiency is generally attained. In the junior classes I have frequently to point out a deficient knowledge of the Tables, making the work slow, and so lessening the amount of practice, besides increasing the mental strain on the children. If the subject is taught properly to young children little brain work will be required; they can, therefore, the sooner without risk leave the Infants' Class, if ever placed in it, and the sooner reach the higher classes—a matter of importance when one considers the age at which most children leave school. In regard to Numeration and Notation, also, a want of thoroughness in the instruction is often observable.

Perhaps in no other obligatory subject is there so much difference in the extent and quality of the instruction given at different schools as in Grammar. In some this subject is thoroughly and soundly taught from the beginning, in others the knowledge gained in the course of a year is almost inappreciable. Some teachers seem to assume that it cannot be taught, and only attempt to teach it superficially. In my opinion it is less worry to the teacher, as well as less strain and more interest to the pupil, to teach the subject intelligently from the first.

Geography is generally known very fairly in Class III.; on the whole, fairly in Classes IV. and V.; not well in VI., except in the particularly good schools. It is generally only in these that any considerable number are enrolled in Class VI., and in middling schools there is a tendency to neglect a small class. I sometimes find that no attempt has been made to keep up in Class VI. the pupils' knowledge of the map of the world attained in Classes III. and IV.

The knowledge of the text-book on Agriculture is seldom more than middling. There are no agricultural schools or school gardens in this district.

About forty schools presented pupils in Book-keeping; the answering was satisfactory in about a fourth of these, mediocre or poor in the rest. Sufficient attention is seldom given to the neatness of the writing and ruling of the sets.

Pupils were presented for examination in Drawing in eleven schools, being a slight increase on previous years; the proficiency was fair on the whole, and generally showed improvement. Music, Hullah's system, was presented in five schools, Tonic Solfa in six. The proficiency was indifferent in two cases, good or fair in the others, and distinctly improved in two. Music, as well as Drawing, shows an increase, and some other schools will probably introduce the subject.

Of other extra and optional subjects pupils were presented in Domestic Economy, Kindergarten, Latin, and Physical Geography, but Algebra and Geometry only were at all common. Upwards of thirty schools were examined in the former, the answering being generally fair. Geometry was presented in fewer cases, and the proficiency is seldom quite satisfactory; very often the steps in the proof are not clearly defined or perceived by the pupil; he does not quote his authority at each step; if a proposition consists of two parts proved independently he is unable to prove one without going through both; any change from the positions in which he has previously seen the lines and points will nonplus him; if he has been in the habit of writing out proofs he cannot prove orally, and *vice versa*.

Industrial Education.—The industrial education in this district, except so far as concerns *Agriculture*, is confined to that of the girls in the various branches of *Needlework*. Some thirty of the ordinary schools are under male principals without provision for instruction in needlework of the girls attending; as a rule these are small schools, a workmistress being appointed wherever the attendance admits; except in one or two mountainous localities some school providing for the subject is within the reach of all. As a rule the proficiency is satisfactory; darning in senior classes is often not so, and I frequently have to explain to new teachers the Programme's requirements for knitting in Classes V¹ and V². In one school good needlework is a speciality, mainly through the interest taken in it and practical attention given to it by the Manager's wife; a large proportion of the pupils annually receive prizes for work shown at exhibitions in Cookstown and other places. The number of schools which have not been exempted from the Alternative Scheme for Sixth Class is small, and decreasing; the sections selected by the schools working on this Programme were commonly A^1, A^2, A^3, or some other, mainly or entirely of the needlework kind; the proficiency in the selected sections was not always good, or in proportion to the time given to them, while the literary portion of the Programme was also not well prepared; the number of schools concerned, however, was scarcely large enough for a general statement.

The 1892 Act is not operative in this district as regards compulsory attendance; and the practical abolition of school fees has not, so far as I can ascertain from inquiries in various localities, had any appreciable affect on the attendance. Under ordinary circumstances attendance varies with the efficiency of the instruction; in schools of low efficiency there will be an annual average of only about half the number enrolled, while in good ones it may reach seventy per cent. In good schools also punctuality in morning arrival is observable; all or almost all the pupils who will be present on the day arrive before the time for commencement of work.

In addition to the ordinary causes which make the attendance of most National School children irregular, the occurrence of epidemics very frequently affects it seriously. There was scarcely a month of last year in which some locality of the district was not suffering from some disorder, not only affecting the attendance of those actually ill but deterring others from attending for a considerable period. Thus, scarlatina was prevalent in three different localities, diphtheria in one, measles in five. At one school, where in the preceding year sixty-eight were qualified for examination, only forty-six made the required attendance last year, in consequence of a succession of epidemics; the teachers, nevertheless, preferred to have the examination in the month fixed, as on the whole the most advantageous course.

In regard to the order of the schoolrooms, I find a difficulty in persuading some teachers to make the pupils use the pegs provided for suspension of caps, &c. Some schools have no provision of the kind, but this is a matter easily and cheaply remedied. I have sometimes to remind teachers that the school-room is a sitting-room, and that they should not set to the pupils a nasty example of expectorating on the floor; I fear a teacher who requires such a hint will not be much improved by it. Of course such cases are exceptional; many of the rooms are at all times clean and comfortable.

I am glad to report that in conducting Results' Examinations I have little trouble in securing honesty of work; attempts at collusion are seldom made and are easily checked.

The School Bank system has not been introduced here.

I have the honour to be, Gentlemen,

Your obedient servant,

J. M'K. WARREN, Inspector of National Schools

The Secretaries,
    Education Office.

Mr. W. PEDLOW, B.A., District Inspector.

Belfast, March, 1893.

GENTLEMEN,—In accordance with instructions I beg to submit to you a General Report on the state of National Education in this District. Geographically it may be described as the southern half of the Antrim side of Belfast, Ballynafeigh and Rosetta on the Down side, and a tract of country varying from four to eight miles in breadth, extending to within a distance of three miles from Dromore, and seventeen miles in length.

The schools under my inspection may be classed as follows :—

3 Model School Departments.
1 Model Evening School.
1 Poor Law Union School with two Departments.
1 Convent School.
1 Ordinary Evening School.
130 Ordinary Day Schools.

Of these schools, 78 are in the City of Belfast, 1 in Lisburn, 3 in Hillsborough, and the others in rural localities. The Belfast schools are large, the rural schools small; some of them, with difficulty, maintain an attendance of 30 pupils, and only 7 have an average attendance above 70.

During the past two years aid has been granted by the Board to five new schools in my district, four of which are in Belfast. One school was divided into two separate departments, two were amalgamated into one, and another, owing to insufficient attendance, became inoperative.

Schoolhouses.—With a single exception the schoolhouses in the Belfast portion of my District are all well built and well ventilated. A few are overcrowded and too small, but, in most cases, allowing eight square feet for each child, the space elsewhere is more than sufficient for the attendance. The one bad schoolhouse would not be in existence could a suitable site be obtained. The efforts of Managers to provide healthy accommodation for the children are highly praiseworthy; and, in procuring funds for enlargements, structural improvements, and keeping premises in proper repair, they spare no pains. Where additional accommodation is required it is usually provided, and, where this is not the case, additional ground cannot be procured owing to surrounding buildings. The following schools have been enlarged or have undergone extensive structural improvements at local expense since I took charge of this District in 1893 :—St. Mary's, Bank-street; St. Joseph's, Slate-street; St. Peter's, Raglan-street; St. Brigid's Infant School, Brook-street; Lower Falls; Morpeth-street; Excise-street; St. Paul's, Lemon-street; Hutchinson-street, No. 1; Clogher; Edenticullo; and Carryduff. In the course of my inspections I have pointed out some defects in common to many non-vested schoolhouses. They are nearly all used for many purposes, in addition to teaching, and have usually one large rectangular room designated the "main school." The fault in construction is the size of this main room. It should be smaller and the class-rooms larger and more numerous. Large rooms are, no doubt, the best for public meetings, but probably the worst for schools. It is difficult

F

Appendix C.
Reports on
State of
Schools.

Mr. W.
Fallon,
District
Inspector.

Belfast.

Class-
rooms

to maintain proper discipline and order in a room where there are more than 100 children. The necessary noise of so many at work is, to some extent, distracting. It is accompanied by an amount of disorder difficult to check, so rare on the teachers, and an encouragement to thoughtlessness and inattention on the part of the pupils. I have, from time to time, suggested the erection of moveable partitions to provide class-rooms, and, when consulted about the erection of schools in Belfast, have advised Managers to adopt the rectangular shape for the main room with a class-room at one side, and to have the main room of such length that an additional class-room could be cut off by a moveable partition. This means two class-rooms and a fair sized schoolroom. Class-rooms cannot well be dispensed with where music is taught or when there is a large attendance of young children. For collective work, which I believe should be encouraged, they are most valuable. My experience leads me to conclude that the number taught with the greatest advantage in a single schoolroom varies from about 80 to 100.

Premises.

Few of the city schools have play-grounds. Most of them have only yards. Although the closets are necessarily near the houses they are kept in excellent order, they are properly and regularly flushed, and there is always a good supply of water for all purposes. It is satisfactory to record that during the past two years not a single school under my supervision in Belfast had to be closed owing to sickness, whilst in the rural parts of my District two were closed for a length of time last year, owing to an epidemic of measles.

Health.

Health.—I have given suggestions to Managers and teachers regarding the health of children, but chiefly to the latter. I pointed out when opportunity arose the importance of ventilation, of physical exercise, of cleanliness, and the precautions which must be taken to prevent children suffering from an infectious disease attending school. In all Infant Schools there has lately been a great extension of drill, action songs, and manual occupations, which tend to make Infant life happy. Teachers are, I am glad to say, becoming daily more alive to their usefulness and importance, and to the fact that when well conducted they make school popular and attendance regular. Within the last eighteen months dumb-bell exercises, pole exercises, and calisthenic drill have been introduced to many schools. They are well conducted by trained extern teachers, and before the ordinary arrangements of time table have been begun or after they are completed. Parents appreciate these health exercises, and teachers know that this appreciation is of importance to them. At all my inspections I have given encouragement to physical training which is so essential to city life.

Compulsory attendance.

Compulsory Attendance.—Compulsory attendance in my District applies only to Belfast, and to one school in Lisburn. When first enforced in January, 1894, the number on rolls was somewhat enlarged, and a few schools were partially disorganised through the admission of grown up children who had never before been taught. This was only temporary, but good teachers accounted for failures at Results Examinations by the introduction of these children who had been waifs and strays. Two facts came forcibly under my notice in localities where the Act extensively operated. One was a marked increase in attendance, and the other a marked decline in proficiency. The totally neglected who should have been taught, received attention at the expense of others who had been regularly at school from an early age. In four localities teachers complained that after compulsion had been enforced parents were more inclined to take their children from school after passing Fourth Class. The Education Act of 1892 applied to seventy six schools in this district, and the following statistics will show how they have been affected:—

Appendix C.

Reports on State of Schools.

Mr. W. Prinlose, District Inspector, Belfast.

1892.		1894.	
Total average on Rolls for year ended 31.12.92	12272	Total average on Rolls for year ended 31.12.94	12352
Total average attendance for year ended 31.12.92	10476	Total average attendance for year ended 31.12.94	11543
Number examined at these schools in 1892	10105	Number examined at these schools in 1894	10579

These figures show that whilst there is only an increase of about 100 on rolls, there is an increase of over 1,000 in average attendance. This does not denote the total increase, for three large schools, capable of accommodating 1,000 children, have been opened during the last twelve months, and have reduced the attendance at those tabulated. Estimating the attendance at these schools at 600, which, I believe, is about correct, the attendance would be increased by 16 per cent, where compulsion is in force.

School Fees.—The competition of free schools with others allowed to charge an excess rate has almost completely abolished the payment of school pence. Where a large rate was insisted on, the children left and went to neighbouring schools. Fees are now more difficult to obtain, as the labourer and mechanic understand nothing about partial abolition, and know that total abolition is the rule. Exclusive of the Model School, all Infant Schools are free. A few ordinary day schools charge a small excess rate, and only one charges a high rate. At this school the fees for last year amounted to over £130, and the excess rate was over 14s. The average attendance, however, decreased from 240 in 1893, to 180 in 1894, and the staff was reduced by two assistants during 1894. To charge a high rate in a school surrounded by others free makes that school a select one, and practically not thoroughly open for the admission of all whom it should benefit. This is, I think, objectionable, but the evil corrects itself. It is, however, well known that in Belfast, and particularly in its suburbs, wealthy parents send their children to National Schools, and should, no doubt, contribute liberally towards their education, but the children are sent to them, not to avoid payment, but simply because these schools are considered to give the best instruction for mercantile purposes. I shall now give some statistics regarding the schools of my District in which attendance is optional, and fees have been wholly or partly abolished. These schools number 51, and the statistics are as follows:—

Effect of charging school fees.

No charge in non-compulsory localities through abolition of school fees.

1892.		1894.	
Total average on Rolls for year ended 31.12.92	3284	Total average on Rolls for year ended 31.12.94	3153
Total average attendance for year ended 31.12.92	2419	Total average attendance for year ended 31.12.94	2507
Number examined at these schools in 1892	2683	Number examined at these schools in 1894	2774

These figures show that where compulsory attendance does not exist, matters remain much the same as they were. Rural schools are, and have been for years, attended by the children of farmers, shopkeepers, and tradesmen, and to them a small fee was not a matter of importance. The towns, and chiefly Belfast, have absorbed the labourers, and whilst

Appendix C.
Report on
State of
Schools.

Mr. W.
Graham,
District
Inspector.
Belfast.

Classifica-
tion of
children.

the country population has declined, poverty has diminished. The poorer classes are those whom the abolition of fees will benefit, and they, as far as my District is concerned, are to be found in Belfast. It will therefore be easily understood how it is that as regards the country I have no appreciable change to report in attendance or condition of schools consequent on the abolition of fees.

Classification.—The compulsory clauses of the recent Education Act have raised the numbers in junior classes without a proportionate increase in senior classes. The numbers qualified for Results Examinations in the different classes are as follows:—

Infants	.	.	.	3,561
I.	.	.	.	1,983
II.	.	.	.	1,981
III.	.	.	.	1,987
IV.	.	.	.	1,498
V.	.	.	.	1,300
VI.	.	.	.	779
VII.	.	.	.	613

It will be seen from this table that the percentage of pupils qualified for examination in junior classes was 68·1, and in senior classes 31·9. In 1884 the percentage of pupils examined in junior classes was 72, and in senior classes 28, whilst in 1887 it was, leaving out decimals, exactly the same as at present.

Teachers
and their
classifica-
tion.

Teachers.—The following table gives the number of teachers in this District, and their classification. From it are excluded returns for the Convent school in charge of a Community, and for evening schools where teachers are employed as assistants in day schools.

Class	Principals		Assistants		Totals	
	Male.	Female.	Male.	Female.	Male.	Female.
I.	22	22	9	6	31	8
II.	13	10	1	6	14	16
III.	23	14	8	61	31	61
IV.	11	5	24	109	35	104
Totals.	79	44	41	187	114	231

This table shows that there are 345 classed teachers in the District, that more than half of the principals have obtained First Class Certificates, and that the majority of the assistant teachers are female. Managers exercise a wise discretion in appointing female assistants. They are more amenable to order than male assistants, are not so liable to change from school to school, and treat the children with more gentleness and toleration. I have the greatest confidence in this large body of teachers. They are always willing to adopt suggestions for improvement, ready to learn all successful methods of imparting knowledge, anxious to please, and ready to admit faults when pointed out. They have difficulties to contend against, which I pointed out to Managers and others. Amongst them I may mention the high classi-

Female
assistants
more
suitable
than male
assistants
for mixed
schools.

Difficulties
that Belfast
teachers

cation of the children for their ages caused by rapid promotion, the daily interruption of work after play time caused by what might be properly termed dual attendance, the imperfect construction of some of the buildings, and the necessarily large number of subjects provided for by a short schoolday. The competition of school against school and the pressure of parents make promotion too rapid. The play half-hour is too short for the children to go home and get dinner, so they return late, and sometimes do not return at all.

Ordinary City Schools.—These may be divided into Infant schools, Senior schools, and schools with separate Infant departments. In Infant schools too little collective or simultaneous work is done. At reading and repetition of poetry I have up to the present found the children taken individually. The teacher rarely reads for their initiation. The importance of Object Lessons has not been properly estimated, and teachers have yet to learn their value as a means of training the mind. I have drawn special attention to these lessons, and now find that from six to twelve are prepared for examination. The English code requires thirty. Kindergarten occupations will I believe before long form a part of the programme in every Belfast Infant School. Twelve schools have already introduced the Kindergarten system. In these schools I have brought under notice the importance of carefully training the eye to correct observation by means of drawing, building, and other suitable occupations; of encouraging the thinking powers by means of simple stories, and of introducing calisthenic exercises so as to pleasantly vary the monotony of reading and spelling, which in my early days of inspection formed the principal work of a junior school. With reference to senior schools I have already pointed out the main defect. Owing to the shortness of the school day the time for each subject is inadequate. As city children never have to travel long distances, and as Singing and Drawing are generally taught inside schoolhours, the work could be conveniently commenced at nine, instead of ten, and this arrangement would afford ample time for all subjects. A few schools have already commenced work at 9, and others at 9.30. I visited them at 9 and 9.30, and found most of the pupils in attendance. Senior schools through insufficient time throw overboard sub-heads and especially Explanation and Mental Arithmetic. I attribute this not to any mercenary feeling but to the short school-day. I have no doubt that the time spent by the children under supervision in comfortable schoolrooms is too short, and that too much time is spent in wandering through the streets under no control.

Rural Schools.—Many of the rural schools are badly attended, and indifferently taught. A few schools with a pretty good attendance are honourable exceptions and well conducted. The bad attendance is partly caused by the scarcity of labourers, as farmers have to make their children who should be at school do farm work. Managers find it impossible to get good teachers for small schools near Belfast. The men of ability have energy enough to make their way to profitable fields of labour, and by doing so benefit the town at the expense of the country. I have found no really good teacher in charge of a school having an average attendance of 30 or thereabouts, and I regret to state with reference to small schools that my Results Reports generally have been of an unsatisfactory nature. The decline in the rural population has rendered the amalgamation of small schools desirable, or the erection of larger schools in more convenient centres to supersede them; but I see no tendency in either direction.

Appendix C.

Reports on State of Schools.

Mr. W. Pedlow, District Inspector, Belfast.

Model school : its work and usefulness.

Model School.—No school in my District commands such esteem as this one. Its work is extensive, thorough, and discharged by a faithful staff of teachers, highly classed, skilful, and loyal to the Board. The staff employed is 3 Principals, 21 Assistants, 33 Pupil Teachers, and 11 Monitors. The Principal Teachers have First of First Class Certificates, as have also 14 of the Assistants. The average attendance for last Session year was 947·8, and the number of pupils examined 943, of whom 249 were in Sixth Class. In this Institution I need hardly say that the ordinary English subjects suitable for business life are successfully taught. The preparation of senior boys in Book-keeping receives marked attention. A Handicraft Class, which seems to be popular, has been well conducted for a number of years, and a Cookery Class has now been commenced in which over 90 pupils are enrolled. The Arithmetic, Geometry, and Algebra courses fully cover the requirements of a University Matriculation Examination. In the Girls' school Industrial work is making rapid progress. Ordinary sewing has been reported as excellent. Scientific dressmaking is taught to advanced pupils, as also the cutting out and making of underclothing. I cannot speak in too praiseworthy terms of the efforts of the Head Mistress to make the Industrial Programme practically useful, appreciated, and suitable for the locality. The pupil teachers and monitors at the termination of their training scarcely ever fail to find employment in schools. In July last 30 were examined on Third Class Teachers' Papers and 29 passed. In the Boy's department, where study at the boarding establishment is under supervision, there has been only one failure during the last nine years. In the ordinary city schools very few boys can be procured suitable for monitorship. The Model School steps in to supply this defect, and when male assistants are wanted that establishment can provide them.

Convent school.

Convent School.—This school is situated in Sussex-place, and surrounded by poor streets. The Sisters of Mercy in charge of it have exercised a beneficial and refining influence over the children, and have taught them to value the comfort of cleanliness, to respect those in authority, and to be orderly and systematic in their daily occupation. My last report on this school was most favourable, and the highest merit Capitation Grant was paid.

Workhouse school.

Workhouse School.—Both departments of this school are well taught, and the girls receive instruction in Music and enjoy the benefits of healthy calisthenic drill. It would be advantageous to give the boys practical lessons in Agriculture on the Workhouse grounds, and to establish a Class in Handicraft.

Under the different heads of Results Programme I shall briefly refer to proficiency.

Too little collective reading in schools.

Reading.—Reading may be described as distinct, but without style or expression. It is chiefly taught in large drafts. I have often counted more than thirty in a draft for Reading, the time being thirty minutes for the lesson. With such a number little progress could be made by individual teaching. I have advised collective reading in class-rooms, the pupils to be taken in groups of from three to six. Such reading should not be solely depended on, and it is only conducted beneficially when the teacher reads well in the first instance for the imitation of the pupils. It modulates the voice and obliges the pupil to attend to the stops.

Writing : deterioration owing to disuse of copy-book.

Writing.—I can report the writing as good up to and including Fourth Class. It deteriorates in First stage of Fifth as the daily use of copy-books in that Class ceases. Children who remain at school until

...they pass in Sixth Class can, however, owing to constant practice on
paper, write well. In Fifth Class I have pointed out the necessity for
frequent comparison between the exercises and head-line copies. I often
find the head-line copies fairly written, and the exercises carelessly.

Arithmetic.—No subject has given me more trouble at incidental
visits and Results Examinations than Arithmetic. I have frequently
referred to objectional methods of teaching the subject in my Minutes
on schools, in Observation Books, and in conversations with teachers.
These are chiefly finger counting and other ways of adding and subtracting by one at a time, in junior classes, and the constant use of test
cards instead of books in all classes. In senior classes these test cards
are a means of teaching Arithmetic rather by the solution of a series of
puzzles than by an education of the mind to think how rules may be
applied to the working of questions. I trust that before long finger
counting will be banished, and the use of Arithmetical books become
more common. Teaching by cards is simply cramming, but so far as
results are concerned it is successful cramming.

Spelling.—This subject is well taught in junior classes. Mis-spelled
words are very common in the composition of both stages of Fifth, and
are sometimes met with in the letters of Sixth Class. This indicates
that improvement is desirable in these classes.

Grammar.—Teachers have informed me that they had not time for
Grammar. If they had informed me that they were unable to give
instruction in the subject I would have been less surprised. Want of
time in some schools and want of skill in others have contributed to
make the results unprofitable. No subjects on the Pupil's Programme
are worse taught in this District than Grammar and Explanation, and
where I find the one good so too is the other. Even where Grammar
is well taught it is not made use of to teach the children to speak correctly. I have brought under notice grammatical mistakes constantly
used by children, sometimes by teachers, of frequent occurrence, and so
few that they could easily be corrected, and banished from any school.

Geography.—I find the classes generally well prepared in this subject;
but the instruction too frequently seems to end in a more effort of the
memory, aided by maps, without much intellectual development.

Needlework.—I cannot praise the teachers on their efforts to take
advantage of the Industrial Programme, or to make technical and
manual work useful and suitable. Although failures in ordinary
needlework are few, I must state that the sewing is very slowly done.
An hour is given to needlework daily, but the importance of literary
subjects compared with industrial is considered so great, that although
the hour is given to the pupils, it is not given by the teachers. I have
again and again seen the work without supervision. That meant that
the children wasted their time, or spent it in talk. They managed to
keep quiet and not to interrupt other work. Improvement will, I
hope, gradually take place, but I am afraid not much can be done until
the Training Colleges produce properly qualified industrial instructors.

Extra and Optional Branches.—Singing especially, according to the
Tonic Solfa system is excellently taught; so too is Drawing. A
Belfast school that omitted these subjects from its Programme could
not maintain an attendance. They are pleasing to the children and a
relief from mental strain. They are taught in all schools in which the
teachers have certificates. The other extra and optional branches
extensively taken up are Book-keeping, Algebra, and Geometry. When
classes are presented for examination in these branches I usually find
them well prepared.

Appendix C

Reports on
State of
Schools.

Mr. W.
Pedlow,
District
Inspector

Belfast.

Objection-
able
methods of
teaching
arithmetic.

Test cards

Spelling.

Obstacles to
the teach-
ing of
grammar.

Geography.

Sewing
slowly done.

Literary
subjects
considered
more
important.

Singing and
drawing.

Other extra
and
optional
subjects.

Appendix C.

Reports on
State of
Schools.

*Mr. W.
Penlow,
District
Inspector.*

Belfast.

Monitorial
teaching
tests.

School
banks.

Inspectors'
assistants.

Suggestions
given to
teachers.

Monitors.—The selection and examination of monitors form a very responsible portion of the Inspector's work. There are now 180 monitors under my supervision. The suggestions given by me from time to time have mainly been directed to improve their methods of teaching and to make them prepare beforehand notes for special lessons. No part of a monitor's examination is I think so important as the teaching test.

School Banks.—I regret to state that no advantage has been taken of the School Bank system. Thrift is by many parents inculcated in children, not through the medium of schools, but by accounts in the Post Office Savings Banks. It would, I think, be profitable to have suspended in every school a mounted tablet pointing out the advantages of the system. This in itself would from time to time bring the subject of forethought and thrift under the notice of Managers, Teachers, and pupils, and might suggest to the Inspector during his examination the desirability of saying a word in season.

Inspectors' Assistants.—I have been assisted by Mr. Honan at the Results Inspections in most of the large town schools. His help has been very valuable to me, as the classes entrusted to him have always been thoughtfully, carefully, and discreetly examined. Mr. Clements gave me occasional help, and examined the Handicraft in two large schools. His suggestions for improving this important technical branch and encouraging teachers to take it up have, I believe, been appreciated.

I shall conclude this Report by quoting a few suggestions which I have given to teachers whilst in this District. They are as follows :—

To aim at thorough work rather than a comprehensive programme.

To pay special attention to junior classes, so that failures or mere pass marks in any subject may be few, bearing in mind that by so doing, the work in senior classes will be rendered easy.

To avoid too rapid promotions, or the placing of children in classes for which they are unfit. (I have known this to be frequently done to prevent a child leaving one school and going to another).

To maintain discipline and order by kindness, and to resort to corporal punishment only under most exceptional circumstances.

To depend on the work done in school rather than on home lessons, but to encourage the latter by making them easy and such as a child could learn alone.

To keep their schoolrooms comfortable, warm, and clean, and thus encourage regular attendance.

To consider the capabilities and aptitudes of their children, and not to visit with reproach those whose natural abilities are below the average.

To encourage the learning of special subjects, such as Drawing, Music, Mathematics, Fancy Needle-work, by senior boys or girls, should they evince a taste for them.

I take this opportunity of thanking the Managers for their courtesy and kindness, and the teachers for their efforts to give me all the assistance in their power at Results Examinations.

I have the honour to be, Gentlemen,

Your obedient servant,

W. PENLOW, District Inspector.

The Secretaries,
    Education Office, Dublin.

Appendix C

Report on State of Schools.

Mr. H. M. Beatty, District Inspector.

Newtownards. The district.

Mr. H. M. Beatty, ll.d., District Inspector.

Newtownards,

February, 1805.

Gentlemen,—I have the honour to submit the following report on the state of the National Schools in the Newtownards District, of which I took charge in January, 1893.

The District includes those portions of the County Down which lie East, North, and North-west of Strangford Lough. It includes, moreover, what may be roughly described as the Ballymacarrott Division of Belfast, extending on the East of the River Lagan from Sydenham on the North to Ormeau Park on the South. Within its bounds are situated three towns of considerable importance—Newtownards with over 9,000 inhabitants, Bangor with 4,000, and Holywood with 3,000; three towns of minor importance—Comber, Donaghadee, and Portaferry; and eleven villages, ranging in population from 100 to 600 inhabitants.

From an educational point of view, Newtownards, Bangor, and Holywood are much the most important. They are the most populous; they are increasing in population; and, moreover, being under Town Commissioners, are liable—and alone liable—to the requirements of Compulsory Education. As to the other towns and villages, their population is not only small but (except in the case of Donaghadee) decreasing; and the same remark applies to the rural districts generally.

This decrease in population and its causes exercise a very serious influence on the schools, and must be borne in mind, if they are to be accurately judged. In many cases the decrease is due to emigration to America or Australia; but it is also frequently due to migration into Belfast. The former cause affects the pupils; the latter, both pupils and teachers. The monitors, who, to the number of from thirty to forty, complete each year their five years' course, if capable and ambitious, aim at obtaining an assistantship in one of the large schools of Belfast, where an assistant's income is frequently larger than that of a principal in a country school. The work to be done is larger in amount and more monotonous, as year after year the assistant may be confined to the teaching of a single large class; but the worry inseparable from the supervision of a multiplicity of small classes is avoided; and a teacher who seeks to rise has a great advantage through being in touch with changes and openings in the teaching staff, by means of chance conversations and the perusal of advertisements in the newspapers. Full advantage of these facilities is taken in Belfast; and accordingly the changes in the teaching staff are incessant. City and country schools compared.

This perhaps forms one of the most striking characteristics of city, as distinguished from rural schools. In the latter, the teacher appointed at eighteen or twenty may remain till his retirement from service at sixty or sixty-five. In Belfast, the principals alone are permanent; the assistants continually change. This district is peculiarly well placed for a comparison between city and rural schools; the number of children in attendance being tolerably equally divided between schools of the two classes. As to the comparative efficiency, the city schools are not merely the better, but show a distinct tendency to improve. However poor a city school may be at its beginnings, it shortly becomes as it were assimilated to the higher standard around. For this there are

Appendix C.
Report on
State of
Schools.

Mr. H. M.
Saville,
District
Inspector.

Newtown-
ards.

several reasons. There is, in the first place, the emulation among the members of the staff. An inefficient teacher involves to some extent the entire school in his disgrace, and is met with a gentle pressure of such a kind as to lead him either to improve his methods or to resign his post. A teacher in a remote school has no opportunity of improving his methods except through books or his own personal experience; in the larger schools (such as are generally found only in a city) the teachers serve as a whetstone, one to another, in sharpening the energies and the wits. The principal however is the centre round which the whole revolves. Nothing is more striking than the uniformity of the high standard maintained under capable principals amid the fluctuations of assistants, good, middling, and indifferent. When an assistant is inefficient with one class, he is tried with another; when inefficient in all, his teaching is supplemented by another assistant or by the principal himself. From these facts, it will be seen how many advantages city schools possess in the race for educational results; and in this connexion should be pointed out an arrangement of schools, which is, I believe, rarely found in other parts of Ireland—the conjunction of an infant and a senior mixed school. Boys' and girls' schools side by side are common enough everywhere, and the triple arrangement of boys', girls', and infant schools is not uncommon; but several of the most important schools in this district are arranged into a mixed senior school and a mixed infant school.

Mixed
senior
schools.

This arrangement is necessitated to a certain extent by local circumstances in the following way. Owing to the large number of employments here open to young men in offices and places of business, the number of boys who complete their monitorial term and supply the vacancies for male teachers is small, and very much smaller than the corresponding number of girls. Now, if 400 children are to be taught, and if they are divided between a boys' school and a girls' school, the staff according to scale will be: one male principal and one female, four male assistants and four female, five male monitors and five female: in all ten men and ten women. But if the 400 children are divided between a Senior and Infant School, the staff may consist of one male principal and one female; eight female assistants, and ten female monitors. The arrangement of the teaching staff is rarely so one-sided as this; it is found convenient to have one male assistant and one male monitor. But it is evident that this arrangement dispenses with the necessity for male teachers to a very large extent. Now, as I have pointed out, this, owing to lack of candidates, was unavoidable. But the arrangement has also intrinsic advantages; even apart from the fact that it is cheaper, owing to the lower salaries of female teachers. The classes are larger and labour is thus economised.

Ordinary
type of
mixed
school.

There is, however, one advantage in the conjunction of a Senior and an Infant School, which seems to give it a clear superiority. It is only under this system that special Infant schools can become widely spread. In very few localities will the number in attendance warrant the threefold division of the schools into boys', girls', and infants'. It is otherwise if schools be merely cut into two parts.

Infant
schools.

Nor is this bifurcation applicable only to towns. In two villages of only five or six hundred inhabitants the arrangement has been adopted: with the result that two of the schools are among the best of the district. As to Infant schools—I may say that I have learned much in regard to education since taking charge of the Newtownards district; but, on the subject of Infant schools their capabilities, advantages and requirements, I have learned nearly all the knowledge I possess; and one lesson above all others I have learned—that they are incalculably useful.

To realise their usefulness it is only necessary to compare the position of, say, one hundred infants, as they are taught and trained in their own school; and their lot, when they form merely a fraction of two schools, one for boys, the other for girls. In the latter case they are huddled wherever there may be room. They are taught their letters and the reading of simple words, generally by an inexperienced monitor. Possibly, in order to meet the requirements of the programme, they may at the last moment be taught to sing a song or to distinguish on a pictorial sheet an elephant from a horse. In a separate Infant school, they are under training of various kinds—songs, action songs, drill, object lessons —during almost the entire day. The advantage is still greater if the training takes the more elaborate and systematic form which is known as the Kindergarten. It is much to be regretted that the latter cannot be adopted to any large extent in this district, owing to the want of abundant space, without which effective training in gifts, occupations and still more games is impossible. Only two schools in Ballymacarrett and three outside have adopted it.

The question of insufficient space is one which is assuming alarming proportions in Ballymacarrett. With hardly an exception the schools are overcrowded; and, owing to the increase in population and the action of compulsory education, the evil becomes daily more accentuated. In some cases, children must have been deterred from schooling simply by want of accommodation. This is certainly suggested by the fact that new schools are crowded almost immediately, while the surrounding schools maintain their numbers as before. Four schools opened within the past two years, or slightly over, have already an attendance of 1,100; and one of them has an attendance of over 500.

While the average attendance at the schools in Ballymacarrett and within the municipal boundary was for the past year 7,100, the accommodation provided was for barely 6,000; and it is hardly necessary to point out that the attendance on many days of the year is far in excess of the average attendance. In fact, under a system of compulsory attendance, the accommodation might fairly be fixed according to the number on rolls. According to that standard, the insufficiency of school space becomes still more glaring, the number of children on the rolls of the Ballymacarrett schools at the end of the past year being 9,500, for nearly forty per cent. of whom therefore there are no school places available. It must be admitted that there exists an earnest desire to cope with this serious deficiency, not merely among managers, but in the community generally. But in a locality, where the population is mainly, almost exclusively, composed of the working classes, the expense of sites and building is a serious barrier, and the requirements of the borough authorities in regard to playgrounds act as a still further deterrent. All new schools within the municipal boundaries must now be provided with a play-ground once and a half as large as the school building—a most beneficent regulation, which will nevertheless greatly increase the cost of providing schools.

The question of accommodation becomes naturally more important under a system of compulsory attendance; as under this system the average attendance tends to approximate more and more to the number on rolls. This has been the effect so far in the four localities in which I have been able to observe its action. In increasing the number on rolls its action has been very slight; in rendering the attendance more

Reports on State of Schools
Mr. H. M. Bonin, District Inspector, Newtownards.
Unfairness of Infant schools
Insufficient accommodation.
Compulsory versus school attendance.

Appendix C.

Reports on State of Schools.

Mr. H. M. Beatty, District Inspector.

Newtownards.

Decrease in Infant schools.

uniform and regular its influence has been very considerable. In the localities here subject to its influence, while the number on rolls has increased three per cent., the average attendance has increased by twenty per cent. within the past year. This is especially remarkable in the case of infant schools; where, although the number on rolls has actually fallen off to the extent of seven per cent., the average attendance has increased in almost precisely the same proportion.

This falling off on the rolls of infant schools is curious, and will illustrate the usual experience that every large advance is accompanied by some minor reactionary movement. I am told that parents, finding that they must send their children to school at certain ages, as it were recoup themselves by sending them only at those ages. In fact they take the legal minimum for their private maximum of schooling. Accordingly very junior pupils and very senior pupils attend less than before; while in the main body of the school there is a regular and systematic attendance established. In many cases no doubt the withdrawal of children who are by age exempt is necessary in order to fill the places for home duties of those who are bound to attend school.

As I have stated above, legal compulsion exists in only four localities of this district—Newtownards, Holywood, Bangor, and Ballymacarrett. But a stimulus in the form of prizes for regular attendance has been applied in two localities with very successful results. In one school the average attendance has thus been increased twenty per cent. in a single year. At the same time, it should be remembered that such prizes exert their greatest force where it is least needed—in the case of children who would otherwise attend well. The careless children are out of the race almost from the commencement, and therefore regard it with indifference. Now these are the children who above all others need a stimulus; and they can only be reached by the long arm of compulsion.

Abolition of school fees.

From compulsory to free education is an easy transition, the latter being, it is generally held, the corollary of the former. In this district, of 148 schools, 44 are entitled, in accordance with the provisions of the Irish Education Act, to continue the charge of school fees to their pupils; but only thirty have actually done so. Three of these are rural and twenty-seven urban schools. The tendency of the abolition of school fees has generally been to produce a prolonged attendance in the higher classes of children, who, in order to save the payment of fees, would otherwise have left at an earlier stage. In the case of children, who had been previously admitted free, I am told that the effect has been less satisfactory; as these children, in return for what was then an exceptional favour, had exerted themselves to do credit to the school by regular attendance and good answering. In one respect the effect has been altogether good, in the position of independence which it has secured for teachers. In remote localities, the dependance of teachers for a portion of their livelihood on ignorant and exacting parents, frequently led to the toleration of breaches of discipline and to the undeserved promotion of pupils.

School savings banks.

In August, 1893, a circular was issued from the Education Office, in which the advantages of establishing school savings banks were pointed out; and the code of instructions issued by the Post Office as to the method of working these banks was quoted. I regret that this circular has apparently aroused very little attention. So far as I have been able to ascertain, the only bank established in the District in consequence of the circular was in the Newtownards Model School at my own suggestion. This has been carried on with satisfactory success. There are at present thirty-five children in connection with it; and in a few cases

the savings amount to nearly one pound. Some children bring a penny
almost every morning; the others, as they happen to have the deposit
ready. Seven of the children leave their deposit cards, with the stamps
gummed in the spaces, in the charge of the Head Master. Seven others
buy the stamps from him but keep the cards themselves. The others
simply come to him when they require a fresh card.

Of the subjects of the Programme—Writing and Arithmetic are well
taught. Spelling also receives on the whole adequate attention.

Grammar is generally a weak subject and rarely taught with much
intelligence.   Indeed it is a most unusual thing to find grammar
thoroughly satisfactory. Probably this is in part due to its abstract
character and intrinsic difficulties. To take the case of the definitions
of the parts of speech :—It seems almost impossible to embody them in
any form, which would be within the comprehension of children, so
brief as to be readily available, and at the same time so comprehensive
as to cover the various uses.

Geography, so far as map-pointing goes, is fairly satisfactory; but
the amount of really useful knowledge possessed by the children is extremely small.   It is a common experience to find children who can
point out unimportant features on the map, who still imagine that France
is water and the Red Sea land; children who can point out Ceylon or
Cuba but cannot point out Ireland. Recently a child of First Stage of
Fifth Class in a fairly-taught school informed me in his letter that "Belfast
is a very large city." It is nearly as large again as Saintfield" (a village
of six hundred inhabitants). A grotesque misconception like this would
be impossible if children were taught to proceed from what they have
actually seen in their own neighbourhood to what they have not seen;
thus bearing with them the actual facts of physical and political geography, which they have gathered in their daily life, as a gauge of what
they can only realise from descriptions and illustrations.

Reading I have left as the last of the ordinary subjects, because it
requires a more detailed notice. Before coming to this District I was
hardly in a position to realise how unsatisfactory this subject can be.
But in the schools of Ballymacarrett it is not an uncommon thing to
meet a child, who has previously attended an English or Scotch school.
They can easily be recognised from their reading: not so much even from
the clearness of articulation as from what may, in musical phraseology,
be called "attack." These children brace themselves for the reading, as
if they had considered what was before them, and had realised the
meaning of the sentence or paragraph as a whole. The reading of our
pupils is at best but the enunciation of separate words. Modulation and
expression are almost unknown, even when the reading is accurate.
And this it is not as a rule.

Reading has been for so many years, as witnessed by Inspectors'
reports, so backward in this country, that one might be tempted to regard
it as beyond cure. But this is not so. Its backwardness is due to the
fact that the importance of the subject is not realised. A class taken
at random will probably show one-fourth of the children without reading books. Children who have books do not follow the reader. This in
itself is a serious drawback; for a child will learn nearly as much in
following his neighbour's performance as in his own turn of reading.
Again, it is only in a very few schools that care is taken to see if
children understand what they read. This alone is sufficient to
account for an absence of intelligence and expression in the reading.

Appendix C.
Reports on state of Schools.
Mr. H. M. Smith, District Inspector.
Newtown-ards.

Much could be accomplished by means of simultaneous reading. In the first place, a teacher can thus employ twenty children as readily as two. The children also gain confidence and animation in their delivery. An incitement moreover is offered to them to keep their eyes constantly, and not intermittently, fixed on their reading books. If simultaneous reading be preceded by a sample paragraph from the teacher, if the chorus be guarded from falling into sing-song, and if the teaching be checked frequently by individual tests, much may be accomplished. The main difficulty in the way is the want of numerous class-rooms, so thoroughly separated from the other rooms, as to shut in the noise of many voices.

Simultaneous reading. Simultaneous repetition of poetry can also be used with equal advantage, and in much the same way. The repetition in chorus of poetry of a stirring character will frequently increase the enjoyment and appreciation of the children.

Drawing. Drawing is taught in seventy schools—nearly half the total number. This is satisfactory, and it is still more satisfactory that the number shows an increase during the past year of nine schools. Many teachers have used enlarged copies of the drawing book samples, which can be exhibited before the class. This system of drawing from a large copy hung at a distance has several advantages. It compels the children to judge by the eye and not by the measurements of a pencil or rule. The same copy can be worked over and over on successive loans of drawing paper, till perfection is attained. It also gives much greater opportunities for teaching of the subject, as opposed to mere supervision.

Singing. The number of schools where singing is taught has also increased. The number is 66, as against 61 in the previous year. The system of Hullah is adopted in 43; the Tonic Sol-fa system in 23. Undoubtedly children can be taught to take the notes more readily and surely under the latter system, and probably it is the better for them. The songs, however, provided in the book generally used, are of a very uninteresting character. To the children of National schools the power of taking notes at sight, which they will hardly ever utilize, will be a poor compensation if they are not trained in some small way to appreciate the elevating and refining beauties of good music, or to sing from ear some beautiful melodies.

The voices in this part of the country are generally harsh, and therefore all the more credit is due to the teachers for the success which has attended their efforts. The notes are generally true, and in some schools the time of the school songs would do credit to a trained choir.

Needle-work. The needlework instruction in this district is generally most efficient, and shows progress. The use of coloured thread I have found very advantageous, as exhibiting the stitches more plainly. Its use might be extended with advantage even to the examinations of teachers and monitors. This would lead to its introduction into the schools, and would facilitate an accurate judgment of the work.

Monitors. The number of monitors in the district is 179, a number which is likely to be larger in the future. This conclusion is warranted by comparing the numbers in the following table :—

Monitors in Fifth Year,	.	.	.	22
Do.	Fourth Year,	.	.	.	16
Do.	Third Year,	.	.	.	34
Do.	Second Year,	.	.	.	41
Do.	First Year,	.	.	.	17

The labour inseparable from the selection, examination, and supervision of this array of monitors, is greatly lightened by the care with
which they are trained and taught. Among the fifty-five monitors of
third and fifth years examined in July, 1894, there occurred only four
failures. The instruction in the course for first, second, and fourth
years is equally effective and careful.

The classification of the teachers is high. There are 367 employed
in the 248 schools of the district, and their classification is as follows:—

I.,	.	.	.	11
I.,	.	.	.	63
II.,	.	.	.	141
III.,	.	.	.	152
				367

The long array of third class teachers is principally made up from
the female assistants in the large schools who have not as yet served a
sufficient time to qualify for second class. Their desire for improvement
is however evidenced by the fact that I have been able to recommend
twenty-three female candidates for second class for the coming July
examinations.

The fact that I have recommended eleven male candidates for first
division of first class will show that the male teachers are equally
anxious for progress.

Progress is indeed observable in almost all directions. The number
of schools has during the past year been increased by four, and the
number of children examined, which was, in 1893, 13,200, was in the
year just passed 14,800.

I cannot close this report without a word of thanks to the teachers
for the courteous attention which they have given to suggestions for
the improvement of the schools, and the zeal with which they have
proceeded to carry them out.

I have the honour to be, Gentlemen,

Your obedient servant,

H. M. DEATY, I.N.S.

The Secretaries,
   Education Office,
      Dublin.

Appendix C.

Reports on State of Schools.

Mr. J. Murphy, District Inspector.

Enniskillen.

Mr. J. MURPHY, District Inspector.

Enniskillen, March, 1895.

GENTLEMEN,—In compliance with your instructions, I beg to lay before you my third General Report on the state of elementary education in this district.

Area of Inspection

The area of inspection work, which lies within the Counties of Fermanagh, Cavan, and Leitrim, has remained unchanged since the year 1888. Since my last report, which was furnished in 1892, three small schools have been closed—one as being held in an unsuitable house, and two as not being needed. On the other hand, two new schools have been taken into connection, one of which, the Wattlebridge Temporary, will supply a long-felt need for a school available for children living in the islands that dot Lough Erne to the south of Newtownbutler. A vested house will shortly supersede the temporary building in which this school is at present held, bringing the number of vested school-houses up to a total of 40.

Application has further been made for a Building Grant for a vested house to take the place of the temporary school-house at Cross Roads, while in North Fermanagh the Parish Priest of Garrison, desirous of building a much-needed school in a locality hitherto unprovided with school accommodation of any kind, and failing to obtain a site from the landlord, has wisely had recourse to the benefits of the Irish Education Acts of 1892 and 1893, and succeeded in satisfying the Local Government Board of the justice of his claim.

State of vested school-h.uses.

The vested houses are, with two exceptions, in a satisfactory state—the Mullaghfad (No. 1) School is not provided with out-offices, and the Crogy School-house I consider, in its present state, altogether unfit for the purposes of education. It is a damp, dismal building, standing on the outskirts of a bog. The school-rooms are low and wretchedly lighted, and pools of stagnant water are to be found immediately underlying the boarded floors—in fact the house could scarcely be in a more unsatisfactory state than it is at present.

State of non-vested school-houses.

Most of the non-vested houses are substantial buildings, in good sanitary condition, and as a rule, in satisfactory repair, and I am glad to say that a school unprovided with out-offices will soon be a thing of the past in this district. There are at present only eleven such schools, and I am confident that in these cases the deficiency will shortly be supplied.

School-rooms.

Speaking generally, the school-rooms are clean, warm, and comfortable. I have seldom to complain of neglect of ventilation, and good fires are kept up in the winter months. Not a few teachers aim at something more than this, and endeavour by good taste and simple device to give their schools a bright and cheerful appearance, and to impress upon the minds of their pupils ideas of order and neatness, which they may carry into home life. But when I say "not a few," I mean "not many," and I must confess to some disappointment at the slow progress made in this direction, notwithstanding the many hints and suggestions I am constantly offering, both orally and in the form of written observations. Improvement by dint of official remonstrance I find to be a slow process, and I am afraid the fault must be laid with the local managers. An active and intelligent management is absolutely necessary to infuse into school life those warm and brightening influences which are an essential part of education, and yet cannot be defined within the strict limits of official requirements.

The town of Enniskillen is well provided in the matter of school accommodation. Besides the Model School, with its three departments, there is the Convent School, conducted by classed teachers; Forthill Mixed, St. Michael's Male, and two other schools situated in the back streets, and intended for the children of the poorest class. The Model School is in a flourishing condition, and I am glad to say that the solid work done here is well appreciated, and that the school is able to hold its own, notwithstanding the existence of the Porters and other high-class schools in the town.

The Compulsory Education Act, which came into operation at the beginning of last year, has not affected the attendance at the town schools to any great extent. A considerable increase in the number on rolls was to be expected, as it was well known that there were a number of children in the town who had never set foot in a school of any kind. But in place of this expected increase, the school-rolls actually show a slight falling-off during the year. On the 1st January, 1894, there were 977 pupils on the rolls of the town schools, and on the 1st January, 1895, there were only 974.

There is some improvement, on the other hand, as regards regularity of attendance. The average annual attendance for 1894 shows an increase of 8 per cent. on that of the previous year. But it is a question whether this increase will be maintained. Dread of prosecution induced parents to send their children more regularly to school during the past year; but they are beginning to find out that the Attendance Committee is mild in its composition and slow to act. In no case as yet has a penalty been inflicted, and I agree with the teachers in their opinion that so long as the law is administered thus leniently no real or permanent improvement will be effected.

In the country schools the attendance is very little better than it was three years ago, as the following table will show:—

—	No. on Rolls last day of Rortn? Year.	No. examined.	Percentage.
1892. . . .	4,975	4,725	67%
1893. . . .	10,530	7,140	667
1894. . . .	10,025	7,024	867

I have taken some trouble to gather the opinions of teachers as to the effect of the abolition of school fees in October, 1892, and I find that the almost universal experience is, that no sensible effect has been produced. Not a few complain that parents are becoming more careless than ever, now that they have nothing to pay for the education of their children. It is painfully evident that the National School is looked upon by many parents as a purely Government institution conducted by a Government official—one of themselves who, by some chance or

G

Appendix G
Reports on
State of
Schools.

Mr. J.
Murray,
District
Inspector.

Possibilities.
other, has been lifted into a position in their midst, out of which he manages to make a tidy living with little labour. People who think in this way send their children to school as a compliment, and, I am afraid, sometimes keep their children from school to spite the teacher. This strangely distorted view of a parent's duties and a teacher's does, added to a carelessness which is hard to eradicate, constitute the main obstacle in the way of regular attendance; and I am strongly convinced that the more a school shows itself in the character of a popular institution under intelligent local management, the less will this view obtain. Attendance and efficient work act and re-act upon each other. This I have often noticed in a marked degree where a change for the better has taken place in the teaching staff; and in general I have found that improved organization, and the importation into school life of anything tending to brighten it, and relieve the dull monotony of the daily routine, invariably result in an improved attendance.

Teaching staff.

The classification of the Teaching Staff is higher than it was three years ago, as will be seen by the following table :—

—	I.	I².	II.	III.	Total
1891, ...	8	11	78	84	271
1894, ...	8	19	84	71	277

This improvement is due mainly to the substitution of trained for untrained teachers, and is only in a small measure the result of Class promotion. Two promotions to the First Division of First Class, and seven to Second Class, is the full district record for the years 1892, 1893, and 1894.

The schools are small as a rule, quite a large number of them being aided under the special provisions of the Irish Education Act, 1892; and teachers in charge of these small schools, once they have secured the benefits of training, naturally look for more remunerative appointments. Changes are comparatively frequent—a trained teacher often being replaced by an inexperienced monitor or pupil-teacher lately chosen; and it is to this cause principally I ascribe the fact, that a large number of the teachers of this district are in the lowest class. More than fifty-two per cent of the teachers are still untrained, but many of them are beyond the age at which a course of training could be expected to be of much service.

Monitors.

The Monitorial Staff—29 in all—is larger than it has been for some years. Only four completed their course during the last three years; and of these only one is as yet in charge of a school. I consider the present staff of monitors an unusually intelligent one, and several of them show signs of special promise.

General proficiency.

I cannot record any very marked improvement in general proficiency. Improvement is going on, no doubt, but it is necessarily very gradual: the older and untrained members of the Teaching Staff work on antiquated lines from which it is hard to move them; and with them, irregular attendance is an insurmountable obstacle to good results. On the other hand, a creditable number of the younger teachers—and these not all trained—are doing work, which could scarcely be improved upon.

Reading is satisfactory as a rule; it is distinct and fairly intelligent, Appendix C.
and more than this is not to be expected. Explanation of subject-
matter is receiving increased attention, but in many schools the time
devoted to this important exercise is very small, and in these schools I
almost always find the answering slow, halting, and uncertain. Poetry
is in general fairly recited. Recitation of poetry is a most valuable
help towards acquiring a distinct and intelligent style of reading, and
I encourage simultaneous repetition, for this reason, as much as possible.

A good standard of writing is kept up in most of the schools. As I
remarked in a previous report, even where the penmanship cannot be
described as good, it is nearly always legible. The Civil Service hand
is becoming very popular; it has a marked character, which is easy
to imitate, and not difficult to retain. Written exercises are receiving
closer attention, and I generally find them carefully worked and neatly
preserved.

Letter-writing continues to improve by dint of steady insistence on
the all-important place it holds in the Results Programme.

Arithmetic is carefully taught, and with creditable success. The
proficiency in this subject is often high in the junior classes, even
where there is notable failure in more advanced work. Mental Arithmetic does not receive the attention it deserves.

Spelling is generally good in First and Second Classes, but too often
poor in Third, Fourth, and Fifth; and I ascribe this defect altogether
to two causes, viz.: Indistinct articulation in Oral Spelling, and careless
supervision of transcription and dictation exercises. The working of
the first of these two causes is seen most plainly in the dictation exercise of Third Class, which is often a complete failure, even where the
pupils, when tested orally, might be pronounced good spellers. I am
constantly reminding teachers that oral spelling is in itself a mere preparation; and that the oral test—taking the subject in its only practical
aspect—is in reality no test at all.

In the better schools of the district the proficiency in Grammar is
creditable, but in many the subject is taught with little system; and,
as I remarked in a previous report, passages for parsing are taken at
random from the Lesson Books without much reference to the Programme laid down for the classes, or to the capabilities of the pupils.
Exercises in the form of sentences for correction are seldom given,
although such exercises are, with composition, the only practical
written tests in applied Grammar.

I notice some improvement in Geography, which is being taught with
more reference to the maps than it used to be. Teachers are beginning
to provide their pupils with small hand-maps. Geography is often made
the subject of home lessons; and it is most desirable that the weary
task of committing to memory long lists of towns, rivers, &c., should be
converted from unprofitable rote-work into interesting and valuable
labour by constant reference to the atlas or the pocket-map. The Programme for Sixth Class is an extended one, and good results can be
secured only where the attendance is regular. In view of the fact that
a large number of children leave school before they reach this class, I
am of opinion that some knowledge of the Geography of Great Britain
should be acquired in Fifth Class.

Very little intelligent instruction is given in Agriculture; the prescribed chapters of the text-book are occasionally learnt, or rather committed to memory, but it is very seldom indeed that I find the subject
effectively taught.

Appendix C.

Reports on State of Schools.

Mr. J. Xxxx xxx's District Inspector. Enniskillen.

Book-keeping.

Book-keeping is occasionally taken up, but I rarely meet with good answering; the instruction given is not practical, or of a nature to be of much real service to the pupils.

Extra.

As a rule the teachers of this district confine themselves to the compulsory subjects of the Results Programme; and in view of the extreme irregularity of the attendance in many of the schools, they do wisely in not attempting too much. Algebra is perhaps more generally taught than any other extra; it is a favourite with pupils, and is easily taught. I have seldom to examine in Geometry.

Drawing.

The number of schools in which Drawing is taught is increasing every year. At present it is taught in 29 schools, but this number is capable of immediate expansion to 46, this being the number of teachers holding certificates of competency to teach the subject. I have been able during the last three years to induce some of the younger and more energetic teachers to seek certificates at the July Examinations, and a fair number of them have succeeded. Drawing, in my opinion, should be a compulsory subject for Queen's Scholars, and it should further be obligatory in all schools in which the certificate is held. I often find excellent results produced, even where the teacher himself is anything but a skilful draughtsman. The black board is never used apparently, although the graduated lesson on a model slowly developed upon the board under the hand of the teacher is a most useful one. A drawing manual for teachers would be a valuable addition to the books on the Board's list.

Singing

Vocal Music is taught in only 6 schools, although there are in the district 32 teachers holding certificates of competency to teach it. This almost total absence of singing in the schools I look upon as such a notable deficiency, that I think some decided steps should be taken, with a view to develop musical taste and talent in the country.

I would advocate the formation of Saturday Singing Classes at district centres, and especially at centres such as Enniskillen, where Model School classrooms would be available. In schools conducted by teachers regularly attending a singing class, with a view to obtaining the usual certificate, I would recommend a small capitation fee to be paid for two years on the satisfactory singing by ear of a certain number of songs, exclusive of theoretical or other text. This would be a most valuable encouragement to the spread of school music, while the small fee awarded would meet the expense of attendance at the Singing Class. As in the case of Drawing, I think certificated teachers, who, without sufficient reason, neglect to teach singing in their schools, should forfeit their certificates.

Needlework.

A slow, but very perceptible improvement is being effected in Needlework. The instruction is more practical than it used to be, and a large number of well-made articles of dress are turned out annually. Shirt-making and woollen work receive special attention, and, in schools where the Industrial Programme is in operation, well-finished shirts, woollen petticoats, shawls, gloves, etc., are not unfrequently shown by girls in both stages of Fifth Class at the end of the Results year.

In 45 mixed schools Needlework is not taught at all, as the required average attendance of 20 girls cannot be maintained.

Industrial programme.

I am glad to say that the Alternative Scheme for girls of Sixth Class is largely adopted in the district: only 13 schools are exempted, and some of these are exempt for the current year only.

The following table shows the branches selected during the last three years and the number of schools in which each branch has been taught:—

Appendix C.

Reports on State of Schools.

Mr. J. Harpur, District Inspector.

Enniskillen.

CLASS A:—		CLASS B:—	
(1) Dress-making, &c., in	35 schools	(1) Lace-making in	5 schools
(2) Baby Clothes, &c., in	17 "	(2) Mountmellick work in	11 "
(3) Knitting and Crocheting in	69 "	(3) Art Needlework in	1 "
(4) Little Boys' suits, &c., in	1 "	(4) Artificial Flower-making in	1 "

It will be seen that the branches generally selected are Sub-heads I. and III. of Class A. The articles made under these heads are intended for home wear, so that the need of a market for them is not felt. In places where special industries exist—and they do exist in this district—Managers should insist upon their being taught, when practicable; and workmistresses only should be appointed who are competent to teach these industries.

There is still a considerable amount of opposition to the Industrial Programme, and I do not believe that parents, or indeed the majority of Managers, have any real idea of its requirements. It has frequently been my duty to point out the advantages of the Alternative Scheme to Managers applying for exemption from the compulsory rule; and, in many cases, I have found an impression existing that, under the Scheme, the whole school-day would be devoted to needlework.

Unfortunately the vagueness of the Literary Programme helps to spread this impression. In my opinion the Literary Programme should be clearly defined, and should include a restricted but thoroughly practical course of Commercial Arithmetic and Geography. A literary course running somewhat on the lines of elementary Civil Service examinations would give to the much-abused Alternative Scheme an aspect attractive to many with whom the Scheme is now unpopular.

There is at present a very promising display of industrial activity in certain parts of the district from which most useful results may be expected. About eighteen months ago a Crochet Lace Class was started in Lisnaskea; but owing, I understand, to the incompetency of the teacher, it quickly fell through. In September last a new class was formed under the auspices of the Irish Industrial Association and is now in a flourishing condition. It is held in a workroom kindly lent by the local Secretary, Mr. Cassidy. No fees are charged, and the enterprise is, practically, self-supporting. There are already 89 members on the Day Class list, while 40 have joined a Night Class intended principally for school-going children who cannot attend during the day. I had an opportunity of visiting the Day Class when it had been about two months in operation, and I was very much struck with the large amount of varied and advanced work on hand. A valuable feature of this industry is that the demand for good work is, as yet, in advance of the supply, so that orders have not to be waited for. A local agent buys in the work and pays for it every Saturday. Large collars bring in about £1 each, while sets are sold at from 1s. 3d. to 7s. each. For lace, four inches in width, from 10s. to 15s. per yard is given, and 1s. per yard for lace an inch wide. The class has not yet, of course, arrived at the highest standard of proficiency; but, even now, I am informed a good worker can earn from 10s. to 15s. a week. Lace, to the value of nearly £200 has been made since the formation of the class in September last.

Local Industries.

Crochet Lace.

I am glad to say that this promising industry has crept into four schools in the neighbourhood of Lisnaskea, and really nice lace is now worked at the Tully, Moorlough, and Mullanvram schools by the girls of Sixth Class.

Appendix C.
Reports on
State of
Schools.

Mr. J.
Murphy,
District
Inspector.

Enniskillen.

Innishmac-
mint lace.

Lace making has been taught in the parish of Innishmacsaint since the year 1867, and still survives; although, owing to a very limited market, there is not at present any prospect of a large development of the industry. There are, I understand, about twenty members in the class, which meets from time to time at the Rectory, Renmore; and Miss L. MacLean, who introduced the work into the district, continues to give it her unremitting attention. Unfortunately the demand for Innishmacsaint lace is not increasing, and the orders, which come chiefly from private sources, do not give continuous occupation even to the small number at present attending the class at Denmore. It is a great pity this excellent work is not more encouraged. I have been shown samples of trimming which is sold at £4 a yard. The following is the award given to this lace as exhibited at the recent Chicago Exhibition:— "This lace is a faithful and accurate reproduction of Venetian Needle Point. The design is beautiful, and the execution very skilful; indeed, the high relief imparting a rich and elegant effect." A specimen of this lace was worked for me a couple of years ago under the Industrial Programme in one of the schools of the parish.

Sprigging.

A good deal of Sprigging is done in the neighbourhood of Derry-gonnelly and Killyclogher. Local agents supply the work from Belfast, and for some time orders have been practically unlimited. The agents in Derrygonnelly are now supplying about 200 hands with work, and I am told that an expert can earn about a shilling a day. It is comparatively easy to acquire skill in this branch of industry, and I am surprised to hear that no girls of a school-going age are working at it. I occasionally get sprigging done under the Industrial Programme, but in general it is very little encouraged in the Schools.

In view of the existence in the district of remunerative industries, which a ready market renders capable of further development, it is highly desirable that teachers should be afforded increased facilities for industrial training. As I suggested in the case of Singing, the Model School at the district centre might be utilised for Saturday classes, at which teachers would have an opportunity of giving mutual aid to one another, while experts could be engaged to give instruction in the special branches to which I have referred.

Handicraft.

Handicraft is not taught at present in this district, although six teachers hold certificates.

Discipline.

I have very little fault to find with the order preserved in the schools: the children seem to be well under the control of the teachers, and behave themselves very creditably when under examination. I often remark, however, a want of smartness and precision in class movement, which is the result of insufficient attention to the numerous little details of school discipline during the year.

Drill.

Improvement in this matter could be easily effected by the introduction of Drill into the daily routine. This I have advocated in previous reports. Trained teachers should be required to carry out a limited, but well-defined course of drill in their schools. The day should begin and end with a few simple physical exercises and a march round, accompanied, if possible, by song. These exercises, repeated at change of lesson and performed with precision, would necessarily command the instant attention of the whole school. The effect would, in fact, be somewhat similar to that produced by the alarm of a clock, and the time occupied about the same.

The School Bank system has, I regret to say, met with a very cold reception in the district. It has been introduced into the Enniskillen Model School and one rural school. In the rural school it has had little success, but in the Model School it has fallen upon good soil, and promises, when fully established, to thrive vigorously. Most teachers say that it would be useless to establish a bank, looking to the difficulty of getting parents to give their children what will pay for their school books. In view of this general opinion on the part of the teachers, I am afraid there is little hope of the system being largely adopted, until the Local Managers take the matter in hand, and give it that encouragement, without which all such schemes must fail.

Annual C. *Reports on Sale of Schools.* *Mr. J. Murphy District Inspector.* *Enniskillen.* *School banks.*

I have the honour to be, Gentlemen,
Your obedient servant,
J. MURPHY, District Inspector.

The Secretaries,
    National Education Office, Dublin.

Mr. J. B. SKEFFINGTON, LL.B., District Inspector.

Mr. J. B. Skeffington, District Inspector. Downpatrick.

Downpatrick, February, 1895.

GENTLEMEN,—I have the honour to furnish the following general report on this district :—

Schools.

The school district has continued unaltered in area and boundaries for the past few years; nor has there been any considerable change in the number of schools. But one of the oldest and most notable has become inoperative. Partly through the master's leaving without notice for a better school in Belfast, after absence for a year in training; partly from lack of clerical, congregational, or industrial support, available for other National Schools in the town equally efficient and well conducted; the oldest National School in Downpatrick, though favoured with excellent rooms, furniture, and appliances, gradually dwindled, and is now closed. Such cases naturally suggest considerations as to (a) whether a first class teacher should not provide at least a second class substitute while in training; (b) whether teachers should be permitted to take other schools during the period of three months' notice; (c) whether other managers should be allowed to employ them, without the consent of former manager, pending the three months period.

One rather important school has been added, illustrating another powerful tendency, so far triumphant—the absorption by the National system of schools from other primary systems. I allude to the Bryansford Road National School, Newcastle, the inclusion of which leaves few, if any, important schools not under the Board within the limits of this district.

One small school restored, and two evening schools suspended, complete the list of changes.

The school buildings are in general fairly suitable, and in many cases excellent; nor is there any lack of appreciation of physical comfort or sanitary requirements, and the evidences of improvement, and still more of the spirit of progress, are satisfactory. One new vested school has recently been erected—Loganney N.S.—which has superseded one of the worst old schoolhouses in the county, and now furnishes

Buildings.

Appendix G.
Reports on
State of
Schools.

Mr. J. B.
Skeffington,
District
Inspector.

Down-
patrick.

an example and model that will stimulate further efforts. Great, indeed, is the contrast between the old thatched, clay-floored room, with its rickety desks, without a spot of playground or appurtenant offices, and the substantially built house, school-room, and class-room (with galleries), ample playground, and out-offices of approved construction. How different must be the healthfulness of pupils and teachers, how much greater the facilities for intellectual, physical, and social training; not to speak of the effect on the tastes and aspirations of the parents, tending in so many ways to uplift the people of this backward locality to a higher standard. This school, and that of Tullaree, erected a year or two earlier, are visited and admired by clergymen and managers of other schools, and thus a spirit of generous rivalry is aroused. Hence, application had been made for a grant to build new vested schoolhouses in Castlewellan, where they are much required. Additional class-rooms are projected for the Annsboro' schools. The schoolhouses at Magheramayo have undergone considerable structural improvements. At Ballyroney a spacious class-room has been erected. Ballymacarrett N.S. has been raised, roofed, floored, and almost rebuilt, and Annalinebigo much improved. In Downpatrick, a large class-room has been provided for the John-street Monastery N.S.; and the Governors of the Southwell Charity have erected a spacious, lofty, and well-equipped school-room to supersede the *Down M.* N.S, which was situated on a town thoroughfare, and had no attached playground. Many minor improvements have also been effected in various schools, as new floors, porches, wainscoting, &c.

Unsuitable
buildings,
etc.

But, notwithstanding, there are still some school buildings which are unsuitable as to structure or situation; several have no grounds outside their four walls for appurtenant offices; in other cases these closets are too close to the schoolhouses, partly from this same limitation of space; while too often, from want of flushing arrangements, these out-buildings are not in such a state as sanitation and cleanliness would require. Indeed, the structure of each closets is not always sufficiently adapted to schools attended by children of various ages. As regards most of these defective buildings, the evil is felt by the local parties; in some cases efforts have been made, and in others are likely to be made, to remedy defects; and I have no doubt a few years more will bring about further substantial improvements.

Managers.

I regret to state that the changes of managers have been rather numerous in the past few years, about one-third of the schools in the district having experienced changes in this respect; in the great majority of cases from deaths, but in about a dozen instances through changes of clerical managers chiefly; in a few cases there have been two changes, that is, three managers in succession during the period; all these changes, as well as those far more numerous changes next to be mentioned, requiring the execution of new agreements.

Teachers.

The changes in the *personnel* of the teaching staff have amounted to over a hundred individual changes of teachers, extending to seventy-five schools, more than half the list: of these over sixty schools have changed their principal teachers, and a third of these more than once, in a dozen cases more than twice, in a few instances there were more than three changes; which means that three or four teachers have been successively in charge of one school, with, in some cases, the farther change of a substitute during the training of the teacher. It need scarcely be said that changes so numerous are not calculated to promote the success of the schools concerned, nor to further the progress of education. In some cases, of course, changes were inevitable; thus twelve teachers died, and a dozen more retired on pension or gratuity; over twenty others went to business, or married and undertook domestic duties; but still the majority (over sixty) were changes pure and simple from one school to another in this or other districts. Of the new teachers supplying the places thus vacated, the majority (about sixty) were also from other schools; more than half the remainder came direct from the Training Colleges, the others being ex-monitors or pupil teachers.

In a few of the above cases, where young teachers had clearly missed their vocation, it was a benefit to the country and a kindness to themselves to turn their efforts in other directions; also where old and useless teachers could retire on pension, it was equally beneficial to induce them, however unwilling, to do so. And in both these classes of cases material advantages have accrued to the localities, in the increased efficiency of the schools. For it need scarcely be repeated how important is the office of the teacher in a locality, not only intellectually and morally, but also materially and financially; since on the teacher largely depends whether the *pupils* (the future *people*), will turn out dull, slow, and unimproving, or on the contrary, bright, intelligent, and successful in life, whether at trades, business, or professions.

But while admitting all this, it must be confessed that too frequent and unnecessary changes are in many ways unsatisfactory, and tend to retard rather than to favour educational progress. Thus, the Results period is usually broken, the newcomer has no great interest, professional or pecuniary, in the first examination, the extra subjects taught may not be to his taste, he may complain of the neglect or of the injudicious promotions of his predecessor, their plans and methods of teaching may differ, &c. And with regard to suggestions, hints, and exemplification of methods by the Inspector, he has commonly to begin *de novo*; in many cases to explain the methods of keeping the school records, of making up averages, &c.; to indicate the essential items of the programme, to point out defects in time tables; to illustrate the teaching of reading, explanation, tables, grammar in its various stages, and geography, especially as to map teaching. Thus, it is clear, there is much sameness and repetition in successive rounds of inspection and examination.

About a dozen schools have lost assistants through fall of averages, or by those leaving who had held under the 50 scale; on the other hand, half this number have gained assistants; while in most cases their loss was partially compensated by the appointment of workmistresses, the number of whom has very considerably increased; girls generally attending better and remaining longer at schools where some needlework is taught.

Appointments of workmistresses (including changes) have become so frequent, that their examination, involving one or two days for each, has become a considerable item; and a great saving of time would be effected, if these examinations could be taken up in July, when a long day is devoted to needlework by all female candidates. Appointments and changes would then be made with a view to this, and candidates (commonly resident dressmakers) would be found to work on such terms, as there are generally several applicants for each vacancy. In connection with this, it seems strange that classed and even trained teachers have to undergo a re-examination as workmistresses, even where they have long taught needlework as assistants to all classes for the Results programme. Now while the present scales of averages for monitors and assistance are maintained (with the facilities for training), there will likely be a large number of classed female candidates unemployed, who would be preferred as workmistresses could they be appointed without re-examination, which could be dispensed with by having the needlework executed in July, by monitors, etc., examined by directresses of this branch, and certified accordingly. These ex-monitors would be much better acquainted with the details of the needlework programme for the various classes, often puzzling to the mere dressmaker, who has also generally very confused ideas as to the industrial programme. The classed workmistress would also be familiar with the routine of school classes; and might not be unwilling to assist in some of the other school work, or might even be able to teach singing or drawing for results; besides, her pronunciation and expression, as well as her mode of teaching needlework, would generally be superior to those of extern workmistresses.

There are too many small schools, in which the average is generally near the minimum, and below it in periods of depression, owing to severe weather, and consequent prolonged field work, or prevalence of various diseases that affect children. These small schools are seldom of a high grade, but are often convenient to the pupils, who now go to school so young, and unfortunately leave so early; in most cases, too, they minister to the desire for Congregational schools, perhaps a development of the denominational idea, on account of the utility of the building for social and religious reunions, as well as for other obvious advantages of an analogous sort. The managers (chiefly clergymen) and the teachers have indeed a ready remedy for small attendance in the common panacea of compulsion, which they desire to have extended to the rural localities, as seemingly their only hope for the resuscitation of those small schools.

The only part of this district to which the Compulsory Act has so far applied is the town of Downpatrick; and here it has been effectively carried out under a strong committee, including W. Healy, Esq., J.P., ex-inspector; W. Russell, Esq., solicitor; the Rector, Ven. Archdeacon Price; Rev. R. H. Semple, M.A.; J. Tate, Esq., J.P.; &c. This committee has from the beginning worked harmoniously with the Town Commissioners, who pay the School Attendance officer and the secretary. The action of the officer in visiting schools, reporting to the committee, taking a census of the pupils, and warning defaulters, is allowed to have materially strengthened the hands of the teachers and managers, and has relieved them from the tasks of visiting careless parents and looking after truants; duties formerly so efficiently performed, that the total increase of pupils could not be great. The attendance has however become steadier, and the few who were unamenable to advice and remonstrance, have, through threat and fear of punishment, been compelled to attend school, to their own great advantage, and furnishing an example useful in preventing others from relapsing into truancy.

Compulsion would doubtless assist the small rural schools, and benefit many neglected children of careless parents, of whom the number in rural localities must be considerable. And if the age and standard of proficiency to be attained before leaving school were higher, the advantage to the schools and the benefit to the children would be pro-

portionally greater. For Fourth Class pupils of tender years may not
long retain their ability to read and write; but were they compelled to
pass in Fifth Class they would have greater facility in these arts, and
be therefore much more likely to practise them, and would have learned
the important forms of epistolary correspondence.

Among the causes that interfere with the attendance at the great
majority of schools, one of the chief is field-work; in spring the planting of potatoes, in summer weeding, and saving the hay and flax crops,
and in autumn the corn harvest earlier, and the potato gathering
later; and when the weather is showery (as it was in 1891) the former
is prolonged and the later extended, so that most of the pupils cannot
return till December; while in 1893 the warm dry summer and short
early harvest benefited the schools proportionately. Epidemics among
the children have also, from time to time and in restricted areas, considerable effects, not only on the attendance of pupils, but also through
the closing of schools by advice of sanitary officers. Thus in 1892 in-
fluenza in January and measles in the summer caused the closing of
twenty-four schools (one sixth of the whole) for from one to three
weeks. In 1893 not half so many cases of such closing occurred, but
some ten schools were closed for two or three weeks from scarlatina
and dread of diphtheria. The past year, however (1894) was much
worse in this respect, quite a number of schools having to close from
one to three weeks, as well as suffering in their attendance from the
prevalence of measles.

The number of school days shows a rather wide margin of difference
in various schools, and especially in the number of days included for
average attendance, varying from under 200 to near 210, a difference of
forty or forty-five school-days, that is eight or nine weeks in the year or
over two months. Of course fifty-two weeks give 200 school-days in the
year, even allowing (besides Sunday) one full day of each week, Saturday
being a new holiday now almost universal outside the Board's Model
Schools, though why it should be utterly discarded for school purposes
is not quite clear, and it should be kept in view as a reserve that may
be drawn on in, case some sort of industrial or artistic work should
require to be carried on with the senior pupils. Thus even 240
school-days leave four weeks for vacations, &c., in the year, which in
many cases would probably be sufficient. But 230 school-days would
leave six weeks for vacations, &c., surely ample for all reasonable purposes. Even 220 school-days (about the average) seems to leave an
excessive margin of idleness for the pupils; but when only 200 days or
under are included, unless the circumstances are very exceptional, the
children would seem to have special facilities for forgetting much they
may have learned, as well as for acquiring habits of carelessness as to
school going. Nor do I believe that such long and frequent closures
are satisfactory to the parents of the children in the majority of cases.
I think teachers can too readily close their schools; and if some part
of the payments awarded to schools depended on the number of days
included in the average, or rather on the number of days the school was
kept working, closing would not be so frequent, the steady workers
would be encouraged, and I believe a good many more pupils would
qualify for results, and be better prepared than at present. And if
small attendances might be excluded from averages, the stipulated fifty
days per quarter, or 200 per year, being reserved, one strong inducement to
unnecessary closing of schools would be removed, namely, the fear of
bringing down the average by including periods of low attendance.

Appendix C.

Reports on State of Schools.

Mr. J. B. Skeffington. District Inspector.

Downpatrick.

School fees.

When the regulations for the abolition of school fees under 6s. per annum came into operation, some twenty-three schools in this district had fees slightly over that rate, but only about a dozen had excess fees of 1s. to 4s. a year per pupil, and in nearly all cases it was found judicious to drop the excess fee, and to make the schools entirely free. This measure was a great relief to many parents, though a few preferred to seem to pay for the education by school fees, but that was only a small fraction of the cost, and they do pay indirectly by taxation; a consideration which also meets the objection of some, that when parents paid fees they valued the education, for they may easily be shown that they do pay by taxation, whether they avail of the instruction or not; and, on the contrary, if they do not obtain their share of the instruction, they are losing something that they help to pay for in taxes. Another objection allied to this was, that when the child paid its fee on Monday, it would attend all week to get the value of the penny; this is counterbalanced by cases where pupils missed a day or two in the beginning of the week, and would not attend the other two or three days when they had to pay the week's fee. Undoubtedly it must make the task of inducing pupils to attend school much easier for teachers and pleasanter to parents, while managers have now much less reluctance in urging pupils to attend. The teachers, too, even where the fees were over the present allowance, have gained in most cases an equivalent in the mode of payment by bulk sums quarterly, instead of in dribbles, of which they had to keep numerous minute accounts, often difficult to collect; as well as a further balance in the freedom from the element of repulsion in demanding fees from pupils reluctant to attend at all, not to speak of the large increment of 20 per cent to class salaries at the same time.

School banks.

The school bank system introduced in connection with the abolition of school fees has not (I regret to say) been extensively taken up in this district, though tried to some extent; in at least nine schools there are some 200 depositors of from 1s. to 10s. each, or some £50 to £60 in all; most of these are rural schools, though the system would seem better adapted to the weekly wage earners of towns. Some of the teachers stated they had tried the experiment, but found no disposition to avail of its advantages. Teachers, however, find it easier now to induce pupils to purchase books, and other school requisites, since the abolition of school fees.

Proficiency.

In estimating the proficiency from results proved, two considerations should be adverted to—first that failures at Results and noughts on Marking Paper do not (as might be supposed) imply absolute ignorance on the part of the pupil, nor total neglect on the part of the teacher; for if the pupils answer one-fourth of the questions, or even a third of them, they would be marked failures, yet this amount of knowledge might be far above pure ignorance, both as concerns utility to pupil and effort of teacher. Secondly, it is to be remembered that a failure in a higher class might easily be equal to a pass in a lower class, and so again the cipher may not indicate absolute ignorance; thus a pupil who fails to pass in Writing in Fifth Class might pass freely in Fourth—one who gets a nought for Geography in Sixth Class might have considerable and useful knowledge of the maps of the World, Europe, and Ireland. For both these reasons, it is plain that there is much useful work done that does not appear from Results marks, and that, therefore, the Examiner or Inspector will be in a much better position to judge of the total worth of a school than he could be from a mere scrutiny of Results passes.

Reading.

In Reading I think there is improvement, though distinctness of utterance and clearness of expression are still difficult to obtain.

Inaccuracy in small words is too common, and seems to arise from Appendix C.
carelessness and inattention, which would be checked by variety and Reports on State of Schools.
interest in the subjects, especially as to the earlier books. The more
advanced books seem in vocabulary and matter somewhat difficult for
the pupils of our schools. If indeed it were feasible, I should Mr. J. A. Carrington District Inquiries.
like to see various sets of reading books adapted to the tastes of
different schools.   And above all, seeing how important are the
school lessons of pupils, how long they may remain in the memory, how Down-patrick.
they may influence their whole ideas and after life, I should like to see
a special set of lessons or books, designed to teach children their
duties to one another, to parents, to elders—lessons which might
save them from having to learn at the dear school of experience the
consequence of words, acts, omissions; which might save them in after
years from the bitter fruit of regret; build up before them models of
character, of devotion to duty, of constancy, perseverance, providence;
teach self-restraint, and warn against self-indulgence and selfishness.
These aims should be accomplished by aid of fables, stories, history, poetry,
and all the forms and varieties of composition that could gain the attention
and impress the memory.   I am aware that already there is a considerable amount in our books of such lessons as I allude to; but I think
there should be almost complete sets of books of this sort, seeing, as
Dr. Johnson says, that "the first requisite is the religious and moral
knowledge of right and wrong."

The sets of copybooks provided for our schools are now so numerous, Writing.
various, and withal excellent, that only due care and practice are needed
to produce good results.   Accordingly, the proficiency is up to a very
fair standard, and might be higher if attention was always paid to the
headlines, and less careless scribbling allowed. In letter-writing
there is very considerable progress both as to form and facility of
expression; and yet a good deal more might be done to correct grammatical errors, &c.

Arithmetic is pretty successfully taught, when its difficulties are Arithmetic.
duly considered; but in the junior classes it is very hard to contend
against the use of mechanical aids in teaching Addition tables. Finger-
counting, nods, dots, strokes, &c., seem such natural devices for over-
coming the initial difficulties of remembering the sum of every two
digits, and of extending the table to several digits successfully, that
they are repeatedly condemned only to re-appear again; yet, there is no
time better spent, nor effort more judiciously exerted than in learning
to add properly a column of figures, though many teachers (even some
trained) do not seem to give due weight to this apparently small but
really very important matter.   It is hardly necessary to point out how
much of the time and labour expended on this subject depends on our
multitudinous standards of weights and measures, with their various
divisors, whole and fractional; how much of all our School Arithmetic
is taken up with Reduction, Weights, Measures, Practice, &c., nearly
all of which would disappear in a uniform system, such as the metric
system.   Yet it is strange to reflect that six or seven centuries have
been too short to unify these manifold irregularities, for we find Magna
Charta by its 35th Clause declaring that "There shall be one standard
of measures and one standard of weights throughout the kingdom."
Surely progress has been rather slow in this department, considering
the waste of time and of energy, the errors and confusion arising from
this source; and how much real knowledge of Numbers and of Mathematics generally children might acquire if the years now wasted (as
may be said) over these tables and their applications were free to be
more profitably used.

So far as regards oral spelling of difficult words, and fair writing of dictation exercises, much time and a great deal of effort are applied, and with very fair success ; perhaps the four words *the, they, there* and *their,* give rise to more errors than ten times the number of other words ; yet their proper use, depending *generally* on whether a noun or a verb follows, seems easy enough to teach ; and the correct use of such small words is far more important than accuracy in spelling difficult words, of perhaps doubtful orthography, and rare occurrence.

Grammar does not seem a favourite subject in the schools ; the fee is small, the labour of learning and teaching considerable, and the application not very obvious in the earlier stages.   Still even the elements may be used to develop the intelligence of the pupils, as well as to aid in the correct use and spelling of words.   I have frequently found in the earlier stages, the use of words not sufficiently attended to in determining the part of speech ; and in the higher classes an analogous error of neglecting practically the Syntax of words, which accounts for many failures in Parsing ; and in this respect even trained teachers are not blameless ; yet such practical application of Syntax aids much in grasping the meaning and drift of sentences.   I should expect good from a fuller and more explicit programme, illustrating perhaps the degree of proficiency expected in each class.

Perhaps a similar remark would apply to Geography.   I mean the utility of a more detailed programme, setting forth definitely the standard of knowledge to be aimed at in each class, and perhaps more re-arrangement of the programmes for Fifth and Sixth Classes.   The book and the maps are the two competing factors in the teaching of Geography ; competing I say, for one or other is apt to have an undue share ; nor are authorities quite in unison either as to their order of precedence, or how far we are to depend on the map, or how deep to dive into the book, which of its numerous facts and figures we are to remember, or if we are to use it as a work of reference chiefly ; hence an ill-defined programme is apt to grow vague or be variously interpreted.   But no programme will serve those who do not attend to it.   I was told lately by a First Class trained teacher, that the programme was to "show the map" instead of to "know the map," and accordingly he taught to show places merely, not to describe situation.

Agriculture is taught in nearly all schools under masters, and often with success so far as answering questions on the text book, and probably that is of some consequence where the pupils and their parents have a practical acquaintance with the subject matter.

Book-keeping was taken up in some twenty schools, and fairly understood so far as personal and real accounts ; but bill transactions seem rather beyond the grasp of Sixth Class pupils, who have not the requisite practical familiarity with them.

Drawing has been taught in nearly forty schools with very fair success ; copies mounted on large sheets suspended before the class are very useful, giving a practical turn to the Drawing, and enabling the teacher (if he will) to give class instruction on the method of Drawing, also preventing measuring and tracing on the drawing copy book.   Outline drawing and shading are useful in "training hand and eye," and in aiding pupils to "observe and compare," as "Dawes' Hints" long ago inculcated in its useful lessons, which are indeed only applications of the Pestalozzian system, the origin of which may be traced to Locke.

But other branches of Drawing are far better adapted to the mechanical Trades and Arts ; thus Geometrical Drawing, involving the use of compasses, scales, set squares, and protractors, forms the basis of Engineering, Mechanical, and Architectural Drawing, and being also exten-

sively useful in Arts and Trades, might well be substituted for Freehand
Drawing where desired. It is scarcely necessary to refer to Isometri-
cal Drawing, so useful in some trades, to Perspective as an essential aid
to object and picture Drawing, or to Orthographic Projection, so useful
in the higher parts of office work.

Geometry was taken up in some twenty schools, but the difficulty of
making up both Euclid and Mensuration prevents this subject from
being generally adopted, as few boys seem to have naturally the ability
to follow, at an early age, the reasoning of Euclid, or few teachers seem
able to develop this power in their pupils. Hence practical Geometry
or Mensuration, might be taken instead of Euclid, being also much
more suitable and useful from a practical point of view ; while the
mere changes of symbols in working the elementary rules of Algebra
without equations, seem by no means so useful, though easily learned,
and sometimes better worked than Arithmetic in Fifth and Sixth
Classes.

Vocal Music has been taught in about thirty schools, and in case
of Tonic Solfa often with much success, while in teaching Hullah's system
there does not yet seem enough of the singing of scales, chords, and
intervals, which constitutes so large a part of Tonic Solfa practice.

Very few other extras are taken up, and in only a few schools. These
are Latin, French, Trigonometry, Physical Geography, Domestic
Economy and Kindergarten ; the last in the excellent Infant Department of the Convent School in Downpatrick is carried out to its full
extent and well applied.

I have the honour to remain, Gentlemen,

Your obedient servant,

J. R. SKEFFINGTON, District Inspector.

The Secretaries,
    National Education, Ireland.

MR. J. STEEDE, LL.D., District Inspector,

Dundalk, February 26th, 1895.

GENTLEMEN,—I have the honour to forward this General Report on
this District for the year 1894, for the information of the Commissioners
of National Education.

The District comprises nearly the entire of the County Louth, a
portion of the County Meath south of Drogheda for a distance of
about nine miles, and small portions of the Counties of Armagh and
Monaghan. It contains the important towns of Drogheda and Dundalk,
and a few small ones—Ardee, Dunleer, Louth, and Crossmaglen.
Fishing is carried on in a few places on the east coast, of which
Baltray, at the mouth of the Boyne, and Clogherhead are the most
important.

Appendix C.

Reports on
State of
Schools.

Mr. J.
Sheridan,
District
Inspector.

Dundalk.

There were 130 schools in operation at the end of the year, classed as follows:—

Poor Law Union,	. . . .	
Infant,	. . . .	
Convent,	. . . .	
Ordinary Male,	. . . .	
Do. Female,	. . . .	
Do. Mixed (boys and girls),	. . . .	
	Total,	130

Numbers
and class of
schools.

Excluding the Poor Law Union and Convent Schools, the remainder are held in 84 schoolhouses. Classifying these, and taking a moderate standard of what a schoolhouse ought to be, 50 may be considered good or excellent, and 10 must be regarded as bad, and therefore require either to be superseded by suitable houses, or to be improved by structural alterations so as to make them at all fit for the purposes of Education. Some of these will shortly be replaced by new vested houses, and others may after some time, but there is no expectation of any change with regard to three of them.

The school-
houses.

Play-
grounds.

Less than half of the schoolhouses are provided with suitable and adequate playgrounds. In rural districts the road or adjacent fields are used for the purpose, evidently not a desirable arrangement. The want of a playground is acutely felt by two large schools where no substitute for one is to be had; and is not only injurious to the education of the pupils, but a source of danger to their health.

Out-offices,
light and
ventilation.

Eleven schoolhouses, in which 15 separate schools are held, have no out-offices attached to them—a state of things which should not be permitted to exist. The out-offices attached to 35 other schoolhouses are objectionable, owing either to situation or to defective construction. Again, in consequence of structural defects, such as low ceilings and windows, the latter being also occasionally insufficient in number, the light is inadequate and the ventilation defective in about 23 schoolhouses. Well-lighted, properly ventilated, warm schoolrooms, with suitable and adequate recreation grounds, must greatly assist the teachers in the discharge of their important duties.

School
furniture.

The furniture of a schoolroom includes desks, blackboards and easels, a clock, and educational and ornamental tablets and pictures. In many of the old schoolhouses the desks are faulty in structure, very long, very broad, of too great a slope, and otherwise objectionable. There will generally be found in all the schoolrooms maps of the World, Europe, and Ireland; and in the greater number, other maps, large or small. In too many cases the clock is broken, and with its handless dial, hangs in a slovenly position on the wall. This leads to the consideration of the tidiness of schoolrooms. It seems strange how teachers will allow their schoolrooms to have an untidy appearance in other respects—the tablets soiled and torn, the maps not suspended on pulleys, dusty books of all kinds on the desks, tables, and window sills; the door wanting a latch; the heading of the desks hanging off for want of a few nails, &c. Disregard to these (some of them apparently little) things will interfere much with the usefulness of a school. I regret to say there are schoolrooms of this character in the District, and I trust they will become fewer. A tidy and clean schoolroom, well furnished, with everything kept in its proper place, and everything done at the proper time, must have an educational effect on the pupils, training them into habits of cleanliness, neatness, order and punctuality.

Tidiness of
the school-
room.

Improve-
ments by
managers.

I have much pleasure in referring here to the efforts of the managers to improve their schoolhouses by structural alterations or by the erection of new houses. As an example of the former I may mention Termonfeckin schoolhouse. Originally an old chapel, it has been used as a schoolhouse with separate rooms for boys and girls respectively. About a year ago it was greatly improved at a very considerable outlay, and the girls' schoolroom is now well lighted, properly ventilated, warm, and commodious. The manager would have preferred to build a new house, but, unfortunately, could not get a site. Belpatrick, Cartown, Dromin, and Phillipstown schoolhouses have had improvements effected on them. A non-vested house has been erected at Ballewstown at a cost of over £300, to supersede an old and unsuitable one. A vested house has been erected at Kilsaran to take the place of a most objectionable one. In Dundalk a vested schoolhouse, to accommodate 500 children, is in course of erection, and applications have been made for aid to build two large vested houses in Drogheda, on the north and south sides of the Boyne respectively. A vested house will, probably, be built at Collon, where it is urgently required before the close of the year. The manager of Crossmaglen schools has, with the Board's aid, added a class room furnished with Kindergarten desks and a suitable gallery to the Infant schoolroom. The manager of Clogherhead and Hackstown schools has been trying, for some years, to build a vested house to supersede these schoolhouses. The rev. gentleman has had difficulties about the site, and has had to put in force the act for compulsorily acquiring sites for schoolhouses. This is necessarily a slow proceeding, but he hopes to be able to commence building in a few months. Ballymakenny non-vested house is to be improved immediately by means of a loan from the Board of Works. It will thus be seen that the managers generally are anxious to do what they can to have suitable schoolhouses.

Excluding workmistresses, there were 162 teachers in the district at the end of the year; of these, 39 were assistant teachers. Of the principal teachers, nearly one half are in the Second Class, one third in First Class (two divisions), and the remainder, nearly one fifth, in the Third Class. It is evident from these numbers that the Third Class teachers are rapidly diminishing, and that when those now in the service retire, there will, practically, be only two classes, viz., First and Second, the former having two divisions. This is due to the Training Colleges. It were, however, much to be desired that First Class teachers should exhibit first-class work in their schools. There are, I regret to say, many First Class teachers in this district who have not produced results in their schools commensurate with their classification. Such teachers should, unless in exceptional circumstances, teach with efficiency (a) the ordinary branches of the School Programme; (b) Algebra, Geometry, and Mensuration to intelligent pupils of the Fifth and Sixth Classes; Book-keeping to pupils of town schools, and Agriculture to those in rural schools, if the latter subjects are included in those for their own classification. Besides, if they possess certificates of competency to teach Freehand Drawing and Singing, these branches should also for them be included in the ordinary school curriculum. In a former General Report I stated, as my opinion, that Elementary Freehand Drawing and Singing should be taught in every National School. With regard to the former, there should be no difficulty in teaching it, as any teacher can be trained to teach elementary Freehand Drawing, as well as Writing. It is different with the teaching of Vocal Music; for, except a teacher, before going to training, has a musical ear and voice so as to be able, at least, to sing the common chord correctly, there is little likelihood of his so profiting by his course of training as to enable him to be awarded a certificate of competency to teach singing. I have dwelt more at length on this subject in a former General Report.

Appendix G.
Reports on State of Schools.

Mr. J. Bundy, LL.D., District Inspector.

Dundalk.

The Teachers.

H

Appendix C.   The efficiency of some teachers cannot but be impaired by having
Reports on   farms or other pursuits in addition to their schools.
Scale of
Salaries.   Ten teachers have to walk daily to and from their schools distances
    varying from seven to nine miles; yet, to their credit be it said, they
Mr. J.   are punctual in attendance, and generally efficient in the discharge of
Garvin,   their duties. This physical labour, if continued, must have an injurious
TT.B.   effect on their constitutions.
District
Inspector,   Teachers who have proved themselves to be inefficient, and who, if
Dundalk.   males, have reached sixty, and if females, fifty-five years of age, should
Teachers'   apply for a pension, and should not continue to keep the condition of
extern em-   education backward in their several schools. Managers with inefficient
ployments.   teachers are almost powerless to effect improvement. Such managers
Resignation   can, it may be, largely increase the attendance, but it will be only for a
of ineffici-   short time, the inefficiency of the teacher not affording any inducements
ent teach-   to the pupils to continue to attend. Many instances could be cited
ers.   where a change from an inefficient to an efficient teacher has completely
    altered the character of a school for good.

Residence.   Residences are connected with twenty-three schoolhouses, of which
    three were erected by means of loans from the Board of Works. Some
    others are urgently required, and one, at least, will shortly be erected.

Abolition of   The abolition of school fees has been a great boon to the teachers.
school fees.   Besides other advantages it has removed a source of friction between
    parents and teachers, which was often injurious to education. The
    attendance of the pupils has not, however, been affected by it. The
    abolition of school fees ought to facilitate the raising of funds to
    provide maps, &c., but in a few cases only have such funds been forth-
School   coming. The establishment of School Savings Banks, too, has been a
Savings   failure as far as this district is concerned, only one such bank to my
Banks.   knowledge having been established. Unless the managers take up this
    idea of School Savings Banks, and, with the assistance of the teachers,
    carry it into practice, it will be hopeless to expect them to be
    established. To show what little things will come to—in 1893, the
    autumn being favourable, the pupils of two schools in this district
    during their vacation gathered as much blackberries as sold for £40;
    and I have been informed that a few years before that they collected as
    much as sold for £50. The establishment of School Savings Banks
    would be extremely useful in training children to thrifty habits.

Compulsory   The Compulsory Attendance Act, applicable to Drogheda, Dundalk,
Attendance   and Ardee, has not been adopted by the municipal authorities of those
Act.   towns. In the two former towns the Act could not be put in force for
    want of school accommodation. After a short time this will no longer
    be so, when the new schoolhouses referred to above shall have been
    built. And then, it is to be hoped, there will be no obstacle to the
    carrying out of the Act. There seems to be little doubt that in the
    towns named above the operation of the Act is much required. In
    rural districts the managers are generally influential enough to compel
    the children in their parishes to attend school, and, if the teachers be
    efficient, they will continue to do so.

Results   The School Programme prescribes the minimum amount of work for
fees.   each class. To stimulate the teachers in their work, as well as to in-
    crease their salaries, Results Fees were introduced. The proportion of
    these Results Fees to the teacher's entire salary varies with the classifi-
    cation of the teacher and the school attendance. They bear a less pro-
    portion to the salaries of the Second Class teachers, and a far less pro-
    portion to those of the First Class teachers than they do to the Third
    Class teachers' salaries. Therefore, the stimulus to work given by

Results Fees is least in the case of First Class teachers, and greatest in the case of Third Class teachers. This may perhaps be the cause why so many First Class teachers do not produce better results. It is well known that if a teacher goes through his school duties in a perfunctory, *laissez-faire* kind of way, the Results' Fees will amount to a respectable sum. If such a teacher, on the other hand, performs his duties with attention, zeal and efficiency, the amount of the Results Fees will be considerably increased. Now, it is this increase which is the real measure of a teacher's earnest work; and in the case of highly classed teachers, it bears a comparatively small proportion to his entire salary. There is therefore a temptation for such teachers to do the minimum amount of work, but I am glad to be able to say there are some honourable examples of the contrary in this district. Again, it is well known that there are some parts of the School Programme, such as Explanation, Mental Arithmetic, &c., for which no Results Fees directly accrue. Some of these (called sub-heads) are generally not attended to. This, I need scarcely say, is not only a great mistake, but a suicidal policy. It is not education in the highest sense of the term, but, to a large extent, cramming. Not long since I examined a well taught school of nearly seventy pupils. In consequence of sickness, inclement weather, and other circumstances the attendance for the last two months was very bad, so much so, that it was intended to postpone the examination. It took place however, at the fixed time, when to my agreeable surprise and to that of the teacher there were very few ciphers on the marking paper. This result was due to good sound teaching; had this been wanting, the failures would have been numerous. The ill effects of this neglect are observed especially in examining in Grammar. Technical terms are not understood, and the "reason why" is not known. The neglect, too, of some parts of the School Programme for which Results Fees are directly paid is I fear due to the fact that the fee for such subjects is small; the teacher forgetting that the entire of his salary, including Results Fees, is paid for teaching all the branches of the School Programme according to the best of his ability, e.g. the fee for a pass in Needlework in Second Class is only sixpence, but surely the teacher should consider that this sixpence is only a part, and in the case of a first class teacher, a small part of the portion of her salary paid for teaching Needlework to Second Class.

Having made these general remarks I shall now make some particular observations on the schools and their examinations.

The Poor Law Union Schools are two in number; the attendance in each is happily small; each contains two departments for boys and girls respectively, and those for the girls are under the care of Nuns.

There is one Monastery School taught by teachers of the De La Salle order of Monks. This school is in other respects regarded as a Model National School.

There are five Convent Schools. One conducted by the Sisters of Charity is a Male Infant School with an Industrial School for junior boys attached. Two of the remaining four are large and very important schools; one of them, under the care of the Sisters of Mercy, has an Industrial School for girls attached, the other is under the care of the Presentation Order of Nuns. The remaining two, conducted by the Sisters of Mercy, although not so large, are yet important schools.

There are also two ordinary Infant Schools; one for boys, the other for boys and girls combined. Both are very well taught. Infant Schools of this kind might with great advantage be established in other parts of the district.

H 2

Appendix C.

Reports on State of Schools.

Mr. J. [illegible] LL.D. District Inspector.

Dundalk.

Extra branches in ordinary schools.

Referring next to the one hundred and twenty-one ordinary schools, the following are the extra branches taught and the number of schools in which pupils were presented for examination in each branch, respectively:—Drawing, ten schools; Vocal Music, seven; Algebra, five; Geometry and Mensuration, seven; Book-keeping, eighteen; Physical Geography, two; and Domestic Economy, one; in addition to three schools where the Alternative Scheme of Industrial Work was adopted, necessitating the teaching of Domestic Economy. Whatever be the cause, the teaching of these very useful optional subjects is very limited. As I have before observed, elementary Freehand Drawing should not be more difficult to be taught than Writing. The programmes of proficiency in Algebra, Geometry and Mensuration, and Book-keeping are very definite, and there should therefore be no difficulty in teaching these subjects to intelligent pupils of the Fifth and Sixth Classes. If there be not time to do this during school hours, surely it would not be too much to utilise the half hour from 9½ to 10 o'clock for the purpose.

Alternative Scheme of Industrial work.

The Alternative Scheme of Needlework is taught in seven of these schools as well as in one of the Convent Schools. As this scheme is under the consideration of the Commissioners, I shall not further refer to it.

Kindergarten.

Kindergarten is taught in one of the two Infant Schools, and in the infant departments of four of the Convent Schools. In three of these latter the accommodation for teaching it is too limited. The successful teaching of Kindergarten requires a class-room large in proportion to the attendance.

Reading.

The number of passes in Reading at Results examinations in proportion to the number examined is large. The defects observed in reference to this branch (which includes explanation and repetition of Poetry) have been so often pointed out in general reports, and the proposed remedies for them suggested, that I think it quite unnecessary to refer to them here. These defects are found in this district, but not, perhaps, to a greater extent than in former ones of which I had charge.

Writing.

The Writing of the first four classes is generally very good. The copy books are clean and the head lines carefully imitated. The blackboards on which the copies are written for First Class pupils are in most cases permanently and suitably ruled, an arrangement which has been found most useful in teaching these pupils to form their letters with uniformity and legibility. Letter-writing is taught to the Fifth and Sixth Classes. In teaching it to the former class three points are attended to, (a) the form of the letter, (b) the social relation of the addressee and the writer, and (c) the subject matter which should be as simple as possible. The Sixth Class pupils write a more extended letter on some useful subject. With regard to this class, the teacher might have a list, say of twenty subjects, on each of which the pupils are prepared to write a letter on the day of the examination. The proficiency attained in Letter-writing is generally very fair.

Arithmetic.

The programme of Arithmetic for the first three classes being so very definite, the percentage of passes to the numbers examined is generally satisfactory. The proficiency exhibited in the senior classes is very fair. I have already referred to the neglect of Mental Arithmetic, to which may be added neglect of the prescribed exercises in Compound Addition.

Spelling.

In the First and Second Classes the words at the heads of the lessons in their reading books are generally correctly spelled by the pupils, but the spelling of phrases taken from the same books, or even from the pieces of poetry the Second Class pupils had learned for repetition, is not at all good. It sometimes happens that very few failures appear for the spelling for which Results Fees are paid, while the character

of the phrase spelling is noted as bad or middling. The Third Class
write from dictation on slates, and the senior classes on paper.

In order that the Third Class pupils be taught Grammar successfully
they must know the meanings of the words which they refer to the
different parts of speech. If for no other reason than this alone,
Grammar should continue to be taught to this class. The programme
of the Fourth Class Grammar is so very definite that it is surprising
there should be any failures in this branch ; yet the general answering
is only middling, a result due probably to want of carefulness in teaching,
and to the imperfect learning and explanation of the home lessons
in it. The Fifth and Sixth Classes parse suitable passages on paper.
At incidental visits I have frequently found unmarked errors in Grammar in the pupils' exercise books. And in any school where this
prevails, failures in Grammar at Results Examinations may be expected.
Again, in the Fifth Class, the pupils are often ignorant of "reason why,"
e.g., why a verb is in the singular number—why future tense I &c. If no
parsing exercises were given to the pupils to be written in their exercise
books but those which had previously been gone over in class ; if, when
written, errors were marked, and after having been explained, the exercises were re-written correctly, there would be very few failures at the
Results Examinations. A pupil thus taught for two years in Fifth Class
would find no difficulty in passing in Sixth Class Grammar after promotion.

With suitable maps, the "Introduction to Geography" on the
Board's list as a text book, and systematic teaching, there should be
very few failures in Geography in the Third, Fourth, and Fifth Classes.
The proficiency, although very fair, might be much better. The Sixth
Class pupils, in some schools, are taught to draw very good maps of
Ireland.

Although a large result fee is paid for a pass in Agriculture the
subject is not successfully taught. That this is not always the case is
proved by the fact that in a few schools a good proportion of those examined in it pass. In former general reports I have stated what I
thought were the causes of this, and have also indicated what might be
done to make the teaching of it more effective. I therefore do not
think it necessary to do so in this report.

It is singular that Book-keeping is not successfully taught. The programme of the required proficiency for Fifth Class, both stages, is definite and simple ; and if pupils passed creditably in these stages, they
would have no difficulty in attaining the required proficiency for a pass
in Sixth Class. In many cases the pupils are left to write out the sets
without proper explanation of the several entries. Even a trial balance
is, in numerous cases, not understood.

Needlework, without doubt, is a most important branch of school
education for girls. Greater attention has been lately given to it. As
a consequence of the careless manner in which it is sometimes taught,
it is no uncommon occurrence at incidental visits, as well as at Result
Examinations, to find girls in the Fifth and Sixth Classes not using
their needles and thimbles properly. Within the last two years I have
seen two monitors in their third year not able to do so. This has
occurred from allowing children in the Second and Third Classes to sew
without thimbles, and even when they have thimbles, allowing them to
use them improperly. I have frequently got teachers to read the following statement in Miss Jones's book, which is on the Board's list :—
" It is not natural to them (the pupils) to use a thimble, or to move
the thumb as described, but till they do so they cannot be said to be
able to work."

Appendix C.

Reports on
State of
Schools.

Mr J.
Steele,
F.D.
District
Inspector,
Dundalk.

I invariably examine the Fifth and Sixth Classes in the cutting out of the articles of apparel prescribed for them severally on the programme, and also in darning. The pupils of the Fourth and higher Classes have for exhibition on the day of the examination finished articles, often tastily worked, of the prescribed kind. In connection with cut-

Cutting-out. ting out, there is one school in this district where the manager got a long and broad board hinged to the wainscoting, at a height of about three feet from the floor. When not in use this board bangs down against the wall, where it occupies very little space. When the time for cutting out comes, the lower part of this board is lifted up, the legs are placed in position, when it affords a very convenient and suitable table for use in teaching the pupils how to cut out their different articles of dress. Another manager has promised to put up similar structures in his schools.

The School Accounts. The school accounts, with very few exceptions, are honestly kept. In numerous cases extreme accuracy is attained by properly checking the books with each other.

The Managers. The managers in the district, as a rule, take great interest in their schools, visiting them frequently, and carrying out any suggestions which they see may benefit the cause of education. I have much pleasure in gratefully acknowledging their courtesy and kindness to me since I took charge of the district in 1893.

I have the honour to be, Gentlemen,

Your obedient servant,

J. STEELE, District Inspector.

The Secretaries, &c., &c., &c.

Mr. P.
Newell,
District
Inspector,
Westport.

Mr. P. NEWELL, District Inspector.

Westport, February, 1896.

GENTLEMEN,—In accordance with your recent instructions, I beg to furnish a General Report on Westport District.

Limits and character of District. Since I was directed to take charge about three years ago, no change has been effected in its dimensions. It is thus confined exclusively to Mayo, except on the south-west, where it crosses into Galway, and embraces such well-known localities as Maamtrasna, Leenane, Kylemore, and Boffin. On the north and east there is nothing to distinguish it from the majority of rural districts in Ireland. The land is of average quality, and the inhabitants are fairly comfortable. On the north-west the District comprises the remote island of Achill, a place that of late has gained more than ordinary notoriety. In this as in other tracts along the shores of Clew Bay the land is of inferior quality, and the population rather congested. Fishing, notwithstanding the proximity of the sea, is unfortunately but little practised. A large number of the adult population of both sexes are in the habit of migrating to England and Scotland early every summer for the purpose of earning what will afterwards tide them over the winter months at home. Even boys and girls of school-going age not unfrequently join their relations on these expeditions.

School-houses. Repairs. For several years past the number of schools in the District has been steadily increasing. There are at present 153 in operation. Within next half-year or so, a few more are sure to be added. The wants of nearly every locality in the way of school accommodation will then have been pretty well supplied. Most of the existing houses are in good order. A few non-vested buildings of an indifferent type still remain. Their number is, however, rapidly diminishing. Nearly all *Appendix C.* houses erected for some years past have, I regret, been vested in *Reports on* trustees, and very few in the Commissioners. As a result, mishaps of *State of Schools.* every kind, such as slates blown off, windows broken, &c., are often left a long time unattended to. What was thus slight at first soon becomes *Mr. F. Knеell, District Inspector, Westport.* serious, and ultimately entails considerably increased outlay.

With adequate school accommodation and capable teachers, the attendance of pupils is sure to be fairly regular, and their proficiency in the main satisfactory. In both respects improvement is being effected. In *Attendance. Compulsory Education.* both, however, there is room for further progress. As a remedy for irregular attendance nearly all concerned are agreed as to the necessity for some kind of legal compulsion. In this regard the Education Act of 1892 is still inoperative here. The compulsion need not necessarily be of a severe or oppressive character. The mere fact of parents and children being aware of its existence could in most cases be quite sufficient to attain the object in view. At present great numbers of pupils who could be at school remain away on the slightest pretext. The parents are generally more to blame than the pupils.

Most of the Managers here are clergymen, and with very few exceptions take a lively interest in their schools. In many cases their efforts are invaluable in the way of stimulating children to greater regularity. Good teachers are also very successful in the same direction. In spring and autumn their difficulties are of course considerably increased, because of so many scholars having to stay at home in connection with field operations. An efficient teacher, however, generally manages to have a respectable proportion of his pupils qualified for the Annual Examination. An inefficient teacher, on the other hand, has usually a large percentage of defaulters. A good school never fails to attract; a bad one with equal certainty repels. The remedy for irregular attendance is thus to some extent in teacher's own hands.

It might have been reasonably expected that the recent abolition of *Fees and Savings Bank scheme.* fees would lead to improved attendance. This is not, however, the case. In no school here do I find that the attendance has been perceptibly affected in consequence. The apparent anomaly is no doubt due to the fact that in very few places were fees rigidly enforced, even before the enactment of 1892. This was notably so in country schools, where I suspect there was often a good deal of unreality about some of the fees represented as paid. For a similar reason the Savings Bank Scheme has been disappointing. Fees were usually paid quarterly here, and generally by parents in person. Very seldom was the money transmitted through the children. In some cases, too, no fees at all were exacted, for the very good reason that parents were quite unable to pay. In neither case did any fees pass through the hands of the pupils. Their ability to establish a banking account has accordingly been very limited in the past, and remains so even at present. I spoke to several Managers and teachers as to the merits of the scheme. In very few cases, however, did I find any disposition to adopt it. The objection usually made was that only a small percentage of the scholars were likely to be possessed of the needful pence and halfpence to render even a modest beginning possible.

Regular attendance results as a rule in improved proficiency. Even *Proficiency of pupils. Classification of teachers.* in indifferent schools pupils with 150 days or so usually acquit themselves very well at the annual examination. It is not however enough. For satisfactory proficiency, something more than mere attendance is required. Good teachers are essential. The great majority of existing

Appendix C.
Reports on State of Schools.

Mr. F. Newell, District Inspector, Westport.

schools are well conducted; only a very small number badly. For the latter little hope is left except in change of staff. There is however an intermediate group—schools neither well nor ill-conducted. Most of them are under Third Class teachers but would notwithstanding soon improve if teachers only endeavoured to raise their own classification. Some already show a laudable desire in this direction; others however are unaccountably remiss. Many teachers work hard in the schools and yet do little or nothing to improve their own classification. In case of elderly teachers this I know is no easy matter. I refer however to those under middle age, many of whom have continued in Third Class for years and seem satisfied to remain there. Improved classification in such cases would inevitably mean better schools and of course much larger incomes.

Restriction on appointment of Third Class teachers to principalships.

As an additional incentive to higher classification and improved proficiency I think it desirable that some restriction should be placed on the appointment of Third Class teachers to Principalships in cases where First or Second Class candidates are forthcoming. At present a large number of important schools are under the charge of lowly-classed and indifferent teachers, while highly classed and capable teachers have only unimportant schools or mere assistantships. This is scarcely a satisfactory state of things. The past cannot now be undone. It need not however be perpetuated. Some reform in the direction indicated would I am sure be welcomed by all concerned and would produce immediate and lasting good.

Reading.

Reading in nearly every school receives a reasonable amount of attention. In several it is well taught. The subsidiary branches, explanation and poetry, are however often neglected. They do not carry fees. This is the obvious cause. As long as the present Results system exists it cannot be expected that work which pays and work which does not will receive equal attention. A fee for one or both of these branches would be sure to produce improvement. In case of girls in the higher classes it is I think desirable that the free use of suitable books on Domestic Economy, Hygiene, and kindred subjects, be allowed in lieu of Readers hitherto commonly employed.

Writing.

In Penmanship the progress made is on the whole satisfactory. Letter-writing or Composition is also pretty well attended to. In some cases, however, I am not satisfied with the proficiency. Want of practice is the general cause of weakness. Next to Reading it is the most important branch of the school course. Very few persons can dispense with it in after life, hence the desirability of having it as well taught as the circumstances of the different schools will admit.

Arithmetic, Spelling, Grammar and Geography.

In Arithmetic, Spelling, Grammar, and Geography, a reasonable amount of instruction is generally imparted. In some schools the proficiency is highly creditable, in most very fair, in only a few indifferent. Of the four Grammar is the subject in which most failures occur. This is quite intelligible. With teachers and scholars it is the least popular because of its abstruse and conventional character. To enable pupils to speak and write correctly should be the principal object in teaching it. In neither does it, however, succeed to any appreciable extent; perhaps under the circumstances it might be made optional instead of obligatory without any injurious result.

Agriculture.

Agriculture is very fairly taught. It is much to be regretted, however, that there are not better facilities for teaching it practically. A good deal of advantage no doubt arises from the subject even as at present taught. The advantage would, however, be considerably increased if every school had a plot of ground attached where practical

Instruction on the various topics dealt with in the Text-book could be carried out. In mixed schools the subject is frequently taught to girls. They often acquit themselves quite as well as the boys. I doubt, however, whether the time so spent could not be often better employed.

Music and Drawing are taken up in only a limited number of schools. The number I am glad to say is gradually increasing; want of certificates is the principal obstacle. In nearly every school where introduced the progress made is gratifying.

Handicraft is, I regret, taught in only one school. At last examination about 25 pupils were presented. All appeared to like the work, and acquitted themselves satisfactorily. At first the teacher had a good deal of difficulty to contend with. He had to provide the various appliances. Since then, however, he has had the satisfaction of seeing his efforts rewarded.

The hour a day devoted to Needlework during the past few years has led to considerable improvement. In no school, however, do I find the teachers anxious to have this interval extended. In Sixth Class, girls who are properly attended to for an hour a day should, at the end of a year, or at least two, be thoroughly capable of making a large number of articles of wearing apparel, besides being expert at sewing and knitting. With this most parents and pupils are satisfied. Many girls, too, have opportunities for supplementing at home the industrial instruction received at school. Hence the difficulty of getting the new scheme more extensively adopted. Funds for supplying the requisite materials are also scarce. The absence of any local employment in which the increased industrial skill could be turned to account is another serious obstacle.

In Castlebar Convent the new programme was tried for a year and then given up. In neither the Westport nor Newport Convent were the nuns at any time satisfied as to its suitability. In both these schools the old programme has accordingly been taught without interruption. In addition, however, the senior girls receive instruction in dressmaking and sewing machine. The dressmaking is taught after the most approved method, and is an unqualified success. There is thus an increased amount of industrial work combined with the usual number of literary branches. The result in the instances in question is eminently satisfactory.

In some parts of the district Irish is still largely spoken. In such localities the difficulties of teaching young children are of course greater than elsewhere. A working knowledge of English has to be imparted first. It is only then that the other subjects of the Programme can be profitably taken up. In ordinary localities the children come to school with a tolerable knowledge of English beforehand. The trouble and delay of learning the medium of instruction as well as the instruction itself are thus obviated. The difficulties of teaching Irish speaking pupils are however sometimes exaggerated. They are often less real than imaginary. As evidence, if such is needed, I will instance two schools quite near each other in the most Irish-speaking part of the district. In each there are two teachers and a large juvenile attendance. The circumstances of both schools are as nearly alike as possible. Neither is of very long standing, pupils all know Irish and till they begin coming to school seldom hear any other language. In each there is usually a large number of infants for examination. In one school the answering is invariably good, in the other quite indifferent, though strange to say the classification of the teachers in the latter is considerably higher than that of those in the former. The former school is however worked with

Appendix C.

Reports on State of Schools.

W. F. Sewell, District Inspector. Westport.

Music and Drawing.

Handicraft.

Needlework.

New scheme for Sixth Class.

Dressmaking.

Irish.

greater industry and skill. This I am satisfied is the sole cause of the disparity.

In only a small number of schools in the district are pupils taught Irish. This I regret. It might be taught in many more without in the least exceeding due bounds. Only a few teachers possess certificates. Where Irish is chiefly spoken however is in the poorest parts of the district. In such places accordingly only a small percentage of the pupils ever reach the higher classes. This of course lessens the advantage of having certificates. Apart altogether from the pecuniary question, more teachers might reasonably be expected to take an interest in the language. Many of them speak it already. It has been in a sense their mother tongue. To such the difficulty of obtaining certificates must be very slight. The Commissioners have considerately allowed a liberal fee for passes. It is rather surprising more advantage is not taken of the boon. Permission to teach the subject to pupils of all classes would not I am sure be judicious. Amongst senior pupils however, and especially those who have colloquial knowledge already, a few half-hours a week devoted to reading and writing the language could scarcely be better employed.

I am, Gentlemen, your obedient servant,
    P. NEWELL, District Inspector.

The Secretaries,
   Education Office, Dublin.

Mr. J. MORAN, LL.D., District Inspector.

Trim, County Meath, 28th February, 1894.

GENTLEMEN,—I have the honour to submit, for the information of the Commissioners, the following General Report on the Trim District, for the year 1894.

The district extends over the greater part of Meath, and includes portions of Cavan, Westmeath, and Kildare. Forming part of the great central plain of Ireland, the surface is either level or slightly undulating. In the Cavan portion of the district the locality is populous, the land poor, and the majority of the pupils are children of small farmers. Throughout the county Meath—and the same may be said to a less extent of Westmeath and Kildare—the holdings are mainly large grass farms. The population is in consequence scattered far apart; and the majority of the pupils attending school are children of herdsmen and small farmers. One may travel sometimes for miles through these large farms without meeting any house but that of the herd. The schools are scattered far apart; and the attendance at each is small.

Within the district are the towns Trim, Navan, Kells, Athboy, and Oldcastle.

In Trim we have the Model School (boys' department only), the Convent school, St. Patrick's, and the two poor law union joint schools. In October, 1893, the able and energetic head master of the Model School was appointed professor of the Marlborough-street Training College. I am happy to be able to state that he is worthily succeeded as head master by Mr. O'Regan, the former assistant. The school maintains the high degree of efficiency in which it was placed by Professor Peyton. We have now two assistants, five pupil-teachers, and two monitors. The attendance has considerably increased, owing to the operation of the Compulsory Act of 1892. The average attendance for 1892 was 105; for 1893, 113; and for 1894 it was 132.

The following optional and extra subjects are taught with great success :—
Vocal Music, Drawing, Book-keeping, Algebra, Geometry and Mensuration, Physical Geography, Latin and French.   The pupils of this fine school receive an excellent education ; and it affords me much satisfaction to find that its excellence is fully appreciated by the parents and the pupils.   It is quite usual to see children of tender years arriving at the Model School gate at half-past eight in the morning.

It is considered unnecessary to refer to the other schools in Trim, which are all in a very satisfactory state.

Navan has two Convent National Schools, a boys' school and a mixed school under Protestant management at Flower Hill.   The attendance at these schools has increased considerably by the operation of the Compulsory Act of 1892.   I am happy to be able to report that all these schools are in a most satisfactory state as regards proficiency, moral tone, order and discipline.

Besides the Christian Brothers' school for boys at Kells, there are two schools in connexion with the National Board—the Convent school, and the Parochial school under Protestant management.   The answering in these schools is excellent.

In Navan and in Trim the Compulsory Act of 1892 is in full force.   In the former town there have been some prosecutions under the Act ; but in Kells no steps have been taken beyond the adoption of the Act and the formation of an attendance committee.

The Endowed Schools at Oldcastle maintain the satisfactory state of proficiency to which I referred in my General Report for 1892.   The only points now calling for remark are the introduction of Kindergarten in the infant school, the erection of suitable out-offices at a cost of £100, and the annual award of £30 per annum in prizes of £5, £4, £3, £2, and £1 for boys, and the same for girls.   When examining for results in the month of May, I arrange to supply the Governors with a list of the candidates in order of merit.   Perhaps I should also state that an industrial department has been established in connexion with the girls' school, and a workshop for teaching handicraft in connexion with the boys' school.   The governors liberally supplement the salary paid by the Commissioners to the industrial teacher, and they pay a fair rate of salary to an experienced teacher of handicraft.   In addition to the monitors paid by the Commissioners, other pupils called "governors' monitors" are paid small salaries out of the endowment.   These appointments and the prizes awarded each year entice a large number of expectant pupils to remain at the school far longer than is usual.   The result is a very large Sixth Class in each school—more than 100 qualified by attendance for examination.   The educational advantage thus gained is to some extent counterbalanced by the burden of a Sixth Class so large and unwieldy on the teaching power of the school.

The number of schools in operation is 140, classified as follows :—

> 1 Model School (boys' department only),
> 4 Convent schools,
> 2 Poor Law Union schools,
> 2 Poor Law Union joint schools (at Trim),
> 131 Ordinary National schools.

Since the date of my last General Report (in 1892) very little change has taken place in the district.   Besides the two joint Poor Law Union schools at Trim, Balrathbury, a small school under Protestant management, has been taken into connexion.   The separate schools for boys and girls at Boyerstown, Hilberry, and Woodpole have been amalgamated into mixed schools, owing to insufficient average attendance.

Appendix C.

Reports on State of Schools.

Mr. J. MacDILL, District Inspector.

Trim.

Education Act of 1892

Oldcastle schools.

Numbers and classification of schools.

Changes in schools.

Appendix C.
Reports on
State of
Schools.

Mr. J.
Moran.LL.D.
District
Inspector.

Trim.

Classifica-
tion as to
proficiency.

The 140 schools in the district may be classified as follows, in regard to the proficiency and general state of the schools :—

5 very good, or excellent,
58 good,
32 very fair,
19 fair,
14 middling,
5 poor,
4 very poor.

It will be seen from the above analysis that the district is in a satisfactory state. The schoolhouses are, with a few exceptions, comfortable, and in a fair state of repair. No new schoolhouses to replace old ones have been erected since the date of my taking charge of this district on the 1st October, 1889 ; but arrangements are in progress for the erection of a suitable house to replace the unsatisfactory one in which the Frains male and female schools are conducted. The school rooms are, as a rule, commodious, properly ventilated, and kept warm and comfortable by suitable fires, provided mainly by contributions from the pupils.

Industrial Programme. The Industrial Programme is taught in a large proportion of the schools in which female teachers or workmistresses are employed ; but I regret to say that it is not popular with the parents or with the teachers. Applications for exemption are frequent. Having recently forwarded to the Commissioners a memorandum on this subject, it is considered unnecessary to go more into detail on the present occasion.

Kindergarten. Kindergarten is successfully taught in the four Convent schools, in St. James's infant school at Athboy, and in the infant school at Oldcastle.

Handicraft. Handicraft is taught in two schools, viz., St. James's male school, Athboy, and the Oldcastle boys' school.

Vocal Music. Vocal Music is taught at the Trim Model School, in the four Convent schools, and in several other schools whose teachers hold certificates. The proficiency in this optional subject is satisfactory at the Model School—where it has been only recently introduced—good in the Convent schools and at Oldcastle, and fairly satisfactory in the rural schools.

Drawing. Drawing is taught at the Model School, in the four Convent schools, and in the rural schools where the teachers have certificates. With reference to these two subjects (Singing and Drawing), I beg to say they are taught, I believe, in all the schools whose teachers hold certificates ; and in the cases in which the teachers have recently obtained certificates, arrangements are in progress for a commencement. It will be my duty to attend to this matter in all such cases.

Book-keeping. Book-keeping, Algebra, Geometry and Mensuration, Sewing Machine and Dressmaking, and Physical Geography are taught in several schools with a fair degree of success.

Agriculture. Agriculture has received a large amount of attention of late. The answering in this subject is comprehensive and accurate. Owing to the increased attention paid to it by the teachers, it has become a favourite subject with the pupils.

Reading. Reading is fluent and easy, especially in the senior classes ; but the repetition of poetry is still hurried and inaccurate. The subject-matter and the explanation of words and phrases are in very many cases defective. The new Fifth Book seems to have effected a considerable change for the better in the answering in that class.

Writing is taught with a varying degree of success; in some schools
it is very good, in others middling, and in a few cases poor.

Spelling and Geography receive a large amount of attention; and
the answering in these subjects is satisfactory—except, of course, in
the few middling or indifferent schools.

I regret I cannot say the same for Grammar, which is the weakest
subject of the entire programme.

Arithmetic is well taught in nearly all the schools. No other subject
receives so much attention, especially in schools taught by male teachers.
In some of the schools taught by female teachers, not highly classed, the
arithmetic is weak in the senior classes.

I regret to say I have observed no improvement in the regularity of
the pupils' attendance consequent on the abolition of school fees. In
the great majority of the schools of this district the teachers had been in
receipt of little more than a nominal amount of school fees previous to
the Act of 1892. Even the pupils, whose parents could afford to pay,
gave very little to the teachers. They seem to have followed the example of the very large proportion of pupils whose parents could ill
afford to pay school fees.

I have observed before that the operation of the Compulsory Act of
1892 has materially increased the attendance in Navan and Trim; but,
in the rural schools, no improvement is observable. This irregularity
of attendance is the great drawback to the success of the schools as
educational establishments for the great mass of the people; and, so far
as I can observe, there can be no remedy except a comprehensive system
of compulsory education extending to every part of the country.

I have examined schools in October, November, and December, in
which several pupils, especially boys, have been presented for examination in the senior classes after having attended on little more than 100
days during the entire year. An examination of the roll-book will show
that these boys had attended well enough in the early portion of the
results year; but, with the exception of an occasional day, had been
absent for several months previous to the date of examination. It is,
of course, impossible for any teacher to gain much credit for the answering of such pupils. After the hay-making comes the harvest, and then
the potato gathering. It may be said that this is necessary; but I am
fully aware the pupils could attend school at frequent intervals occasioned
by wet weather or other causes. It would be tedious and uninteresting
to enumerate the various causes of irregularity of attendance. If children
were compelled to attend on 150 days, ample time could be found, even
in the most exceptional cases.

My relations with the Managers continue to be most friendly. I have
found them courteous and obliging and ready to adopt any suggestion
for the welfare of the schools. I was able to report, after a residence of
more than ten years in Belfast, that no difference or misunderstanding
had, during that time, interfered with the harmony and good feeling
that existed between the Managers and myself; and, I hope, I may be
able to leave Trim with the same record.

The School Bank system has not been availed of except in the Trim
Model School. The parents of the vast majority of the pupils have little
money to spend, and, therefore, very little to spare. In the Model
School, owing to the exertions of the head master, the system has been
successful. There are now nearly forty depositors, some with pretty
considerable amounts.

The teachers of this district compare favourably with those of any
other in which I have been engaged. They are, in every respect, a most

Appendix G
Reports on
State of
Schools.

Mr. J.
Moran, LL.D.
District
Inspector.

Truim.

Classifica-
tion of the
teachers.

respectable body of public servants. The degree of comfort and respectability in which they can now live, as compared with former times, is
most pleasing to all persons interested in the education of the people.
Recent legislation has raised considerably the status of the teacher. In
a fairly large school he has now a good income; and, I am happy to say
that, with very few exceptions, he amply deserves all he gets.

The classification of the teachers here has, of late years, been considerably raised. The following synopsis represents the classification of
the teachers, excluding the Convent and Poor Law Union schools:—

I.	.	.	.	.	19 Teachers.	
I²	.	.	.	.	16	
II.	.	.	.	.	71	
III.	.	.	.	.	31	
		Total	.	.	137	

I have the honour to be, Gentlemen,

Your obedient servant,

JOHN MORAN.

The Secretaries.

Mr. W. P.
Headen,
B.A.,
District
Inspector.

Dublin.

District.

Mr. W. P. HEADEN, B.A., District Inspector.

South Dublin.

GENTLEMEN,—I have the honour to submit the following general
report upon the condition and progress of Elementary Education as
given in the National schools of District 37 during the year 1894.

This district, of which I have had charge since the 1st March, 1892,
is of triangular shape, the base extending along the Midland Great
Western Railway line from Dublin to Kilcock, and the vertex being
situated at Hollywood, a small village in the north-west of the county
Wicklow. It thus includes a large area in the south-west of the city
and county of Dublin, with six baronies in the east of the county
Kildare, and a narrow strip of the county Wicklow, occupying the
north-western slope of the Wicklow mountains. The townships of
Rathmines, Rathgar, and Inchicore, with the large county town of Naas,
and the villages of Maynooth, Kilcock, Clane, Celbridge, Blessington, and
Tallaght, are within its boundaries. The schools are distributed over
this extensive area with due regard to the educational wants of each
locality, and in ample numbers, so far as the rural parts are concerned.
They include almost every variety, from the large Convent school in
the city with daily attendance of over 1,000 pupils, to the small and
remote country school that with difficulty maintains an average of 30.
In the rural parts the school-going population consists almost exclusively
of the children of farmers. They are as a rule docile, orderly, well-
mannered children, comfortably dressed and well-fed, but not generally
remarkable for brilliancy of parts or diligence in application to lessons.
Most of my city schools are located in the poorest parts, so that a large
number of the children are recruited from the labouring class. Uncertainty of employment with the parents, actual want in some cases,
with their inevitable consequence, disorganised homes, are painfully
reflected in the irregular, and even more conspicuously in the late and
unpunctual attendance of this class of children. It will thus be seen
that the progress of the schools is mainly due to the efficient and admirable work of the teachers of the district, and that the co-operation

Distribu-
tion of
schools.

on the pupils' part is, from one cause or another, neither hearty nor effective in general.

When I took charge of this district three years ago, there were 112 schools in operation. The following changes have occurred since then. On the 1st March, 1892, a grant was made to St. Kevin's evening school in Cuffe street. On the 1st March, 1893, St. Peter's M. F. and Infant schools in Whitefriar street, were transferred from District 40A, and on the 1st May following Warrenmount Convent schools were also transferred from the same district to mine. These formed an important addition as they increased the number of pupils on the rolls of my district by considerably more than two thousand. On the 1st September, 1893, a grant was made to Naas M. evening school; and on 1st November, 1893, the commodious and well appointed school erected by the Jewish Community was taken into connexion.

A handsome schoolhouse erected by the Wesleyan body on the Naas Road, Inchicore, was taken into connexion on the 1st April, 1894, and grants were made to the Rathmines Township school from the 7th August, 1894. On the other hand Kill M. N. S. was struck off the Rolls on the 15th December, 1893, owing to the small attendance, and the manager's desire to amalgamate the Boys' and Girls' schools under the principalship of a female teacher. There are consequently in operation at present 120 schools, classed as under :—

- 11 Convent Schools.
- 104 Ordinary
- 2 Poor Law Union Schools.
- 3 Evening Schools.

120

The school buildings throughout the district may be described in every sense as satisfactory on the whole. Due provision for lighting, ventilation, and warmth, is maintained; and occasional suggestions of mine, as to the erection of a porch, the repairing of old desks, or the providing of new ones, etc., are cheerfully adopted and efficiently carried out by the managers. In some rural parishes, notably those of Kilcock and Caragh, the schools are kept in excellent order and repair. It is a pleasure to visit one of the schools in the parish of Kilcock. Cleanliness and neatness characterise everything within and around. All the Convent schools are, without exception, maintained in the highest possible condition of repair. Those in the city, and more especially those attached to the Training College, Baggot-street, are equipped with every appliance —class-rooms, galleries, work-rooms, kindergartens, etc.—for carrying on the work of primary education in the most complete and systematic manner. Some of the city schoolhouses take high rank from architectural and aesthetic points of view. St. Mary's National schools, Rathmines, for example, are admirable examples both within and without of the ideal schoolhouse. The handsome pile of buildings, with commodious residences for three principal teachers adjoining, and surrounded by grounds tastefully planted with flowers, are objects of universal admiration. Ample floor space within and extensive playgrounds at the rere are provided for an attendance of over 600 pupils. Last autumn extensive alterations were effected in St. Patrick's Male National school attached to the Training College, Drumcondra. Additions were made regardless of expense, so as to form three schools instead of one, with a view to afford the teachers in training the opportunity of seeing in operation, and occasionally assisting in the

Appendix C
Reports on
State of
Schools.

Mr. W. P.
Brazier,
District
Inspector.
Dublin.

teaching of, schools of graded sizes, organised on the most approved systems, and conducted by most competent staffs. These buildings are symmetrically grouped in a handsome pile, and are exceedingly fine. In a remote part of the district—Allenwood—the manager has replaced an old vested schoolhouse, which had gradually fallen into disrepair, by a substantial, commodious, and pretty school-house constructed of iron lined with wood, and interlined with felt, and affording accommodation for over 200 pupils. This case is a striking example of the extent to which an efficient teacher and an attractive school-room can influence the attendance of the pupils. The year before the present teacher was appointed, 1800, the average attendance at this school was thirty, and the number of pupils examined for Result Fees three. Last year the average attendance was 98·3, and the number of pupils examined for Results Fees 127, and I may add that their answering in all subjects was highly satisfactory. At Donadea, another remote part of the district, the old schoolhouse, which was merely an old barn or out-office of some kind extemporised for the occasion, has been replaced by a handsome little building erected out of local resources, and neatly equipped in every detail. The work of improvement is, at the present moment, in vigorous progress. In Whitefriar-street, Very Rev. John Hall, o.s.a., aided by the Commissioners of National Education, is erecting magnificent schoolhouses at a cost of nearly £7,000, in addition to the very large expense incurred in purchasing the site, to accommodate 1,500 pupils. The design—one of the last works of the late eminent architect, J. L. Robinson, Esq.—is of the most complete and modern character. Each of the three schoolhouses will be fitted with class-rooms, galleries, teachers' rooms, and lavatories, and ample playgrounds will also be provided. Very Rev. Canon Connolly, p.p., St. Kevin's, is also, with the aid of the Commissioners, building schoolhouses at Blackpitts at a cost of over £2,000. This will meet a pressing want, and provide two well-equipped schools— a senior and a junior— for the boys of this densely populated locality. The building is a very fine one, and both it and the one last referred to are rapidly approaching completion. I regret to have to add that two or three schoolhouses continue to exist which are quite unsuitable as to building, furniture, and every detail, but I have reason to expect that these will soon be replaced by new and well-appointed houses.

Poor Law
Union
schools.

In the classification of schools given above, two fall under the head of Poor Law Union schools, and three under that of Evening schools. The former are those of Naas Poor Law Union and Celbridge Poor Law Union. The Naas Poor Law Union school is taught by lay teachers, who discharge their duties with the highest efficiency; the Celbridge Poor Law Union school is conducted by a Sister of Charity, the excellence of whose work is manifested by the superior proficiency of the children, their neatness of dress and good manners, the cleanliness and order of the schoolrooms, and the decoration of its walls with pretty pictures, nicely framed and glazed by one of the bigger boys. This school, I am pleased to say, is one of the few exceptions I had in mind when writing the preceding paragraph. The Evening Schools are

Evening
schools.

SS. Michael and John's Male, and St. Kevin's Male in the city, and Naas Male in the town of Naas. They are doing as much good as the average Evening school anywhere, and that in my experience is generally limited and disappointing. In my remaining remarks I shall exclude from consideration these five schools, as well as the two that have been taken into connexion recently, and I shall deal only with those that were examined for Results Fees within the year 1894. These consist of

11 Convent and 109 ordinary schools. Of these, one was examined by my Head Inspector, two by Mr. M'Millan, Junior, District Inspector, and the remaining 110 by myself, efficiently aided from time to time by Mr. William Hartley.

The eleven Convent schools are ably conducted by the members of the several communities, those in the city employing in addition 54 lay assistants, the great majority of whom are classed under the Board. In the ordinary schools, 199 classed teachers were continuously engaged during the year 1894, of whom 108 had received a course of training in a recognised Training College, and the remaining 91 were untrained. Of the entire number 102 were principal teachers, and 97 assistants.

The following tables show the classification of both :—

Appendix C.
Reports on State of Schools.
Mr. W. P. Hartes, District Inspector, Dublin.
Teachers.
Classification of the teachers.

I.—Principals

Class	Males		Females	
	Trained.	Untrained.	Trained.	Untrained.
I¹,	5	—	9	1
I²,	8	—	8	2
II¹,	13	6	16	8
II²,	3	1	3	—
III¹,	6	9	3	6
III²,	—	—	—	2

II.—Assistants.

Class	Males		Females	
	Trained.	Untrained.	Trained.	Untrained.
I.	7	—	6	3
II.	8	6	16	12
III.	—	9	2	21

Both these tables will bear favourable comparison with similar tables from any other districts in Ireland. From them it may be seen that over thirty-two per cent. of the principal teachers rank in Class I., over fifty-one per cent. in Class II., and less than seventeen per cent. in Class III. Taking both principals and assistants together the corresponding percentages are twenty-four, forty-seven and twenty-nine respectively. Again, of the principal teachers, sixty-eight per cent. have been trained, and of the assistants, forty per cent. Whether from the point of view of high classification, or of the superior advantages which training confers, the managers of this district deserve public commendation for the respectability of the staffs employed by them in their schools. While I have no hesitation in saying, not merely as the result of any *a priori* reasoning, but from my own practical experience, that the work done by the trained teacher is, as a rule, more effective and of higher quality than that of the average untrained teacher, I feel bound to state at the same time that there is a large number of technically untrained teachers in my district who are doing work equal to that of any trained teacher in Ireland. I say *technically* untrained, because using the term in a broader sense, they have been trained more strictly and properly than many of those who pass through college, that is, they have been trained not to pass examinations merely, but trained in the actual practice of teaching during a long term of years, aided and encouraged throughout by the counsel and example of a class of teachers unequalled for zeal and self-sacrificing devotion. I refer to a number of my female teachers who rank in the highest classes and who were trained as monitors in the large Convent schools of the district. The teachers on the whole are doing their work faithfully and efficiently. The proficiency of their schools as shown in the following paragraph establishes this fact beyond controversy. Unhappily, however, there are a few cases, but the fingers of one hand would more than suffice to count them, in which the teaching is indifferent and the results do not approach a respectable standard.

At the Results Examination of every school I invariably compile certain statistics which are of use to me, not so much in determining the relative position of the school as compared with other schools, as in determining its progress or retrogression as compared with itself the previous year. These statistics include, (a.) the number of classed pupils examined; (b.) the number of possible passes in ordinary literary branches, viz, reading, writing, arithmetic, spelling, grammar, and geography; (c.) the number of actual passes assigned; (d.) the number of those last which were "No. 2" or more passes; and (e.) the number of pupils who qualified for promotion to a higher class by passing in reading, writing, and arithmetic. I make out two sets of these statistics, one for the entire number of classed pupils, and one for the senior classes alone, viz, Fourth, Fifth, and Sixth. I make out the latter set, because while in some cases the percentages from the first set are high, those from the latter set are low. The junior classes are numerically much larger than the senior, but the teaching in this division of the school is almost purely mechanical and becoming more so every day, while in the senior classes the teaching, to be effective, must be of a higher and more intellectual order. Hence I like to correct and fortify my judgment in all cases by a sort of tape rule applied to this last kind of work done by the teacher as it is the best criterion of his real worth. I have totted these statistics into a table which I give below, and a glance at it will suffice to show how successfully the teachers of this district are doing their work:

—	(a.) Number of pupils examined	(b.) Number of passes attainable	(c.) Number of actual passes obtained	Percentage of (c.) to (b.)	(d.) Number of "No. 2" passes	Percentage of (d.) to (c.)	(e.) Number of Pupils promoted	Percentage of (e.) to (a.)
All Classed Pupils.	7,761	22,512	20,522	91.1	10,884	27.9	4,187	57.9
Senior Classes.	1,770	14,468	14,558	87.9	4,226	25.9	1,520	57

The actual passes obtained by the classed pupils of the district in ordinary literary branches were 91·1 per cent. of the total passes available, and of these pupils 87·9 per cent. qualified at Results Examination for promotion to a higher class. The corresponding figures for the senior classes are equally creditable.

Reading comes first in order of importance. This is the one subject in which perhaps there is least actual teaching. The teachers in too many cases are satisfied if the pupils read with tolerable mechanical accuracy. They scarcely ever correct bad intonation, wrong grouping of words, or neglect of pauses. The result is, that in all such cases, the reading is wanting in intelligence, and the direct consequence of this is the lamentable failure of the pupils when questioned on explanation. In my opinion, the universal and long-continued complaint regarding explanation is due not so much to the fact that the teachers neglect to question the pupils on the matter and phraseology of their lesson, as that they neglect to teach them to read it intelligently. This is strikingly apparent when such a pupil is questioned on a sentence he has just read. If he is not wholly silent, his answer usually wears one or other of two complexions: either he fails to recognise the question as bearing on the text, and tries to call back some answer that he fancies he has heard, or he ejaculates a phrase from the sentence read which has no intelligent bearing on the point. In a large number of my schools, however, reading is taught with excellent care and success, and in these schools it is very pleasing at examinations to observe that the reader is not merely a sort of phonograph, but that his lips are giving intelligent expression to what his mind is grasping as he passes from line to line. The repetition of poetry, which I have always regarded as one of the most effective helps to good reading, is not attended to with satisfactory general care. A few schools, however, form notable exceptions, and in these the poetic pieces are recited with much taste and faultless accuracy.

Penmanship in all classes and in all schools of the district is good. The admirable series of headline copy-books everywhere in use have relieved the teachers of much of the labour of teaching this useful branch. In First Class, too, the teachers are careful to set before the children phrases and sentences neatly written between lines on the blackboard, and they everywhere insist on the pupils' exact imitation on the slate of shape, slope, and filling of spaces. Letter-writing is making much slower progress. I am pleased, however, to be able to state that it is improving. I notice from year to year more care in writing in the address and date, and in the correlation of beginning and end, the disappearance of vulgarisms and bad spelling, and the arrangement of the matter in short sentences. Where the Alternative Industrial Scheme is adopted by Sixth Class girls they are prepared during the year to write long letters, extending frequently over three pages of foolscap, on at least twenty different subjects, dealing chiefly with matters geographical, commercial, or industrial. A list of these subjects is handed to me on the morning of examination, and I select two or more, according to the size of the class. In many cases these girls write beautiful letters, and even assuming that this letter is written from memory, which is scarcely possible to the entire extent, I regard it as of excellent educational value, inasmuch as it is but one of more than twenty, all of which are at hand for similar reproduction.

Arithmetic yields creditable results on the whole. The teachers do their best to teach it well. Unhappily in this work they rely too much on cards and texts and too little on blackboard explanation. Tables are satisfactorily learnt, but notation and mental arithmetic are largely neglected. The importance of the last-mentioned exercise in smartening the pupils and improving their general intelligence should commend itself to the teacher as an effective means of helping this work.

Oral spelling in First and Second Classes is good; and in all cases the meanings of the words arranged in the vocabularies at head of the Second Book lessons are carefully learnt. In Third Class, failures in

I 2

Appendix C.

Reports on State of Schools.

Mr. W. P. Madden, District Inspector, Dublin.

Explanation.

Repetition of poetry.

Writing.

Letter-writing.

Arithmetic.

Notation and mental arithmetic.

Spelling.

Th. rules.

dictation are frequent, less so in Fourth, and in Fifth and Sixth Classes the pupils as a rule pass well in this subject. The teachers in general are faithful in the practice of dictation and transcription on alternate days with their Third and higher Classes, and they make an honest attempt to revise the exercises, and point out all mistakes with a view to their correction.

I am pleased to notice from year to year slow but steady progress in the important subject of grammar. I have never ceased to regard it as one of the few branches of strictly intellectual study as opposed to those which are largely mechanical. It teaches a child to think, and even if it has no further value, this is one of great importance. Complaints have been made from time to time that the programme is not definite enough here, too difficult there, and so on ; but all my teachers thoroughly understand it now, and attain much success in teaching it. In examination I invariably use the Reading Book of the class as the text of my parsing sentences :—Simple parsing in Third Class with reasons assigned for the classification of every word, using words and sentences of simple meaning and construction ; Etymological parsing in Fourth Class ; and Syntactical parsing of graduated difficulty in Fifth and Sixth Classes. I would certainly welcome the addition to our programme of Analysis for Sixth Class pupils.

Geography shows creditable general proficiency. In this branch, also, scarcely any cases now occur in which the teacher misunderstands the requirements of the programme. Pointing out on the maps is wonderfully improved in all schools ; and in the sub-heads of the programme, such for example as the explanation of the terms "Latitude and Longitude" in Fifth Class, the pupils are in all schools prepared to illustrate on the map the application of the terms employed. In one item—the drawing of an outline map of Ireland by Sixth Class pupils—there is, however, a general absence of progress.

Particulars as the remaining subjects of the programme taught in this district, including those which are optional and extra, are given in the following table :—

Subject.	Number of Schools in which taught.	Number of Pupils Examined.	Number who Passed.	Percentage of Passes.
Agriculture,	27	410	228	67·1
Needlework,	90	3,626	3,157	87·2
Book-keeping,	28	688	570	8·
Tonic Sol-Fa,	27	2,109	1,810	85·1
Hullah,	8	807	620	87·1
Drawing,	81	1,864	1,620	87·2
Geometry and Mensuration,	7	43	31	82·7
Algebra,	11	170	128	73·7
Dressmaking and Sewing Machine,	5	133	108	77·3
Cookery,	3	98	66	67·7
Domestic Economy,	4	74	60	81·1
Physical Geography,	4	50	27	54·
Piano,	10	79	74	92·0
French,	4	65	50	87·1
Latin,	3	11	4	87·7
Handicraft,	1	2	2	100·
Kindergarten,	19	3,263	3,576	91·3

A few of the subjects above-named require more detailed reference.

Agriculture is taught only in those rural schools which are conducted by a master. The number of pupils presented is small, and the answering a little better than middling. Three causes are in my opinion responsible for this latter fact, 1st—the general absence of plan or method in teaching the boys to read intelligently their ordinary Reading Books tells against them unmistakably when they try to gather from their prosy agricultural class book the gist of its dry facts and philosophic principles; 2nd, the phraseology and general treatment of the subject in the text book in use are too difficult, so that teachers are in many cases tempted into the use of catechisms; 3rd, with rare exceptions no attempt is ever made to render the subject interesting to the pupils, either by blackboard or other illustrations, by collections of soils or grasses or plants, or by reference to the processes going on beneath their very eyes in the farms and gardens around them.

Plain needlework is the most successfully taught industrial branch in our National Schools. Since the enforcement of Rule 9, requiring one hour a day to be given to it by all girls from Second Class upwards wherever a female teacher is employed, nothing has been more satisfactory than the great and universal progress made in sewing and knitting. From the table above it is seen that 3,495 girls were examined in these branches during the year 1894, and that over 90 per cent. passed. The programme has been graduated with excellent judgment for each class, and in addition to the execution of certain specified descriptions of sewing, as stitching, patching, buttonholes, etc., the girls of Fourth and higher Classes are required each to exhibit on examination day a specified article of dress wholly made by herself during the previous year. This rule is invariably complied with, and it is particularly pleasing to see how gratified the children are when these articles of dress are distributed to them for exhibition. In some of the larger schools the work is by no means limited to the articles named on the programme. These are generally supplemented by others according to the taste and requirements of the pupils.

This naturally brings me to make a short reference to the industrial programme framed a few years ago as an alternative to the ordinary literary programme hitherto prescribed for Sixth Class girls. The conception of this scheme was admirable from the theoretic point of view, but the practical working out of it was impeded by difficulties of such varied and unexpected character, that it may almost be said to have failed in this district. During the year 1894 I found it adopted in only sixteen of my schools out of a total number of eighty-four in which plain needlework and knitting are efficiently taught. It may be interesting to discuss briefly some of the causes referred to above of the failure of this scheme. From the teachers' side they are chiefly two—1, difficulty of providing material for work; and 2, difficulty of disposing of finished articles. The Industrial Programme requires a minimum of two and a quarter hours daily to be devoted to industrial work. This necessitates a constant supply of material to keep the pupils occupied or they will develop habits of laziness, gossiping, &c. The teacher is unable out of her own resources to provide this supply, the girls are unwilling to bring it, and the managers as a rule are indisposed to help. Again, if the teacher or others supply material there is no market for the finished article by which they might hope to be even partially recouped. From the pupils', or rather the parents' side, there is a sort of inherent national prejudice against learning

Appendix C.

Reports on State of Schools.

Mr. W. P. Hanna, District Inspector, Dublin.

Agriculture.

Needlework.

Garments.

Industrial scheme.

Its failure.

Causes of failure.

Appendix C.
Reports on
State of
Schools.

Mr. W. F.
Head..,
District
Inspector.
Dublin.

anything of the name of "work" in a school. The school is associated in their minds exclusively with the idea of books and intellectual training, and even the very humblest class are on this account unwilling to take up cordially the Industrial Programme, and they remain at home from school instead. This, of course, is unfortunate, and I am in hopes that before long, the people will be educated into the wisdom of acceptingly gladly industrial teaching of every sort in the school as the golden key to comfort and independence in after life. There is, however, a further difficulty which deserves consideration when we come to determine the propriety of making this industrial scheme compulsory. Sixth Class girls, as a rule, in town or country, are not recruited from the humblest, or even to any great extent from the humble ranks of life. Such children leave school before they reach Sixth Class, the pupils of which, in country places, are the daughters for the most part of respectable farmers, and in towns, of independent shopkeepers. It is questionable, therefore, whether these children, so

Should be
optional.

long as they are received as pupils in our National schools, should not be left free to choose for themselves according to their parents' advice, between the Industrial and the Literary Programme, and to adopt that one most in consonance with their own present tastes and future prospects.

Suggestion.

Furthermore, the establishment by aid of national, local, or philanthropic resources of one or more central depots which would supply material to all schools applying for it, and make a small payment for the finished article which they would undertake to dispose of, would do more towards encouraging the growth of industrial occupations than any programme whatever enforced by penal regulations.

Vocal
Music.

Vocal Music is taught in thirty-five schools, twenty-seven of which adopt the Tonic Sol-Fa method. The superior efficiency of this method in teaching children to sing has been triumphantly established, if any doubt had ever existed, by the results of the public competition between the schools of Dublin during the last two years. I regret that this humanising branch of education is not more generally taught. I give it every possible encouragement, and I am pleased to say that it has been taken up in eight new schools since I took charge of the district, and two or three more are this year trying it for the first time. "Every child," writes John Ruskin, "should be taught from its youth to form its voice discreetly and dexterously, as it does its hands, and not to be able to sing should be more disgraceful than not to be able to read or write."

Drawing.

Drawing is taught with very fair general success in twenty-four schools. The number of schools, and the number of pupils, are entirely too few. Drawing, which is the foundation of all technical education, should be taught in every primary school. As a training of the hand and eye it is superior to any other means available. Every child who can write should learn to draw, and with a view to bringing about this

Should be
obligatory.

necessary reform (1) every teacher who passes through a training college should be required to take up this branch as part of the obligatory course; (2) in every school in which a teacher certificated in Drawing is employed, he or she should be compelled to teach it; (3) in every school in which more than one teacher is employed the manager should be required to keep at least one who is qualified to teach Drawing. Further, I am of opinion that Drawing should be intro-

and made
a subject
for second
class pupils.

duced as a subject of examination for Second Class pupils in our schools. These pupils might get a pass for drawing lines and simple rectilineal figures or ornament on chequered paper. This would form the connecting link between Kindergarten and Freehand Drawing, and would make the course unbroken and complete.

Of the schools of this district thirteen are Infant schools, and there are besides eleven regularly organised Infant departments attached to the Convent schools. In nineteen of these Kindergartens are established and most successfully conducted. With the truly fascinating gifts of the Kindergarten proper are associated musical drill, object lessons, and singing; and the system as a whole is attended with the most gratifying results. Some modified system of Kindergarten should be introduced into all schools in which infants are taught; and object lessons should be regularly given in every school to pupils of the junior classes. They cultivate the habit of observation, increase the vocabulary, enlarge the information, and impart facility of expression. The proper cultivation and development of the senses and instincts of children endow them with resources of far more value from the formative and truly educational standpoint than any other regimen of their entire school course.

From the 1st January, 1892, the schools of this district, with the exception of twenty, were ordered to admit all children free. These twenty were authorised to charge a reduced rate of school fees, but many of them have voluntarily given up this privilege. The result of this abolition of school fees has been to increase the attendance to a small extent in the urban schools, but it did not in anywise affect the attendance at the rural schools. In the following table I give (a) the entire number on rolls on the last day of results year, (b) the number who qualified for admission to Results Examination by making at least 100 attendances within the year, (c) the number of these actually present and examined, and (d) the average daily attendance for the year. A study of these figures will prove interesting.

—	Number of Schools.	(a) Total No. of Pupils on Rolls.	(b) No. who Qualified for Admission to Examination.	(c) No. actually Examined.	(d) Average Attendance for Results Year.
All Schools (exclusive of Poor Law Union and Evening),	103	29,439	21,327	11,850	11,310·6
Urban Schools, . . .	68	24,674	8,084	7,852	8,077·2
Rural Schools, . . .	69	4,885	3,611	1,827	1,283·4

By *Urban Schools* is meant those situated in the city and townships empowered by the Education Act to appoint school attendance committees for the purpose of administering its compulsory clauses.

This table establishes two or three important facts. In the first place, while the average attendance of the 69 rural schools is 63·8 per cent. of the total number on rolls, the average attendance of the 48 urban schools is only 59·9 per cent. of the corresponding total. Or taking another view of it, while the number of pupils who qualified for admission to Results Examination in the rural schools is 72·4 per cent. of the total number on rolls, the number who qualified in the urban schools is only 60 per cent. of the corresponding total. Th—

facts are significant, and establish with much force the absolute necessity of compulsion in these urban districts. My opinion is that compulsion is unnecessary in rural districts. The average attendance in the rural parts of my own district is 68·8 per cent of the total number on rolls, as stated above, but owing to the fact that teachers are in the habit of retaining on their rolls for months many names of pupils who have finally left their schools, this percentage is considerably lower than what the facts of the case guarantee. With a compulsory system in operation for years in England the average attendance for last year in that country was barely 77·8 per cent of the total number on rolls; so that our rural schools do not lag far behind, and when the poverty of our country, the greater distance of the schools, and other circumstances are considered, it will be admitted that our percentage is as high as any compulsory scheme could hope to make it. With urban districts the case is entirely different. Not only is the average proportionately lower, but the number who qualify for examination is lower still, and lowest of all is the number actually examined. In rural schools 70·0 per cent of the total number on rolls were present on examination day and examined; in urban schools the percentage was only 55·1, that is, more than 15 per cent lower than in country schools. Or putting the same fact in another light, while the number actually examined in rural schools last year was 7·2 per cent higher than the average attendance, the number actually examined in urban schools was 8 per cent lower than the average attendance. These two evils, viz., the low average attendance, and the relatively smaller number present at examination have their origin in somewhat different causes. The low average is due to absolute neglect or indifference on the parents' part, the result perhaps of poverty in some cases; the smallness of the number present at examination arises from several causes, of which I may mention one or two. In urban districts many children *emigrate*, that is, after having made the requisite number of attendances they start off to another school for the most trifling reason. Again, if a pupil is indifferently prepared and not likely to pass, he either voluntarily stays away on examination day, or, as I regret to say I have found in some cases, he is directed to absent himself by the teacher.

Before concluding, I must make a brief reference to the monitors of the district. Two hundred and thirty-one monitors are at present employed in its schools. They are classified as under :—

Year of Service.	Males.	Females.
Fifth	1	34
Fourth	8	27
Third	6	50
Second	5	52
First	14	49
Total,	30	201

They are all giving good service and being trained for the profession of teaching with excellent care and efficiency. As a proof of this I may

state that at the annual examinations last July, twenty-five monitors in
their final year presented themselves for classification, and twenty-four
were classed as teachers on a high average percentage. Twenty-six
monitors in their third year presented themselves for examination at
the same time, and every one of them passed most creditably.

I regret to say that no attempt has been made to establish a School
Bank in connexion with any school in this district.

In conclusion, I feel pleased to be able to state that the primary
education of this district is in a healthy condition and making steady
progress, that the teachers, as a body, are earnest, faithful, and efficient;
that the managers without exception are deeply interested in the
practical welfare of their schools; and that both with them and the
teachers my relations have been of the happiest character since I came
to Dublin.

> I have the honour to be, Gentlemen,
>
> Your obedient servant,
>
> W. P. HEADEN,
>
> District Inspector.

The Secretaries,
National Education Office, Dublin.

Mr. W. A. BROWN, B.A., District Inspector.

Portarlington, February, 1895.

GENTLEMEN,—I beg to submit for the consideration of the Commissioners a report on the state of the schools in the district of which
Portarlington is the official centre.

A similar report was submitted two years ago. The inspection area
remains the same as it was then, and includes the greater part of
Queen's County—all but the baronies in the south-east and south-west—
the eastern half of King's County, and portions of parishes in Kildare,
Meath, and Westmeath.

The district is extensive, but is conveniently worked by the arrangements of the Great Southern and Western Railway.

Four new schools have been added, the most important of which is
St. Brigid's, Tullamore, previously conducted by the Christian Brothers.
This school employs seven classed teachers. There has been a good deal
of activity among the school managers in the matters of repairs to the
schoolhouses, the enlargement of existing buildings, and the erection of
new buildings. There are still some cases in which local effort is hard
to rouse, and for which the greater stimulus of direct official pressure
may become necessary. Speaking generally, however, there is decided
improvement in the condition of the buildings, and a readiness to act
on reasonable suggestions.

The most important new schoolhouses are two in Abbeyleix, which
now possess three vested schools (one being in connection with a
Convent), and has the distinction of being better supplied with school-
buildings and premises than any other town in the district. The
liberality of Lord de Vesci, who is patron of two of these schools, deserves

Appendix C.
Reports on State of Schools.

Mr. W. A. Brown, District Inspector.

Personallington.

recognition. In my previous report prominence was given to the state of the schoolrooms in respect of cleanliness, neatness, etc., and the criticism was not very favourable. A period of two years' gradual progress has done a good deal to remove what cannot but be considered as a reproach to those who have so much to do with the training of the children attending the National Schools. In the past the perfunctory observance of the Rules of the Commissioners relating to cleanliness, order, etc., and the neglect of these Rules, resulted in a condition of things which even a lenient judgment would condemn. It is creditable to the teachers that in almost every case there has been appreciation of suggestions that tended to effect improvement in the matters referred to. There are still floors untroubled by the scrubbing brush, porches and schoolrooms that witness a daily struggle for cap and cloak, not distinguished during school-hours by the individualising relation of separate position, and naked walls that "clamour for decoration"; but there are many floors that are kept clean, cloak rooms that are orderly, and walls well furnished with maps and picture tablets.

Necessity for inspection as distinguished from examination.

Under the existing system Results Fees are given solely for the state of the school, as it is indicated by the record of marks assigned in the various subjects of the programme. Fees are not payable for discipline or condition of schoolrooms. The material and moral conditions of school life have not a money value. Doubtless due regard to these conditions is required of the teacher, and neglect of them is an offence, but they have not the positive encouragement of a merit grant. The importance of inspection of the school as distinguished from examination of the pupils immediately follows from this. It is doubtful whether inspection is strict enough—it might demand much more without being exacting—while it is certain that not more than the lower limit of the actual demand is reached.

Improvement in discipline and order.

Improvement in discipline and order has to be reported. Increased attention has been given to class formation and to the demeanour of the pupils in their school occupations. An appreciation of appearances and form has been making its way, evidenced not only by the improved state of the schoolrooms, but by the more orderly bearing and movements of the pupils. My experience is that the value of systematic class movements and regularity in all the arrangements both as to the position of the pupils when at work, and the disposal of apparatus, has not been thoroughly understood in the schools.

The progress to which I have referred is, however, hopeful, and with increased experience of the advantages of order and system in the greater ease and effectiveness of work, and in the educational value of the wisely regulated restraints of discipline, the improvement will become a permanent condition.

Character of schools as to efficiency.

There are few schools in this district which, either for the amount of work done or its quality, are entitled to be placed in the highest rank. Steadiness and regularity rather than exceptional energy and power are characteristic of the work. If there has not been progress marked by a large increase in the number of schools to be classed as excellent, there has been a decrease in the number to be classed as bad, and considerable improvement in those of the more comprehensive class that lies between these two. The improvement has been indicated by more favourable records of marks at the annual examinations for Results Fees, as well as by the adoption of methods that tend not only to give the pupil a knowledge of facts, but also the reason of the thing.

It is sometimes hard to impress the truth that a method which is fundamentally sound, appealing to the intelligence and awakening

interest, is as rapid as it is admittedly ultimately more effective. Efforts
to bring about a wider appreciation of this principle have met with
success.

There can be no doubt that the want of continuity in the instruction of
the pupils caused by irregularity of attendance tends to throw even the
best teacher off his balance, and leads him to adopt not what he ap-
proves as excellent, but what he finds productive of a certain definite,
measurable, result.

The schools here are, as a rule, small, employing one teacher; the
services of a workmistress being availed of in most of those attended
both by boys and girls. The smaller the staff of teachers the greater
obviously is the necessity for the systematic distribution of effort, and
for such arrangements as shall necessitate the constant, active occupation of the pupil. The time-tables are now, generally speaking, satisfactory. The least skilfully arranged of them would produce good
results if carried out with energy and ingenious adaptation of means to
ends. One sees too little previous preparation for the work of classes
not under the immediate supervision of the teacher; too few devices for
besetting the indolent pupil with a succession of inevitable tasks. The
desk lessons are the idle pupil's delight, and the degree of activity found
in the desks at any period of the day may be taken as a measure of the
usefulness of the school, and of the ability of the teacher as an organiser.
The loss of time caused by failure to make work in the desks effective
is serious, and a more careful consideration of this question is what
is chiefly required in the schools that are of inferior merit.

The attendance of the pupils in the winter months is good. This fact
partly explains the difference between the average attendance of the
pupils, and the average number of children on the registers of the
school. This difference amounts to about forty per cent. It is in the
winter months that the overcrowding such as it is, and its actual amount
is very slight, occurs. In these months the teacher renews acquaintance with the grown boy or girl not now required at home; such pupils
are a severe trial of the teacher's patience, coming back after a long
interval, almost as ignorant as they were at the corresponding period of
the previous year, and with increased awkwardness in adapting themselves to school work. As much is done for this class of pupils as can
be done. Irregularity of attendance is the great obstacle to be overcome,
and frequent inquiry among the pupils as to its causes impresses one
with the difficulty of ascertaining to what extent it is remediable without unduly restricting parents desirous of turning to profit the physical
capacity of their children. This applies more particularly to districts,
such as that to which this report refers, in which tillage is largely
practised.

The compulsory clauses of the Irish Education Act of 1892 apply to
three towns in this district, viz.: Mountmellick, Maryboro', and Tullamore. In the first two towns the local authority would not consent
to raise from the rates the small amount needed to carry out the provisions of the Act. In Tullamore, however, the Town Commissioners
took the matter up at once, an influential School Attendance Committee
was formed, and its duties have been performed with fairly good
result.

There are only ten schools in the district in which, by the provisions
of the Education Act of 1892, school fees are payable, and in all but one
of these the rates are merely nominal. The abolition of school
fees has not affected the attendance of the pupils, because the scale of
fees in the past was not oppressive, and in most of the schools there were

Appendix C.
Reports on
State of
Schools.

Mr. W. J.
Brown,
District
Inspector.
Forwarding-
tes.

School
banks.

Ages and
antecedents
of pupils.

Evil effects
of neglect.

Reading.

Writing.

numbers of pupils who paid nothing, the Manager having power to admit the children of the very poor gratuitously. The teachers rather than the parents have benefited by the abolition of fees. In many schools supplies of maps and apparatus have been bought with collections from the pupils, made expressly on the grounds that it was reasonable to expect the parents to contribute to the proper equipment of the school, since they have not to pay for the instruction of their children. The teachers, however, appear to think that there is little change in the attitude of the parents.

The scheme for the establishment of School Savings Banks for the encouragement of thrift among the pupils has not been successful in this district.

The Results Examinations of the schools bring under notice two matters in which the teachers do not take sufficient care, viz. :—the ascertaining of the correct ages of the pupils, and the obtaining of the antecedents of pupils who have come from other schools. From time to time children are presented for examination in the infant class as seven years old who are obviously nine, and similar errors are to be found in the higher classes of most of the schools. The ages entered are scarcely ever too great. Failure to appreciate the importance of accuracy, as well as an apparently too implicit reliance on the statements of parents, chiefly contributes to the incorrect returns of ages. Appeal to the parish register has in every disputed case confirmed my decision. It should not be impossible to devise some plan for correctly recording the ages. The clergyman of the parish, who is nearly always the school manager, would, as a rule, willingly supply the necessary information —this is being done in a number of the schools—but reference to the official register might reasonably be made easy for official purposes, and until there is an obligation on the teacher to ascertain the exact ages of the pupils, and to keep in the school evidence of the ages for official reference, there can be no certain reliance placed on the returns.

Carelessness in ascertaining a new pupil's previous school history, besides causing delay in reporting on the school, is often prejudicial to the pupil, as it is found that he has been prepared for examination in the same class as that in which he had already passed in another school. The harm done in such cases is the greater, when, as usually happens, an account of the pupil's antecedents is obtained only a few days before the annual examination, that is, at the end of the school year. It should be obligatory on the teachers to obtain the school history of new pupils within a fortnight of the date of their admission. I will now briefly comment on the instruction in the branches taught in the schools.

The Reading is not very good. My impression is that it is inferior in this district as compared with many others. The work required to make the average pupil of an elementary school a good reader is considerable. Such a pupil has so much to be got rid of before the positive qualities of good reading can find room. More might be done, however, in this branch. The pupil's reading is too little like the teacher's best attempts at the "lights and shades of a musical intonation," because these attempts are too little heard. The valuable exercise of requiring the pupil to express orally the substance of a passage read—a most useful introduction to written composition—is not practised.

The repetition of poetry as it is carried on is an exercise of memory—not much more.

Penmanship is improved in the junior classes ; more care is taken to teach the pupils than was formerly taken. The writing lesson is apt to degenerate for want of close supervision.

Composition in the form of letter-writing has improved. A good many *Appendix C.* of the letters are well expressed and give evidence of instruction; but the importance of this branch has not yet been fully realized, nor have the limits of what is possible to be done in it been reached in the schools. Progress in penmanship is not very evident in the latter part of the pupil's career, and the fee gained for writing does not often indicate improvement, but rather a fixed condition already paid for. If this is the case, it might be suggested that the Results Fee in writing should be determined much more by the quality of the composition than of the penmanship. I believe that more advantage to the pupil is to be expected from regulations that would necessitate increased attention to composition than from any other minor change in the programme of instruction.

The results in Arithmetic vary little from year to year. The subject is taught, as a rule, for an hour daily, that is, twice as long as any other literary subject. A better knowledge of the tables has caused the almost entire disappearance from the junior classes of methods of counting that were more primitive than successful.

For purposes of criticism, Grammar and Geography may be dealt with together. Both subjects suffer from irrational treatment, more especially in the first stages of instruction. There are too few preliminary lessons dealing with the object of the new branch with the simplicity of art that conceals its hand while it stimulates curiosity, and with little use of technical terms gives pleasing exercise to reasoning powers or imagination. The pupil is too roughly handled—made to experience the unpleasantness of swinging blind-fold in mid-air, instead of being gradually and skilfully led up to the unknown. He is too suddenly confronted with the new element. On that element travel he must, but his first steps might be on an easy slope, and he might be "coaxed," not driven. The two questions—what is a map, and what are the parts of speech—seldom receive proper treatment in any class.

There has been more progress in Grammar than in Geography. The results in the Geography of the highest class are not good. The course is extensive, and the attendance of the pupils of this class is often unsatisfactory.

Spelling is well enough taught, but it is disappointing to frequently find gross errors in spelling perpetuated by want of care in the correction of the written exercises, particularly parsing and composition.

The improvement in Needlework in the last few years, that is, since the introduction of the rule that an hour daily shall be given to this branch, has been unquestionable. The sewing is much more careful, and the quantity of clothing made much greater. As a rule, the children supply material for the work sufficient to satisfy what is required in each class. In many cases much more than this is done—the number of garments made corresponding to the skill of the teacher as an instructor in needlework, and her power of influencing the pupils and their parents.

In the case of a few schools the interest taken by local ladies in the needlework is of such advantage as to suggest that an extension of voluntary effort from local sources might be attainable. Such an extension is more likely to lead to improvement in this industrial branch than more stringent official regulations regarding it. The time given to needlework, which in this district is one fourth of the whole

Appendix C.
Reports on State of Schools.
Mr. W. A.
Browne, District Inspector.
Particular.

time given to secular Instruction, is sufficient, and the teachers are, with few exceptions, sufficiently skilful. The stimulus and support of local aid, consisting in the supplying of materials, the giving of orders and the encouragement of skill by inspection of work done, and by a system of rewards to the pupils, would include almost all that is needed in the schools. Encouragement of this kind is given by individuals and parochial associations, but only in a few schools. Much more could be done in this direction by the managers of the schools. Too much is left to official initiative, which in this matter might be supposed to have satisfied reasonable demands by the determination of a standard of instruction, and the providing of a system of testing the work done, and rewarding the teachers. In one respect needlework is under a disadvantage compared with the literary branches of the school programme, namely, that the Inspector, though able to judge of the merit of the work, cannot make his examination so instructive as is possible in the literary branches. The criticism of the needlework must to a considerable extent be destructive—a statement of defects without the suggestion that results from a practical experience. Whatever may be the complete remedy for this, the local effort to which I have referred includes among its advantages the positive element of instruction which the existing system of examination does not fully supply.

Cookery.

Practical Cookery is taught in two schools, the Convents at Clara and Tullamore. The examination consists in the individual testing of the pupils in the making of simple dishes and in ordinary cooking operations, supplemented by questions on the theory of the subject. The results are satisfactory. The instruction is careful and judicious. This branch is of course better suited to town schools or large country schools than to the smaller country schools. It can be very effectively taught in Convent schools in which there is a large staff from which to select a suitable instructor.

In one of the schools referred to above, a close range is used for the work of the class; in the other, an open grate such as is to be found in the homes of the children. Greater advantage to the pupils is likely to result from the use of the more limited appliances that correspond to those used in their own homes, than from the more perfect, but more costly apparatus of modern cookery. Among other things there is less likelihood of the reaction on a disappointment when the resources of wealth have to be exchanged for the inconveniences of straitened circumstances. Practical Dairying continues to be successfully taught in Clara Convent school.

Vocal Music.

Vocal Music is being taught in seventeen schools, eleven of which are Convent schools, and Drawing in thirteen. This does not indicate an increase in the number of schools in which these subjects are taught. There is still a considerable number of certificated teachers who have not taken up either of these branches.

Drawing.

Drawing is found the more difficult of the two, and it appeals less than singing to the sympathies of the parents. In most of the ordinary schools in which only one teacher is employed, and four hours are given to instruction in the secular subjects, it would be found difficult to give effective instruction in both music and drawing without special arrangements for work before or after ordinary school hours. One of the two branches, however, might be provided for within these hours, and singing would be the most popular. Of course in the schools in which needlework is taught, that is in 99 out of 140 in this district, one hour daily is taken from the four hours now devoted to secular instruction, so that

it would appear that a slight increase of working hours, including Appendix O.
possibly some time on Saturday, which is now a *dies non*, would become Reports on State of Schools.
necessary in most cases.

The facts at any rate are, that the great majority of the pupils of the Mr. W. A. Brown, District Inspector.
elementary schools are growing up ignorant of singing and drawing,
and that a large number of the teachers can teach these subjects and are
not teaching them.

The text-book on Agriculture is read in the schools, and used as a Reading-book.
task book for home lessons. The success of the pupils in this subject is Agriculture.
but moderate.

Book-keeping, Geometry, Mensuration, and Algebra are taught in a
few schools with success.

The Kindergarten system is followed in eight Convent schools, and
the results are satisfactory.

Clara Convent school deserves special praise for the excellent work
done in the Infants' department in which Kindergarten is a leading
feature. The condition of this school generally is very creditable.

The attainment of greater efficiency in the schools is to be expected How to secure efficiency.
from more systematic and accurate performance of the work actually
being done rather than from more ambitious attempts at subjects that
are not obligatory. To one whose duties give an intimate knowledge
of the difficulties that the teachers of our National schools have to contend against, appreciation of merit is pleasanter than the language of
sober criticism. A review of the educational work of a district discloses
a good deal that is imperfect, and something that is perfunctory and
even positively unsound; but viewed in its entirety the merit of the
work done in this district is very considerable; and it is pardonable in
closing a report that deals with the education of about fourteen
thousand children to allow a feeling of the magnitude and usefulness
of what the teachers have effected to shut out a knowledge of shortcomings, and to give more prominence to the good that has been done
than to the imperfections that have missed a greater goal.

I am, gentlemen,

Your obedient servant,

W. A. BROWN.

The Secretaries,
Education Office, Dublin.

MR. I. CRAIG, B.A., District Inspector.   Mr. I. Craig, District Inspector. Tipperary.

Tipperary, February, 1895.

GENTLEMEN,—I beg to submit the following as my general report The district.
on the state of National Education in this district for the year ending
28th February, 1895.

No change has taken place in the outline of the district since my
last report in 1893. It is about thirty miles long, and thirty-eight
broad, the Great Southern and Western Railway runs almost through
the middle of it, and Knocklong is its geographical centre. It contains
three good business towns, Tipperary, Kilmallock, and Mitchelstown,
besides several prosperous villages. The occupation of the people being

Appendix C.
Reports on State of Schools.

Mr. J. Craig, District Inspector.

Tipperary.

Number of schools.

chiefly pastoral, no tillage to speak of and no manufactures, the labouring portion of the population has regular employment at seed-time and harvest only, and at other periods of the year little or none. Hence the large attendance of senior pupils, who continue coming to school because there is nothing else for them to do.

The number of schools in operation throughout the year was:—

113 Ordinary National Schools, average attendance.	.	.	7277
5 Convent	"	"	7072
1 Monastery	"	"	1145
2 Poor Law Union.	"	"	1277
1 Industrial under the Act.	"	"	478

Accommodation.

These 122 schools provide accommodation for 13,070 children, allowing eight square feet for each pupil, but the number on rolls for the year was 12,280. There are fifteen schools where the accommodation is decidedly insufficient. This overcrowding is not, as might perhaps be supposed, a consequence of the compulsory clauses of the Education Act, 1892. In this district these clauses apply to the borough of Tipperary only, but as yet nothing further than the formation of a school committee has been attempted. Were the provisions of the Act judiciously enforced, it is my belief that the attendance at the town schools would be considerably augmented, and the accommodation to meet the increase is ample.

New Schools.

Within the past two years four large vested school-houses have been erected, two at Nicker, and two at Ballylanders. The male school at Hospital has been enlarged, refitted, and remodelled at a cost of over £600, and placed in charge of Christian Brothers of the De La Salle order. A large grant has recently been sanctioned to build in connection with the Convent at Doon, while another is at present under consideration to replace the existing unsuitable schools at Cappawhim. Application has also been made on behalf of the two schools at Garryshane, and the manager of the schools at Bilboa has obtained a site, preparatory to replacing those existing there. The managers of Ayle M. and F., Derk and Shrawell have also promised to build at each of those places, though as yet no decided steps have been taken.

School buildings.

Ninety of the present school-houses may be said to be in good repair, twenty-five middling, and seven bad. In thirty-four cases, owing to want of premises, there are no out-offices, and twenty-nine of the schools have no playgrounds.

Sanitation, warmth, &c.

Most of the vested houses are satisfactory as regards sanitation, &c., but a great number of those non-vested are excessively damp. In winter, water may be seen running down the walls; and maps, tablets, &c., are very soon discoloured and destroyed. In many cases this is not due to insufficient heating of the room alone, but in a great measure to defects in the construction of the building. Proper attention is too seldom paid to the due warmth of the school-room. In severe weather it is not too much to expect that a fire should be lighted and brightly burning at half-past nine in the morning; it is then that it is most needed, when the children, many of whom have long distances to come, are dropping in to school. Instead of this, the lighting of the fire is too often postponed until a few minutes before ten o'clock, when it is hurriedly and of course badly done. The consequence is that, when the regular business of the day commences, the temperature of the room is so low as to prevent the work being carried on with any degree of comfort. Where possible, the ventilation of the room is, on the whole, fairly well attended to, but in many of the old houses it is out of the question, owing to structural defects. Managers are fully alive to the

Appendix C.

Reports as to State of Schools.

Mr. J. Coss, District Inspector.

Tipperary.

Furniture, apparatus, &c.

supreme importance of providing healthful schoolhouses, and during the past six years no fewer than eighteen vested buildings have been erected.

In fully two-thirds of the schools the furniture is good, and middling in the others. An adequate supply of sale stock is kept on hands by the teachers, and maps and other schoolroom appliances are fairly well provided. In most schools there is a time-piece of some description, but in very few indeed does it remain long in working order. Damp and frost are the most frequent causes assigned, and in remote places teachers have to wait until an itinerant clockmaker appears before the damage can be repaired.

Discipline, &c.

It is in discipline and the tone of the school generally that the trained teacher shown to most advantage; indeed, I may say that, with few exceptions, the teachers bestow upon them the attention which their importance demands. Prompting, copying, and the like, are practically unknown on the day of the Results Examination, and the pupils are both orderly and obedient. I can confidently assert that the arrangements of the majority of the schools in this district are such as to promote truthfulness, habits of neatness, good manners, and good behaviour amongst those attending them.

Attendance.

In the year 1892, the number on rolls was 12,177, and the average attendance 7,884. For the year 1894, the corresponding numbers were 12,280 and 6231·5. A consideration of these numbers shows a decided improvement in the regularity of the attendance, which would have been still greater had it not been for the exceptionally wet summer and the extreme severity of the weather since Christmas. Ninety of the schools have been entirely free of school fees since the 1st October, 1893, and 32 partially so, but in these latter fees are charged in only 16 cases. This fact explains the increased attendance, as the compulsory clauses of the Education Act are, so far as this district is concerned, inoperative.

Teachers' residences.

There are 13 residences built from private sources, which accommodate 15 teachers, and 10 of them are rent free. In addition to these, 19 have been built under the Teachers' Residences Act. These give accommodation to 21 teachers, but only two are free to the occupants. Many teachers here with young families find it impossible to get suitable dwellings, and some of them are very badly housed. To such, the official residence would be a great boon, and now that sites can be compulsorily acquired, there is no reason whatever for the inconvenience to which many most efficient teachers are put.

Classification of teachers.

The following figures show the classification of the teachers in 116 of the schools:—

—	Principals	Assistants
Class I. , , , ,	23	1
Class II. , , ,	62	10
Class III. , , , ,	31	49
Total .	116	60

In addition to the staff above referred to, there are the nuns engaged in three Convent schools, six classed teachers in the Workhouse schools, and also four workmistresses.

K

Appendix C.

Reports on
State of
Schools.

Mr. I. Craig,
District
Inspector

Tipperary.

In 1892 the classification of the teachers was: —

	Principals.	Assistants.
Class I.	22	2
Class II.	57	17
Class III.	77	49
Total. . .	116	68

From these tables it will be seen that there is a slight improvement in classification within the past two years. During that time only eight teachers presented themselves for promotion, and five were successful. Upon a cursory perusal of the statistical sheets, I find that the majority of second and third class teachers, whether principals or assistants, are over 40 years of age, and most of them married. Many of these and notably some who are only in third class, are first rate teachers, but with them it is practically useless to urge reading for higher classification, as, after a hard day's work in the school-room, they have little energy left for the systematic study necessary to success at the annual examinations.

Trained teachers.

About 34 per cent of the teachers have undergone a course of training. Their numbers for the several classes are given below :—

	I.	II.	III.	Total.
Males, ...	13	19	2	34
Females, . . .	13	15	2	30
Total, . . .	26	34	4	63

Masters.

Twenty-six were trained in Marlboro'-street College, sixteen in St. Patrick's, nineteen in Baggot-street, and two in the De La Salle College. Two years ago the number of trained teachers in this district was sixty. Of monitors there are at present 115, forty-six males and sixty-nine females. They have been chosen by examination from amongst the best pupils in Fifth and Sixth Classes in the schools where they have been appointed, and the competition is sometimes very keen. The result of their examination is abundant proof of the care expended upon their training. Last July, out of seventeen third year monitors, thirteen passed a creditable examination and were retained for two years additional. Sixteen were examined at the close of their fifth year of service, and fourteen succeeded in obtaining classification.

The school accounts.

I have every reason for stating that the accounts are, on the whole, honestly kept. The incidental visit is the surest means of checking the correctness of the daily entries in roll and report books. I have paid at least one of these to 115 different schools, and the total number of such visits is 230. In only three cases, did I find any serious irregularity in the accounts. In one, a pupil was deliberately marked present though absent, and in the other two, the rolls were not called in proper time

It is not unusual, however, to find the register in arrears, and an occasional neglect of the use of the leave-of-absence book may be met with. So much of the income of a school now depends on the average attendance between three and fifteen, that it is absolutely necessary to have the ages of children correctly ascertained upon their admission. I certainly think that some teachers are not as careful as they should be in this respect when enrolling the infants.

With regard to the literary aspect of the schools and the general proficiency of the pupils, I am glad to be able to say that steady progress is being made.

The infant departments in connection with the convents at Tipperary, Hospital, and Doon continue to be efficiently conducted, and in each the Kindergarten system is in full operation. The Tipperary M. Infant, Emly Infant, and Kilfinane Infant schools, the only infant schools in the district, are as well taught as ever, but Kindergarten exercises are taken up in the last named only. In all other cases, the infant class is found to be well prepared, but little is attempted beyond the usual programme.

Failures in reading are rare. Some few teachers totally neglect explanation, but in the majority of schools this is far from being the case, and I believe that this important sub-head is every day receiving more attention. The required pieces of poetry, even when well committed to memory, are only indifferently recited.

In the Fourth and lower classes writing is good. Many teachers do not seem even yet to know that this subject in the Fifth and Sixth Classes includes, not only penmanship, but also the ability to write a short letter on any simple subject, and failures in these classes are frequent. I certainly think that letter-writing is badly taught in a great many schools. Many Fifth Class children know neither how to begin nor how to end a letter. Mistakes in spelling are numerous, and besides being freely interspersed with provincialisms, the letter is mostly in one long sentence from start to finish. The required number of written exercises is always forthcoming on the day of the examination, but a glance through them will often discover many uncorrected mistakes.

Nearly every child passes in arithmetic in the classes up to Third, inclusive, and there are few failures in the Fourth and First stage of Fifth. Since the issue of the last set of cards in May, 1894, I notice a very perceptible falling off in the number of boys who pass in the Fifth Class, second stage, though the change has made no apparent difference in the hitherto good answering of the girls. The proficiency in the Sixth Class is usually satisfactory. The knowledge of tables and notation is good, but more practice at mental arithmetic would be advisable.

Spelling in the First and Second Classes is excellent. In the remaining classes the proficiency in dictation is satisfactory.

It is usual to find grammar intelligently taught in the Third Class. Although the course in Fourth Class is definite and not extensive, still it is only in the best schools that the pupils are well prepared. There is plenty of guess work in the syntactical parsing of the Fifth and Sixth Classes, in most cases arising from want of thought; yet the proficiency, generally speaking, is very fair.

I have every reason to be satisfied with the teaching of geography, so far as that part of it is concerned on which the payment of results fees is made. In some cases the minor parts of the programme, such as definitions of the physical divisions of land and water, the elements of

Appendix C.
Reports on State of Schools.
Mr. I. Craig, District Inspector.
Tipperary.
Proficiency.
Infants.
Reading.
Writing.
Arithmetic.
Spelling.
Grammar.
Geography.

Appendix C.
Rep: 2:1 on
State of
Schools.

Mr. L. Craig,
District
Inspector.

Tipperary.

Agriculture

mathematical geography, &c., are overlooked until the approach of the Results Examination; and map drawing, as heretofore, receives little or no attention, judging from the attempts pupils of Sixth Class make in drawing an outline map of Ireland.

The pupils are well prepared in the principles of agriculture as treated of in the practical farming. The teaching of this subject is compulsory, and the result fees for a pass are liberal, but the knowledge imparted of this science, which under-lies all farming operations, seems to confer no practical ability. Boys in the Fifth and higher classes show a minute acquaintance with the rules laid down for the proper management of a cottage garden, yet in every direction here nothing appears to be grown in gardens except potatoes and cabbage. And so it is with the treatment of live stock in winter. Every boy for instance can tell you, when under examination, that dairy cows during this season should get a daily allowance of roots in addition to hay. The usual practice, however, is to grow no roots, to allow the cows to run dry early in winter, and to feed them on hay exclusively. It is beyond doubt that if the teaching of agriculture is to benefit the staple industries of our country, it must be made more practical.

This district comprises portions of the Unions of Tipperary, Mitchelstown, Kilmallock, and Limerick, in each of which a very large number of labourers' cottages has been erected within recent years. To each of these cottages half an acre of ground is attached, and where cultivated at all the plot is entirely confined to the growth of potatoes and cabbage. Now, if there were an acre of ground in connection with each country school, and if the teacher were required to give his pupils a practical training in cottage gardening, unquestionably the experience thus acquired at school would sooner or later make itself felt at home.

Mr. Hartland, the well-known Cork seed merchant, has taken a practical step towards the improvement of cottage gardening in the Cork Union, by offering seeds free of charge and awarding prizes for the best cultivated plots. The first of these competitions took place in 1894; twenty-eight competitors entered and the result was most encouraging. The gentleman who acted as judge in his report says that if this practice were more universal, the "labourers' cottages of the country, instead of being eyesores, would be among the prettiest objects in it—training schools of thrift and taste—home lessons for the rising generations."

Needle-
work.
Industrial
columns.

The programme in needlework is very fairly taught and seldom neglected.

During the past year, 224 Sixth Class girls were examined on the alternative scheme. The branches taken up, in addition to plain needlework and shirtmaking, were dressmaking, &c., crocheting of caps, wraps, &c., and in a few cases, Mountmellick work. This programme, although intended to benefit the class of children attending National Schools, does not seem to be appreciated by their parents, who appear to think that one hour out of the school day is quite sufficient to devote to needlework and kindred subjects. In most cases the teachers have to supply material used by the girls during the year, and afterwards to dispose of the finished articles as they best can.

Drawing.

Freehand drawing is taught in every school where the teacher holds the necessary certificate, and the number of such is twenty, showing an increase of five in two years. In nineteen schools, 936 pupils were examined during the past year; in three the proficiency was excellent, good in ten and bad in only one. Geometrical drawing I have never met with, and it is a matter for regret that it is not taught, as the subject is one of great practical utility.

The introduction of vocal music proceeds very slowly. Four years ago it was taught in fifteen schools and now the number is only sixteen. Hullah's method is adopted in thirteen cases, and tonic sol-fa in the remainder.

Subjoined is a table showing the number of schools in which extra and optional branches, other than those already mentioned, were taken up, together with the total number of pupils examined in each subject.

Subjects.	No. of Schools.	No. of Pupils Examined.
Algebra, . . .	33	315
Geometry, &c., .	31	245
Book-keeping, .	21	491
Sewing Machine, &c. .	13	189
Physical Geography, .	12	133
Girls' Reading Book, &c.,	7	100
French, . . .	5	63
Instrumental Music, .	8	88
Irish, . . .	1	83

Referring to the adoption of School Banks, I have spoken to many school managers and teachers on the subject, but in no single instance has one of these been started here. I have no doubt that, if the system were established in even one case, the example would speedily be followed by others.

I am, gentlemen, your obedient servant,

ISAAC CRAIG, District Inspector.

The Secretaries,
  Education Office
    Dublin.

Mr. P. SHANNON, District Inspector.

Kilkenny, February, 1895.

GENTLEMEN,—In compliance with your instructions, I beg to submit, for the information of the Commissioners, a general report upon this district, of which I have been in charge since 1st April, 1892.

There have been no changes in the area and boundaries of the district since the last general report was made upon it by my predecessor, and not many in its circumstances in other respects. Three new schools have been recognised by the Commissioners since then, viz.:— Poulacapple, three miles south of Callan, Kells Parochial, and Wandesforde. The latter two are only new as National Schools: Kells

Appendix C.
Reports on
State of
Schools.

Mr. P.
Strmmon,
District
Inspector,

Kilkenny.

Parochial was formerly connected with the Church Education Society; and the Wandesforde School in Castlecomer has been in existence many years, supported by the Wandesforde family, but not connected with any Board or Society.

Two schools have been transferred from the charge of lay teachers to that of members of religious orders, viz.:—Thomastown Infant, now conducted by Nuns of the Order of Mercy, and St. Bridget's Male School, Bagnalstown, which has been placed under the Brothers of De la Salle. In each case, the change has been followed by a considerable increase in the attendance.

Changes in
schools.

Only one new schoolhouse has been built since 1892—the Callan Boys' School, which had become very dilapidated, has been replaced by a very handsome and commodious building. There are several schools still in the district which, on account of their state of repair or defective accommodation, are unfit for their purpose; but in most of them repairs and improvements would suffice to render them suitable. In a few other cases, however, the structures are so bad that new houses are imperatively required; and in two of the worst of these cases, grants have been obtained from the Commissioners for this purpose. In connection with this matter, I may mention one difficulty managers have met with in trying to avail themselves of these grants. The condition upon which they are given is, that one-half the amount of the grant should, in each case, be raised locally to build the school according to the plans and specifications of the Board of Works. The amount of the grant depends upon the size of the building and the accommodation it is to afford, and is regulated according to a scale laid down in the Rules of the Commissioners. In no case in this district have the managers been able to build the schools as required for the amount laid down by the Board of Works as sufficient. Thus a school estimated by them to cost £300, viz., £200 to be given from the public funds, and £100 to be raised locally, cannot as a matter of fact be built for that sum; it will really cost £50 or more additional.

Building
grants.

In this district there are about thirty schools which give sufficient light, ventilation, and space accommodation, but which have structural defects that interfere with their usefulness. The side walls are too low, the windows are too near the floor, and thus maps and tables cannot be properly suspended. In most of these schools, too, the desks are clumsy and unsuitable. They were built many years ago, when the requirements of school building were not properly understood, and were, no doubt, looked upon with satisfaction when completed, and they are now too good in many respects to be entirely condemned. These schools are, in this respect, a difficulty to Managers and Inspectors. In connection with this subject, I may point out one minor defect in schools lately built by the Board of Works, or according to their plans. The fireplace is placed at the end wall in a line with the door; and generally there is a rostrum placed on a platform fixed next the wall between the fireplace and the door. This is very uncomfortable and inconvenient, and has no advantage that I can see to recommend it. The utility of having a rostrum seems to be very questionable; a table in all cases would be much better.

Character
of school-
houses.

Twenty-one schools have no out-offices, and forty-three have no premises or playgrounds. As almost all the latter are rural schools, the want of these grounds is but of trifling consequence. The deficiency as regards offices is more serious. Most of the schools which are without them belong to the class to which I have referred as being

Premises,
out-offices,
&c.

built when the requirements of schoolhouses were not properly under- ^(marginal: Appendix C.)
stood; and in many of them, unfortunately, the defect cannot now be ^(marginal: Reports on State of Schools.)
remedied, or, if remedied, only at considerable trouble and expense.

The importance of having well-built, comfortable schoolhouses, always
apparent to those experienced in the practical working of schools, must ^(marginal: Mr. P. Skerrett, District Inspector.)
become a matter of general public concern when the operation of the
Irish Education Act of 1892 is taken into account. Unless schools are ^(marginal: Kilkenny.)
of this character, the compulsory clauses of the Act cannot be carried
into practical effect. This naturally suggests the question of its ^(marginal: Irish Edu-cation Act, 1892.)
operation, or probable operation, in this district. Though the district
contains the cities or towns of Kilkenny, Callan, Castlecomer, Bagnalstown, Leighlinbridge, Durrow, and Borris, the provisions of the Act at
present only apply to three of these—Kilkenny, Callan, and Bagnalstown,
as they only have municipal authorities. No objection was raised in any
of these places at first to the Act, and very representative and excellent
committees were formed to administer it. But the Corporation of Kil- ^(marginal: School committees.)
kenny finally determined, for reasons which it is outside my province to
discuss, not to proceed further in the matter. The committees of Bagnalstown and Callan met, and elected the necessary officers. Uncertainty
as to their power to raise the funds required prevented further action;
and so we are left to conjecture as to how the Act would work in this
part of the country.

As the main object of the Act was to secure regular attendance at
school of all children of a school-going age in this country, I am
naturally led to give my opinions on this subject as regards my district.
Nearly every child in it is attending school; the city of Kilkenny,
perhaps, furnishes most of the exceptions. But of course there is con- ^(marginal: Irregularity of attend-ance.)
siderable variation in the regularity of their attendance. Very many
never make the number of attendances (100) per annum which would
qualify them for examination to earn Results' Fees; many qualify one
year, but fail to do so the next, and so on. It is with such children
the Act is intended to deal, and, no doubt, the numbers for examination
and the Results' Fees for the teachers will be considerably increased
should it come into operation generally.

While dealing with this subject I am bound to state that the Managers
of the schools have nothing to reproach themselves with under this
head. With scarcely an exception, they watch over the schools most
carefully, look after the absent children, and do everything they can
with them and their parents to get them to attend. The Most Rev. Dr.
Brownrigg, R. C. Bishop of Ossory, takes an intense interest in the
educational requirements of his Diocese. When visiting his various ^(marginal: Attendance.)
parishes, he calls to the schools when practicable, and in all cases he
gets the centesimal proportion of average attendance to number on
rolls submitted to him. This naturally has a most stimulating effect.

But of course there are some things that managers cannot do; and
hence there is a great deal of irregularity in many cases.

In comparing the attendances in 1884 and 1894, respectively, of 129
schools—the number in the district records of this centre which were connected with it at both periods—I find that the yearly average has increased
in 26, decreased in 47, and remained stationary in 56. I do not take
into account any increase or decrease of less than 10 per cent.; and in
six or seven cases lately, six schools had to be placed on the capitation
system, the yearly average having gone permanently below 30. These
figures no doubt show at first sight a retrogressive character as regards
attendance at school; but in reality it is not so. The population has
been steadily declining during the decennial period under reference;

Appendix C.

Reports on State of Schools.

Mr. P. Thassam. District Inspector.

Kilkenny.

Epidemics, &c.

and but for the efforts of the managers to which I have borne testimony, the falling off in the averages would have been far greater. I am sure but for these efforts almost every one of the fifty-six schools where the averages are stationary would have to be added to the forty-seven where they have decreased; and the latter would have been far lower down in the scale.

I may mention, as an additional cause of lowered averages, the epidemics of illness which have unfortunately prevailed in most parts of this district. It appears remarkable how these spread in the rural localities, where the houses are far apart, and the general conditions are sanitary. When the epidemic is manifest, the schools are generally closed; but I believe the mischief is then done. The disease appears to be communicated by the children to each other in the schools before its public manifestation.

I do not think that the abolition of school-fees, which has practically been effected by the Act of 1892, has had any appreciable effect upon the average attendance in the schools under my charge. I am not aware that even a single child was prevented from attending, before 1892, by the exaction of fees; if unable, or even unwilling to pay, the children were still admitted.

Proficiency.

I now proceed to offer some observations respecting the proficiency in the various subjects of the Programme.

Reading.—I notice that in the last General Report of the Commissioners, just issued, for the year 1893, every Inspector who refers to this subject—and I believe every one of them who has contributed to its pages does so—finds fault with the proficiency in it, and more especially as regards explanation; and the same remark applies to almost every report issued for years past. I regret to say this report can form no exception. The faults which are so prevalent elsewhere, indistinctness and neglect of explanation, are to be found in too many of the schools here. The reason is very obvious. No branch of the school programme

Limited amount of time given to reading.

receives less attention, judging from the time tables, than this, the most important one. This is especially the case in the senior classes. In the schools where reading is defective, half an hour per day is the time allotted to it at the outside; in some only a quarter of an hour; I have occasionally met cases where the time is even less. Only the mechanical part can be attended to under such circumstances, and that very imperfectly. Little or no attempt is made to develop the sense of what is read; at the Results' Examination even the poetical pieces, selected by the teachers themselves, and with the entire year to study them, are either not understood at all, or very imperfectly. In all such cases I point out the defect in the time table to the teachers; they admit the facts, say they must give time to other subjects, and in most instances promise to make the necessary changes. In about one-fourth of the cases so dealt with I have found subsequent improvement.

Writing.

The proficiency in Writing is generally fair; I have noticed improvement in it during the past year.

Arithmetic.

I believe progress in Arithmetic is lower—at least in the senior classes—than in most districts in Ireland. The failures in these classes are more numerous here than I have experienced elsewhere. The schools which are thus defective are mainly in charge of Third Class teachers; and I think the cause is want of accuracy from defective teaching in the lower classes. At desk arithmetic the children of those classes are either idle from want of text-books, or of proper supervision. Exercises are generally set on a black board placed before them; but these are few in number, and the work of the pupils is not adequately checked, and copying is not prevented. Thus pupils who may pass in First and Second Classes, or with difficulty in Third Class, fail when promoted to the higher classes.

Pupils of the Second Class fail more frequently in spelling than those of the other classes. The difficulty of the spelling programme of Second Class when compared with that of First Class is greater than in that of any other class when compared with the class below it. The passes in this branch in the other classes reach an average standard.

I cannot report favourably upon the proficiency in Grammar. The answering according to the Programme is generally poor, and there are few attempts made to correct grammatical errors in speaking and writing. The local vulgarisms are reproduced, apparently without causing any notice; even in letters, otherwise fair, of Sixth Class pupils, phrases, such as 'I does,' 'We goes,' &c., are prevalent.

A reasonable amount of proficiency is reached in Geography. In at least half the schools, however, there is not a proper supply of pointers. Sometimes a piece of bough or bush is used; sometimes a partly used up cane; and sometimes the roller of a map. As regards maps, the schools are generally fairly supplied with the more useful ones; though sometimes those in use, especially the map of the world, are so dilapidated and defaced as to be all but useless. I must state, however, that in most of the cases where I have drawn attention to this defect, it has been remedied.

Judging from the results of the examination in Agriculture, its study in the schools here is neither intelligent nor calculated to serve the pupils in after life. This mainly arises from the neglect of explanation adverted to in my remarks on reading. The pupils are supposed to have text-books of their own, but many do not get them. The teacher, therefore, does not, as a rule, follow a uniform plan in giving instruction. He does not teach it altogether as an ordinary reading book, nor does he confine himself to oral teaching or lectures, but combines both methods. It must be recollected, too, that the phraseology of the text-book is by no means suitable for pupils of Fourth or Fifth Classes. Then, also, the teachers rarely illustrate their instruction by reference to the actual work in the fields around them.

In the great majority of the schools the instruction in Needlework is satisfactory, but in the few where it is not, it is, as a rule, very bad; there seems to be no medium. Where it is unsatisfactory, the defect arises from an insufficient supply of materials and from not giving 'lessons' on the subject. The teachers of these schools simply give the pupils the implements and materials, and tell them to sew, work a button-hole, &c., as if capacity and power in this branch were inherent in girls.

The extra, or optional subjects, most frequently presented in this district are Geometry, Algebra, Music, Drawing, and Book-keeping. I occasionally examine in Physical Geography, French, and Girls' Reading Book; and in one school (Garryhill) there are classes where a very respectable proficiency in Greek and Latin is exhibited. The percentage of passes obtained in the other branches named is respectable: the practice I found prevailing in other districts of presenting pupils that the teacher knows to be all but ignorant of them does not exist to any great extent here.

I believe the number of schools where the alternative scheme for girls in Sixth Class is adopted is larger in this than in any other district in Ireland. This is mainly due to the efforts of my predecessor who had the encouragement and powerful assistance of the Most Rev.

Appendix C.

Reports on State of Schools.

Mr. P. Skinner, District Inspector.

Efficiency.

Spelling.

Grammar.

Geography

Agriculture.

Needlework.

Extra branches.

Industrial education.

Appendix C.
Reports on State of Schools.
Mr. P. Gleeson, District Inspector.
Kilkenny.

Dr. Brownrigg in developing it. Except in two cases, however, it is not connected with local industries, and thus one of the beneficial results the scheme was intended to produce has been only partially accomplished. The two cases referred to are, however, very remarkable. They are the Convents of the Presentation Order, and of the Order of St. John of God, both in Kilkenny. In each of these large workrooms have been erected and furnished with looms, wheels, and warping mills, for linen weaving. At these occupations, which, though comparatively small, are yet a great object of desire, a considerable number of girls earn wages. It is remarkable that, though the demand for domestic servants in Kilkenny is great, and the wages are comparatively high, it is very difficult to obtain them. Girls and young women will work eight or nine hours daily at the looms—girls who are fairly skilled at the work—for 5s. or 6s. per week, who will not become servants for the same wages, with board and lodging in addition. These Convents turn out linen goods of various degrees of fineness, towelling, sheeting, cambric handkerchiefs, shirtings, &c., and the demand for them is on the whole good. The sale is partly local, and partly in Dublin and England. There are contracts for sheeting and towelling with two work-houses, and were the very excellent qualities of the goods manufactured more generally known, I am sure the sale would be largely increased.

The Alternative scheme.

Even in the schools where there is no sale for the goods produced the Alternative Scheme may be pronounced successful. The teachers state the parents object to it in some instances: it is popular enough however, and for various reasons, with the girls. The branches of the Industrial Programme generally selected are dressmaking, knitting and crocheting, Mountmellick work, and lace making. In most schools there is quite a respectable show of articles at the Results' Examination; and these are then taken home by the girls. The lamp-stands, tea-cosies, toilet-covers, &c., which thus impart an air of neatness and refinement to their homes, must help to remove prejudices against the scheme.

Defects of Instruction.

The principal defects I have found in connection with the working of the scheme are in reading and cutting-out. In quite too large a number of schools the girls read without intelligence the industrial text-books nominally studied through the year, and fail to answer when questioned on the subject matter of them. This serious defect arises partly from the insufficient time and attention given to the subject, and partly from the neglect of explanation in the lower classes. In cutting-out both teachers and pupils too often proceed without any system; and in after life what they learn under this head in school will be of little or no use to the latter. I have pointed out this to the teachers: and I have also explained to them that much more attention can be given to the literary portion of the Sixth Class programme without interfering with progress in the industrial portion. I have reason to expect that defects under these heads will sensibly diminish.

Music and Drawing.

There are about twenty schools in this district in which music is taught, and drawing is taught in about the same number. As these include the convent schools, the number of pupils who receive instruction in these branches is comparatively large. Those presented are generally fairly proficient. I am sorry that in Sixth class scarcely any ever attempt object drawing.

Discipline.

Discipline of Pupils.—I can report in a satisfactory manner upon this important branch of education. In nearly every school, the pupils are quiet and respectful in their demeanour: though a rigid disciplinarian might object, in some cases, to their mode of standing in class, moving from place to place, &c.

School Savings Banks.—I regret to say only two schools in this district have depositors among their pupils in these Savings Banks. They are Garryhill male and female, county Carlow. Twenty-five boys and three girls have commenced this example of thrift; the nucleus of the fund in each case is the premium given by Mr. Ponsonby, the patron of the school.

There is here, as in nearly every district in Ireland, a supply of candidates for the post of monitor, more than equal to the demand, especially in the case of female vacancies. In every school where there is an average of 40 or above, a claim is made for the appointment, as if numbers were the only consideration. Teachers are very inconsistent on this point. Each will admit that there are too many monitors in the service, that they are of no use where the principal does not show a good example of organization and method in his school; but each will press for the appointment of one in his particular school, for special reasons which he is sure to find. He will agree that the total number should be lessened, provided he gets the number he thinks his average attendance entitles him to; and he naturally persuades the Manager to press these views on the Inspector and the Commissioners. The following table shows the successes and failures of each class of monitors at the annual examinations of 1893 and 1894:—

Appendix C.

Reports on State of Schools.

Mr. P. Sheppard District Inspector.

Kilkenny.

Banks.

Monitors.

1894.

C.—(Monitors of 5th Year).

	Males.	Females.
Passed,	8	11
Failed,	1	8

D.—(Monitors of 3rd Year).

	Males.	Females.
Passed,	4	77
Failed,	4	4

1893.

C.—(Monitors of 5th Year):

	Males.	Females.
Passed,	8	8
Failed,	1	8

D.—(Monitors of 3rd Year).

	Males.	Females.
Passed,	4	11
Failed,	8	4

Appendix C.
Reports on
State of
Schools.

Mr. P.
Shannon,
District
Inspector.
Kilkenny.

School
exami-
nation of
monitors.

The subject in which the answering of these monitors, especially those in their last year of training, is weakest and the failures are most frequent is Lesson Books. Even when the monitor passes in this subject, the percentage of marks is often but little over the minimum. In schools where the general answering is good, and explanation is properly attended to, the answering of the monitors in Lesson Books is as good as in any other branch of their programme, showing plainly the main cause of the failure in this important subject at the July examination.

At the school examinations of monitors of first, second, and fourth years I find the results generally satisfactory, with one remarkable exception. I have been astonished to find, seeing how many years the present monitorial programme has been in operation, a large number of teachers ignorant that they have to select subjects for their monitors in teaching tests, and that monitors in fourth year are required to have notes of lessons. Even when the latter are prepared, they are in the majority of cases meagre and all but worthless. By neglecting the practical part of the monitorial programme in method, teachers not only injure the monitors, but also impair greatly the condition of their schools. Monitors of the fourth year, teaching systematically from notes, under the supervision of their principals, can be almost as effective as assistants, and their work is rendered more interesting to themselves and the pupils. The principals in too many cases aim rather at making them scholars than teachers.

School
accounts.

The school accounts are honestly kept, under some temptations to falsification. I have met only one serious case of the latter since I took charge of the district. But there is often carelessness shown, especially in the preparation of the documents for the results examination. These are sometimes not completed in time; and the correction of erroneous entries takes up considerable time. The inquiries as to the antecedents of pupils admitted from other schools are rarely made when the pupils are admitted; and the information hastily procured just on the day of the examination is too often erroneous.

Managers.

Two managers, distinguished even among the great number of their colleagues in this district, who are remarkable for their zeal in education, by the interest which they always took in their schools and teachers, died during the past year—Rev. James Shortall, P.P., Freshford, and Rev. John M'Grath, P.P., Ballyragget. Their successors, I am happy to know, will follow in their footsteps in this respect.

I remain, Gentlemen, your obedient servant,

P. SHANNON, District Inspector.

The Secretaries,
Education Office.

Mr. W. R.
Connelly,
District
Inspector.
Youghal.

Mr. W. R. CONNELLY, B.A., District Inspector.

Youghal, 1st March, 1894.

GENTLEMEN,—In compliance with your request, I beg to submit a general report upon my district for the year 1894.

No. of
schools.

The number of schools, previously 130, has nominally increased by one —an infant school at Cappoquin for boys till now attending the Convent of Mercy. At a short distance the well-appointed schoolroom of the Industrial Institution for young boys, certified under the Industrial Act, and conducted by the Sisters of Mercy, has been opened for the re-

ception of outsiders. There has also been recently recognised a tem- *Attendance &*
porary structure for a period of twelve months at Camphire, close to *Reports on*
the Blackwater, as the parish priest of Cappoquin proposed to erect a *State of*
suitable school for boys and girls in the neighbourhood. *Schools.*

The present condition of the schools displays no great change since *Mr. W. B.*
my last report, two years ago. They have pursued the even tenor of *Chamblin,*
their way, marked by little that has been eventful, maintaining a *District*
standard of literary and industrial attainments well above the average, *Invader.*
making some progress, and seldom falling back. The learning acquired *Verbal.*
from book work is of the same generally satisfactory nature now as *Literary*
then. Reading has improved, because it has been found that the ex- *condition*
amination in it is perhaps somewhat probing, and that a pass is neither *of schools.*
obtained easily nor as a matter of course. Needlework is, as usual,
properly done, and those industrial branches which are followed in Convent schools are also fairly creditable.

Much beyond the obligatory subjects is not thought of; nor is their
absence subject for regret. An ordinary boy or girl in a country district who has been grounded adequately in reading, grammatical composition, ciphering, some geography and agriculture, has received a very
fair preparation for life, so far as it can be got from books.

In the Convent schools Singing, chiefly by the Tonic Sol-Fa method, *Convent*
and drawing are taught, and in a few schools Physical Geography, and *schools.*
occasionally Algebra, Geometry, and Book-keeping are prosented. But
these subjects occupy no great attention, and may pass with the remark
that they are fairly taught. The school day can advantageously be
devoted to proper teaching of the ordinary branches, and if they are
taught properly the time can be fully occupied.

It is attention to discipline in its broadest view which differ-
entiates the Convent schools from all others. There are eight such schools
in this district. The literary and industrial work is almost always
well prepared. In them are gathered the girls of the towns in which
they are situated. Whether intellectually or morally the results
obtained are substantial, the latter lasting for life. These schools
stand out in so far as they really fulfil the end for which a school is
intended—the formation of character and preparation of a girl for the
world. The moral training she receives becomes part of herself and
remains as she grows up. The silent presence of refinement and
decorum, coupled with the subjugation of the less worthy parts of
human nature—ever present in the person of their superiors, whom
they respect in a way different from their regard for the ordinary lay
teacher, united as it generally is in this district to ability to teach well—
cannot but impress the youthful mind in an especial manner. This
influence and the affection of girls for their convent in after years is
shown by the bond which still brings them to their old haunts whether
in the form of religious exercises, or singing classes, or other ways. It
is only the fact to say that these convents are performing a noble work
successfully.

As regards the school structures at the time of my last report more *School*
than a third were built by State aid. Three non-vested schools have *buildings.*
since been replaced by commodious well-appointed buildings vested
in trustees; and two other vested schools have been enlarged and furnished with entrance porches to serve as cloak-rooms. The number of
really unsuitable houses is now very small. But any such houses
should scarcely be allowed to remain in receipt of grants. And there
are not a few others which though permitted to pass as fair could be
much improved. Some of these latter being vested schools built long

Appendix G.
Reports on State of Schools.
Mr. W. R. Connolly, District Inspector, Youghal.

ago—of the plainest and most rudimentary description—houses with four substantial walls, but with small windows, unsatisfactory fireplaces, and doors opening straight on to the open without porch, cloakroom, or protection from the wind and rain. Nothing is done to make them comfortable. There is little practical control over these houses, which once established and placed under grants are left to take care of themselves. Written suggestions in the observation book of the school would meet with dilatory or no response. Possibly such unfavourable remarks would only meet the eye of the teacher. His duty does not extend to the maintenance of the house, and he not improbably is hardly anxious to submit them to the unwilling eye of the manager. To bring such proposals before him, in conversation or by letter, is a source of embarrassment unless he is ready to recognise their desirability, and there is no practical means of enforcing suggestions. But if the department withdrew their grants in the event of houses remaining uncomfortable after reasonable notice, children would not for long shiver and be unhappy to the detriment of their health and studies in inadequate buildings.

Teachers.

The teachers of the district perform their duties, whether masters or mistresses, with very fair regularity and success. They are well ordered—in apparently comfortable circumstances—but are not fired with any high ambition to improve their educational status as I remarked in my last report; so now whatever desire is evinced for promotion to a higher class is to be found amongst those who are already in the lower division of the first class or in the second, and an appreciable portion of these candidates are trained teachers. Far too many are in the third class and are satisfied to remain there.

Teachers' residences.

Some four new teachers' residences are in contemplation, three in the parish of Aghada, the parish priest of which has, since his advent to the parish, built with State aid seven schools to replace unsuitable structures, and one teacher's residence. When these projected houses are built there will be seventeen residences in the district. One house, however, where master and mistress are married, sometimes serves for two schools. Other schools are provided with residences not built by State aid, and though it were to be wished that the facilities for building were more extensively availed of, still I am not aware that, as a rule, teachers are unsuitably accommodated.

School accounts.

The school accounts are as usual written with care and cause little trouble upon examination. The teachers show their anxiety to maintain their accuracy. I may here add that in other respects, as well as account keeping, whether at the annual inspection or occasional visits, I have seldom to remark any serious irregularity. The time table is, perhaps not always observed strictly to the letter in the case of every class, but it is substantially followed, and the arrangements on the form are indicative of the work of the day.

School savings bank.

I took occasion two years ago to refer to a small venture undertaken in the Lismore Convent—the only instance in the district—the establishment of a School Savings Bank. A year ago the bank was in a fairly satisfactory condition, but the convent would have been glad of more depositors. Now it is doing well, and exciting much interest among the infant and more juvenile part of the school. It is being taken up with vigour, more money is deposited, and, what is more important, the number of depositors is greater. There are 115 child depositors in a school of 168 in average attendance. Two years ago the number of depositors was only 33.

Singing is taught in the Convent Schools, sometimes particularly well, according to the Tonic Sol-fa system. Two or three convents show exceptional merit, especially Queenstown, where the results are of the first order. The method is simpler than the old staff plan, and gives children a more certain grasp of what they are doing.

Great encouragement and assistance has been given by the Rev. E. Gaynor of the Congregation of Missions resident in Cork. He has placed his services gratuitously at the disposal of various Convent Schools, not only in this district but, I believe, elsewhere, and has achieved singular results—in measure due to the merits of the system, but not less to his knowledge, his way of handling a class, the noticeable influence he is capable of exercising over the pupils, and the enthusiasm and ambition which he infuses.

The Irish Education Act of 1892 so far as regards compulsory attendance is in force in only one of the four towns which come under its operation. In Youghal, Lismore, and Midleton the catholic boys attend the schools of the Christian Brothers, and as these are not in receipt of Government Grants the local authorities have not put the Act in operation. At Queenstown the Presentation Brothers have large National Schools. The attendance committee have appointed an attendance officer who is assiduous in the performance of his duty, and has appreciably raised the number taught by the monks. In the Convent School he has not been so successful, though the girls are free from the manifold distractions of a seaport town to which boys are subject. No prosecutions have yet been ordered, but the committee contemplate less leniency in future. In the remaining four schools of the locality the attendance had previously been so satisfactory as to admit of little improvement.

The number of monitors has of recent years been considerably reduced in accordance with the policy of the Commissioners based upon the ample supply of qualified teachers to fill vacancies, and the difficulty experienced by monitors at the close of their period of service in winning teacherships and the consequent disappointment and diversion from other pursuits. The great majority of monitors are girls, partly because the Convents which have the largest schools are the chief applicants. I do not know that teachers are specially anxious for their services, except in the case of their own children. They are of no great use as members of the teaching staff for the first years of their term, and just when they become really useful their term expires; while the teacher has had the trouble of training them with the possibility of a loss of gratuity in the event of their failing to pass the necessary examinations. Unless a school is conducted by a thoroughly competent teacher who can adequately form a monitor, its interests are not particularly served by his presence.

In conclusion it may be said that the schools perform an essential though unobtrusive part in the life of the community. Like the vital portions of the human frame it is only when disease is present that their presence is felt. As in health the vital organs are ever silently, actively, peacefully fulfilling their functions without which death would ensue, so also is education quietly, persistently, beneficially ministering to the present and future well-being of the people.

I am, gentlemen, your obedient servant,

WILLIAM CONNELLY, District Inspector.

To the Secretaries,
Education Office.

Appendix C.

Reports on
State of
Schools.

Mr. J.
Dickie,
District
Inspector.

Rathkeale.

Mr. J. DICKIE, B.A., District Inspector.

Rathkeale, February, 1895.

GENTLEMEN,—I have the honour to submit, in accordance with the terms of your letter, dated 4th December last, a General Report on the state of education in this district.

A similar report was furnished by me, barely two years ago, in which I dealt fully with the various aspects of the National Schools under my charge. I do not, on this occasion, purpose to enter on so minute an examination of them.

The district remains in extent the same as at the date of my previous report. An Evening School, at Newcastle West, to which I alluded then, has been discontinued, a change of teachers having removed the personal influence which, rather than any desire for instruction, contributed to its success.

The improvement in school accommodation, on which I also remarked, has continued, and, with the completion of two excellent vested houses at Ardagh, and the replacement of Mount Pleasant School by two new schools, little further remains to be done in that direction.

An addition to the number of teachers' residences, built by loan or grant, is also to be noted. A neat and comfortable house has been erected at Rookchapel, the educational value of which, in that wild region, is not confined to the accommodation which it affords the teacher.

It will readily be admitted that the character of the population in a given locality is a most important factor in shaping the education which, under any system, their children receive. I may then be pardoned if I descant at some length on the social characteristics of the people among whom, for more than five years past, my lot has been cast.

The only industry of this portion of the country is agriculture, or rather grazing. Farms are generally small and of about the same size. Owing to the scarcity of tillage the lot of the labourer is extremely precarious. Most of the light work entailed on a dairy farm is done by the sons and daughters of the occupier. There are few yearly engagements for the labourer and, therefore, he rarely has settled or continuous employment. Hence, one is struck when passing through the country, by the number of idle men to be seen at street corners in villages. The population, then, is almost of one quality, a comparatively small proportion of labourers and a large mass of farmers who, whatever their means, differ very little in manner of life or education and not at all in dress. Among such a people there is, properly speaking, no middle class (it will be understood that the town element in my district is so small as not to materially affect these conclusions) and, therefore, no class directly interested in their work sufficiently well educated or informed to criticise the work of the teachers. This fact constitutes a very serious bar to progress. Possibly a similar state of things obtains in many rural districts of Ireland. To put the matter briefly, the teacher is not sustained, urged on, and guided in his work by an intelligent public opinion. The parents of the school children are, as a rule, entirely unable to gauge their progress in the various subjects, though they know the names of these, and, as in the case of the industrial scheme, resent the omission of any of them from the programme. Time after time have I been amazed at the public estimation in which

Appendix C.

Reports on State of Schools.

Mr. J. Fleckia, District Inspector. Rathkeale.

schools are held which, if situated in other communities, would scarcely compete successfully for pupils. The chance expressions of the Inspector and the usually more guarded remarks of the manager are factors which qualify this ignorance, but, for obvious reasons, neither party speaks very plainly or publicly on the subject.

Side by side with this inability to appreciate good work, exists a widespread respect for the teacher's position, and a confidence in the National system and its administrators and officers which is, to say the least, impressive. It may be said that it is quite an Utopian ideal to expect the parents of pupils at our primary schools to exhibit an intelligent interest in their progress, but the National schools of Ireland occupy a peculiar position. Owing to the paucity of secondary schools they are largely availed of by the professional, mercantile, and other well-to-do classes, and it is just this admixture of the children of the better class which gives tone to the school and makes the good as well as the bad teacher feel that he is not only working for a test, annual or incidental, to be applied by an official who usually keeps his views to the manager and his own department, but that his energy or his remissness are equally under the public eye.

A word now as to the upper classes. As a body, the gentry of this part of the country appear to be indifferent to the educational interests of their poorer neighbours. Their zeal for education, even amongst their own class is extremely limited. The number of books sold in the county must be surprisingly small; and during the whole period which I have spent here I cannot recall a single instance of a lecture on secular subjects having been delivered in my district. There are of course some brilliant exceptions. I have in my mind two families, the members of which regularly visit the schools near them, to the immense advantage of both teachers and taught.

The peasantry are a fine race, especially in the east of the county, civil, good-natured, and, above all, humorous. Despite the very depressed state of their only industry, there is a large amount of material prosperity. One seldom sees ill-fed or ill-clad children, and the bright-faced, if somewhat slow, boys and girls that are to be seen in most of the schools render the duty of visiting them not an unpleasant one.

The period which has elapsed since my last report has been one of steady progress. An experience of some years has enabled me to distinguish between the good and the barren ground in making suggestions. There are many teachers in this district who are producing really good work by methods not the best approved. But these methods are their own, they can use them to best advantage, and, as long as that is so it would seem a questionable gain to eliminate them by outside pressure. There are, of course, well defined principles on which all successful teaching must be conducted, but as regards the lesser minutiæ of school keeping I cordially agree with a remark which I lately noticed in a report on this subject, that teaching is really a fine art, and that one man will produce excellent work on lines which, if followed by another man, would eventuate in failure. Allowance must be made for the personal element. There are also teachers in this, as in every other district in Ireland, on whom all suggestion is wasted. The inveterate habits formed by years of careless work it is now quite impossible to change. For most of these advancing age will provide a remedy. For one or two some sharper means would seem to be desirable.

Appendix C.

Reports on
State of
Schools.

Mr. J.
Fleming
District
Inspector.
Rathmines.

Of the 117 schools in my district about twenty have attained a very
high standard of efficiency. Perhaps ten may be characterised as bad.
The remainder are fairly well conducted. There is scarcely any school
in the district to which the term wholly inefficient can be applied.

The school accommodation is, as I have already remarked, ample for
the population. But the care with which the buildings are kept leaves
much to be desired. I do not now speak of the infrequency and
inadequacy of repairs, on which I had occasion to comment severely in
my last report. Such matters involve outlay, and the collection of the
necessary funds entails a quite disproportionate expenditure of energy.
The more the tax-spending departments do for the people, the less they
seem to do for themselves. But a room can be kept clean without
expense, and simple decoration of walls and arrangement of tablets do
not necessitate any outlay. Still cases occur not infrequently when at
incidental visits I find the room in disorder, and the floor littered with
the dust and debris of previous days. On such occasions I invariably
criticise severely. The educational value of a well ordered room is very
great, and the carelessness which removes this means of improvement
is worthy of severe censure. And I have sometimes to complain of
insufficient heating of schoolrooms. Much of the expense of this is
probably in the last resort borne by the teacher, but, even so, leaving
aside the question of his personal comfort, an enlightened economy
should teach him that a warm and cheerful room will increase the
attendance of pupils, and make his work less laborious and more
effectual. Such points as these are those on which a manager can speak
with most authority. To his supervision properly belong what may be
termed the domestic arrangements of the school, as apart from the
technical. Many managers assume this discretion, but many, on the
other hand, leave all such matters to the inspector, who sometimes, to
deal adequately in the space of a few minutes with all irregularities,
would need to be Argus-eyed and brazen-voiced.

Of the discipline in the schools I can speak favourably. Discipline,
strictly so called, is good throughout the greater portion of the district.
But its complement, order, is not so frequently found. Teachers, as a
rule, find little difficulty in dealing with the children of this part of the
country, for gentleness is a marked trait in their character. That order
is not so good is to be attributed to the fact that the majority of the
teachers are untrained. The power to preserve really good discipline
is perhaps an even rarer quality than the highest teaching capacity.
Firmness, strength of will, and also, let me add, sympathy will enable
one teacher to accomplish with a simple look what another will scarcely
effect after repeated commands. The penalty which the teacher, less
endowed personally, has to pay for that deficiency is the attainment of
the same end with many times the labour. Experience shows that
bad discipline generally accompanies, as indeed it is a cause of, bad
teaching. Cases occur, however, where a school which has during the
year been conducted with fair discipline, but laxness of order and
organization, shows very favourably at Results Examination. The
teacher of such a school finds himself at the end of the year in as good
a position as his neighbour who, say, has always maintained perfect
discipline, and whose school runs like a well-regulated machine. But
how different the training which the pupils of each receive! The
proficiency of both schools is the same, not so the *efficiency.* In both
schools a certain amount of knowledge has been assimilated, but the
education given in the better-disciplined school has, in addition, conferred
habits of regularity and obedience, which will remain factors of the
man's life, when nothing, perhaps, remains of the knowledge but the

power to read a newspaper and the ability to write his name. Yet the *Appendix G*
only advantage which the better teacher gains thereby is the approbation *Reports on State of Schools.*
of his official superiors, opening to him the way to promotion, the
possibilities of which he may have already exhausted. It is for this
reason that I hold strongly that such efficiency as I have described *Mr. J. Nicholl, District Inspector.*
should receive direct recognition in the shape of a special grant, graduated
according to merit. *Rathkeale.*

Excluding those employed in Convents there are in this district 160
classed teachers. Of these just two-fifths are trained. This is not, considering the nature of the district, an unsatisfactory proportion. The proportion,
too, grows more favourable year by year. Managers are very averse to
giving principalships to untrained teachers. I can only recall two
exceptions to this rule, and in each case a promise to undergo training
as soon as possible was made a condition of the appointment. And
the next few years will greatly change the *personnel* of the staff of
teachers, a number of whom are approaching the retirement age. The
advantages of training are undoubted. Style, order, and precision are
generally found in the schools of the teachers recently trained. Add
to this, an enlarged view of men and things and a becoming *esprit de
corps*, and the benefits which these institutions confer will be apparent.
They are the teachers' universities.

Complaint has often been made in my hearing by managers and
teachers that certain of the colleges reject all applications from placed
teachers who are only third class. The directors of the colleges pre-
sumably consider that no teachers of any capacity for improvement
remain in the lowest class. Perhaps they are right. But it would, I
submit, be more conducible to progress if the higher step in promotion,
from II'. to I'., were made conditional on the success of the candidate's
school. Let me illustrate what I mean. The colleges, or some of them,
accept only candidates of second class or higher. The teacher then
who wishes for promotion, being in third class, applies to his inspector,
and on fair proficiency is allowed to compete at the district examination
for second class; this obtained, he goes to training, and obtains first
class, quite irrespective of the condition of his school; but were he a
candidate for first class at the district examination, a much higher
standard of school keeping would be required. This difficulty he avoids
by securing the higher step through the training colleges, and therefore
is sometimes promoted through a mere presumption of improvement.

There are now 70 monitors in the district, a reduction of 7 on the
number serving two years ago. The appointment of these young
persons is left entirely to me by the managers, and I find abundance of
good material. Attention is very generally paid to their teaching and
training by the teachers, and on the whole I have little fault to find
with their progress. They are not, however, subjected to written
examination frequently enough. One half of these "apprentices" are
going on steadily towards a profession for which they will be declared
competent, but which they will never actually reach. The bitter cry of the
disappointed is not so much in evidence in this district as it formerly
was, but the grievance is still keenly felt.

A simple remedy would be to raise the standard for certificates so as
to make the disproportion between supply and demand less marked.
The question of outside candidates for training and subsequent classification invites comment too. It is generally admitted that the best
preparation for a teacher's work is service as a monitor. The admission
then of numbers who have not served that apprenticeship to the profession is very like an interference with vested interests, and the matter

Appendix C.
Reports on State of Schools.
Mr. J. Diskin, District Inspector.
Rathkeale.
School Banks.
Abolition of school fees.
The Education Act.
Increased attendance.

is rendered more grievous by the fact that often these non-monitor candidates are preferred to those who obtain certificates by the normal path.

The action of the Commissioners in offering facilities for the establishment of School Banks has not, so far, commended itself to local parties in this district. Of the wisdom of this praiseworthy attempt to combat one of our national vices no two opinions can be held, but there are several reasons why the scheme should be taken up but slowly. In the first place the very novelty of the idea proved a great hindrance; moreover its working would seem (the objection is absurd, but I have no doubt such a view exists) to pass the limits which indicate the domain of State interference in private matters. There are, I am informed, a large number of School Banks amongst the primary schools of France and Belgium, and the system has been found very successful in England too. I do not know, however, how many years have been necessary to the production of these results, nor do I know what inducements are held out to the teachers concerned by the various departments.

When urging the adoption of the scheme I have been met with this objection—"Oh, but no payment is proposed for that, we have our hands full in attending to those branches on which our salary depends." I could not but acknowledge the force of this argument, and must here record my opinion that so long as results payments are calculated on literary proficiency alone, neither discipline, nor intelligence, nor culture, any more than the reform just treated of, will receive the attention it otherwise would. We cannot in these times expect official praise, even when joined to the approval of a good conscience, to balance the more substantial inducements of pecuniary recompense.

I should notice here that the abolition of school fees has had but little effect on the schools. Managers were always so considerate with reference to poor parents that the cost of education was little felt. The real relief afforded was to the teachers, who now obtain at least the same amount with no friction or trouble. Many of them now endeavour to obtain from their pupils small contributions towards purchase of maps or similar appliances, a practice which I always approve of, for, apart from the pecuniary help afforded to the teachers (on whom in this district the cost of such apparatus almost invariably falls), such a custom gives the pupils a healthy interest in the article bought.

The Compulsory Act of 1893 only applies to one small portion of my district, the township of Rathkeale. Early in the year 1894 a school attendance committee was formed, comprising representatives of every denomination. An officer was appointed who, for financial reasons, undertook to regard his new duties as pertaining to the municipal post which he already held, and to perform them without any additional stipend. This officer has regularly visited the schools during the year, and personally warned defaulting parents. But for various reasons—the fear of being involved in costs, which they had no funds to meet, the desire to have their first case free from the somewhat elastic exceptions of the Act, and, I suspect, the wish to keep in line with the various southern towns who oppose its operation—the committee have up to the present undertaken no actual prosecutions. The result, however, of merely holding the Act *in terrorem* over offenders has been to increase the proportion of attendants to roll-names in the schools concerned from 66 per cent. in 1893 to 76 per cent. in 1894. Some deduction is to be made from these numbers on account of sickness prevalent in 1893, but enough remains to show the effect of such legislation. Most of this increase was effected in the early part of the year, and, unless prosecutions are soon commenced, things may be expected to return to their normal condition. As regards punctuality of morning attendance, the schools of this district do not compare favourably with those of other counties. One prominent cause of this is the number of creameries in the country. Many of the pupils must convey the morning's "meal" of milk to these factories before going to school. Consequently they put in an appearance just in time for roll-call, thus losing almost a quarter of the day. But, quite apart from this, there is a good deal of unpunctuality. In Newcastle West, for example, the children of well-to-do shopkeepers may be seen often strolling to school about 10.30, and of the nuns there, in self-defence, are obliged to lock the doors of the schools at an early hour.

I shall now treat of the various subjects on the Programme, more especially with reference to the progress made since my last Report, and first, Reading claims remark. Mechanical reading is very well done in almost every school in the district, i.e, the pupils read so as to be understood. A reasonably high standard in this subject will ensure its being well taught with the limitations of which I shall shortly speak. I always so shape my examination that, to obtain success, each portion of the text must be taught, and it is very rarely, indeed, that I now meet with such "tricks of the trade" as the leaving out of a particular lesson or the confining the instruction to the prose portions of the book. As regards intelligent reading, and more particularly explanation of subject matter, there is no need for me to swell the chorus with which all my colleagues deplore the absence of the one and the fashionless of the other. We are told "there is no time to teach it," or, with more candour, "it does not pay to teach it." This inability to understand what is read is much more apparent in the senior classes, possibly because many of the juniors practically commit their reading to memory, and thus answer better when questioned on them. Let me here observe that explanation of subject matter is not so easy as an outsider might fancy. To explain the various phrases in a lesson and the drift of the same to a class of varying abilities, with due economy of time and language, is a task which taxes the power of arrangement, and, still more, the energy of the average teacher.

The question of readers here demands some attention. On one point the opinions of all well-informed persons coincide. The unapproachable cheapness of the Board's books is a great boon to the poor children who crowd many of their schools. As for the matter of the books, despite some uncommon and bookish words, such as "faint," "main," etc., the readers provided for the junior classes are admirably suited to the needs of the pupils. Those available for the higher classes would be much improved by the insertion of more narrative matter. The ultimate object of the reading course is not only to teach the pupil the art of reading, but also, to some extent, to inspire him with a taste for reading. Now, it is narrative that attracts most minds at any stage of their development, and this element is not sufficiently represented in the Fifth and Sixth Books. The Sixth Book is a collection from the finest prose and the noblest poetry in the language, but it is not too much to say that the matter therein contained is, to a great extent, beyond the mental reach not only of pupils but also, in many cases, of teachers. I only once saw a pupil reading a Sixth Book to himself with interest, and the incident was so uncommon as to form, as it were, an island in my experience.

A taste for reading would seem, indeed, to be a very unusual outcome of education in a National School. I frequently question senior pupils as to what books they have read, and I find that, except in two or three

Appendix C.

Reports on State of Schools

Mr. J. Drohan, District Inspector.

Rathkeale.

Punctuality of attendance.

Reading.

Reading books.

Appendix C.
Reports on State of Schools.

Mr. J. Dickie, District Inspector.

Rathkeale.

town schools, their reading is entirely confined to school books. To such pupils reading for pleasure is unknown. It should be understood that these remarks refer only to my present district and my own experience. I now dismiss the subject with the reflection that this is one of the many points in which a leaven of culture, which may be defined as the pursuit of knowledge, for its own sake, and, with conscious pleasure in its acquisition, would do much to raise the tone of the instruction, and this leaven might be obtained by some system which would take into account the individual quality as well as the numerical quantity of the work done.

School Libraries.

It seems strange that so little attention has been given to the question of school libraries. In higher class schools a taste for reading cannot be allowed free scope, for its indulgence would choke regular progress, but one would imagine that one of the chief objects of a primary school should be to evoke and foster that taste. I would, therefore, like to see a few simple books placed at the disposal of each teacher for the use of the senior pupils.

Writing.

In Writing I can report a marked and general improvement. The subject is easy to teach, and in schools where the writing is bad it may be at once inferred that it is not taught. The use of Mr. Foster's Civil Service Series is universal in this district.

Letter-writing.

Letter-writing, too, is on the whole good. The number of subjects on which the pupils' general information enables them to write freely is somewhat limited, but, any subject fairly known is well treated. I do not approve of the practice of giving pupils specimen letters in copy books. Its results are two-fold; the pupil either uses language to which he does not attach any precise ideas, or he regards his letter, which should be either didactic, descriptive, or historical, as an exercise in fiction, not an instrument for giving or asking for information.

Spelling.

Spelling does not call for much remark. The subject is generally well taught. A somewhat higher standard might be adopted in Sixth Class with advantage. For some years I have entirely discountenanced transcription in this class. The practice, though recommended in the manual, seems a pure waste of time.

Arithmetic.

The proficiency in Arithmetic is generally satisfactory, but this proficiency is not gained in the best way. I rarely find, on entrance to a school, the master with the time-honoured chalk in his hand. Constant drilling on "cards" enables the pupil to attain the answer in a certain number of cases by a process which he does not understand. I need not here repeat what I said in my last report about the deplorably preposterous answers which are often presented by pupils who successfully pass the test. Such blots are, I suppose, inseparable from a system which aims at the greatest instruction of the greatest number. The conditions of a "pass" which are well known to teachers might be made somewhat harder, for, while in good schools the most of the examples set are properly worked, in poor or indifferent ones, the minimum standard is so nearly touched that it is, with regret, that the Inspector puts down the mark which ensures the fee. Mental arithmetic is, generally, well treated throughout the District. I never examine a school without testing this branch, which, I consider, one of the most important of the collaterals of the programme. A habit of "counting up" or doing work in Addition or Subtraction, by repeating the table inaudibly till the required combination was found, was common some time ago in some of the schools. This species of calculation, which is not Arithmetic at all,

but a sort of mental hall-framework, I declined to regard at all as a basis
for a "pass." It has now entirely disappeared. I have to note here
the very unsatisfactory way in which many teachers conduct the lesson
termed "Desk Arithmetic." The pupils sit languidly in the desks, the
teacher's attention being engrossed elsewhere, and work, three or four
perhaps, from the same book. The lesson is, to a great extent useless,
unless each pupil has a book, and, in the junior classes, at least, is subjected to the active supervision of the teacher.

Grammar is being very much improved. It is a subject which pre-
sents many difficulties, so many, indeed, that I have often thought that
its successful teaching lies somewhat outside the province of the ordinary
primary school. It is so disheartening to an inspector to find the senior
pupils not only unable to parse properly, but showing plainly, by their
efforts to analyse the sentence, that they simply do not understand the
meaning of the words. But, as I find increased attention on the
teacher's part producing its natural result, increased proficiency, I do
not now so frequently lean to such a pessimistic view. I still think,
however, that the subject might be made an optional one. The
permission to drop the teaching of the branch would be availed
of only by the poorer class of schools, and these institutions, by
contracting their programme and concentrating their teaching power,
would, on the whole, do much better work. The subject is both
an art and a science. It is the art of using language correctly, but it
is also, in a humble way, the science of language. Its advantages as an
art are not always apparent, for however successful the grammatical
instruction may be, the language of the pupils remains what it has
grown to, through the intercourse and environment which the locality
affords. But, as a science, and treated as such, its value does not depend
solely on the knowledge or correctness which its cultivation may impart,
but also on its training of the intellectual faculties. The worst is that
the branch is not often so taught. Teachers highly classed and well
informed have gravely argued with me that the value of teaching in
this subject should be measured by a quantitative, not a qualitative
test. Thus, out of six words, if three are parsed correctly, a pass should
be given, irrespective of the ignorance which the treatment of the other
words may exhibit. Such a method of examining in a homogeneous
and interdependent subject like parsing would be absurd, for by it it
is quite conceivable that a pupil who would fail if tested in third
class programme would pass in sixth class. My experience has convinced me that the subject should not be begun sooner than in fourth
class. The work done in third class is to a great extent rote work
combined with guessing. Only the verb and the noun are recognised
by mental analysis. The other parts of speech are distinguished by an
effort of memory. An unknown word is usually classed as an adverb.
The frequency with which *were* is confounded with *where*, and parsed
as the latter, shows how much memory has to do with third class
grammar. Exceptions to the foregoing estimate, of course, exist, but
my opinion is that the training in guessing, and what I may term
"want of intellectual candour" which the "preparation" of third class
grammar gives to pupils, leaves its mark in the child's subsequent
school career. Besides, is it reasonable to expect pupils of eight or
nine to grasp the import of the definitions. No, on the grounds I have
stated, and for the further reason that multiplication of classes and
subdivision of subjects is undesirable, I should be glad to see some
re-arrangement of the various standards in this subject. In fourth
class, owing to the fact that most teachers have now grasped the meaning

Appendix C.
Reports on
State of
Schools.

Mr. J.
Birrel,
District
Inspector.

Rathkeale.

of the programme, good work, all things considered, is being done. But it is in the two subsequent classes, 5ᵃ and 5ᵇ, that I notice the greatest improvement. I could point to schools in which a few years ago, in order to avoid complete failure the parsing test would have had to be confined to the stereotyped combination, subject, transitive verb and object, where now any reasonably hard sentence would be done. As to sixth class, I cannot report favourably on the proficiency, the cause being the very common inability of the pupils, as at present taught, to understand the more difficult passages of the book.

Geography.

Progress has been made in geography. More tint maps are now in use, but the number is still far too small. More prominence might, I think, be given to America. It is a common experience to find pupils well acquainted with Zanzibar or the Gulf of Cavea, but unable to point out Boston or Philadelphia. Atlases are seldom used. The use of a globe of some kind should be made obligatory in all schools.

Agriculture.

Fairly good results are obtained from the teaching of the Agricultural Text-book. Perhaps 55 per cent. of those presented pass. I think I notice more intelligence in the answers than formerly, or it may be that the teachers have become better acquainted with my methods. I always endeavour to ensure that the simple principles of the various rotations are mastered. The remark has often been made that many portions of the manual require to be re-written or re-arranged, and I think there are grounds for this criticism. Circumstances, too, have much altered the aspect of Agriculture since the book was written. In the South, at least, of Ireland tillage seems likely soon to become a lost art, and dairying is mostly done by machinery. The East Lothian six years' course has but an academic interest for the boy whose father measures his farm by its number of milk-stock, and speaks of any ploughed field as a "garden." The almost complete absence of leguminous crops from the horticultural economy of this district has often struck me. Beans I have never seen, and peas are confined to the gardens of the gentry. The little care which the farming class in some portions of Ireland expend on the gardens of their homesteads is a strange fact, and eloquent of more social deficiencies than one. Objection is made to the teaching of Agriculture as too theoretical. No other sort of instruction is practicable in a National School. Nor is it at all certain that a widely extended system of school farms, with the accompanying expenditure of public money, would effect the improvement so confidently claimed for it. Our countrymen do not take so kindly to State leading-strings as some of the continental nations. The way must be shown by themselves. The man who first has the capital, the energy, and the public spirit to demonstrate what I believe to be a fact, that the only serious obstacle to the growing of flax in the South of Ireland is the question of labour, will have done more service to Irish Agriculture than a number of school farms. "Flaxed-out" Ulster has to go to Belgium for raw material for her mills. Why not to Limerick or Tipperary?

Needle-
work.

Needlework may be regarded as good. The number of schools in which excellent work is produced is not large, but neither, on the other hand, are there many in which the work is bad. Some few teachers appear, I really don't know why, quite unable to secure good sewing. Possibly they are not able to sew properly themselves. I regret to say there is still room for improvement. At the examination each subdivision of the programme is tested, and, if the proficiency in any one is utterly bad, I decline to give a pass. The adherence to this standard has secured proper attention to each, and cutting-out is now as regularly taught as sewing. I also see in the course of my inspections a large amount of garments made by the pupils.

The Industrial Scheme remains in much the same position as at the date of my last report. The number of schools in which it is in operation is slightly less. No fresh opening has in any direction been found for the disposal of the finished work, and hence the amount exhibited at examination is reduced to a minimum. Composition is rarely up to a satisfactory standard. That more industrial training for the girls in our schools is desirable is generally agreed, the problem is how to give that industrial training without materially lessening the literary instruction. As I lately addressed to you, in common with my colleagues, a memorandum dealing with this subject, I shall not further criticise the progress made, nor indicate the difficulties in the way of any such scheme. I shall merely observe that there is also involved, when it is proposed to produce in schools any work usually sold in shops or made in workrooms, a question of trade jealousy—no trivial consideration in times when every handicraft calls aloud for "protection," and the making of a door mat in a prison may wreck a Government.

Extra subjects are little taught in my district. It is not found that the taking up of such branches merely for the purpose of making fees is remunerative, and I seldom find an addition to the school programme for which there is no local demand. Drawing and Vocal Music are the two most useful branches of the kind, and in pursuance of official instructions I urge their adoption wherever at all practicable. But the number of new schools into which they have been introduced since my last report is very small. The proficiency in Drawing I consider disappointing, and I am endeavouring to improve it by the suggestion of black-board teaching and the use of large charts. In Music, for which there exists both considerable aptitude and taste, the results of instruction are generally very good. I have held for some time that the institution of a smaller Results fee for singing alone without theory would be an improvement. My experience is that the theoretical part of the subject is laboriously "crammed" in the few days or weeks immediately prior to the examination, and forgotten in as short a period subsequent to the same.

Advanced Dressmaking is nowhere taught here, but many pupils incidentally learn the use of the sewing machine in school.

Domestic Economy is sometimes taken up, but the whole programme is rarely known.

Physical Geography I examine in, perhaps, ten times in the course of the year. The subject, as presented in the only book available, is generally well known though not, perhaps, understood.

Algebra and Geometry are sparingly taken up; the first more frequently than the second. The proficiency in Algebra is very fair; in Geometry bad. The latter subject requires thorough treatment, and for an oral test, no cramming is of any avail. False reasoning is fatal, the utmost an examiner can admit is assumption.

French is now taught in two convent schools; the instruction is thorough.

Cookery is taught with much success in Rathkeale convent. Latterly, too, I understand, the Charleville nuns have started a class; the subject is of great importance.

As I have already indicated, the evil of indiscriminate teaching of extra branches, merely for Results fees, does not exist in this district,

Appendix C.
Reports on
State of
Schools.

Mr. J.
Dickie,
District
Inspector.
Rathkeale.

Undue
promotions.

but, speaking generally, some more stringent regulation on the matter is required. In a good school the more subjects taught the better; in a poor one, the dissipation of the teacher's time and energy produces a general bad result.

I regret to have to say that the evil of promoting pupils, irrespective of "pass," has, up to recently, been quite too common in this district. Now, mis-estimation of a pupil's attainments, no doubt, occurs from time to time at examination. Accidental failures are as common as accidental passes. No system of examination can be otherwise than generally, or on an average, correct, least of all a test which is applied to young children, and special reasons for promotion may, in some cases, exist; therefore, any hard-and-fast rule on the matter is undesirable; but when I find that three-fourths of the rejected pupils are promoted, and, on investigation, discover that none of these pupils have been informed that they failed, I say that such conduct, on the teacher's part, is a fraud on both parents and pupils; for, to recur to my observations in the beginning of this report, the promotion or non-promotion of the pupil is the only test of his progress which the parents, as a rule, are able to apply; but, if the result of examination is kept back, how can they apply this test? I have, for some time back, exerted myself to stop this evil of indiscriminate promotions and, I think, with success.

The tone of the schools is very fair. I have, from time to time, met with cases of extensive mendacity which, to a stranger unacquainted with the country, would seem to indicate a much lower tone than it really points to. Such unveracity is the result of fear; and, it is also to be noted, that the masses here, while as a body scrupulous in personal honesty, deal often quite loosely with facts, especially in conversation with officials.

The
training of
Infants.

The question of training of Infants is now receiving much attention. In this district there are five infant schools, and some notion of each will not be misplaced. Number 1 is a convent school conducted with striking energy and sympathy. Needless to say its success is remarkable. Number 2, also a convent school, compares unfavourably with Number 1, as regards discipline and variety of Kindergarten instruction. Number 3 is conducted by two teachers no longer young, on whom the most strenuous efforts of the Inspector have to be expended to impress them with the duty of discipline and physical training. Numbers 4 and 5 are in the hands of teachers industrious enough, but whose work is chiefly valuable on the side of literary proficiency. In the first two only of these schools is Kindergarten taught. I think that the Commissioners might, for the future, decline to recognise any appointment to an infant school where the proposed teacher is unable to give instruction in this branch. Without it the work of an infant school might, to all intents and purposes, be limited to two hours daily.

School
accounts.

I have not for the past two years met with any serious case of falsification, and I believe that the school accounts are fully and completely kept.

To sum up, the work done in the schools is substantial and effective. The Results system is slowly but surely eliminating the poorer type of teachers. Under it there is simply no room for the inefficient. Whether the best work as surely takes first place is, perhaps, questionable. Some modification, such as special grants for discipline and intelligence, or culture, would, as I have hinted in the course of this report, tend more to foster individual excellence, the slight encouragement offered to which seems to me to be a weak point in this system. Something, too, to make less prevalent what I shall term "groove-teaching," owing to which the alteration of the position of a map for purposes of examination is a grievance, the putting of a question in reverse order an injustice, and the change of Inspector a catastrophe. Any modification of this kind would have the further advantage of obviating the strain of the Results Examination by lessening the pecuniary importance of each "pass."

In conclusion I have to add that my relations with most of the Managers of the district continue to be most cordial.

I am, Gentlemen, your obedient servant,

J. DICKIE, District Inspector.

The Secretaries, Education Office.

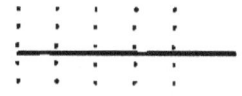

Mr. J. J. HYNES, M.A., District Inspector.

Mallow, 18th February, 1895.

GENTLEMEN,—I beg to submit to you, in compliance with instructions, a General Report upon the District (No. 56) of which I have been in charge since March, 1892.

The District comprises the Baronies of Fermoy and Barretts, with part of the Baronies of Duhallow, Barrymore, Condons and Orrery, all in the County of Cork. It contains several places of historic interest, not the least interesting of which is Kilcolman Castle, near Doneraile, the residence of Edmund Spenser—from 1586 to 1589—where he wrote the greater part of the "Fairy Queen," and received visits from the famous Raleigh. The Awbeg, styled by the Poet the Mulla—

"Amongst the melly shade,
Of the green alders, by the Mulla's shore,"

flows near.

The District does not contain any very large centres of population. There are only three towns with more than 2,000 inhabitants, viz. :— Fermoy, 6,454 ; Mallow, 4,439 ; and Mitchelstown, 2,467. There are, comparatively, few factories, and the bulk of the people are engaged in agricultural pursuits. The greater part of the land is of good quality, well watered and picturesquely wooded. The farms, as a rule, are large ; the cultivation is fairly skilful, and the farmers and the labouring class seem well to do. The general character of the attendance at the schools is regular, subject of course to the periodic ebb and flow at the spring and harvesting seasons. There are, also, other fluctuations caused by severity of the weather or by epidemics, which, occurring as they sometimes do at the eve of the annual Inspection, occasion great loss to the teachers. In the poorer localities a year rarely passes without some visitation of this kind, more or less marked.

Appendix C.
Reports on
Scale of
Schools.

Mr. J. J.
Burke,
District
Inspector.
Mallow.

For some years past there has been a steady decline in the population owing to emigration, and there has been a corresponding decrease in the attendance at our schools. Several schools have, in consequence of the falling off in their averages, ceased to be entitled to the services of an assistant. I am inclined to think, however, that we have, at length, reached low-water mark and that there will soon be a turn of the tide. The craze (for it really amounted to a sort of madness) for emigration is dying out. People are beginning to discover that the conditions of life, for the working class at least, are improving at home and changing for the worse abroad. It is dawning upon them that a man, with sobriety and industry, can live as happily in his native land as in many of their fancied El Dorados.

Number and classification of schools.

The number of National Schools at present in operation in the District is 113, which may be classified as follows:—

Ordinary,	.	.	.	.	.	103
Convent,	.	.	.	.	.	5
Monastery,	.	.	.	.	.	1
Workhouse,	.	.	.	.	.	3
Industrial,	.	.	.	.	.	1
Total,	.	.	.	.	.	113

These are amply sufficient for the requirements of the public. In fact, there is no part of the District in which children do not enjoy reasonable facilities for education. Elementary instruction is, practically speaking, confined to the National Schools, as there are only three non-national schools within the area referred to, to wit, the Christian Brothers' Schools at Fermoy, Mitchelstown, and Doneraile. Grants have been lately withdrawn from Rathcoole Female National School and Wallstown Female National School, as, judging from the small attendance which they attracted, they were not needed. The Kilhumia National School, which had been closed for some years, was re-opened on the 1st October, 1893.

Efficiency of the schools.

Speaking generally, the standard of efficiency is high. There are many excellent schools, and but few decidedly bad ones. In some cases, too, there are extenuating circumstances, such as inadequate accommodation, failing health of teacher, &c., &c., connected with these latter, which go a long way to excuse their shortcomings. In the better class of schools the tone is business-like, the discipline effective, without being in the least overstrained, the order perfect, and the teaching intelligent and thorough.

Convent schools.

In this connexion I cannot refrain from saying a few words about the convent schools of the district, which are admirably conducted. The sisters in charge pay special regard to the manners of the pupils, and the deportment of the children at examination is always most exemplary. Great pains are also taken with the industrial training of the girls. The proficiency in sewing and knitting is very creditable. The specimens of needlework exhibited at the last inspections of the Fermoy and Mitchelstown Convent Schools were remarkably good. Vocal music is almost made a speciality. The Tonic Sol-Fa system has been recently introduced into all the convent schools, and the charge has been attended with the best results. The taste and neatness, evident on every side, in the school-rooms and in the trimly-kept grounds, add greatly, in my opinion, to the educational value of these establishments

Another excellent school, which deserves special mention, is the Ballyhooly Female National School. I have never examined a better, rarely, if ever, as good a school. The principal, Mrs. Twohill, is a trained teacher, ranks in the first division of first class, and has seen long service under the National Board. She has repeatedly been awarded the Carlisle and Blake premium for her efficient discharge of her duties, and her school is in every sense a model one.

Appendix C. Reports on State of Schools. Mr. J. J. Hynes, District Inspector, Mallow.

Of the unsuccessful schools the two most common types are those in which discipline is lax and those in which it is overstrained. The latter is, I think, the more objectionable, because in it all the natural gaiety of the children, instead of being kept within due bounds, is entirely repressed, and their intelligence is stunted. Such schools are usually conducted by painstaking teachers, who are nervous and over-anxious. In their desire to avoid that cardinal sin disorder, they run into the opposite extreme. In vitium ducit culpae fuga, si caret arte.

Baldwandy F. N. S. Common types of unsuccessful schools.

Much remains to be done before the school buildings of the district can be pronounced satisfactory. Many of them (the great majority) leave little to be desired, but some are quite unfit for teaching purposes. The Kilcullen school-house, for instance, has not a redeeming feature. It is far from the high-road, and the approach is through an ill-kept lane, which in wet weather is ankle-deep in mud. The structure is old and crazy. It does not afford sufficient accommodation, and is kept in very poor repair. There is serious over-crowding in the boys' room. A new house is urgently needed. The Manager promised to have one erected, and a site was actually selected. But there now appears to be some difficulty concerning the title, and the matter is at present in abeyance.

School buildings.

New houses are also required at Ballindangan and at Kildinan, and will, I am informed, be soon provided.

The Lahara school-house is in a very poor state, but the Manager has undertaken to have the necessary repairs executed before next annual inspection.

The lighting and ventilation of the following schools are very defective :—Gortroe Male and Female National Schools, Firmount Female National, Ballykerwick Female National School, Whitechurch Female National School, Glenville Female National School, Minane Female National School, Blarney (Old) National School. I have received promises, however, that better accommodation will be provided before long for the Gortroe and Minane National Schools.

Lighting and ventilation defective.

There is considerable overcrowding at Araglen Male and Female National Schools, Vicarstown Female National School, Mallow Convent National School (Junior department). The Vicarstown school-house and premises are in a very unsatisfactory condition, but I am hopeful that they will be put to rights soon, as an active Manager, who takes a great interest in education, has been recently appointed.

Overcrowding.

The Ballyclough and the Ballygaddy school buildings present a neglected appearance. I have repeatedly urged upon the Manager the necessity for repairs, but hitherto without effect. The amount of my time occupied in writing to Managers and in waiting upon them with a view to having repairs executed, is very considerable indeed. When State aid is granted to a school, it is on the express understanding (except in the case of schools vested in the Commissioners) that the people of the locality will keep the buildings in fit and proper order, and the local parties should be kept strictly to their compact. If notice be called to serious defects, and if they be not remedied within a reasonable time, say six months from the date of such notice, grants should be immediately suspended. This would be only fair to teachers, pupils, and officials. It is high time to adopt a firm attitude in this matter, as the system of compulsory education, which has hitherto been tried only in towns, will, it is reasonable to suppose, be soon extended to rural schools. It would obviously be unjust to enforce attendance at schools in which due regard is not paid to the health and comfort of the children.

Four schools are unprovided with out-offices, viz. :—Araglen Male and Female, Raheen, Ballindangan Male, while the offices at Vicarstown Male, and Ballindangan Female, have been suffered to fall into extreme disrepair. In the case of several of the older schools the offices are much too near (often adjoining) the school-house. This, I need hardly say, is most unsanitary. In one case (Grange (1) National School), the air of the school-room became in consequence so much vitiated that the Manager, at my urgent and repeated request, had the structure taken down and re-erected at some distance from the school.

A good many improvements have been recently affected. I must mention in particular the new houses erected at Castletownroche and at Carrignavar. These are very fine structures. They are a great boon to the teachers and the pupils, who previously laboured at a great disadvantage, and form an ornament to the villages in which they are situated. They are vested in trustees, and have been built according to the plans furnished by the Board of Works (with slight modifications, as regards external decoration, in the case of the Carrignavar house).

The Board of Works' plans are admirable in all points save two—the fireplaces and the windows. The former are much too large, and are placed under cavernous chimneys, which carry off the greater part of the heat. Fuel is now so dear that it is a matter of urgency to practise economy in using it. I strongly recommend that stoves or slow-combustion grates be substituted for these wasteful fireplaces. The windows, again, are constantly getting out of order. They are so arranged that the upper half, which is on hinges, can be made to open inwards by means of a cord and a quadrant. Now these cords and quadrants are a never-ending source of trouble. The wood, too, sometimes swells, and then the window must be left open or left shut for good. All this would be obviated by the old-fashioned sash, sliding up and down by means of side weights, which is much less liable to get disarranged, and enables the room to be more thoroughly ventilated.

A very considerable addition has been made to the Knocksouliths schoolhouse, which was before far too small for the attendance. Progress was seriously retarded by overcrowding, and the apartments were draughty and badly ventilated. There is now ample accommodation, and the rooms are very comfortable. A fine porch (with cap-racks and receptacles for fuel) has been provided.

A new schoolhouse is at present in course of erection at Donerail, where it was much needed, and substantial improvements have been made (at local expense) at the Blarney (3) National School, and the Kingston National School. Numerous other necessary works of a minor nature have likewise been carried out.

The praiseworthy efforts of the Board to secure for its teachers comfortable houses have not been attended with much success in this district. Only twenty schools have residences attached, which were erected by State aid. It is surprising that the favourable terms offered have not been more largely availed of. It is true that thirteen other schools have residences (some of them of a miserable description) connected with them, which were provided from local funds, and that many of the teachers, who are unmarried, prefer to live with their friends or in lodgings; but, excluding all these, there are numerous cases in which suitable dwellings are urgently needed, and in which the necessary steps are not taken, sometimes owing to the difficulty in procuring sites, but in general on account of the apathy of the parties who should be most interested in the matter.

It is greatly to be regretted that more attention is not paid to the school plots. It is rare indeed to find any care or taste displayed in keeping them. With a little care and an extremely trifling outlay they could be transformed from neglected looking spaces into ornamental pieces of ground. The slovenly habits of our cottagers are notorious. Their ill-kept plots (which it is rank euphemism to style gardens) are simply eye-sores. In my opinion, our school grounds should set them an example of something better. The convent schools in this respect are a conspicuous exception to the general run of schools. Their grounds are kept with scrupulous neatness. The Castlelyons Male National School can likewise boast of a very well kept plot, which, in fact, is a model of what a cottage garden should be. To Mr. Heffernan, the present teacher, the sole credit of this is due.

The same want of neatness, so often evident in the grounds, appears occasionally in the school-rooms. It was not at all unusual to find maps and tablets hanging awry, floors badly swept, windows uncleaned, and dusting neglected. But, by sheer dint of harping on the subject, a marked improvement has, I think, been effected. An effort at making the school-room look tasteful, so far from being the exception, is now quite the rule. A little decoration of an effective, but inexpensive, kind is generally attempted. This was at first done solely in deference to my wishes, but now nearly all the teachers in the district see, I believe, the importance of it. Their early surroundings leave an indelible impression on the minds of children. How important then must it be that their memory of the school-room, in which so much of their time was spent, should be associated with ideas of neatness and taste! It is surprising how much a little coloured paper, judiciously used in binding tablets, &c., brightens an apartment. A good many of the teachers at first seemed to me to labour under a sort of colour-blindness, which prevented them from seeing dust or cobwebs, but this peculiarity of vision has, I am happy to say, almost completely disappeared.

As a body, the teachers of this district are earnest and well-conducted. The readiness with which they comply with my suggestions, and the desire which they evince at time of inspection to facilitate my work, are very gratifying. I feel much pleasure in testifying to their invariable politeness. Their relations with pupils and their parents are very harmonious. Discipline is well enforced, but the teachers avoid harshness or severity. The best proof of this is the fact, that during the three years I have been in charge of the district, no complaint has reached me concerning their treatment of the children entrusted to their care. Their accounts, as a rule, are kept with scrupulous care, and are satisfactory both as regards neatness and

Appendix C.
Reports on
State of
Schools.

Mr. J. J.
Byrne,
District
Inspector.

Mallow.

accuracy. Cases of falsification are extremely rare. Their classification is high. There are 160 classed teachers who rank as follows:—

First Class,	.	.	.	.	61
Second Class,	.	.	.	.	71
Third Class,	.	.	.	.	28
Total,	.	.	.	.	160

Classification of Teachers.

No less than 12 are in the first division of first class, and at the approaching July examinations half a dozen others will be candidates for that distinction. Of those ranking in the lowest class, a considerable number are newly appointed teachers, who have not yet had time to gain promotion. As the old teachers (most of them untrained) gradually drop out, their places in most cases are taken by young persons who have spent two years in a training college. Thus slowly, but surely, an immense change for the better is being effected. The principle of classification has not been adopted in the convent schools, and the sisters in charge labour under the disadvantage of not having been trained. They make up, however, to a great extent for these drawbacks by their zeal and superior intelligence.

Monitors.

The office of monitor is not, I am sorry to say, very much coveted. When a vacancy occurs, candidates are not as numerous as I should wish. Very often the most intelligent and best qualified pupils will not accept the appointment. As the ranks of the teachers are so largely recruited from the staff of monitors, this is greatly to be regretted. The reasons for it are twofold—first, the smallness of the remuneration; and, secondly, the fact that a large number of monitors, on the expiration of their term of service, fail to obtain further employment in National Schools.

Training of monitors.

Great pains are taken with the training of monitors. They are examined so frequently, that any want of application on their own part, or of care on the part of their teachers, cannot escape notice long. In their third and fifth years they are summoned to the teachers' examinations, which are held annually in July, and are subjected to very searching tests. In addition to this, their progress in the practical work of the school, in teaching and examining classes, &c., is tested by the Inspector at some one of his visits during the first, second, and fourth years of service. There was only one failure amongst the monitors of this district who attended the last July examinations. Some of the candidates scored upwards of seventy per cent., and over eighty per cent. was assigned to one. This I consider a very creditable record.

The pupils.

Compared with the children in other parts of Ireland where I have been in charge, the pupils of District 56 appear to me to be much above the average in intelligence. Their nice manners and pleasing faces are also greatly in their favour. Even in the poorest localities they turn out on days of inspection scrupulously clean, and dressed with surprising neatness.

Compulsory Education Act.

The Compulsory Education Act, which came into force on the 1st January, 1894, has been put into operation in Mallow alone. The local authorities in Fermoy, the only other town to which the provisions of the Act would apply, declined to take any steps towards the appointment of a school attendance committee, pending some arrangement by which the Christian Brothers' Schools of the country should receive the benefit of State aid. The schools in Mallow affected by the measure are—Mallow Convent N.S., Mallow Monastery N.S.,

and Mallow Mixed N.S. I here append the average attendance at
each of these for the four quarters of 1893, before compulsory education was introduced, and for the corresponding periods of 1894, since
its introduction.

Appendix C.

Reports on
State of
Schools.

Mr. J. J.
Byrne,
District
Inspector.

Mallow.

		Mallow Convent National School.	Mallow Monastery National School.	Mallow Mixed National School.
March Quarter, 1893,	. . . . .	887·4	249·9	47·4
June „ 1893,	. . . . .	313·1	227·9	84·3
September „ 1893,	. . . . .	336·6	217·6	44·5
December „ 1893,	. . . . .	331·7	240·6	47·7
March Quarter, 1894,	. . . . .	311·7	231·8	63·7
June „ 1894,	. . . . .	332·7	257·3	57·8
September „ 1894,	. . . . .	313·0	231·3	64·9
December „ 1894,	. . . . .	321·7	235·9	47·3

A marked change for the better is noticeable in the case of Mallow
Mixed N.S., but the other schools have been very little affected. The
results so far do not appear very encouraging. A comparison, however,
between the averages of 1893 and those of 1894 is to some extent
misleading. The former year was exceptionally (I may say phenomen-
ally) fine and free from epidemics. This circumstance, so favourable
to the attendance of children at school, would have a much greater
effect in the case of schools, such as the Mallow Convent N.S., and the
Mallow Monastery N.S., the bulk of whose pupils belong to the poorest
class. A longer trial is necessary before we can pronounce positively
as to the efficiency of compulsion, so far as this district is concerned.
I feel confident that much benefit will accrue from it, and I hope that
the provisions of the Act will be soon extended to rural schools.
There is not, I believe, any danger that the Act will be harshly
administered. The Mallow committee are exercising their functions
with the greatest moderation. Their attendance officer is very active.
A number of parents have been warned by him. Four parents, who
proved inattentive to his representations, were summoned before the
magistrates, who cautioned them against further delinquency. But up
to the present only one fine (1s. and 1s. 6d. costs) has been imposed.

Abolition of
school fees.

The abolition of school fees, in 1892, although a most welcome
reform to the poorer class of parents and to the great majority of the
teachers, whom it released from the irksome task of collecting school
pence, has not influenced, to any appreciable extent, the attendance at
our schools. Of course, the reason of this is obvious; the teachers were
never exacting in the matter of payments, in fact, showed the greatest
consideration, and never, to my knowledge, demanded fees from any
but those who were well able to pay.

Alternative
scheme.

The Alternative Scheme for girls of Sixth Class has been adopted to
a very limited extent. It has not, so far, become very popular with
parents, and one has not to look very far for an explanation. I think I
am not wrong in ascribing a fair share of the want of success of the

M

Appendix G.

Reports on
State of
Schools.

Mr. J. J.
Fynes,
District
Inspector.

Mallow.

Teachers'
view of the
scheme.

scheme to a peculiarity of the Irish character—a tendency to set a higher value on literary instruction than on any technical or manual training. Objectors to the scheme have also urged, when discussing the matter with me, that a very extensive industrial course is included in the ordinary Results Programme—sufficient, in fact, in the case of most of the girls, for all the requirements of everyday life, while, at the same time, due attention is paid to Arithmetic, Grammar, and Geography.

The teachers, too, it must be confessed, have not taken up the scheme cordially. Those who have not given it a trial are influenced, to some extent, at least, by the novelty of the matter, and I do not attach much importance to their opinion. I regret to find, however, that some who have adopted the Industrial Programme complain that it entails a good deal of expense on them, especially in poor localities, in the way of providing materials, and that it does not attract as many girls to Sixth Class as the Literary Programme did. I also hear pretty general complaints that it unavoidably imports an element of disorder into the schools. Of course, as might have been expected, the teachers who have the most successful schools were the least inclined to undertake the new Programme. They might suffer, they thought, and could not benefit by the change.

Industrial
training
under the
ordinary
programme.

Plain sewing, knitting, and cutting-out are very efficiently taught under the ordinary Results Programme, but the practical application of the teaching is not always attended to. The pupils should be required to keep their own garments properly patched and darned. I sometimes, at incidental visits, see girls out at elbows and wearing torn pinafores. It never seems to occur to them, until I call attention to the matter, that it is discreditable to them and to the school to leave them unmended. This sort of work has a double advantage—it trains the children to habits of neatness, while that dreadful stumbling-block—cost of materials—is reduced to a minimum.

School
banks.

Three School Banks have already been established. The teachers of the following schools, Ballygiblin Male, Ballygiblin Female, and Barrack-hill, were the first to introduce the system. The experiment, so far, has been fairly successful. Parents and pupils seem interested in it, and the number of depositors and the amount deposited are rather encouraging. The teachers of four other schools have promised to take the matter in hands at once, and I expect that before very long almost every school under my charge will have a bank connected with it. Much benefit will, I feel sure, accrue from this movement, tending, as it does, to counteract the want of thrift and the improvident habits of our people.

The number of schools in which Drawing and Vocal Music are taught (two branches the importance of which in the school curriculum can hardly be overrated) is steadily on the increase. In Drawing the results are only pretty fair, but the proficiency in Singing, especially in the convent schools (all of which have adopted the Tonic Sol-fa system) is highly creditable. The Mallow and the Fermoy convents are the most successful. Their advanced pupils render very difficult harmonised pieces with a sweetness and precision that speak well for the natural aptitude of the children, and the great care with which they are trained.

Reading.

It is to be regretted that teachers do not aim at a higher standard in Reading and in Recitation. In many cases mere verbal correctness seems to be the summit of their ambition, and if this be attained, due emphasis, rate of speaking, and tone of voice are quite disregarded. Monotonous reading is, in consequence, very common, and not unfrequently the reading is also hurried and indistinct. I find myself constantly harping on this theme, and on neglect of explanation, which is closely linked therewith. Children, whose attention is engrossed with the mere mechanical difficulties of reading, and who never give any heed to the sense, may, by imitating a good reader, learn, in a parrot-like fashion, to read intelligibly, but their reading can never be really intelligent. To prove this, it is only necessary to set before children trained in such a fashion a lesson, however easy, that is new to them, and observe how devoid of emphasis, expression, and intelligence their reading of it will be.

Spelling is well taught. In general the Dictation Exercises are sufficient in number, they are carefully corrected, and last, but not least, the corrections are, so to speak, "driven home" by the pupils having to re-write a number of times in correct form all mis-spelt words. These corrections furnish teachers with quiz on manual of questions for use on "Revision Day." It is greatly to be desired, I think, that Spelling, Penmanship, and Composition should be grouped into one branch, to be styled "Letter Writing," in the case of Sixth Class.

A great deal of time and attention is devoted to ciphering, and the results therein are highly satisfactory. There seems indeed to me a tendency to attach undue importance to it. In some schools I cannot help looking on it as a kind of idol of Juggernaut, crushing out of existence beneath the wheels of its chariot other hardly less deserving branches. But although so much value is set on the working of abstruse problems—"mere tricks to show the nimrods of human brain"—mental calculation, the arithmetic of every-day life, is held in undeserved contempt, so often the fate of what is useful, but unpretending. It is not at all unusual to meet children, who could work correctly difficult sums in Involution and Evolution, unable to answer simple questions like these:—"If a cwt. of hay cost 2s. 6d., what will be the price of a ton?" "What will 3 stone of sugar cost at 3½d. per pound?" By sheer dint of urging the matter I have effected some improvement, but it will, I fear, be a considerable time before I can pronounce the verdict "satisfactory" in reference to this part of the Programme.

I observe a marked change for the better in Letter-writing. The attempts at composition are often feeble enough in VI Class, but the pupils of the more advanced classes (especially Sixth) display considerable facility in expressing their ideas. The form of the letters and the penmanship are in the great majority of cases satisfactory.

Considering the intrinsic difficulty of the subject, the results in Grammar are fair. Analysis of sentences might, I think, with advantage be substituted for parsing of Sixth Class.

I am also fairly well pleased with the proficiency in Geography. In the new text-books some interesting or noteworthy fact is mentioned in connexion with each of the more important towns. This is a decided improvement. Blank maps for examination purposes have been provided in almost all the schools of the district, and much benefit has been derived from their use.

Agriculture is receiving considerable attention, but except in the Castlelyons Male National School, which has a school-garden attached, the instruction is confined exclusively to theory. The children in general acquire a very thorough acquaintance with the principle of the rotation of crops, with cottage gardening, poultry keeping, rearing

M 2

Appendix C. Reports on State of Schools.

Mr. J. J. Hynes, District Inspector.

Mallow.

Extra branches.

of live stock, dairy management, systems of drainage, and with the effects of lime and manure. It is difficult to estimate the amount of practical good which results from the information thus imparted, but I am strongly of opinion that a great deal of the credit due for the marked improvement that has been effected in Irish farming within the last twenty years (an improvement which the most casual observer cannot fail to observe) belongs to our teachers.

Pupils are occasionally presented in Book-keeping and in the following extras :—Physical Geography, Geometry, Algebra, and Instrumental Music, but these branches do not call for any special remarks. The results in them are for the most part very fair.

I make it a point, especially at incidental examinations, to study carefully the written exercises (home and school). Nothing reveals more unerringly the earnestness of the staff and the merits of the teaching than the manner in which the work is attended to. I have seldom ground for any serious complaint. Generally speaking, the number of exercises is sufficient, and the correction is thorough and systematic.

I am, Gentlemen, your obedient servant,

JAMES J. HYNES, District Inspector.

The Secretaries,
N. E. Office.

Mr. M. Kernan, R.I., District Inspector.

Cork.

Mr. M. KERNAN, R.I., District Inspector.

Cork, 5th February, 1893.

GENTLEMEN,—In compliance with the instructions contained in your letter of 12th December last, I beg to submit, for the information of the Commissioners of National Education, the following, my first General Report, upon the state of Education in the Cork District.

Since I took charge of this district on the 1st March, 1892, it has been increased by the addition of thirty schools, chiefly within the City of Cork and suburbs, so that it now comprises all the schools in the city, with the exception of the Model schools, and extends along the northern bank of the River Lee, a distance of sixteen miles, and on the south it extends almost from Queenstown Harbour to Clonakilty Bay, a distance of thirty-three miles.

In addition to the City of Cork, it contains the important towns of Bandon and Kinsale.

The population of this extensive district is 125,000. To meet the educational wants of this large population there are 155 schools in connection with the Board, and four large schools in the City of Cork conducted by the Christian Brothers, which do not receive any aid from the State. This report has reference to the National schools only, as I have not had an opportunity of estimating the worth of the work done in the schools in charge of the Christian Brothers.

Schools.

The National schools may be divided as follows :—
   3 Poor Law Union schools,
   8 Convent schools.
   4 Monastery schools.
 134 Ordinary schools.
   6 Evening schools.

With the exception of those in the City of Cork, which have an average attendance of 200 scholars daily, the Poor Law Union schools are small and not important. The total attendance of Kinsale and Bandon Poor Law Union schools is only twenty, and these twenty are only in junior classes. The Cork Poor Law Union schools are divided into three departments, male, female, and infant, each in charge of a skilful and efficient staff of teachers, so that the pupils attending these schools are receiving an excellent education, which will, to some extent, enable them to overcome many of the exceptional difficulties which they will have to encounter when engaged in the battle of life.

The system of boarding out children, which is in great favour at the Poor Law Boards, greatly reduces the attendance at these schools.

Of the eight Convent National schools, four are in the City of Cork, one in Blackrock, one in Crosshaven, one in Bandon, and one in Kinsale. These Convent schools have almost entire charge of the education of the Roman Catholic girls in the towns. Four of these Convent schools are conducted by Nuns of the Presentation Order who devote themselves exclusively to teaching; these ladies undergo a course of training by their own Order to fit them for the office of teacher. One of the Convent schools is conducted by the Sisters of Charity and two by the Sisters of Mercy. The ladies of these Orders, in addition to teaching, nurse the sick, visit the poor in their own homes, and dispense charities in various ways; however, I must say they do not allow the discharge of these duties to interfere in the least with their duties as teachers. They generally avail themselves of the opportunities afforded them by visiting to see, in their own homes, the children who are irregular, and exhort them to attend school more regularly.

The Convent school at Blackrock is conducted by Ursuline Nuns, and is attended only by the poorer classes—children of fishermen, labourers, &c.

In each of the four large Convent schools in Cork, in addition to the Nuns, there is a large staff of lay assistants, nearly all of whom are classed and some highly classed.

The average daily attendance at all the Convent schools in Cork District is 4,147, and 4,190 were examined for Results fees.

The special features of the education given at Convent schools have been so often written, that I shall content myself with saying that the moral and intellectual training given to the pupils attending the above schools is of the highest order, many of the best features of which cannot be tested by examination.

There are four schools taught by Brothers of the Presentation Order—three in Cork and one in Kinsale. Two of these schools are paid by capitation, and two by classification, as in ordinary National schools. I find the schools in which the principle of classification is adopted by far the best taught. I do not observe that these schools possess any distinctive feature. In all lay assistants are employed. The average daily attendance at these schools is 1,913, and the number examined for Results fees is 1,923.

The great disadvantage which the members of this Order labour under is want of training. They have not been able to avail themselves of the advantages of any of the Training Colleges. The Rev. Superior is doing his utmost to supply this want, but so far has not been successful. This is a very serious matter in an Order that has so many young members.

I now come to treat of the 134 ordinary National Schools—33 of these are in the City of Cork, 6 in Bandon, and 1 in Kinsale. The remaining

Appendix C.
Reports on
State of
Schools.

Mr. M.
Fenelon,
District
Inspector,
Cork.

School
accommoda-
tion.

New school
buildings.

Evening
schools.

Compul-
sory
education.

Average
attendance.

104 meet the educational requirements of a large rural population, and are so distributed that almost every child of school-going age is within reasonable distance of a school. A pleasing feature in Cork schools is that in general there are separate schools for boys and girls, and when this is not the case a female assistant or workmistress is employed, so that in every locality there is suitable industrial teaching for girls.

In the rural districts and smaller towns there is ample school accommodation, and I am satisfied that all the children attend school, however irregularly; but in the City of Cork there must be a large number of the Roman Catholic population who do not go to school, and for whom there is not sufficient accommodation. In passing from one school to another in the city one day, a distance of half a mile, I counted 100 children of school-going age who were running idle about the streets.

The work of building schools is, however, seriously engaging the attention of Managers. Within the past three years new schools have been erected at Eason's Hill, Tremleth's-lane, and Blackpool. At present there are in course of erection new school buildings to replace the miserable school of St. Francis in Kyle-street, and the nuns of St. Fintan's Convent are building a new school to provide accommodation for the infant boys. The Board have also given grants to build two schools for boys, one in Bandon and one in Kinsale. These schools will be built before the end of the present year. Two new vested schools, one for boys and one for girls, at Farran, will be opened before May. About three additional schools—one in Bandon, one in Kinsale, and one at Oysterhaven—would fully meet the requirements of the district.

There are six evening schools, all in the city, in operation at present. Many, if not most of the pupils attending these schools, are mere children, and should be attending a day school.

The Compulsory Education Act applies to three towns in the district—Cork, Bandon, and Kinsale; but I regret to report that no steps have been taken by the local authorities in these places to put the Act in force. In Cork and Bandon absolutely nothing has been done; in Kinsale a committee was appointed, but never met.

—	1892	1893	1894
Average attendance of all Schools in Cork, . . .	6,594	6,501	6,567
Do. do. in Bandon, . .	7,077	7,141	7,093
Do. do. in Kinsale, . .	687?	711	737?

In Bandon and Kinsale there has been no considerable increase in the number of children attending school. I believe there are very few children of school-going age in these two towns who are not attending school, and even if the Compulsory Education Act were put in force the attendance would not be much increased. In Cork there has been a slight increase, but when we take into account the large population, the increase is trifling, and it is evident that the non-school-going portion of the population have not been affected. Within the past three years four new schools have been built in the City of Cork, and have now attendances equal to the extent of their accommodation. Many of the pupils came from non-National schools, attracted by these new schools.

I observe in some cases the tendency in Cork is to enlarge existing *Apprentice.*
schools rather than to build new ones. From an educational point of
view I regard this as a mistake—(1) Many of these schools are too
large already ; (2) the children are drawn from too large an area, and
this tends to irregular attendance ; (3) there is no emulation among
different schools ; (4) the children of careless parents more easily escape
observation.

With regard to the aims of the teachers, I cannot say much is
attempted beyond what is prescribed in the Results Programme. The
moral qualities—truth, honesty, and freedom from vice of all kinds—are
carefully and successfully cultivated.

I have much pleasure in reporting, for the information of the Commissioners of National Education, that the teachers of this district are a
zealous, industrious, and highly efficient body of public servants ; that
they discharge their important duties with ability and success, and that
they are held in high esteem in their respective localities. Only one
instance has come under my notice of a teacher having a misunderstanding with a considerable number of the parents in his locality. An
unerring sign of the satisfactory manner in which the teachers are
discharging their duties, and of the high esteem in which they are held,
is to be found in the small number of changes which take place in the
teaching staff of the different schools. If we except four schools that
are under the management of the Cork School Board, and two other
schools commanding an average attendance of less than thirty pupils,
there have been no changes in the principal teacherships of the schools
of this district, except in the case of two deaths, and one who was
dismissed by order of the Board. When a vacancy occurs the Manager
invariably appoints the most eligible candidate. Other things being
equal, a preference is given to candidates who are qualified to teach
Vocal Music and Drawing.

The following Table shows the classification of the principal teachers
in charge of schools and of the assistants :—

—	Males.	Females.
I.	11	8
I.	16	11
II.	81	62
III.	2	1
III.	16	14
III.	—	—

ASSISTANTS.

—	Males.	Females.
I.	—	8
I.	8	4
II.	11	11
II.	10	3
III.	21	86
III.	4	3

Appendix C.

Reports on State of Schools.

Mr. M. Kiveau, District Inspector, Cork.

Residences.

Monitors.

School banks.

The assistant teachers, who are classed 3⁰ and 3³, have either obtained their promotion or classification within the past twelve months.

The principal teachers, classed 2³, have not been considered deserving of promotion on account of the state of their schools.

The average incomes of the principal teachers is £103 and that of the assistants is £58. The incomes of the conductors of schools that are paid by capitation are not included in this calculation.

With regard to residences, I do not know of more than two cases where teachers have not comfortable homes at a short distance from their schools. Twenty-four principal teachers have residences under the Act; twenty-two have residences free, which were provided by their managers; six have a sum of £30 a year in lieu of a free house; and the others, with the exceptions above referred to, have suitable residences.

There are at present serving in the schools of this district 201 monitors, 59 males and 142 females. A much smaller number would more than suffice to fill up the vacancies in the teaching staff. In the Convent schools alone there are upwards of 100. In some of the Convents where lay teachers are employed, the conductors are enabled to fill up vacancies in their staff from their monitors; and again, some of the monitors find their way into the teaching profession by other channels. The monitors trained in Convents are generally able to teach music and drawing. A small proportion of those trained in the ordinary National schools make their way into the teaching profession by first passing through one of the Training Colleges.

The number of males is not excessive, and those who pass their final examination and obtain provisional classification in general procure appointments either as assistants or as substitutes for teachers in training.

The number who obtain provisional classification at the termination of their five years' course would be from twenty-five to thirty each year.

I know of only one school with a savings bank established for the pupils. It is an excellent institution, giving the pupils a valuable training in thrift and economy. I brought this matter under the notice of some of the managers and teachers. They expressed themselves warmly in favour of it, but so far as I can learn they have taken no steps to introduce it into their schools. In some schools, where the pupils would be in the best position to establish a school bank, I learn that their parents periodically lodge in the Savings Bank Department of the Post Office sums to the credit of their children. This of course serves the same purpose, but it does not possess the same educational advantages.

The payment of school pence weekly was always confined to a very few schools, school fees generally being paid by the quarter or the half year. In some of the schools I observe many of the children, instead of bringing lunch from home, purchase buns and fruit at the school door. I have pointed out to the teachers of these schools the great advantage of a savings bank when the children are able to spend so many pennies.

During the year ended 28th February, 1895, I examined 134 schools for Results fees, and the remaining thirty were examined by unattached District Inspectors who were from time to time employed in the Cork district. The number of pupils examined by me was 14,193, and the number examined by other Inspectors was 848.

The average attendance of all the schools in this district is 16,601, and the average number of pupils examined for Results fees in each of the ordinary National schools of the district was 77.

I now come to the consideration of the different subjects of the Results Programme.

Generally the reading is fluent and the words are correctly grouped. Pronunciation, especially in the smaller schools, is not correct. The teachers do not take sufficient pains to make their pupils pronounce their words correctly. In the Junior classes the pupils can readily give the meanings of the difficult words and phrases that occur in their reading lesson. In the Senior classes explanation of the subject matter does not receive sufficient attention. In schools where there is only one teacher, and the number in each of the Senior classes is comparatively small, the teacher is obliged to conduct the reading lesson of two or three classes in the same half hour. It is impossible for such a teacher, however competent or well disposed he may be, to devote sufficient time to the explanation of the subject matter of each class. The pieces of poetry required by the Programme are always well prepared, but only in a few schools are they repeated with taste and expression. I have from time to time impressed upon the teachers the necessity of teaching their pupils to read the pieces of poetry correctly before requiring them to commit them to memory.

Writing is well taught in all the schools to the Junior classes. In a few schools I find the head-line copies of Senior classes only middling. The required number of head-line copies and exercises is always submitted to me on the day of examination. I find few instances in which these exercises are not carefully corrected by the teachers. I should say that, in some schools, an undue proportion of the exercises of pupils in Fifth and Sixth classes is mere transcription. However, a good proportion of these exercises are on arithmetic, grammar, geography, dictation, and letters on various subjects.

The exercises which I receive on the day of examination are always well written and free from blots.

In examining the head line copies at the end of the year I found that the writing lesson had been carefully taught. Defects were pointed out by the teachers, and the copies supplied were suitable to the capacities of the pupils.

Within the past three years I have observed a great improvement in the letters I receive from the pupils at the Annual Examinations for Results Fees. The form of epistolary correspondence is well understood in all our schools, and the subject-matter is treated with a fair amount of skill and intelligence, but the pupils do not know when they come to the end of a sentence, and, further, instances of pronunciations and bad grammar are frequent. I sometimes find in sentences of Sixth class pupils a pronoun of the first person nominative to a verb of the third person—"I does be doing," &c. These same pupils would be able to analyse and parse a most difficult sentence, yet when writing or speaking their own language they never think it necessary to observe the rules of grammar.

In order to check these blunders I would suggest that the examination for a pass in grammar should not only require the parsing of a sentence correctly, but also that the pupils should be required to correct and amend a sentence in which there is a grammatical error.

Arithmetic, which is one of the most important and difficult subjects in our school course, is well taught in almost all the schools in Cork District. No teacher could lay claim to success or efficiency, either in the eyes of the Board or in those of the parents of his pupils, if his school broke down in arithmetic at the annual examination. In the Junior classes, where a thorough knowledge of the addition, subtraction, and multiplication tables enables the pupils to work the exercises usually set; I find cases of failure rare. In the Senior classes, where the questions set are much more difficult, and for solving them a higher degree of intelligence is required, failures are more numerous; however, I should say upon the whole the number of failures does not amount to 10 per cent. of those examined.

The different rules are carefully explained by the teachers and well understood by the pupils. The teachers also give their pupils ample practice, as I find mistakes or blunders in working out sums are rare. More attention should be given to mental arithmetic in the second stage of fifth and sixth classes.

I would suggest that a short course in Mensuration should be added to the programme in arithmetic for boys of second stage of fifth and sixth classes. This would better define the distinction between the programmes for boys and girls in three classes.

Spelling

The oral spelling of pupils of first and second classes is excellent. The third, which is the lowest class required to write a dictation exercise, has greatly improved within the last three years. Formerly the number of failures in third class was greater than the number of passes, now the proportion of failures is not much less than in the fourth and fifth classes. In senior classes the dictation exercise is fairly good in all our schools. Oral spelling is also good in third and higher classes. The pupils of these classes can not only spell the difficult words that occur in their lessons, but they are able also to give the meanings.

Grammar

In the great majority of schools grammar is fairly well taught, and the different classes are well up to the requirements of their respective programmes. But there is a considerable minority of schools in which the teaching of this subject is not satisfactory, and some of those are taught by teachers who are highly classed, and who are otherwise skilful and efficient. Whether this want of success in teaching grammar is due to want of skill, or that sufficient time is not devoted to it, I am at a loss to determine. I greatly fear the requirements of the programme are not understood by some of these teachers, and they are satisfied with quite too low a standard. Derivations are only middling, and the home lessons are not well prepared in many schools. As I stated in a former part of this report, I would recommend that to obtain a pass in grammar a pupil should be required both to parse a sentence and to correct a sentence in which there was a grammatical error.

Geography

The answering of third and fourth classes in geography is excellent, and fifth class, both stages, good; and sixth class fair. It is to be regretted that the geographical reading lessons commenced in the Third Book were not continued in Fifth and Sixth Books. These lessons give an interest to the study of local geography, which our present mode of teaching it can never evoke. I would suggest that instead of requiring the pupils of fifth and sixth classes to point out places on the map and describe their relative positions, that a skeleton map be put into the hands of these pupils, and that they be required to mark the positions of places. This, I think, would more accurately fix upon the minds the actual position of places, and it would serve as an introduction to drawing maps. The sub-heads of this subject are in general fairly well taught.

Agriculture

Agriculture is taught in all the rural schools which are in charge of masters, and in some of the town schools. The answering of the pupils is in general good. In the rural districts the boys, especially of the sixth class, have so much practical knowledge that the class book is used *Appendix.* with interest and intelligence. It is strange that in a district like Cork, which extends thirty miles through an agricultural district, there is not attached to any school a school garden, a model farm, or a dairy, although some of the teachers have farms which they cultivate profitably.

Book-keeping is taught in all the town and in a few of the rural schools, which are in charge of highly classed teachers. The answering is upon the whole good. In fifth class, both stages, the sets prescribed by their respective programmes are neatly written out, and the entries are well understood. In the sixth class also the fifth and sixth sets are carefully written, but the entries in the sixth set are in many cases not well understood. The complicated bill transactions dealt with in the sixth set render it difficult to be understood by mere school boys. Would a bank account added to the accounts of the fifth set not meet the requirements of modern trade?

As I stated in a previous part of this report, the schools of this district are so arranged that all the girls attending school are receiving instruction in Needlework. The proficiency in plain sewing and knitting is good. Cutting-out is only middling. This important branch has not hitherto received sufficient attention. In some of the Convent schools scientific dressmaking is taught. I cannot say much for the cutting-out as I very rarely see either teacher or pupil wearing a dress that she has cut out herself.

The Alternative Scheme, or Industrial Programme for the instruction of girls of Sixth class.—Within the past three years four schools that had obtained exemption, gave up the Literary for the Industrial Programme, and only two schools in which the Industrial Programme had been adopted have applied for permission to return to the Literary Programme. I was glad to learn from the teachers in whose schools the Industrial Programme had been adopted, that it was growing in favour with the parents of the children attending these schools, and that now most of the material required in school is supplied by the parents. The instruction given under this programme is sound and practical. This programme is at present in force in fifty-two schools of the Cork district. As a general rule it has not been adopted in the city schools.

Two of the four large Convent schools in Cork have not adopted it. In schools attended by considerable numbers of children, whose parents belong to the middle class in society, this programme has not found favour.

As a means of fostering local industries this scheme has not, as it is worked at present, carried out the intentions of its framers. The large schools have not assisted the smaller ones, as it was originally intended they should do. Each teacher, in selecting subjects, makes her selection of such as please herself without reference to what the other teachers in the same locality are doing. In some of the large Convent schools—notably Kinsale—the work done by the pupils readily found a market. In fact, the agents of some large manufacturers called upon the conductors of these schools and offered to provide material and pay a reasonable price for the work done. If the schools in the neighbourhood of Kinsale had been associated with the Convent in carrying out this programme, they would of course have obtained remunerative prices for the work done in their schools, and the work would have attained a much higher standard of excellence.

Drawing is taught in thirty-three schools. In the larger schools, especially those that have classes in connection with the Science and Art Department, the proficiency is high, very often quite in advance of the requirements of the programme. In the smaller schools the results are not so satisfactory, and in a few instances the instruction is valueless. In Kinsale Convent the pupils turn their knowledge to practical account by making patterns for the lace manufactured there.

Vocal Music is taught in forty-one schools. Hullah's system has been almost entirely superseded by the Tonic Sol-fa. In thirty of these schools the singing is excellent; in SS. Peter and Paul's female school especially, the proficiency is quite beyond the requirements of the programme. The pupils of Fifth and Sixth classes in this school can sing difficult music at sight. An attempt was made in 1894 to get up a public competition among the elementary schools in Cork, and the Corporation offered a liberal sum to be distributed as prizes, but it failed, as a sufficient number of competitors did not come forward.

Geometry and Mensuration is taught in thirty-four schools; in twelve of these courses of first, second, and third years are taught. Mensuration does not receive sufficient attention. The answering in Geometry is in general good.

Algebra is taught in forty-four schools; answering on courses of first and second year is good; answering on third year course is middling.

Physical Geography is taught in twelve schools; proficiency is very fair.

Girls' Reading Book and Domestic Economy are taught in six schools as an extra branch. The answering is generally very good. In most of the schools in which the Alternative Scheme has been adopted, one or other of these subjects is taught as a reading lesson.

Sewing machine and dressmaking are taught in twelve schools. The dressmaking has been greatly improved of late years.

Practical Cookery is taught in all the Convent schools, and SS. Peter and Paul's female in the City of Cork, and in Kinsale Convent. The course of instruction is eminently practical and valuable.

French is taught in eight schools—courses of first and second years. Pupils readily translate the portions of the works prescribed from French into English; translation from English into French and French Grammar are not well understood.

Kindergarten exercises are taught to infants in twelve schools. The pupils are always well up to the requirements of the programme on this subject.

Latin is taught in two schools only—courses of first and second years; answering is good.

Physical Science, Electricity and Magnetism, Light and Sound, and Hydrostatics are taught in two schools.

The course of instruction in these subjects consists chiefly of experiments, which are carefully explained by the teachers and well understood by the pupils.

School Accounts are neatly and honestly kept. I only found one case of falsification of accounts during the past three years.

I have the honour to be, Gentlemen, your obedient servant,

M. KENNAN, District Inspector.

The Secretaries,
Education Office.

(A) REPORT upon INDUSTRIAL INSTRUCTION, by the Directress of Needlework, Miss PRENDERGAST.

Appendix C.
Reports on State of Schools.
Report on Industrial Education.
Miss Prendergast.

June, 1895.

GENTLEMEN,—I have the honour to lay before you a short report on the state of industrial education during the past year.

These twelve months have not been fruitful in incident. I have not any doubt that industrial education advanced, if slowly, yet steadily, in some directions during this past year, but I have a disappointed hope to mourn. One event to which I looked forward with eager expectation for a long time has not come to pass—pressure of work in the Office has prevented for this year also the revision relating to the examination of teachers and monitresses. It is still possible for them to pass into the Board's service, or continue in it, utterly ignorant of the branches of needlework which they are, by rule, required to teach for an hour daily to all pupils above first class; the Inspector, who has full discretion in other matters, has in this no power to exclude even utterly incompetent candidates, and that many such receive the pay of the Commissioners I am obliged to believe when I appraise the specimens of sewing, knitting, darning, cutting-out, and dressmaking, produced at the July examinations each year.

The specimens executed in 1894 showed little improvement upon those of previous years—indeed, in a good many districts the percentage of satisfactory work in sewing and cutting-out fell below that of 1893. The subjects in which improvement was visible were darning and dressmaking. The gradually extending employment of a system has worked a beneficial change in the state of the latter subject, which is one possessed of interest for girls; and where a system has been taught one could generally see that carelessness or thoughtlessness, not actual ignorance, was the cause of failure. It is pleasant to be able to chronicle some extension of knowledge in this useful subject. But sewing is a distinctly more important branch, and the present condition of sewing among monitresses, as exhibited in their July examinations' work, is certainly far from satisfactory.

Work of monitresses at last examinations.

There are, of course, exceptions to every rule, and they gleam out here, too, like gems among the rubbish, in the form of finely-worked and finished specimens which it is a pleasure to examine; but they are rare—too rare. Common, on the other hand, are the hopelessly faulty productions of candidates whose ambition seems to rise no higher than the acquisition of the art of cobbling. What patches they devise; what clumsy gathers, pitchforked into crooked bands; above all, what buttonholes! It is irritating to remember that the industrial instruction of future generations of school-children may be at the mercy of these incompetents. Of all the branches of needlework in which candidates are examined, sewing shows least improvement during the past five years: yet the monitresses examined at end of third year must, for part of that time, have sewed for an hour daily. One wonders how they can have contrived to do so little. Darning has made some progress during the past twelve months as regards knowledge of the proper method, which seems better understood; but carelessness in execution often destroys the value of the work, even where a correct plan has been followed. To begin with, a total want of judgment is often exhibited in regard to the use of materials; the cotton web supplied to candidates is darned with wool—wool,

Darning.

sometimes thick enough to be fit for knitting a petticoat, sometimes fine enough to be used in embroidery. In the first case, the darn forms a clumsy excrescence; in the second, it fills the hole in the web with a cobweb-like fabric, without either substance or endurance. In either case it is wholly out of place, "like to like" being the principle suitably followed wherever there is question of the repair of a garment—wool to wool, cotton to cotton, silk to silk. Then, knots are made on the thread—the darn is worked entirely on the surface not to candidate without putting the stitch *under* the edge of the hole at all and so a thick border of web is left around that under side to form such a wedge as might easily blister the foot of any wearer of a sock so repaired. Or the woof-threads, in crossing, are run through instead of over and under, the warp-threads, splitting them, and injuring not only the appearance, but the durability of the darn. This is, perhaps, the commonest fault of all; but it is common enough, too, to find, after a couple of running stitches have been taken, the loops cut close all round the hole, so that a little stretching, such as must occur in drawing a stocking on or off, will pull the darn to pieces. This work is absolutely worthless. Of little worth is another class of darn, so sparely crossed that it is as full of holes as a sieve.

In the numerous cases wherein utter ignorance prevails, the tendency is always to ignore the fact that darning is intended as a means of repair for holes worn in stocking-web material, and that such material is, therefore, so thinned around the actual hole as to require strengthening by *run* darning stitches, these stitches being continued until the worker gets beyond the weak and rubbed spot, and finds a stronger portion of the web on which to take hold. Ignorant workers of this kind place a square of solid darn exactly over the hole, attached by single stitches to the thin part round it, from which the strong new work is liable to be rent by the friction of a few hours' wear. This mistake is encouraged by a plan which I find adopted in many schools—that of teaching darning upon calico—about as unsuitable material as could be found for the purpose. The calico being new, and giving strong hold to a single stitch, no running into the material around the darn is attempted; no loops are left to allow for the shrinkage of the new wool or cotton, when the already-shrunk sock or stocking goes to the wash, and, if the darn so produced remains in being at all, it remains as the centre of a mass of puckers. Old web—the sounder portions of discarded stockings, vests, etc., is within the reach of almost every teacher, and makes most suitable material for practising this subject.

In the Training Colleges I observe a general advance in needlework, though room for improvement still exists. The advance is, perhaps, most marked in Marlborough-street College, and least in Our Lady of Mercy. Sewing in all three colleges was nearly on a level; but the highest percentage of "good" and "excellent" work was produced by the students in Kildare-place. The quantity of "excellent" was, however, less than last year, and the quality of the "good" more mixed. Defective buttonholes, in all colleges, often reduced to the "middling" class sewing which, had these been better worked, might have ranked as "good." The best knitting—78 per cent of "excellent" and "good" —came from Church of Ireland College, where careful attention, with most satisfactory results, had evidently been bestowed upon this branch during the year. Dressmaking was highly successful, both in Our Lady of Mercy and Marlborough-street, average of passes being 98 and 91 per cent, and the great bulk of these either "excellent" or "good" ones.

Cutting out, in all colleges, I am sorry to say, was by no means so correct as one would wish to see it, and the defects most common—such as that of making the fronts so much too wide that, instead of simply allowing room for buttoning, they overlapped by four or five inches across the chest—appeared to me to be due to want of thought and attention on the part of the candidates. I am quite certain that the instructions given them on this subject, by the mistresses of work, would, had they been intelligently followed, have produced a very different result; but the best seed cannot bear good fruit in an unfertile soil. Immediate reward, in the shape of good marks to swell their total, not being forthcoming, a sense of duty to the children whose industrial instruction they hope to have in hands is not strong enough, in many cases, to secure the application necessary for enabling the student to acquire a thorough knowledge of the various branches of needlework. They have much to do, "extras" as well as obligatory subjects to acquire; and, until needlework has been made, by rule, an essential, and one carrying tempting marks, it is not in human nature to give it its just due.

Many feminine industries are connected with the use of the needle, and when, some years since, the Commissioners of Education offered to the Sixth Class girls attending their schools the benefit of the Alternative Scheme, they were giving them a measure of technical training which has not, so far, been appreciated as it deserved to be. Large towns have not, as a rule, adopted it with goodwill. Girls likely to become telegraphists, book-keepers, etc., are, of course, justified in devoting themselves to such branches of education as will best further them in their chosen way of life; but their numbers are comparatively small. Many who disdain to avail themselves of the technical training offered by the Alternative Scheme are destined to gain their living by their hands. But the "common" sense is wanting which would teach them that the earlier the training of those hands begins, the better. The proverb which tells us that a penny saved is a penny gained, is not a popular one in Ireland, if it were more so the country would be wealthier. As it is, people seem ashamed to save—perhaps still more ashamed to be thought to do it. The Alternative Scheme is very popular in some parts of the country, where parents, in a body, have become aware of its usefulness. Conductors of schools in these places tell me that a remarkable change for the better in the outward appearance, not only of their pupils, but of members of their pupils' families, is the result of the work taught and done in the school. With material obtained at wholesale rates from the Board's stores and with the girls' own labour, clothing becomes cheap and plentiful, and personal neatness is encouraged and made possible. Habits of thrift and of industry are inculcated together. It is an insertion of the thin edge of the wedge, an endeavour to implant in one-half of the rising generation the seeds of those qualities which make nations prosperous.

In consequence of the want of favour shown the scheme in some localities, it has, of late, been debated whether it might not be wise to abandon it, as condemned by public opinion; but I hope that this will not be done. It has, I think, too many possibilities of good in it to be lightly laid aside. Pruning is, doubtless, needed, and compromise may be, also; two subjects required instead of three, and less time, in proportion, devoted, making the teaching of the much prized arithmetic possible, and its fee payable—these changes are worthy of consideration, and the scheme would certainly gain much in general popularity were they made. I have ascertained so much as this by inquiries in schools. It would be a sad pity to abandon it before it had been given due trial

Appendix C.
Reports on State of Schools.
Report on Industrial Education.
Miss Province-ssel.
Progress of Industrial Departments.
and every reasonable chance of becoming a success, and it would, surely, seem a backward step to take, that of throwing overboard a scheme of technical instruction, just now, when other countries are doing their best to further such education in their schools.

That under proper supervision, Irish girls are capable of attaining excellent skill in manual occupations is proved by the record of the Industrial departments, which, in a good many instances, carry on and perfect the work of the Alternative Scheme. A review of the present position of these Departments may not be without interest. The total number now recognised by the Board is fifty-four. The number of pupils attending as recorded in notes taken for reports, averages one thousand three hundred and forty-two. Some of these are pupils who have passed twice in Sixth Class, and now spend part of their school day in the work-room; some are externs, who are occupied there according to their own convenience and desire, for periods of time varying from two to nine hours; and some—the least numerous contingent—are the monitresses of the schools, whose instruction is given by the special Industrial Teacher. Extern pupils generally attend with a view to qualifying themselves for situations as nursery maids having care of children's wardrobes), sewing maids (in hotels or large private houses), machinists and general working hands (in the workrooms of shops and warehouses). They receive, through the Industrial Department, knowledge which enables them to earn their bread in a better way than would be open to them without such instruction, besides acquiring habits of industry, mental activity (for few kinds of needlework can be successfully done without the co-operation of mind with body), and personal neatness; and they are also enabled, while passing through this apprenticeship to usefulness, to earn sums of money which either lessen the cost of their maintenance at home, or else remove it altogether. One department—that attached to the Convent School, Chapel-street, Newry—pays, on an average, as much as £1,800 yearly in wages to these girl workers; other schools follow, with smaller, but still important sums—£800, £600, £400.

Progress of lace-making.
The department at Carrickmacross, attached to the Bath and Shirley School, was, for many years, the centre of the lace industry which so powerfully helps to banish poverty from that district. Its two teachers were always ready to instruct workers, provide them with designs, copied for use, and negotiate for orders and sales. The character of the lace rose, and a combination of the two distinctive styles, guipure and appliqué, initiated by the principal Industrial teacher, produced a remarkably good effect, and was awarded first prize by the Judges at the Royal Dublin Society's Show, a couple of years ago. Shortly after this, however, the Home Industries Association established an agency of its own in Carrickmacross, and desired all workers anxious to sell their lace to deal direct with the agent; and, in this way, the best workers, old pupils of the Industrial Department, have been withdrawn from it, and its powers of usefulness sadly curtailed. It seems a pity that such a check should have been given to its progress just when that seemed most assured.

Departments in which lace is the principal industry carried on might be supposed to have taken "Excelsior" for their motto, for their aim is year by year, to advance in their delicate art, and produce more and more perfect and beautiful specimens of it. The affiliation of these schools to S. Kensington has done much to improve design in general, and to draw out individual talent for its production. Most of the patterns worked are now produced in the schools, either by gifted members of the communities conducting them, or by senior pupils, whose talent has been cultivated by a special artistic training.

The old-established lace-making centres, Youghal, Kenmare, New
Ross, Kinsale, etc., continue to produce lace of the highest quality, which
they are always seeking to perfect still further; and those more recently
founded are making rapid strides towards excellence. The flat needle-
point made in Killarney had reached a high standard of merit when I
last visited there; some of the workers, still young girls, promise to
become remarkably skilled. This class has made great progress during
the few years which have elapsed since the foundation of the Industrial
Department. In the Presentation Convent School, Killarney, excellent
"reticella" lace is made, and, also, English Point, of which a flounce
was ordered for Lady Aberdeen. The same Order of Nuns in Kilkenny
(I find recorded in notes of my last visit) have done a great deal with
Limerick lace, of a rich, heavily-worked character, suited for church
use, and this subject has made a decided advance in Canal-street Convent
National School, also. It is taught, too, in Golden-bridge Convent
National School, where the Sisters hope to make it a success.
Carlow Presentation Convent has a class of young pupils in training
for the working of flat needle-point.

In the last-mentioned Department a great deal of useful work of very
good quality is produced; and, for the same merit, a high one, I should
like to mention other schools having Departments attached, such as
Ennis, Gort, Oughterard, Stradbally (County Waterford), Stradbally
(Queen's County), Oldcastle National School, Cashel, Kinsale,
Clonakilty, Kilrush, Newtownsmith (Galway), Ballyshannon, Carrick-
on-Suir (Mercy and Presentation Convents), and Navan. There are
some specialities produced in these schools, such as the "Clare
Embroidery" of Ennis, of some pretty and delicate work, a combination of
embroidery and smocking, applied principally to children's garments,
which are made and finished with great taste and neatness. This work
was started at the school by Mrs. Vere O'Brien, who encourages it by
her interest and advice, and by procuring many orders for the Department. A fashionable children's outfitting house in London takes many
of the pretty smocks, and some have even been purchased by Her Royal
Highness Princess Beatrice, for her own little daughters' wear.
Ecclesiastical embroidery, in gold and silver, on sets of vestments, is a
prominent feature in the work of Gort and Stradbally (County
Waterford) Convent National Schools; guipure lace and drawn-thread
work in Oughterard; art embroidery on linen is beautifully done by
senior pupils in Newtownsmith; embroidery of a slightly different
character is very good in Convent of Mercy, Carrick-on-Suir. Bulgarian
embroidery in three colours is well done in Cashel Convent, whence it
is sent to a business house in London; drawn-thread and cut-linen work
are of fine quality in Kinsale; and excellent Mountmellick is produced
in Kilrush and Navan.

Besides these advanced branches, a large quantity of homely, but
very useful work is sent out from Industrial Departments. Nearly all
of them now teach dressmaking and some do so with great success;
an immense number of shirts and other articles of underclothing are
completed each year, and the pupils knit and crochet piles of warm
petticoats, vests, jerseys, jackets, caps, shawls, babies' bonnets, cloaks,
frocks and boots, gloves, slippers, mufflers, and other warm things;
some for sale, but the most for their own and their relatives' use.
Speaking generally, Industrial Departments have, in the last few years,
much increased in usefulness, and in the quantity and quality of the
work produced in them. Twenty of them are presided over by lay
teachers, some of whom are old in the Board's service, while others,

N

active and efficient, are but recently appointed; the remaining thirty-four Departments are in charge of Nuns. To these latter belong nearly all the conspicuously successful ones, those remarkable either for high quality or large quantity of the work produced, and for the amount of solid benefit conferred upon the pupils.

To the help and improvement of these girls the Sisters devote themselves with admirable energy, patience, and self sacrifice. Even the brief time allowed them for necessary relaxation is, often, ungrudgingly devoted to the advancement of the work of their Department, the writing of necessary letters, the keeping of accounts. In some large workrooms, where many extern pupils are receiving instruction and earning wages other Sisters have to give time and help, to enable the Nun in special charge to cope successfully with her volume of work. This is the case in Ballyshannon Convent National School, which though a very recently founded Department, has rapidly developed into a large and still growing one. A considerable knitting industry is carried on here.

Nearly all the extern pupils attending special industrial classes are ex-pupils of the schools.

Some of the Departments in charge of lay teachers are not so active by any means as one would desire to see them; but these dark spots, too, have a use of their own. They serve to throw up more brilliantly the high lights of the picture, and give value to its half lights; and it would be unreasonable, I suppose, to demand, like Queen Elizabeth, one painted without shadow.

I have the honour to be, Gentlemen,

Your obedient servant,

M. PRENDERGAST,

Directress of Needlework.

To the Secretaries.

NATIONAL SCHOOLS HAVING SPECIAL INDUSTRIAL DEPARTMENTS.

(5.)—SYNOPSIS of REPORTS by DISTRICT INSPECTORS on SCHOOL DEPARTMENTS coming within the provisions of Rule 53 (Industrial Instruction), viz.:—

(a.) In National Schools whose managers desire that special provision be made for the instruction and training of Externs, as well as female pupils who have passed through the Sixth Class, in embroidery and other advanced kinds of needlework or other approved branches of industrial instruction for females, a salary dependent upon the circumstances of the case may be awarded to a Special Industrial Teacher thoroughly qualified to organize and conduct such instruction.

(b.) Such Teacher will be charged with the general supervision of the entire Industrial Education in the School, including the plain needlework, &c., prescribed in the programme of the several classes, and will be personally responsible for the efficient instruction and training of a Special Industrial Class composed of extern young women, and such pupils as may have passed through the ordinary literary course of the School.

(c.) Each member of the Special Industrial Class must be engaged in receiving Industrial instruction daily, for such time as in consideration of the nature of the industry pursued may be deemed adequate.

(d.) The recognition of a Special Industrial Teacher will not relieve the ordinary female teachers of the School from the obligation of giving efficient practical instruction under the supervision of the Special Industrial Teacher, in plain needlework, &c., to the pupils of the school classes as prescribed in the programmes, and particularly to the girls of the Sixth Class, under the Alternative Scheme approved for that class.

(e) To warrant the recognition of a Special Industrial Teacher, there must be a separate work-room suitably furnished and used for the instruction of the Special Industrial Class. The instruction, however, of the several classes in needlework, &c., and of the Sixth Class in the Alternative Scheme, may be carried on wholly or partly by the teachers in this work-room.

(f.) The remuneration of the Special Industrial Teacher from the Commissioners is limited to the personal salary awarded to her, but the Commissioners strongly recommend that such salary be augmented from local sources by the Patron or Manager of the School.

(g.) In every Industrial Department, a separate Roll Book, and separate Daily Report Book, must be kept for the Special Industrial Class.

DISTRICT 5.—BALLYSHANNON CONVENT.

INDUSTRIAL DEPARTMENT.

This Industrial Department has been in operation since November, 1893. The number of pupils on the roll was 33, of whom 28 were externs, and the number present on the day of inspection was 31; engaged at machine knitting, dressmaking, shirt and underclothes making, and grafting and pressing. The work material is supplied partly by the community and partly by the local shop-keepers. A portion of the made garments is returned to the shop-keepers, and the remainder is supplied on private orders. The garments supplied on private orders are sold. The pupils receive from 1s. 6d. to 8s. per week.

DISTRICT 8.—CRUMLIN ROAD CONVENT, BELFAST.

INDUSTRIAL DEPARTMENT.

This Industrial Department has been in operation for more than a quarter of a century, and the teacher is proficient in the various branches of dressmaking, knitting, crocheting, lace-making, sprigging, and art needlework; she also possesses the necessary knowledge of drawing and understands its application to scientific dress cutting and tracing patterns for embroidery.

There were 26 pupils on the rolls, of whom 13 were externs; and on the day of inspection 22 of those pupils were found engaged on the various branches indicated, with very satisfactory results.

N 2

The proficiency of the pupils of the literary school in plain needlework, knitting, &c., is good, and very good in the various branches of the Alternative Scheme.

The work material is supplied to some extent by the pupils, but mainly by the community, and the finished work is either given to poor children or used by the pupils.

DISTRICT 19.—CANAL STREET CONVENT, NEWRY.

INDUSTRIAL DEPARTMENT.

This Industrial Department has been in operation since 1853, and the teacher is well qualified in all branches of needlework, including dressmaking, cutting out, plain sewing, knitting, crochet and crewel work, lace making (Limerick and point), embroidery, ecclesiastical work, satin stitch, drawn linen work, hem stitching, and veining.

The number on the rolls was 54, of whom 47 were externs, and 38 were present on the day of inspection engaged on fine underclothing in silk, linen, &c., lace making, and ecclesiastical embroidery. This was for the most part work that had been recently ordered, some of it was completed and ready for despatch, and some still in the hands of the the workers. A few of the less experienced girls were engaged in work requiring not so much skill, such as ordinary underclothing and men's shirts.

A few of those who give orders supply the material: in other cases it is supplied by the community. The finished work is sold in England, in the Colonies, and locally. The pupils receive from 1s. to 10s. per work according to the ability of the worker. The amount paid in wages annually is about £800. The proficiency in needlework of the pupils and monitors in the literary school is good, and the Alternative Scheme is successfully carried out. A number of Sixth Class pupils and monitors were presented in sewing machine and scientific dressmaking: they showed good skill in this useful branch.

DISTRICT 19.—ROSTREVOR CONVENT.

INDUSTRIAL DEPARTMENT.

This Industrial Department has been in operation since 1867. The teacher is qualified to teach all branches of plain sewing, cutting out and dressmaking, also Limerick and point lace, Mountmellick work, embroidery, knitting, crochet and crewel work.

There were 9 pupils on the roll (7 being externs), of whom 8 were present on day of inspection engaged at various articles of fine underclothing in response to an order from a lady in London.

Some of the ladies giving orders for work send their own material; in all other cases material is supplied by the community. The finished work is sold in England and locally in cases where it is not made up to order.

The pupils receive 2s. 6d. to 7s. 6d., or 10s. per week according to ability.

The pupils of the literary school showed on the whole very fair proficiency in the various requirements of the results programme in needlework. Only one Sixth Class girl was presented in the Alternative Scheme; she displayed evidence of having had sufficient practice in the industrial branches. The monitors are proficient in needlework, and superior work is done by the extern members of the industrial class.

District 28.—St. Joseph's Convent, Longford.

Appendix C.
Reports on State of Schools.

Industrial Department.

This Industrial Department has been in operation since 1861. The industrial teacher is competent to give instruction in plain and fancy needlework, knitting (by hand and machine), macrame, Berlin woolwork, Mountmellick and art needlework. There are 56 pupils on the rolls (including 18 externs), of whom 23 were present on the day of inspection engaged at shirtmaking and machine knitting, Mountmellick work and art needlework.

St. Joseph's Convent, Longford, Industrial Department.

Mr. O'Cain.

The material for shirtmaking is supplied by Johnson's shirt factory, of Mullingar, and the finished shirts are returned. The community supply material for articles of hosiery and the Sixth Class pupils supply their own materials.

A commission is paid for shirtmaking by Johnson of Mullingar. Articles of hosiery are made to order—the Sixth Class pupils retain their own finished work. Payment is made at the rate of from 2s. to 6s. per week according to proficiency. The proficiency of the pupils of the literary school in needlework, cutting out, &c. is satisfactory.

District 29.—Kells Convent.

Kells Convent, Industrial Department.

Dr. Mura.

Industrial Department.

The Industrial Department has been in operation since September, 1890. The teacher was educated at Cabra, where she received instruction in all kinds of needlework from trained and well-qualified teachers.

There were twenty-one pupils on the Rolls (including four externs), of whom twenty were present on the day of examination engaged at dressmaking, shirtmaking, Mountmellick work, crewel work, fancy knitting, crocheting, baby clothes, darning, repairs, &c.

The community supply materials for clothing for the orphanage, and shopkeepers in town send materials to be made up. The finished work is kept by the nuns (for orphanage) or paid for by the shops sending the material. Pupils make up their own material for their own use. The extern pupils are paid 3s. to 4s. per week according to work done.

The proficiency of the pupils of the literary department in plain needlework, knitting, &c., was satisfactory.

District 29.—Navan (N) Convent.

Navan (N) Convent, Industrial Department.

Dr. Hara.

Industrial Department.

This Industrial Department has been in operation since January, 1892. The teacher is a highly qualified nun who was educated at Sion Hill Dominican Convent, Blackrock, County Dublin.

There were thirty-two pupils on the Rolls (including twelve externs), of whom thirty-one were present on the day of examination, engaged, with good results, at shirtmaking, ladies' underclothing, dressmaking, knitting, crochet, crewel work, Macrame lace, Mountmellick work, &c.

Appendix C.
Reports on
State of
Schools.

The work material is supplied by the nuns, and the finished work is disposed of to the friends of the community; the pupils receive from 1s. 6d. to 5s. per week according to efficiency and dexterity.

The proficiency of the pupils of the literary school in needlework, knitting, &c., was fairly satisfactory.

King's
Inns-street
Convent,
Industrial
Department.

Mr.
Barrelow.

DISTRICT 30.—KING'S INNS-STREET CONVENT, DUBLIN.

INDUSTRIAL DEPARTMENT.

This Industrial Department has been in operation since April, 1888. The teacher can instruct in all kinds of plain and fancy work, dress making with use of sewing machine, children's tailoring, designing. She holds a certificate from the Scientific Dress Cutting Association. There were forty pupils on the Rolls, none of them being externs, and thirty-nine were present on the day of examination engaged on the branches specified above. The work material is supplied principally by the pupils themselves—the rest by the nuns—the pupils retain the garments made from the materials which they supply—the others are disposed of in charity. None of the work is sold.

The proficiency of the pupils of the literary department in plain needlework, knitting, &c., was satisfactory.

Oughterard
Convent,
Co. Galway,
Industrial
Department.

Mr. B'riys.

DISTRICT 34.—OUGHTERARD CONVENT, CO. GALWAY.

INDUSTRIAL DEPARTMENT.

This Industrial Department has been in operation since October, 1889. The teacher is well qualified to teach dressmaking, woollen, and crochet work, Mountmellick work, lace, guipure, and English point, embroidery, sprigging, drawn thread work, and the use of the knitting machine. There were 19 pupils on the Roll (9 externs), of whom 17 were present on the day of inspection engaged at guipure lace, Mountmellick work, wool work, and drawn-thread work. In every case, even in those of pupils engaged in lace-making, the work was being executed deftly and with intelligence.

The work material is supplied by the community, and the finished work is disposed of partly by sale in the locality and partly by orders. The pupils receive from 1s. 6d. to 4s. per week. The general proficiency of the pupils of the literary school in plain needlework, knitting, &c., was excellent.

Newtown-
smith
Convent,
Co. Galway,
Industrial
Department.

Mr. Welply.

DISTRICT 34.—NEWTOWNSMITH CONVENT, CO. GALWAY.

INDUSTRIAL DEPARTMENT.

The Industrial Department has been in operation since July, 1856. The teacher was trained in a boarding school attached to another convent, and a book-binder from Dublin was specially engaged to instruct her and a class at the same time. The branches taught are book-binding, shirtmaking, dressmaking, glovemaking (i.e., knitting of gloves), woollen crochet, knitting, guipure lace, Macrame, cut work, embroidery, drawn-thread work, Mountmellick work, crewel work, leather work, fret work, watch guards, Hungarian embroidery, Glengarry work.

There were 30 pupils on the Roll of the Industrial Department (10 being externs), of whom 11 were present on the day of inspection. Two pupils were engaged at guipure lace-making and drawn thread work, and 9 pupils at book-binding in the room specially devoted to that purpose. Several specimens of newly finished work in each kind were exhibited.

The work material is purchased and the finished work is disposed of locally by sale. The pupils receive from 2s. 6d. to 4s. per week. The needlework of the literary department, except in the Sixth Class, is below the average proficiency, owing to the want of efficient supervision and to the time (9.30 to 10.30 o'clock, a.m.) devoted to instruction in this branch, when a full attendance of pupils cannot be ensured. The pupils of Sixth Class displayed a satisfactory knowledge of their needlework programme as well as of the special industrial branches selected under the Alternative Scheme. In the other industrial branches, already enumerated, considerable technical skill has been attained.

DISTRICT 40.—BLACKROCK CONVENT, CO. DUBLIN.

INDUSTRIAL DEPARTMENT.

The Industrial Department has been in operation since 1868. It is in charge of a classed teacher who has studied and practised all the branches of her work under professional teachers. The branches taught are scientific dressmaking, woolwork, shirtmaking, underclothing, knitting, and Mountmellick work. There were 17 pupils on the Roll (including 11 externs), of whom 12 were present on the day of inspection engaged at shirtmaking, wool work, and Mountmellick work. The work material is supplied partly by the children and partly by the community. The pupils retain their finished work; the rest is given to the poor.

The proficiency of the pupils of the literary department in plain needlework, knitting, &c., is generally very good.

DISTRICT 42.—GORT CONVENT, COUNTY GALWAY.

INDUSTRIAL DEPARTMENT.

This Industrial Department has been in operation since June, 1891. The teacher has over twenty years experience in various places under the community. The branches taught are weaving, embroidery, knitting, shirtmaking, sewing machine, advanced dressmaking, and Mountmellick work. There were sixteen pupils on the Roll (including one extern), all of whom were present on the day of inspection, engaged, with satisfactory results, on the various branches indicated. The work material is supplied by the community, and the finished work is sold in Ireland, England, and South Africa; the pupils receive from 3s. to 5s. per week.

The proficiency of the pupils of the literary school in plain needlework, knitting, &c., and in the Alternative Scheme branches (weaving and Mountmellick work) is in every way satisfactory. The sister in charge (Industrial Teacher), two work mistresses paid by the community, and a weaver form the staff which is quite sufficient.

DISTRICT 44.—CARLOW PRESENTATION CONVENT.

INDUSTRIAL DEPARTMENT.

This Industrial Department was established in 1868, and re-organised in 1889. The teacher being a member of the community, has had a long experience at, and a natural taste for, industrial work. The branches taught are underclothing, dressmaking, lace-making, shirt-making, knitting, and crocheting, and clerical garments. There were twenty-nine pupils on the Roll (including seventeen externs), of whom seventeen were present on the day of inspection engaged at dressmaking, lace-making, underclothing, knitting, and crocheting.

The work material is partly bought, and partly supplied by the community, and the finished work is disposed of by sale in London, and to local shopkeepers. The pupils receive from 1s. to 4s. per week, according to proficiency.

The proficiency of the pupils of the literary department in plain needlework and knitting was of a satisfactory character. The teaching power is adequate.

DISTRICT 44.—STRADBALLY CONVENT, QUEEN'S COUNTY.

INDUSTRIAL DEPARTMENT.

This Industrial Department has been in operation since January, 1890, under a teacher who has been trained from girlhood in most of the branches taught, and has received special training in the remainder. The branches taught are ladies' fine underclothing, baby linen, shirt-making, crocheting, plain and fancy aprons, pinafores, underskirts, plain and embroidered, sprigging and marking on handkerchiefs, Mountmellick work, crewel work, and knitting. There were twenty-eight pupils on the Roll (including twenty-two externs), of whom twenty-two were present on day of inspection, engaged at Mountmellick work, dressmaking, underclothing, shirtmaking, embroidery, crochet work, crewel work, and fancy aprons.

The work material is supplied by the community, and the finished work is disposed of by means of a saleswoman. Payment is made to the pupils in kind, and varies according to the proficiency displayed. The proficiency of the pupils of the literary department in plain needle-work, knitting, &c., was good. The teaching power is adequate and efficient.

DISTRICT 45.—ENNIS CONVENT, CO. CLARE.

INDUSTRIAL DEPARTMENT.

This Industrial Department has been in operation since April, 1891, under a teacher qualified in the various branches of needlework, knitting, dressmaking, and fancy work.

The number of pupils on the roll was 28 (including 16 externs), of whom 20 were present on day of inspection, engaged at Mountmellick work, shirtmaking, Clare embroidery, and needlework.

The work material is supplied by the community, and the finished work is sold: the pupils receive the profit remaining over after paying

cost of material. The proficiency of the pupils of the literary department in plain needlework, knitting, &c., is good. The externs are earning some small amounts, which help to afford them a respectable livelihood, and there is a ready sale, particularly in the early portion of the
year, for the articles made.

District 45.—Kilkee Convent, Co. Clare.

Industrial Department.

This Industrial Department has been in operation since January,
1892, under a qualified teacher, the branches taught being crochet,
Mountmellick work, point lace, silk embroidery, macrame work, all
branches of needlework, dressmaking, and cutting-out, shirtmaking,
and crewel work. There were 41 pupils on the rolls (including 32
externs), of whom 15 were present on the day of inspection, very efficient
work being done at dressmaking, fancy work, crochet, and point lace.
The work material is supplied partly by the community and partly by
the pupils, and of the finished work some is sold, some kept by the
pupils for their own use, and some given by the community to poor
children. After recouping the cost of materials, the pupils get the
balance in proportion to the amount of work done.

The pupils of the literary school are well prepared in plain needlework, knitting, &c., and the teaching power is adequate.

District 45.—Kilrush Convent, Co. Clare.

Industrial Department.

This Industrial Department has been in operation for 36 years. It is
conducted by a qualified teacher, the branches taught being crochet,
Mountmellick work, point lace, silk embroidery, macrame work, all
kinds of needlework, dressmaking, and cutting-out, shirtmaking, and
crewel work. There were 43 pupils (including 33 externs) on rolls, of
whom 23 were present on the day of inspection engaged at dressmaking,
embroidery, and lacemaking.

The work material is supplied partly by the community and partly
by the pupils, and of the finished work some is kept by the pupils for
their own use, and some given by the community to poor children.
After recouping cost of materials, the pupils get the balance in proportion to amount of work done.

The pupils of the literary department are well prepared in the various
branches coming under the head of needlework, and the Industrial programme is satisfactorily carried out in Sixth Class. The teaching power
is adequate.

District 49.—New Ross Convent (1), Co. Wexford.

Industrial Department.

This Department has been in operation since January, 1891, and is
conducted by a teacher with a thorough knowledge of the various
industrial subjects taught, viz., rose-point lace, flat-point lace, Spanish
point lace, guipure lace, crochet and Mountmellick work.

The number of pupils on the rolls (including 42 externs) was 41, of whom 29 were present on the day of inspection engaged on the branches indicated above.

The work material is supplied by the nuns, and the finished work is disposed of by sale to merchants in London, Paris, and New York. The workers receive from 4s. to 10s. per week. The proficiency of the pupils of the literary department in plain needlework, knitting, &c., is fair. The industrial programme has been taught with fair success as regards the subjects woollen and crochet work and macramé work.

The number of girls and adults employed in the Industrial Department varies from 25 to 35; as a proof of their skill it may be mentioned that some of them obtained first prizes at the Kirkby Lonsdale and Royal Dublin Society's Exhibitions of work. The teaching power is adequate.

DISTRICT 48.—YOUGHAL CONVENT, Co. CORK.

INDUSTRIAL DEPARTMENT.

This Department has been in operation since June, 1889. The branches taught are Youghal lace, dressmaking, and art needlework.

The number of pupils on the roll (including 83 externs) was 38, of whom 30 were present on the day of inspection engaged on the branches indicated above.

Part of the work materials is bought by the pupils, and part is supplied by the community—some of the finished work is sold, including all the lace, and some is kept by the pupils for their own use. The lace workers receive from 2s. to 10s. per week.

Adequate work was shown in plain sewing, knitting, &c., by the pupils of the literary department.

DISTRICT 47.—ST. PATRICK'S CONVENT, KILKENNY.

INDUSTRIAL DEPARTMENT.

This Industrial Department has been in operation since June, 1891. The branches taught are plain needlework in all its branches, crocheting in wool and cotton, knitting, lace making, macramé work, and ecclesiastical embroidery.

The number of pupils on the roll (including 22 externs) was 35, of whom 29 were present on the day of inspection, engaged with satisfactory results at the various branches indicated above.

The work material is supplied by the nuns, and the finished work is disposed of by sale, locally, and by orders from other places. The pupils receive from 1s. to 6s. per week, according to the proficiency of the worker.

The proficiency of the pupils of the literary department in plain needlework, knitting, &c., was satisfactory; the work done is much appreciated, and the teaching power is adequate.

DISTRICT 47.—PRESENTATION CONVENT, KILKENNY.

INDUSTRIAL DEPARTMENT.

This Industrial Department has been in operation since 1888, under a duly qualified teacher. The branches taught are plain and fancy needlework, dressmaking, knitting, crocheting, lacemaking (Limerick, torchon, macramé) and ecclesiastical embroidery.

There were sixty-three pupils (including thirty-three externs) on the rolls, of whom sixty-two were present on the day of inspection, engaged with very satisfactory results on the branches enumerated above.

The work material is supplied by the community, but bought by the pupils; the finished work is sold to pupils and others—the pupils receiving from 3s. to 6s. per week. This department continues to make satisfactory progress: a large number of children and young women receive at once industrial instruction and payment; the instruction may be the means of earning a respectable livelihood hereafter, and the present wages are a sensible help to their families. There is a considerable local demand for the work, especially in dressmaking, and for the laces made there is a good demand from other places in Ireland. This is especially the case as regards ecclesiastical embroidery.

District 53.—Carrick-on-Suir Convent, Co. Tipperary.

Industrial Department.

This Industrial Department has been in operation since January, 1880, and is conducted by a teacher well qualified in the various branches taught. The number of pupils on the rolls (including fourteen externs) was twenty-two, all of whom were present on the day of inspection engaged at shirtmaking, dressmaking, knitting stockings by hand and machine, crewel work and marking.

Some of the work material is supplied by the community, some by local traders, and some by the pupils. Of the finished work, some is given to the poor, and some returned to the traders—the pupils receive from 3s. to 6s. per week.

Needlework and knitting are taught to the pupils of the literary school in a very satisfactory manner.

The teaching power of the department is sufficient.

District 54.—Castleisland Convent, County Kerry.

Industrial Department.

This Industrial Department has been in operation since September, 1893. The branches taught are dressmaking, making-up of underclothing, knitting, crocheting of all kinds, crewel embroidery, baby clothes, and little boys' suits.

There were 58 pupils (including 39 externs) on the rolls, of whom 33 were present on the day of inspection engaged in a satisfactory manner on the various branches specified above.

The work material is supplied by the manager, who is the Superioress of the Convent, and the finished work is sold, the pupils receiving what can be afforded after cost of materials and expenses of sale have been discharged; the nuns make no profit on the sales.

The proficiency of the pupils of the Literary Department in plain needlework, knitting, &c., was moderate; the teaching staff is adequate.

DISTRICT 54.—MOUNTMELLICK CONVENT, COUNTY KERRY.

INDUSTRIAL DEPARTMENT.

This Industrial Department has been recognised since January, 1892.
The branches taught are embroidery, quiltmaking, designs for table-
covers, coseys, afternoon-tea cloths, sachets, fire-screens, Mountmellick
work, &c.

There were 31 pupils (including 16 externs) on the rolls, of whom
24 were present on the day of inspection engaged on the various branches
indicated.

The work material is supplied partly by the nuns, but principally by
private families ; the finished work is disposed of partly by sale, and
the rest is returned as manufactured articles to those who supplied the
raw material. The pupils receive from 1s. 6d. to 8s. per week, according
to the quality of the work done.

The proficiency of the pupils of the Literary Department in plain
needlework, knitting, &c., was good, and the teaching power is adequate
and efficient.

DISTRICT 55.—DONERAILE CONVENT, COUNTY CORK.

INDUSTRIAL DEPARTMENT.

This Industrial Department has been in operation since June, 1891,
and is in charge of a teacher who is proficient in cutting-out, dressmaking, and all kinds of plain needlework, and who has a fair knowledge of fancy work. The number of pupils on the rolls (including 14
externs) was 22, of whom 13 were present on the day of inspection
engaged at dressmaking, shirtmaking, flowermaking, crewel work,
macramé work, and knitting, with very good results. The work
material is supplied partly by the Community, and some by the public
who pay for the work done for them ; the finished work is given either
to the owner, or in charity to the poorer pupils and to others. The
payment varies (according to the amount of work executed) from 1s. to
2s. per week.

The proficiency of the pupils of the Literary School in plain needlework, knitting, &c., is good, and the teaching staff is adequate.

DISTRICT 56.—MITCHELSTOWN CONVENT, COUNTY CORK.

INDUSTRIAL DEPARTMENT.

This Industrial Department has been in operation since June, 1893,
and is conducted by a teacher who is competent to teach all kinds of
plain needlework, and many branches of fancy work.

The number of pupils on the roll (including 20 externs) was 48, of
whom 33 were present on the day of inspection engaged, with good
results, at dressmaking, shirtmaking, ladies' underclothing, crewel work,
Berlin woolwork, Mountmellick work, embroidery, knitting, and crochet.

The work material is supplied by the Community gratis to poor
children, at cost price to others ; and, as regards the finished work, some
is retained by the pupils who have purchased the materials, the rest is
given in charity to poor children. None of the work is sold.

The proficiency of the pupils of the Literary Department in plain
needlework and knitting is good, and the teaching power is adequate.

DISTRICT 59.—SKIBBEREEN CONVENT, COUNTY CORK.

INDUSTRIAL DEPARTMENT.

This Industrial Department has been in operation since 1860. The branches taught are knitting and crochet work, dressmaking, Mountmellick work, and fine underclothing.

There were 27 pupils (including 5 externs) on the rolls, of whom only 4 were present on the day of inspection. Of the work material, some is supplied by the Community and some by the pupils; the finished work is given to the poor.

The proficiency of the pupils of the Literary Department in plain needlework, knitting, &c., was fair.

REPORT on the MODEL FARMS and AGRICULTURAL SCHOOLS by the Superintendent of the Agricultural Department, Mr. CARROLL.

GENTLEMEN,—I beg to submit my report upon the Agricultural Department for 1894.

The progress of this department has been satisfactory.

The agricultural institutions at Glasnevin and Cork have had a fair number of pupils in attendance.

The agricultural schools and schools to which gardens are attached, have made fair progress. At some of these schools I can report considerable improvement.

The department for dairy instruction has been very successful. The creameries visited by the instructor appointed for the purpose of inspecting and giving instruction in creameries, appear to have derived considerable benefit from the visits of the instructor.

The system of itinerant dairy instruction given by skilled instructors, appears to be very successfully extending, and I am hopeful that this most useful branch of industrial instruction will before long have wide spread developments.

In respect of the agriculture of the country generally, the vicissitudes of the potato crop, the barley crop, pork production, and the dairy, during the year have had most interest for the Irish farmer.

The periodically recurring disease has, in 1894, done considerable damage to the potatoes in many parts of Ireland.

The country was not uniformly subjected to the evil influence of this blight, but several districts suffered severely.

The origin of the disease, and the method by which it is renewed from year to year, are still subjects that may be classed as unsettled, and until laborious scientific investigation shall have definitely set at rest speculation upon these points, we cannot calculate upon complete preventive or remedial measures being available.

It is satisfactory, however, to note that during 1894 the preventive system devised by M. Alené Girard has been eminently successful in Ireland, and there is evidence sufficient to prove that when properly applied the sulphate of copper preparation, *bouillie Bordelaise*, is an almost complete preventive of the potato blight.

In many parts of the country complete freedom from disease was assured through the careful application of this preventive, whereas

Appendix O.
Reports on
State of
schools.

Mr.
Carroll,
Superin-
tendents of
Agricul-
tural De-
partment.

several cases of non-success of the *bouillie Bordelaise*, through the absence of intelligent direction in application of the mixture, have come under my notice.

I have frequently stated my opinion—1st, that the dressing must be applied before the disease makes its appearance; 2nd, that every effort should be made to give a fine coating of the mixture to the upper surfaces of the potato leaves; 3rd, that if the upper surfaces of the potato leaves are coated with the mixture there will be no necessity for dressing the under surfaces of the leaves.

I am of opinion that the danger to the tubers consists in allowing the fungus spores to attack the leaves from above, and that the disease reaches the tubers of the plant through spores being produced upon the undersides of the leaves, and thence falling upon the ground to be washed through the earth to the immature tubers.

In several instances I have noticed ineffectual spraying of potatoes resulting from attempts made to direct the spray towards the undersides of the leaves. When fine mould (the aerial Hyphae of the fungus) appears on the underside of the leaves, the disease has got hold of the plant and dressings as preventive are almost valueless.

For Ireland the potato crop and its proper cultivation are matters of first importance, and every effort should be made to enable the farmers of backward districts to cultivate the crop so that satisfactory results may be secured.

Change of seed and the ensuring that varieties true to name shall be grown will do much in this direction.

When one considers the large sums of money that are annually expended in the purchase of potatoes for planting in Ireland, and the haphazard way in which the trade in importing seed is carried on, it would appear that some systematic method of dealing with this question at home would be desirable. I have in previous reports stated my opinion that the interchange of potatoes for seed in Ireland would be found to be satisfactory.

Experiments made upon the farms of agricultural schools in different parts of Ireland with seed potatoes grown in the county Dublin as against imported Scotch seed potatoes have shown that there was really no difference in the produce. I believe that there are in this country all the conditions necessary for the useful interchange of seed potatoes.

Experiments to test these points have already been carried out in the Agricultural Department of the Commissioners. These experiments will be continued.

The Barley Crop.— For some considerable time the cultivation of barley was profitably carried on in various districts of Ireland. The farmers of land suitable to it had the most hopeful expectations. Latterly, however, prices for this grain gave way, and it was supposed that barley growing in Ireland must dwindle as in the case of wheat growing. At the present time the growth of barley in Ireland is precarious, and the question of its continuance or abandonment is seriously debated.

Various causes are assigned for this depression, such as the use of matters other than barley in brewing; the importation of foreign barley from various countries; the want of due care on the part of our Irish farmers in the cultivation of the crop; and especially the want of care in preparing the grain for market.

Some attempts will be made by way of experiment at the farms of the Commissioners to determine points that have been discussed recently as to successful or profitable cultivation of barley in Ireland.

The main questions to be decided will be (1) as to the influence of change of seed upon productiveness in the crop; (2) whether manuring for barley should be done by means of a preceding manurial crop or through the media of artificial manures applied directly to the crop in its cultivation; (3) the amelioration of the soil either by drawings of salt, or through the application of lime for the crop.

There is unquestionably on the part of maltsters a desire for home-grown barleys in preference to those of foreign growth, but in consequence of a fickle climate, and probably of want of skill in treating home-grown barley, our present position in the growing of barley is that although we should produce as good or perhaps a better grain, we do not put it upon the markets in as good condition as that of foreign growth.

The swine industry of the country has been gradually declining, and the outlook of this very important business is at present gloomy.

The improvement in the breeds of pigs in America along with the large production of Indian corn in that country has done much to depress our Irish trade. A new competitor, also, has recently appeared in the Danish farmers and bacon curers, so that an industry that has been regarded hitherto as peculiarly Irish is almost threatened with extinction.

The growth of the bacon trade in Denmark is one of the evidences of the forethought of the people of that country, and a result of care on the part of the Government. It is not long since the Danish bacon trade was confined to Germany. The quality of the Danish pigs and pork was so low that the English markets were not available to Danish bacon. Now this is all altered. Some of the highest priced bacon on the London market comes from Denmark, and the bacon curers of Ireland have to contend against an improving manufacture, so that unless there is a fair measure of improvement in this country on the part of the breeders and feeders of swine, along with a corresponding improvement in the systems of manufacture, the Irish bacon trade must decline.

There is every reason for hope, that with improved methods this very important industry may be retained, but our farmers and especially the small occupiers who are really the pork producers must endeavour to improve their methods (1) by keeping the best stock; that is, the most suitable for the markets, and (2) by producing in the most economical way the meat that can be converted to the most valuable bacon.

Experiments upon breeds and upon systems of feeding pigs have been carried out at Glasnevin and at the Munster Dairy School. These will be continued and arrangements are being made to co-operate with the Bacon Curers' Association of the South of Ireland, with a view of carrying on experiments in pig feeding in order to promote more effectively the means of dealing with this very important agricultural work.

The dairying industry of Ireland during 1894 was certainly in a depressed condition, and although there have been strong and persistent efforts made to raise the condition of dairying in Ireland to a profitable state, the competition of foreign produce renders the problem one of much difficulty.

Co-operation in dairying will do much to improve the position of farmers, and although systematic co-operation is at present confined to creameries, I consider that there are districts in Ireland within which creameries would not be successful, and where a system of co-operation in the marketing of butter upon the Normandy system would be suitable.

The instruction in dairying which is now available through the Agricultural Department of the National Education Commissioners will, if availed of, do much service in promoting improvement in butter production in places where cows are held only in small numbers by small

Appendix C.

Reports on State of Schools.

Mr. Carroll, Superintendent of Agricultural Department.

farmers, and already it may be noted that there is a growing desire for information in districts so circumstanced in the Province of Ulster.

The Instructor appointed by the Commissioners for the purpose of visiting creameries has been fully occupied during the year. His work has been mainly in the direction of giving instruction in the testing of milk for adulteration, and in giving information as to dealing with difficulties arising from high temperature during summer weather.

The itinerant instruction in dairying which has been recently organized was availed of in the Counties of Cork and Kerry to some considerable extent. At Newmarket and Kingwilliamstown there were classes held, and the attendances at the instruction were very large.

I feel confidence in stating that as the benefits of this instruction become known there will be a large demand for the services of Dairy Instructors.

I should like to see the system of dairy instruction that is prescribed for rural National Schools, under qualified female teachers, more generally adopted by managers. The girls of the higher classes should have opportunities for acquiring a knowledge of the principles and practice of improved dairying. I believe that great improvement in knowledge of dairy management may come through instruction given to the young people of the agricultural classes. It is extremely difficult to persuade a peasant of mature years that the methods practised by him during a long period are not perfect.

There are many districts in Ireland in which there are small farmers who keep few cows, and where the systems of dairying are extremely careless. In such districts the practice of dairying cannot be profitable. I should like to see the National Schools made use of in the evenings for instruction to young persons in dairying, and I shall recommend that a trial of such instruction be made in certain districts.

The classes for instruction to creamery managers that were established at Glasnevin and at the Munster Agricultural School have been successful. I am strengthened in the opinion that these classes are necessary, and that considerable improvement in creameries will come through a well considered plan of instruction and practical training for persons who intend to take positions as managers of creameries.

THE ALBERT NATIONAL AGRICULTURAL INSTITUTION.

During the year the students who attended at this institution were as follows:—

1.—*The young men (Queen's Scholars) who are in training for teacherships of National Schools.*

   (a.) From the Marlborough-street Training College,   96

   (b.) From the Church of Ireland Training College,   33

I have again to urge the desirability of providing instruction in the sciences that bear upon Agriculture for teachers who are to be engaged in the instruction of youths in this branch.

A very small acquaintance with the agricultural classes of Ireland is sufficient to indicate what beneficial results would follow if the school teachers would take up a course of Elementary Science in connexion with the instruction of their pupils in Agriculture.

At our Agricultural institutions an enormous amount of effort is imparting instruction is lost through the want of grounding in Elementary Science in those who enter.

How pleasant, for instance, would the teacher of Agricultural Chemistry find his duty if he could be certain that his now class had mastered the

elementary principles of this subject. It is really pitiable to note
the time spent by our lecturers in doing work that should have been
completed by the schoolmaster before the pupil's left school.

It appears to me that until the teachers of our National Schools make
themselves better acquainted with the science ancillary to Agriculture, a
due measure of success in Agricultural education will not be attained.

2.—THE MALE AGRICULTURAL PUPILS.

The number of pupils who attended during the year was:—

Free by Competitive Examination,   .   .   .   23

Paying Intern Students, ...   16

During the Agricultural Session of 1891, the conduct and application
to business of the pupils were most satisfactory.

There has been no material change in the course of studies. The
object of combining scientific with practical instruction has been carried
on as carefully as possible, and every effort is made to fully establish
in the minds of the pupils the conviction that of all the Industrial arts
Agriculture is the one that is most helped by scientific study.

Fortunately the Professors at this Institution are all men who are
engaged in practical work of such character as has relation to Agriculture. Each of these Lecturers has a keen perception of the requirements of an Agricultural Education, and if we could present them with
pupils well prepared in the elements of the various scientific subjects
taught, our educational results would indeed be great.

The students have a considerable advantage in being taken to the
Royal Botanic Gardens occasionally for instruction in Botany, and they
thus obtain a practical instruction that makes the teaching interesting
and real. Again, in the Natural History Department, a good deal of
time is given to practical work. Lessons on the use of the microscope
will, it is hoped, cultivate a taste for scientific enquiry.

The Veterinary instruction is illustrated by natural preparations and
models of such a character as are to be found in the best veterinary
schools, and this subject, which has such interest for the agriculturist, is
made especially interesting and practical here.

In Agricultural Chemistry and Geology the pupils are fortunate in
having the services of a Professor whose reputation is world-wide;[*] and
certainly the time spent and pains taken in giving instruction in this
department afford evidence of his enthusiasm.

3.—FEMALE DAIRY STUDENTS.

This Department of the Institution continues in a flourishing condition. At the session—

January 6 to February 20,   .   .   20 pupils attended.

November 6 to December 20, .   .   34 ,,   .

The pupils were most attentive and industrious.

The course of instruction was made more thorough during the Sessions
of 1891. Many of the Dairy students of the Glasnevin and Munster
Establishments are now engaged in creameries; it was thought desirable
to widen the scope of instruction, and milk-testing upon different
systems of modern introduction was a subject to which considerable
attention was given.

In addition to butter-making the making of different varieties of
cheese was taught, and although at the present time cheese-making is

[*] Dr. M'Weeney.

Appendix O.

Reports on
State of
Schools.

Mr.
Carroll,

Superin-
tendent of
Agricul-
tural De-
partment.

The Albert
Agricul-
tural Insti-
tution.

not practised to any extent in Ireland, it may be hoped that at some future period it will be introduced as a profitable industry.

The Examinations at the close of the Sessions for female dairy pupils showed very good results, and in the competition in butter-making there was considerable skill manifested.

THE FARM.

The farm has yielded good results in the produce of the crops and in the profit from the year's farming. The health of the farm stock has been excellent, and altogether a very satisfactory year's operations may be reported.

The fluctuations that are so trying in ordinary farming do not as a rule affect our system of farming at Glasnevin, and the results of farming here must not be looked upon as criteria of general farming throughout the whole of Ireland. With good markets for all produce and a large demand for milk which is sold at a high price in Dublin, the profits of farming at Glasnevin should be considerable, and there ought not be much variation from year to year.

The stock kept upon the farm during the years noted was :—

—	1894.	1893.	1892.
Horses, ...	8	6	7
Cows, ...	50	51	45
Young Cattle, ...	18	23	39
Sheep, ...	44	46	49
Pigs, ...	80	57	58

The produce of the following crops in stones (14 lbs.), was :—

—	1894.	1893.	1892.
Wheat, ...	230	250	270
Oats, ...	943	638	627
Barley, ...	890	808	714
Mangold, ...	6,800	4,881	4,080
Swedes, ...	3,320	8,250	4,080
Potatoes, . . .	681	1,000	1,250
Cabbage, . . .	4,100	1,800	4,750

—	1893.	1894.
	£ s. d.	£ s. d.
The Farm Profits were, . . .	741 6 7	738 13 6
Rent, ...	679 10 1	677 10 1
The Valuation of Farm Stock, . .	3,106 5 6	5,057 4 7

Several important experiments were carried out upon the farm during the year. These are recorded later.

The experiment as to manurial value of different foods when fed to sheep is interesting.

In this experiment two results may be gauged :—(1) The increase in the weight of mutton produced by the use of food additional to swedes and hay; and (2), the influence of these foods on the grass upon which the foods were consumed.

The experiments will be carried on for some years in order to test whether the plants in the pasture will be influenced in respect of variety by the artificial foods consumed by stock.

The experiments upon pig-feeding were instituted for the purpose of testing the value of separated skim milk under different conditions of being given sweet or sour.

The use of separated milk as food for calves and pigs has at present considerable interest for farmers, and experiments in its use will be carried out at the Glasnevin and Munster Farms of the Commissioners.

Experiments upon the continuous use of artificial manures upon grass have been continued during 1894. These experiments have considerable educational value for the pupils of the Institution.

Experiments upon the use of sulphate of copper as a preventive of potato disease were carried out and are reported. It may be taken that this preventive remedy has passed its experimental stage. The experience of its use in 1894 throughout Ireland has made it perfectly clear that, when properly applied, sulphate of copper is almost a complete preventive of potato blight.

Munster Agricultural and Dairy National School.

This School has had a year of considerable success.

The applications for entrance of dairy students are always in excess of what the School can accommodate, and the number of pupils attending is now quite as many as can be properly instructed.

Arrangements are made for a good supply of milk and cream additional to what the farm produces, and thus the pupils have the necessary material for manual training.

There has been an increase in the number of young men attending as agricultural pupils, and it is hoped that this class will in point of number continue to increase.

The opportunity which this School offers to its pupils for passing through the competitive examination to free places in the Glasnevin Institution appears to induce farmers to send their sons to the Munster Agricultural School in increased numbers. As a rule, the pupils of the Munster Agricultural School are successful in the competition.

The Munster School, being situated in a dairying district, its instruction is mainly in the direction of dairy farming, and although a large proportion of the farm is devoted to tillage, this tillage has for its object the providing of food for dairy cows.

The Governors of the Agricultural Institute, which was recently founded under a scheme of the Endowed Schools Commission, continue to aid this Institution upon the same conditions as the late local committee. The ladies' committee has also during the year given valuable service in the supervision of the comfort of the dairy pupils, and in promoting the efficiency of the teaching.

Appendix C.

Reports on
State of
Schools.

Mr.
Carroll.

Superintendent of
Agricultural Department.

The
Munster
Agricultural and
Dairy
School.

The
ordinary
Agricultural
Schools.

The numbers who attended during the year were:—

MALE PUPILS.

Session, 21st August to 20th December,		.		.		21

FEMALE PUPILS.

First Session,	.	.	.	.	.	83
Second Session,	.	.	.	.	.	28
Third Session,	.	.	.	.	.	34

Experiments were carried out upon the farm during the year. The report of Mr. Smyth, the Superintendent, is appended.

THE ORDINARY AGRICULTURAL SCHOOLS.

My visits of inspection to these Schools were made regularly during the year.

The results of examinations showed in several cases considerable improvement, and I believe that the teachers generally are taking pains to make the teaching effective.

The Industrial classes, in which pupils are paid a small sum for their work done upon the School farm, are in operation in many of these Schools. The option given to Managers under recent Treasury sanction of having the practical instruction given for three hours on Saturdays instead of half an hour each day, will, I think, promote efficiency in these classes.

Some experiments were carried out upon the School Farms (under local managers) to test the efficiency of sulphate of copper as a preventive of potato disease ; reports are given herewith.

I am devising a scheme for approval by which experiments might be carried out upon the farms of those Agricultural Schools. They offer a good means for carrying out experiments that should have much value for agriculture in Ireland.

They have variety in soil ; they are situate in districts of different climates; and they present excellent machinery for carrying on agricultural experiments of various kinds. Already very valuable experiments in potato cultivation have been carried out; and with moderate outlay very useful work may be accomplished through the agricultural schools and school gardens of the Commissioners.

I have arranged for the coming year that varieties of potatoes for seed shall be sent to those schools, the produce of which will be distributed in the neighbourhood of the schools.

I hope to propose shortly, for the consideration of the Commissioners, the scheme for the further utilisation of the Agricultural Schools as experimental stations.

I remain, Gentlemen, your obedient servant,

THOMAS CARROLL.

Appendix A.
Reports on State of Schools.

Mr. Carroll.

Superintendent of Agricultural Department.

APPENDIX A.

EXPERIMENTS CARRIED OUT at the ALBERT AGRICULTURAL INSTITUTION, 1894.

ON ARTIFICIAL MANURES applied to GRASS.

Area of each plot = 5 perches.   Grass cut on 9th July, 1894.

No. of Plot.	Manure.	Quantity of Manure Applied.		Yield of Grass per Plot.		Yield per Acre.			
		Stones.	Lbs.	Stones.	Lbs.	Tons.	Cwts.	Qrs.	Lbs.
1	Sulphate of Soda,	1	11	21	13	6	19	2	14
2	Peruvian Guano,	–	23½	27	3	7	6	3	12
3	No manure,	–	–	29	–	6	13	–	–
4	Mineral Superphosphate,	2	11	23	–	6	13	–	–
5	Common Salt,	10	–	29	–	6	8	–	–
6	Kainit,	–	17½						
	Sulphate of Ammonia,	–	6½	47	–	6	6	–	–
	Mineral Superphosphate,	–	6½						
7	Farm Yard Manure,	60	7	34	13	6	29	–	12
8	Kainit,	3	10½	34	11	3	15	–	16
9	Sulphate of Lime,	9	–	31	6	6	6	2	24
10	No Manure,	–	–	18	6	6	16	1	20
11	Nitrate of Soda,	–	13	31	1½	6	6	1	20
12	Sulphate of Ammonia,	–	8½	29	11	8	29	–	18
13	Quick Lime,	4	–	18	13½	3	7	1	4
14	Kainit,	2	32½	40	–	12	–	–	–
	Mineral Superphosphate,	2	6½						
15	Nitrate of Soda,	–	6	27	–	6	8	–	–
	Mineral Superphosphate,	2	6½						
16	Sulphate of Ammonia,	–	6½	23	–	6	13	–	–
	Mineral Superphosphate,	2	6½						

ON THE USE OF SULPHATE OF COPPER AS A PREVENTIVE OF POTATO DISEASE.

Dressed Potatoes, about 3½ acres, on 19th July, 1894.
Raised on 8th October, 1894.

YIELD PER ACRE.

Tons. Cwts. Qrs. Lbs.
Undressed,   11 3 0 8 sound.
              2 13 1 19 diseased.
Percentage Diseased = 18·97.

Tons. Cwts. Qrs. Lbs.
Dressed,   16 11 0 0 sound.
             1 0 0 0 diseased.
Percentage Diseased = 7·70.

Appendix C.

Reports on State of Schools.

Mr. Carroll.

Superintendent of Agricultural Department.

EXPERIMENTS to test the FOOD and MANURIAL VALUE of LINSEED CAKE, COTTON SEED CAKE, and MAIZE in the feeding of SHEEP upon pasture land. SWEDISH TURNIPS and HAY being given to the SHEEP folded upon the pasture.

On 14th September, 1894, sheep were put into plot of grass on Experimental Ground, 5 in each division, fed as follows:—Turnips at the rate of about 12 tons per acre, rye grass hay *ad lib.*, and artificial food as stated below.

The grass was cut on 19th and 20th June, 1895, and weighed as grass and afterwards as hay.

No. 1.			No. 2.		
5 Sheep, marked on side A.			5 Sheep, marked on side A. A.		
Commenced feeding with Linseed Cake on 2nd October, 1894, 5 lbs. for lot per day, at £9 10s. per ton.			Commenced feeding with Cotton Cake on 2nd October, 1894, 5 lbs. 4¼ ozs. for lot per day, at £9 12s. per ton.		
	Cwts. Qrs. Lbs.			Cwts. Qrs. Lbs.	
Live weight, 14 Sept., 1894,	8	1	0	Live weight, 14 Sept., 1894,	7 3 14
Do. 13 Nov., 1894,	9	3	14	Do. 13 Nov., 1894,	9 0 14
Increase,	.	1	1	14	Increase,	. 1 1 0
Weight of grass .	.	23	0	21	Weight of grass .	. 21 3 21
Do. of hay .	.	10	2	14	Do. of hay .	. 13 2 0

No. 3.			No. 4.		
5 Sheep, marked on side A. A. A.			5 Sheep, not marked, fed on Turnips alone.		
Commenced feeding with Indian Corn, 7 lbs. 1½ oz. per day for lot, at 4s. per ton.					
	Cwts. Qrs. Lbs.			Cwts. Qrs. Lbs.	
Live weight, 14 Sept., 1894,	7	0	0	Live weight, 14 Sept., 1894,	7 1 21
Do. 13 Nov., 1894,	8	3	14	Do. 13 Nov., 1894,	7 0 14
Increase,	.	1	0	14	Increase,	.. 0 1 21
Weight of grass, .	.	18	2	7	Weight of grass,	. 23 3 14
Do. of hay .	.	9	1	21	Do. of hay .	. 12 3 0

EXPERIMENTS with SKIM MILK in the FEEDING of PIGS.

Experiment with Skim Milk in the feeding of pigs. Six (6) pigs were selected for the purpose, 3 fed on sour, and 3 on sweet skim milk.

Experiment commenced on 7th July, 1894.

—	No.	Weight at Commencement.		Weight at End.		Increase.	
		Stones.	Lbs.	Stones.	Lbs.	Stones.	Lbs.
Lot No. 1.	*1	8	—	10	0	1	8
	2	9	—	10	0	1	0
	3	7	4	8	4	1	—
		24	4	29	0	4	4

EXPERIMENTS with SKIM MILK in the FEEDING of PIGS—*continued.*

Experiment commenced on July 7th, 1894—*continued.*

—	No.	Weight at Commencement.		Weight at End.		Increase.	
		Stones.	Lbs.	Stones.	Lbs.	Stones.	Lbs.
Lot No 2.	*1	9	—	9	4	—	4
	2	6	13	9	4	2	6
	3	10	9	11	4	1	2
		25	—	29	12	3	12

Experiment ended on 9th August, 1894.

Each lot was fed altogether with 1,970 quarts of milk.

* Pig No. 1, Lot No. 1,   .   . 10 stone 9 lbs. live weight.
  Pig No. 1, Lot No. 2,   .   . 6 stone 4 lbs. live weight.

  29 stone 13 lbs. live weight.

Sold to Mr. Shaw at 44s. per cwt. Dead weight, 4 cwt. 3 qrs. 26 lbs. = £1 18s. 8d.

28th November, 1894.

Experiments with Skim Milk in the feeding of pigs. Four lots of three pigs each were selected, and fed as follows :—

No. of Lot	Particulars of Feeding.	Weight on 28th Nov., 1894.			Weight on 2nd Jan., 1895.			Increase.		
		Cwt.	Qrs.	Lbs.	Cwt.	Qrs.	Lbs.	Cwt.	Qrs.	Lbs.
1	Potatoes alone cooked, 5 stones per day, for lot, .	6	1	13	6	2	7	9	—	23
2	13 quarts Separated Milk & Wash: 4 stone Potatoes, per day, for lot, .	3	2	14	9	0	11	3	—	—
3	13 quarts Separated Milk (Sour): 4 stone Potatoes, per day, for lot, .	6	—	—	7	0	0	2	2	5
4	13 quarts Separated Milk : 4 stone Potatoes and 1½ lb. Maize Meal, boiled, .	3	3	—	4	0	7	2	3	7

Appendix C.
Reports on
State of
Schools.
——
Mr.
Carroll,
Superintendent of
Agricultural Department.
——

REPORT on EXPERIMENTS at the MUNSTER AGRICULTURAL AND
DAIRY SCHOOL.

The following are results of some experiments carried out during the
year 1894. The efficacy of the "Bordeaux Mixture" was again tested.
On the 13th July, before the blight appeared, a two per cent. solution
was sprayed with the Eclair machine over the foliage on plots of the
potato crop; and some plots got a later second dressing.

The effect was so marked as to attract frequent notice and inquiries,
the dressed part being green, when the rest were withered by disease.

The effect on the crop is shown by the following summary. Part of
the field was planted with seedlings which were very much blighted, so
the Champions near there—the east plot—were also greatly diseased.

CROP PER ACRE.

	CHAMPIONS				REICE		
	Not Dressed.		Dressed.		Not Dressed	Dressed.	
	West Plot.	East Plot.	Once.	Twice.		Once.	Twice.
	cwt. lb.	cwt. lb.	cwt. lb.	cwt. lb.	cwt.	cwt. lb.	cwt. lb.
Large, . .	185 50	133 37	180 23	221 19	144	167 1	129 105
Small, . .	29 103	31 78	22 40	83 23	11	17 3	86 89
Diseased, . .	9 111	62 16	1 32	8 20	44	9 6	9 48
Total,	221 40	226 7	208 97	287 18	211	193 10	225 3

In order to trace the course of the spores which occasion the disease in the tubers, and dod if they could be arrested on the way, part
of drill planted with Flounders was covered with cotton wadding applied
as closely as possible round the stems. On raising the crop, 10th
October, 0·7 per cent. of the tubers were diseased on the covered part,
and 24·7 per cent. on the uncovered crop.

Pig-feeding.—Four pigs were fed on separated milk only, for two the
milk was sweet, for the other two sour.

FOOD.	Weight of Two.			Posted 11 Sept.	Dead Weight.	Percentage in Live Weight.
	21 July.	6 Aug.	18 Sept.			
	lbs.	lbs.	lbs.	lbs.	lbs.	lbs.
8 Gallons Sweet Separated Milk each per day, . .	845	335	359	359	281	78·3
8 Gallons Sour Separated Milk each per day, . .	824	623	324	328	225	78
Daily increase of each—						Total increase.
Sweet Milk, . . .	—	2·7	—	1·44	—	274
Sour, . . .	—	2·17	—	1·33	—	442

Appendix C.

Reports on State of Schools.

Mr. Carroll.

Report in-cident of Agricul-tural De-partment.

Experiments on mixed food.   Four lots of two pigs each.

Food to each Pig daily.	Average weight.				Dead weight.	Per-centage.
	27th July.	14th Aug.	30th Aug.	17th Sept.		
	Lbs.	Lbs.	Lbs.	Lbs.	Lbs.	Lbs.
4 lbs. Pollard and 15 lbs. Sweet Separated Milk,	85	120	130	152	126	771
Daily increase,	—	16	113	1·	—	—
for whole period,	—	—	—	124	—	—
4 lbs. Pollard and 15 lbs. Sour Separated Milk,	82	107	146	157	129	759
Daily increase,	—	109	16	173	—	—
for whole period,	—	—	—	161	—	—
4 lbs. Indian Meal and 15 lbs. Sweet Separated Milk,	82	126	151	14th Sept. 177	134	737
Daily increase,	—	109	175	123	—	—
for whole period,	—	—	—	171	—	—
4 lbs. Indian Meal and 15 lbs. Sour Separated Milk,	85½	157	167½	190½	144½	709
Daily increase,	—	34	212	123	—	—
for whole period,	—	—	—	601	—	—

	Percentage increase.			Percentage increase.
Pollard and Sweet Milk,	778	Indian Meal and Sweet Milk,	871
Pollard and Sour Milk,	971	Indian Meal and Sour Milk,	1182

Experiments with Potatoes and other food.   Eight pigs in 4 lots.
Age on 30th Nov., 170 days.

Lot.	Food.	Average weight.			Remarks by Messrs. Shaw and Son.
		30th Nov.	27th Dec.	22nd Jan.	
		Lbs.	Lbs.	Lbs.	
1	10 lbs. Potatoes; 10 lbs. Sweet Separated Milk,	151	152	212	Very choice; well laid; right depth of fat.
	Daily increase,	—	9	177	
	do. (whole period),	—	—	12	
	Percentage increase,	—	—	679	
2	10 lbs. Potatoes; 10 lbs. Sour Separated Milk,	153	173½	185½	Very choice.
	Daily increase,	—	12	12	
	do. (whole period),	—	—	75	
	Percentage increase,	—	—	675	
3	10 lbs. Potatoes; 1 lb. Indian Meal; 9 lbs. Separated Milk,	152½	169	227	Perfect finish.
	Daily increase,	—	75	146	
	do. (whole period),	—	—	112	
	Percentage increase,	—	—	679	
4	10 lbs. Potatoes,	144½	170	184	Lean back; mag-nesium fatty.
	Daily increase,	—	18	10	
	do. (whole period),	—	—	157	
	Percentage increase,	—	—	271	

Lots 1 and 2 got 10 lbs. Milk additional from 9th January.
Lots 3 and 4 got 8 lbs. Potatoes additional from 9th January.

ANDREW SMYTH.

Appendix C.

Reports on Basis of Schools.

Mr. Carroll,

Superintendent of Agricultural Department.

REPORTS on the SPRAYING of POTATOES with COPPER SULPHATE
SOLUTION at CLARE and GARRYHILL NATIONAL SCHOOLS.

Clare Agricultural National School,
Castlederg, Co. Tyrone.

The following are particulars of the dressing of the potatoes with the
solution of the sulphate of copper and lime in 1894. The crop here
consisted principally of Champions and Irish Whites. Both varieties
grew very luxuriantly, rather more so than what is considered desirable
for a good crop of tubers. On July 24th the Champions and part of
the Irish Whites were sprayed with the solution of sulphate of copper
and lime in the proportion of 8 lbs. of the sulphate of copper to 5 lbs. of
lime and forty gallons of water. Just at this time the disease appeared,
when nearly all the potatoes in this part of the country were not more
than half grown. Wet weather set in immediately, and the disease
spread rapidly. The beneficial effects of the dressing soon became
visible, even to persons passing the road. When the weather became
fine again the dressed portion was still growing green, and in the undressed portion the leaves were all gone. A second dressing similar to
the first was again applied about August 12th. It was considered useless at this stage to apply any dressing to the portion which was left
undone at first. This preserved them growing green till September,
when those in the hollow part of the field were killed by frost. When
the storing came it was found that while there were very few diseased
potatoes in any part of the field, those in the dressed portion of the Irish
Whites were much larger than in the undressed portion. The Champions
were a remarkably good crop, and the best potatoes for the table I ever
saw, which could not possibly have been the case if their growth had
been stopped at the time the disease appeared.

JOSEPH WHITTON, Teacher.

GARRYHILL AGRICULTURAL SCHOOL.

The potato crop in this district in the year 1894 was a very poor
one. A heavy frost in May checked their growth very considerably
and as the blight appeared here before 1st August the potato crop was
almost a failure. I applied a dressing of sulphate of copper and lime
to the crop on school farm with very satisfactory results. The application
was made about the middle of July, before the blight appeared. The
yield per acre was 9 tons 16 cwt., including 1 ton 11 cwt. diseased. On
an undressed plot the total yield per acre was 7 tons 9 cwt. of which 1 ton
8 cwt. was diseased. This bears out the results of previous experiments
on this farm, that most advantage is to be looked for in the direction of
increased produce, the potatoes remaining green and maturing the
tubers long after the blight has shown itself.

MALACHY RYAN, Teacher.

Appendix C.
Reports on
State of
Schools.
Mr.
Carroll,
Superin-
tendent of
Agricul-
tural De-
partment.

APPENDIX B.—ALBERT FARMS.

(a.) ALBERT LARGE FARM.

BALANCE SHEET for Twelve Months ending 31st March, 1895.

EXPENSES.	£	s.	d.	RECEIPTS.	£	s.	d.
To Amount of Valuation at com-mencement of year,	2,776	10	1	By Amount Dairy Produce,	2,103	10	2
„ Outstanding Debts,	159	11	6	„ Cattle,	622	2	6
„ Milk, Intermediate Farm; Milk, Small Farm,	451	19	10	„ Sheep,	187	8	9
„ Cattle purchased,	559	19	3	„ Pigs,	685	18	2
„ Sheep purchased,	288	11	11	„ Wheat,	88	0	3
„ Potatoes,	6	0	7	„ Oats,	7	0	6
„ Labour,	845	9	10	„ Barley,	56	6	5
„ Seeds,	99	1	3	„ Potatoes,	141	9	8
„ Manures,	56	9	9	„ Hay and Straw,	83	10	1
„ Implements,	171	8	10	„ Service of Sires,	1	0	2
„ Horse Shoeing,	92	11	4	„ Miscellaneous,	29	8	1
„ Harness,	9	8	8	„ Outstanding Debts,	157	6	11
„ Feeding Stuffs,	388	6	11	„ Estimated proportion of Ex-penses in connexion with delivery of Milk—Small Farm,	6	7	6
„ Oil and Medicine,	12	17	0	„ Do. Intermediate Farm,	15	13	4
„ Expenses to Fairs,	24	11	6	„ Intermediate Farm, Miscel-laneous,	163	14	3
„ Miscellaneous,	56	9	0	„ Small Farm, Miscellaneous,	51	6	0
„ Coal for Engine,	26	0	0	„ Garden,	11	17	6
„ Small Farm, Miscellaneous,	62	9	6	„ Poultry Department,	62	2	5
„ Intermediate Farm, Miscel-laneous,	122	13	6	„ Rent Experimental Ground,	30	7	6
„ Poultry Department,	17	17	8	„ Keep Superintendent's Horse,	25	0	0
„ Dairy School,	206	19	1	„ Rent Albert Lodge,	56	0	0
„ Rent,	651	7	4	„ Valuation at close of year,	2,586	19	10
„ Balance,	356	19	8				
Total,	£8,623	0	9	Total,	£8,623	0	9

Appendix C.
Reports on
State of
Schools.

*Mr.
Carroll*,
Superin-
tendent of
Agricul-
tural De-
partment.

(b.) Albert Intermediate Farm.

Balance Sheet for the Twelve Months ending 31st March, 1895.

Expenditure.	£ s. d.	Receipts.	£ s. d.
To Amount of Valuation at commencement of year, .	337 19 11	By Cash received for Twelve Months, viz :—	
„ Labour, ...	44 8 0	Milk, ...	105 1 4
„ Rents, ...	6 4 0	Cattle, ...	115 1 3
„ Manures, ...	3 7 0	Pigs, ...	3 19 9
„ Cattle, ...	58 4 8	Oats, ...	49 3 0
„ Rent, ...	71 6 0	Hay, ...	40 7 1
„ Feeding Stuffs, . .	39 7 9	Miscellaneous, . .	31 4 1
„ Large Farm (Transfers),	103 14 3	Small Farm (Transfers),	6 4 4
„ Small Farm do.	18 0 0	„ Amount of Valuation at close of year, . .	616 3 11
„ Expenses in connexion with Delivery of Milk,	14 13 4		
„ Fuel for Cooking, .	3 6 0		
„ Balance in favour of Manage- ment, . . .	373 19 11		
Total, . .	£997 16 2	Total, . .	£997 16 2

(d.) Albert Small Farm.

Balance Sheet for the Twelve Months ending 31st March, 1895.

Expenditure.	£ s. d.	Receipts.	£ s. d.
To Amount of Valuation at the commencement of year, .	153 16 8	By Cash received during the Twelve Months, viz :—	
„ Labour, ...	11 2 8	New Milk, . . .	139 16 6
„ Rents, ...	7 11 5	Cattle, ...	40 3 0
„ Manures, ...	3 1 3	Pigs, ...	4 4 0
„ Feeding Stuffs, . .	6 16 8	Potatoes, . . .	1 8 0
„ Large Farm (Transfers),	31 8 0	Oats, ...	13 11 0
„ Intermediate Farm (Trans- fers), . . .	8 6 0	„ Amount of Valuation at the close of the year, .	201 7 6
„ Rent, ...	16 14 3		
„ Expenses in connexion with Delivery of Milk,	5 7 5		
„ Fuel for Cooking, .	3 6 0		
„ Balance in favour of Manage- ment, . . .	107 8 0		
Total . .	£221 8 3	Total . .	£221 8 3

Appendix C.

Reports on
State of
Schools.
—
Mr.
Carroll.

Superin-
tendent of
Agricul-
tural De-
partment.
—

APPENDIX C.

BALANCE SHEET of MUNSTER MODEL FARM for Twelve Months, ending 31st March, 1895.

EXPENSES.	£	s.	d.	RECEIPTS.	£	s.	d.
To Amount of Valuation at the commencement of the year,	1,297	6	0	By Amount of Cash received during the year, viz. :—			
„ Labour,	348	10	0	Dairy produce,	418	6	11
„ Cattle,	340	7	0	Butter from bought Cream,	415	14	11
„ Horses	31	10	0	Cattle,	78	15	0
„ Pigs,	80	15	10	Horses,	7	10	0
„ Manures,	44	6	0	Pigs,	76	13	3
„ Poultry,	1	0	0	Roots,	53	10	0
„ Seeds,	26	13	2	Garden Produce,	22	14	7
„ Feeding Stuffs,	65	4	3	Poultry,	18	13	0
„ Implements,	127	3	7				
„ Smithwork,	9	16	3	Training Department:—			
„ Cream for Educational pur- poses,	425	13	7	Loss on bought Cream,	131	6	5
„ Miscellaneous,	55	6	1	„ Farm Milk,	122	12	0
„ Rent,	270	0	0	Labour for Establishment,	169	6	2
„ Profit and Loss, being gain on the year's transactions,	130	0	2	By Amount of Valuation at end of year,	1,447	12	3
	3,193	**3**	**5**		**3,193**	**3**	**5**

Mr. GOODMAN, Examiner in Music.

GENTLEMEN,—In compliance with your instructions I beg to submit my Report on the examinations in Music in the Training Colleges, Practising Schools, and other National Schools for the year 1894.

My chief official work for the year has been in connection with the preparation of the Music Papers required for the July examinations; the holding of the practical examinations in Vocal and Instrumental Music of the Queen's Scholars in the Training Colleges; the examination of the pupils of the various Practising Schools; the marking of the papers of Queen's Scholars, and of the acting teachers and candidates seeking certificates in Vocal Music; the examination of the acting teachers seeking certificates in Instrumental Music; the examination in singing of such teachers in and about Dublin as had passed in the July Papers; the reporting upon the various musical matters submitted to me from the office, from time to time during the year; and last, but not least, the visiting the ordinary schools in Dublin and the neighbourhood.

The examination in Music of the Queen's Scholars is of two kinds: first an examination in actual singing, and afterwards an examination in the Theory of Music. In all the Training Colleges Vocal Music still continues to be taught on the Tonic Sol-fa system. The mode of examina-

Appendix C.
Reports on
State of
Schools.

Mr.
Goodman,
Examiner
in Music.

Practical
examina-
tion.

Examina-
tion in
Theory of
Music.

tion for the Board's Certificate is practically the same as that in use for the certificate of the Tonic Sol-fa College. Each candidate is examined individually, and is required—(1) to point on the Modulator the notes of certain school songs, solfaing as he points ; (2) to read certain rhythms, beating time as he does so ; (3) to sing from the Examiner's pointing on the Modulator an exercise including transitions or changes of key ; (4) to Sol-fa and afterwards to vocalise a piece of music never seen before ; and (5) to tell the names of certain notes played on an instrument.

Besides this examination in practice each candidate must also take the Paper in Theory, in which, in addition to the general theory of the subject, ability to translate from the Tonic Sol-fa notation into the staff, and from the staff into Tonic Sol-fa, is expected. From this it will be seen that the musical examination of the Queen's Scholars is, so far as it goes, of a thoroughly practical and useful character.

During the month of June I held the practical examinations in the different Training Colleges. In all 225 Queen's Scholars—116 males and 109 females—presented themselves for examination. The numbers in each Training College were :—

Numbers
examined.

—				Males	—				Females
St. Patrick's,	,	.	,	53	Baggot-street,	,	,	.	46
Marlborough-street,	.	.	43	Marlborough-street,	,	.	22
De La Salle,	.	.	17	Kildare-place,	.	.	41
Kildare-place,	,	.	4					109
				116					

Proficiency
exhibited.

The proficiency exhibited by the Queen's Scholars was on the whole of a satisfactory, though scarcely of a brilliant kind. Brilliant results are, indeed, not to be expected, even with the most efficient teaching, so long as the great majority of the students continue to come up to the Training Colleges without any previous practice whatever in singing. Of all the students who began their course of training in Baggot-street College in September, 1893, I was informed that only two had learnt to sing while at school. And if such could have been the state of things in the principal Female Training College, matters, I am afraid, must have been still worse in this respect in the Colleges for males. At my examination I found the sight singing in Kildare-place to be particularly good. But this only confirms what I have said. For in Kildare-place, and there only at present, does ability to sing count as one of the subjects of examination for entrance. This being so, the students prepare themselves in the subject before coming into the College, and when the Examiner comes later with the sight tests that cause so much trouble elsewhere, he finds they give very little trouble here. This, however, applies only to the female students of the College. The male students, from a musical point of view, are much the same as those in the other Training Colleges.

Musical
condition of
Queen's
scholars on
admission.

This question as to the musical condition of the Queen's Scholars on their entrance into the Training Colleges is at the root of the whole subject of musical instruction in the National Schools of the country. No one who has not had experience of it can form an idea of what a painful, laborious, and all but hopeless task it is to have to teach singing to adults who have never had "voice" or "ear" developed in early youth. Even when, by dint of hard, persevering work, some progress

Appendix C

Reports on State of Schools.

Mr. Goodman, Examiner in Music.

has been made, a few weeks' vacation or cessation from singing will, with such a class, undo almost all previously done. And this, no doubt, is partly the reason why so many Queen's Scholars who have obtained certificates in music fail to teach the subject in their schools. Many of them, perhaps, have barely scraped through the examination, and if they do not keep up their practice by proceeding immediately to teach, they find themselves after a time quite unequal to the task of giving a correct musical "pattern" to their pupils, and so lose heart and abandon the subject altogether. Nevertheless the only way to improve matters and to develop something of "voice" and "ear" in those coming to the Training Colleges is to have singing—even of the most elementary kind—in as many as possible of the schools throughout the country. For this reason I, for one, would gladly see singing "by ear" recognised in National Schools. If only soft, sweet singing were always insisted on, singing "by ear" could not possibly do harm, and would certainly do good. The first and most important result would be that the pupils of schools where singing of the kind had been practised, would be found, on entering into the Training Colleges, to have acquired the power of correctly imitating musical sounds, and to possess a certain readiness and quickness in vocal matters generally which are sadly wanting at present.

Singing by ear.

Tonic Sol-fa has now been taught in the Training Colleges for a period of about ten years. During this time a considerable number of Queen's Scholars must have obtained at least such proficiency in it as would have enabled them, if so disposed, to teach the moderate requirements of the Board's programme. From the reports of the Inspectors it may be seen that Tonic Sol-fa is steadily gaining ground in the schools of the country. But there is no information published by which anyone interested in the matter may discover the precise number of schools in which the system is taught. In the last report of the Commissioners, it is stated that 1,100 National Schools presented pupils for examination in Vocal Music. This number, however, includes schools using the Hullah or Fixed Do method as well as those using Tonic Sol-fa. The Hullah system is no longer taught in the Training Colleges. Consequently those who have passed through the Training Colleges will, if they undertake to teach singing at all, almost certainly do so according to the Tonic Sol-fa system. The development of Tonic Sol-fa in Ireland will, therefore, be almost entirely the work of the Training Colleges. As a means of showing the course of this development I would beg to suggest that in the General Report of the Commissioners for each year, besides the total number of schools presenting Vocal Music as a subject of examination, the numbers be also given of the schools using each of the two recognised systems—Tonic Sol-fa and Hullah. And if, in addition, further information could be supplied as to the number of Boys' schools and the number of Girls' schools in which each system is in use, it would aid very much those interested in the matter in tracing the musical work of the Training Colleges.

Tonic Sol-fa.

Returning to the July examination, I have to report that the answering on the Theory Paper was on the whole good. In all 223 papers were taken by Queen's scholars, 220 in Tonic Sol-fa, and 3 in Hullah. Outside the Training Colleges 394 papers were returned. Of these 188 were in Tonic Sol-fa—126 of them coming from female and 62 from male candidates. The remaining 206 were in Hullah—161 coming from female, and 45 from male teachers and candidates. In these numbers are included the "D" papers taken by monitors, monitresses, and candidates for training.

Appendix C

Reports on
States of
Schools.

Mr.
Goodman,
Examiner
in Music.

July
examina-
tion.

Answering
on Theory
of Music.

Counting all the papers returned, the numbers taking the two systems were :—

—	Tonic Sol-fa.	Hullah.
Training Colleges, . . .	226	6
Districts, ...	182	294
	418	299

I have already given details as to the answering on these papers in the report which I had the honour to submit immediately after the examination in August last. I shall only repeat here that the answering of the acting teachers outside the Training Colleges in the theory of both Tonic Sol-fa and "Hullah" was generally very fair, and that the answering on the "D" papers was generally poor.

Instrumen-
tal Music.

Great attention is now given in all the Training Colleges to the subject of instrumental music. In each of the Training Colleges in Kildare-place and in Baggot-street there is an excellent organ on which the more advanced players are permitted to practise. In the same two Colleges, and also in the Female Training College, Marlborough-street, the Piano is taught to a limited number of students. It is, however, the Harmonium which is chiefly studied in all the Training Colleges. And everything considered, it is perhaps the most useful instrument for ordinary school teachers to be able to play. In a place like a Training College it is only a very limited time, indeed, that can each day be devoted from other subjects to the practice of instrumental music. But the students as a rule are very earnest, and make the most of whatever time is allowed them for practice. Very great proficiency, however, cannot be expected for various reasons. Nevertheless the best students, after two years' regular instruction and practice, attain to a fairly respectable standard of performance; many of them being able to play easy masses, church services, hymn tunes and the like, in a satisfactory manner. And there can be no doubt but that the ability to do this much will ultimately have an effect on the School Music of the country.

Examina-
tion of the
Practising
Schools.

Besides the examination of the Queen's Scholars, it is also my duty to examine the pupils of the Practising Schools attached to the Training Colleges. There are fourteen such schools, nine of them being in connection with Marlborough-street, two with Kildare-place, and one with each of the other Training Colleges. With the exception of two of the smaller schools in Marlborough-street and the Boys' School in Kildare-place, where no pupils were presented for examination, singing continues to be taught efficiently in all these schools. In the Practising School at Waterford it is taught by teachers who have only recently completed their course of training, and who studied the subject with myself when students of the Drumcondra and Marlborough-street Training Colleges.

Competi-
tion in
Public
Singing.

My visits to schools, other than Practising Schools, have been mainly in connection with the Public Singing Competition in Dublin. This Competition, which I trust will become an event of annual occurrence with us, came off for the second time in June last. As in the preceding year, it was conducted under the auspices of the Governors of the Royal Irish Academy of Music. The conditions of the Competition were much the same as before, but in order to encourage fresh schools to take upon themselves the work of preparation each year, it was arranged that those schools which should obtain the First Prize in any

one year should not be eligible to compete for the two years immedi- Apparatus C
ately following. This regulation I found to be very generally approved
of by the teachers. Reports on
State of
Schools

A Public School Singing Competition is comparatively easy to work
up for the first time. It is much more difficult to have it a second time. Mr.
Goodman,
Examiner
in New.
The teachers who have tried their fortune in the first, and have failed,
often feel very sore and disappointed over their want of success, and in
their vexation vow they will never more have anything to do with an
affair of the kind. After a while this bitter feeling passes away, and
the teacher, if possessed of ambition, soon begins to feel a wish
to go in and try again. In some instances this was the case last year,
but in my visits to the schools I found ambition to be only too often
wanting. Here was a splendid opportunity for teachers who were
anxious to distinguish themselves and their schools in a most conspicuous and public manner. And yet few appeared anxious to avail themselves of it. All would, no doubt, compete if they were only sure of
winning the prize; but the fear of being beaten by others was sufficient to keep more than one prominent school from entering, notwithstanding that I tried everywhere to impress upon the teachers the idea
that the great object of the Competition was not so much to give a
money prize to the teacher as to improve and raise the standard of
performance amongst the children.

Ten National Schools ultimately determined on preparing for the Schools
competing
Competition. These schools I kept visiting from time to time, helping
the teachers where necessary in their work of preparation. Due notice
was given the Academy of Music of the intention of these ten schools to
compete; but on the eve of the Competition four of them—two Boys'
and two Girls' schools—retired, leaving only six in the field. The six
comprised five Girls' and one Boys' school. The five Girls' schools were—
King's Inns-street Convent, Manor-street Convent, Kingstown Convent, Loretto Convent, Stephen's-green, and the Girls' Central Model
School, Marlborough-street; the Boys' school was No. 1 Central Model,
Marlborough-street.

The Competition for Boys' schools was the first to take place. It Boys'
schools.
came off in the Concert Room of the Royal Irish Academy of Music,
Westland-row. For this Competition there were only three entries—
namely, Marlborough-street Model, and the Schools of the Christian
Brothers, St. Mary's-place and Synge-street. The Judges were—Mr.
A. L. Cowley, London, as Tonic Sol-fa expert, Mr. Joseph Robinson,
and Mr. Thomas Mayne.

Each choir had to sing a prescribed part song arranged for three Tests
employed.
treble voices, a similar piece of its own selection, also a sight test in
two parts, and had further to write down the notes of an ear test played
on the harmonium.

The Competition for Girls' schools took place in a much more public Girls'
schools.
manner in the Ancient Concert Room on Thursday, June 27th. The
proceedings were followed with keen interest and enjoyment by the large
audience which filled the building to overflowing. Amongst those
present were the (late) Right Hon. Sir Patrick Keenan, the Most Rev.
Dr. Donnelly, Bishop of Canea, Mr. W. R. Molloy, the Rev. D. Petitt,
a number of Catholic Clergymen, Christian Brothers, and others
interested in the music of the primary schools. There were also present
the musical students of all the Dublin Training Colleges, for whom the
day's performances must have been an admirable model lesson.

The Judges were the same as on the preceding day. Seven Girls' schools Judges and
tests.
had originally entered for the Competition, but two had withdrawn,

F

Appendix C.
Reports on
State of
Schools.

Mr.
Goodman.
Examiner in
Music.

so that only five appeared on the day of battle. Their performances were of a very high character, and elicited the constant applause of the audience. The part singing was particularly good, both in the prescribed piece—Lord Mornington's *Come, Fairest Nymph*, arranged for three treble voices—and also in the different pieces of their own selection. There were two sight tests, a more difficult one in two parts printed in the Tonic Sol-fa notation, and an easier one in the staff notation. With but one exception both these tests were admirably sung by all the competing choirs. What seemed, however, to please the audience most was the writing down of the ear test, consisting of a short musical phrase played twice on the harmonium. This the classes took down and sang immediately to the Sol-fa syllables in almost every instance with surprising readiness and accuracy. When all the tests had been gone through by the five competing choirs the Judges retired to consider their awards. During the interval the choir of the Christian Schools, St. Mary's-place, which had obtained first place in the Boys' Competition of the preceding day, sang some part songs.

Opinion of
one of the
Judges.

Mr. Cowley, who is Superintendent of Music in the Board Schools, London, in the address which he delivered in announcing the awards, congratulated the schools on the great progress they had made during the last ten years. The singing of the best choirs was excellent, and the performances on the whole nearly as good as those in London. Indeed, he said, as regards the majority of the London schools, the singing there that day was better than they could produce under similar circumstances.

The Competition was the great musical event of the year in the Dublin schools. For months it had been looked forward to, in school circles, with anxious expectancy. Its effect from a musical point of view has been immense, especially in those schools which undertook to prepare for it. But there is scarcely a music teacher in the schools of Dublin and the neighbourhood who has not received new lights from seeing what even mere school children can be brought to do. The standard of performance, especially in the Girls' schools, has been raised, and considerably raised, and an excellence in part and sight singing obtained which a few years ago was unknown.

General
effects of the
Competi-
tion.

But while the Competition has shown the excellence of the singing of the Girls' schools, it has also shown the inferiority of the Boys' schools in this subject. In the London schools it would seem the boys are, if not better than, at least quite equal to, the girls in singing. Our last Competition has however conclusively shown that, as compared with the Girls' our Boys' schools are simply nowhere. This is an important matter. I shall not dwell upon it now, but hope to direct attention again to it on another occasion.

Amongst those who appeared to follow the doings of the children at the Competition with particular interest was the late Resident Commissioner of National Education, Sir Patrick Keenan, with whom indeed originated the idea of these Competitions. He expressed himself as greatly pleased with the performance of the different choirs. By his death in November last music in Ireland has lost a staunch patron, and Irish musicians a kind friend.

I am, Gentlemen, your obedient servant,

P. GOODMAN.

The Secretaries,
    Office of National Education,
        Marlborough-street.

APPENDIX D.

(L.)—LITERARY CLASSIFICATION of the PUPILS who attended School once or oftener within the last Fourteen Days of the Month immediately preceding the Results Examinations in 1894.

District and Groups.	Infants.	Class I.	Class II.	Class III.	Class IV.	Class V.	Class VI.	Class VII.	Total.
1. Letterkenny,	2,258	2,070	1,887	1,591	857	633	318	375	11,880
2. Londonderry,	1,947	2,145	3,790	1,691	1,113	541	48	48	12,372
2A. "	783	488	374	351	530	186	147	343	3,158
3. Coleraine,	2,356	1,458	1,459	1,512	1,823	763	511	685	14,846
4. Ballymena,	2,138	1,451	1,631	1,890	1,146	119	626	633	20,157
5. Donegal,	2,607	1,989	1,194	1,268	1,617	819	573	688	9,358
6. Rathbane,	2,709	1,661	1,848	1,380	841	800	374	188	8,880
7. Castlederg,	3,003	1,480	1,800	1,586	1,080	718	441	480	8,953
8. Belfast, North,	1,187	8,006	5,134	3,697	8,883	1,408	384	719	23,358
8A. Carrickfergus,	3,187	1,645	1,803	1,489	1,188	841	421	877	14,877
9. Belfast, South,	4,308	2,483	8,796	2,578	1,860	1,303	343	488	16,044
9A. "	1,848	1,001	704	680	861	334	348	313	4,631
10. Newtownards,	0,488	2,848	2,547	3,847	1,851	1,307	347	686	14,363
11. Lurgan,	4,648	1,783	1,673	1,848	1,159	810	448	688	11,138
12. Sligo,	2,373	1,423	1,380	1,691	1,357	871	638	737	10,089
13. Enniskillen,	2,876	1,307	1,180	1,116	873	576	877	476	8,881
14. Omagh,	3,489	1,380	1,300	1,864	888	730	448	813	8,818
15. Dungannon,	3,880	1,681	1,648	1,853	1,653	783	498	613	14,179
16. Armagh,	2,811	1,915	1,814	1,105	1,671	773	631	708	9,873
17. Downpatrick,	2,307	1,468	1,533	1,378	1,364	812	388	820	16,183
18. Monaghan,	1,787	1,833	1,533	1,861	1,633	886	403	348	8,848
19. Newry,	3,859	1,879	1,804	1,613	1,341	821	488	803	10,846
20. Ballina,	9,653	1,688	1,897	1,788	1,360	883	458	611	11,448
21. Ballaghaderreen,	3,538	1,637	1,715	1,676	1,445	1,488	784	748	23,661
22. Boyle,	3,378	1,538	1,378	1,787	1,686	833	633	658	8,489
23. Cavan,	6,888	1,844	3,380	1,884	1,188	838	514	618	9,838
24. Ballieborough,	3,388	1,483	1,497	1,688	1,337	847	445	588	15,847
25. Dundalk,	8,788	1,800	1,848	1,840	2,188	868	473	813	11,711
26. Westport,	3,884	1,884	2,688	1,850	1,641	1,488	613	641	12,862
27. Roscommon,	2,878	1,674	1,611	1,681	1,616	1,670	348	778	31,833
28. Longford,	2,738	1,871	1,680	1,468	1,183	613	639	711	10,733
29. Trim,	8,888	1,590	1,800	1,178	1,017	779	601	648	9,848
30. Dublin, North,	8,888	1,685	2,680	1,488	1,448	883	503	603	17,483
30A. "	1,880	688	676	441	373	171	114	88	4,838
31. Ballinasloe,	3,448	1,883	1,468	1,418	1,318	834	818	883	9,838
32. Tuam,	8,788	3,187	3,191	2,048	2,676	1,381	779	743	14,880

LITERARY CLASSIFICATION of the PUPILS who attended School once or
oftener within the last Fourteen Days of the Month immediately preceding the Results Examination in 1891—*continued.*

District and Centre.	Infants.	Class I.	Class II.	Class III.	Class IV.	Class V.	Class VI.	Class VII.	Total.
33. Mullingar,									
34. Galway,									
34A. ,,									
35. Ballinasloe,									
36. Parsonstown,									
37. Dublin, South (I).									
38. Listowel,									
39. Dublin, South (II).									
40A.									
41. Portarlington,									
42. Cork,									
43. Templemore,									
44. Athy,									
45. Ennis,									
46. Tipperary,									
47. Kilkenny,									
48. Youghal,									
49. Waterford,									
50. Wexford,									
51. Limerick,									
52. Rathkeale,									
53. Clonmel,									
54. Tralee,									
55. Millstreet,									
56. Mallow,									
57. Killarney,									
58. Bantry,									
59. Dunmanway,									
60. Cork,									
60A.									
Grand Total,									
Per-centage,									
Per-centage,									

APPENDIX E.

APPENDIX E.

TABLE No. 1.—Classification of 8,500 National Schools in regard to cleanliness of School-rooms and Children, also Out-Offices.

District and Centre	Out-Offices				School-rooms			Children			Total Number of Schools
	Good	Middling	Dirty	None	Good	Middling	Bad	Good	Middling	Bad	
1. Londonderry.	80	18	3	10	127	91	9	130	80	–	168
2. Londonderry.	128	54	0	3	111	83	1	03	80	6	159
3a. „	31	4	–	1	34	4	.	33	5	–	8
3. Coleraine.	111	30	6	14	108	61	8	134	25	–	159
4. Ballymena.	56	48	10	36	78	73	6	63	63	1	147
5. Donegal,	70	21	4	45	60	65	3	85	63	–	143
6. Strabane,	76	53	8	80	80	66	13	108	28	10	188
7. Cadirdawan,	146	83	1	8	117	38	2	117	85	5	163
8. Belfast, North.	118	16	4	–	128	10	–	84	36	–	189
8a. Carrickfergus,	128	17	4	8	181	21	–	123	37	–	188
9. Belfast, South,	101	10	8	–	148	15	7	191	1	–	153
9a. „	23	13	–	–	34	14	3	30	0	6	48
10. Newtownards,	146	2	–	–	141	7	–	148	0	–	318
11. Lurgan,	94	80	6	8	150	6	3	149	9	–	153
12. Sligo,	67	26	10	13	77	45	11	91	43	5	129
13. Enniskillen,	104	25	4	13	110	21	4	129	28	–	153
14. Omagh,	191	15	8	8	118	25	3	139	25	6	149
15. Dungannon,	98	43	–	9	94	30	–	111	33	–	147
16. Armagh,	81	40	61	2	119	30	6	120	27	9	163
17. Downpatrick,	70	40	15	8	80	33	1	113	28	–	141
18. Monaghan,	118	4	0	20	109	18	2	148	–	1	148
19. Newry,	88	83	4	6	87	70	3	72	64	–	146
20. Dublin,	71	23	7	30	91	37	0	96	28	7	146
21. Sutherland,	118	3	7	16	129	11	1	131	16	1	167
22. Boyle,	88	3	•	80	140	16	8	167	•	–	177
23. Cavan,	70	41	2	32	116	38	–	08	80	–	146
24. Enniscorthy,	76	28	6	88	130	13	6	103	40	3	116
25. Dundalk,	80	16	0	15	94	36	7	98	70	6	137
26. Westport,	122	0	–	19	148	78	–	139	23	–	146
27. Roscommon,	88	4	6	63	113	21	6	113	21	2	138
28. Longford,	83	25	16	17	73	67	6	109	34	1	153
29. Trim,	118	91	–	6	229	16	6	127	9	–	146

Table No. 1.—Classification of 8,500 National Schools in regard to cleanliness of School-rooms and Children, also Out-Offices—*continued.*

District and Centre	A Out-Offices				B School-rooms			C Children			Total Number of schools
	Good	Middling	Bad	Exec.	Good	Middling	Bad	Good	Middling	Bad	
29. Dublin, North,	168	13	–	6	113	16	–	117	12	–	129
30. „ „	34	9	–	–	37	6	–	35	8	–	43
31. Ballinasloe,	67	23	3	26	90	19	11	76	65	0	179
32. Tuam,	115	13	–	9	123	10	1	150	7	–	157
33. Mullingar,	80	61	18	19	108	16	21	103	13	21	168
34. Galway,	76	30	22	17	91	11	30	90	43	–	133
34a.	23	8	–	3	38	6	–	30	7	–	46
35. Ballinasloe,	59	30	20	23	53	64	23	49	80	13	160
36. Parsonstown,	64	20	6	23	110	22	3	123	23	–	115
37. Dublin, South, 1.	83	22	6	9	107	9	1	107	9	1	117
38. Listowel,	91	19	7	7	60	22	0	91	31	6	128
41. Dublin, South, 2.	91	38	3	11	70	43	18	82	61	6	144
41a. „ „	31	4	–	–	20	7	–	23	2	–	23
42. Portarlington,	90	33	6	12	160	30	10	83	14	10	144
43. Cork,	91	18	6	13	100	23	10	117	20	–	133
44. Thurles,	66	10	8	60	68	37	2	67	27	3	127
45. Athy,	101	21	2	10	97	30	18	153	10	–	148
46. Ennis,	83	10	4	30	63	22	3	115	8	–	127
46. Tipperary,	60	26	2	91	63	31	8	67	54	1	128
47. Kilkenny,	116	6	8	81	231	13	6	133	13	1	154
48. Youghal,	103	13	6	6	80	33	8	70	19	4	137
49. Waterford,	101	10	6	13	83	23	3	111	20	2	139
50. Wexford,	81	17	7	24	83	73	4	90	65	6	120
51. Limerick,	80	19	18	18	81	23	0	87	36	1	115
52. Rathkeale,	73	30	–	6	74	27	7	83	18	1	113
53. Clonmel,	30	61	18	13	82	14	6	76	40	3	119
54. Tralee,	80	34	4	14	78	31	2	80	51	–	111
55. Milltown,	85	84	1	8	71	21	–	79	37	6	113
56. Mallow,	71	20	6	8	63	37	8	90	19	–	123
57. Killarney,	81	16	10	1	73	10	11	78	60	11	137
58. Bantry,	90	18	6	13	87	21	6	100	13	–	188
59. Dunmanway,	84	35	3	10	76	37	18	19	19	4	123
60. Cork,	118	12	3	8	127	10	1	157	23	–	148
61. „ „	19	7	8	7	61	6	2	24	8	–	23
Total,	**5,887**	**1,876**	**374**	**1,406**	**5,173**	**1,903**	**568**	**6,457**	**1,538**	**181**	**8,600**

TABLE No. 2.—Classification of 8,500 National Schools

District and Centre.	No. of Schools Returned.	A. Building, Repairs, &c.			D. Furniture and Apparatus.		
		Good.	Middling.	Bad.	Good.	Middling.	Bad.
1. Letterkenny,							
2. Londonderry,							
3.							
4. Coleraine,							
5. Ballymena,							
6. Donegal,							
7. Strabane,							
8. Castlewellan,							
9. Belfast, North,							
9A. Carrickfergus,							
9. Belfast, South.							
10. Newtownards,							
11. Lurgan,							
12. Sligo,							
13. Enniskillen,							
14. Omagh,							
15. Dungannon,							
16. Armagh,							
17. Downpatrick,							
18. Monaghan,							
19. Newry,							
20. Ballina,							
21. Swineford,							
22. Boyle,							
23. Cavan,							
24. Ballyborough,							
25. Dundalk,							
26. Westport,							
27. Roscommon,							
28. Longford,							
29. Trim,							
30. Dublin, North.							
31.							
32. Ballinamore,							
33. Tuam,							
34. Mullingar,							
35. Galway,							
36.							
36. Ballinasloe,							
37. Parsonstown,							
38. Dublin, South, 1.							
39. Listowel,							
40. Dublin, South, 1.							
40A.							
41. Portarlington,							
42. Gort,							
43. Templemore,							
44. Athy,							
45. Ennis,							
46. Tipperary,							
47. Kilkenny,							
48. Youghal,							
49. Waterford,							
50. Wexford,							
51. Limerick,							
52. Rathkeale,							
53. Clonmel,							
54. Tralee,							
55. Millstreet,							
56. Mallow,							
57. Killarney,							
58. Bandry,							
59. Dunmanway,							
60. Cork,							
61.							
Total,	8,500	6,029	1,788	683	6,808	1,079	613

in regard to heads indicated in the following Table:—

C. Premises, Playgrounds, &c.				D. Space Accommodation.			E. Supply of Books and other Requisites.			Districts.
Good.	Middling.	Bad.	None.	Good.	Middling.	Bad.	Good.	Middling.	Bad.	
[illegible]	[illegible]	[illegible]	[illegible]	[illegible]	[illegible]	[illegible]	[illegible]	[illegible]	[illegible]	[illegible]
4,642	1,065	627	1,528	6,765	1,505	440	6,650	1,637	227	

APPENDIX F.

REPORT of the NATIONAL SCHOOL TEACHERS' (Ireland) PENSION FUND, under the Act 42 & 43 Vict. cap. 74, for the Year ended 31st December, 1894.

1. The fifteenth year of the operation of the Act ended on the 31st December, 1894.

2. The fluctuation of numbers on the Pension Establishment under the Act was as follows :—

	MALES.					FEMALES.					Total both sexes
	3rd Class.	2nd Class.	1st Class.	1½ Class.	Total.	3rd Class.	2nd Class.	1st Class.	1½ Class.	Total.	
On the Books on the 31st December, 1893. First appointed in 1894. Re-appointed in 1894. Promoted into Class, 1894. Depressed from Class above, 1894.	2,670 173 61 — 2	1,880 — 16 33 1	416 — 4 37 —	159 — 1 6 —	4,800 365 62 3,118 8	2,371 600 79 — 1	1,461 — 14 72 —	240 — 9 15 —	128 — 3 3 —	4,480 — — — 3	10,370 E1 125 — 8
	3,118	1,872	411	157	6,690	2,855	1,557	280	134	4,798	11,65
Removed from Establishment on account of Age, or receipt of Pension or Gratuity. Quitted the Service, 1894. Promoted out of Class, 1894. Depressed to Lower Class, 1894. Died, 1894.	23 25 68 — 80	34 33 37 9 18	14 18 8 1 3	4 3 — — —	60 130 113 8 61	40 150 79 — 80	35 21 14 8 10	18 8 8 1 1	5 — — — —	67 180 — 7 8	125 83 228 4 71
Remained on Books, 31st December, 1894. Maximum Number allowed by the Act .	2,850 3,170	1,850 1,850	410 415	159 145	4,800 4,800	2,870 2,370	1,550 1,550	750 250	130 150	4,600 4,600	9,130 9,130

3. The Model School Teachers who have availed themselves of the supplemental privilege conferred under Rules 37 to 43, are as follows :—

	Males.	Females.	Total.
On the Books, 31st December, 1893. Joined in 1894.	62 5	71 1	129 6
Total . .	87	14	141
Removed from Establishment on account of Age, or on receipt of Gratuity, or award of Pension in 1894. Died in 1894. Resigned or Dismissed, 1894.	9 . .	4 . .	7 . .
On the Books, 31st December, 1894.	54	60	144
Maximum Number allowed. .	.	.	659
Supplemental Pensions :	£ s. d.	£ s. d.	£ s. d.
Amount payable 31st Dec., 1893. Granted in 1894. Ceased in 1894.	248 7 8 77 3 0	405 16 5 144 11 6	653 3 8 122 5 6
Amount Payable on 31st Dec., 1894.	668 16 8	549 6 4	1,175 3 5

APPENDIX G.

I.—List of One Hundred and Fifty-eight Vested Schools on the Suspended List at end of year 1894.

County.	Diocese	Parish.	Roll No.	School.		How vested.
Antrim,	8	Armoy,	1200	Breen,	m.	v. v.
Do.,	8	Tullyrusk,	3557	Dundrod,	f.	v.c.
Do.,	-	Shankill,	0653	Crevilill,	t.	v.v.
Do.,	8a	Killead,	7814	Ballskill,		v.c.
Cavan,	23	Annagh.C.W.	129	Corlurgan,	m.	a.
Do.,	-	Kildrumsherdan,	145	Corsnary,		v.v.
Do.,	-	Do.,	114	Do.,	f.	v.v.
Do.,	-	Urney,	157	Comboyogue,	m.	v.v.
Do.,	-	Do.,	188	Do.,	t.	v.v.
Do.,	-	Annagh,	3370	Kilnaleck,		v.v.
Do.,	-	Kildrumsherdan,	11206	Killasherdra,	t.	v.v.
Do.,	-	Drumlummon,	138	St. Joseph's,	a.	v.v.
Do.,	-	Do.,	184	Do.,	t.	v.v.
Do.,	-	Crosserlough,	13019	Crosserlough,	f.	v.v.
Do.,	24	Laragn,	3190	Laittmen,	t.	v.v.
Do.,	-	Drungnos,	3320	Oslaw,	t.	v.v.
Donegal,	3	Muff,	2980	Tore,	f.	v.c.
Do.,	-	Fahan, Lower,	6824	Tullydish,	f.	v.c.
Do.,	5	Killevmyan,	4421	Ballyshannon,	f.	v.c.
Down,	17	Bright,	4743	Bright,	m.	v.c.
Do.,	-	Kilclief,	18672	Kilclief		v.v.
Fermanagh,	13	Gallow,	291	Drumberry,		v.v.
Do.,	-	Magheraculmoney,	288	Tulnacorgay,		v.v.
Do.,	-	Aghavea,	11552	Brookboro',	m.	v.c.
Londonderry,	3	Killowen,	3097	Kilowen-street,	m.	v.v.
Do.,	7	Tamlaght O'Crilly,	3486	Drumgarner,	t.	v.v.
Do.,	-	Upper Cumber,	3496	Gleanndale,	m.	v.c.
Do.,	-	Maghera,	3396	Lammaroy,	t.	a.
Monaghan,	18	Tydavnet,	1773	Knockatallon,	t.	v.v.
Do.,	-	Do.,	4653	Tullyeratemsin,	t.	v.v.
Do.,	-	Ematris,	10450	Corravessan,	t.	v.v.
Do.,	-	Drumsnatt,	10453	Drumsheray,	t.	v.v.
Do.,	24	Magherose,	347	Carrickmacross,	f.	v.v.
Tyrone,	2	Donaghedy,	1260	Donaghedy,	f.	a.
Do.,	8	Badoney, Upper,	3678	Letterbuoy,	f.	v.c.
Do.,	14	Kilskeery,	3777	Feglish,	f.	v.v.
Do.,	-	Cappagh,	390	Carrigans, Lower,		v.v.
Do.,	-	Clogher,	398	Kalen,	m.	v.v.
Do.,	-	Errigle Keerogue,	413	Glascoll,	m.	v.v.
Do.,	-	Clogher,	1090	Kalen,	t.	v.v.
Do.,	-	Donaghedy,	2456	Blackfort,	t.	v.c.
Do.,	-	Cappagh,	3544	Reyheag,		a.
Do.,	-	Clogher,	11441	Fivemiletown,		v.c.
Do.,	18	Kilreret,	418	Dunamore,	t.	v.v.
Do.,	-	Pomeroy,	1142	Altmore,		v.c.
Do.,	-	Kildress,	1370	Stewartsmardra,		v.v.
Clare,	42	Dysart,	1254	Mayrhea,	m.	a.
Do.,	-	Kilmoon,	3198	Cahorballag,	m.	v.v.
Do.,	-	Do.,	3199	Do.,	f.	v.v.
Do.,	45	Drumelliba,	448	Newtownsashpoale, tn.		v.v.
Do.,	-	Do.,	5514	Do.,	t.	v.v.
Do.,	51	Oloolea,	4480	Kilkishen,	m.	v.v.
Do.,	-	Do.,	4489	Do.,	t.	v.v.
Cork,	53	Killashlual,	2809	Dromleigh,	t.	v.v.
Do.,	-	Omerea,	3130	Canovee,	m.	v.v.
Do.,	-	Canovee,	8486	Canovee,	t.	v.v.

L.—List of One Hundred and Fifty-eight Vested Schools on the
Suspended List at end of year 1894—*continued.*

County.	No.	Parish.	Roll No.	School.	How vested.
Cork,	55	Drishane,	1690	Millstreet (1),	. V.S.
Do.,	–	Nohavaldaly,	5244	King-William's-town, m.	V.S.
Do.,	–	Do.,	5245	Do.,	V.T.
Do.,	56	Britway,	5964	Britway,	V.S.
Do.,	–	Desertsale,	4125	Shanbeg, m.	V.T.
Do.,	–	Blarney,	1542	Blarney,	V.T.
Do.,	–	Kilshanig,	3930	Kilpadder,	V.S.
Do.,	–	Desertale,	11570	Ballyvacane, m.	V.S.
Do.,	–	Carrigtuohill,	12517	Ulster and Carig, m.	V.T.
Do.,	58	Marmrat,	3119	Carrstranen, m.	A.
Do.,	–	Do.,	9143	Do.,	L.
Do.,	–	Skibbereen,	5141	Skibbereen (4),	V.S.
Do.,	–	Ardfield,	10037	Ardfield,	V.T.
Do.,	–	Castlehaven,	5716	Castletownsend, m.	V.G.
Do.,	–	Do.,	5717	Do., f.	V.G.
Do.,	–	Kilmoen,	13507	Ballyvortane,	V.S.
Do.,	–	Tullagh,	1978	Sherkin Island,	V.P.
Kerry,	59	Killeentierna,	10958	Lixnaw,	V.E.
Do.,	–	Killarney,	9121	Gortamakeel,	V.P.
Do.,	54	Dingle,	1778	Dingle,	V.S.
Do.,	–	Killiney,	9191	Cualagregory, m.	V.T.
Do.,	–	Do.,	9192	Do.,	V.S.
Do.,	–	Ballinahaglish,	5453	Gun, f.	V.T.
Do.,	55	Kilcummin,	2905	Rushrow,	V.T.
Do.,	57	Killarney,	1909	Gortaguilane,	V.T.
Do.,	–	Killiney,	9155	Filemore, m.	V.T.
Do.,	–	Do.,	9194	Do.,	V.T.
Do.,	–	Templenoe,	5143	Greaghanlagh,	V.G.
Do.,	–	Kilcrohan,	5256	Inam, f.	V.G.
Do.,	–	Do.,	10059	Lauderdaisk, f.	V.G.
Do.,	58	Kenmare,	7950	Kenmare, f.	A.
Limerick,	59	Kilfinny,	1960	Kilfinny, m.	V.S.
Do.,	–	Do.,	1967	Do., f.	V.S.
Do.,	59	Ballingarry,	2210	Ballingarry, f.	V.P.
Tipperary,	56	Cloughprior,	2076	Carney, m.	V.T.
Do.,	–	Borrisokane,	5694	Kyle Park, m.	V.G.
Do.,	57	Templemore,	10453	Ardmore, m.	V.S.
Do.,	55	Roscrea and Athnowen	12760	Leggamstown,	V.S.
Do.,	–	Do.,	9450	Ballynasarse,	V.G.
Waterford,	59	Tallow,	5690	Kilmolf, m.	A.
Do.,	–	Do.,	4316	Ballyduff,	V.T.
Do.,	59	Mothell,	4157	Coolnahorna,	V.T.
Dublin,	59	Rathmichael,	5295	Ballycorus, m.	V.G.
Kildare,	57	Cloncurry,	1497	Newtown,	V.S.
Do.,	–	Donaghcumper,	5451	Abbey,	V.G.
Do.,	44	Donadea,	5719	Levitstown,	V.T.
Kilkenny,	47	Grange,	760	Church Hill,	V.S.
Do.,	–	Powerstown,	1151	Skeoughvosteen,	V.T.
Do.,	–	St. John's,	8415	St. John's,	V.T.
Do.,	–	Do.,	10659	St. John's Preparatory m.	V.T.
Do.,	59	Listerling,	1977	Mullinakill,	V.S.
King's,	59	Drumcullen,	2414	Thomastown,	V.T.
Do.,	41	Kilfidh,	829	Tullamore, m.	V.S.
Longford,	55	Columkill,	2373	Clonee,	V.S.
Louth,	54	Drumshallon,	1305	Kellystown, m.	A.
Do.,	–	Ballybranigan,	1355	Walshestown, m.	V.T.
Do.,	–	Termonfeckin,	5304	Cartown,	V.S.
Do.,	–	Ardee,	5385	Ardee Monastry, m.	V.T.

I.—List of One Hundred and Fifty-eight Vested Schools on the Suspended List at the end of year 1894—*continued.*

County.	District.	Parish.	Roll No.	School.	How Vested.
Meath,	25	Kilsharvin,	1176	Mount Hanover,	l.	V.T.
Do.,	25	Clonalvy,	2089	Clonalvy,	m.	V.T.
Do.,	29	Donaghmill,	1827	Batterstown,		V.V.
Do.,	—	Oaklestown,	8147	Oaklestown,	f.	V.V.
Do.,	—	Kilskeer,	8813	Carnlea,	l.	V.T.
Do.,	—	Clonarduff,	4409	Tullaghanstown,		V.T.
Do.,	28	Trim,	4390	Phillerstown,		V.V.
Queen's,	44	Tullmoy,	1635	Luggacurren,	m.	V.C.
Do.,	—	Killabban,	4779	Killabban,	f.	V.C.
Westmeath,	33	Ballyloughloe,	939	Mount Temple,	m.	V.V.
Do.,	—	Do.,	1206	Do.,	l.	V.V.
Do.,	—	Ballymore,	1313	Newbrisay,	m.	V.T.
Do.,	29	Castlepollard Delvin,	2158	Crowenstown,	m.	V.T.
Do.,	41	Rahugh,	2906	Rahugh,	l.	V.T.
Wexford,	49	Hook,	11895	Loftus Hall,	l.	V.E.
Do.,	50	Ballybeg,	1491	Oakbally,	l.	V.T.
Do.,	—	Horetown,	8937	Courtnacuddy,	m.	V.G.
Do.,	—	Carrick,	20780	Barntown,	f.	V.V.
Do.,	—	Marshalstown,	12740	Marshalstown,	m.	V.T.
Wicklow,	46	Rathdrum,	5850	Rathdrum,	l.	V.C.
Galway,	26	Ballinakill,	1319	Tully,		V.T.
Do.,	34	Kilcommin,	1787	Oughterard,		V.C.
Do.,	—	Moyrus,	8566	Marvey,	f.	V.C.
Do.,	—	Oranmore,	6789	Maclough,	m.	V.V.
Do.,	34a	Oranmore,	4507	Oranmore,		V.C.
Do.,	35	Abbey,	590	Brierfield,	l.	V.T.
Do.,	—	Lickerig,	1019	Lickerig,	f.	V.V.
Do.,	—	Loughrea,	1011	Loughrea,	l.	V.T.
Do.,	—	Kilconnell,	12910	Woodlawn,	m.	V.T.
Do.,	43	Killimmoury,	1338	Killalaus,	l.	V.T.
Do.,	—	Do.,	1870	Do.,	l.	V.T.
Do.,	—	Killanaheagh,	4781	Gort,	l.	V.C.
Mayo,	30	Crossmolina,	4810	Kishmond,	m.	V.T.
Do.,	—	Do.,	4011	Do.,	l.	V.T.
Do.,	—	Turmore,	12636	Fanford,	l.	V.T.
Do.,	21	Kilmainemoy,	8031	Swinford,	l.	V.T.
Do.,	26	Kilfidan,	1618	Newtownlavrown,		V.T.
Do.,	—	Aughaval,	2823	Murrisk,	m.	A.
Do.,	—	Burrishoole,	4651	Newport Pratt,	l.	A.
Roscommon,	65	St. Peter's,	6192	Derrynark,	l.	V.T.
Do.,	—	Cure,	1603	Carrick,		V.T.
Do.,	22	Kilbixie,	2494	Cartabor,	l.	V.T.
Sligo,	20	Kilbroumtannaghan,	4489	Castlerock,		V.T.
Do.,	21	Cloonoughill,	12808	Bunninaddea,	l.	V.T.

Ia.—List of Eleven Vested Model School Departments,[1] amalgamated with other Departments of same School.

County.	District.	Roll No.	School.		Parish.		How Vested.
Cavan,	34	6514	Bailiebore' Model,	l.	Bailieborough,		V.C.
Tipperary,	58	5635	Clonmel	f.	Clonmel,		V.C.
Waterford,	46	6976	Waterford	l.	St. John's,		V.C.
Dublin,	41a	4089	Glasnevin,	f.	Glasnevin,		V.C.
Kildare,	44	6515	Athy	l.	St. Michael's,		V.C.
Kilkenny,	47	6968	Kilkenny	l.	St. Patrick's,		V.C.
King's,	34	7251	Parsonstown	l.	Birr,		V.C.
Meath,	29	6691	Trim	f.	Trim,		V.C.
Do.,	—	5693	Do.		Do.,		V.C.
Wexford,	50	7768	Enniscorthy	l.	St. Mary's (Enniscorthy),		V.C.
Galway,	34a	6216	Galway	l.	Rahoon,		V.C.

[1] The Boy departments of the Infant Department of Dunmanway Model School was rebuilt.

II.—List of Two Hundred and Ninety-one Vested Schools, towards the erection of which the Commissioners had sanctioned Grants, but which had not come into operation on 31st December, 1894.

County.	District.	Parish.	Roll No.	School.	Number of Pupils to be accommodated.			Sanctioned.
					Males.	Females.	Total.	
Ulster.								
Antrim,	7	Rashurkin,	14511	St. Patrick's,	m.	190	—	190	Y.C.
"	"	Do.	14512	Do.	f.	—	100	100	Y.C.
"	8a	Larne,	14513	North End,	m.			200	Y.Z.
"	9	Shankill,	14774	Maiow,				200	Y.Z.
"	4	Do.	14573	Do.	Inft.			200	
Armagh,	11	Sergon,	13711	Aghnamullen,		160	100	260	Y.P.
"	"	Shankill,	13712	Silverwood,		40	40	80	Y.Y.
"	16	Derrynoose,	14325	Derrymaco,	m.	100	—	100	Y.Y.
"	"	Do.	14326	Do.	f.	—	100	100	Y.Y.
"	21	Creggan,	13673	Cregganduff,		60	40	100	Y.Z.
Cavan,	23	Annaclife,	13790	Kilnarry,		60	62	122	Y.Z.
"	"	Dean,	14576	Larkin,		40	40	80	Y.Z.
"	"	Lurch,	14780	Cliffonia,	m.	90	—	90	Y.Z.
"	"	Do.	14781	Do.	f.	—	60	60	Y.Z.
"	24	Skervech,	13812	Nelagh,		60	40	100	Y.Z.
"	"	Annaheen,	13711	Largan,		41	40	81	Y.Z.
"	"	Knockbride,	14216	Knockbride,		40	40	80	Y.C.
"	"	Ennishmore,	14220	Corban,	m.	60	—	60	Y.P.
"	"	Do.	14221	Do.	f.	—	60	60	Y.Z.
"	"	Ellishere,	14811	Derryham,		51	60	108	Y.Z.
"	"	Knockbride,	14809	Hackhagarro,		60	60	120	Y.Z.
"	51	Knowley,	14471	Tirvelan,		40	50	170	Y.Y.
Donegal,	1	Tullygaten,	13152	Illy,		60	60	120	Y.Z.
"	"	Inishkeel,	14001	Beagh,		40	50	90	Y.Z.
"	"	Kilmacrenan,	14101	Termon,		75	75	150	Y.Z.
"	"	Mevagh,	14277	Glen,		60	60	120	Y.Z.
"	"	Templecrone,	14215	Mullaghduff,		60	60	120	Y.Y.
"	"	Tullaghobegley,	14242	Derrybeg,	m.	75	—	75	Y.C.
"	"	Do.	14243	Do.	f.	—	75	75	Y.C.
"	"	Crannull,	14342	Letterkenny,		150	—	150	Y.C.
"	3	Moville Lower,	14352	Moville,	m.	160	—	160	Y.Z.
"	"	Inangh,	14348	St. Patrick's,	m.	60	—	60	Y.Z.
"	"	Culdaff,	14321	Coolkenny,	m.	60	—	60	Y.Z.
"	"	Moville, Lower,	14352	Bredagh Glen,		60	60	120	Y.Z.
"	5	Inver,	14378	Drumnabrath,		60	60	120	Y.Z.
"	"	Innishlongo,	14452	Lagley,		40	40	80	Y.Z.
"	"	Johnstakshat,	14531	Bundoran Convent,		80	110	250	Y.Z.
"	"	Kilear,	14565	Crona,		60	20	64	Y.Z.
Down,	10	Greyabbey,	14117	Ballyrolery,		60	60	120	Y.C.
"	"	Knocklurde,	14551	Lagan Village,	m.	125	—	125	Y.Z.
"	"	Do.	14552	Do.	f.	—	125	125	Y.Z.
"	10	Killead,	13810	Barbs,		40	40	80	Y.Z.
"	"	Do.	14569	Brackney,		40	40	80	Y.Y.
"	"	Do.	14573	Kumejobragh,		84	15	100	Y.Y.
Fermanagh,	12	Galloon,	13611	Drumionet,		60	60	75	Y.Y.
Londonderry,	2	Templemore,	14318	Derry,	m.			166	Y.Y.
"	"	Do.	14319	Do.	f.				Y.Y.
"	3	Formoyle,	14454	Ballinleen,		40	40	80	Y.Z.
"	7	Maghera,	13500	Listamuch,				80	Y.Z.
"	"	Magherafelt,	14616	Fahlill,	m.			200	Y.Z.
"	"	Do.	14617	Do.	f.				Y.Z.
Monaghan,	16	Morkre,	14595	Mullyash,		40	40	80	Y.Y.
"	"	Tydavret,	14644	Hamiltappy,		60	60	120	Y.Y.
"	"	Aghnamallen,	14510	Annoy,		80	80	80	Y.Z.
Tyrone,	15	Pomeroy,	14455	Kerrih,		60	60	120	Y.Z.
Munster.								
Clare,	42	Inchicronan,	14550	Ballornan,	m.	75	—	75	Y.Y.
"	"	Do.	14500	Do.	f.	—	75	75	Y.Z.
"	"	Feakle,	14453	Killero-an-Oir,		50	50	100	L.Z.

II.—List of Two Hundred and Ninety-one Vested Schools—*continued.*

County.	District.	Parish.	Roll No.	School.	Number of Pupils to be accommodated.			How vested.
					Males.	Females.	Total.	
MUNSTER—*con.*								
CLARE—*con.*	43	Tulgramey,	1178	Tulgramey, m.	75	—	75	V.T.
"	—	Do.	1471	Do. f.	—	75	75	V.T.
"	—	Kilferan,	1036	Kilferan,	40	40	80	V.T.
"	43	Kilnihill,	1826	Lackea, m.	150	—	150	V.T.
"	—	Do.	1227	Do. f.	—	150	150	V.T.
"	—	Kilnasry Davikes,	1242	Mulluck, f.	—	75	75	V.T.
"	—	Kilchreest,	1196	Island View,	60	60	120	V.T.
"	—	Kilfenar,	1323	Kilfenar, m.	15	—	75	V.C.
"	—	Do.	1704	Do. f.	—	75	75	V.C.
"	—	Kilfeush,	1213	Scattery Island,	Special plan for	45	V.T.
"	—	Inagh,	1440	The Spags,	60	50	110	V.C.
"	—	Kilrushry,	1449	Kilrushry,	75	—	75	V.T.
"	—	Do.	1302	Do. f.	—	75	75	V.T.
"	—	Kilmurragh,	1824	Termone,	60	60	120	V.T.
"	—	Inagh,	1332	Inagh, m.	75	—	75	V.T.
"	—	Do.	1455	Do. f.	—	75	75	V.T.
CORK.	63	Drishane,	1330	Hill-street, m.	350	—	350	V.C.
"	—	Do.	1331	Do. f.(?)	—	—	—	V.C.
"	56	Kilnoe,	1237	Kilnoe, m.	125	—	125	V.C.
"	—	Do.	1281	Do. f.	—	125	125	V.C.
"	—	Kilcrumper,	1452	Derryvira,	40	40	80	V.T.
"	—	Lackington,	1370	Ballinguvry,	150	—	150	V.T.
"	36	Kilcoe,	1353	Cape Coral, m.	60	—	60	V.C.
"	—	Do.	1311	Do.	—	—	60	V.C.
"	76	St. Anne's, Shandon,	1712	Blackpool, m.	Special plan for	360	V.T.
"	—	Do.	1713	Do. f.				V.T.
"	—	St. Molinne,	1105	St. John's (Kinsale),	400	—	400	V.T.
"	—	Aglish,	1431	Farran, f.	125	—	125	V.T.
"	—	Do.	1432	Do. f.	—	125	125	V.T.
"	—	Kinure,	1546	Oysterhaven, m.	60	—	60	V.T.
"	—	Do.	1347	Do. f.	—	60	60	V.T.
"	—	St. Nicholas,	1364	St. Joseph's Convent, m. inf.	250	—	250	V.T.
"	—	Holy Trinity,	1610	St. Francis, m.	Special plan for	300	V.T.
"	—	Do.	1611	Do. f.				V.T.
"	50A	Marmullane,	1450	St. Mary's,	300	—	300	V.T.
"	—	Caheriag,	1404	Ammount, m.	75	—	75	V.T.
"	—	Do.	1407	Do. f.	—	75	75	V.T.
KERRY.	54	Oughtdeland,	1121	Oughtdeland Convent, inf.	100	100	200	V.T.
"	—	Ballynaclogh,	1299	Longhmaclor,	40	40	80	V.C.
"	—	Ballymacelligott,	1374	Rumpus, m.	50	50	100	V.G.
"	—	Kilgarvan,	1449	St. Brendan's,	60	60	120	V.T.
"	—	Kilcolman,	1572	St. Joseph's (Millstreet, Co. Kerry), m.	200	—	200	V.T.
"	57	Knockane,	1344	Drish,	50	50	100	V.T.
"	—	Dromod,	1751	Derrinane, f.	50	50	100	V.T.
"	—	Killarney,	1434	Fairhill, m.	300	300	600	V.C.
"	—	Caher,	1330	Cooknore,	40	40	80	V.C.
"	—	Knockane,	1404	Gortderk,	30	30	60	V.G.
"	—	Tualist,	1863	Gurrane,	50	50	100	V.C.
LIMERICK.	20	Abbeyfeale,	1416	Foals View, m.	50	—	50	V.T.
"	—	Do.	1417	Do. f.	—	50	50	V.T.
"	45	Doon,	1632	Doon Convent, m.	—	150	150	V.C.
"	61	Fedamore,	1087	Fedamore, m.	100	—	100	V.T.
"	—	Do.	1058	Do. f.	—	100	100	V.T.
"	—	Murrere,	1409	Murgret, m.	100	—	100	V.T.
"	—	St. Michael,	1680	Sexton-street Convent, inf.	Special plan for	400	V.T.
"	80	Limerick,	1673	Ardagh, m.	125	—	125	V.T.
"	—	Do.	1678	Do. f.	—	125	125	V.T.
"	—	Ballingurry,	1335	St. Joseph's, inf.	Special plan for	300	V.T.

II.—List of Two Hundred and Ninety-one Vested Schools—*continued.*

County.	District.	Parish.	Roll No.	School.	Number of Pupils to be accommodated.			How vested.
					Males.	Females.	Total.	
MUNSTER—*con.*								
Tipperary, .	43	Brickendown,	14266	Marlhurshill, . . m.	60	60	120	V.T.
"	"	Oughterleague,	14424	Knockavilla, . .	75	–	75	V.T.
"	"	Do.	14427	Do. . . L.	–	75	75	V.T.
"	"	Killea,	14410	Killea, . . .	60	–	60	V.T.
"	"	Do.	14461	Do. . . L.	–	60	60	V.T.
Waterford, .	42	Do.	14455	Ballake, . .	50	50	100	V.A.
"	"	Do.	14568	KC'an, . . .	40	40	80	V.A.
"	"	Kilrossn,	14679	Butlerstown, . .	75	–	75	V.A.
"	"	Do.	14680	Do. . . L.	–	75	75	V.A.
LEINSTER.								
Carlow, .	41	Ballon,	14129	Ballon, . . . m.	120	–	120	V.T.
Dublin, .	47	Old Leighlin,	14166	Sligo, . . .	40	40	80	V.T.
"	50	St. Paul's,	14519	St. Gabriel's, . m.				
"	"	Do.	14519	Do. (Cowper-street, m. inf.), . f. inf.			770	V.T.
"	"	Do.	14550					
"	"	St. Thomas'	14514	East Wall, . . m.	175	–	175	V.T.
"	"	Do.	14525	Do. . . L.	–	175	175	V.T.T.
"	"	St. George's,	14565	St. Joseph's, m. sur.				
"	"	Do.	14586	Do. m. ppy.			700	V.T.
"	"	Do.	14687	Do. m. inf.				
"	"	Chantref,	14664	Havck-road, inf.			100	V.T.
"	57	Lucan,	14442	Lucan Convent, .			400	V.T.
"	"	St. Catherine's,	14548	St. Kevin's, . .	460	–	460	V.T.
"	"	St. Peter's,	14556	St. Peter's (White-friar-street), . m.				
"	"	Do.	14557	Do. . . L.			1400	V.T.
"	"	Do.	14544	Do. inf.				
"	"	Stillorgan,	14546	Blackrock, . . L.			800	V.T.
"	"	St. Mark's,	14438	St. Andrew's, . m.			1200	V.T.
"	"	Do.	14539	Do. . . L.				
Kildare,	44	Kilmoagh,	14418	Bigstown, . .	40	40	80	V.T.
Kilkenny,	47	St. Mary's,	13265	Kilkenny Convt. inf.	100	100	200	V.T.
"	"	Killalea,	14285	Ballyline, . .	40	40	80	V.T.
"	"	Dysart,	14826	Hamiltown, . .	60	60	120	V.T.
"	48	Tullaghea,	14419	Mulhanhill, . .	30	30	60	V.T.
"	"	Dysartmore,	14646	Toflegive, . .	40	40	80	V.T.
Longford,	20	Templemichael,	14281	Clonahard, . .	40	40	80	V.T.
"	"	Columbkille,	14592	St. Joseph's, . m.	60	–	60	V.T.
"	"	Do.	14593	Do. . . L.	–	60	60	V.T.
"	"	Granard,	14304	Killmana, . .	40	40	80	V.T.
"	"	Oughal,	14485	Gowendough, . .	125	–	125	V.T.
"	"	Do.	14436	Do. . . L.	–	125	125	V.T.
"	"	Killoe,	14479	Ennybeg, . .	60	60	150	V.T.
"	"	Do.	14481	Edenmore, . . m.	75	–	75	V.T.
"	"	Do.	14481	Do. . . L.	–	75	75	V.T.
"	"	Do.	14456	Glannagh, . .	60	30	100	V.T.
"	23	Tashinay,	14612	Colehill, . . m.	100	–	100	V.T.
"	"	Do.	14673	Do. . . L.	–	100	100	V.T.
Louth,	23	Kilsaran,	14607	Kilsaran, . . m.	150	–	150	V.T.
"	"	Do.	14608	Do. . . L.	–	150	150	V.T.
"	"	Clogher,	14296	Callystown, . .	125	–	125	V.T.
"	"	Do.	14293	Do. . . L.	–	125	125	V.T.
"	"	Ballymascanlan,	14237	Faughart, . .	30	30	60	V.T.
"	"	Grosson,	14540	Greerhouse, . .	60	60	120	V.T.
"	"	Callen,	14578	Callen, . . m.	75	–	75	V.T.
"	"	Do.	14579	Do. . . L.	–	75	75	V.T.
"	"	Dundalk,	14641	Castletown-road, .	250	–	250	V.T.
"	"	Do.	14651	Do. . . L.	–	250	250	V.T.
Meath,	24	Kentstown,	14318	Carrickleck, . .	50	50	100	V.T.

II.—List of Two Hundred and Ninety-one Vested Schools—*continued.*

County.	District.	Parish.	Roll No.	School.	Number of Pupils to be accommodated.			How vested.
					Males.	Females.	Total.	
LEINSTER—*con.*								
Queen's	41	Aghaboe,	14338	Grantstown Manor,	50	50	100	V.E.
"	"	Borris,	14156	Maryborough,	60	80	140	V.E.
"	"	Clonenagh,	14477	Kirness,	50	50	100	V.V.
Westmeath,	52	St. Feighin's,	14450	St. Feighin's, m.	75	—	75	V.E.
"	"	Do.	14451	Do. f.	—	75	75	V.E.
"	41	Rathconrath,	14615	Rathconrath Conv.,	—	256	256	V.V.
Kildare,	49	Kilbeggan,	14491	Kilbeggan Convent,	—	250	250	V.V.
		St. Mary's,	14544	St. Joseph's (New Ross) Convent	special places		400	V.V.
	50	St. Margaret's,	14593	Curraclee,	56	50	160	V.E.
	"	Ballybeckard,	14588	Balgaykeen,	60	50	120	V.V.
Wicklow,	49	Ballytain,	14587	Aughrim, m.	75	—	75	V.E.
"	"	Do.	14588	Do. f.	—	75	75	V.E.
"	"	Do.	14415	Ballyoreen,	30	30	60	V.E.
"	"	Baltinglass,	14583	Baltinglass Convent,	—	200	200	V.E.
"	44	Donaghmore,	14496	Davidstown,	20	40	60	V.E.
CONNAUGHT.								
Galway,	97	Kilkyne,	14219	Windfield, m.	100	—	100	V.E.
"	"	Do.	14219	Do. f.	—	100	100	V.E.
"	"	Do.	14283	Ballaghlea,	50	50	100	V.V.
"	93	Boyounagh,	12711	Cashel, m.	75	—	75	V.V.
"	"	Do.	12712	Do. f.	—	75	75	V.V.
"	"	Moylough,	14250	Moylough, m.	150	—	150	V.V.
"	"	Do.	14251	Do. f.	—	150	150	V.V.
"	"	Abbeyknockmoy,	14584	Brierfield, m.	100	—	100	V.E.
"	"	Do.	14585	Do. f.	—	100	100	V.E.
"	"	Kilconly,	14555	Tobberea, m.	123	—	123	V.E.
"	"	Do.	14556	Do. f.	—	125	125	V.E.
"	"	Killererin,	14555	Lissandusky, m.	125	—	125	V.V.
"	"	Do.	14556	Do. f.	—	125	125	V.T.
"	"	Do.	14550	Garra, f.	—	60	60	V.T.
"	"	Cong,	14554	Cargurve,	40	40	80	V.T.
"	34	Moyrus,	14391	Glynsk,	30	30	60	V.T.
"	"	Ballinakill,	14430	St. Patrick's (Tully),	50	50	100	V.V.
"	"	Killeany,	14415	Clongaaneve, m.	75	—	75	V.T.
"	"	Do.	14449	Do. f.	—	75	75	V.T.
"	"	Inishmore,	14553	Oatquarter,	100	100	200	V.T.
"	"	Killannin,	14559	St. Anne's, m.	75	—	75	V.E.
"	"	Do.	14561	Do. f.	—	75	75	V.E.
"	"	Lettermore,	14559	St. Anne's, f.	75	—	75	V.E.
"	"	Do.	14564	Do. f.	—	75	75	V.E.
"	85	Lickmolasy,	14159	St. Joseph's Convent,	—	200	200	V.E.
"	"	Aughrim,	14423	Aughrim, m.	75	—	75	V.E.
"	"	Do.	14424	Do. f.	—	75	75	V.E.
"	"	Kilconnell,	14577	Kilconnell, m.	75	—	75	V.E.
"	"	Do.	14578	Do. f.	—	75	75	V.V.
"	"	Clonkeenkerrill,	14583	Shanballard,	40	40	80	V.E.
"	42	Derrybrien,	14123	Derrybrien,	50	50	100	V.E.
"	"	Ardrahan,	14642	Ballyglass,	50	50	100	V.G.
"	5	Rossinver,	14501	Rossinver,	40	40	80	V.T.
Leitrim,	12	Inishmagrath,	13977	Tarmon, m.	75	—	75	V.T.
"	"	Do.	13978	Do. f.	—	75	75	V.V.
"	81	Kilmakilde,	14718	Kilcaire, m.	60	60	120	V.E.
"	"	Cloone,	14588	Oughteil, m.	100	—	100	V.V.
"	"	Do.	14589	Do. f.	—	100	100	V.V.
"	"	Drumreilly,	14470	Corravoohia,	40	40	80	V.V.
"	"	Do.	14518	Slievenakilla,	40	40	80	V.T.
"	"	Kiltoghert,	14580	St. Joseph's (Shanamoury)	40	40	80	V.E.
"	"	Do.	14479	St. Mary's (Aughagrahan),	50	50	100	V.E.

II.—List of Two Hundred and Ninety-one Vested Schools—*continued*

County.	District.	Parish.	Roll No.	School.	Number of Pupils to be Accommodated			Registered
					Males.	Females.	Total.	
CONNAUGHT—con.								
Mayo,		26	Kilmaine.	13849	Attymachugh,	60	—	60	V.S.
"		—	Do.	13810	Do.	—	60	60	V.S.
"		—	Kilcommon,	13862	Glencorrib,	—	—	—	V.S.
"		—	Do.	14162	Barnatra.	75	75	150	V.S.
"		—	Do.	14193	Doohoma,	60	—	60	V.S.
"		—	Dawnomoy,	14240	Ballycastle,	75	—	75	V.S.
"		—	Do.	14291	Do.	—	75	75	V.S.
"		—	Kilgarvan,	14301	Bunaveagha,	30	30	60	V.S.
"		—	Kilgarvan,	14418	Belfield,	125	—	125	V.S.
"		—	Do.	14419	Do.	—	125	125	V.S.
"		—	Crossmolina,	14420	Enaghbeg,	—	60	60	V.S.
"		—	Kilmore Erris,	14443	Inishkea Island, North.	30	30	60	V.S.
"		—	Kilmoremoyle,	14471	Cartagh,	55	55	110	V.S.
"		21	Killedan,	14473	Cancoerry.	60	60	120	V.S.
"		—	Kilmovee,	14530	Kilkelly,			110	V.S.
"		27	Burrishoole,	13653	Kilmeen,	100	75	75	V.S.
"		—	Roslea,	13868	Roslea.	100	—	100	V.S.
"		—	Do.	13820	Do.	—	100	100	V.S.
"		1	Aughaval,	13787	St. Patrick's, Lecanvey,	60	60	120	V.S.
"		—	Burrishoole,	13915	Rossgalliss,	60	60	120	V.S.
"		—	Mayo.	14206	Mayo,	125	—	125	V.S.
"		—	Do.	14202	Do.	—	125	125	V.S.
"		—	Islandeady,	14245	Beltra,	40	40	80	V.S.
"		—	Templemore,	14328	Strade,	75	—	75	V.S.
"		—	Do.	14370	Do.	—	75	75	V.S.
"		—	Aglish,	14410	St. Angela's P. Convent, Castlebar,				V.S.
"		—	Do.	14411	Do.				
"		—	Islandeady,	14437	St. Patrick's, Carramoal,	50	50	100	V.S.
"		—	Bohola,	14537	Lismirane,	100	—	100	V.S.
"		—	Manulla,	14544	Manulla,	75	—	75	V.S.
"		—	Do.	14545	Do.	—	75	75	V.S.
"		—	Ballyvary,	14654	Derrew,	40	40	80	V.S.
"		83	Annagh,	14281	St. Joseph's, Derryloran,	125	—	125	V.S.
"		—	Do.	14302	Do.	—	125	125	V.S.
"		—	Kelton,	14467	Newbrook,	75	75	150	V.S.
"		—	Kilmacshoy,	14524	Garrfarden,	100	—	100	V.S.
"		—	Do.	14526	Do.	—	100	100	V.S.
Roscommon,		21	Tibohine,	14592	Neelick,	150	—	150	V.S.
"		—	Do.	14563	Do.	—	150	150	V.S.
"		27	Oran,	14345	Lissaniska,	60	—	60	V.S.
"		—	Glennamaddy,	14368	Lakeview,	50	50	100	V.S.
"		—	Kilkeevin,	14601	Glanoran,	75	—	75	V.S.
"		—	Do.	14602	Do.	—	75	75	V.S.
"		26	Elphin,	14502	Drumnardiley,	75	75	150	V.S.
"		23	Creagh,	14010	Creagh,	75	—	75	V.S.
"		—	Do.	14021	Do.	—	75	75	V.S.
Sligo,		12	Ahamlish,	14109	Breaghwy,	100	—	100	V.S.
"		—	Do.	14110	Do.	—	100	100	V.S.
"		—	St. John's,	14585	Quay street,	400	—	400	V.S.
"		—	Calry,	14587	Drumcastial,	50	50	100	V.S.
"		—	St. John's,	14636	Carrarue,	100	—	100	V.S.
"		—	Do.	14637	Do.	—	100	100	V.S.
"		20	Castleconnor,	14081	Stackane,	60	60	120	V.S.
"		—	Easkey,	14567	Easkey,	75	—	75	V.S.
"		—	Do.	13928	Do.	—	75	75	V.S.
"		31	Kilmacteige,	14380	St. Michael's,	75	75	150	V.S.
"		23	Toomore,	13995	Tonah,	40	—	40	V.S.
"		—	Kilmacallan,	14113	Glen,	75	—	75	V.S.
"		—	Do.	14114	Do.	—	75	75	V.S.
"		—	Shragagh,	14230	Arigna,	60	—	60	V.S.
"		—	Emlfad,	14461	Liscarney,	60	—	60	V.S.

III.—List of Eighty-seven Building Cases brought into operation during the year 1894.

County	District	Roll No.	School	Parish	Rent raised	Managers	
Antrim	9	15748	Sandy Row	Shankill	V.C.	Rev. Ed. Nazleton	Meth.
"	—	18750	Do. inft.	Do.	T.C.	Do.	Meth.
"	4	14443	Ringsatown m.	Drummaul	T.T.	Rev. Hugh Magorian, P.P.	R.C.
"	—	14114	Do. f.	Do.	T.T.	Do.	R.C.
Armagh	14	14373	Newtownhamilton	Newtownhamilton	T.T.	Rev. P. Kerley, P.P.	R.C.
"	—	14485	Cullyhanna m.	Cullyhanna	T.T.	Do.	R.C.
"	—	14406	Do. f.	Do.	T.T.	Do.	R.C.
Cavan	51	14296	Comma	Kiramley	T.T.	Rev. P. O'Reilly, P.P.	R.C.
"	21	14533	Killyclare	Drumgoon	T.T.	Rev. J. A. R. Boyd	Pres.
"	—	14538	Sharrock	Killare	T.T.	Very Rev. J. O'Connor, P.P.	R.C.
"	—	14216	Mullagh m.	Mullagh	T.T.	Rev. L. Carroll, P.P.	R.C.
"	—	14217	Do. f.	Do.	T.T.	Do.	R.C.
Donegal	1	14224	Largaboyne	Killygarvan	T.T.	Rev. J. J. Gallagher, P.P.	R.C.
"	3	14249	Malin	Clonca	T.C.	U. M. Harvey, Esq.	R.C.
Down	19	14929	Bingvan	Kilkeel	T.C.	Rev. W. M'Mordie, M.A.	Pres.
"	16	14514	Portaverin (?)	St. Andrew's	T.T.	Rev. A. Whitley	Pres.
"	17	14191	Legnagay	Dromgoolanl	T.T.	Rev. J. Lowry, V.G.	R.C.
Londonderry	9	14360	Kilgort m.	Learmount	T.T.	Rev. K. M'Keen	R.C.
"	—	14261	Do. f.	Do.	T.T.	Do.	R.C.
"	5	14346	Desertzon m.	Dungiven	T.T.	Rev. E. Loughry	R.C.
"	—	14347	Do. f.	Do.	T.K.	Do.	R.C.
Monaghan	24	14061	Farmoyle	Aughnamullen	T.T.	Very Rev. P. Canon M'Kone, P.P., D.D.	R.C.
Tyrone	14	14372	Omagh Convent	Drumragh	T.T.	Very Rev. B. M'Namee	R.C.
"	—	14469	Aughafad	Donaghmoy	T.C.	Very Rev. Canon Duffy, P.P.	R.C.
"	15	14158	St. Patrick's Convent	Donagh	T.P.	Right Rev. Monsignor Byrne, P.P.	R.C.
Cork	42	14265	Gurtown	Kilbrimy	T.T.	Rev. M. M'Gurran, P.P.	R.C.
"	15	14111	Crook m.	Kilbultgorm	T.T.	Rev. D. Hayes, P.P.	R.C.
"	—	14112	Do. f.	Do.	T.T.	Do.	R.C.
"	2	14270	Uandumbridge	Tangraney	T.C.	Rev. J. Bremnham, P.P.	R.C.
"	41	14542	Kilmurry	Kilmurry	T.T.	Rev. R. H. Little, P.P.	R.C.
Cork	44	14042	Carrignavar f.	Dunbullogue	T.T.	Very Rev. Canon Hegarty, P.P.	R.C.
"	43	14255	Dlrreenlamane	Schull	T.T.	Rev. J. O'Connor, P.P.	R.C.
"	47	14265	Sherkin Island m.	Tullagh	T.C.	Rev. M. J. Brophy, P.P.	R.C.
"	43	14247	Cloln m.	Kilmamagh	T.C.	Rev. J. Beazley, P.C.	R.C.
"	—	14248	Do. f.	Do.	T.P.	Do.	R.C.
"	—	14255	Ballydehob m.	Schull	T.T.	Rev. J. O'Connor, P.P.	R.C.
"	—	14258	Do. f.	Do.	T.K.	Do.	R.C.
Kerry	47	14776	Glanmore	Kilcrohane	T.C.	Rev. J. J. Martin	R.C.
"	—	14155	Farranfaugh	Do.	T.C.	Daniel O'Connell, Esq.	R.C.
"	—	14796	Kilnahelin l.	Dromod	T.T.	Rev. M. O'Reilly, P.P.	R.C.
"	—	14555	Baslaghdeinagh	Prior	T.C.	Rev. A. Murphy	R.C.
"	28	14573	Tooreemard	Sneem	T.C.	Rev. J. Neligan, P.P.	R.C.

III.—List of Eighty-seven Building Cases brought into operation during
the year 1894—*continued.*

County.	District.	Roll No.	School.	Parish.	How Vested	Managers.	
Limerick,	49	14181	Ballygrennan, . m.	Robertstown, .	V.T.	Very Rev. M. Dunn,	R C
„	–	14192	Do. . l.	Do. .	V.T.	Do.	R.C
„	46	14283	Ballylanders, m.	Ballylanders,	V.T.	Rev. T. Cullen, P.P.,	R.C
„	–	14308	Do. l.	Do. .	V.T.	Do.,	R.C
„	–	14231	Nicker, m.	Grean, .	V.T.	Rev. John Sullivan, Adm.,	R.C
„	–	14232	Do. l.	Do. .	V.P.	Do.,	R.C
Carlow,	67	14029	Ballymurrin, . l.	Clonygoose, .	V.C.	Rev. J. Banaghan, P.P.,	R C
Kildare,	44	14391	Castledermot, l.	Castledermot, .	V.T.	Rev. M. Walsh P.P.,	R.C
Kilkenny,	47	14975	Galtas, m.	Callan, .	V.T.	Very Rev. M. Howley,	R.C
Longford,	28	14528	Legan, m.	Killoe, .	V.P.	Rev. B. Malone, P.P.,	R.C
„	–	14529	Do. l.	Do. .	V.P.	Do.	R.C
„	–	14366	Stonepark, m.	Templemichael, .	V.T.	Rev. J. Atkinson, Adm.,	R.C
„	–	14387	Do l.	Do. .	V.T.	Do.,	R.C
Queen's,	41	14590	Abbeyleix, South,. l.	Abbeyleix, .	V.C.	H. C. Fitzherbert, Esq.,	E.C
Westmeath,	38	14382	Kinnegad, m.	Kilbixy, .	V.T.	Rev. M. Fitzsimons, P.P.,	R.C
„	–	14383	Do. l.	Do. .	V.T.	Do.,	R.C
Wexford,	39	14284	Davorstalla, . m.	Bantow, .	V.C.	Very Rev. P. Ouam	R.C
						Shirihan, P.P.	
„	–	14285	Do. l.	Do. .	V.T.	Do.	R.C
Galway,	42	14820	Sonna, .	Killererankeen, .	V.T.	Rev. J. Cunningham,	R C
„	27	14273	Lisheencullia, m.	Boyounagh, .	V.T.	Rev. T. Walsh, P.P.,	R.C
„	–	14874	Do. l.	Do. .	V.T.	Do.	R.C
„	–	14257	Kilmore, .	Killerernan, .	V.T.	Rev. John Glenn, P.P.,	R.C
„	–	14408	Ougagh, m.	Killynn, .	V.C.	Do.	R.C
„	54	14491	Ard, m.	Moyrus, .	V.T.	Rev. M. M'Hugh, P.P.,	R.C
„	–	14492	Do. l.	Do. .	V.T.	Do.	R.C
„	42	14394	Kilbennety, m.	Kilbennety, .	V.T.	Rev. J. O'Farrell, P.P.,	R.C
„	54	14278	Knockrooe, m.	Donaghpatrick, .	V.T.	Very Rev. P. Cusa	R.C
						Hanssy, P.P.	
„	–	14401	Do. l.	Do. .	V.P.	Do.	R.C
„	25	14443	Innisheen, l.	Raffin, .	V.T	Rev. E. Lavelle, Adm.,	R C
„	24	14961	Lettermore, .	Killannin, .	V.T.	Rev. J. Conolly, P.P.,	R.C
Mayo,	29	13843	Raheengh, .	Crossmolina, .	V.T.	Very Rev. J. H. O'Brien,	R.C
						P.P.	
„	28	14728	Carrowgarrett, m.	Balnia, .	V.T.	Rev. John O'Grady, P.P.,	R.C
„	–	14790	Do. l.	Do. .	V.P.	Do.	R.C
„	29	14183	Glennaun, .	Moygownagh, .	V.T.	Rev. P. A. M'Lenald,	R.C
						P.P.	
„	32	14288	Largaboy, . m.	Balsa, .	V.C.	Rev. Robert Fraser,	R.C
						P.P.	
„	–	14289	Do. l.	Do. .	V.T.	Do.	R.C
„	26	13954	St. Brigid's (Derry xierly,	Aughavale, .	V.T.	Rev. P. M'Tiria, Adm.,	R.C
„	70	14285	Kilmore Erris, m.	Kilmore Erris, .	V.T.	Rev. M. Morrally, P.P.,	R.C
„	–	14409	Richmond, m.	Crossmolina, .	V.T.	Rev. J. M. O'Hara, P.P.,	R.C
„	–	14492	Do. l.	Do. .	V.T.	Do.	R.C
„	29	14248	Christ Church (Castlebar).	Aglish, .	V.C.	Rev. W. Crane Dyke,	R.C
Roscommon,	27	14397	Enfield, .	Ballintubber, .	V.T.	Rev. James Fulmer,	R.C
						P.P.	
Sligo,	31	14394	Bunsin, m.	Kilmacowen, .	V.T.	Rev. B. Quinn, Adm.,	R.C
„	72	14441	Kilmacowen, m.	Kilmacowen, .	V.T.	Rev. J. M'Dermott, C.C.,	R.C
„	–	14442	Do. l.	Do. .	V.T.	Do.	R.C

IV.—LIST of FORTY-EIGHT NON-VESTED SCHOOLS taken into connexion in 1894.

County.	Dis. Int.	Roll No.	School.	Parish.	Manager.	Rel.
Antrim, -	8	14528	William-street,	Shan kill,	Rev. R. Crawford Johnson	Meth.
"	4	14543	Conner (T),	Conner,	Rev. Canon Fitzgerald,	R.C.
"	5	14503	Rev. Brownrigg,	Shankill,	Mr. H. Reed,	Pres.
"	8a	14612	St. Aidan's,	" Do.	Rev. J. Northbridge,	R.C.
"	—	14615	" "	" Do.	Do.,	R.C.
Armagh, -	16	14508	Grove,	Ballymore,	Rev. A. R. Foy, M.A.,	Pres.
"	11	14567	Achnamanna,	Angus,	Rev. K. M'Larran, P.P.,	R.C.
"	15	14562	Cohors,	Tinburre,	Very Rev. L. Byrne, P.P.,	R.C.
"	16	14573	Darrykervill,	Tartaraghan,	Rev. M. O'Brien, P.P.,	R.C.
Donegal, -	1	14532	Inishinbo Island,	Tobingobugly,	Rev. J. M'Farlane, P.P.	R.C.
Down, -	9	14527	Knockbrocken,	Drumbo,	James White, esq.,	Pres.
"	10	14530	Brown Moravian,	Knockbrede,	Rev. T. B. Hallowsites,	Pres.
"	19	14577	St. Patrick's (Newry)	Newry,	Rev. W. Henry, R.A.,	R.C.
"	20	14527	St. Matthews, m. inf.	Kanonbrede,	Rev. J. Browning, P.P.,	R.C.
"	—	14512	Ravensnorth,	Holywood,	Rev. T. B. Hallowsites,	Pres.
"	—	14528	Orphand Island,	Downpadire,	Rev. W. V. Hamilton,	Pres.
Fermanagh, -	18	14521	Stranafaley,	Aghavea,	Rev. W. H. Bradley,	P.C.
Londonderry, -	2	14519	Oamus,	Camas juxta Bann,	Rev. F. Torrens, B.A.,	Pres.
"	2	14520	St. Columban, inf. C. Convent	Templemore,	Rev. H. M'Mountain,	R.C.
"	—	14529	" "	Do.	Do.,	R.C.
Monaghan, -	18	14523	Drumsloe,	Killanvre,	Rev. J. T. Tarleton,	R.C.
"	—	14542	Largy, inf.	Clasm.	Very Rev. Canon O'Neill, P.P.	R.C.
Kerry, -	64	14529	St. Edward's (Tralee)	Tralee.	Rev. J. W. B. Campbell,	Meth.
"	80	14540	Kilmoghrim,	Kilmoghrim,	Rev. R. Brolly,	R.C.
Waterford, -	62	14533	Oamphire,	Lismore and Mogh ullop,	Rev. T. M'Donnell, P.P.	R.C.
"	—	14537	Crypmquin Convent, inf. m.	Lismore West,	Do.,	R.C.
Carlow, -	60	14562	Barnahask,	Batrugh,	Ven. Archdn. Ardshdl,	R.C.
Dublin, -	87	14529	Ad'lside-road,	St. Marthins,	M. R. Robertson, esq., J.P.	Jew.
"	44	14529	Beerytown,	Booterstown,	Rev. T. R. Barry, B.A.,	R.C.
"	87	14508	Jackburn, Central,	St. Jude's,	Rev. T. A. M'Kee, B.D.,	Meth.
"	50	14530	Grandison,	Clontarf,	Rev. J. W. Morryn,	R.C.
"	40	14527	Dalkey (T),	Dalkey,	Rev. W. H. Kerr, M.A.,	R.C.
"	87	14527	Rathmines Township,	St. Peter's,	Rev. S. M. Harris, B.A.,	R.C.
King's, -	41	14523	St. Brigot's, m.	Kilbride,	V.Rev. H. Baher, P.P., P.P.	R.C.
"	—	14524	Rhode, m.	Ballynare(Rhan,	Rev. J. Kelly, P.P.,	R.C.
"	—	14571	Oorton,	Hamhill,	Rev. J. T. Aguew,	Meth.
Louth, -	23	14519	Mask Grange, inf.	Carlingford,	Rev. H. Murphy, P.P.,	R.C.
Westmeath, -	32	14545	Rathowen (T),	Rathaspia,	Rev. H. St. George, M.A.,	R.C.
"	42	14561	Athlone,	St. Mary's,	Rev. R. G. D. Campbell, B.D.	R.C.
Wicklow, -	44	14543	Arklyan,	Ardayne,	Rev. A. R. Bor,	R.C.
"	49	14523	Darrynoin,	Kilbride,	Rev. J. Hale,	R.C.
"	—	14556	Lenark,	Derrylossary,	Rev. W. Scobie, M.A.,	R.C.
Galway, -	25	14504	Laughrun, m. (T),	Loughrea,	Rev. J. Fallon, R.C.,	R.C.
"	82	14529	Oamgarrer,	Ross,	Rev. M. Mullaly, P.P.,	R.C.
Leitrim, -	81	14516	Mohanvogagh,	V.Kinbride,	Rev. H. Bowman, A.B.,	R.C.
Mayo, -	20	14545	Balfarred,	Balfarred,	Rev. J. P. Connolly, P.P.	R.C.
Sligo, -	22	14527	Kanh,	Tumwater,	Rev. A. Callaghan, C.C.,	R.C.
"	20	14514	Dromroin,	Kilmorahigan,	Rev. R. Bowen,	R.C.

V.—GENERAL SUMMARY of OPERATION, BUILDING, and SUSPENDED SCHOOLS in connexion on 31st December, 1894.

County.	In Operation.	Building.	Suspended.	Total.	County.	In Operation.	Building.	Suspended.	Total.
Antrim,	673	5	4	682	Kildare,	107	1	4	112
Armagh,	272	6	–	278	Kilkenny,	167	8	6	182
Cavan,	287	13	12	312	King's,	154	–	3	157
Donegal,	423	16	3	443	Longford,	111	13	1	125
Down,	405	5	2	423	Louth,	104	10	4	118
Fermanagh,	178	1	3	183	Meath,	161	1	3	151
Londonderry,	297	5	4	307	Queen's,	124	3	2	129
Monaghan,	180	5	3	195	Westmeath,	134	4	5	143
Tyrone,	575	1	13	589	Wexford,	165	3	6	174
Clare,	251	19	7	277	Wicklow,	124	5	1	130
Cork,	733	21	20	784	Galway,	424	23	13	460
Kerry,	350	11	14	383	Leitrim,	202	10	–	212
Limerick,	261	10	2	274	Mayo,	449	27	7	483
Tipperary,	320	5	6	631	Roscommon,	239	9	3	251
Waterford,	139	4	4	147	Sligo,	311	13	2	726
Carlow,	81	3	–	83					
Dublin,	315	17	9	331	Total,	8,565	291	149	8,961

* Including unassigned Model School Departments.

VI.—LIST of ONE HUNDRED and TWENTY-FOUR SCHOOLS to which Building Grants have been made during 1894.

County.	District.	Parish.	Roll No.	School.	Number of Pupils to be accommodated.			Class vested.
					Males.	Females.	Total.	
Antrim,	7	Rashorkin,	1451	St. Patrick's, m.	100	–	104	v.c.
"	–	Do.	1452	Do. f.	–	100	140	v.c.
"	6a	Larne,	1453	North Rnd.,	special	per day	200	v.v.
"	9	Shankill,	1454	Malone,		–	200	v.v.
"		Do.,	1456	Do. infte.		–		
Cavan,	22	Lara,	1456	Larkem,	45	40	108	b.v.
"	34	Killinkere,	1461	Derrybane,	50	50	100	v.v.
"		Teechbride,	1460	Greaghgowra,	60	60	120	v.v.
"	22	Lara,	1450	Cliff. Rns.,	40	–	60	v.v.
"		Do.	1461	Do.		60	60	v.v.
Donegal,	5	Inismagrath,	1453	Bundoran Convent,	60	160	250	v.v.
"	–	Kilcar,	1456	Crove,	30	30	60	v.v.
"	1	Conwall,	1400	Laterrkanny, m.	130	–	130	v.v.
"	9	Cabhiff,	1431	Coolhenny, m.	60	–	60	v.v.
"		Do.	1432	Do. f.	–	60	60	v.v.
"		Meville, Lower,	1435	Breimgh Glen,	50	50	100	v.v.
Down,	10	Knockbreda,	1455	Lagan Village, m.	125	–	125	v.v.
"	–	Do.	1452	Do. f.	–	175	135	v.v.
"	19	Kilkeel,	1453	Ben kuary,	40	40	60	v.v.
"		Do.,	1478	Monaydarragh,	50	50	100	v.v.

VI.—List of One Hundred and Twenty-four Schools, to which Building Grants have been made during 1894—*continued.*

County.	District.	Parish.	Roll No.	School.	Number of Pupils to be accommodated.			How erected.
					Males.	Females.	Total.	
Londonderry,	7	Maghera,	12560	Lissamuck,	Special	place for	50	V.T.
"	—	Maghera-felt,	14616	Fairhill,	—	—	200	V.T.
"	—	Do.	14617	Do.	—	—		V.T.
Monaghan,	24	Aughnamullen,	14510	Anney,	80	40		V.T.
"	18	Muckno,	14355	McDyrah,	40	40	80	V.T.
"	—	Tydavnet,	14461	Bernakeppy,	60	60	120	V.T.
Clare,	43	Kilmurry,	14424	Turmen,	60	60	120	V.T.
"	—	Inagh,	14521	Inagh,	75	—	75	V.T.
"	—	Do.	14522	Do.	—	75	75	V.T.
"	42	Tomgraney,	14170	Tomgraney,	74	—	74	V.T.
"	—	Do.	14571	Do.	—	75	75	V.T.
"	—	Kilfenora,	14638	Killenan,	40	40		V.E.
Cork,	60	Kilmeen,	14516	Oysterhaven,	60	—	60	V.T.
"	—	Do.	14547	Do.	—	60	60	V.T.
"	58	Inchigeela,	14560	Ballingeary,	150	—	150	V.T.
"	60	St. Nicholas,	14504	St. Joseph's Convent, industrial.	250	—	250	V.T.
"	—	Holy Trinity,	14410	St. Francis,	Special	place for	300	V.T.
"	—	Do.	14411	Do.	—	—		V.T.
Kerry,	57	Knockane,	14509	Gortbee,	30	30	60	V.A.
"	54	Kilmalough,	14573	St. Joseph's (Milltown, co. Kerry),	100	—	100	V.T.
Limerick,	23	Abbeyfeale,	14516	Fenis View,	60	—	60	V.T.
"	—	Do.	14517	Do.	—	60	60	V.T.
"	22	Ballingarry,	14285	St. Joseph's, industrial.	Special	place for	500	V.T.
"	21	St. Michael,	14290	Sexton-st. Convent, ind.	—	—	400	V.T.
"	43	Doon,	14572	Doon Convent,	—	400	400	V.T.
Waterford,	40	Kilsha,	14353	Ballake,	50	50	100	V.C.
"	—	Do.	14352	Kilbae,	18	40	58	V.C.
"	—	Kilrossanty,	14572	Ballenstown,	75	—	75	V.C.
"	—	Do.	14580	Do.	—	75	75	V.C.
Dublin,	39	St. Paul's,	14549	St. Gabriel's (Cowper-street),	Special	place for	770	V.T.
"	—	Do.	14549	Do.	—	—		V.T.
"	—	Do.	14550	Do.	—	—		V.T.
"	—	St. Thomas,	14514	East Wall,	175	—	175	V.T.
"	—	Do.	14515	Do.	—	175	175	V.L.
"	37	St. Peter's,	14558	St. Peter's (Whitefriar-street),	Special	place for	1349	V.T.
"	—	Do.	14557	Do.	—	—		V.T.
"	—	Do.	14558	Do.	—	—		V.T.
"	30	Clontarf,	14564	Howth Road,	—	—	108	V.T.
"	40	Stillorgan,	14565	Blackrock,	—	—	600	V.T.
"	—	St. Mark's,	14558	St. Andrew's,	—	—	1600	V.T.
"	—	Do.	14629	Do.	—	—		V.T.
"	30	St. George,	14665	St. Joseph's,	—	—	700	V.T.
"	—	Do.	14566	Do.	—	—		V.T.
"	—	Do.	14667	Do.	—	—		V.T.
Kildare,	44	Kilcoagh,	14643	Bigstone,	40	40	80	V.T.
Kilkenny,	67	Dysart,	14625	Smithstown,	80	80	160	V.T.
"	68	Tullaghan,	14649	Muckalee,	80	80	160	V.T.
"	—	Dysartmoon,	14648	Tullaghur,	40	40	80	V.T.
Longford,	28	Killoe,	14554	Edenmore,	75	—	75	V.T.
"	—	Do.	14555	Do.	—	75	75	V.T.
"	—	Kilcahan,	14556	Glangoagh,	50	50	100	V.T.
"	23	Tashiny,	14675	Calsdill,	100	—	100	V.T.
"	—	Do.	14676	Do.	—	100	100	V.T.

R

VI.—List of One Hundred and Twenty-four Schools to which Building Grants have been made during 1894—*continued.*

County.	District.	Parish.	Roll No.	School.	Number of Pupils to be accommodated.			How used.
					Males.	Females.	Total.	
Louth,	25	Creggan,	14544	Overthane,	60	60	120	v.v.
„	—	Collan,	14678	Callan,	75	—	75	v.v.
„	—	Do.	14579	Do.	—	75	75	v.v.
„	—	Dundalk,	14641	Castletown-road,	120	—	250	v.v.
„	—	Do.	14681	Do.	—	240	240	v.v.
Queen's,	41	Clonaugh,	14677	Brincell,	50	50	180	v.v.
Westmeath,	33	Rochfortbridge,	14688	Rochfortbridge Convt. f.	—	250	250	v.v.
Wexford,	49	St. Mary's,	14544	St. Joseph's (New Ross) Convent,	Special	plus two	480	v.v.
„	50	Ballyhackard,	14663	Ballaghkeen,	65	60	125	v.v.
Wicklow,	40	Ballytina,	14667	Aughrim,	75	—	75	v.v.
„	—	Do.	14653	Do.	—	75	75	v.v.
„	—	Do.	14615	Ballywreen,	50	60	60	v.v.
„	—	Baltinglass,	14653	Baltinglass Convent,	—	200	200	v.v.
Galway,	34	Inishmore,	14582	Onicpartar,	100	100	200	v.v.
„	32	Kilmely,	14538	Tobbrew,	125	—	125	v.v.
„	—	Do.	14584	Do.	—	125	125	v.v.
„	34	Kiliasin,	14590	St. Anne's,	75	—	75	v.v.
„	—	Do.	14591	Do.	—	75	75	v.v.
„	35	Killererin,	14655	Farranderg,	125	—	125	v.v.
„	—	Do.	14654	Do.	—	125	125	v.v.
„	42	Arbraham,	14643	Ballyglass,	30	30	162	v.v.
„	52	Kilbennin,	14652	Curra,	—	60	60	v.v.
„	—	Cong,	14654	Carapurra,	40	60	86	v.v.
„	55	Inishmore,	14659	St. Ronan's,	75	—	73	v.v.
„	—	Do.	14660	Do.	—	75	75	v.v.
„	35	Clonkeenkerrill,	14683	Shanballard,	40	40	80	v.v.
Leitrim,	31	Drumreilly,	14518	Silverstonhill,	60	61	120	v.v.
„	—	Killargbert,	14659	St. Joseph's (Shannacarry),	40	40	86	v.v.
„	—	Do.	14670	St. Mary of (Aughavranta)	50	50	103	v.v.
Mayo,	29	Crossmolina,	14528	Enagbbeg,	60	60	120	v.v.
„	28	Kilmaenbeg,	14584	Gurtjerdan,	100	—	100	v.v.
„	29	Babole,	14587	Lisnairanet,	100	—	100	v.v.
„	—	Do.	14588	Do.	—	100	100	v.v.
„	—	Manulla,	14644	Manulla,	75	—	75	v.v.
„	—	Do.	14545	Do.	—	75	75	v.v.
„	20	Kilmore Erris,	14563	Inishen Island, North,	60	30	66	v.v.
„	21	Kilmeln,	14678	Corcobarry,	60	60	120	v.v.
„	28	Ballyovey,	14654	Derrew,	40	40	60	v.v.
„	21	Kilmurra,	14550	Kilxally,	Special	plus two	162	v.v.
„	29	Kilcummin,	14671	Courogb,	50	40	100	v.v.
„	22	Kilmaenbeg,	14676	Gurtjerdan,	—	168	168	v.v.
Roscommon,	21	Tibohine,	14592	Monfah,	156	—	150	v.v.
„	—	Do.	14598	Do.	—	150	150	v.v.
„	27	Kilkeevin,	14591	Cloonten,	75	—	75	v.v.
„	—	Do.	14609	Do.	—	75	75	v.v.
Sligo,	12	St. John's,	14553	Quay-street,	400	—	400	v.v.
„	23	Kilfree,	14561	Lisnamay,	30	30	60	v.v.
„	19	Calry,	14547	Drumnabol,	50	50	100	v.v.
„	21	Killaraght,	14559	St. Michael's,	75	75	150	v.v.
„	12	St. John's,	16559	Carrarce,	100	—	100	v.v.
„	—	Do.	14557	Do.	—	100	100	v.v.

VII.—List of Twelve Struck-off Schools restored to Roll
during 1894.

County.	Dist.	Roll No.	School.	Parish.
Antrim, . .	4	2545	Seymour's Bridge,† . .	Drummaul
Cavan, . .	23	1463	Shannon,† . . L	Annagh
„ . .	"	7827	Drumbride,† . . L	Ballintemple.
Donegal, .	2	10579	Sheriff's Mountain, . .	Templemore.
Fermanagh, .	13	5487	Lisblake, . . .	Killesher.
Tipperary, .	43	13751	Clonmen, . . L	Clonmen.
Dublin, . .	59	6313	Josephian,* . evening	St. George.
Kilkenny, .	47	7674	Dunbell,† . . .	Dunbell.
Meath, . .	24	5509	Edengora,† . . L	Kilmainhamwood.
„ . .	20	11040	Kilbeg, . . L	Kilbeg.
Westmeath, .	33	5994	Ardnagrath,† . . L	Drumraney.
Wexford, .	43	7864	Killurk, . . .	Selskar.

* This School has a separate Roll Number.
† Struck off and restored to Roll during 1891.

VIII.—List of Three Suspended Schools re-opened during 1894.

County.	Dist.	Roll No.	School.	Parish.	How vested.
Kerry, . .	29	8830	Rocktown, . . L	Killorglin, .	V.T.
„ . .	31	9251	Lismullick, . . L	Tralee, . .	V.T.
Dublin, . .	68	1296	Stillorgan,* . . .	Stillorgan.	V.C.

* Subsequently placed on Non-Vested Roll as 6 struck off Roll. Lease expired.

IX.—List of Eleven Schools placed on Suspended List during 1894.

County.	Dist.	Roll No.	School.	How vested.	Parish.	Reason for placing School on Suspended List.
Cavan, .	73	13539	Cramerlough, . L	V.V.	Cramerlough, .	Average insufficient.
Londonderry, .	7	5296	Lettermoy, . L	A.	Machera, .	Do.
Cork, .	59	1275	Shorkla Island, .	V.T.	Tullogh, .	Do.
„ .	6	15437	Ballygorteen, . m.	V.V.	Kilnora, .	Do.
Tipperary, .	30	5034	Kyle Park, . m.	V.C.	Derrinlahane, .	Amalgamated with 2034.
Louth, .	25	2063	Ardee Mount, m. l.	V.T.	Ardee, .	Average insufficient.
Queen's, .	44	4779	Kilahbee, . L	V.C.	Kilahbee, .	Do.
Galway, .	85	12910	Woodlawn, m.	V.T.	K. Samnell, .	Superseded by 14400 & 14402
Mayo, .	30	4011	Richmond, .	V.V.	Crossmolina,	Average insufficient.
Roscommon, .	22	2494	Cartober, . L	V.T.	Kilakin, .	Do.
Sligo, .	91	15250	Bannickstan, . L	V.T.	Ghesreeghill.	

X.—List of Ninety-three Non-vested Schools struck off the Rolls during 1894.

County.	District.	Roll No.	School.	Parish.	Reason for striking School off Roll.
Antrim,	4	3455	Seymour's-bridge,	Drummaul,	Average insufficient.
″	5	7253	Soulbane-m. m.	Glenakill,	″
″	9a	8053	Ledge Mill,	″	″ School house is bad repair.
″	7	13319	St. Paul's, temply.,	Rasharkin,	Temporary existence ceased.
″	6	42	Randalstown, m.	Drummaul,	Superseded by 14143.
″	—	5583	″ f.	″	″ 14444.
Armagh,	10	4380	Newtownhamilton,	Newtownhamilton,	Superseded by 14332.
″	11	16406	Portadown Convent, Inft.	Drumcree,	Amalgamated with 12441.
″	12	4205	Ballard, f.	Loughgilly,	Inoperative.
″	16	5830	Callyrivers,	Cullyhanna,	Superseded by 14484-5.
Cavan,	23	7102	Lackew, m.	Denn,	Average insufficient—School very insufficient.
″	7	1347	Drumbride, f.	Kilbriatemple.	Average insufficient.
″	—	1483	Slanmore, f.	Armagh,	″
″	51	1152	Garrela,	Templeport.	House unsuitable.
″	—	8270	Common,	Kinawley,	Superseded by 14788.
″	24	4623	Killycara,	Drumgoon,	″ 14328.
″	—	8052	Shercock,	Killann,	″ 14336.
″	31	7456	Lequanrugim,	Templeport,	Unsatisfactory character of Teacher.
″	24	4371	Lough Ramer,	Loughan,	No longer under control of recognised Manager.
″	23	1385	Drumbride, m.	Kilbriatemple,	Amalgamated with 7387.
″	24	7201	Mullagh, m.	Mullagh,	Superseded by 14815.
″	—	8815	″ f.	″	″ 14717.
″	—	10854	Tullinchim,	Drumgoon,	Teacher and recognised.
Donegal,	2	2380	Walla,	Clonoha,	Superseded by 13943.
″	6	8737	Ardara, (3)	Killybegs,	Low average and falsification of registers.
Down,	16	12162	Ringlan,	Kilkeel,	Superseded by 14722.
″	17	1283	Legitamary,	Dromgooland,	″ 14191.
Fermanagh,	13	5708	Drumluggus,	Devenish,	House the property of Teacher.
Londonderry,	7	11185	Moneymore, Inft.	Artrea,	Average insufficient.
″	—	292	Ballymoney, (1),	″	Teacher insufficient.
″	2a	7305	Myroe, f.	Tamlaght Finlagan,	Amalgamated with 7908.
″	3	14703	Dungiven, m.	Dungiven,	Superseded by 14796.
″	—	5856	″ f.	″	″ 14797.
Monaghan,	24	12463	Clones an Dion,	Aughnamullen,	Superseded by 14881.
Tyrone,	14	5328	Omagh Convent,	Drumragh,	Superseded by 14372.
″	7	781	Aughafad,	Badoney,	″ 14463.
″	15	410	Derganum, m.	Drumglass,	″ 14455.
″	—	411	″ f.	″	″ 14456.
″	16	5454	Rem rion,	Coppagh,	House unsuitable. Teacher insufficient.
Clare,	43	5362	Cree,	Kildallysown,	Superseded by 14111-2.
″	51	7004	Killmurry,	Kilmurry,	″ 14843.
″	42	7220	Ballyvarry, m.	Killaloe,	Average insufficient.

X.—LIST of NINETY-THREE NON-VESTED SCHOOLS struck off the ROLLS
during 1894—*continued.*

County.	District.	Roll No.	School.	Parish.	Reason for striking School off Roll.
Cork,			Carrigroe,	Drydeliagan,	Superseded by 14073.
„				School,	„ 14555.
„			Wallstown,	Wallstown,	Average insufficient.
„			Clain,	Kilmurough,	Superseded by 13567-8.
„			Rathcormk,	Dunaghmore,	Average insufficient. Teacher incompetent.
„			Ballydaluh,	Sohall,	Superseded by 14275.
„			„	„	14108.
Kerry,			Glenmum,	Kilcrohane,	Superseded by 13073.
„			Kevetark,	Kilereghten,	Used as class room for Mixed School.
„			Commanleonmm,	Molraheen,	Superseded by 14185.
„			Kinlaghmenmk,	Prior,	„ 14063.
Limerick,			Murnbrymart,	Robertstown,	Superseded by 14101-2.
„			Ballywolocs,	Ballyleaders,	„ 14393.
„					„ 14504.
„			Nicker,	Grean,	Superseded by 14231.
„					„ 14232.
„			Ardagh,	Ardagh,	} To be superseded by 14275-6.
Carlow,			Ballyneartin,	Clonygame,	Superseded by 14402.
Dublin,			Finglas,	Finglas,	Ceased to be conducted as a National School.
„			Ballforgan,	Ballforgan,	Inoperative.
Kildare,			Castledermot,	Castledermot,	Superseded by 14531.
„			Kill,	Kill,	Amalgamated with 1978.
Kilkenny,			Dunbell,	Dunbell,	House out of repair.
„			Culhun,	Culhun,	Superseded by 14273.
Longford,			Legygh,	Killoe,	Superseded by 14853.
„					14239.
„			Slanepark,	Templemichael,	„ 14581.
„			„	„	14037.
Louth,			Flekhstown,	Drumphellon,	Average insufficient.
Mayo,			Killagrille, (1)	Mayhelagaa,	Average insufficient.
„			Edeagorra,	Kilmaindan	
				West.	
Queen's Co.			Abbeyleix, South,	Abbeyleix,	Superseded by 14598.
Westmeath,			Arduagrak,	Drunraney,	Average insufficient.
„			Kiltaageal,	Killucan,	Superseded by 14567.
„			„	„	14805.
Wexford,			Dunmorath,	Batmary,	Superseded by 14284-5.
Galway,			Killmore,	Kilkegann,	Superseded by 14537.
„			Ard,	Moyrus,	„ 14631-2.
„			Kawelcroom,	Dunaghpatrick,	„ 14276.
„					„ 14601.
„			Rundmurk,	Rollis,	„ 14441.

X.—List of Ninety-three Non-vested Schools struck off the Rolls
during 1894—*continued.*

County.	District.	Roll No.	School.	Parish.	Reason for striking School off Roll.
Mayo,	28	3353	Carrowgowna, m.	Bohola, .	Superseded by 1473.
„	„	9735	„	„	„ 14730.
„	„	10880	Loughhaxran, m.	Kealoguan,	Average insufficient.
„	29	6540	Moygownagh, .	Moygownagh, .	Superseded by 14165.
„	32	11335	Lotranhey, .	Bekan, .	„ 14730-9.
„	39	6546	Kilmore Erris, .	Kilmore Erris, .	„ 4836.
„	28	12857	Two Mile, .	Aglish, .	„ 14336.
Sligo,	21	1688	Banada, m.	Kilmactigue, .	Superseded by 14364.
„	13	8841	Kilmacowen, .	Kilmacowen, .	„ 14441-2.

XI.—List of Twelve Building Grants cancelled during 1894.

County.	District.	Roll No.	School.	Parish.	Man vested	Reason for cancelling Grant.
Donegal, .	9	14433	Cockhoney, .	f.	GnидаK, .	v.v.	Plan rejected.
Down, .	10	14355	Portavogie, .	c.	Ballyhalbert,	v.v.	Do. do.
Tyrone, .	13	14114	Gortreagh, .	.	Kildrem, .	v.v.	Not proceeded with.
Clare, .	51	13613	Kilkerry, .	.	Kilmurry, .	v.v.	Plan rejected.
„	49	14083	Gortyclare, .	.	Oughtmama, .	v.v.	Not proceeded with.
Tipperary, .	45	14297	Rankan, .	.	Movalliss, .	v.v.	Do. do.
Waterford, .	49	14203	Kilha, .	.	Kilrea, .	v.c.	Superseded by new Grant.
Leitrim, .	51	14102	Shannagarry, .	m.	Kilkeghort,	v.v.	Do. do.
„	„	14321	„	c.	„	v.v.	„ do.
Mayo, .	28	14439	Derrinnan, .	f.	Bohola, .	v.v.	Plan rejected.
Roscommon, .	27	14117	Lissalehey, .	c.	Oran, .	v.v.	Do. do.
Sligo, .	13	13853	Dromard, .	.	Dromard, .	v.v.	Superseded by new Grant.

XII.—Cancelled Building Grants restored to Roll during 1894.

County.	District.	Parish.	Roll No.	School.	Number of Pupils to be accommodated.			
					Males.	Females.	Total.	
Nil.	—	Nil.	—	Nil.	—	—	—	—

APPENDIX H.

I. (a.)—List of One Hundred and Fifty-six Workhouse Schools in connexion on 31st December, 1894, with the Total Number of Pupils on Rolls and the Average Daily Attendance of Pupils, as returned for the Year ended 31st December, 1894.

District	Roll No.	County and School	Total No. of Pupils on Rolls	Average Attendance	District	Roll No.	County and School	Total No. of Pupils on Rolls	Average Attendance
		ANTRIM.					**LONDONDERRY.**		
8	6699	Ballymoney,	31	23	9	3841	Londonderry,	45	18
4	3852	Ballycastle,	19	8	24	0487	Limavady,	29	14
–	3843	Ballymena,	54	37	8	7381	Coleraine,	41	22
3a	3643	Larne,	54	24	7	30523	Magherafelt,	40	23
–	6314	Antrim,	51	23	4		Total,	154	78
9	8016	Belfast,	775	234					
7		Total,	1,853	302			**MONAGHAN.**		
					18		Monaghan,	15	15
		ARMAGH.			–		Clones,	18	15
11	11800	Lurgan,	18	13	–		Castleblayney,	33	20
16	10412	Armagh,	58	24	24		Carrickmacross,	33	24
19	16798	Newry,	70	9	4		Total,	164	76
3		Total,	99	43					
							TYRONE.		
		CAVAN.			6		Castlederg,	8	4
23	8420	Cavan,	47	24	–		Strabane,	57	29
24	5447	Bailieborough,	27	15	14		Omagh,	43	23
–	3644	Cootehill,	15	7	15		Clogher,	25	16
31	6810	Bawnboy,	21	15	–		Dungannon,	25	8
4		Total,	110	44	6		Total,	179	82
		DONEGAL.					**CLARE.**		
1	4921	Milford,	23	10	42		Scariff,	11	9
–	4375	Letterkenny,	5	4	–		Ennistymon,	41	28
2	7714	Glenties,	18	5	–		Tulla,	24	14
5	4313	Donegal,	29	7	–		Ballyvaughan,	18	12
6	6359	Ballyshannon,	23	11	45		Corofin,	21	14
–	12764	Stranorlar,	10	12	–		Ennis,	139	104
7		Total,	153	49	–		Kilrush,	62	37
					–		Killadysert,	50	22
		DOWN.			8		Total,	330	220
10	3250	Newtownards,	49	29					
11	5016	Banbridge,	17	14			**CORK.**		
17	10570	Downpatrick,	27	15	49	3167	Midleton,	60	29
19	11620	Kilkeel,	24	15	–	6171	Youghal,	50	24
4		Total,	117	72	44		Kanturk,	62	48
					–		Macroom,	24	17
		FERMANAGH.			46		Millstreet,	38	29
13	10795	Enniskillen,	56	24	–	7249	Fermoy,	43	17
–	11896	Lisnaskea,	16	13	–	3841	Mallow,	36	16
14	11424	Irvinestown,	16	14	–	6218	Mitchelstown,	31	23
3		Total,	90	51					

WORKHOUSE SCHOOLS— *continued.*

District.	Roll No.	County and School.	Total No. of Pupils on Rolls.	Average Attendance.	District.	Roll No.	County and School.	Total No. of Pupils on Rolls.	Average Attendance.
		CORK—*continued.*					**CARLOW.**		
58	4811	Bantry,	28	18	64	11154	Carlow,	44	28
—	3983	Castletown,	11	7					
—	6146	Schull,	7	6		1	Total,	44	20
59	3417	Skibbereen,	43	28					
—	3563	Dunmanway,	28	16			**DUBLIN.**		
—	5943	Clonakilty,	30	30					
60	3543	Cork,	477	212		3144	Balrothery,	88	18
—	4935	Kinsale,	18	11	39	7187	Dublin, North,	570	243
—	8123	Bandon,	32	21	63	3285	Rathdown,	138	61
	17	Total,	1,040	544		5	Total,	712	440
		KERRY.					**KILDARE.**		
86	4316	Listowel,	79	46	37	3135	Naas,	65	31
34	8880	Tralee,	104	40	—	6334	Celbridge,	26	20
—	5394	Dingle,	60	21	64	5860	Athy,	45	18
67	4341	Killarney,	101	61		3	Total,	150	74
—	4206	Cahersiveen,	19	12					
56	4670	Kenmare,	20	18			**KILKENNY.**		
	6	Total,	373	214	43	6721	Urlingford,	25	13
					47	6347	Castlecomer,	89	54
		LIMERICK.			—	3379	Callan,	47	19
					—	3887	Kilkenny,	87	67
85	3096	Kilmallock,	111	76	—	6276	Thomastown,	44	17
51	8655	Limerick,	254	189		5	Total,	243	160
62	3040	Newcastle,	18	20					
—	3415	Rathkeale,	65	30			**KING'S.**		
—	6018	Croom,	33	21	56	7385	Parsonstown,	48	22
	5	Total,	532	316	61	3394	Edenderry,	13	5
					—	8446	Tullamore,	34	9
		TIPPERARY.				3	Total,	105	36
38	3418	Roscrea,	38	24					
—	3319	Nenagh,	33	19			**LONGFORD.**		
—	6031	Borrisokane,	17	16		3489	Longford,	57	25
43	3547	Thurles,	83	54	25	3556	Granard,	48	22
46	8142	Tipperary,	180	76	53	6311	Ballymahon,	29	20
43	3283	Cashel,	45	47		3	Total,	134	67
—	3443	Clogheen,	47	52					
—	3346	Carrick-on-Suir,	67	35					
—	12363	Clonmel,	63	25			**LOUTH.**		
	9	Total,	532	307					
						3377	Dundalk,	61	30
		WATERFORD.			28	3382	Ardee,	43	23
49	3418	Lismore,	24	18	—				
47	12221	Dungarvan,	64	50		2	Total,	104	53
—	2636	Waterford,	281	90					
—	6743	Kilmacthomas,	27	17					
	6	Total,	396	185					

WORKHOUSE SCHOOLS—*continued.*

District	Roll No.	County and School.	Total No. of Pupils on Rolls	Average Attendance	District	Roll No.	County and School.	Total No. of Pupils on Rolls	Average Attendance
		MEATH.					**GALWAY—***con.*		
29	8410	Kells,	14	5	35	5397	Loughrea,	20	18
—	8044	Oldcastle,	20	7	—	5408	Mountbellew,	11	10
—	14036	Trim District, m.	59	92	—	5734	Portumna,	21	14
—	14104	Do., f.	119	77	—	7010	Ballinasloe,	57	39
					47	5379	Gort,	21	11
	4	Total,	243	171		10	Total,	307	228
		QUEEN'S.							
41	4315	Mountmellick,	45	21			**LEITRIM.**		
—	10810	Abbeyleix,	38	80	12	3650	Manorhamilton,	80	20
	2	Total,	83	51	29	8413	Mohill,	56	27
					31	3333	Car.-on-Shannon,	51	30
		WESTMEATH.				3	Total,	187	77
32	5830	Mullingar,	62	24					
—	5369	Delvin,	29	21			**MAYO.**		
85	3274	Athlone,	51	30	20	8349	Ballina,	45	35
	3	Total,	122	75	—	8474	Belmullet,	13	11
					9241	Killala,	4	4	
		WEXFORD.			21	4285	Swinford,	28	28
45	3520	New Ross,	131	74	22	4242	Castlebar,	15	10
30	3549	Wexford,	70	55	62	4727	Westport,	48	20
—	3674	Enniscorthy,	60	51		8117	Ballinrobe,	24	15
—	10534	Gorey,	30	30		6143	Claremorris,		
	4	Total,	331	179		8	Total,	187	143
		WICKLOW.					**ROSCOMMON.**		
48	3325	Rathdrum,	51	19	62	3289	Boyle,	47	33
—	3679	Shillelagh,	80	30	37	8572	Roscommon,	39	26
44	13103	Baltinglass,	17	10	—	4833	Castlerea,	41	27
	3	Total,	90	49	—	6121	Strokestown,	33	19
						4	Total,	160	105
		GALWAY.							
27	9733	Glennamaddy,	12	10			**SLIGO.**		
32	4443	Tuam,	60	27	19	3534	Sligo,	55	38
34	3361	Galway,	90	60	69	4590	Dromore West,	13	6
—	4375	Clifden,	18	9	21	9215	Tobercurry,	28	11
—	3472	Oughterard,	15	15		3	Total,	98	48

[SUMMARY

SUMMARY of WORKHOUSE SCHOOLS in CONNEXION.

No. of Schools	County.	Total No. of Pupils on Rolls	Average Attendance.	No. of Schools	County.	Total No. of Pupils on Rolls	Average Attendance.
7	Antrim,	1,038	392	3	King's,	108	46
5	Armagh,	48	48	3	Longford,	134	60
4	Cavan,	110	60	2	Louth,	104	85
7	Donegal,	133	62	4	Meath,	248	171
5	Down,	117	72	2	Queen's,	62	54
4	Fermanagh,	50	51	5	Westmeath,	122	73
4	Londonderry,	154	73	4	Wexford,	215	172
4	Monaghan,	104	70	3	Wicklow,	98	45
5	Tyrone,	173	83				
49	Total for Ulster,	2,029	881	36	Total for Leinster,	2,325	1,457
8	Clare,	530	239	10	Galway,	407	229
17	Cork,	1,248	584	5	Leitrim,	107	72
8	Kerry,	373	214	6	Mayo,	197	145
5	Limerick,	572	316	4	Roscommon,	159	153
6	Tipperary,	553	322	3	Sligo,	63	42
4	Waterford,	826	155				
				28	Total for Connaught,	941	592
49	Total for Munster,	5,102	1,800	49	Schools in Ulster,	2,029	881
				49	„ in Munster,	5,103	1,800
1	Carlow,	44	28	36	„ in Leinster,	2,325	1,457
3	Dublin,	743	458	28	„ in Connaught,	644	592
5	Kildare,	150	74				
5	Kilkenny,	242	180	185	Gross Total,	8,411	4,735

I. (b.)—The number of TEACHERS employed in these SCHOOLS on 31st December, 1894, according to the Returns received from the different Clerks of Unions is set forth in the following Table:—

Class.	Principals.		Assistants.		Total.		Total.
	Males.	Females.	Males.	Females.	Males.	Females.	
Unclassed,	8	14			8	14	22
3d,	7	9		9	7	18	25
3d,	45	77	7	12	52	89	141
3d,	4	7	2		6	9	15
2d,	17	28	1		18	28	47
1d,	1	5			1	5	6
1d,	1				1		1
Total,	79	155	10	21	89	176	245
	234		31				
Gross Total,					245		

* In addition to the above, twenty-six departments were conducted by nuns, viz., Youghal, Skibbereen, Limerick, Clonmel, Thurles, Celbridge, Callan, Gorard, New Ross, Galway, Carrick-on-Suir, Thomastown, North Dublin, Enniscorthy, Mohill, Trim, Tullamore, Macmine Junction, Dundalk, Ardee, Ballymahon, Athy, Fermoy, Bantry, Cork, and Bonmiller.

II.—LUNATIC ASYLUM SCHOOLS in connexion on 31st December, 1894.

County.	District.	Roll No.	School.	Parish.	Total No. of Pupils on Roll.	Average Attend.
Dublin,	30	5,853	Richmond, m.	Grangegorman,	246	196
Ditto,	—	5,636	Ditto, f.	Ditto,	273	260

III.—CONVENT AND MONASTERY SCHOOLS.

(a.) Convent Schools paid by Capitation; (b.) Convent Schools paid by Classification; (c.) Monastery Schools paid by Capitation; (d.) Monastery Schools paid by Classification; (e.) Summary according to Religious Orders; and (f.) General Summary.

(a.)—TWO HUNDRED AND SIXTY-ONE CONVENT NATIONAL SCHOOLS PAID BY CAPITATION.

Province and County.	District.	Roll No.	School.	Religious Order of Community.	Total No. of Pupils for whom on the Year ended 31st Dec. 1894.	Average Daily Attendance of Pupils (Male and Female) for Year ended 31st Dec. 1894.
ULSTER.						
Co. ANTRIM,	8	1010	Crumlin-road,	L	Sisters of Mercy,	482	248
"	—	13568	St. Catherine's,	L	Dominican,	635	381
"	—	10171	Castle-street (Lisburn),		Sacred Heart,	721	189
"	—		do.,		do.,		
"	—	14167	do.,		do.,	114	34
"	—	13463	Star of the Sea,	L	Sisters of Mercy,	401	208
"	—	14188	St. Joseph's, Crumlin-road,		do.,	764	68
"	9	6354	St. Malachy's,	L	do.,	625	514
	7				Total,	3,517	1,809
Co. ARMAGH,	11	9719	Edward-street,	L	Sisters of Mercy,	623	414
"	—		do.,		do.,	287	161
"	16	8230	Mt. St. Catherine,		Sacred Heart,	430	212
"	—	10850	Keady,	L	Poor Clares,	253	155
"	19	7608	Canal-street,	L	Sisters of Mercy,	349	205
"	—	16878	Magherafelt,	L	do.,	261	156
	3				Total,	2,413	1,383
Co. CAVAN,	23	8186	Cavan,	L	Poor Clares,	321	214
"	—	10178	Ballyjamesduff,	L	do.,	109	35
"	—	11749	Belturbet,	L	Sisters of Mercy,	700	183
"	24	13093	Cootehill,	L	do.,	119	82
	4				Total,	868	468
Co. DONEGAL,	3	2633	Slanebeg,	L	Sisters of Mercy,	118	47
"	—	2278	Moville,	L	do.,	197	100
"	—	10658	St. Patrick's,	L	do.,	176	90
"	5	7503	Ballyshannon (2),		St. Louis,	227	159
"	—	1371	Bundoran,	L		185	101
	5				Total,	591	472
Co. DOWN,	17	10253	Mt. St. Patrick,	L	Sisters of Mercy,	328	297
"	18	244	St. Clare's,	L	Poor Clares,	700	81
"	—	8725	Rostrevor,	L	Sisters of Mercy,	155	91
"	—	13733	Warrenpoint,	L	do.,	139	100
	4				Total,	1,588	683
Co. L'DERRY,	2	6168	St. Columb's (2),		Sisters of Mercy,	673	404
"	—	14603	do.,	L	do.,	306	107
"	—	11498	do.,	W.	do.,	371	132
"	7	8312	St. Patrick's (2),	L	do.,	584	343
"	—	14007	St. Mary's, Magherafelt,		Immaculate Conception,	190	100
	5				Total,	2,045	1,115
Co. MONAGHAN,	24	13699	Carrickmacross,	L	St. Louis,	377	176
	1				Total,	377	126

(a.)—Two Hundred and Sixty-one Convent National Schools paid by Capitation—*continued.*

Province and County.	Physical	Roll No.	School.	Religious Order of Community.	Total No. of Pupils on the Rolls during the Year ended the 31st March, 1894.	Average Daily Attendance during the Year ended the 31st March, 1894.
ULSTER—*cont.* Co. Tyrone,	6	10110	Strabane,	Sisters of Mercy,	651	533
"	14	14275	Omagh,	Loretto,	688	167
"	15	13487	Loy,	Sisters of Mercy,	192	175
"	—	15314	Cookstown,	do.,	308	188
"	—	14468	St. Patrick's,	do.,	445	331
	6			Total,	1,333	1,038
MUNSTER. Co. Clare,	42	8523	Killaloe,	Sisters of Mercy,	162	43
"	—	10944	Ennistymon,	do.,	539	144
"	—	12872	Tulla,	do.,	343	388
"	43	7316	Ennis,	do.,	508	388
"	—	11560	Kildysart,	do.,	171	16
"	—	13074	Kilrush,	do.,	676	545
	6			Total,	2,483	1,398
Co. Cork,	48	412	Midleton,	Presentation,	733	473
"	—	8623	Youghal,	do.,	719	387
"	—	8576	Queenstown,	Sisters of Mercy,	697	388
"	—	7419	St. Mary's (Carrigtwohill),	Poor Servants of the Mother of God and the Poor,	207	117
"	52	15459	Bandon,	Sisters of Mercy,	146	178
"	—	1641	Charleville,	do.,	290	228
"	—	18051	St. Joseph's,	Presentation,	406	446
"	53	2378	Millstreet,	Sisters of Mercy,	261	156
"	—	18645	Macroom,	do.,	274	152
"	—	10220	Kanturk,	Presentation,	380	146
"	54	9240	Fermoy,	do.,	260	152
"	—	4528	Doneraile,	Sisters of Mercy,	444	152
"	—	4630	Mallow,	do.,	208	152
"	—	11855	Ballyvourney,	Presentation,	114	111
"	55	12787	Mitchelstown,	Sisters of Mercy,	897	588
"	—	9141	Bantry,	do.,	110	114
"	56	13372	St. Patrick's,	do.,	846	558
"	—	1274	Ardagh (I.),	do.,	450	374
"	—	7651	Clonakilty,	do.,	421	152
"	—	8450	Skibbereen,	do.,	256	152
"	—	15591	St. Mary's,	Sisters of Charity,	745	152
"	—	15692	Do.,	do.,	741	688
"	60	4179	Kinsale,	Sisters of Mercy,	691	888
"	—	6257	Bandon,	Presentation,	1,734	588
"	—	6155	St. Finbar's,	do.,	1,212	388
"	—	15596	St. Vincent's,	Sisters of Charity,	758	588
"	—	14600	St. Joseph's,	Sisters of Mercy,	1,399	888
"	60A	14105	Clarence-street,	Presentation,	1,315	888
"	—	6046	Blackrock,	Ursuline,	153	88
"	—	5474	Passage West,	Sisters of Mercy,	848	888
	30			Total,	17,391	9,469
Co. Kerry,	30	4543	Listowel,	Presentation,	656	488
"	—	11845	Lixnaw,	do.,	914	188
"	—	17218	Ballybunion,	Sisters of Mercy,	193	185
"	54	1835	Milltown,	Presentation,	910	188
"	—	6215	Castleisland,	do.,	681	188
"	—	2550	Moyderwell,	Sisters of Mercy,	771	444
"	—	18915	Tralee (?),	do.,	458	274
"	57	18040	St. Gertrude's,	Loretto,	70	6
	6			Total,	3,101	1,876

(G.)—Two Hundred and Sixty-one Convent National Schools paid by Capitation—*continued.*

Province and County.	District.	Roll No.	School.	Religious Order or Community.	Total No. of Pupils for any whole Number on Roll during the Year ended 31st Dec., 1894.	Average Daily Attendance of Pupils (those only) for the Year ended during that period.
MUNSTER—*con.*						
Co. Limerick, ..	59	7439	Abbeyfeale, .. £	Sisters of Mercy, .	259	212
,,	46	9416	Limerick, .. £	do.,	551	193
,,	—	13330	Hospital, .. £	Presentation,	460	367
,,	51	550	SS. Mary and Munchin's, £	Sisters of Mercy,	921	583
,,	—	6143	Fevy-square, .. £	Presentation,	709	490
,,	—	5547	Sexton-street, .. £	Presentation,	1,354	354
,,	—	6530	St. John's-square, .. £	Sisters of Mercy,	516	469
,,	—	8756	Adare, .. £	do.,	146	91
,,	—	10684	Ma. St. Vincent's, £	do.,	316	174
,,	—	11137	Bruff, .. £	Faithful Companions of Jesus,		
,,	—	13459	St. Mary's, m. £	Sisters of Mercy,	348	154
,,	—	14189	St. John's, m-Leb.	do.,	297	147
,,	57	6632	St. Catherine's, £	do.,	295	184
,,	—	5543	St. Anne's, .. £	do.,	351	216
,,	—	10975	St. Joseph's, Leb.	do.,	188	148
,,	—	12716	Ballingarry, .. £	do.,	371	168
	19			Total,	7,469	4,663

Co. Tipperary, ..	93	9143	Airhill, .. £	Sacred Heart,	215	215
,,	—	7387	Nenagh, .. £	Sisters of Mercy,	548	386
,,	—	13371	Borrisokane, .. £	do.,	169	147
,,	45	6488	Borrisoleigh, .. £	do.,	160	123
,,	—	6068	Thurles, .. £	Presentation,	621	437
,,	—	9407	Templemore, .. £	Sisters of Mercy,	446	373
,,	—	10873	Ballingarry, .. £	Presentation,	176	88
,,	—	11751	Tonagh, .. £	Sisters of Mercy,	181	63
,,	46	6430	Tipperary, .. £	do.,	498	217
,,	53	581	Cashel, .. £	Presentation,	437	230
,,	—	4133	Clogheen, .. £	Sisters of Mercy,	108	47
,,	—	7353	Drangan, .. £	do.,	285	173
,,	—	5503	Fethard, .. £	Presentation,	437	237
,,	—	10123	Cahir, .. £	Sisters of Mercy,	230	220
,,	—	10437	Ballyporeen, £	do.,	128	127
,,	—	11879	Carrick-on-Suir, .. £	Presentation,	745	444
,,	—	12369	Marlow-street, £	Sisters of Charity,	782	383
,,	—	13467	St. Joseph's (Carrick-on-Suir), £	Sisters of Mercy,	344	184
,,	—	13158	Clogheen, Leb.	do.,	115	79
,,	—	13404	New Inn, .. £	do.,	133	83
	20			Total, .	6,853	4,020

Co. Waterford,	48	6532	Cappoquin, .. £	Sisters of Mercy,	230	188
,,	—	14697	do., Leb.	do.,	86	66
,,	—	10811	Lismore, .. £	Presentation,	133	132
,,	40	11540	Kilmacthomas, £	Sisters of Mercy,	130	86
,,	—	11044	Waterford, .. £	Presentation,	462	243
,,	—	12007	Ferrybank, .. £	Sacred Heart,	228	107
,,	—	12067	Dungarvan (2), £	Presentation,	360	212
,,	—	12354	Star of the Sea, £	Sisters of Charity,	620	147
,,	—	13480	St. Joseph's, £	do.,	1,204	677
,,	—		do., wri.		241	74
,,	—	6530	Portlaw, .. £	Sisters of Mercy, .	234	181
,,	—	7036	St. John's (W), £	Ursuline,	548	383
,,	—	11371	Dunmore, East, £	Sisters of Mercy,	145	94
,,	—	11925	Stradbally, .. £	do.,	160	107
,,	90	12160	Clonmel, .. £	Presentation,	613	383
	14			Total, .	5,485	3,364

(a.)—Two Hundred and Sixty-one Convent National Schools paid by Capitation—*continued.*

Province and County.	District	Roll No.	School.	Religious Order of Community.		
LEINSTER.						
Co. Carlow,	44	435	Carlow,	f.	Presentation,	441	257
"	—	10010	do.	infts.	Sisters of Mercy,	214	171
"	—	13507	Tullow,	f.	Brigidine,	356	161
"	47	1925	Bagnalstown,	f.	Presentation,	453	257
	4				Total,	1,484	840
Co. Dublin,	60	1145	King's Inns-st.,	f.	Sisters of Charity,	1,517	964
"	—	5035	George's-hill,	f.	Presentation,	900	410
"	—	8033	Manor-street,	f.	Sisters of Charity,	1,078	455
"	—	11595	Baldoyle,	f.	do.	236	147
"	—	2460	Cabra,	f.	Dominican,	175	61
"	—	13418	Harlicar-street,	f.	Sisters of Charity,	2,455	1,177
"	—	18627	Mount Sackville,	f.	St. Joseph's,	134	64
"	36a	215	Lucan,	f.	Presentation,	261	86
"	37	2910	Baggot-street,	f.	Sisters of Mercy,	3,934	1,855
"	—	7632	Leeson-lane,	f.	Loretto,	1,100	443
"	—	7546	Golden Bridge,	f.	Sisters of Mercy,	970	583
"	—	7883	Chandal'm,	f.	Presentation,	303	140
"	—	11064	Weaver's-square,	f.	Sisters of Mercy,	1,574	801
"	—	12471	Our Lady's Mount,	f.	Sisters of Charity,	911	910
"	—	13611	Warrenmount,	f.	Presentation,	1,785	841
"	40	791	Blackrock,	f.	Sisters of Mercy,	341	510
"	—	1085	Booterstown,	f.	do.	885	189
"	—	6520	Kingstown,	f.	Dominican,	1,564	179
"	—	11357	Mount Anville,	f.	Sacred Heart,	160	77
"	—	11934	Sandymount,	f.	Sisters of Charity,	449	181
"	—	12508	St. Anne's,	f.	do.	377	145
"	40a	729	Loretto,	f.	Loretto,	157	66
"	—	7189	Dalkey,	f.	do.	294	141
"	—	7898	Glasthule,	f.	Sisters of Mercy,	315	300
"	—	11659	Townsend-street,	f.	do.	1,413	657
"	—	13812	St. Joseph's, Terenure,	f.	Presentation,	449	242
	28				Total	20,112	9,734
Co. Kildare,	37	775	Maynooth,	f.	Presentation,	903	146
"	—	1161	Clane,	f.	do.	179	81
"	—	3346	Naas,	f.	Sisters of Mercy,	450	240
"	—	11976	Kilcock,	f.	Presentation,	254	141
"	44	771	Kildare,	f.	do.	576	147
"	—	2105	Newbridge,	f.	Immaculate Conception,	245	124
"	—	11743	Great Connell,	f.	do.	189	63
"	—	11856	Kilcullen,	f.	Sacred Heart,	311	162
"	—	13373	St. Michael's (Athy),	f.	Sisters of Mercy,	660	357
	9				Total,	2,794	1,451
Co. Kilkenny,	47	846	Kilkenny,	f.	Presentation,	645	85
"	—	9184	Gowran,	f.	Brigidine,	164	55
"	—	10478	St. Patrick's,	f.	St. John of God,	405	263
"	—	10835	Castlecomer,	f.	Presentation,	893	388
"	—	11175	Thomastown,	infts.	Sisters of Mercy,	170	172
"	—	13874	Callan Lodge,	f.	do.	674	193
"	49	5457	Mooncoin,	f.	Presentation,	188	117
	7				Total,	2,832	1,440

(s.)—Two Hundred and Sixty-one Convent National Schools paid by
Capitation—*continued.*

Province and County.	Classes.	Roll No.	School.		Religious Order of Community.		Total No. of Pupils on the Rolls within the Year ended 31st Dec., 1803.	Average Daily Attendance of Pupils (Girls' and Infants') for the Year ended 31st Dec., 1803.
LEINSTER— *continued.*							
King's Co.	36	8220	Birr,	L.	Sisters of Mercy,		873	231
"	—	8915	Frankford,	L.	do.,		233	139
"	—	12403	St. Synagh's (Banagher)	L.	Sacred Heart,		306	115
"	41	825	Killien,	L.	Presentation,		144	101
"	—	9380	Tullamore,	L.	Sisters of Mercy,		770	625
"	—	7471	Portarlington,	L.	Presentation,		332	173
"	—	13118	Clara,	L.	Sisters of Mercy,		341	158
	7				Total,		2,457	1,467
Co. Longford,	28	12842	St. Joseph's,	L.	Sisters of Mercy,		574	291
"	—	18345	Granard,	L.	do.,		374	115
"	33	5065	Ballymahon,	L.	do.,		190	143
	3				Total,		1,038	814
Co. Louth,	25	641	Drogheda,	L.	Presentation,		763	442
"	—	5387	Dundalk (B),	L.	Sisters of Mercy,		1,418	793
"	—	8445	Ardee (?),	L.	do.,		238	150
"	—	10475	Drogheda,	L.	Sisters of Charity,		403	210
	4				Total,		2,600	1,513
Co. Meath,	23	8052	St. Mary's,	L.	Sisters of Mercy,		418	301
"	19	683	Navan (1),	L.	Loreto,		845	249
"	—	7472	Do. (2),	L.	Sisters of Mercy,		804	413
"	—	10118	Trim,	L.	do.,		578	176
"	—	12844	Kells,	L.	do.,		447	207
	5				Total,		2,812	1,500
Queen's Co.,	41	1558	Ballyroan,	L.	Brigidine,		128	68
"	—	7185	Mountmellick,	L.	Presentation,		531	187
"	—	7481	Borris-in-Ossory,	L.	Sisters of Mercy,		184	94
"	—	12343	Castletown,	L.	Brigidine,		310	110
"	—	13287	Maryborough,	L.	Presentation,		341	212
"	—	13815	Abbeyleix,	L.	Brigidine,		303	168
"	44	13887	Stradbally,	L.	Presentation,		290	151
	7				Total,		1,787	1,023
Co. Westmeath,	38	854	Mullingar,	L.	Presentation,		482	273
"	—	6874	Rochfort Bridge,	L.	Sisters of Mercy,		172	95
"	—	8672	Moate,	L.	do.,		344	148
"	36	13417	St. Mary's,	L.	Sacred Heart,		518	197
"	41	13178	Kilbeggan,	L.	Sisters of Mercy,		397	171
	5				Total,		1,843	884

(a.)—Two Hundred and Sixty-one Convent National Schools paid by Capitation—*continued.*

Province and County.	District.	Roll No.	School.	Religious Order of Community.	Total No. of Pupils on the rolls within the Year ended 31st Dec. 1893.	Average No. on the rolls for the Year.
LEINSTER—*cont.*						
Co. Wexford,	48	887	New Ross (1),	f.	Carmelite,	474	256
"	"	8047	Do. (3),	f.	Sisters of Mercy,	533	168
"	"	10629	Ramsgrange,	f.	St. Louis,	131	65
"	50	953	Wexford,	f.	Presentation,	568	48
"	"	5654	Newtownbarry,	f.	Faithful Companions,	172	108
"	"	3214	Gorey,	f.	Loretto,	735	163
"	"	4249	St. Mary's,	Inf.	Sisters of Mercy,	354	260
"	"	6258	Presentation Convent, Enniscorthy.	f.	Presentation,	872	277
"	"	6921	Templeshannon,	f.	Sisters of Mercy,	574	297
"	"	11351	Foulks,	f.	Sr. John of God,	486	378
"	"	11786	Ramsgrange hill,	f.	Sisters of Mercy,	213	101
"	"	12946	Wexford (3),	f.	do.,	291	159
	13				**Total,**	4,616	2,463
Co. Wicklow,	48	8237	Delgany,	f.	Carmelite,	69	66
"	"	7180	Bray (3),	f.	Loretto,	439	286
"	"	10102	St. Michael's,	f.	Sisters of Mercy,	128	73
"	"	10418	Wicklow,	f.	Dominican,	647	368
"	"	13873	Arklow,	f.	Sisters of Mercy,	412	289
"	44	873	Baltinglass,	f.	Presentation,	215	153
	6				**Total,**	1,820	345
CONNAUGHT.						
Co. Galway,	82	12254	Tuam,	f.	Presentation,	576	184
"	"	12250	Do. (3),	f.	Sisters of Mercy,	456	231
"	84	1013	Baboon,	f.	Presentation,	376	283
"	"	4575	Newtownparish,	f.	Sisters of Mercy,	732	363
"	"	11343	Carm,	f.	do.,	82	66
"	"	13190	Clifden,	f.	do.,	214	108
"	"	13439	Oughterard,	f.	do.,	382	264
"	34A	12361	Claremorris,	f.	Sisters of Charity,	101	84
"	"	13351	Creamore,	f.	Presentation,	163	261
"	85	6634	St. Vincent's,	f.	Sisters of Mercy,	494	376
"	"	6850	Ballinasloe,	f.	do.,	629	394
"	"	12371	St. Joseph's,	f.	do.,	233	135
"	"	11237	Kinvara,	f.	do.,	229	141
"	66	13288	Gort (2),	f.	do.,	274	168
	14				**Total,**	4,033	2,571
Co. Leitrim,	20	13770	Mohill,	f.	Sisters of Mercy,	584	165
"	21	12844	Carrick-on-Shannon,	f.	Marist,	377	195
"	"	13814	Ballinamore,	f.	Sisters of Mercy,	223	102
	3				**Total,**	847	462
Co. Mayo,	20	14175	St. John's (Foxford),	f.	Sisters of Charity,	128	79
"	"	14849	Do.,	Inf.	do.,	141	129
"	21	7719	Swinford,	f.	Sisters of Mercy,	511	173
"	"	13902	St. Fra. Xavier's,	f.	Sisters of Charity,	369	198
"	22	12284	Castlebar,	f.	Sisters of Mercy,	485	372
"	"	12255	St. Patrick's,	f.	do.,	705	356
"	"	13517	St. Joseph's,	f.	do.,	365	141
"	23	13253	Mt. St. Michael's,	f.	do.,	607	248
"	"	13503	Ballinrobe,	f.	do.,	460	231
	9				**Total,**	4,394	1,683

(a.)—Two Hundred and Sixty-one Convent National Schools paid by Capitation—*continued.*

Province and County.	Dist.	Roll No.	School.	Religious Order of Community.	Total No. of Pupils on Rolls	Average attend.
CONNAUGHT— *cont.*						
Co. Roscommon,	29	10529	Abbeytown,	Sisters of Mercy,	323	161
"	37	6308	St. Mary's (Strokestown),	do.,	319	157
"	—	7233	Roscommon,	do.,	415	236
"	—	16052	Abbeyartton,	do.,	258	131
"	35	13133	St. Ann's,	do.,	471	281
"	"	7771	St. Peter's,	do.,	478	271
"	"	12754	St. Joseph's, Summerhill,	do.,	133	72
	7			Total,	2,837	1,403
Co. SLIGO,	13	13246	St. Patrick's,	Sisters of Mercy,	717	444
"	—	13546	Do., m. inft.,	do.,	213	124
"	—	14158	St. Vincent's,	Ursuline,	113	57
"	21	11887	Banada,	Sisters of Charity,	175	63
	4			Total,	1,218	740

SUMMARY OF CONVENT SCHOOLS PAID by CAPITATION.

No. of Schools.	County.	Total No. of Pupils on Rolls	Average attendance.	No. of Schools.	County.	Total No. of Pupils on Rolls	Average attendance.
7	Antrim,	2,617	1,396	3	Longford,	1,028	610
6	Armagh,	2,415	1,395	6	Louth,	2,890	1,613
4	Cavan,	869	481	7	Meath,	2,312	1,301
5	Donegal,	991	672	5	Queen's,	1,742	1,073
3	Down,	1,380	635	3	Westmeath,	1,441	872
—	Fermanagh,	—	—	12	Wexford,	4,118	2,167
5	Londonderry,	2,046	1,115	6	Wicklow,	1,620	943
1	Monaghan,	227	170				
4	Tyrone,	1,034	1,032	34	Total for Leinster,	44,803	23,570
35	Total for Ulster,	12,542	6,391	16	Galway,	5,863	2,651
				3	Leitrim,	897	462
6	Clare,	2,492	1,295	9	Mayo,	3,866	1,954
30	Cork,	17,981	9,442	7	Roscommon,	2,437	1,403
9	Kerry,	3,151	1,876	4	Sligo,	1,218	740
12	Limerick,	7,443	4,043	47	Total for Connaught,	15,979	7,142
23	Tipperary,	6,845	4,020				
14	Waterford,	4,483	2,554	35	Schools in Ulster,	12,542	6,391
				94	" Munster,	42,797	23,552
94	Total for Munster,	42,727	23,540	34	" Leinster,	44,803	23,570
4	Carlow,	1,434	898	47	" Connaught,	15,979	7,142
28	Dublin,	20,112	9,764				
8	Kildare,	4,794	1,454	261	Gross Total of Convent Capitation Cases,	115,944	61,125
7	Kilkenny,	2,532	1,439				
7	King's,	3,457	1,657				

B

(h.)—TWENTY CONVENT NATIONAL SCHOOLS PAID BY CLASSIFICATION.

Province and County.	District.	Roll No.	School.	Religious Order of Community.			
ULSTER.							
Co. ARMAGH,	11	12441	Portadown,	£	Presentation,		250	122
"	16	—	Do.,	T	do.,		76	23
"		11782	Middletown (J),	L	St. Louis,		166	97
	2				Total,		521	273
Co. FERMANAGH,	13	13401	Enniskillen,	£	Sisters of Mercy,		851	178
	1				Total,		851	178
Co. MONAGHAN,	16	250	Monaghan,	£	St. Louis,		873	288
	1				Total,		873	288
MUNSTER.							
Co. CORK,	58	12762	Castletown,	£	Sisters of Mercy,		227	127
"	60	18910	Crosshaven,	£	Presentation,		820	183
	2				Total,		547	310
Co. KERRY,	54	433	Dingle,	L	Presentation,		328	343
"	43	843	Tralee,	L	do.,		773	418
"	65	12742	Rathmore,	L	do.,		397	141
"	57	13442	Caherdaniel,	L	do.,		408	238
"	—	13061	Killarney,	L	do.,		452	270
"		13331	Do. (3),	L	Sisters of Mercy,		453	273
"	46	8730	Kenmare,	L	Poor Clares,		444	273
	7				Total,		4,635	1,802
Co. WATERFORD,	48	1238	Tallow,	£	Carmelite,		143	104
"	49	11481	Dungarvan,	£	Sisters of Mercy,		260	177
"	—	13473	Do.,	L	do.,		269	153
	3				Total,		672	439
LEINSTER.							
Co. KILDARE,	41	11586	Rathangan,	£	Sisters of Mercy,		288	152
	1				Total,		288	152

(*b.*)—TWENTY CONVENT NATIONAL SCHOOLS PAID BY CLASSIFICATION.—*continued.*

Province and County.	District.	Roll No.	School.		Religious Order of Community.	Total No. of Pupils on the Rolls within the Year ended 31st Dec., 1894.	Average Daily Attendance of Pupils for the Year ended 31st Dec., 1894.
LEINSTER— *continued.*							
Co. Longford, .	39	6345	Newtownforbes, .	f.	Sisters of Mercy, .	153	91
,,	1				Total, .	153	91
CONNAUGHT.							
Co. Mayo, .	29	5018	Ballina, . . .	f.	Sisters of Mercy, .	313	149
,,	—	12431	Do., . . .	f.	do., . . .	331	130
	2				Total, . .	644	279
Total Convent Classification Schools.	20				Gross Total of Convent Classification Cases, .	6,887	3,835

(*c.*)—THREE MONASTERY NATIONAL SCHOOLS PAID BY CAPITATION.

Province and County.	District.	Roll No.	School.		Religious Order of Community.	Total No. of Pupils for any time on the Rolls within the Year ended 31st Dec., 1894.	Average Daily Attendance of Pupils for the Year ended 31st Dec., 1894.
MUNSTER.							
Co. Cork, .	60	5699	Gt. George's-street, .	m.	Presentation, .	480	274
,,	,,	5699	Douglas-street, .	m.	Do., .	1,124	480
	2				Total, . .	1,604	754
Co. Kerry, .	54	3635	Milltown, . .	m.	Presentation, .	163	128
,,	1				Total . .	163	128
Total Monastery Capitation Schools.	3				Total of Monastery Schools paid by Capitation, .	1,767	882

(d.)—Thirty-seven Monastery National Schools paid by Classification.

Province and County.	District.	Roll No.	School.	Religious Order of Community.	Total No. of Pupils on the Rolls on the last school-day of the year 1894.	Average Daily Attendance of Pupils for the Year ended 1894.
ULSTER.						
Co. Donegal,	1	1215	Letterkenny, m.	Presentation,	106	77
	1				106	77
Co. Down,	17	9429	John-street, m.	Brothers of the Christian Schools,	114	77
	1			Total,	114	77
MUNSTER.						
Co. Cork,	48	1397	St. Joseph's, Cove (1) m.	Presentation,	654	267
"	"	1502	Do. (2), m.	do.,	249	284
"	56	12519	Mallow, m.	Patrician,	452	289
"	59	476	St. Patrick's (Dunmanway), m.	Brothers of the Christian Schools,	282	157
"	60	1612	Kinsale (1), m.	Presentation,	873	228
"	—	12175	Greenmount, m.	do.,	601	617
	6			Total,	3,543	1,897
Co. Kerry,	57	1788	Killarney, m.	Presentation,	353	174
	1			Total,	353	174
Co. Limerick,	48	6543	Hospital, m.	Brothers of the Christian Schools,	304	144
	1			Total,	390	144
Co. Tipperary,	53	13814	Fethard, m.	Patrician,	385	113
	1			Total,	803	113
Co. Waterford,	48	13560	St. Stephen's, m.	Brothers of the Christian Schools,	761	835
"	—	—	Do. ery.	do.,	310	61
	1			Total,	1,071	395
LEINSTER.						
Co. Carlow,	46	691	Tullow, m.	Patrician,	178	62
"	47	13165	St. Bridget's, m.	Brothers of the Christian Schools,	304	161
	2			Total,	482	223
Co. Kildare,	44	12747	Kildare, m.	Brothers of the Christian Schools,	149	74
	1			Total,	169	74
Co. Kilkenny,	47	13565	St. Patrick's, m.	Brothers of the Christian Schools,	189	197
	1			Total,	169	167

(d.)—Thirty-seven Monastery National Schools paid by Classification—*continued.*

Province and County.	Number.	Roll No.	School.		Religious Order of Conductors by.	Total No. of Pupils on rolls ...	Average daily ...
LEINSTER—*con.*							
King's Co.,	85	12870	St. Brendan's, Clara.	m.	Presentation,	231	171
"	41	4285		m.	Franciscan,	444	209
	2				Total,	675	380
Co. Louth,	25	2794	Ardee,	m.	Brothers of the Christian Schools,	275	149
	1				Total,	275	149
Queen's Co.,	41	916	Castletown,	m.	Brothers of the Christian Schools,	76	33
"	—	7654	Oats street,	m.	Patrician,	203	101
	2				Total,	279	134
Co. Westmeath,	35	12984	St. Mary's,	m.	Marist,	263	144
"	—	13756	Do., prop. m.		do.,	214	126
	2				Total,	477	270
CONNAUGHT.							
Co. Galway,	27	12422	Killartin,	m.	Franciscan,	142	78
"	30	12509	Carry,	m.	do.,	116	54
"	34	1014	Galway,	m.	Patrician,	297	193
"	—	12973	Nun's Island,	m.	do.,	146	85
"	—	11906	Galway,	m. inft.	do.,	162	70
"	5..	11765	Carraheg,	m.	Franciscan,	163	74
	6				Total,	1,123	531
Co. Leitrim,	81	14494	St. Mary's (Carrick-on-Shannon).	m.	Presentation,	211	113
	1				Total,	211	113
Co. Mayo,	21	13709	St. John's (Ballaghaderreen),	m.	Brothers of the Christian Schools,	220	110
"	26	12971	Treaderer,	m.	Franciscan,	133	41
"	—	12927	Eeraw,	m.	do.,	53	37
"	—	13160	Bangasetty,	m.	do.,	63	46
"	—	13347	St. Patrick's,	m.	Brothers of the Christian Schools,	317	135
	5				Total,	885	434
Co. Roscommon,	27	17564	Highlake,	m.	Franciscan,	83	44
"	32	12247	Granlahan.	m.	do.,	189	77
	2				Total,	275	122
Total Monastery Classification Schools,	37				Gross Total of Monastery Classification Class,	3,380	4,923

(e.)—Summary according to Religious Orders—Convent National Schools.

Religious Order	Capitation Schools	Classification Schools	Total
Sisters of Mercy,	143	8	151
Presentation,	51	7	58
Sisters of Charity,	19	—	19
Sacred Heart,	8	—	8
Loretto,	6	—	6
Poor Clares,	4	1	5
St. Louis,	3	2	5
Brigidine,	5	—	5
Dominican,	5	—	5
Immaculate Conception,	5	—	5
Ursuline,	3	—	3
Carmelite,	2	1	3
St. John of God,	3	—	3
Faithful Companions of Jesus,	1	—	1
St. Joseph,	1	—	1
Marist,	1	—	1
Poor Servants of the Mother of God and the Poor,	1	—	1
Faithful Companions,	1	—	1
Total Convent National Schools,	**261**	**20**	**281**

Monastery National Schools.

Religious Order	Capitation Schools	Classification Schools	Total
Brothers of the Christian Schools,	—	11	11
Presentation,	3	8	11
Franciscan,	—	8	8
Patrician,	—	7	7
Marist,	—	3	3
Total Monastery National Schools,	**3**	**37**	**40**
Grand Total—Convent and Monastery National Schools,	**264**	**57**	**321**

(f.)—General Summary—Schools and Attendance.

	Paid by Capitation			Paid by Classification			Total		
	No. of Schools	Total No. of Pupils on Rolls	Average Daily Attendance	No. of Schools	Total No. of Pupils on Rolls	Average Daily Attendance	No. of Schools	Total No. of Pupils on Rolls	Average Daily Attendance
Convents,	261	118,044	61,126	20	6,897	3,846	281	119,941	65,072
Monasteries,	3	1,767	682	37	9,390	4,972	40	11,157	4,804
Total	264	114,811	61,807	57	14,887	8,878	321	130,900	70,880

* The number of Convent Capitation Schools in receipt of the 12s. grant was 255, and the number in receipt of the 11s. grant was 11 ; of this latter number 7 are Convents which have been only recently added, and which are provisionally paid at the 11s. rate. Of the 3 Monastery Capitation Schools, 2 are paid at the 12s. rate and 1 at the 11s. rate.

IV.—List of Ninety-nine Island Schools in connexion on 31st December, 1894.

County.	Dist.	Roll No.	Name of School.	County.	Dist.	Roll No.	Name of School.
Antrim,	4	9372	Rathlin Island.	Galway,	34	8818	Killeany, &c.
				Ditto,	"	10292	Garumna,
Down,	18	14589	Copeland "	Ditto,	"	11616	Kilbronaghy,
				Ditto,	"	11748	Lettermullen Island.
Donegal,	1	4729	Gola "	Ditto,	"	11845	Islandeady Island.
Ditto,	"	3164	Tory "	Ditto,	"	11936	Inishbarra
Ditto,	"	3775	Owey "	Ditto,	"	12339	Inishmaine Islands.
Ditto,	"	3496	Rutland "	Ditto,	"	12533	Do.
Ditto,	"	5829	Inishfree "	Ditto,	"	12546	Kilmurry, Arranmore
Ditto,	"	6571	Arranmore (1)	Ditto,	"	12567	Onaght, Island.
Ditto,	"	9791	Inishbofin	Ditto,	"	12567	Oney Island.
Ditto,	"	10371	Cruit	Ditto,	"	12517	Maree
Ditto,	"	11849	Arranmore (2)	Ditto,	"	12561	Annaghvane
Ditto,	"	13392	Inishmeane	Ditto,	"	12641	Inishnark
Ditto,	"	14623	Inishfedin	Ditto,	"	12750	Furnish
Ditto,	2	6280	Lusk	Ditto,	"	12920	Inishkerre
Ditto,	"	14244	Inishduff	Ditto,	"	12844	Inishnaquerre
				Ditto,	"	12701	Roundi(Garumna Isl.)
Fermanagh,	6	8002	Devenagisulum	Ditto,	"	13030	Mannagh's Island
Ditto,	"	11633	Nun	Ditto,	"	13043	Inishkrone
Ditto,	15	7632	Gubb Island.	Ditto,	"	13386	Tashee (Garumna
Ditto,	"	11837	Inishmore Island.				Island).
				Ditto,	"	12849	Lettermullen, or
Clare,	45	6448	Canny "				Lettermore Island.
Ditto,	"	10319	Scattery "	Ditto,	"	13116	Myalsh
Ditto,	"	13818	Low "	Ditto,	"	13572	Inishlean Island, &c.
				Ditto,	"	13622	Do.
Cork,	48	8195	Heir Island	Ditto,	"	13416	Lettermullen Island
Ditto,	"	8318	Spike "	Ditto,	"	13534	Turmeen, Garumna
Ditto,	56	4903	Long "	Ditto,	"	13577	Do. Island
Ditto,	"	7255	Hare "	Ditto,	"	13588	Derre,
Ditto,	1	7452	Lasconto	Ditto,	"	13659	Lettermore Island.
			Crove, m. Bear	Ditto,	"	14185	Inishterbet
Ditto,	"	7453	Do. f. Island.	Ditto,	"	14536	Inishbecket
Ditto,	"	7454	Ballinakilla	Ditto,	"	14638	Dynish Island.
Ditto,	"	13130	Dursey Island.				
Ditto,	"	13632	Whiddy	Mayo,	16	14364	Inishkea Island.
Ditto,	16	4531	Cape Clear, m. Clear	Ditto,	26	5527	Silvermore
				Ditto,	"	5598	Duvena, Achill
Ditto,	"	5291	Roangurmore Island.	Ditto,	"	5669	Dooega, Island.
Ditto,	"	5537	Cape Clear, f., Clear	Ditto,	"	5659	Saccarry, Achill
				Ditto,	"	5617	Valley Island.
Ditto,	"	4529	Sherkin Island, f.	Ditto,	"	5116	Inishbark Island.
Ditto,	"	14085	Do.	Ditto,	"	5647	Ballinstoeth Achill
				Ditto,	"	10214	Soyle Island.
Kerry,	54	5237	Blasket Island	Ditto,	"	12150	Inishmurray Manor
Ditto,	57	7357	Knight's-town, m.	Ditto,	"	13174	St. Colman's,
							Inishturk Island
Ditto,	"	7598	Do. f.	Ditto,	"	13177	St. Brigid's, Clare
Ditto,	"	10731	Coravog, m. Valen-	Ditto,	"	13211	St. Patrick's, Clare
Ditto,	"	10732	Do. f. tia	Ditto,	"	13357	Collatemore
Ditto,	"	10510	Ballyhearty, m. Island.	Ditto,	"	13668	Doogh m. Achill
			Do. f.	Ditto,	"	13410	Do. f. Island.
Ditto,	"	14650	Do. f.	Ditto,	"	13761	Achill Beg Island.
				Ditto,	"	13806	Inishmore
Dublin,	50	6125	Lambay Island.	Ditto,	"	13577	Inishahole
				Ditto,	"	14839	Do. f.
				Sligo,	12	8618	Coney
				Ditto,	"	9847	Inishmurray

V.—List of Thirty Industrial Schools (under the Act) in connexion with recognised National Schools on 31st December, 1894.

Roll District No.	District	County	School	Religious Order of Conductors	Total No. of Pupils on Roll	Average Paid Attendance
11782	18	Armagh,	Middletown,	Sisters of St. Louis,	33	41
340	—	Monaghan,	St. Martha's, Monaghan,	Do.,	45	48
14118	8	Tyrone,	St. Catherine's, Strabane,	Sisters of Mercy,	85	70
7313	45	Clare,	Ennis,	Do.,	44	53
4576	48	Cork,	St. Coleman's, Queenstown,	Do.,	41	43
4428	56	"	Mallow	Do.,	48	46
7851	50	Cork,	Glanmire (St. Aloysius),	Do.,	131	103
6414	60	"	Passage West, Cork,	Do.,	78	71
1873	54	Kerry,	Pembroke Arms, Tralee,	Do.,	70	69
13801	57	"	St. Joseph's House, Killarney,	Do.,	109	91
1069	31	Limerick,	St. Vincent's, Limerick,	Do.,	191	65
3407	43	Tipperary,	St. Augustine's, Templemore,	Do.,	80	45
4063	—	"	St. Louis, Thurles,	Presentation Sisters,	43	38
6132	46	"	Tipperary,	Sisters of Mercy,	60	54
581	55	"	St. Francis, Cashel,	Presentation Sisters,	113	88
1765	40	Dublin,	Booterstown,	Sisters of Mercy,	120	104
6346	26	Longford,	Our Lady of Succour, Newtownforbes,	Do.,	194	75
6587	26	Louth,	Dundalk,	Do.,	88	84
10457	—	"	House of Charity, Drogheda,	French Sist. of Charity,	114	88
6482	33	Westmeath,	Mount Carmel, Moate,	Sisters of Mercy,	43	38
11040	54	Wexford,	St. Michael's, Wexford,	Do.,	42	38
12430	54	Galway,	Oughterard,	Do.,	71	53
4312	—	"	St. Anne's, Galway,	Do.,	51	44
13180	—	"	Clifden,	Do.,	110	49
6832	25	"	St. Bridget's, Loughrea,	Do.,	68	54
6529	—	"	Ballinasloe,	Do.,	163	86
1268	26	Mayo,	St. Colembers, Westport,	Do.,	148	121
7128	27	Roscommon,	St. Monica's, Roscommon,	Do.,	149	—
1264	83	"	St. Joseph's, Athlone,	Do.,	113	—
13240	12	Sligo,	St. Lawrence's, Sligo,	Do.,		
				Total,	3,637	1,884

VI.—List of Forty-five Evening Schools in operation on 31st December, 1894.

Position	Roll No.	County	School	District	Roll No.	County	School
R	71	Antrim,	Cromwells,	29	7187	Cavan,	Keelagh,
J	6545	"	Belfast Model,	—	10564	"	Clonervid,
—	13632	"	St. Paul's,	—	12819	"	St. Joseph's,
11	9710	Armagh,	Edward Street Convent,	2	1698	Donegal,	St. Eugene's,
—	11475	"	St. Peter's,				
—	12288	"	Carma-street,				
—	10141	"	Portadown Convent,				
—	13664	"	Eaky,	11	4811	Derry,	Gilford Mill,
13	2897	"	Marbury,	—	4812	"	Do.,
14	7366	"	Tullyroan,	17	8746	"	Killyloey,
—	10478	"	Charlestown,	—	10723	"	Drumloam Mills,

* This Evening School has a separate Roll Number.

VI.—List of Forty-five Evening Schools in operation on 31st December, 1894—*continued.*

D. dist.	Roll No.	County.	School.	Dist.	Roll No.	County.	School.
3	14053	Londonderry	St. Columb's Hall. *	30	8867	Dublin	St. Michan's.
–	3634	„	Carlmkey.	–	5540	„	West Dublin Model, m. *
				–	6518	„	Jamephian. *
4	11586	Tyrone	Son Mills.	37	14846	„	St. Joseph's.
13	14487	„	Loy Convent. *	37	744	„	SS. Michael and John.
–	5184	„	Rasa.	–	14162	„	St. Kevin's. *
–	4144	„	Mullinahone.	40	6378	„	Inchicore Model, m.
				40a	763	„	Central Model, m.
60	9996	Cork	Blackpool, m.				
–	11297	„	SS. Peter and Paul's, m. Du. L	37	11677	Kildare	Naas. m.
–	11958	„					
–	18404	„	St. Vincent's Convent.				
–	14044	„	St. Mary's, Brown's Hill.	32	1676	Mayo	Ballindine. m.
–	13722	„	St. Finbar's. *				
49	12442	Waterford	St. Joseph's Convent.	15	1669	Roscommon	Ballyboy.
–	13467	„	St. Stephen's Monastery.	–	5248	„	Drumport.

◆ This Evening School has a separate Roll Number.

VII.—List of Seventy-two Vested Schools to which Grants for Teachers Residences have been made (from the Act coming into operation in 1875 to 31st December, 1894).

County.	School.	County.	School.	County.	School.
Armagh,	Townmill, N. T. Hamilton.	Cork,	Coonbella.	Longford,	Clonmore.
Ditto,	Camvilla.	Ditto,	Wolvertown.	Ditto,	Langford.
		Ditto,	Chimneyfield.	Meath,	Kildana.
Cavan,	Derrylesagh.			Ditto,	Baconsgrove.
		Kerry,	Derryagalby.		
Donegal,	Milford.	Ditto,	Portinagre.	Queen's,	Abbeyleix, North.
Ditto,	Amlagh.	Ditto,	Drummacurra.		
		Ditto,	Glanmore.	Wexford,	Carrickbyrne.
Down,	Downshire.	Ditto,	Knockaherry	Ditto,	Court.
		Limerick,	Ballyelaghan.		
Fermanagh,	Brookborough.	Ditto,	Manigay.	Wicklow,	Laskea.
Ditto,	Tempo.	Ditto,	Bruree.		
Ditto,	Mullinahartilla.	Ditto,	Mamun.	Galway,	Lettergush. m.
Ditto,	Immarus.			Ditto,	Duss. L
Ditto,	Mallack.	Tipperary,	Curryclogher.	Ditto,	Cloondoyle.
				Ditto,	Garrusa.
L. Derry,	Garvu.	Waterford,	Falshiery.	Ditto,	New Inn.
		Ditto,	Ballinvella.	Ditto,	Leam.
Tyrone,	Drumoyla.	Ditto,	Ballydaff. L	Ditto,	Trust.
				Ditto,	Otaght.
Clare,	Scropel.	Carlow,	Rathoma.	Ditto,	Kilbony.
Ditto,	Clenadrum.			Ditto,	Lsishaur.
Ditto,	Kilbaha.	Dublin,	Ringsend.	Ditto,	Islahmaina.
		Kildare,	Kilberry.		
Cork,	Kilooma.			Leitrim,	Drumakera.
Ditto,	Kingwilliamstown, m.	Kilkenny,	Graba.		
Ditto,	Gurrus. L	King's,	St. Cronan's.	Mayo,	Knanks.
Ditto,	Mallow.	Ditto,	Sean.	Ditto,	Loughmama.
Ditto,	Clonakilty. m.	Longford,	Moydow.	Ditto,	St. Colman's, Inishturk.
Ditto,	Knockacrubotha.	Ditto,	Mileshen.	Ditto,	Aglish.
				Ditto,	Kilkelly.

VIII.—LIST of NAMES of FIFTY-TWO* SCHOOLS in which SPECIAL GRANTS of SALARY in aid of INDUSTRIAL INSTRUCTION were available, under Rule 52, for Year ended 31st December, 1894.

County.	Dis-trict	Roll No.	School.	County.	Dis-trict	Roll No.	School.
Antrim.	3	7018	Crumlin-road, Convt.	Waterford,	59	15020	Stradbally, Convent.
Donegal.	5	7593	Ballyraine	Carlow,	44	866	Carlow.
Down,	18	5725	Rostrevor	Dublin,	30	1149	King's Inns-street Convent
„	—	7568	Canal-street, „	„	37	2010	Harpur-st., Convent.
Monaghan,	24	3617	Carrickmacross	„	—	7646	Golden-bridge, „
Clare,	43	7518	Ennis, Convent.	„	—	1106	Weaver's-square, „
„	—	15374	Kilrush, „	„	40	721	Blackrock, „
„	—	11609	Kildis, „	„	1965	Booterstown, „
				„	40a	15912	Terenure Convent.
Cork,	48	3828	Youghal, „				Genasi Model.
„	55	10282	Kanturk, „	Kilkenny,	47	806	Kilkenny Convent.
„	58	2288	Doneraile, „	„	—	10478	St. Patrick's, „
„	—	12791	Mitchelstown, „				
„	70	8420	Rathkeale, „	Longford,	22	12942	St. Joseph's, „
„	—	7651	Clonakilty, „ (E.)	Meath,	29	7472	Navan, „ (P).
„	69	4372	Kinsale, „	„	—	12960	Kells, „
Kerry,	61	343	Tralee, Convent.	„	—	12480	Oldcastle „
„	—	6213	Cumlade and „				
„	—	13520	Moyderwell „	Queen's,	44	13347	Stradbally.
„	47	13391	Killarney, „				
„	54	8220	Kenmare, „	Wexford,	43	867	Kas Ross, „ (I).
Limerick,	61	8730	Adare, Convent.	„	60	12943	SS. Mary's (Wexford), „
„	63	9992	St. Catherine's, Convent.	„	„	5891	Templeanouse, „
„	—	8509	St. Anne's, Convent	Galway,	84	4315	N.T. Smith, Convent
Tipperary,	52	861	Cashel, „	„	—	12489	Oughterard.
„	—	5943	Fethard, „	„	85	9692	SS. Vincent's, „
„	—	11872	Carrick-on-Suir, „	„	49	13268	Gort.
„	—	13197	„	Mayo,	31	13262	St. Francis Xavier, „

* Fifty of these are Convent Schools.

IX.—HALF-TIME PUPILS ATTENDING NATIONAL SCHOOLS.

(Extract from Appendix to Commissioners' Rules. Edition 1891.)

The Commissioners having had under consideration the case of factory children who attend National Schools for half time, have decided that the following attendances qualify such pupils for presentation for fees to the teachers at the annual results examinations, viz. :—

200 days of 2 hours a day,
135 days of 3 hours a day,
100 days of 4 hours each day,
80 days of 5 hours each day,
66 days of 6 hours each day,

The teachers shall adopt such a system of marking half-time pupils who attend for more than four hours, as will afford a means of check on the accuracy of the records.

* The time fixed must be two or more complete hours. Fractions of an hour cannot be included.

LIST of ONE HUNDRED and FIFTY-ONE National Schools attended by HALF-TIME pupils in 1894—the number of such HALF-TIME pupils on the Roll, and the average daily attendance of HALF-TIME pupils.

County	Dist.	Roll Number	School	Total Number of Half-time pupils on Roll	Average daily attendance of Half-time pupils
Antrim,	5	6634	Balnamore,	42	10
"	"	11137	Liscolman,	17	4
"	"	2367	Guy's,	104	30
"	"	7747	Do.	79	34
"	"	7952	Harryville (2),	17	4
"	"	7367	Do. (1),	23	8
"	"	12345	Ballymoney-road,	21	7
"	3	12599	Do.	17	3
"	"	1224	Edenderry,	232	44
"	"	1776	Cromlin,	4	1
"	"	4226	Cinkers,	43	14
"	"	4134	Do.	88	11
"	"	5784	Seamen's Friend Society,	114	31
"	"	6292	Old Park,	20	6
"	"	7319	Wolfhill,	110	42
"	"	7533	Moorhead,	70	18
"	"	8055	Springfield,	61	11
"	"	8816	Ligoniel Village,	77	14
"	"	8904	Wolfhill Mill,	39	15
"	"	8464	Old Lodge Road,	9	2
"	"	8985	Do.	17	3
"	"	3840	Carnmoney-road,	52	18
"	"	9851	Do.	98	35
"	"	10675	Oromilla-road,	192	43
"	"	11125	Do.	224	58
"	"	10535	Holywood,	83	34
"	"	10659	Do.	43	27
"	"	10915	Jennymount,	236	38
"	"	10645	St. Catherine's,	66	24
"	"	10831	Milfort Mill,	68	24
"	"	10971	Castle-street Convent,	5	2
"	"	11605	Hilden,	896	117
"	"	11442	Greencastle,	93	19
"	"	11613	Do.	36	14
"	"	11149	St. Mark's,	95	24
"	"	12936	Edenderry,	637	75
"	"	12419	Star of the Sea,	185	63
"	"	13145	Cavehill-street,	167	43
"	"	12991	St. Patrick's Ch.,	163	66
"	"	14128	St. Joseph's Convent,	246	84
"	"	77	Whitehouse (1),	112	14
"	"	2849	White Abbey,	45	17
"	"	2450	Do.	47	17
"	"	4564	Monkstown,	41	13
"	"	6430	Carey Mills,	9	1
"	"	6634	Woodburn (1),	21	8
"	"	7237	Dougb,	12	7
"	"	7920	Do.	23	13
"	"	6298	Barneskill,	103	95
"	"	11438	Wembey,	52	16
"	"	11465	Whitehead (2),	1	1
"	"	11712	Ballysloan,	23	7
"	"	11713	Do.	16	5

Ltst of One Hundred and Fifty-one National Schools attended by
Half-time pupils in 1894, &c.—*continued.*

County,	Dist.	Roll Number.	School.					Total Number of Half-time pupils on Roll.	Average daily attendance of Half-time pupils.
Antrim,	8A	11221	Parkgate,					6	2
"	"	11476	Millbrook,					11	5
"	"	12317	Tyrage,					6	2
"	"	14157	Whitewell,					10	4
"	J	47	Dunmurry,				B.	62	12
"	b	4714	Do.				L.	13	9
"	N	6325	St. Mary's,				B.	40	11
"	"	6295	Do.				L.	83	31
"	R	6212	Campbell's-row,					516	141
"	"	6924	Hutchinson-street (1),					9	2
"	T	11160	Linfield Mill,					282	74
"	"	16536	Workman Memorial,					166	29
"	U	14155	Lambeg Village,					21	4
"	"	12089	St. Peter's,				B.	78	17
"	"	7540	Do.				L.	334	61
"	"	13833	Derriaghy,					15	4
"	7A	6581	Earl-street,				B.	60	16
"	"	7382	Millard,				L.	74	18
"	"	6568	Mark-street,				L.	63	10
"	"	9718	Milford,				W.	67	14
"	"	12047	York-road,					189	48
Armagh,	11	6244	Portadown,					2	2
"	"	12890	Edgerstown,					64	25
"	16	5174	Markethill,				f.	5	3
"	"	7447	Darkley,					19	10
"	"	6640	Do.				L.	17	9
"	"	6166	Mullavilly (1),					7	4
"	"	6220	Mount St. Catherine's Convent,				B.	13	10
"	"	4403	Tandrugee,				B.	11	8
"	"	6404	Do.				L.	9	6
"	"	8702	Milford,					19	10
"	"	11720	Tinnaamore,					16	8
"	"	12845	St. Patrick's,				B.	7	4
"	"	12865	Mullavilly,				W.	71	10
"	"	13112	St. Josseh's,				f.	6	4
"	"	13115	Do.					12	7
"	18	12073	Drumnahre,				B.	62	25
"	"	6236	Bambrook,				L.	30	15
"	"	6227	Do.					90	29
"	"	7303	Canal-street Convent,					44	10
"	"	11879	Ballybot,					75	29
"	"	13869	Magheraabely Convent,					70	23
"	"	13911	Do.						
Down,	8	10348	Largymore,					120	32
"	"	11729	Ballyjames,					9	3
"	"	11436	Ravernette,					19	4
"	"	13463	Blaris,					10	6
"	10	3574	Mill-street,					11	3
"	"	4657	Newtownards (2),					7	2
"	"	6603	St. Mathew's,				L.	5	1
"	"	6441	Newtownards (1),					320	88
"	"	11576	Bannbridge,					5	1
"	"	1863	Anna-street,				B.	9	3
"	"	9084	Do.				L.	3	3
"	"	10414	Lagan-village,					16	3
"	"	11542	Glenawall-street,					11	3
"	"	11896	Comber Spinning Mill,					48	15

List of One Hundred and Fifty-one National Schools attended by Half-time pupils in 1894, &c.—*continued.*

County.	Dist.	Roll Number.	School.		Total Number of Half-time pupils on Roll.	Average daily attendance of Half-time pupils.
Down,	10	12191	Castlegardens,		55	51
"	"	12590	Newtownards,		16	4
"	"	12531	Do.	z.	23	12
"	11	4811	Gilford Mill,	z.	40	19
"	"	4812	Do.	z.	34	17
"	"	11455	Seapatrick,		60	24
"	17	1244	Annahoe,	m.	24	10
"	"	1455	Do.	f.	19	5
"	"	2745	Shrigley,		57	23
"	"	4543	Lisnafirret (Killyleagh),		30	13
"	"	6024	Killyleagh,		27	10
"	"	10793	Drumnasoo Mills,		67	23
Tyrone,	6	7131	Drumnabrey,		7	2
"	"	11597	Sion Mills,	z.	51	91
"	"	11557	Do.		22	18
"	13	407	Gortalowry,		22	8
"	"	410	Dungannon,	z.	15	6
"	"	411	Do.		10	7
"	"	2251	Brackaville,		14	4
"	"	2253	Do.		4	4
"	"	8164	Ley Old,		4	1
"	"	8651	Ley,	m.	4	1
"	"	10179	Moshure,	z.	4	2
"	"	10179	Do.		4	2
"	"	11171	Annaghmore,		15	5
"	"	11939	Derrylomn,	m.	8	4
"	"	11917	Do.	f.	8	1
"	"	11767	John-street,	m.	4	3
"	"	11953	Do.		2	1
"	"	12440	Lower Market,		7	2
"	"	12256	Gortgonis,		4	3
"	"	13114	Cookstown Convent,			
Cork,	56	5500	Blarney,	m.	4	1
"	60	7028	Do.	z.		1
"	"	14103	Clareen-street Convent,		47	7
Waterford,	49	7228	Mayfield,	m.	3	1
"	"	7221	Portlaw Convent,		4	5
Louth,	13	851	Drogheda Convent,		23	21
Meath,	"	945	St. Mary's,	m.	6	10
Mayo,	29	14176	St. John's Convent,		8	4
			Total—151 Schools,		4,783	2,494

APPENDIX I.

AGRICULTURAL SCHOOLS ON 31ST DECEMBER, 1894.

I.—AGRICULTURAL SCHOOLS under the exclusive MANAGEMENT of BOARD.

No.	County.	Roll No.	School.	Post Town.	Area of Farm.	
1	Dublin,	—	Albert Training Institution,	Glasnevin,	A. R. P.	
2	Cork,	6735	Munster (Cork),	Cork,		
3	Fermanagh,	11071	Enniskillen School Garden	Enniskillen,		13

II.—AGRICULTURAL SCHOOLS under LOCAL MANAGEMENT.

No.	County.	Dist. No.	Roll No.	School.	Post Town.	Area of Farm.	Date on which last Literary Results Period ended.
						A. R. P.	
1	Armagh,	16	4371	Tanlakey,	Poyntzpass,	7 9 20	94. 4 .
2	Ditto,	16	4325	Drumbanagher,	Ditto,	4 9 20	31 . 3 . 94
3	Cavan,	12	4397	Maungh,	Blacklion,	16 0 0	30. 6 . 91
4	Donegal,	5	9659	Barnesmore,	Donegal,	3 1 0	22. 2. 94
5	Ditto,	1	4705	Doah vey,	Derrybeg,	15 0 0	34. 5. 94
6	Fermanagh,	13	3961	Carrick,	Lisbellaw, Enniskillen,	27 2 1	30 6 94
7	Londonderry,	2	6365	Park,	Park, Derry,	11 0 18	31 3. 94
8	Monaghan,	16	4321	Cormore,	Monaghan,	48 2 20	31 . 3 94
9	Ditto,	—	7230	Ballintroppy,	Scotstown,	12 3 19	32. 12. 33
10	Tyrone,	15	10173	Rockarb,	Rockarb, Moy,	4 3 1	31 . 5. 94
11	Ditto,	—	4788	Parkanaur,	Dungannon,	16 0 0	29. 9. 94
12	Ditto,	6	5488	Clare,	Coalisland,	20 3 20	29. 6. 94
13	Clare,	51	448	Parteen,	Limerick,	2 1 10	30. 4. 94
14	Ditto,	42	10336	Tubber,	Tubber, Gort,	16 3 85	29. 9. 94
15	Ditto,	43	6341	Scropul,	Mullough,Milltown-Malbay,	10 0 0	31. 3. 94
16	Cork,	59	5700	Glanbrue,	Leap,	77 0 0	31. 1. 94
17	Ditto,	—	10783	St. Edmund's,	Dunmanway,	5 0 20	31. 1. 94
18	Kerry,	67	7815	Dirreendarragh,	Kenmare,	8 2 0	31. 1. 94
19	Ditto,	66	6891	Lansdowne,	Ditto,	7 0 0	31. 1. 94
20	Ditto,	67	6301	Sneem,	Sneem,	7 0 0	31. 1. 94
21	Ditto,	—	8543	Ballinakelligs,	Cahersiveen,	11 0 0	31. 1. 94
22	Ditto,	56	11748	Glantanes,	Kenmare,	8 0 0	31. 0. 94
23	Limerick,	82	1467	Killacolla,	Bruree,	16 0 0	31. 1. 94
24	Carlow,	47	5803	Garryhill,	Bagnalstown,	11 2 20	31 . 3. 94
25	Kilkenny,	49	13420	Clanmore,	Piltown,	8 0 0	31 . 1. 94
26	Ditto,	53	6169	Piltown,	Ditto,	7 1 20	31. 1. 94
27	Ditto,	48	5241	Woodstock,	Inistioge,	8 0 0	31. 7. 94
28	Westmeath,	53	801	Ballivalley,	Delvin,	6 2 0	30. 4. 94

II.—Agricultural Schools under Local Management—*continued.*

No.	County.	Dist. No.	Roll No.	School.	Post Town.	Area of Farm.			Date on which last Literary Results Period ended.
						A.	R.	P.	
29	Galway,	57	18880	Ballyroe,	Williamstown, Castlerea,	8	1	0	31 . 1 . 94
30	Mayo,	30	15793	Carrageen,	Knockmore, Foxford,	10	3	33	31 . 8 . 94
31	Ditto,	30	11141	Kilmore,	Swinford,	7	1	7	23 . 2 . 94
32	Ditto,	31	14712	Derrinalla,	Bunninadden, Ballymote,	3	0	12	31 . 5 . 94
33	Ditto,	31	10848	Kinaffe,	Swinford,	5	0	0	31 . 10 . 94
34	Ditto,	52	5190	Lahard,	Hollymount, Mayo,	7	3	0	29 . 2 . 94
35	Ditto,	20	5236	Lissalisha,	Knockmore, Foxford,	5	0	0	31 . 3 . 94
36	Ditto,	90	6042	Carrowmore Palmer,	Rathkealan, Balllna,	3	1	0	30 . 4 . 94
37	Ditto,	20	11920	Callow,	Foxford,	1	2	16	31 . 8 . 94
38	Ditto,	21	12620	Newtownbrowne	Kiltimagh,	1	3	23	31 . 7 . 94
39	Roscommon,	28	10218	North Yard,	Strokestown,	3	1	0	31 . 5 . 94
40	Ditto,	57	12964	Ballymurray,	Ballymurray, Roscommon,	20	0	6	31 . 1 . 94
41	Sligo,	13	9665	Doonfin,	Skreen, Sligo,	8	0	0	31 . 3 . 94
42	Ditto,	20	4106	Kilvrahattin,	Templeboy, Ballisodare,	11	1	38	31 . 8 . 94
43	Ditto,	12	10473	Colry,	Barr, Sligo,	1	3	0	30 . 4 . 94
44	Ditto,	19	8138	Ballintrasna,	Dromard, Ballisodare,	9	3	25	29 . 2 . 94

III.—School Gardens under Local Management in connexion with Board.

No.	County.	Dist. No.	Roll No.	School.	Post Town.
1	Armagh,	16	9771	Lisdrumchor,	Markethill.
2	Cavan,	23	12564	Clonervid,	Loughduff.
3	Ditto,	—	11834	Ballybane, Upper,	Ballybane.
4	Donegal,	6	8280	Convoy,	Convoy, Raphoe.
5	Ditto,	9	9035	Dromlag,	Stralane.
6	Down,	11	83	Magheraharry,	Moira.
7	Londonderry,	3	12391	Ballagh,	Dungiven.
8	Ditto,	—	6531	Articlave,	Coleraine.
9	Monaghan,	22	10934	Rerne,	Drumvalley, Clones.
10	Ditto,	14	14574	Halltory,	Halltory.
11	Tyrone,	2	9865	Lurgbash,	Gortin.
12	Ditto,	14	4713	Aughadarragh,	Augher.
13	Cork,	66	1867	Cloddelymot,	Fermoy.
14	Ditto,	56	4567	Adrigole,	Bantry.
15	Ditto,	60a	13976	Clogheen,	Cathedral, Cork.
16	Kerry,	51	1389	Doon,	Kenmare.
17	Ditto,	57	4483	Masterygihy,	Waterville.
18	Limerick,	52	7723	Issagun,	Croom.
19	Tipperary,	63	5328	Mortyke,	Thurles.
20	Carlow,	47	11347	Kilgraney,	Bagenalstown.
21	Dublin,	30	6850	Portrane,	Donabate.
22	Kilkenny,	49	11692	Inistioge fn,	Thomastown.
23	King's,	61	8960	Ballycommon,	Tullamore.
24	Wicklow,	60	11383	Knockanarry,	Knockanarry.
25	Ditto,	—	1119	Castletown,	Enniskerry.
26	Galway,	—	9772	Loughcutra,	Loughcutra, Gort.
27	Ditto,	52	14700	Farm,	Ballymoe.
28	Ditto,	52	14660	Behan,	Ballyhaunis.
29	Sligo,	13	4837	Tubbercurriane,	Skreen.
30	Ditto,	20	3807	Ballymote,	Ballymote.

APPENDIX K.

TEACHERS' INCOMES FOR THE YEAR 1893.*
I. PRINCIPAL TEACHERS.

Table showing the average income of 6,942 Principal Teachers for the year 1893, distinguishing their classes and the sources from which their incomes were derived.

From this Return are excluded Teachers of Model Schools, Teachers of all Schools paid by capitation, Teachers who moved from school to school within the year, and Teachers who did not give service during the entire year.

AVERAGE INCOME OF PRINCIPAL TEACHERS.

Class of Teachers.	Number of Teachers included in Return.	Average Parliamentary Grant.	Average Local Aid.	Total (Average.)
		£ s. d.	£ s. d.	£ s. d.
Male—				
I.	404	128 3 5	13 5 3	141 8 5
II.	810	109 19 0½	5 15 1½	115 14 4
II.	1,924	80 1 4½	4 12 5	84 13 9
III.	1,179	73 7 4½	2 13 8¼	75 6 1½
Total.	4,117	—	—	—
Average of all Classes.	—	90 4 5	6 1 6½	97 4 11½
Female—				
I.	504	115 15 8	4 8 0½	120 7 8¼
II.	408	92 11 8½	4 1 6½	96 13 ¼
II.	1,533	71 8 4½	4 9 8½	75 18 1
III.	615	60 10 1½	3 4 4½	64 19 4½
Total.	2,560	—	—	—
Average of all Classes.	—	76 17 8½	9 17 6½	80 15 3

II. ASSISTANT TEACHERS.
The following Table shows the *average* income of 684 Male and 1,970 Female Assistant Teachers.

—	Male.	Female.
	£ s. d.	£ s. d.
Parliamentary Grant.	60 7 0½	49 10 1
Local Aid.	2 7 4½	7 2 5
Total (average).	62 14 6	50 12 6

* Arrears of Capitation (Residual portion of "School Grant" under the Act for 1892, payable within that year, but the payment of which was unavoidably deferred till 1893, are included.

APPENDIX L.

QUESTIONS proposed at Examinations of Teachers and Monitors,
July, 1894.

Appendix L.
Exami-
nation
Questions.
State
Teachers.
A' Papers.

I.—MALE TEACHERS.

METHODS, SCHOOL ACCOUNTS, COMMISSIONERS' RULES.—60 Marks.

Two hours allowed for this paper.

N.B.—*Only five questions to be attempted.*

Mr. DOWLING, Head Inspector.
Mr. M'GLADE, District Inspector.

1. Propose a series of questions suited to lead your pupils to grasp the meaning of the following passage, adding such explanation as would probably be necessary on the part of the teacher—

"The oak leviathans, whose huge ribs make
Their clay creator the vain title take
Of lord of thee, and arbiter of war;
These are thy toys, and, as the snowy flake,
They melt into thy yeast of waves which mar
Alike the Armada's pride, or spoils of Trafalgar."

12 marks.

2. Write notes of a lesson on *artificial manures*, or on *the balancing of accounts*.
12 marks.

3. Describe fully the proper position and construction of out-offices for mixed schools; and state the precautions necessary to prevent them from being a source of ill-health.
12 marks.

4. Break up the question—"How is rain caused?"—into a series of easier questions with a view to eliciting from your pupils the desired answer.
12 marks.

5. Give the substance of the rules that restrict teachers in the matters of (a) occupation out of school hours; (b) place of residence; and (c) attendance at meetings.
12 marks.

6. How may home tasks be made to supplement school instruction in Reading, Dictation, Grammar and Geography?
6 marks.

7. What hints on the mode of successfully committing to memory do you consider it desirable to give to your pupils?
6 marks.

8. What is the difference, as to class promotion, in case of extra branches that have only one examination, and of those having a series of examinations? State the exception to the general rule.
6 marks.

9. What exercises in Third or Fourth Class might be made subservient to the subsequent teaching of letter-writing or composition?
6 marks.

10. "A time-table is to a school what grammar is to a language." Explain this statement fully.
6 marks.

T

ARITHMETIC.—100 Marks.

Two hours and a half allowed for this paper.

N.D.—Only five questions to be attempted.

Mr. STRONGE, Head Inspector.
Mr. DEWAR, District Inspector.

1. Show that if, in any number with an even number of digits, say eight, the last digit be taken away and placed in front, the sum of the number thus formed and the original number will be divisible by 11.
20 marks.

2. A person buys five shares in a company at 40; next year the price is 45, and every succeeding year there is a fall of 4; each year he sells out one share, and finds at the end that he has neither gained nor lost. What interest did the company pay?
20 marks.

3. One vessel contains 19 gallons of water, another contains 11 gallons of wine; one gallon is taken from each and is then poured into the other; this is done three times. How much wine and how much water will the vessels then respectively contain?
20 marks.

4. An up train, 88 yards long, travelling at the rate of 35 miles an hour, meets a down train, 110 yards long, at 2 o'clock, and passes it in 6 seconds; at 13½ minutes past 2 o'clock the up train meets a second down train, 154 yards long, and passes it also in 6 seconds. At what time will the second down train overtake the first?
20 marks.

5. Explain fully (a) why the fraction $\frac{3}{7}$ must produce a pure circulating decimal; and (b) why the fraction $\frac{13}{8}$ must produce a mixed circulating decimal.
20 marks.

6. A person buys an article, and sells it so as to gain 6 per cent. If he had bought it at 8 per cent. less, and sold it for one shilling less, he would have gained 15 per cent. Find the cost price.
10 marks.

7. A and B run a mile, and A wins by 80 yards. A and C run over the same course, and A wins by 30 seconds. B and C run, and D wins by 5 seconds. In what time can A run a mile?
10 marks.

8. If the difference between the interest and the true discount on a sum of money for 4 months, at 2¾ per cent., is £4½, what is the sum?
10 marks.

9. Find the greatest number which will divide 5,053; 23,947; 28,367; and 925,933; and leave remainders 13, 7, 17 and 1 respectively.
10 marks.

10. A parasang, which is the road measure of Persia, is equal to 3⅔ kilometres; a kilometre equals 39,370 inches. Calculate the number of parasangs contained in a degree, the length of which is 365,000 feet.
10 marks.

GRAMMAR AND DERIVATIONS.—60 Marks.

Two hours allowed for this paper.

Appendix L.
Exami-
nation
Questions.
Male
Teachers.
5ᵗʰ Paper

N.B.—*Only five of these questions, of which the starring exercise must be one, are to be attempted.*

Mr. PURSER, Head Inspector.
Mr. DICKIE, District Inspector.

1.   *Welcome,* dear Rosencrantz and Guildenstern !
Moreover *that* we much did long to see you,
The need we have to use you did provoke
Our hasty sending. *Something* have you heard
Of Hamlet's transformation ; so call it,
Sith nor the exterior nor the inward man
Resembles *that* it was. *What* it should be
More than his father's *death,* that thus hath put him
So much from the understanding of himself,
I cannot dream of : I entreat you *both,*
That, *being of* so young days brought up with him,
And *sith* so *neighboured* to his youth and haviour,
That you *vouchsafe* your rest here in our court
Some little *time.*

Paraphrase the above passage, and parse the words in *italics.*

20 marks.

2. Give a general and a particular analysis of the following passage :—

Slanders, sir, for the satirical rogue says here that old men have grey beards, that their faces are wrinkled, and that they have a plentiful lack of wit, together with most weak hams, all which, sir, though I most potently believe, yet I hold it not honesty to have thus set down.

12 marks.

3. Write notes on the italicised words in the following :—

(a.) O me, what hast thou done !
(b.) No, *faith,* not a jot.
(c.) This *likes* me well : these foils have all a length.
(d.) If *that* his Majesty *would ought* with us.   10 marks.

4. What classes of words have come to us *from* Latin ; through what medium have they come to us, and for the most part since what date ?
10 marks.

5. Name the three kinds of contracted sentences, and give examples.
8 marks.

6. Give the derivation of *witch, lady, bridegroom.*   6 marks.

7. Explain the metrical structure of the sonnet. How does Shakespere's sonnet differ from the general form ?   5 marks.

8.   Where nothing save the waves and I
May hear our mutual murmurs sweep.

Discuss the anomalous construction which these lines contain.
8 marks.

9. An adjective and its cognate adverb if joined to the same verb convey different shades of meaning. Explain.   5 marks.

10. Discuss the grammatical propriety of each of the following sentences :—

(a.) You or I am right.
(b.) He or I is right.
(c.) It is I who is right.   5 marks.

T 2

Appendix L.

Exami-
nation
Questions.

- *Male
Teachers.*

A' Papers.

PENMANSHIP. — 10 Marks.

Half an hour allowed for this exercise.

Your penmanship will be judged from the neatness and accuracy with which you copy the following passage :—

Forlorn ! the very word is like a bell
To toll me back from thee to my sole self !
Adieu ! the fancy cannot cheat so well
As she is famed to do, deceiving elf.
Adieu ! adieu ! thy plaintive anthem fades
Past the near meadows, over the still stream,
Up the hill-side ; and now 'tis buried deep
In the next valley glades :
Was it a vision, or a waking dream ?
Fled is that music : do I wake or sleep ?

When Paradise Lost first appeared, though it was not neglected, it attracted no crowd of imitators, and made no visible change in the poetical practice of the age. Milton stood alone and aloof above his times ; the bard of immortal subjects, and, as far as there is perpetuity in language, of immortal fame. The very choice of those subjects bespoke a contempt for any species of excellence that was attainable by other men.

GEOMETRY AND MENSURATION.—100 Marks.

Two hours and a half allowed for this paper.

N.B.—*Only five questions to be attempted.*

Only geometrical solutions will be accepted, and only the propositions of Euclid may be assumed.

Mr. SULLIVAN, Head Inspector.
Mr. KELLY, District Inspector.

1. If two figures be homothetic, the lines joining corresponding angular points are concurrent.   20 marks.

2. If a circle be described touching a semicircle and its diameter, the diameter of the circle is a harmonic mean between the segments into which the diameter of the semicircle is divided at the point of contact.   20 marks.

3. The distances between the vertices of a triangle and its orthocentre are respectively the doubles of the perpendiculars from the circumcentre on the sides.   20 marks.

4. If the sum of two arcs A C, CB of a circle be less than a semicircle, the rectangle AC·CB contained by their chords is equal to the rectangle contained by the radius and the excess of the chord of the supplement of their difference above the chord of the supplement of their sum.   20 marks.

5. Two opposite sides of a quadrilateral field are parallel, but not equal, the remaining sides are equal. The parallel sides are 420 links and 640 links respectively, each of the other sides is 580 links. It is required to cut off half an acre by a line parallel to the side which is 420 links. Find the distance of such parallel from the side which is 420 links.   20 marks.

6. If from the point of contact of a tangent to a circle a chord be drawn cutting the circle, the angles made by these lines are respectively equal to the angles in the alternate segments of the circle. Prove this by the method of limits.   10 marks.

7. To inscribe in a given triangle the maximum parallelogram having a common angle with the triangle.   10 marks.

8. If lines drawn from any point in the plane of a figure to all its angular points be divided in the same ratio, the lines joining the points of division will form a new figure similar to the original figure.
                                                                  10 marks.

9. Two triangles, which have one angle in one equal to one angle in the other, and the sides about these angles reciprocally proportional, are equal in area. Prove.   10 marks.

10. A corner of a cube is cut off by a plane which meets the edges at distances of 6, 8, and 10 inches, respectively, from their common point. Find the volume of the piece cut off. Explain your work. 10 marks.

ENGLISH COMPOSITION.—50 Marks.

Two hours allowed for this subject.

N.B.—*Only one subject to be selected.*

Mr. PURSER, Head Inspector.
Mr. DALTON, District Inspector.

1. School rewards and punishments.
2. Scott as a lyrical poet.

ALGEBRA.—100 Marks.

Two hours and a half allowed for this paper.

N.B.—*Only five questions to be attempted.*

Mr. STRONGE, Head Inspector.
Mr. PEDLOW, District Inspector.

1. A ship has two pumps, one of which could pump out the hold in a hours less than the other. She springs a leak, through which the water flows at a constant rate, such that, with the first pump only at work, the hold would fill in b hours, with the second only at work in c hours. Find the time occupied in filling the hold, neither pump working, and prove that if $a = b - c$, the ship cannot sink   20 marks.

2. Solve—
$$x^{\frac{pq}{p+q}} = \left\{\left(\frac{a^3-b^3}{a^3+b^3}\right)\left(a^{\frac{1}{p}}+a^{\frac{1}{q}}\right)\right.$$
                                                                  20 marks.

3. Prove that—
$$\frac{(x^2-y^2)^2 + (y^2-z^2)^2 + (z^2-x^2)^2}{(x-y)^2 + (y-z)^2 + (z-x)^2} = (x+y)(y+z)(z+x).$$
                                                                  20 marks.

Appendix L.

Exami-
nation
Questions.

Male
Teachers.

A' Papers.

4. Find the values of x and y which satisfy

$$\sqrt{x} - \sqrt{y} = \sqrt{x}(\sqrt{x} + \sqrt{y})$$

$$(x+y)^2 = 2(x-y)^3. \qquad \text{20 marks.}$$

5. Between what limits must $\dfrac{a^2 - 2a + 4}{a^2 + 2a + 4}$ lie for all real values of a?

20 marks.

6. If

$$ax + by + c = 0,$$
$$bx + cy + a = 0,$$
$$cx + ay + b = 0 \ ; \ \text{show that}$$
$$a^3 + b^3 + c^3 - 3abc = 0 \qquad \text{10 marks.}$$

7. Solve the equations—

$$x + y = 10$$

$$\sqrt{\frac{x}{y}} + \sqrt{\frac{y}{x}} = \frac{5}{2} \qquad \text{10 marks.}$$

8. If the arithmetic mean between two quantities x and y be twice the geometric mean, prove that

$$\frac{x}{y} = \frac{2 + \sqrt{3}}{2 - \sqrt{3}} \qquad \text{10 marks.}$$

9. Simplify

$$\frac{1 + \sqrt{-1}}{1 - \sqrt{-1}} \times \frac{5 - \sqrt{-3}}{1 + \sqrt{-3}} \qquad \text{10 marks.}$$

10. Resolve into factors—

(1) $a^2b - bx^2 + a^2x - x^3$.

(2) $a^2 - b^2 - c^2 + d^2 - 2(ad - bc)$.

10 marks.

HISTORY.—40 Marks.

One hour and a half allowed for this paper.

N.B.—Only five questions to be attempted.

Mr. Downing, Head Inspector.
Mr. Rogers, District Inspector.

1. Give the dates at which a number of petty states were united to form the monarchies of—(a.) England; (b.) Norway, and (c.) Russia. Give the name of the first monarch in each case.　8 marks.

2. When and by whom was the "Union of Calmar" effected; and when and by whom was it broken?　8 marks.

3. Relate four incidents in the life of Charles XII. of Sweden; and mention the occasion and date of his death.　8 marks.

4. Name, in order, the sovereigns of England during the 17th century, and mention some important event in each of their reigns.　8 marks.

5. What was the character of the reign of Catherine II. of Russia; against what people did she wage war, and by whom was she succeeded?　8 marks.

6. In what reign, and by what Bill was the right of an English subject to petition his sovereign declared?　4 marks.

7. Who were the two most famous Grecian orators that opposed the encroachments of Philip of Macedon on the liberties of Hellas? How are their respective styles of oratory contrasted?   4 marks.

8. In what year did the Turks gain a footing in Italy, and in what part of the country?   4 marks.

9. Name any five of the important sources or authorities from which modern writers derive their knowledge of Irish History.   4 marks.

10. Enumerate the chief events in the history of the Israelites during the last thirty-eight years of their sojourn in the Wilderness, and mention the change that during this period was effected in their national character.   4 marks.

Appendix L.

Examination
Questions.

Male
Teachers.

A¹ Papers.

GEOGRAPHY.—60 Marks.

Two hours allowed for this paper.

N.B.—*Only five questions, of which the first question must be one, are to be attempted.*

Mr. CONNELLAN, Head Inspector.
Mr. ALEXANDER, District Inspector.

1. Draw a sketch map, as large as your paper will allow, of the five great lakes, and the course of the St. Lawrence, marking the boundaries of the provinces of Canada, and of the States of the Union which lie adjacent, and the towns on the margin of the lakes and river.   12 marks.

2. Give a full description of the Pyrenees under the following heads:— (1) length, (2) summits, (3) branch chains. What rivers drain the northern and southern slopes, respectively?   12 marks.

3. On what geographical fact do the second and third laws of climate depend? Explain your answer, and give illustrations in proof.   12 marks.

4. Write as full a description of Tasmania as you can under the following heads:—Area and population, government, climate, mountains and rivers, principal towns, exports.   12 marks.

5. Write what you know of (a.) "Hanse Towns," (b.) "All the Russias," (c.) "The terraced roof of the World."   12 marks.

6. Enumerate the leading physical features of (a.) Northern, (b.) Middle, and (c.) Southern Germany.   6 marks.

7. Describe the course of the river Rhine from its source to its outflow, naming the countries through which it flows, the towns on its banks, the tributaries which join it, and its branches in Holland.   6 marks.

8. Name the French possessions in and connected with Africa and give their chief towns.   6 marks.

9. Explain why there is no marked system of currents in the northern parts of the Indian Ocean.   6 marks.

10. What and where are—Weimar, Rohilkand, Tiflis, Schreckhorn, Mondego, Yarra-Yarra.   6 marks.

PLANE TRIGONOMETRY.—50 Marks.

Two hours and a half allowed for this paper.

N.B.—*Only five questions to be attempted.*

Mr. SULLIVAN, Head Inspector.
Mr. M'CLINTOCK, District Inspector.

1. Given $A = 60°$, $a = 41$, $b = 45$. Calculate angle B. Is the case "ambiguous"? Explain.

Log sin 60° = 9·93753,
Log 410 = 2·61278,
Log 4500 = 3·65331,
Log cos 15° 0' = 9·97796.   10 marks.

2. In the ambiguous case of triangles, prove that if c and c' be the two values found for the third side of the triangle—

$$c^2 - 2cc' \cos 2A + c'^2 = 4a^2 \cos^2 A.$$

10 marks.

3. A B C is a plane triangle. Prove the following relation—

$$\frac{\cos A}{\sin B \sin C} + \frac{\cos B}{\sin A \sin C} + \frac{\cos C}{\sin A \sin B} = 2$$

10 marks.

4. Trace the changes in the sign and the magnitude of $\sec A - \cos A$ as A changes from 0° to 180°.   10 marks.

5. Prove that the sum of the diameters of the inscribed and circumscribed circles of any plane triangle is equal to—

$$a \cot A + b \cot B + c \cot C.$$

10 marks.

6. If $\tan^2 A = 1 + 2 \tan^2 B$, prove that $\cos^2 B = 1 + \cos 2A$.

5 marks.

7. In any plane triangle ABC prove that—

$$a^2 \sin 2B + b^2 \sin 2A = 2ab \sin C.$$

5 marks.

8. Prove that the length of the line bisecting the angle A of a triangle and meeting the opposite side is—

$$\frac{2bc \cos \dfrac{A}{2}}{b + c}.$$

5 marks.

9. Prove that

$$\cos A - \cos 3A = (\sin 3A - \sin A) \tan 2A.$$

5 marks.

10. In a triangle prove that $2bc \cos A = b^2 + c^2 - a^2$; and hence show how the area of a triangle is found in terms of its sides.   5 marks.

MECHANICS.—50 Marks.

One hour and a half allowed for this paper.

N.B.—*Only five questions to be attempted.*

Mr. SULLIVAN, Head Inspector.
Mr. HOSS, District Inspector.

1. A uniform beam A B, of weight W, free to turn in a vertical plane round a hinge at A, is held, making an angle of 60° with the horizon, by a string BC, in same vertical plane and attached to a point C, in same horizontal plane as A, so that CA = AB; find the tension of the string and show in a diagram the direction of the reaction at A.   10 marks.

2. A body placed on a rough inclined plane whose inclination is α Appendix L Exami-nation Questions. — Male Teachers. A' Papers. is just on the point of sliding down the plane; find the least force sufficient to draw the body up the plane.   10 marks.

3. The circumference of a screw is c, the circumference of the circle described by the power (P) is C; h is the distance between the threads, m the co-efficient of friction, and w the resistance; show that

$$\frac{P}{w} = \frac{c}{C} \cdot \frac{h + mc}{c - mh}.$$ 10 marks.

4. A cube and a wedge are of equal height, the base of the wedge being a square equal in area to a face of the cube. They stand on a horizontal table sufficiently rough to prevent slipping when the table is tilted, and the sides of the faces on which they rest are parallel to the edges of the table. Find the angles of elevation of the table when these bodies, respectively, topple. Give diagrams in elucidation of your answer.   10 marks.

5. Find the line of quickest descent to a given line AB, which is not horizontal, from a given point P above the line.   10 marks.

6. "The co-efficient of friction is equal to the tangent of the angle of friction." Prove.   5 marks.

7. A beam AB, whose weight is W, has one end B, supported by a string, while the other end A rests on a smooth horizontal table. Show that in the position of rest the string must be vertical, and find its tension.   5 marks.

8. A line is drawn parallel to a diagonal of a square, and cutting off one-fourth of the square; find the distance of the centre of gravity of the remainder of the square from the centre of gravity of the whole square.   5 marks.

9. State and explain Newton's third law of motion, taking as your illustration the case of a horse drawing a body forwards by means of a rope.   5 marks.

10. Forces of 2lbs. and 3lbs., respectively, act along the sides of an equilateral triangle on a body placed at the vertex. Find the magnitude and the direction of the resultant.   5 marks.

HYDROSTATICS AND HYDRAULICS.—50 Marks.

One hour and a half allowed for this paper.

N.B.—*Only five questions to be attempted.*

Mr. CONNELLAN, Head Inspector.
Mr. ROSS, District Inspector.

1. A child's balloon with an inelastic cover is filled to one-third its capacity with air at atmospheric pressure, and is then placed under the receiver of an air-pump. If the receiver has four times the capacity of the barrel show that during the 5th stroke the balloon will be fully distended.   10 marks.

2. A vessel in the shape of a pyramid, 5 feet high and with a base 4 feet square, is filled with water. Find the pressure on the base. Compare this pressure with the weight of the water, and explain the difference between them.   10 marks.

3. Find the barometric pressure inside the receiver of an air-pump after 15 strokes, the cylinder of the air-pump being $\frac{1}{4}$ of the volume of the receiver and tube, and the original barometric pressure being 20·5 inches. Explain your work.   10 marks.

Apparatus L.
Exami-
nation
Questions.

Male
Teachers.

A' Pupils.

4. The length of the suction tube in a common pump is 33 feet and the entire stroke of the piston is 6 feet. The piston starts from the bottom of the barrel and at the end of the first stroke the water has risen 12 feet in the tube. Compare the sectional area of the barrel with that of the tube, the water barometer being 34 feet.   10 marks.

5. Give the laws which govern the ascent and depression of liquids in capillary tubes.   10 marks.

6. How is it that a light rod of very small diameter takes the horizontal and not the vertical position when floating in water?
    5 marks.

7. How are the specific gravities of liquids found by means of the hydrostatic balance?   5 marks.

8. Describe any experiment which will exhibit the upward pressure of liquids.   5 marks.

9. A solid cube of metal, the edge of which is 3 inches and whose specific gravity is 7, is wholly immersed in water, and is supported by a string attached to it. Find its apparent weight in water.   5 marks.

10. A body of uniform density weighing 12 lbs. floats in a liquid with one-third of its volume above the surface. Find the force sufficient to keep this body just wholly submerged.   5 marks.

———

HEAT AND THE STEAM ENGINE.—50 Marks.

One hour and a half allowed for this paper.

N.B.—Only five questions to be attempted.

Mr. CONNELLAN, Head Inspector.
Mr. ROSS, District Inspector.

1. A lead bullet falls from such a height that on striking the ground its temperature is raised 4 degrees. Assuming that all the heat is expended in raising the temperature of the bullet, taking the specific heat of lead as 0·0314, and Joule's equivalent in metres as 424; find (a.) the height from which the bullet falls; (b.) the velocity acquired.
    10 marks.

2. Give Dulong and Petit's method of determining the absolute expansion of mercury. Show that the expansion of the envelope is eliminated in this method.   10 marks.

3. State the laws of vapour formation. What is a saturated vapour? Into a vacuum in a barometer tube minute successive quantities of ether are introduced; describe and account for what happens.   10 marks.

4. A tall cylindrical glass vessel full of water at 15° C, and having a thermometer inserted in the water near the top and one near the bottom, has round its middle part a collar of melting ice. State and account for the indications of the thermometer as the temperature falls.
    10 marks.

5. What is the distinction between an *expanding* and a *non-expanding* engine? To which should a high pressure engine belong, and why?
    10 marks.

6. At what temperature is the number on the Fahrenheit and Réaumur thermometers the same? Prove.   5 marks.

7. On what circumstances does the amount of heat given out by a body in a very short time depend? Construct a formula from which the quantity emitted may be determined.   5 marks.

8. Explain how the waste of power in the ordinary application of the
"governor" is remedied in the Corliss engine.   5 marks.

9. What is meant by "specific heat"? State how you would determine the specific heat of oil.   5 marks.

10. Explain the following formula:—
"Water at 0°=ice at 0°+latent heat of liquefaction."   5 marks.

*domestic.
Examination
Questions.
Male
Teachers.
A' Papers.*

LIGHT AND SOUND.—50 Marks.

One hour and a half allowed for this paper.

N.B.—*Only five questions to be attempted.*

Mr. Conellan, Head Inspector.
Mr. Heenan, District Inspector.

1. A candle at a distance of 120 centimetres from a lens forms an
image on the other side of the lens at a distance of 200 feet. Required
the nature of the lens and its focal distance. Explain your work by
means of a diagram.   10 marks.

2. What is meant by (a) the refracting angle of a Prism, and (b)
the minimum deviation?
Deduce a formula by means of which the index of refraction may be
determined when the refracting angle and the minimum deviation
are given.   10 marks.

3. Describe the mode in which air vibrates in an open organ pipe
sounding its fundamental note.   10 marks.

4. Give Newton's formula for calculating the velocity of sound in
gases. Explain why the velocity is not affected by pressure.
10 marks.

5. Show how the magnitude of an image may be calculated when
the distance of the object, its magnitude, and the radius of the mirror
are given.   10 marks.

6. Prove that short sighted persons have an advantage over long
sighted persons in the use of telescopes.   5 marks.

7. A thick plate of glass is interposed obliquely between a candle and
the eye of an observer. Will the candle be seen in its true position?
Explain fully, and illustrate your answer by a diagram.   5 marks.

8. Explain the terms—*Myopy, aplanatic, achiosial, optical centre.*
5 marks.

9. What is meant by the Chromatic scale? On what principle is it
constructed? What are its advantages and disadvantages? 5 marks.

10. What purposes are served by the wooden body of a violin in the
production of musical sounds?   5 marks.

MAGNETISM AND ELECTRICITY.—50 Marks.

One hour and a half allowed for this paper.

N.B.—*Only five questions to be attempted.*

Mr. Sullivan, Head Inspector.
Mr. Keenan, District Inspector.

1. Describe the method of duplex telegraphy which is based on the
principle of *Wheatstone's Bridge.*   10 marks.

2. State Lenz's Law relative to induction.   10 marks.

3. Describe the *Jablochkoff Candle*. Explain why alternating currents are used in its production.　　10 marks.

4. What are the special defects and advantages of Leclanché's battery? Of what does an element consist? Compare the electromotive force of an element of Leclanché's with that of a Daniell's.　　10 marks.

5. Explain the principle of Abel's machine for applying the electric discharge to the firing of mines.　　10 marks.

6. If a platinum and a gold plate are immersed in pure nitric acid, no current is produced; but on adding a small quantity of hydrochloric acid a current is excited. Account for these facts.　　5 marks.

7. Show how a bar of soft iron may be magnetised by the action of the earth. Can a steel bar be magnetised in the same way? Explain.　　5 marks.

8. Given a wire of which l, c, s represent respectively, length, specific conducting power, and cross section; find the length of another wire which would offer the same resistance to an electric current, and whose specific conducting power is c', and cross section s'.　　5 marks.

9. "The magnetic action of the earth on a magnetised needle may be compared to a *couple*." Show that this is the case.　　5 marks.

10. A person standing on an insulating stool touches a prime conductor. Describe the effects which follow, and account for them.　　5 marks.

INORGANIC CHEMISTRY.—50 Marks.

One hour and a half allowed.

N.B.—*Only five questions to be attempted.*

Mr. DOWNING, Head Inspector.
Mr. CHAMBERS, District Inspector.

1. Give the symbol for ammonia sulphate; state how it is prepared on a large scale; and mention two uses for which it is employed.　　10 marks.

2. How are the metals which are not precipitated by any general re-agent separately detected?　　10 marks.

3. Describe the process of *cupellation*.　　10 marks.

4. Describe the ammonia-soda process of manufacturing Na_2CO_3, and mention the one disadvantage of this process as compared with the older method of Leblanc.　　10 marks.

5. How may pure iron in the form of a powder be obtained? When obtained how must it be preserved; and why?　　10 marks.

6. Give the chemical description of a *glass*.　　5 marks.

7. Note the scientific names, and the symbols for :—Calamine, iron pyrites, lunar caustic, cinnabar, and sal-ammoniac.　　5 marks.

8. How may you detect the presence of lead in water?　　5 marks.

9. Describe fully the mode of preparing and collecting nitrous oxide.　　5 marks.

10. By what test may you ascertain whether a certain liquid is a solution of potassium iodide?　　5 marks.

ORGANIC CHEMISTRY.—50 Marks.

One hour and a half allowed for this paper.

N.B.—Only five questions to be attempted.

Mr. Downing, Head Inspector.
Mr. Skeffington, District Inspector.

1. How is alizarin artificially obtained; and why does the discovery of its mode of preparation mark an era in the history of applied chemistry?
10 marks.

2. Give a diagram of the apparatus required, and describe the manipulation for the production of chloroform from chloride of lime and spirits of wine.
10 marks.

3. Give the general formula for hydrocarbons of the paraffin group; and describe one method of obtaining a paraffin, giving the explanatory equation.
10 marks.

4. How is each of the following effected; and what is the product in each case?—

    (*a*) acetous fermentation;
    (*b*) lactic fermentation.
10 marks.

5. Give the empirical, and the constitutional formula for acetic acid, and explain the significance of the latter.
10 marks.

6. Describe how lead oleate is prepared, and mention any use made of it.
5 marks.

7. Point out what causes the difference in various kinds of soap; namely, hard, soft, transparent, marine.
5 marks.

8. If strong sulphuric acid be mixed with strong formic acid, what decomposition of the latter will take place on the application of gentle heat? Illustrate your answer with an equation.
5 marks.

9. What change takes place in cane sugar in the presence of yeast?
5 marks.

10. How may you prepare a solution of albumen? What change takes place in this solution on the application of heat? What elements are always found in albumen?
5 marks.

AGRICULTURAL CHEMISTRY.—50 Marks.

An hour and a half allowed for this paper.

N.B.—Only five questions to be attempted.

Mr. Downing, Head Inspector.
Mr. Skeffington, District Inspector.

1. What constituent of flour supplies the animal with material for the fibre of the muscles; and what constituent of flour supplies material for the animal heat?
10 marks.

2. Name all the substances to be found in cow's milk, and give approximately the proportion of each of these substances to be obtained from 10 gallons of that liquid.
10 marks.

3. Describe the use of starch as food, and mention three other substances that serve the same purpose as starch.
10 marks.

4. Compare the chemical composition of linseed or rape-seed with that of peas or beans.
10 marks.

5. Describe fully how chlorine may be prepared and collected, and how its various peculiar qualities may be illustrated experimentally. Give a diagram of the apparatus needed.
10 marks.

Appendix L.

Examination Questions.

Male Teachers.

A' Papers.

6. Point out the uses of the gluten, fat, and saline matters in the food of animals.   5 marks.

7. Compare dried figs, dried dates, and apples as articles of food with wheaten bread and potatoes.   5 marks.

8. What substances are found in the ash or incombustible part of grain, and which are the most important of these substances?   5 marks.

9. Of what is soot found to consist, and to which of its ingredients does it principally owe its value as a manure?   5 marks.

10. Contrast the properties of Hydrogen, Oxygen, and Nitrogen.   5 marks.

ENGLISH LITERATURE.—60 Marks.

One hour and a half allowed for this paper.

N.B.—*Only five questions to be attempted.*

Mr. NEWELL, Head Inspector.
Dr. MORAN, District Inspector.

1. Hamlet has been accused of *irresolution*; discuss the justice of this, quoting passages from the Play.   12 marks.

2. *Captain.*—"We go to gain a little patch of ground
   That hath in it no profit but the name."

How does Hamlet in a subsequent soliloquy spur himself on to avenge his father's death by reflections on this example "gross as earth"?   12 marks.

3. In what terms does Hamlet reply to his mother in Act I., when she requests him to "cast his nighted colour off," and not "for ever seek his noble father in the dust"?   12 marks.

4. Write explanatory notes on :—

   (a) "For they are brokers—
       Not of that which their investments show,
       But mere implorators of unholy suits."
   (b) "So tell him with the occurrents more and less,
       Which have solicited—the rest is silence."
   (c) "This is the imposthume of much wealth and peace."   12 marks.

5. "Bass Harold, bard of brave St. Clara."
   Describe the poetical education that this bard had enjoyed.   12 marks.

6. How does the first clown (or grave-digger) endeavour to prove that Ophelia "drowned herself willingly"?   6 marks.

7. Describe the foreign mercenaries who had joined the English for the attack on Branksome Castle.   6 marks.

8. "The harp's wild notes, though hush'd the song,
   The mimic march of death prolong"—

Quote the succeeding lines in which the poet describes the music of the dirge.   6 marks.

9. Explain the following :—

   (a) "And recks not his own rede."
   (b) "An anchor's cheer in prison be my scope."
   (c) "The mouse-trap. Marry, how? Tropically."   6 marks.

10. What flowers does Ophelia mention in her madness, and what does she say of each?   6 marks.

SPHERICAL TRIGONOMETRY.—50 Marks.

Two hours and a half allowed for this paper.

N.B.—Only five questions to be attempted.

Mr. Sullivan, Head Inspector.

Mr. M'Clintock, District Inspector.

1. If secondaries be drawn from the extremities and the middle point of the base of an isosceles spherical triangle, to any arc of a great circle, through the vertex, the tangents of the intercepts between the perpendiculars and the vertex, will be in arithmetical progression. Prove.
10 marks.

2. Show that—

$$\tan^2 \tfrac{1}{2} s = \tan \tfrac{1}{2} s \, . \, \tan \tfrac{1}{2} (s-a) \tan \tfrac{1}{2} (s-b) \tan \tfrac{1}{2} (s-c).$$
10 marks.

3. In a right-angled spherical triangle, C being the right angle, prove that

$$\sin a \tan \tfrac{1}{2} A - \sin b \tan \tfrac{1}{2} B = \sin (a - b).$$
10 marks.

4. If in latitude $l°$ north, the sun's declination is $d°$ north, find an expression for the sun's amplitude.   10 marks.

5. In a spherical triangle prove

$$\sin^2 \tfrac{1}{2} c = \sin^2 \tfrac{1}{2} (a-b) \cos^2 \tfrac{1}{2} C + \sin^2 \tfrac{1}{2} (a+b) \sin^2 \tfrac{1}{2} C.$$
10 marks.

6. In a spherical triangle, given the sum of the sides equal to two right angles, prove

$$\cot a \cot b = \sin^2 \tfrac{1}{2} C.$$
5 marks.

7. ABC is a right-angled spherical triangle, C being the right angle. Prove that

$$\cos A = \cos a \sin B \text{ and}$$
$$\cos c = \cot A \cot B.$$
5 marks.

8. Assuming

$$\cos C = \frac{\cos c - \cos a \cos b}{\sin a \sin b} \cdot \cdot \cdot$$

find, by means of the Polar triangle, the corresponding expression for $\cos c$.   5 marks.

9. Prove

$$\cos \tfrac{1}{2} A = \sqrt{\left\{ \frac{\sin s \sin (s-a)}{\sin b \sin c} \right\}}$$

The ordinary expression for $\cos A$ may be assumed.   5 marks.

10. Given a, b and C of the spherical triangle ABC, show how A, B and c may be found.   5 marks.

REASONING.—50 Marks.

One hour and a half allowed for this paper.

N.B.—Only five questions to be attempted.

Mr. Downing, Head Inspector.

Mr. M'Alister, District Inspector.

1. Refer to its proper mood and figure the following syllogism, giving your reasons:—

"The natives of Ugogo are not cannibals. Mabruki is a cannibal, therefore Mabruki is not a native of Ugogo."

Give your opinion as to the validity of this syllogism.   10 marks.

2. How may E be converted; and why? Give an example, not in more arbitrary symbols.   10 marks.

3. Supply the missing premiss in the following enthymems, (a) so as to make the argument valid; and (b) so as to make it invalid; and in the latter case, describe the nature of the fallacy:—" Anarchists should not be allowed to address the public, because by so doing, they embarrass the Government."   10 marks.

4. What forms do the fallacies of "illicit process" and "undistributed middle" assume in conditional syllogisms?   10 marks.

5. Take Hume's apparent argument against miracles; and give a parallel case, leading to an obviously false conclusion. In what consists the fallacy in this case?   10 marks.

6. Why is the minor premiss of a dilemma frequently stated first?   5 marks.

7. Discuss the use of the fourth figure, and show by an example how it may be reduced to the first.   5 marks.

8. Explain what is meant by "contingent matter"; and give an example.   5 marks.

9. If the major term of a syllogism be the predicate of the major premise, what do we know about the minor premise?   5 marks.

10. What is a sorites? Explain why the first proposition only of a sorites may be particular, and only the last may be negative.   5 marks.

METHODS, SCHOOL ACCOUNTS, COMMISSIONERS' RULES.—60 Marks.

Two hours allowed for this paper.

N.B.—*Only five questions to be attempted*

Mr. Downing, Head Inspector.
Dr. Bateman, District Inspector.

1. On the following passage, propose a series of questions suitable to test and develop the intelligence of your pupils, adding such explanation as would probably be necessary on the part of the teacher —

"All those arts which are the natural defence of the weak are more familiar to this subtle race than to the Ionian of the time of Juvenal, or the Jew of the dark ages. What the horns are to the buffalo, what the paw is to the tiger, what the sting is to the bee, deceit is to the Bengalee. Large promises, smooth excuses, elaborate tissues of circumstantial falsehood, chicanery, perjury, forgery, are the weapons, offensive and defensive, of the people of the Lower Ganges."   12 marks.

2. Name the extra branches that may be taught in ordinary National Schools within the ordinary school-hours; and state fully the conditions on which Results Fees are allowed for them.   12 marks.

3. Taking the 12th proposition of the First Book of Euclid for purpose of illustration, point out in order the several steps of the solution as you would require them to be distinguished by a pupil.   12 marks.

4. Suppose a school to have an average attendance of 27 in Cl. Inf.; 16 in Cl. I.; 12 in Cl. II.; 10 in Cl. III.; 6 in Cl. IV.; 4 in Cl. V¹.; 3 in Cl. V².; 3 in Cl. VI. and 3 in Cl. VI¹., with a staff consisting of the Principal, one Assistant, and two Paid Monitors. Describe fully how you would carry out the following time-table arrangements—

1 to 1.30 o'clock.—Jun. Div., Reading; Mid. Div., Dictation; Sen. Div., Geography.   12 marks.

5. Discuss the question of the extent to which a teacher should aim at making school work pleasant for the pupils. 12 marks.

6. Why may it be improper and even unjust to punish a pupil for an error in his work or answer? 6 marks.

7. Describe in detail the amount of home work which it is proper to assign daily to a Sixth Class pupil. 6 marks.

8. During the time, suppose half an hour, assigned on the time-table to one lesson, in how many divisions, classes, or drafts should the teacher personally instruct? What further duty devolves on him in the meantime? 6 marks.

9. How may the Rolls be made to yield an efficient check on the monthly summaries of attendances in the Report Book? 6 marks.

10. Mention four conditions necessary to secure good penmanship. 6 marks.

Appendix L.
Annual Examination Questions.
Male Teachers.
A Papers.

ARITHMETIC.—100 Marks.

Two hours and a half allowed for this paper.

N.B.—Only five questions to be attempted.

Mr. STRONGE, Head Inspector.
Mr. DEWAR, District Inspector.

1. In a sum in Long Division the dividend is 564178, and the three successive remainders are 484, 263, and 316. Find the divisor and the quotient. Explain your work. 20 marks.

2. A can do a piece of work in 6 hours, B in 5 hours, and C in 4 hours. They all commence working together; but B leaves off one hour before the work is finished and C one hour and a half before the work is finished; in what time will the work be completed? 20 marks.

3. A person pays a rate of 3s. 4d. in the pound on one property, and of 2s. 3d. upon another. If both properties were rated at 2s. 11d., he would pay the same total as before, but if the rate were lowered to 2s. 10d. he would gain £9 11s. 3d. What is the rateable value of each property? 20 marks.

4. How many times is the greatest number of 3 digits in the scale 4 contained in the greatest number of 4 digits in scale 5? 20 marks.

5. State and prove the rule for reducing a vulgar fraction to a decimal,

   (a.) when the decimal terminates;

   (b.) when the decimal recurs. 20 marks.

6. Convert 17 from radix 9 to radix 12. 10 marks.

7. When the discovered figures of a cube root are greater in number by 2 than those remaining to be discovered, how are we able to obtain the latter by division only? Show this by an example. 10 marks.

8. Insert two harmonic means between ½ and ⅕. 10 marks.

9. A servant whose half-yearly wage is £8 10s. allows it to remain unpaid for 2½ years. How much will he be entitled to receive at the end of that time, compound interest being allowed at the rate of 4½ per cent. half-yearly? 10 marks.

10. A cube contains 2·370 yards. Find (1) its edge, (2) its diagonal, (3) the cost of painting its outside at 1½ shillings per square foot. 10 marks.

Appendix L.

Examination Questions.

Male Teachers.

A Papers.

GRAMMAR AND DERIVATIONS.—60 Marks

Two hours allowed for this paper.

N.B.—*Only five of these questions, of which the parsing exercise must be one, are to be attempted.*

Mr. PURSER, Head Inspector.
Mr. DICKIE, District Inspector.

1. HAMLET.—*Horatio, thou art e'en as just a man*
   As e'er my conversation coped withal.
   HORATIO.—O, my dear lord,——
   HAM.——   Nay, do not think I flatter,
   For what *advancement* may I hope from thee,
   That no *revenue hast,* but thy good spirits
   To feed and *clothe* thee! Why should the *poor* be flattered!
                    For thou hast been
   As one in *suffering all, that* suffers nothing;
   A *man,* that fortune's buffets and rewards
   Hast ta'en with equal thanks; and *blessed* are those
   Whose blood and judgment are so well co-mingled,
   That they are not a pipe for fortune's finger
   To sound *what stop she please.*

   Parse the words in *italics*; and write a paraphrase of the passage.
                                                        20 marks.

2. Give a general and a particular analysis of the following passage:—

   Be thy intents wicked or charitable,
   Thou comest in such a questionable shape,
   That I will speak to thee; I'll call thee, Hamlet,
   King, father: Royal Dane, O answer me.
                                                        12 marks.

3. What is the strict rule of concord if a pronoun refers to nouns of different genders? Give examples, and some apparent exceptions.
                                                        10 marks.

4. How would you instruct a pupil to parse the following *italicised* words:—

   (a.) He found *his* own hat, but he lost *mine.*
   (b.) That hat is *mine. So* I thought.
   (c.) He is a subject of the *King's.*
                                                        10 marks.

5. Classify conjunctions; and give two uses of *or.*
                                                        8 marks.

6. Give the derivation of *children, mongrel, hale, its, which*; and name the language from which each word comes.   5 marks.

7. Show that English orthography is very anomalous. To what is this due?   5 marks.

8. Discuss the point whether *as* should ever be regarded as a relative pronoun; and illustrate your answer by three suitable sentences.
                                                        5 marks.

9. Distinguish between a vulgarism and a colloquial expression, and give examples of each.   5 marks.

10. To what class of words is the Celtic element in the English language almost entirely confined?   5 marks.

Appendix L.

Exami-
nation
Questions.

Male
Teachers.

A Papers.

PENMANSHIP.—40 Marks.

Half an hour allowed for this exercise.

*Your penmanship will be judged from the neatness and accuracy with
which you copy the following passages:—*

> Forlorn ! the very word is like a bell
>   To toll me back from thee to my sole self !
> Adieu ! the fancy cannot cheat so well
>   As she is famed to do, deceiving elf.
> Adieu ! adieu ! thy plaintive anthem fades
>   Past the near meadows, over the still stream,
>   Up the hill-side ; and now 'tis buried deep
>   In the next valley glades :
>   Was it a vision, or a waking dream ?
>   Fled is that music : do I wake or sleep !

When Paradise Lost first appeared, though it was not neglected, it
attracted no crowd of imitators, and made no visible change in the
poetical practice of the age. Milton stood alone and aloof above his
times ; the bard of immortal subjects, and, as far as there is perpetuity
in language, of immortal fame. The very choice of those subjects
bespoke a contempt for any species of excellence that was attainable
by other men.

GEOMETRY AND MENSURATION.—100 Marks.

Two hours and a half allowed for this paper.

N.B.—*Only five questions to be attempted.*

*Only geometrical solutions will be accepted, and only the propositions of
Euclid may be assumed.*

Mr. SULLIVAN, Head Inspector.
Mr. M'NEILL, District Inspector.

1. Given the base, the ratio of the sides, and the difference of the
squares of the sides of a triangle, construct the triangle.
                                                            20 marks.

2. The rectangle contained by the diameter of the circumscribed
circle and the radius of the inscribed circle of any triangle is equal
to the rectangle contained by the segments of any chord of the
circumscribed circle passing through the centre of the inscribed circle.
                                                            20 marks.

3. Every two consecutive diagonals of a regular pentagon, divide
each other in extreme and mean ratio.   20 marks.

4. If lines be drawn from a fixed point to all the points of the
circumference of a given circle, the locus of all their points of bisection
is a circle.   20 marks.

5. A vessel shaped like the frustum of a cone, is 14 inches wide
at top, 8 inches wide at the bottom, and 15 inches deep. The
vessel is filled with water, and then half the water is poured out. At
what height does the remainder stand in the vessel ?   20 marks.

U 2

6. The volume of a right circular cone is 16 cubic feet; the height is twice the radius of the base; find the area of the whole surface.
       10 marks.

7. Equiangular parallelograms are to each other as the rectangles contained by their sides about a pair of equal angles. Prove. Also give Euclid's enunciation of this proposition.   10 marks.

8. To divide a given line C D *externally* in the ratio of two given lines m and n.   10 marks.

9. If two sides of a triangle, measured from an angle, be cut proportionally, the line joining the points of section is parallel to the third side. Prove.   10 marks.

10. Given the difference of two lines and the rectangle contained by them; find the lines.   10 marks.

ENGLISH COMPOSITION.—50 Marks.

Two hours allowed for this subject.

N.B.—*Only one subject to be selected*

Mr. Purser, Head Inspector.
Mr. Dalton, District Inspector

1. The study of the physical sciences.
2. Speech is silver, silence is gold.

ALGEBRA.—100 Marks.

Two hours and a half allowed for this paper.

N.B.—*Only five questions to be attempted.*

Mr. Stronge, Head Inspector.
Mr. Crosle, District Inspector.

1. A starts from P to walk to Q and back again, and B at the same time starts from Q to walk to P and back again, each walking at a uniform rate. They first meet at a point 13 miles from Q, and 8 hours later they meet again 9 miles from P; find their respective rates of walking, and the distance from P to Q.   20 marks.

2. Given—
$$x + y + z = a,$$
$$x^2 + y^2 + z^2 = b^2,$$
$$a^3 + y^3 + z^3 = c^3 ;$$
find the product xyz in terms of a, b, c.   20 marks.

3. If the squares of $(xy - yz + zx)$, $(yz - zx + xy)$ and $(zx - xy + yz)$ be in arithmetical progression; prove that x, y and z are also in arithmetical progression.   20 marks.

4. Resolve into factors—

(1) $a^4(b^2 - c^2) + b^4(c^2 - a^2) + c^4(a^2 - b^2)$.

(2) $(a^2 - b^2)^3 + (b^2 - c^2)^3 + (c^2 - a^2)^3$.

    20 marks.

Appendix L.

Exami-
nation
Questions.

*Male
Teachers*

A Paper.

5. Solve

$$x + y = a\sqrt{xy}$$
$$x - y = c\sqrt{\frac{x}{y}}$$

  20 marks.

6. Find the condition that m may be a root of $ax^2 + bx + c = 0$, and when this is so, find the other root. 10 marks.

7. If $x + \frac{1}{x} = y$, express $x^2 + \frac{1}{x^2}$ in terms of y. 10 marks.

8. If $x^x = y^y$ show that $\left(\frac{x}{y}\right)^{\frac{x}{y}} = x^{\frac{x}{y} - 1}$; and if $x = 3y$ find the value of y. 10 marks.

9. Solve—

$$\frac{25x^3 - 16}{10x - 8} = \frac{3x(x^2 - 4)}{9x - 6}$$

  10 marks.

10. If $x = b - c$, $y = c - a$, $z = a - b$, prove

$$yz - x^2 = zx - y^2 = xy - z^2 = xy + yz + zx$$

  10 marks.

HISTORY.—40 Marks

One hour and a half allowed for this paper.

N.B.—Only five questions to be attempted.

Mr. DOWNING, Head Inspector.
Mr. NICHOLLS, District Inspector.

1. What was the nature and the period of :—(a) the Confederation of the Rhine, and (b) the Germanic Confederation? 8 marks.

2. When, and in whose person did the line of Charlemagne terminate; and what important empire came then into existence? 8 marks.

3. Name the Plantagenet Kings of England; and account for the origin of this name of a race. 8 marks.

4. What important events in the history of France can you assign respectively to the years 1597, 1799, 1848, 1852? 8 marks.

5. Describe the circumstances, and give the dates of the battles of :—Toulouse, Salamanca, Borodino, and Sadowa. 8 marks.

6. Mention the remark of Herodotus on the effect of the administration of Dejoces, King of the Medes. 4 marks.

7. Describe the fortunes of the English arms in France after 1490. 4 marks.

8. In what directions has Russia extended her dominions during the present century? 4 marks.

9. Describe the circumstances of the battle of Thermopylæ. 4 marks.

10. What other prophecy, besides that of the writing on the wall at Belshazzar's feast, was fulfilled, as an immediate result of the capture of Babylon? 4 marks.

GEOGRAPHY.—60 Marks

Two hours allowed for this paper.

N.B.—Only five questions to be attempted.

Mr. CONNELLAN, Head Inspector.
Mr. ALEXANDER, District Inspector.

1. Draw an outline map of Greece, marking the inlets of the sea, the mountains, the chief towns, and the islands near the coast.
12 marks.

2. (a.) Show by means of a diagram how the latitude can be ascertained when the spectator and the sun are on opposite sides of the equator. (b.) In the southern hemisphere on 21st June, the meridian altitude of the sun is 48°; find the latitude.
12 marks.

3. Describe (a.) New South Wales, and (b.) Queensland, under the following heads :—

Boundaries, area, industrial resources, and chief towns.
12 marks.

4. Name the provinces of Spain. Enumerate its foreign possessions. Describe its surface, climate and soil.
12 marks.

5. Name the most remarkable island chains which form the summits of submarine mountain chains.
12 marks.

6. Name six of the protected States of British India, with their chief towns. Describe the position of each State.
6 marks.

7. Explain the origin of the following geographical names :— Antilles, Tierra del Fuego, Punta Arenas, Tripoli.
6 marks.

8. Refer the following towns to their respective counties ; and name the river or sea inlet on which each is built :—Dornoch, Huntly, Alloa, Maxwelltown.
6 marks.

9. What and where are the following :—(a.) the Gate of India, (b.) "The Brocken," (c.) El Despoblado, (d.) Le Maremme ?
6 marks.

10. In what countries are the following chiefly found :— Platina, Silver, Mercury, Bismuth ?
6 marks.

PLANE TRIGONOMETRY.—50 Marks

Two hours and a half allowed for this paper.

N.B.—Only five questions to be attempted.

Mr. SULLIVAN, Head Inspector.
Mr. M'CLINTOCK, District Inspector.

1. If from two points in a horizontal plane an object not in the same direction be seen at angles of elevation A and C, and if from a third point in the line between the two points, and at distances from them of a and b respectively the object be seen at an angle of elevation B ; find the height of the object above the horizontal plane.
10 marks.

2. $A + B + C = 180°$. Prove that
$$\sin^2 A + \sin^2 B + \sin^2 C = 2 \cos A \cos B \cos C = 2.$$
10 marks.

3. In a triangle, given $a = 26$, $b = 1.06$, and angle $D = 68°$; find A.
Is the case ambiguous? Explain.

Appendix L.

Exami-
nation
Questions.

Male
Teachers.

A Papers.

$$Log\ 260 = 2.41497$$
$$Log\ 106 = 2.02531$$
$$Log\ sin\ 68° = 9.96717$$
$$Log\ sin\ 13°8' = 9.35644$$
$$Log\ sin\ 13°9' = 9.35698$$

10 marks.

4. A statue 12 feet high stands on the top of a pedestal, and at a point in the horizontal plane on which the pedestal stands the pedestal and the statue subtend the same angle, 15°. Find the height of the pedestal.
10 marks.

5. Show that the area of a regular polygon of $2n$ sides inscribed in a circle is a mean proportional between the areas of the inscribed and circumscribed regular polygons of n sides.
10 marks.

6. Prove $\cos 4A = 1 - 8 \cos^2 A + 8 \cos^4 A$.

5 marks.

7. Find the radius of the circle described round a triangle in terms of the sides of the triangle.
5 marks.

8. Prove

$$\cot^2 A - \cot^2 B = \frac{\sin^2 B - \sin^2 A}{\sin^2 A \cdot \sin^2 B}$$

5 marks.

9. Assuming the ordinary expressions for $\sin (A \pm B)$ and $\cos (A \pm B)$ show that $\cos A + \cos B = 2 \cos \frac{1}{2}(A + B) \cos \frac{1}{2}(A - B)$.

5 marks.

10. Prove $\sin^2 A + \tan^2 A + \cos^2 A + \cot^2 A + 1 = \sec^2 A + \csc^2 A$.
5 marks.

MECHANICS.—50 Marks.

An hour and a half allowed for this paper.

N.B.—*Only five questions to be attempted.*

Mr. SULLIVAN, Head Inspector.
Mr. ROSS, District Inspector.

1. A straight uniform bar of length L and weight W has weights P and Q suspended from its extremities: find the distance of the centre of gravity of this system from the extremity to which P is attached.
10 marks.

2. If h be the height of a rough inclined plane, b the length of its base, and μ the coefficient of friction, prove that in pushing a body whose weight is W up the plane the work done is $W (h + \mu b)$.
10 marks.

3. Two projectiles fired with velocities due to the heights h and h' at elevations e and e' strike the same point on the side of the hill on which the gun is placed: find the slope of the hill.
10 marks.

4. A weight of P lbs. hanging freely is raised up by means of a string passing over a fixed pulley a weight Q attached to a single movable pulley whose weight is neglected: find the tension of the string, assuming that the parts of the string are parallel.
10 marks.

5. Prove that if two perfectly elastic spheres whose masses are equal come into direct collision they will exchange velocities.   10 marks.

Appendix L.
Exami-
nation
Questions.

*Male
Teachers*

A Paper.

6. If three equal forces acting on a particle keep it at rest, show that their directions must be equally inclined to each other.   5 marks.

7. How would you show by means of Atwood's machine—

(a.) That when different forces act on the same mass the accelerations are proportional to the forces?

(b.) That when the force is constant the accelerations are inversely proportional to the masses?   5 marks.

8. The algebraic sum of the moments of the two forces which form a couple is constant round every point in their plane, and is always equal to the moment of the couple. Prove.   5 marks.

9. A pound weight rests on a platform which is ascending vertically: find the acceleration of the platform when the pressure of the weight on it is equal to eighteen ounces.   5 marks.

10. Weights of 3 lbs. and 5 lbs. are attached to the extremities of a string passing over a pulley. When the system is in motion find the pressure on the pulley.   5 marks.

HYDROSTATICS AND HYDRAULICS.—50 Marks.

One hour and a half allowed for this paper.

N.B.—*Only five questions to be attempted.*

Mr. Connellan, Head Inspector,
Mr. Ross, District Inspector.

1. Describe the method of finding the specific gravity in each of the following cases, and give the usual formulæ :—

(a.) A body lighter than water.

(b.) A body soluble in water but insoluble in a liquid of known specific gravity.   10 marks.

2. A tube 4 feet in length and closed at one end has 3 feet of its length filled with mercury; it is then placed vertically with its open end just below the surface of a mercury trough. If the barometer stands at 30 inches find the height of the mercury inside the tube.   10 marks.

3. What is meant by error of capacity in a cistern barometer? Give a brief description of Fortin's barometer, explaining the adjustment by which the mercury in the cistern is kept at a constant level.   10 marks.

4. If a mercury barometer, standing at 76 CM., be immersed 4 metres below the surface of a lake, find the height of the column.   10 marks.

5. When a liquid is in contact with a solid, under what circumstances will the surface of the fluid be (a) horizontal, (b) concave, (c) convex? Explain your answer.   10 marks.

6. How can it be shown that the pressure of fluids in motion is diminished by their velocity?   5 marks.

7. How can the specific gravities of bodies soluble in water be determined by means of the specific gravity bottle?

What is the use of the thermometer in this instrument?   5 marks.

8. Describe the "phial of four elements"; and state the principle of the equilibrium of superposed liquid which is experimentally demonstrated by means of it.　　　5 marks.

9. A cube of lead (sp. gr. 11·2) 4 inches in the side is suspended from one end of an equal armed balance and immersed in water: What weight hung from the other end will counterpoise the lead? A cubic foot of water weighs 1000 oz.　　　5 marks.

10. Describe Graham's dialyser. On what principle is it founded?　　　5 marks.

HEAT AND THE STEAM ENGINE.—50 Marks.

One hour and a half allowed for this paper.

N.B.—*Only five questions to be attempted*

Mr. CONNELLAN, Head Inspector.
Mr. ROSS, District Inspector.

1. How much water at 45° C. must be mixed with 11 kilogrammes of crushed ice so that the temperature of the mixture may be 12° C. The latent heat of water is assumed to be 79.　　　10 marks.

2. The specific gravity of mercury at 0° C. being 13·6, required the volume of 5 kilos at 85° C.; coefficient of expansion being $\frac{1}{5000}$.　　　10 marks.

3. State as fully as you can the tests for a good mercurial thermometer. Why is it necessary to take note of the height of the barometer when determining the upper fixed point of thermometer.　　　10 marks.

4. Describe experiments showing the ebullition of water—(a.) below its normal boiling point, (b.) above its normal boiling point. Mention a practical application in the arts that has been made of each of these phenomena.　　　10 marks.

5. What is a compound engine? Describe its peculiar action and advantages.　　　10 marks.

6. Show in a diagram the slide valve of a steam engine, and explain its action: describe by aid of a sketch the piece of mechanism that gives the valve its motion.　　　5 marks.

7. Define specific heat. How would you compare the quantity of heat in a kettle of warm water with that in a red hot poker?　　　5 marks.

8. Explain why boiling is impossible in a closed tube.　　　5 marks.

9. What weight of steam at 100° C. is necessary to raise the temperature of 208 pounds of water from 14° to 82° C.? Explain.　　　5 marks.

10. In a heat engine the quantity of heat received from the source always exceeds the quantity given up to the condenser. How do you account for the difference?　　　5 marks.

LIGHT AND SOUND.—50 Marks.

One hour and a half allowed for this paper.

N.B.—*Only five questions to be attempted.*

Mr. CONNELLAN, Head Inspector.
Mr. KEENAN, District Inspector.

1. Explain fully by means of a diagram how it is that stars are visible to us when below the horizon.　　　10 marks.

2. Prove mathematically that the distances of the conjugate foci from the surface of a mirror are to each other as their distances from the centre of the mirror, whether concave or convex.　　　10 marks.

3. State and prove the principle on which Hadley's sextant is constructed. 10 marks.

4. Air and hydrogen gas are urged in succession with the same force through an organ pipe; compare the sounds produced in each case. Explain the difference. 10 marks.

5. Sound travels through air at 0° C. at the rate of 1,090 feet per second, and through hydrogen at the same temperature at the rate of 4,164 feet per second. What must be the temperature of air in order that sound may travel in it with the same velocity as in hydrogen at 0° C.? 10 marks.

6. What note makes three times, and what note one-third as many vibrations as the fundamental note C? Explain. 5 marks.

7. A person standing in front of a large concave mirror finds that in a certain position his image vanishes. What is that position? Explain your answer by means of a diagram. 5 marks.

8. Name the two laws to which the intensity of the illumination of light on a given surface is subject. 5 marks.

9. Standing on the margin of a smooth lake I see inverted images of objects on the opposite shore. Explain the phenomenon. 5 marks.

10. A string stretched by a weight of 5 lbs. sounds a certain note (Do), what weight will cause the string to sound the 5th note (Sol) of the scale? 5 marks.

MAGNETISM AND ELECTRICITY.—50 Marks.

One hour and a half allowed for this paper.

N.B.—Only five questions to be attempted.

Mr. SULLIVAN, Head Inspector.
Mr. KEENAN, District Inspector.

1. Describe Wimshurst's electrical machine. 10 marks.

2. State Ohm's law and explain the terms used.

"In an ordinary element there are essentially two resistances to be considered." What are the two? 10 marks.

3. What is meant by specific inductive capacity? Describe Faraday's experiment for finding the specific inductive capacity of shellac? 10 marks.

4. Prove that if C and C' are currents producing deflections φ and φ' in a tangent galvanometer, than

$$C : C' :: \tan\phi : \tan\phi'.$$ 10 marks.

5. Give Ampère's theory of magnetism. 10 marks.

6. Describe Henley's Electrometer and the manner of using it. 5 marks.

7. What is meant by *Magnetic Saturation*? Can a bar be magnetised beyond the point of magnetic saturation? Explain. 5 marks.

8. Explain the following terms:—*A Volt, an Ampère, a Coulomb.* 5 marks.

9. If the N. pole of a strong magnet be held at some distance from the N. pole of a weak magnet it will repel it, but if it be pushed up quite close it will attract it. Explain this. 5 marks.

10. Describe the construction and explain the manner of using Volta's Electrophorus. 5 marks.

INORGANIC CHEMISTRY.—50 Marks.

One hour and a half allowed.

N.B.—Only five questions to be attempted.

Mr. DOWNING, Head Inspector.
Mr. CHAMBERS, District Inspector.

1. State the sources from which chromium is obtained; its degree of fusibility; and the uses of its compounds.   10 marks.

2. Describe how oxygen may be obtained from manganese dioxide. Give the formula; and from it calculate the proportion of oxygen to be so obtained; the combining weight of manganese being 55.   10 marks.

3. Give an instance to illustrate the fact that bodies in the nascent state have peculiarly active chemical properties; and state how this is accounted for.   10 marks.

4. How is a concentrated solution of iodine to be prepared?   10 marks.

5. How may you estimate the quantity of CO_2 in a given quantity of air? Describe the construction and use of the necessary apparatus.   10 marks.

6. Required 500 grains of carbon dioxide; how will you obtain it, and from what weight of materials? Take $Ca = 40$: $Cl = 35\frac{1}{2}$.   5 marks.

7. Give the names, with symbols, of the compound radicals of ammonia, sulphuric acid, and sodium carbonate.   5 marks.

8. Name the eight elements of which the primary rocks are mainly composed, arranging them in order, according to the proportion in which they enter into the compositions of these rocks.   5 marks.

9. What two laws apply to the density of elementary gases, and of compound gases respectively?   5 marks.

10. Explain the composition and the action of mortar and of cement.   5 marks.

ORGANIC CHEMISTRY.—50 Marks.

One hour and a half allowed for this paper.

N.B.—Only five questions to be attempted.

Mr. DOWNING, Head Inspector.
Mr. SKEFFINGTON, District Inspector.

1. Describe the apparatus, manipulation, and calculation necessary to ascertain the weight of a given volume of the vapour of any compound; and explain the important information to be derived from this weight.   10 marks.

2. Give the other names, and the symbol, for glycerin; and explain how it is obtained. Give also the name and symbol of the very explosive substance formed from it by the action of a mixture of nitric and sulphuric acids.   10 marks.

3. Describe quinine, including its appearance, properties, and the tests by which its presence may be detected.   10 marks.

4. By what test may the presence of each of the following be ascertained:—aniline, starch, hydrocyanic acid, and strychnine?   10 marks.

5. Explain fully how the quantity of urea in a solution may be estimated.   10 marks.

6. State some of the general characteristics of a glucoside, and name a few examples of this class.   5 marks.

7. What is ethylene; how is it prepared; and what are its reactions with chlorine?   5 marks.

8. Describe caoutchouc under the following heads:—(a) its elements; (b) its solvents; (c) how converted into "vulcanite."   5 marks.

9. Name five essential oils that are isomerides of turpentine.   5 marks.

10. What are amides? Give the names and formulæ of the amides of acetyl.   5 marks.

AGRICULTURAL CHEMISTRY.—50 Marks.

An hour and a half allowed for this paper.

N.B.—Only *five* questions to be attempted.

Mr. DOWNING, Head Inspector.
Mr. SKEFFINGTON, District Inspector.

1. Describe the elements, in their approximate relative proportions, supplied to the soil by Glauber salts, when used as a manure; and explain the action of heat upon the crystals of this substance.   10 marks.

2. What volatile salt of ammonia is found in urine, and how is its escape prevented? Explain the reaction.   10 marks.

3. Describe an experiment to prove that carbonic acid exists in the air, and that quicklime combines with carbonic acid.   10 marks.

4. How would you test for the presence of lime in a soil? Explain fully why you consider this an adequate test.   10 marks.

5. Describe the appearance of sodium nitrate, say where it is obtained, and give the names of its elements, with their relative proportions.   10 marks.

6. Give examples of carbo-hydrates and of albumenoids, and name the elements of which these are respectively composed.   5 marks.

7. What experiment will illustrate how lime removes sourness from the land?   5 marks.

8. State approximately how much carbon is daily thrown off by a cow or horse. Explain how this takes place, and estimate the quantity of starch sufficient to supply this waste.   5 marks.

9. Point out the properties of water that are most important to vegetation, and show how they are so.   5 marks.

10. How much water does a ton of quicklime absorb in slaking?   5 marks.

ENGLISH LITERATURE.—60 Marks.

One hour and a half allowed for this paper.

N.B.—*Only five questions to be attempted.*

Mr. NEWELL, Head Inspector.
Dr. MORAN, District Inspector.

1. Sketch the character of *Polonius*, illustrating your view by quotations from the Play.   12 marks.

2. Write explanatory notes on the following passages :—

(a.) " *A little more than kin and less than kind.*"

(b.) " *I think this inhibition comes by the means of the late innovation.*"

(c.) " *This quarry cries on havock.*"

(d.) " *Let the galled jade wince, our withers are unwrung.*"
     12 marks.

3. Quote, or give the substance of the king's soliloquy, commencing—
   " O, my offence is rank, it smells to heaven."   12 marks.

4. Write notes on the following—

(a.) " *He died with conquering Graeme.*"

(b.) " *A heriot he sought.*"

(c.) " *To make your towers a Ferniost-firth.*"

(d.) " *When English blood swelled Ancram's ford.*"
     12 marks.

5. Give the context in the case of these phrases—

(a.) " *Where are my Switzers.*"

(b.) " *'Tis as easy as lying.*"

(c.) " *Or the blank verse shall halt for it.*"

(d.) " *The lady doth protest too much, methinks.*"
     12 marks.

6. Write brief notes on the following extracts, and state in what connexion each occurs in the Play :—

(a.) " *This lapwing runs away with the shell on his head.*"

(b.) " *As patient as the female dove
When that her golden couplets are disclosed.*"

(c.) " *Shards, flints and pebbles should be thrown on her.*"
     6 marks.

7. What border clans mustered for the defence of Branksome Towers ?
     6 marks.

8. " Each minstrel's war-note loud was blown ;—
   But, ere a gray-goose shaft had flown,
   A horseman galloped from the rear."

State the substance of the tidings which this horseman brought to the English lords.   6 marks.

9. Give Horatio's summary of the events of the Tragedy.
     6 marks.

10. Give the substance of Hamlet's apology and Laertes' reply before they begin to play with the foils.   6 marks.

Appendix I.

*Exami-
nation
Questions.*

*Male
Teachers.*

A Papers.

SPHERICAL TRIGONOMETRY.—50 Marks.

Two hours and a half allowed for this paper.

N.B.—*Only five questions to be attempted.*

Mr. SULLIVAN, Head Inspector.
Mr. M'CLINTOCK, District Inspector.

1. Let θ represent the arc of a great circle joining the middle points of the sides a and b of a spherical triangle. Prove that

$$\cos \theta = \frac{1 + \cos a + \cos b + \cos c}{4 \cos \tfrac{1}{2}a \cos \tfrac{1}{2}b}$$

   10 marks.

2. Find the expression for the area of a spherical triangle in terms of two sides and the angle included by them.   10 marks.

3. In a right-angled spherical triangle, C being the right angle, prove that $\sin (c + a) \sin (c - a) = \sin^2 b \cos^2 a$; and that $\cot A = \cot a \sin b$.   10 marks.

4. In a spherical triangle ABC show that

$$\cot a \sin c = \cot A \sin B + \cos c \cos B.$$

   10 marks.

5. Prove that in a spherical triangle

$$\frac{\cos \tfrac{1}{2}C}{\cos \tfrac{1}{2}c} = \frac{\sin \tfrac{1}{2}(A + B)}{\cos \tfrac{1}{2}(a - b)}.$$

   10 marks.

6. In a spherical triangle $A = 105°$, $B = 45°$, $c = 90°$; calculate the value of $\tan \tfrac{1}{2}(a + b)$.   5 marks.

7. What is meant by the *Polar triangle?* Assuming

$$\sin A = \frac{2}{\sin a \sin b} \sqrt{\left\{ \sin s \cdot \sin (s - a) \sin (s - b) \sin (s - c) \right\}};$$

find, by means of the Polar triangle, the corresponding expression for $\sin a$.   5 marks.

8. The spherical excess of a triangle is 30' 5"; find its area, the diameter of the sphere being 100 feet.   5 marks.

9. Prove that the Polar triangle of a quadrantal triangle is right-angled.   5 marks.

10. Assuming the usual expression for cos A, prove

$$\tan^2 \tfrac{1}{2}A = \frac{\sin (s - b) \sin (s - c)}{\sin s \sin (s - a)}$$

   5 marks.

B Papers.

METHODS, SCHOOL ACCOUNTS, COMMISSIONERS' RULES.—60 Marks.

Two hours allowed for this paper.

N.B.—*Only five questions to be attempted.*

Mr. DOWNING, Head Inspector.
Dr. BATEMAN, District Inspector.

1. With reference to the following passage, show how you would proceed to test and develop the intelligence of your pupils:—

> "There is a green island in lone Gougane-Barra,
> Where Allua of song rushes forth as an arrow,
> In deep-valleyed Desmond, a thousand wild fountains
> Come down to that lake, from their home in the mountains.
> There grows the wild ash; and a time-stricken willow
> Looks chidingly down on the mirth of the billow,
> As, like some gay child, that sad monitor scorning,
> It lightly laughs back to the laugh of the morning."

   12 marks.

2. Give outlines of a lesson on the inflexions of the verb treated inductively.   13 marks.

3. Describe fully an efficient system of getting the letters, required from Fifth and Sixth Classes, written, marked and corrected.
                                                              13 marks.

4. From half-past one to two o'clock: Senior Division—Reading (Grammar on Wednesday) in desks. Junior Division—Writing in desks.

Explain fully how the school is to be worked during this half-hour with a staff of one teacher and one paid monitor; all classes being represented.   12 marks.

5. State fully the requirements of the school programme with regard to mental arithmetic, giving two specimen questions for each class.
                                                              12 marks.

6. Under what circumstances should an *extra instruction* lesson be given to the senior classes? Suggest suitable time arrangements for such instruction.   6 marks.

7. Describe certain physical conditions calculated to interfere with the attention of a pupil, and, consequently, with the benefit derived from the lesson.   6 marks.

8. Give six specimens of matter suitable to enliven a lesson on the Map of the World.   6 marks.

9. What conditions should determine the degree of rapidity of questioning?   6 marks.

10. Explain the difference between the No. 1 and the No. 2 forms of agreement between manager and teacher.   6 marks.

ARITHMETIC.—100 Marks.

Two hours and a half allowed for this paper.

N.B.—*Only five questions to be attempted.*

Mr. STRONGE, Head Inspector.
Mr. DEWAR, District Inspector.

1. (a) The ratio of a less number to a greater is diminished by subtracting the same number from each of them. Give an example in illustration of this theorem and state why it is true. (b) Three sums of money are in the proportion of 2 : 3 : 5, and when each has been reduced by £25 the remainders are in the proportion of 1 : 2 : 4. Find the sums of money.   20 marks.

2. A person has stock in the 3 per cents., which yields £240 a year. He sells out ⅓ of his stock at 87½, and invests the proceeds in railway stock at 174½. What dividend ought the latter to pay that he may thereby increase his income by £101?   20 marks.

3. A train took 15 seconds to pass completely through a tunnel 176 yards long, and 3 seconds to pass the signal box outside the tunnel. Find the length of the train and its velocity in miles per hour. 20 marks.

4. Seven men do ⅘ of a piece of work in 2½ days; how long will 6 boys take to finish it, it being known that 3 men and 5 boys have done a similar piece of work in 9 days?   20 marks.

5. Find the present worth of £105 3s. 4½d. due 3 years hence, reckoning compound interest at 5 per cent. Explain your work.
                                                              20 marks.

6. A person sells £5,000, 3 per cent. stock, and buys 3½ per cents. at 87½. If the increase in his income be £5, what is the price of the 3 per cents.?   10 marks.

7. A map of a plot which is drawn on a scale of an inch to a mile contains 6 feet 6 inches: find the acreage of the plot.   10 marks.

8. Insert 4 geometric means between 1 and 1024, and find the sum of the series so obtained.   10 marks.

9. The telegraph poles on a railway are 88 yards apart. Show that the number of poles passed in three minutes will exactly express in miles per hour the speed of a train.   10 marks.

10. Show how it may be known by inspection that 247104 is divisible without remainder by each of the numbers 3, 4, 6, 8, and 9.   10 marks.

GRAMMAR AND DERIVATIONS.—60 Marks.

Two hours allowed for this paper.

N.B.—*Only five questions, of which the parsing exercise must be one, are to be attempted.*

Mr. Purser, Head-Inspector.
Mr. Murphy, District Inspector.

1.
> *Virtue confessed* in human shape he draws,
> What Plato *thought*, and godlike Cato was;
> No common object to your sight *displays*,
> But what with pleasure Heaven itself surveys—
> A brave man struggling in the storms of fate,
> And *greatly falling with a falling state.*
> While Cato gives his little senate laws,
> *What bosom beats* not in his country's cause?
> Who sees him act, *but envies every deed?*
> *Who hears him groan*, and does not wish to bleed?

Parse the words in *italics*, and paraphrase the passage.   30 marks.

2. Make a general analysis of the following passage:—

A man who, having left England when a boy, returns to it after thirty or forty years passed in India, will find, be his talents what they may, that he has much both to learn and to unlearn, before he can take a place among English statesmen.   10 marks.

3. Discuss the assertion "Strictly speaking, the participles do not in themselves contain any notification of the time to which they refer."   10 marks.

4. Give two prepositions which follow each of these verbs—*attend, divide, thirst, fawn, abide.* Form sentences showing the proper use of each preposition.   10 marks.

5. Trace and account for the different forms assumed by the verb *to be* in its several moods and tenses.   10 marks.

6. Give five exceptions to the first rule of syntax.   5 marks.

7. Construct sentences to show—

(a) The verb having both a direct and an indirect object.
(b) An intransitive verb followed by an objective case.
    5 marks.

8. How is it that the forms *ourself* and *yourself* can be used, but not *themself*?   5 marks.

9. Quote words formed with the prefixes *syn, hyper, anti*; and with the affixes *ee, een.* Give the meaning of each of these prefixes and affixes.   5 marks.

10. Explain clearly the difference between *custom* and *habit, haughtiness* and *disdain.*   5 marks.

PENMANSHIP.—40 Marks.

Half an hour allowed for this exercise.

Your penmanship will be judged from the neatness and accuracy with which you copy the following passages :—

Forlorn ! the very word is like a bell
To toll me back from thee to my sole self !
Adieu ! the fancy cannot cheat so well
As she is famed to do, deceiving elf.
Adieu ! adieu ! thy plaintive anthem fades
Past the near meadows, over the still stream,
Up the hill-side ; and now 'tis buried deep
In the next valley glades :
Was it a vision, or a waking dream ?
Fled is that music : do I wake or sleep ?

When Paradise Lost first appeared, though it was not neglected, it attracted no crowd of imitators, and made no visible change in the poetical practice of the age. Milton stood alone and aloof above his times ; the bard of immortal subjects and, as far as there is perpetuity in language, of immortal fame. The very choice of these subjects bespoke a contempt for any species of excellence that was attainable by other men.

———

DICTATION AND SPELLING BOOK SUPERSEDED.

50 Marks (including 30 Marks for Dictation.)

One hour and a half allowed for this paper.

N.B.—*Only five questions to be attempted.*

Mr. STRONGE, Head Inspector.
Mr. LEMANS, District Inspector.

The passage for Dictation is to be taken from the Sixth Book of Lessons, page 412, from "Thirdly, it is shown" down to "with water or only with air."   20 marks.

1. *Vain, vanity ; secret, secretary ; coal, collier.* Give other similar examples, and explain clearly how these changes arise, and to what tendency they are due.   6 marks.

2. What was the pronunciation in the seventeenth century of *great, Rome, oblige?* Quote the statement of Dr. Johnson regarding the first, and the couplets of Shakespeare and Pope, regarding the other two, in proof of the old pronunciation.   6 marks.

3. What is the origin of the parts of the following words printed in italics :—*Ath*elney, *Mall*imavat, *Cheap*side, *Dal*key, *Arund*el, *Cotswold* ? Write notes on the spelling of the last two words.   6 marks.

Appendix I.

Examination Questions.

Holi Teachers.

B Papers.

4. *Eager, meagre, attitude, enemy.* Show from the present forms of these words that they do not come direct from the Latin. Trace their derivation.   6 marks.

5. Correct where necessary the spelling of the following words, and give reasons for the changes you make :—*dilapidated, despatch, molass, inseparable, benefited, unmanageble.*   0 marks.

6. Why are the following words considered as difficult or irregular in their spelling :—*catarrh, flambeau, southerly*?   3 marks.

7. How does Dr. Sullivan say the following words should be pronounced :—*genuine, advertise, nervous*? Write and accent the words as you would pronounce them.   3 marks.

8. Notice anything peculiar in the spelling of the following words and give their derivations :—*oena, garner, fancy.*   5 marks.

9. Write notes on the italicised letters in the following words :—*could, psalm, vertebræ.*   3 marks.

10. Distinguish between the so-called synonymous terms:—*education, instruction, tuition.*   3 marks.

GEOMETRY AND MENSURATION.—100 Marks.

Two hours and a half allowed for this paper.

N.B.—Only five questions to be attempted.

Mr. SULLIVAN, Head Inspector.
Mr. M'NEILL, District Inspector.

1. The square described on the sum of the sides of a right-angled triangle exceeds the square on the hypotenuse by four times the area of the triangle. (To be proved within the limits of the First Book.)   20 marks.

2. Given two points, one of which is in a given line, it is required to find another point in the given line, such that the difference of its distances from the former points may be given.   20 marks.

3. Two parallel chords of a circle are 24 feet and 20 feet, and the perpendicular distance between them is 10 feet; find the area of the zone which they form.   20 marks.

4. The perimeter of any polygon is greater than that of any inscribed polygon of the same number of sides.   20 marks.

5. Give an *indirect* proof of Proposition 48, Book I.   20 marks.

6. From a given point without a circle to draw a tangent to a circle.   10 marks.

7. The area of a sector is 61·8, and the radius of the circle 19·6; find the length of the arc, also the number of degrees which it contains.   10 marks.

8. Find a point that shall be equidistant from three given points, B, C, and D.   10 marks.

9. To divide a given finite line C D into two segments so that the rectangle contained by the whole line and one segment may be equal to the square on the other segment.   10 marks.

10. Prove that any right line through the intersection of the diagonals of a parallelogram bisects the parallelogram.   10 marks.

BOOK-KEEPING.—50 Marks.

Two hours allowed for this paper.

N.B. —Only five questions to be attempted.

Mr. Connellan, Head Inspector.
Mr. M'Millan, District Inspector.

Balance Sheet on 31st December, 1893.

Liabilities	£ s. d	Assets	£ s. d
1. *Bill payable*—C. Cooke on Self, .97 12 . 6		Cash in hand,	437 13 5
Creditor—Due to R. Smart 316 12 10		Balance of Bank Account,	560 15 6
		50 pipes Port, at £42,	2,100 0 0
		60 butts Sherry, at £40,	2,400 0 0
		Bills Receivable.	
		No. 1. Thomas Nairn on H. Grey, due 6th inst.,	156 13 4
		No. 2. Self on J. Evans, due 10th inst.,	218 15 0
		Thos. Wray's balance,	140 0 0

1894.

		£ s. d
Jan. 2—Bought of R. Smart, 10 butts Sherry, at £40,		400 0 0
,, 4—Received of Thomas Wray his acceptance No. 3, at one month,		100 0 0
,, ,, Paid R. Smart by cheque,		100 0 0
,, 8—T. Nairn's bill No. 1, returned dishonoured—Cash paid for noting, 7s. 6d.,		157 0 10
,, 10—Paid R. Smart—Cheque, £400, Cash, £100—for amount of account, . . £516 12 10		
Less discount, . 16 12 10		516 12 10
,, ,, Received payment of J. Evans' acceptance No. 2,		218 15 0
,, ,, Paid into Bank,		340 0 0
,, ,, Sold J. Evans, 10 pipes Port, at £45, and 10 butts Sherry, at £43,		870 0 0
Jan. 11—Cash paid J. Evans for leakage found to have taken place from a pipe of Port Wine,		6 0 0
,, 23—Sold J. Wray, on three months' credit, 5 butts of Sherry, at £46,		230 0 0
,, ,, Sold J. Ward, 10 pipes Port, at £45, 5 butts Sherry, at £43, less 2½ per cent. discount for cash,		643 10 0
,, 26—Cash received from T. Wray for Wine sold him on 23rd, on which I allow discount—Cash, . £218 10 0		
Discount, . 11 10 0		230 0 0
,, 31—Paid wages,		10 0 0

Journalise these statements with concise but sufficient "narration."

15 marks.

2. Post and close the Ledger Accounts, taking Wine on hand at cost price. Use separate quantity columns in the Wine Account for pipes and butts.   15 marks.

3. Having bought 15 cwt. of sugar for £14 18s. 9d. on credit from Robinson, I find that the weight is short by 20 lbs. Give the Journal entries.   8 marks.

4. Sold John Blake and shipped at his risk goods for £420, which I insured with Richard Young for £460, paying £8 insurance. Give the necessary Journal entries.   8 marks.

5. Renewed my acceptance due this day for £570
 13s. 2d., in favour of Inman & Co., for two months,
 including interest, ... £577 15 8
Journalize.   6 marks.

6. When I draw bills of exchange on my factor, and get them accepted, but do not receive payment, what are the Journal entries?   5 marks.

7. An error has been made in charging William Bell 9s. 8d. per cwt. for sugar sold to him, instead of 13s. 6d. How must the error be corrected?   5 marks.

8. I buy goods from W. Smith for £20 and sell them to J. Barry for £35. He pays me in cash £10 and bill for £15. I pay Barry's acceptance to Smith and cash for balance, he allowing me 5 per cent. discount on cash I pay. Give my Journal entries.   5 marks.

9. William Ross pays into Bank £200 to credit of J. Hamilton, advising him that he does so at request and on account of J. Edwards. Give Journal entries of each of the parties concerned.   5 marks.

10. I pay J. Murray £100, a debt I owe him, he allowing me 5 per cent. What are my entries? What are J. Murray's?   5 marks.

ALGEBRA.—100 Marks.

Two hours and a half allowed for this paper.

N.B.—*Only five questions to be attempted*

Mr. Stronge, Head Inspector.
Mr. Groome, District Inspector.

1. Six gallons of wine are drawn from a cask and replaced by six gallons of water; six gallons of the mixture are then drawn and replaced by six gallons of water. The quantity of wine now in the cask is to the quantity of water as 1 : 19; find how much wine the cask contained at first.   20 marks.

2. Resolve into factors—

(1) $a^2 + acx^2 - b^2x^2 + bcx^3$.

(3) $a^4 - 2(b^2 + c^2)a^2 + (b^2 - c^2)^2$.   20 marks.

3. Solve—

$$2\sqrt{(x^2 - y^2)} + xy = 1.$$
$$\frac{x}{y} - \frac{y}{x} = a.$$ 20 marks.

5. Simplify—

$$\left\{ \frac{(x-1)^3}{x^3-1} + \frac{x^2-2x+1}{x^2-x+1} \right\} \times \left\{ \frac{2x-1}{3+x} - \frac{2+x}{3-x} + \frac{3(3+x^2)}{4-x^2} \right\}.$$

20 marks.

6. The length of a rectangular field is twice its breadth. If 30 yards were added to its length, and 30 to its breadth, its area would be increased by one acre. Find the size of the field.   10 marks.

7. Find the Least Common Multiple of—

$$a^3 - 9a^2 + 26a - 24 \text{ and } a^3 - 11a^2 + 38a - 40.$$

10 marks.

8. Solve—

$$\frac{1+x}{1-x} + \frac{2+x}{1-2x} = 3 - \frac{3(1+x)(2+x)}{(1-x)(1-2x)}.$$

10 marks.

9. Find the values of—

(1) $(a^2 + ab + b^2)(a^2 + b^2) + (a+b)(a^4 + a^2b^2 + b^4)$.

and (2) $x^6 - y^6 + (x-y)(x^2 + 2x^2y + 2xy^2 + y^2)$.

10 marks.

10. Find two numbers such that their sum, product, and the difference of their squares may all be equal.   10 marks.

LESSON BOOKS.—50 Marks.

Two hours allowed for this paper.

N.B.—Only five questions to be attempted.

Mr. SULLIVAN, Head Inspector.
Dr. MORAN, District Inspector.

1. In what year, and under what circumstances did the censorship of the Press cease to be operative in England?   10 marks.

2. Give the substance of Campbell's remarks on any one of the following poets:—*Milton, Pope, Chatterton, Goldsmith.*   10 marks.

3. Explain fully how, in the Holy Land, the permanence and mutual independence of the separate tribes, were secured.   10 marks.

4. Explain the following allusions in Milton's description of Athens —"*This specular mount*." "*Blind Melesigenes*." "*Painted Stoa next*." "*Orators, whose eloquence fulmined over Greece*." "*The Stoic severe*."   10 marks.

5. Give a description of *Ardollen* and its antiquities.   10 marks.

6. "The oldest poets of many nations preserve their reputation, and the following generations of wit, after a short celebrity, sink into oblivion." How does Dr. Johnson account for this?   5 marks.

7. In connexion with the Public Funds explain clearly the following terms:—*Reduced annuities; Consolidated annuities; the Consolidated fund*.   5 marks.

8. Relate briefly the circumstances that led to the desertion of Tara as a residence of the Irish Kings.   5 marks.

9. Explain the words in italics in the following passages, and state in what poem each occurs :—

(a) " The crows and *choughs* that *wing* the *midway* air
　　Show scarce so gross as beetles."
(b) " The *Tanist* be to great O'Neill."
(c) " Let me *languish into life*."
(d) " The *water-wraith* was shrieking."
(e) " Nor *Oun* on his *bosom their image receives*." 　　5 marks.

10. What measures were adopted by Warren Hastings, on assuming the government of Bengal, for relieving its financial embarrassments ?
　　　　　　　　　　　　　　　　　　　　　　　　5 marks.

────────

GEOGRAPHY.—60 Marks.

Two hours allowed for this paper.

N.B.—*Only five questions to be attempted.*

Mr. CONNELLAN, Head Inspector.
Mr. ALEXANDER, District Inspector.

1. Draw an outline map of the " Border Counties " of England and Scotland, marking the boundaries of each county, and indicating with names the positions of the principal towns, rivers and mountains.
　　　　　　　　　　　　　　　　　　　　　　　　12 marks.

2. Where are Cardiff, Glossop, Schaffhausen, Milwaukie, Jubbulpore, Cracow ?
Name some distinguishing circumstance connected with each.
　　　　　　　　　　　　　　　　　　　　　　　　12 marks.

3. (a.) Name the highest summit of the Andes. In what country is it situated ?
(b.) Name the principal mountains on or around the table-land of Quito.　　　　　　　　　　　　　　　　　　　　　12 marks.

4. Give an account of the basin of the " Continental Streams " of Europe and Asia. Name the principal rivers of this system ; and state what is peculiar to this outflow.　　　　　　　　　12 marks.

5. Prove that the zenith distance of the celestial equator is always equal to the sum or difference of the sun's zenith distance and the sun's declination.　　　　　　　　　　　　　　　　　12 marks.

6. Give the position and the geographical designation of Port Victoria, Guadaloupe, Tristan d'Acunha, Guayaquil, Taupo, Mulhacen.
　　　　　　　　　　　　　　　　　　　　　　　　6 marks.

7. On what rivers are the following towns :—Avignon, Prague, Magdeburg, Lucknow, Melbourne, Kiev ?　　　　　　6 marks.

8. Describe the anti-trade winds as to locality, regularity and direction.　　　　　　　　　　　　　　　　　　　　6 marks.

9. Describe the vegetable and animal life of Australia.　6 marks.

10. What are Natron lakes ? State where the chief of them are found.　　　　　　　　　　　　　　　　　　　　6 marks.

AGRICULTURE.—50 Marks.

Two hours and a half allowed for this paper.

N.B.—Only five questions to be attempted.

Mr. CONNELLAN, Head Inspector.
Mr. CASIO, District Inspector.

1. (a) What three functions are performed by combustible matter in the soil?

(b) What are the effects of paring and burning on light land, and on heavy clay land, respectively? Explain.   10 marks.

2. "Artificial manures must be more or less special, according to the class of crop to which they may be applied and the condition of the soil." Give, as fully as you can, the reasons for this statement.

10 marks.

3. In its natural state clay land has three defects. Say what these are, and state the means usually adopted for the improvement of this class of soil.   10 marks.

4. Explain the nature and properties of humus, and describe its mode of action in the case of light and heavy soils respectively.

10 marks.

5. State and discuss the arguments in favour of the shallow draining of heavy clay soil.   10 marks.

6. Describe fully the mode of fattening sheep.   5 marks.

7. What are the four ways in which corn may be sown, and what are the three conditions which perfection in sowing corn requires?

5 marks.

8. State what you know about hard fescue grass as regards its adaptability to certain soils, its productiveness and general usefulness.

5 marks.

9. What is the best artificial top-dressing for grass during the middle of summer, and why?   5 marks.

10. Describe the preparation of the ground for flax, and the proper method of sowing this crop. What is the proper quantity of seed per acre?   5 marks.

MECHANICS.—50 Marks.

Two hours and a half allowed for this paper.

N.B.—Only five questions to be attempted.

Mr. SULLIVAN, Head Inspector.
Mr. ROSS, District Inspector.

1. A certain force acting on a mass of 18 lbs. increases its velocity every second by 3⅓ feet per second, while another force acting on a mass of 20 lbs. increases its velocity every second by 6⅔ feet per second: find the ratio of these forces.   10 marks.

2. Two forces acting in opposite directions have a resultant of 5 lbs., and if they acted at right angles their resultant would be 25 lbs.: find the forces.   10 marks.

3. A uniform bar, six feet long, and weighing 26 lbs., lies on a table with one end projecting two feet beyond the table: find the greatest weight that can be attached to the extremity of the projecting end without causing the bar to overturn.   10 marks.

Appendix L.
Examination Questions.
Male Teachers.
B Papers.

4. State clearly the meaning of each of the symbols in the equation $s = ut + \frac{1}{2} ft^2$. Show that the space described in the nth second by a body falling freely is $\frac{1}{2} g (2n - 1)$.   10 marks.

5. In the system of pulleys in which each string is attached to the weight and all the strings are parallel, show that when there is equilibrium the weight is equal to the power multiplied by $(2^n - 1)$, where n is the number of pulleys.   10 marks.

6. Show that the centre of gravity of the perimeter of a parallelogram coincides with the centre of gravity of the parallelogram.   5 marks.

7. A body known to possess a constant acceleration moves from rest and describes 64 feet in the first 4 seconds. With what velocity will it be moving at the end of the 7th second ?   5 marks.

8. Weights of 10 lbs. and 12 lbs. are placed at the extremities of a weightless rod 24 inches long : upon what point will the rod balance, and what will be the pressure on that point ?   5 marks.

9. With what velocity must a bullet be thrown vertically upwards that it may return to the earth in six seconds ? Find the greatest height attained.   5 marks.

10. Forces of 16 lbs. and 30 lbs. act on a particle at an angle of 60°. Find the resultant, and show that it does *not* bisect the angle 60°.
                    5 marks.

HISTORY.—40 Marks.

One hour and a half allowed for this paper.

N.B.—Only five questions to be attempted.

Mr. DOWNING, Head Inspector.
Mr. J. C. ROGERS, District Inspector.

1. Narrate the circumstances that led to " the Battle of the Baltic "; and comment on Nelson's course of action on this occasion. 8 marks.

2. What bonds held together the States of ancient Greece against their common enemy ; and what institutions contributed materially to their union ?   8 marks.

3. By whom, and when, was Italy recovered from the Goths ; and how was this country subsequently governed ?   8 marks.

4. Trace the origin of the titles " Emperor " and " Czar." 8 marks.

5. What event led to the change of the ancient name of Anglesey ?
                    8 marks.

6. When and by whom were the Picts and Scots united into one Nation ?
By whom and in what year was the Crown of Scotland united with that of England ?   4 marks.

7. Mention any historical event that occurred at Flushing, and another that occurred at Magdala ; giving the date in each case.
                    4 marks.

8. In what European countries has the title *Consul* been given to the head of the State, and at what periods ?   4 marks.

9. What was the full title under which the present King of Sweden was proclaimed ?   4 marks.

10. What important events occurred in the years 1509 and 1690 respectively ?   4 marks.

REASONING.—50 Marks.

One hour and a half allowed for this paper.

N.B.—*Only five questions to be attempted.*

Mr. DOWNING, Head Inspector.
Mr. O'CONNOR, District Inspector.

1. What name do we give to the act of the mind in taking in the significance—(*a*) of a term, (*b*) of a proposition, and (*c*) of an argument; and what names do we apply to defects in each of these cases respectively?
10 marks.

2. "There is no set of men less engaged in dispute and controversy than Mathematicians; who are the most constantly occupied in reasoning." What mistake is this argument used to disprove? State the argument in syllogistic form.
10 marks.

3. "The advantage of technical terms is just like what we derive from the use of any other common terms." Explain this statement fully.
10 marks.

4. State an example in which the cause is employed, as an argument to prove the existence of its effect.
10 marks.

5. Describe any mode of exposing a fallacy to a man who has no knowledge of the technical rules. Illustrate your answer by an example.
10 marks.

6. Of the two processes, abstraction and generalisation, which is dependent on the other, and why?
5 marks.

7. Quote or frame a syllogism in which the reasoning is conclusive, whilst all three propositions are false.
5 marks.

8. Where is ambiguity most likely to occur in a fallacy? Give an example.
5 marks.

9. What are the two apparent exceptions to the rule that the predicate of an affirmative proposition is undistributed? Show that these are merely *apparent* exceptions.
5 marks.

10. When are sound arguments apt to be discarded as fallacious?
5 marks.

COMPOSITION.—50 Marks.

One hour and a half allowed for this subject.

N.B.—*Only one subject to be selected.*

Mr. PURSER, Head Inspector.
Mr. DALTON, District Inspector.

1. Railways.
2. Newspapers.

METHODS, SCHOOL ACCOUNTS, COMMISSIONERS'
RULES.—50 Marks.

Two hours allowed for this paper.

N.B.—*Only five questions to be attempted.*

Mr. DOWNING, Head Inspector.
Dr. BATEMAN, District Inspector.

1. Describe the arrangements for keeping all classes employed, where the staff consists of one teacher and one paid monitor, during half an hour for which the time-table prescribes,—for the junior division, reading, and for the senior division, dictation; all classes being represented
12 marks.

Appendix A.
Examination
Questions.

Male
Teachers.

O Papers

2. During what lesson, in particular, should the pupils stand in drafts of limited size; and why? At what number would you fix the limit in this case?   12 marks.

3. Describe the lines on which instruction on the Map of the World should proceed from the commencement.   12 marks.

4. In what schools, and to what extent should marching be practised? What time should be given to it? What are the points to be attended to, in order to teach pupils to march properly?   12 marks.

5. Describe minutely the daily process of recording the attendance in a National school, and the means to be adopted to secure accuracy.
                                                                      12 marks.

6. What two-fold harm results from permitting the brighter pupils to laugh at the blunders of the dull ones?   6 marks.

7. What use should be made of the scale on a map?   6 marks.

8. Describe fully the occasions on which the Religious Instruction Certificate Book comes into use.   6 marks.

9. When, in a reading lesson, there occurs a word capable of various applications, whether is it preferable to explain all the various significations of it, or to confine oneself to the explanation of its meaning in the passage? Give a reason for your answer.   6 marks.

10. Why should a teacher avoid addressing the school whilst any noise prevails?   6 marks.

ARITHMETIC.—100 Marks.

Two hours and a half allowed for this paper.

N.B.—*Only five questions to be attempted.*

Mr. Stronge, Head Inspector.
Mr. O'Riordan, District Inspector.

1. (a.) Explain the meaning of the terms—*true discount, commercial discount*, and *present worth.*

(b.) The true discount on a bill for three months drawn on August 8th and discounted on August 28th, at 7½ per cent., was £3 18s. 9d. Find the worth of the bill when discounted.   20 marks.

2. By selling tea at 2s. 3d. a pound, a grocer gained $\frac{1}{11}$ of his outlay. What would he have gained per cent., if he had sold the tea for 2s. 6d. a pound?   20 marks.

3. For doing a certain work, A's ability is equal to the joint ability of B and C. If A and B together could do the work in 9⅓ hours, and C by himself in 48 hours, in what time could B alone do it?
                                                                      20 marks.

4. What must be the price of the 3 per cents. in order that a buyer may receive 3½ per cent. interest on his money?   20 marks.

5. Find the amount of £875 at the end of fifteen months at 4 per cent. per annum, compound interest, the interest accruing quarterly.
                                                                      20 marks.

6. Multiply ·03875 of 2 gallons 1 pint by ·025, and divide the product by ·1½.   10 marks.

7. Find a decimal multiplier for converting English into Irish miles.
                                                                      10 marks.

8. Find the square root of $\frac{1}{100}$, and express it as a decimal to 3 places.
                                                                      10 marks.

9. I bought a horse for £75, and sold him by auction, immediately afterwards, at a profit of 20 per cent.: how much did I receive—the auctioneer charging me 7½ per cent. for his services?   10 marks.

10. What decimal of $\frac{1}{100}$ of 2 acres Irish is $\frac{1}{10}$ of 1 acre statute?

GRAMMAR AND DERIVATIONS.—50 Marks.

Two hours allowed for this paper.

N.B.—*Only five questions, of which the parsing exercise must be one, are to be attempted.*

Mr. Pearse, Head Inspector.
Mr. Murphy, District Inspector.

Appendix L.
Examining Questions.
Male Teachers.
C Papers

1.   *Avoid extremes; and shun the fault of such
Who still are pleased too little or too much.
At every trifle scorn to take offence,
That always shows great pride or little sense :
Those heads, as stomachs, are not sure the best
Which nauseate all, and nothing can digest.
Yes let not each gay turn thy rapture move,
For fools admire, but men of sense approve :
As things seem large which we through mist descry,
Dulness is ever apt to magnify.*

Parse the words in *italics.*   20 marks.

2. Write a general analysis of the following :—His resentments so seldom hurried him into any blunder, that it may be doubted whether what appeared to be revenge was anything but policy.   10 marks.

3. Of what may the subject of a verb consist ? Give examples.   10 marks.

4. Justify or correct the following sentences, giving your reason in each case.

    (a) Such expressions sound harshly.
    (b) I had several men died in my ship of fever.
    (c) Be not too tame neither.
    (d) The ebb and flow of the tides were explained by Newton.
    (e) Hoping that I will soon hear from you, believe me, yours truly.   10 marks.

5. Give five derivatives from the Latin root *pono*, I place ; and trace the root-meaning in each of your examples.   10 marks.

6. Give the present tense and the past participle of the verbs of which the following are the past tenses—*lay, wound, bore, flew, durst.*   5 marks.

7. Name the compound personal pronouns, and explain how they are used.   5 marks.

8. On what grounds is the use of the present-perfect tense in the following sentences justified :—

    (a.) Strange events have occurred this century.
    (b.) Cicero has written orations.   5 marks.

9. Explain as to a class the grammatical peculiarities of the italicised words in the following sentences :—

    The patient is one Le Fevre, a lieutenant in *Angus's.*
    'Tis Innisfail, rings o'er the echoing sea.
    Many a *little* makes a mickle.   5 marks.

10. Why must it, under all circumstances, be wrong to say, " will I " ? What forms are allowable ?   5 marks.

PENMANSHIP.—40 Marks.

Half an hour allowed for this exercise.

Your penmanship will be judged from the neatness and accuracy with which you copy the following passages :—

> Forlorn ! the very word is like a bell
> To toll me back from thee to my sole self !
> Adieu ! the fancy cannot cheat so well
> As she is famed to do, deceiving elf.
> Adieu ! adieu ! thy plaintive anthem fades
> Past the near meadows, over the still stream,
> Up the hill-side ; and now 'tis buried deep
> In the next valley glades :
> Was it a vision, or a waking dream ?
> Fled is that music : do I wake or sleep !

When Paradise Lost first appeared, though it was not neglected, it attracted no crowd of imitators, and made no visible change in the poetical practice of the age. Milton stood alone and aloof above his times ; the bard of immortal subjects, and, as far as there is perpetuity in language, of immortal fame. The very choice of these subjects bespoke a contempt for any species of excellence that was attainable by other men.

————

DICTATION AND SPELLING BOOK SUPERSEDED.

50 Marks (including 20 Marks for Dictation).

One hour and a half allowed for this paper.

N.B.—Only five questions to be attempted.

Mr. STRONGE, Head Inspector.
Mr. LEHANE, District Inspector.

The passage for Dictation is to be taken from the Sixth Book of Lessons, page 412, from "Thirdly, it is shown" down to "with water or only with air." 20 marks.

1. Correct the spelling of the following words, giving reasons for your correction :—*accomodate, disipation, camparin, obiesance, rapeedy, feasable.*
6 marks.

2. *Abound, precarious, Norwich, tragedy, endeavour, Dublin.* Give the etymology of these words, referring each to the language from which it is derived. 6 marks.

3. In the case of the following words of unsettled orthography, which spelling do you prefer, and why ?—*Ardour, ardor ; ecstacy, ecstasy ; civilize, civilise ; downfall, downfal ; licence, licence ; thrash, thresh .*
6 marks.

4. (a) Explain clearly why the sound of an English word is of little assistance, as a rule, to the hearer who desires to spell the word; and (b) describe the proper method of teaching spelling. 6 marks.

5. Write the present participles of the following verbs, and show how the rules for spelling apply to each case :—*vary, demur, vie, traffic.*
6 marks.

6. Give the derivation of the following words; point out the changes which have taken place in the forms of the prefixes; and explain the causes of these changes:—*expletion, immortal, suppress.*   3 marks.

7. Write notes on :—' To *file* a bill,' 'to *stand* at bay,' ' to *brood* over.'
    3 marks.

8. The prefixes *in* and *be* have each two distinct meanings. Give examples.
    3 marks.

9. What are the different meanings of :—*Hind, deal, grave* ?
    3 marks.

10. Spell fully the words of which the following are abbreviations :—
e.g., &c., 8vo., Anon.   3 marks.

———

GEOMETRY AND MENSURATION.—50 Marks.

Two hours and a half allowed for this paper.

N.B.—*Only five questions to be attempted.*

Mr. SULLIVAN, Head Inspector.
Mr. KELLY, District Inspector.

1. If a line be divided in extreme and mean ratio, the greater segment will be cut in the same manner by taking on it a part equal to the less. Prove.   10 marks.

2. As a corollary from Propositions IV. and VII., Book II., show that " the square on the sum of two lines plus the square on their difference is equal to twice the sum of the squares on the lines."
    10 marks.

3. The radius of a circle is 10 inches : find the area of each of the three spaces into which it is divided by two parallel chords, each 10 inches.   10 marks.

4. Prove Proposition 6, Book II., by describing a square on half the given line.   10 marks.

5. The bisector of any angle bisects the corresponding re-entrant angle. Prove.   10 marks.

6. Show that the bisectors of the adjacent angles, which one right line standing on another makes with it, are at right angles to each other.
    5 marks.

7. The angle C of the triangle A D C is obtuse, and perpendiculars from A and B to the opposite sides produced, meet these in E and D : show that the rectangle A C, C E is equal to the rectangle B C, C D.
    5 marks.

8. The radius of a circle is 8 feet ; find the area of a sector which contains an angle equal to one of the angles of an equilateral triangle.
    5 marks.

9. If one angle of a triangle be greater than another angle, the side which is opposite to the greater angle is greater than the side which is opposite to the less.   5 marks.

10. What propositions in the First Book prove that triangles are congruent ? What is the hypothesis in each of these propositions ?
    5 marks.

Appendix L.
Exami-
nation
Questions.

Male
Teachers.

0 Papers.

BOOK-KEEPING.—50 Marks.

Two hours allowed for this paper.

N.B.—*Only five questions to be attempted.*

Mr. COSNELLAN, Head Inspector.
Mr. W. J. BROWNE, District Inspector.

1. State of my affairs on 1st January, 1893 :—

		£	s.	d.
Assets.—Cash in hand,		400	0	0
	John Browne,	50	0	0
	Wm. Jones,	30	0	0
	Goods,	00	10	0
Liabilities.—John Sheridan,		250	0	0
	Patrick O'Neill,	100	0	0
	Bills Payable, due 15th Jan.,	45	10	0
6th.	Bought of J. Mulhall, goods,	200	0	0
,,	Sold W. Jones, goods,	80	0	0
,,	Cash paid J. Mulhall (he allowed me £2 discount),	198	0	0
10th.	Sold Wm. Armstrong, goods,	30	0	0
11th.	Received of Wm. Armstrong (I allowed him 3s. discount),	10	17	0
12th.	Bought of Arnott & Co., goods,	130	10	6
,,	Accepted Arnott's Draft at two months for amount of account,	130	10	6
14th.	Sold Patrick O'Neill, goods,	25	0	0
,,	Accepted P. O'Neill's draft on me at two months, for Viz. :—Balance of account, £75, one month's interest, 4s. 8d.	75	4	8
15th.	Paid my Acceptance, due this day,	45	10	6
17th.	Received of W. Jones, cash,	50	10	0
	And his Acceptance for two months, for Viz. :—Amount of account, £110, interest, 8s. 9d.	59	18	9
30th.	Discounted with M'Millan & Co., Jones' Bill,	59	18	9
	Discount,	0	10	6
	Cash received,	£59	8	3

Goods on hand may be valued at £200.
Journalise.   15 marks.

2. Post into Ledger, and balance the different Accounts. 15 marks.
3. I have made the following errors :—

(a). I posted £20 to Dr. side of J. Smith, instead of Dr. side of W. Thomson.

(b). I have journalised cash Dr. to J. Edwards, £37 10s., when it should have been £39 10s.

(c.) Goods Dr. to J. Jones. I have posted this entry correctly, as regards the goods account, but I have made no entry in Jones's account. Show how each error is to be rectified.   8 marks.

4. The sum of the Cr. side of the Stock, as posted at the beginning of the year, exceeds that of the Dr. side by £1,000 ; and the Profit and Loss Account is closed in these words :—To Stock, £351. What is the balance of the Balance Account ?   8 marks.

5. John Miller sold James Rafferty 250 tons of wheat; ten tons were damaged before delivery, and the seller pays the buyer £5 for the loss. How does John Miller journalize the transaction?   6 marks.

6. May 4.   Consigned to W. Rice for Sale on my
   account, three hhds. of Whiskey, £ s. d.
   invoiced at . . . 64 0 0
 „ 5. Paid cost of shipping ditto, . . 1 10 0
 „ 28. Received from W. Rice, account, sales of
   Whiskey, sold for £90, less freight
   £3 10s., and commission £2 5s., . 84 5 0

Post and close the Ledger account for this consignment. On the supposition that Rice sold the whiskey in one lot for cash, give his Ledger account of the transaction.   5 marks.

7. August 4th, sold J. Graham 500 bags of flour, at £2 per bag; received from him my acceptance (cancelled) of the 1st August to him for £600, and his acceptance for remaining £400 at two months. £1,000. Journalize.   5 marks.

8. Journalize the following transactions:—

Jan. 1st.—(a.) Discounted with the Ulster Bank, John Browne's acceptance for £600, and allowed for discount £5. (b.) My acceptance of Smith's draft paid at Ulster Bank this day.   5 marks.

9. I had on hand at the beginning of the year, 200 lbs. of tea, at 2s. per lb. and during the course of my business I sell none of it. When the books are being closed, the price is 4d. in the lb. lower than its first cost. How is the account closed?   5 marks.

10. John Jones accepts my draft on him for £90. I give this when due to W. Stephenson with £30 cash for sugar worth £120. Journalize.   5 marks.

ALGEBRA.—50 Marks.

Two hours and a half allowed for this paper.

N.B.—Only five questions to be attempted.

Mr. STRONGE, Head Inspector.
Mr. FEDLOW, District Inspector.

1. The price of one kind of sugar is 2s. 6d. per cwt. more than that of another kind, and £1 will purchase 30 lbs. less of the first kind than of the second: find the price per cwt. of each kind.   10 marks.

2. Prove—
$$\frac{b}{a+b} + \frac{b^2}{(a+b)(2a+b)} + \frac{b^3}{(2a+b)(3a+b)} = \frac{3b}{3a+b}$$
                10 marks.

3. Find the highest common factor of—
$$(6x^2 - 13xy + 5y^2)\{(x+y)^2 - 1\} \text{ and}$$
$$\{4y^2 - (x^2 - y^2 - 1)^2\}(3x - 2y).$$
                10 marks.

4. Divide—
$$\frac{1}{x^m} - 2 + x^m \text{ by } \frac{1}{x^{\frac{m}{2}}} - x^{\frac{m}{2}}$$
                10 marks.

Appendix L.

Exami-
nation
Questions.

Male
Teachers.

O Papers.

5. Solve—

$$\frac{x+7}{x+8} + \frac{x+9}{x+7} = \frac{5}{2}.$$

10 marks.

6. Solve—

$$1.35x + 0.1y = 13.2$$

$$\frac{x}{3} - \frac{y}{0.4} = 1.75.$$

5 marks.

7. Reduce to its lowest terms the fraction —

$$\frac{15x^2 - 6x^2 + 8}{18x^3 + 3x^2 + 1}.$$

5 marks.

8. Simplify—

$$\frac{1}{x-y} - \frac{1}{x+y} - \frac{2y}{x^2+y^2} - \frac{4y^3}{x^4-y^4}.$$

5 marks.

9. Find the fraction which becomes $\frac{4}{5}$, if 1 be added to the numerator, but which becomes $\frac{1}{2}$, if 1 be added to the denominator.

5 marks.

10. Extract the square root of :—

$$9x^4 - 2x^3 - \frac{161}{9}x^2 + 2x + 9.$$

5 marks.

LESSON BOOKS.—50 Marks.

Two hours allowed for this paper.

N.B.—Only five questions to be attempted.

Mr. SULLIVAN, Head Inspector.
Mr. W. J. BROWNE, District Inspector.

1. Mention circumstances which were favourable to the commercial spirit of the Phœnicians. Give details regarding the route by which merchandise was generally brought from India to Tyre.   10 marks.

2. Enumerate the methods that have from time to time been employed to reduce the National Debt. What is the only proper method?   10 marks.

3. As an exercise in composition write an essay on "Life at Sea," or on "The Mitchelstown Caves."   10 marks.

4. What is the composition of bronze? How does ancient differ from modern bronze? For what purposes was it used in ancient times?   10 marks.

5. In what three ways may an insurer dispose of his share of the profits of the Company in which he is insured?   10 marks.

6. Give a brief account of the life of Dr. Johnson.   5 marks.

7. What is the traditional belief as to the "petrifying qualities" of the water of Lough Neagh? Mention arguments for, and against, the belief in question.   5 marks.

8. Describe the ruins of the Banqueting Hall at Tara.   5 marks.

9. What is spermaceti; where is it procured; and how?   5 marks.

10. Give, in the words of Macaulay, the character of Sir Philip Francis.   5 marks.

GEOGRAPHY.—60 Marks.

Two hours allowed for this paper.

N.B.—Only five questions to be attempted.

Mr. CONNELLAN, Head Inspector.
Mr. ALEXANDER, District Inspector.

1. Draw an outline map of Ireland, as large as your paper will allow; sketch the course of the Shannon and of its tributaries, filling in the boundaries of the bordering counties, and marking the position of all important towns built on the Shannon, or on its tributaries.
12 marks.

2. Explain any method by which a navigator may determine the amount of error of his chronometer, if it should fail to keep exact time.
12 marks.

3. (a) Give an account of Holland under the following heads:—Area, population, government, exports.
(b) Name four chief towns and state some circumstance of note respecting each.
12 marks.

4. In what towns of Great Britain are the following manufactures principally carried on:—Flannel, jute, pins, cutlery? In what county is each town situated?
12 marks.

5. Name the maritime counties of Wales with their chief towns; give the two highest mountains of the Principality; and state the county in which they are situated.
12 marks.

6. Name three rivers between the mouth of the Tweed and Spurn Head, with an important town on each.
6 marks.

7. Where, and for what noted, are Leith, Deptford, Rheims, Sacramento?
6 marks.

8. From what countries do we obtain mahogany, diamonds, cinnamon, respectively?
6 marks.

9. What and where are—Scholdt, Manchooria, Sumatra, Connecticut?
6 marks.

10. Why is the snow line higher on the northern side of the Himalayas than it is on the southern side?
6 marks.

AGRICULTURE.—60 Marks.

Two hours and a half allowed for this paper.

N.B.—Only five questions to be attempted.

Mr. CONNELLAN, Head Inspector.
Mr. CRAIG, District Inspector.

1. What are albuminoids? Of what use are they in the animal system? Name the kinds of food in which they are most abundant.
10 marks.

2. In what three ways do bones act when decaying in a soil?
10 marks.

3. A large field with an undulating surface is to be thoroughly drained. Explain how this should be done.
10 marks.

4. Describe the preparation of the ground for barley, and the proper methods of sowing this crop.
10 marks.

Y

Appendix I.
Examination
Questions.

Male
Teachers

C Papers.

5. Describe the Anglo-American plough, and state its advantages.
10 marks.

6. What are the best ways of fastening cows in stalls? 5 marks.

7. Why is peat the best covering for manure heaps? 5 marks.

8. Write down a six-course rotation suitable for a one-horse farm of a hilly nature, and show why this rotation is specially suited for such a farm. 6 marks.

9. Describe the cultivation of celery. 6 marks.

10. What soils are best suited for pears, cherries, plums, and currants, respectively? 5 marks.

II.—FEMALE TEACHERS.

METHODS, SCHOOL ACCOUNTS, COMMISSIONERS' RULES.—60 Marks.

Two hours allowed for this paper.

N.B.—*Only five questions to be attempted.*

Mr. DOWNING, Head Inspector.
Dr. BATEMAN, District Inspector.

1. What emotions may be made use of, in school, with a view to encouraging the pupils to be more diligent? Show that, when making use of these emotions for this purpose, great care and moderation are, in some instances, necessary. 12 marks.

2. Specify, in order, the different steps to be taken when instructing a class in the cutting-out of a bodice. 12 marks.

3. What duties, in connection with the school, devolve on the teacher outside of the regular school hours? 12 marks.

4. Criticise the following time-table arrangements for Senior division:—Needlework, 10 to 10¾ o'clock; Roll-call; Arithmetic (desk), 11 to 11½; Writing, 11½ to 12; Play; Dictation or Transcribing, 12½ to 1; Reading and Home Lessons, 1 to 1½; Grammar and Geography, alternately, 1½ to 2; Arithmetic (floor), 2 to 2½; Religious Instruction, 2½ to 3; Extra Subjects, 2½ to 3½. 12 marks.

5. Give the substance of the Rule which determines the conditions under which the appointment of a paid monitor is recommended. 12 marks.

6. Suggest twelve subjects of a varied character, suitable for letters by pupils of Sixth class. 6 marks.

7. What are the regulations with respect to the classification and promotion of pupils; and what is the prudent course in those cases in which the regulations leave the teacher an option? 6 marks.

8. Write six questions suitable to test whether your pupils can distinguish which simple rule of arithmetic should be used according to the occasion. 6 marks.

9. Show the evil of attempting to include too much matter in one lesson. 6 marks.

10. Give the substance of the Rules which relate to the inscription required to be placed on every National School-house. 6 marks.

Appendix L.

Examination Questions.

Female Teachers.

A¹ Papers.

ARITHMETIC.—100 Marks.

Two hours and a half allowed for this paper.

N.B.—*Only five questions to be attempted.*

Mr. STRONGE, Head Inspector.
Mr. DEWAR, District Inspector.

1. Show how the process of multiplication can in certain cases be shortened by the use of a complementary number. Find by this means the product of 39,998 and 17,883,246, and prove the result by casting out the nines.   20 marks.

2. A, B and C go into partnership. A is to get 10 per cent, and B 8 per cent of the profits, as managers, and the remaining profits are to be divided proportionally to the capital of each. It is found at the end of the year that the profits are equally divided. Find the ratio between the three capitals.   20 marks.

3. If the interest on £8,825 at 4 per cent, be equal to the discount on £11,119 10s. for the same time and at the same rate, when is the latter sum due?   20 marks.

4. A man wishes to settle on his son a yearly income of £100, clear of an income tax of 8d. in the £1; what sum of money must he invest for this purpose in the 2½ per cent. Consols at 94½?   20 marks.

5. (a.) Explain the difference between a decimal, a decimal fraction, and a vulgar fraction.

(b.) Simplify:—

$$1\tfrac{1}{2} \text{ of } 3\tfrac{1}{4} + 6\tfrac{1}{2} \div 2\tfrac{1}{4} - \left\{ \frac{5\tfrac{1}{2} + \cdot 24 + \cdot 53}{2\tfrac{1}{4} - \cdot 64} \right\}.$$ 20 marks.

6. Find the difference between the banker's discount and the true discount on £129 3s. 7d. due in five months at 7½ per cent. 10 marks.

7. A man travels 60 miles in 3 hours, partly by rail and partly by car; but if he had gone all the way by rail, he would have ended his journey an hour sooner, and saved ¾ of the time he was on the car. How far did he go by car?   10 marks.

8. A quantity of tea is sold for 4s. 7d. per lb., the gain is 10 per cent., and the total gain is £24. What is the quantity of tea sold?   10 marks.

9. If 3 men, 5 women or 8 children could do a certain work in 26½ days; in what time will 3 men, 3 women and 4 children do it?   10 marks.

10. Give examples of short methods of multiplying by 99, 996, 125, and of dividing by 25 and 125.   10 marks.

GEOGRAPHY.—60 Marks.

Two hours allowed for this paper.

N.B.—*Only five questions to be attempted.*

Mr. CONNELLAN, Head Inspector.
Mr. WORSLEY, District Inspector.

1. Draw a map of the Japanese Islands and the opposite coast of Asia, indicating with names the positions of Jeddo, Miaco, Nagasaki, Matsmai.   12 marks.

2. Compare the length of the day and the *periodic time* in each of any two planets, with the length of our day and the *periodic time* of the earth.   12 marks.

3. Give the substance of Elphinstone's description of the South-west Monsoon in India.   12 marks.

T 2

4. What and where are—Taurus, Helsingfors, Bencoolen, Tras-os-Montes, Providence, Curaçao ?   12 marks.

5. Name the thirteen original States of the United States with a town in each.   12 marks.

6. What are the three natural divisions of the mainland of Scotland; and how are they separated from one another ?   6 marks.

7. Define the following terms :—

(a.) Elevation of the Pole; (b.) Right Ascension; (c.) Amplitude; (d.) the Colures.   6 marks.

8. From what countries do we obtain (a.) Amber; (b.) Arsenic; (c.) Sulphur; (d.) Asphalt ?   6 marks.

9. Give a general description of the Atlas mountains.   6 marks.

10. Name three naval stations of France; and mention at least one city of France noted for the production or export of wine, of silk, and of lace, respectively.   6 marks.

PENMANSHIP.—40 Marks.

Half an hour allowed for this exercise.

Your penmanship will be judged from the neatness and accuracy with which you copy the following passages :—

> Darkling I listen : and for many a time
> I have been half in love with easeful Death,
> Called him soft names in many a mused rhyme,
> To take into the air my quiet breath ;
> Now more than ever it seems rich to die,
> To cease upon the midnight with no pain,
> While thou art pouring forth thy soul abroad
> In such an ecstasy !
> Still would'st thou sing, and I have ears in vain—
> To thy high requiem become a sod.

The clouds of his allegory may seem to spread into shapeless forms, but they are still the clouds of a glowing atmosphere. Though his story grows desultory, the sweetness and grace of his manner still abide by him. We always rise from perusing him with melody in the mind's ear, and with pictures of romantic beauty impressed on the imagination.

GRAMMAR AND DERIVATIONS.—60 Marks.

Two hours allowed for this paper.

N.B.—*Only five of these questions, of which the parsing exercise must be one, are to be attempted.*

Mr. Purser, Head Inspector.
Mr. Dickie, District Inspector.

1. So many *journeys* may the sun and moon
   Make us again count o'er, ere love be done !
   But, *wo is me*, you are so sick of late,
   So far from cheer, and from your former state,
   That I distrust you. Yet, though I *distrust*,
   Discomfort you, my lord, *it nothing must.*
   For women fear too much, even as they love,
   And women's fear and love hold quantity ;
   In neither *aught*, or in extremity.
   Now, *what* my love is, proof hath made you know,
   And, as my love is *sized*, my fear is so.

Parse the words in Italics, and paraphrase the passage.   20 marks.

2. Give a general and a particular analysis of the following lines :—

> And I, alas! survive alone,
> To muse o'er rivalries of yore,
> And grieve that I shall hear no more
> The strains that envy heard before ;
> For, with my minstrel brethren fled,
> My jealousy of song is dead.   12 marks.

3. Distinguish between the *impersonal* and *indefinite* use of *it*, and the use of *it* as *formal subject*. Give examples of each.   10 marks.

4. "Two or more nouns or pronouns occurring in the same simple sentence, and referring to the same person or thing, agree in case." Give examples to illustrate (1) the general rule ; (2) the apparent exceptions ; and of each example write an explanation suitable for a sixth class.   10 marks.

5. Name the different parts of a simple sentence, and state in what order they are usually arranged. Why is this order sometimes departed from ? Give examples.   8 marks.

6. Classify subordinate sentences, and write out a complex sentence containing an example of each class.   8 marks.

7. Explain the origin or derivation of *Io, alas, dear me, lord, spinster.*   5 marks.

8. Distinguish between the meaning of the two following sentences :—
(a.) If it rains I will not go. (b.) If it rain I will not go. 5 marks.

9. Explain as to a sixth class the grammar of the italicised words, and their force in the sentence :—

> (a) A few short *hours*, and he will rise
>   To give the morrow birth.
> (b) *'Twere* long to tell what stends gave o'er.
> (c) Then happy, *low*, lie down.
> (d) Go, *get thee* from me.   5 marks.

10. In what metres are the following lines written ? Mark the metres by the usual symbols :—

> (a) O solitude ! where are the charms
>   That sages have seen in thy face ?
> (b) Know ye the land where the cypress and myrtle
>   Are emblems of deeds that are done in their clime ?

          5 marks.

HISTORY.—40 Marks.

One hour and a half allowed for this paper.

N.B.—*Only five questions to be attempted.*

Mr. DOWNING, Head Inspector.
Mr. ROGERS, District Inspector.

1. Mention ten leading events in the history of England from the 13th to the 16th century inclusive, assigning dates.   8 marks.
2. Detail the circumstances under which Cyrus added all Asia Minor to his dominions.   8 marks.
3. On what two occasions did the Turks unsuccessfully attack Vienna ? Give the dates, and mention by whom they were repulsed on each occasion.   8 marks.

Appendix L.
Exami-
nation
Questions.

*Female
Teachers.*

A' Papers.

4. Give an account of the rise of the kingdom of Media, and name three kings who reigned over this kingdom.   8 marks.

5. What led to the abolition of the East India Company, and when did the abolition take place?   8 marks.

6. What reference is made to Parthalon in the legendary history of Ireland? In what annals does this legend appear?   4 marks.

7. To what three powers successively were the Netherlands subject between the end of the 14th and the end of the 16th centuries?
          4 marks.

8. Give an account of the training to which the military superiority of the Spartans was due.   4 marks.

9. What political change occurred in Spain in 1872?   4 marks.

10. Of what ancestry is the reigning King of the Hellenes?
          4 marks.

ENGLISH COMPOSITION.—50 Marks.

Two hours allowed for this subject.

N.B.—*Only one subject to be selected.*

Mr. Purser, Head Inspector.
Mr. Dalton, District Inspector.

1. Fairy tales.
2. A teacher's influence for good.

ENGLISH LITERATURE.—60 Marks.

Two hours allowed for this paper.

N.B.—*Only five questions to be attempted.*

Mr. Newell, Head Inspector.
Mr. Connelly, District Inspector.

1. Sketch the character of *Ophelia*, illustrating your view by quotations from the Play.   12 marks.

2. Discuss the question whether the Queen was an accessory to the murder of her husband.   12 marks.

3. "When sorrows come, they come not single spies,
      But in battalions."
What examples of the truth of this does the King bring forward?
          12 marks.

4. Comment on the following italicised words:—

(a) "With windlasses and with *assays of bias*."
(b) "Be you and I behind an *arras* then."
(c) "Your ladyship is nearer to heaven, than when I saw you last, by the altitude of a *chopine*."
(d)   "Nymph, in thy *orisons*
      Be all my sins remembered."
(e) "Of the *chameleon's dish*: I eat the air promise-crammed."
(f) "You may choose a sword *unbated*."   12 marks.

5. "While thus he spoke, the bold yeoman
      Entered the echoing barbican;"—
Describe this bold yeoman's appearance, dress, and arms.   12 marks.

6. Quote the ballad verse which Hamlet speaks when the court has *Appendix L* broken up in disorder after the representation of the " Play " (The Examination Questions. murder of Gonzago).   6 marks.

7. What two reasons does the King give Laertes for not proceeding against Hamlet after the death of Polonius ?   6 marks.   Female Teachers.

8. Explain the following:—*blackbut-men, lever-darting, morning-horns, kartizan, sorgoon-schrio, pencils.*   6 marks.   A' Papers.

9. In what connexion do the following passages occur :—

   (a) " *Those that are married already, all but one, shall live.*"
   (b) " *Nay an thou't mouth, I'll rant as well as thou.*"
   (c) " *Though this be madness, yet there's method in it.*"

                      6 marks.

10. Quote the line which succeeds each of them—

   (a) " *For all of wonderful and wild* "—
   (b) " *All mourn the Minstrel's harp unstrung* "—
   (c) " *The Harper smiled, well pleased, for ne'er* "—   6 marks.

METHODS, SCHOOL ACCOUNTS, COMMISSIONERS' RULES.—60 Marks.   A. Papers.

Two hours allowed for this paper.

N.B.—*Only five questions to be attempted.*

Mr. DOWNING, Head Inspector.
Dr. BATEMAN, District Inspector.

1. Discuss fully the suitability of the following time-table arrangements for Senior division :—Writing, 10 to 10½ o'clock ; Grammar or Geography, 10½ to 11 ; Preparing Lessons, 11 to 11½ ; Reading and Home Lessons, 11½ to 12 ; Play ; Dictation and Transcribing, alternately 12½ to 1 ; Arithmetic (F.), 1 to 1½ ; Arithmetic (D.), 1½ to 2 ; Needlework, 2 to 3 (four days, letter on Monday).   12 marks.

2. Draw up full notes of a lesson, for the instruction of monitors, on the annual motion of the earth.   12 marks.

3. Explain definitely to what extent school work done on Saturday is recognised towards earning results fees.   12 marks.

4. What preparation is necessary before proceeding with the parsing of a difficult passage ? Take an example, and show how you would deal with it.   12 marks.

5. Describe six "appropriate exercises" for an infant class in an ordinary National School.   12 marks.

6. Describe fully how a teacher may impress on the school her own style of reading.   6 marks.

7. State definitely what *details* it is possible and proper to teach under the head of letter-writing.   6 marks.

8. Describe an effective plan for the revision of written home exercises.   6 marks.

9. Give details as to the manner in which a cloak-room should be fitted up ; and also how provision should be made for cloaks, &c., in case there is no cloak-room.   6 marks.

10. Define what is understood by school organisation ; and name one main object of every system of school organisation.   6 marks.

Appendix L.
Examination Questions

Female Teachers.

A Papers.

ARITHMETIC.—100 Marks.

Two hours and a half allowed for this paper.

N.B.—*Only five questions to be attempted.*

Mr. Strowke, Head Inspector.
Mr. Dewar, District Inspector.

1. (*a*) State and prove the rule for dividing one vulgar fraction by another.

(*b*) Find the value of

$$1\tfrac{1}{3}(3\tfrac{1}{2} - 2\tfrac{1}{3}) \times \left(\tfrac{1\frac{1}{4}}{\frac{3}{3\frac{1}{7}}} - \tfrac{\frac{9}{7}}{1\frac{1}{7}} \right) + 13\tfrac{1}{2}\left(\tfrac{4\frac{1}{3}\frac{7}{7}}{6\frac{1}{3}\frac{1}{7}} + \tfrac{1\frac{2}{3}}{1\frac{1}{4}} \right).$$

20 marks.

2. Two pumps discharging respectively 90 and 110 gallons per minute are employed to drain a well. It is observed that if the smaller pump alone is at work the water sinks 4 inches in 3 minutes, and if both are employed from the first, the well is pumped dry in 2½ hours. Find the depth of the well, and how long the larger pump alone would take to pump it dry.   20 marks.

3. The difference between the incomes derived from investing a certain sum in 5 per cent. stock at 133 and in 5½ per cent. stock at 133 is £2 6*s*. Find the amount invested, and the income resulting from each investment. Neglect brokerage.   20 marks.

4. A person by selling goods, which cost £14 per cwt., at 2*s*. 9¾*d*. per lb., makes 5 per cent. more profit than he would have made if he had sold the goods for £55 15*s*. 3¾*d*.; what was the amount sold?   20 marks.

5. The alloy in a shilling is ¹⁄₁₂ of its weight and the coin would be worth ⁴⁄₅*d*., if it were all made of the baser metal; what would be its exact value if it were all pure silver?   20 marks.

6. An article which costs £18 2*s*. 7½*d*. per cwt. is retailed at 4*s*. 6*d*. per lb., and there is a waste of 7½ per cent.; what is the rate of profit per cent.?   10 marks.

7. In a sum in simple proportion when the product of the second and third terms is divided by the first, the quotient must be of the same denomination as the third term. Explain fully why this must be the case.   10 marks.

8. If the 3 per cents. are at 88⅞, what must be the price of the 5 per cents. that it may be advantageous to transfer from the former into the latter, ½ per cent. commission being charged both on the sale and the purchase of stock?   10 marks.

9. A can run ¹⁄₁₇ of a mile in ⅔ of a minute; B can run ¹⁄₁₅ of a mile in ¾ of a minute; and C ⁷⁄₉ of a mile in ⅘ of a minute. Which is the quickest runner? If A can run a certain distance in 3½ minutes, how long will each of the others take?   10 marks.

10. Two men undertake to do a piece of work for £21 1*s*. 6*d*. One could do it alone in 15 days, the other in 24 days. With the help of a third man they finish it in 6 days. How should the money be divided among them?   10 marks.

GEOGRAPHY.—60 Marks.

Two hours allowed for this paper.

N.B.—*Only five questions to be attempted.*

Mr. CONNELLAN, Head Inspector.
Mr. WORSLEY, District Inspector.

1. Draw an outline map of the South of Europe from Venice to Gibraltar, marking the boundaries of the countries, principal cities, mouths of rivers, capes and sea inlets, and adjacent islands.
12 marks.

2. Describe the phases of the moon and account fully for them.
12 marks.

3. Give a brief geographical account of Belgium, under the following heads:—population, area, provinces, rivers, and towns. 12 marks.

4. Describe the Alpine system of lakes, giving the situation of each lake, and the name of the river which is its outlet. 12 marks.

5. Where are the following towns, and for what is each remarkable—Upsala, Toulouse, Frederickshald, Utrecht, Saragossa, Potsdam ?
12 marks.

6. In what ocean do the trade winds blow most regularly ? Explain the cause of this regularity.
6 marks.

7. Refer the following towns to their respective counties, and name the river on or near which each is situated :—Oldham, King's Lynn, Dudley, Danbury, Haverford West, Sudbury. 6 marks.

8. What and where are—Carinthia, Hainault, Innerleithen, Colonna, Marsala, Orissa ?
6 marks.

9. How far are the following rivers navigable :—Nore, Lagan, Boyne, Bandon ?
6 marks.

10. Name the Baltic provinces of Russia, with the principal town of each.
6 marks.

PENMANSHIP.—40 Marks.

Half an hour allowed for this exercise.

Your penmanship will be judged from the neatness and accuracy with which you copy the following passage :—

Darkling I listen : and for many a time
I have been half in love with easeful Death,
Called him soft names in many a mused rhyme,
To take into the air my quiet breath ;
Now more than ever it seems rich to die,
To cease upon the midnight with no pain,
While thou art pouring forth thy soul abroad
In such an ecstasy !
Still would'st thou sing, and I have ears in vain—
To thy high requiem become a sod.

The clouds of his allegory may seem to spread into shapeless forms, but they are still the clouds of a glowing atmosphere. Though his story grows desultory, the sweetness and grace of his manner still abide by him. We always rise from perusing him with melody in the mind's ear, and with pictures of romantic beauty impressed on the imagination.

GRAMMAR AND DERIVATIONS.—60 Marks.

Two hours allowed for this paper.

N.B.—*Only five of these questions, of which the parsing exercise must be one, are to be attempted.*

Mr. PURSER, Head Inspector.
Mr. DICKIE, District Inspector.

1. Now, Richard *Musgrave*, liest thou here !
  I *ween*, my deadly enemy ;
  For if I *slew* thy brother dear,
    Thou slow'st a sister's son to me ;
  And when I lay in dungeon dark
    Of Naworth Castle, long *months* three,
  Till *ransomed* for a thousand mark—
    Dark Musgrave, it *was long* of thee.
  And, Musgrave, *could'st* our fight be *tried*,
    And thou *wert now alive as I*,
  No mortal man should us divide,
    Till one, or both of us *did die* ;
  Yet, *rest thee*, God ! for well I know
  I ne'er shall find a nobler foe.

Parse the words in italics, and paraphrase the passage. 20 marks.

2. Give a particular analysis of the following :—

    This, in obedience, hath my daughter shown me ;
    And more above, hath his solicitings,
    As they fell out by time, by means and place,
    All given to mine ear. 12 marks.

3. Give six rules for the use of figurative language. 10 marks.

4. What is meant by Iambic Pentameter ? Name two varieties of this metre, and a poem written in each variety. State the peculiarity of each variety. 10 marks.

5. After what verbs is "to" as the sign of the infinitive mood omitted ? When must it be inserted after these verbs ? And what other form of the verb may sometimes replace the dependent infinitive ? Give examples. 8 marks.

6. Write notes on the italicised words :—

    (a) *Be* the players ready.
    (b) God *be* his aid.
    (c) *Belike* this show imports the argument.
    (d) I *sat me* down.
    (e) Go *to*. 5 marks.

7. Account for the form of each of the following words :—

    Cherry, sherry, swine, kine, pea. 5 marks.

8. Distinguish between *accent*, *emphasis*, and *intonation*. 5 marks.

9. Give examples of :—

    (a) The omission of the relative ;
    (b) The relative pronoun performing the double function of a relative and a demonstrative pronoun ;
    (c) A part of sentence forming the antecedent to the relative. 5 marks.

10. "It would be easy to show that the conjunction *that* is really a demonstrative pronoun." Write a note on this statement, and illustrate your remarks by suitable examples. 5 marks.

HISTORY.—40 Marks.

One hour and a half allowed for this paper

N.B.—*Only five questions to be attempted.*

Mr. Downing, Head Inspector.
Mr. Nicholls, District Inspector.

1. What suggested to the Athenians to employ Draco to draw up a code of laws? State the character and the result of his legislation.
8 marks.

2. State when the Turks were at the height of their power; and mention three important steps in their decline.   6 marks.

3. Describe the historical event which gave rise to the phrase—"crossing the Rubicon."   8 marks.

4. What circumstances led to the execution of Charles I.?
8 marks.

5. What events affecting the sovereign authority in Spain occurred in the years—1826, 1828, 1854, and 1863 respectively?   8 marks.

6. In what years were two partitions of the ancient territory of Poland effected; and in what year did the final dismemberment of that country take place?   4 marks.

7. Explain the circumstances under which Alphonso XVI. came to the throne of Spain.   4 marks.

8. What important work was constructed by Mœris, one of the early kings of Egypt?   4 marks.

9. Mention any remarkable incident related of the Roman general Cincinnatus.   4 marks.

10. Give a short description of the condition of Britain at the time of the Roman invasion.   4 marks.

COMPOSITION.—50 Marks.

Two hours allowed for this subject.

N.B—*Only one subject to be selected.*

Mr. Purser, Head Inspector.
Mr. Dalton, District Inspector.

1. Pleasures of reading.
2. Duty.

ENGLISH LITERATURE.—60 Marks.

Two hours allowed for this paper.

N.B.—*Only five questions to be attempted.*

Mr. Newell, Head Inspector.
Mr. Connelly, District Inspector.

1. Give quotations from the Play favouring the view that Hamlet's madness was real.   12 marks.

2. Give the substance of Hamlet's advice to the Players as to elocution, &c.   12 marks.

Appendix L.
Examination
Questions.

Female
Teachers.

A Papers

3. Mention some facts regarding the political history of *Denmark*, *England*, and *Norway*, which may be gleaned from the Play.

12 marks.

4. Explain the portions of the following extracts which are italicised :—

(a) "The clown shall make those laugh whose lungs are *tickle o'
the sere.*"

(b)   "for she may strew
Dangerous conjectures in *ill-breeding minds.*"

(c) "Where it draws blood no *cataplasm* so rare . . . . . can
save the thing from death."

(d) "I once did hold it, as our *statists* do,
A *baseness* to write fair."

(e) "For women's fear and love *holds quantity.*"

(f) "Madam, it so fell out that certain players
We *o'er-raught* on the way." 12 marks.

5. Give the substance of the three stanzas in Fitztraver's song beginning—

"*But soon within that mirror huge and high*"

12 marks.

6. Quote the substance of the Ladye's reply to the herald of Lord
Howard, beginning—

"Say to your Lords of high emprize.'   6 marks.

7. Explain the following :—

Harquebuss, floating wraith, ombre rare.   6 marks.

8. Write notes on—

(a) "*Mobled queen.*"
(b) "*My dearest foe.*"
(c) "*A vice of Kings.*"   6 marks.

9. Comment on the following italicised words—

(a)   "Young Fortinbras   .   .   .
Hath in the skirts of Norway here and there
Shark'd up a list of lawless resolutes"—

(b) "Why do you go about to *recover the wind* of me as if you
would drive me into a toil?"

(c) "Yet here she is allow'd her virgin *crants,*
Her maiden strewments, and the bringing home
Of bell and burial."   6 marks.

10. "When for the lists they sought the plain,
The stately Ladye's silken rein
Did noble Howard hold."

Describe the attire of noble Howard   6 marks.

Appendix L.

Examination Questions.

Female Teachers.

B Papers.

METHODS, SCHOOL ACCOUNTS, COMMISSIONERS' RULES.—60 Marks.

Two hours allowed for this paper.

N.B.—*Only five questions to be attempted.*

Mr. Dowling, Head Inspector.
Mr. M'Glade, District Inspector.

1. Write out notes of a lesson on government in Syntax.
13 marks.

2. At what stage should the pupils begin to use paper in school for Arithmetical exercises? What are the common faults in such exercises; and how are these faults to be corrected?
13 marks.

3. What is the requirement of the school programme for each class in the subject of *cutting-out;* and what are the garments to be exhibited by the girls of each class?
13 marks.

4. What is the rule which determines how the religious denomination of a new pupil is to be ascertained?
13 marks.

5. What is the proper temperature for a school-room; and how should the temperature be regulated? How is proper ventilation to be secured? Give the substance of the Practical Rule that refers to ventilation.
13 marks.

6. Offer some suggestions as to the *manner* of giving a lesson with a view to securing the greatest possible attention of the pupils.
6 marks.

7. Point out the causes and the evil of *unequal classification.* How is this evil to be remedied?
6 marks.

8. Write out the requirements of the programme under heads (b) and (c) of Reading for Classes III., IV., and V¹., respectively.
6 marks.

9. State the circumstances which determine (a) the position of the draft-space in a school-room; (b) the breadth of this space; (c) the number of circles to be traced in it.
6 marks.

10. What entry in the Daily Report Book indicates the degree of regularity of attendance; and how is the calculation for this entry made?
6 marks.

ARITHMETIC.—100 Marks.

Two hours and a half allowed for this paper.

N.B.—*Only five questions to be attempted.*

Mr. Synotch, Head Inspector.
Mr. Dwan, District Inspector.

1. (a.) State and prove the rule for reducing fractions to equivalent fractions having a common denominator.

(b.) Simplify

$$\left(1\tfrac{1}{2} + \tfrac{3}{4} + \tfrac{5}{9}\ \text{of}\ \tfrac{7}{8\frac{1}{4}} - \tfrac{11\frac{1}{4}}{2\frac{1}{4}}\right) \div 2\tfrac{7}{11}.$$

20 marks.

2. If a merchant gain ·142857 of the prime cost of an article by selling it at £2·69, at what price must he sell it to gain 75 per cent.?
20 marks.

Appendix L.
Examination
Questions.

Female
Teachers.

D Papers.

3. If 5 horses require as much corn as 8 ponies, and 16 qrs. last 12 ponies for 64 days, how many horses may be kept 96 days for £41 5s., when corn is £1 2s. per quarter ?   20 marks.

4. A bill of £170 12s. 6d. is drawn on the 22nd December, 1885, at 6 months, and is discounted on the 29th April, at 3¾ per cent. ; how much will the banker retain ?   20 marks.

5. If I buy 10 shares of £20 each at 27½, and sell out at 37½, after receiving a dividend of 15 per cent.; how much shall I gain in all ?   20 marks.

6. A mixture is made of 27 tons of coal at 17s. 9d. per ton, 19 tons at 22s. 6d. per ton, and 11 tons at 19s. 4d. Find the value per ton of the mixture.   10 marks.

7. A drover buys 87 oxen for £1,740. He sells 25 at 7 per cent. profit, and 40 at 12½ per cent. profit ; he loses 3 by disease, and sells the rest at cost price. How much does he gain or lose ?   10 marks.

8. Find the least number which, when divided by 33, 171, and 1,900, will always leave the same remainder, 21.   10 marks.

9. A person paid ·15 of a certain sum to one person, and ¼ of the remainder to another. If at the end he had £38, what had he originally ?   10 marks.

10. Add together ⁵⁄₇ of ·2781 of 3 cwt. 1 qr. 21¼ lbs. ; 5·24 of 3 qrs. 15½ ozs.; and ¾ of ·084 of 12¾ ozs. ; express the answer in ounces and the decimal of an ounce.   10 marks.

GEOGRAPHY.—60 Marks.

Two hours allowed for this paper.

N.B.—*Only five questions to be attempted.*

Mr. CONNELLAN, Head Inspector.
Mr. WORSLEY, District Inspector.

1. Draw a sketch map of the coasts of the Irish Sea, marking the mouths of the rivers that run into it, and the principal islands.   12 marks.

2. What are the principal exports of the following countries :—Brazil, Argentine Confederation, Italy, West Indies ?   12 marks.

3. Give some account of six of the principal cities of Italy, as to historical associations, position and population.   12 marks.

4. Describe the Equatorial current in the Pacific Ocean.   12 marks.

5. What and where are—Shiraz, Corrientes, Benguela, Popocatapetl, Thaiss, Cettinje ?   12 marks.

6. Where are the poles of maximum cold in the Northern hemisphere ? How is their position accounted for ?   6 marks.

7. Describe the river system of China.   6 marks.

8. Describe the course of the tidal wave in the Atlantic Ocean. Why is high water later on the East Coast than on the West Coast of the British Islands?   6 marks.

9. What rivers drain Loch Awe, Lough Conn, Lake Bala ?   6 marks.

10. Describe the positions of the Chagos Archipelago, Botany Bay, Lake Titicaca, Island of Gozo.   6 marks.

Appendix L.

Examination Questions.

French Teachers.

B Paper

PENMANSHIP.—40 Marks.

Half an hour allowed for this exercise.

Your penmanship will be judged from the neatness and accuracy with which you copy the following passages : —

Darkling I listen : and for many a time
I have been half in love with easeful Death,
Called him soft names in many a mused rhyme,
To take into the air my quiet breath ;
Now more than ever it seems rich to die,
To cease upon the midnight with no pain,
While thou art pouring forth thy soul abroad
     In such an ecstasy !
Still would'st thou sing, and I have ears in vain—
To thy high requiem become a sod.

The clouds of his allegory may seem to spread into shapeless forms, but they are still the clouds of a glowing atmosphere. Though his story grows desultory, the sweetness and grace of his manner still abide by him. We always rise from perusing him with melody in the mind's ear, and with pictures of romantic beauty impressed on the imagination.

DICTATION AND SPELLING BOOK SUPERSEDED.

50 Marks (including 20 Marks for Dictation).

One hour and a half allowed for this paper.

N.B.—*Only five questions to be attempted.*

Mr. STRONGE, Head Inspector.
Mr. DALY, District Inspector.

The Dictation Exercise is to be taken from the Sixth Book, page 316, from—"And like snow did they descend," to "and behind them a desert."   20 marks.

1. What is a perfect alphabet? What are the imperfections of the English alphabet? What letters or groups of letters in the following words illustrate these imperfections :—snatch, exotes, honey, though?
                                                                              6 marks.

2. Give three instances of groups of words in regard to the spelling of which modern usage is at variance with Dr. Johnson's authority. Justify as far as possible the modern spelling.   6 marks.

3. Mark the silent letters in the following words, and account in each case for their occurrence :—psalm, abscind, rhythm, malign, schism, palm.   6 marks.

4. Con, over, sub. Group with each of these prefixes a prefix of similar meaning from another language. Refer each prefix to its proper language and quote words illustrating each.   6 marks.

5. Why is the English language particularly rich in synonymes? What are the two chief faults in the employment of synonymous terms? Give two synonymes for each of the following words :—adherent, curious, dark.   6 marks.

Appendix L.
Exami-
nation
Questions.

Female
Teachers.

8 Papers.

6. In the case of each of the first three rules of spelling, give a word exemplifying the rule and a word illustrating an exception to the rule.
3 marks.

7. Give examples of words in which *ent*, *al*, *en* are used (*a*) as prefixes; (*b*) as affixes.
3 marks.

8. Give four examples of common nouns derived from names of places, and two examples of common nouns derived from names of persons.
3 marks.

9. *Pomegranate, malability, dipthong.* Correct the spelling of these words, justifying your correction in each case by reference to the derivation.
3 marks.

10. "In English as in all other languages there are families of words." Explain this statement and give examples of "families of words."
3 marks.

GRAMMAR AND DERIVATIONS.—60 Marks.

Two hours allowed for this paper.

N.B.—*Only five questions, of which the parsing exercise must be one, are to be attempted.*

Mr. Purser, Head Inspector.
Mr. Murphy, District Inspector.

1   'Tis *he* the obstructed paths of sound shall clear,
And *bid* new music charm the unfolding ear.
The dumb shall sing, the *lame* his crutch *forego*
And *leap exulting, like* the bounding roe.
No sign, no murmur, the wide world shall hear;
From every face be wiped off every tear.
In adamantine chains *shall death be bound*,
And hell's grim tyrant *feel* the eternal wound.
As the good shepherd tends his fleecy care,
Seeks freshest pasture, and the purest air;
Thus shall *mankind* his guardian care *engage*,
The promised *father* of the future age.

Parse the words in italics; and paraphrase the passage.
20 marks.

2. Write a general analysis of the following sentence:—Rasselas, who knew not that any one was near him, having for some time fixed his eyes upon the goats that were browsing among the rocks, began to compare their condition with his own.
10 marks.

3. Write the remarks which you would consider necessary for a Sixth Class on the use of the verbs *dare, quoth, wit, worth.*
10 marks.

4. Give two prepositions that follow each of the words—*compare, disappointed, reduce, contend*; and form sentences showing the proper use of each preposition.
10 marks.

5. Show reasons for considering the preposition in the case of compound transitive verbs to be substantially a part of the verb; and mention other ways in which an intransitive verb may become transitive.
10 marks.

6. Explain and illustrate the use of the note of interrogation.
5 marks.

7. What are idioms ? Give two classes of idioms, and two examples of each class.   5 marks.

8. Explain, as to a class, the grammar of the Italicised words :—

 Who chucks at me, to death is *dight*.
 The choughs *show scarce so gross as beetles*.
 An't please your honour.   5 marks.

9. Give general rules for forming the plurals of Latin and Greek nouns in use in our language, with an example under each rule.
 5 marks.

10. Give the derivation of *stipend, scurrilous, ratify, posthumous, precipitate.*   5 marks.

Appendix I.
Examination Questions.
Female Teachers.
D Papers.

LESSON BOOKS.—50 Marks.

An hour and a half allowed for this paper.

N.B.—*Only five questions to be attempted.*

Mr. SULLIVAN, Head Inspector.
Dr. MORAN, District Inspector.

1. *Macbeth.* "I am settled ; and bend up
 Each corporal agent to this terrible feat.
 Away, and mock the time with fairest show :
 False face must hide what the false heart doth know."

Under what circumstances was this speech made ? Explain as you would to a class, "*Each corporal agent,*" "*Mock the time with fairest show,*" "*False face must hide.*"   10 marks.

2. Mention facts which fully establish the early origin of the *Catacombs.* Assign, approximately, a date to their origin.   10 marks.

3. In general the authors who lived in Johnson's early days were wretchedly poor. How does Lord Macaulay account for this fact ; and how does he account for the further fact that Pope, Young, and Richardson were exceptions ?   10 marks.

4. "In making *barley-broth*, most persons violate, to a serious extent the most obvious principles of good cookery and economy." Show fully how these principles are violated in the case in question.   10 marks.

5. What faults does Dr. Johnson attribute to Shakespeare as a writer ?   10 marks.

6. Give a brief description of the peninsula known as Island Magee.
 5 marks.

7. Explain the following extracts from Sir Walter Scott's *Marmion* and *Lady of the Lake* :—

 "E'en such a falcon, on his shield,
  Soar'd noble in an azure field."
 "There morricers, with bell at heel,
  And blade in hand, their maze wheel."
 5 marks.

8. Two conditions are mentioned in the Girls' Reading Book as essential, in order that it may be possible to go near persons suffering from fever, without serious risk of infection. What are the two conditions ?   5 marks.

9. Discuss the suggestion of Petrie that the *Lia Fail* still remains at Tara.   5 marks.

10. Name the principal varieties of the Eagle family, and describe any one variety.   5 marks.

E

Appendix I.
Exami-
nation
Questions.

Female
Teachers

B Paper. .

BOOK-KEEPING.—50 Marks.

Two hours allowed for this paper.

NB.—Only five questions to be attempted.

Mr. Connellan, Head Inspector.
Mr. MacMillan, District Inspector.

1.

		£	s.	d.
Inventory, 1st March, 1893.				
Cash,	. . . .	46	13	6
Sugar—67 cwt, 1 qr., 4 lbs., at 45s. 6d.,				
per cwt.,	. . .	153	1	8
Tea—3 cwt, 1 qr., 12 lbs., at 2s. 6d., per lb.	.	75	0	0
Wine—Port, 6 pipes at £75,	. .	450	0	0
Sherry, 4 butts at £60,	. .	240	0	0
In Provincial Bank,	. . .	250	0	0
Debts due to me—Thom & Co.,	. .	40	0	0
John Williamson,	.	67	10	0
Bills receivable.				
John Smith's acceptance, due 17th				
March,	. . . .	50	0	0
Edward Reid's do., due 15th				
April,	. . .	45	10	0
Warehouse and stores,	.	150	0	0
I owe William Edwardes,	. .	36	10	0
„ Robert Johnston,	. .	80	0	0
Bills payable.				
No. 10—Drawn by Dowley & Co., at 2				
months, dated 10th January,	.	135	12	6
No. 11—Drawn by Todd, Burns, & Co.,				
at 3 months, dated 10th February,	.	50	0	0
2nd March—Received from E. Rambaut invoice				
of brandy, shipped per *Star*, 12				
cases at 50s.,	. .	30	0	0
Freight and charges, .	.	2	10	0
Paid duty on do.,	.	20	0	0
4th „ Paid Robert Johnston by cheque,	.	40	0	0
Drew from bank,	. .	30	0	0
7th „ Sold Todd, Burns, & Co., 20 cwt,				
2 qrs. of sugar at 50s. per cwt.,	.	51	5	0
Journalise the foregoing transactions.		15 marks.		

2. Enter the transactions in the Ledger. Balance and close the Ledger. Goods on hand to be valued as in Inventory.

15 marks.

3. Paid by cheque on Provincial Bank to P. Cotter for goods forwarded to J. & C. Kitts, per their order, . £714 15 0
My commission on which is . 17 17 0
————— £732 12 0

Journalize and explain.

8 marks.

4. May 5. Received from T. Ball his acceptance at 3 months for £405, being the balance of his account £400, with interest, £5. Journalise.

6 marks.

5. Received from John Wallace the account of our sales of wine—

Sale of 6 pipes,	£720	0 0
His commission, 2½ per cent.,	18	0 0
Net proceeds,	702	0 0
My half,	351	0 0

He pays me by a draft on the Provincial Bank for that sum, which I lodge there. Explain these transactions, and give the journal entries. 6 marks.

6. Explain what is meant by "Protest," "Adventure in Company," "Factorage." 5 marks.

7. On which side must the balance (a.) of a bills payable account be, and (b.) that of a bills receivable account? Give reasons for your answer. 5 marks.

8. Specify three distinct kinds of error that may occur in posting into the Journal and Ledger, and state in each case how the mistake is to be corrected. 5 marks.

9. June 14. Received from Ingham & Co., to be sold on their account and risk, cotton invoiced at	£410	0 0
„ 10. Paid freight and charges on Ingham & Co.'s cotton,	131	11 8
„ 31. Sold J. Jackson in one lot Ingham & Co.'s consignment of cotton,	600	0 0
My commission is	15	0 0

Post and close the account for this consignment on the supposition that the proceeds are not transmitted to consignors. 5 marks.

10. Describe fully the method of tracing entries from one book to another. 5 marks.

COMPOSITION.—50 Marks.

Two hours allowed.

N.B.—*Only one subject to be selected.*

Mr. Purser, Head Inspector.
Mr. Dalton, District Inspector.

1. Dress.
2. Savings Banks.

HISTORY.—40 Marks.

An hour and a half allowed for this paper.

N.B.—*Only five questions to be attempted.*

Mr. Downing, Head Inspector.
Mr. Rogers, District Inspector.

1. When, and under what circumstances, did the third great monarchy of antiquity, that is to say, the Macedonian empire, terminate? Give the names of the three chief kingdoms formed out of this territory; and the name of the first sovereign of each. 8 marks.

2 2

Appendix L.
Kxamination
Questions.

*Female
Teachers.*

D Papers.

2. When were Schleswig and Holstein annexed to Prussia? On what grounds were these provinces then severed from Denmark?
8 marks.

3. Which side did the "Grand Alliance" take in the famous Spanish war at the commencement of the 18th century? What was the occasion of this war?
8 marks.

4. Through what crisis in her history was Greece passing in the year B.C. 480? Who was the most famous Athenian of that period?
8 marks.

5. From whom did the Houses of Lancaster and York respectively originate? Why were the civil wars between these rivals called the "Wars of the Roses"?
8 marks.

6. Mention some signs of social and commercial progress in Russia during the reign of the present emperor.
4 marks.

7. Divide the history of the Middle Ages into six periods; mentioning both events and dates.
4 marks.

8. What remarkable reference is made to the Island of Thanet in early English history?
4 marks.

9. From what years has England held possession of :—(a) Australia; (b) Malta ; (c) Cyprus; (d) Mauritius?
4 marks.

10. Explain the historical allusions in the following lines quoted from a well-known poem of Byron's :—

    (a) The King was on his throne,
    (b) A captive in the land,
    (c) The Mede is at his gate !
    The Persian on his throne !
                        4 marks.

C Paper.

METHODS, SCHOOL ACCOUNTS, COMMISSIONERS' RULES.—60 Marks.

Two hours allowed for this paper.

N.B.—*Only five questions to be attempted.*

Mr. DOWNING, Head Inspector.
Mr. M'GLADE, District Inspector.

1. How should the first lessons in Arithmetic be conducted up to the stage at which children understand the addition of abstract numbers? What apparatus will be required ?
12 marks.

2. Give six of the most useful hints as to the proper method of pointing at a map lesson.
12 marks.

3. Describe the manner in which Grammar is to be taught, and define the portion of this subject in which each class should be instructed, in order to meet the requirements of the school programme.
12 marks.

4. What exercise is suggested with a view to add new words permanently to the child's vocabulary ?
12 marks.

5. What entries are to be made each year in the Register, in the case of pupils examined for payment of Results Fees ; and, again, in the case of those not so examined?
12 marks.

6. For what class is each of the following exercises in Needlework prescribed in the school programme:—Plain patching, top sewing, plain darning, knitting a sock completed to the heel, working button-holes, and sewing on gathers ?
6 marks.

7. If a pupil had been absent for a day or two, with what home work would you expect her to come prepared ?   6 marks.

8. What provision would you make for the recapitulation of poetry; and why ?   6 marks.

9. Explain the difference in the nature of the following errors in a written exercise:—'similiar,' and 'durind,' for 'during.' State whether you would mark the latter as an error, or not; and give your reason.   6 marks.

10. Under what circumstances may a school day be excluded from the calculation of the quarterly averages ?   6 marks.

ARITHMETIC.—100 Marks.

Two hours and a half allowed for this paper.

N.B.—Only five questions to be attempted.

Mr. Steaner, Head Inspector.
Mr. Dewar, District Inspector.

1. What are prime numbers?
Find the prime factors of 111,540 ; 42,330 ; and 67,392 ; and thence write down their Least Common Multiple and their Greatest Common Measure.   20 marks.

2. Simplify ·1875 of £5 11s. 8d. + ⅓ of ·81 of 4s. 9½d. ÷ ·001 of £1 0s. 10d., and reduce the result to the decimal of £10 4s. 7d.   20 marks.

3. Find the price of 4½ per cent. stock when an investment of £869 5s. produces an income of £42 15s.   20 marks.

4. A contractor agrees to execute a certain work in a certain time ; he employs 55 men who work 8 hours daily ; when ⅔ of the time is expired he finds that only ⅘ of the work is done.   How many men must he employ during the rest of the time, working 11 hours daily, in order that he may fulfil his contract ?   20 marks.

5. (a) At what rate per cent. will a given sum of money double itself in 30 years at simple interest ?
(b) Explain your work.   20 marks.

6. Find the circulating decimal which will become 9 when multiplied by 3⅞ + 4⅓.   10 marks.

7. A merchant spends £1,036 5s. on equal quantities of wheat at 42s. a quarter, barley at 21s., and oats at 14s.   How much grain will he have ?   10 marks.

8. If 5½ per cent. would be gained by selling 242 yards of silk for £53 3s. 9½d., at what price per yard must the silk be sold to gain 12 per cent. ?   10 marks.

9. What is the true present worth of £276 10s. 5d. due in 219 days at 3½ per cent. per annum ?   10 marks.

10. Make out neatly the following bill of parcels, and sum it up :—
1 tea chest of 43 lbs. at 1s. 7d. per lb. ; 1 barrel of sugar of 5 cwt. at 1½d. per lb. ; ¼ ton of flour at 1s. 3d. per stone ; 100 loaves at 3½d. per loaf, and 1 43-gallon cask of paraffin at 4½d. per gallon.   10 marks.

Appendix L,
Exami-
nation
Questions.

*Female
Teachers.*

O Papers.

GEOGRAPHY.—60 Marks

Two hours allowed for this paper.

N.B.—*Only five questions to be attempted.*

Mr. CONNELLAN, Head Inspector.
Mr. WORSLEY, District Inspector.

1. Draw a map of Lough Neagh and the counties which surround it, giving the full outline of each county.   12 marks.

2. Give proofs of the sphericity of the earth, derived from astronomical observation.   12 marks.

3. What manufactures are carried on in Kilmarnock, Newtowards, Luton, Macclesfield, respectively? In what county is each town situated?   12 marks.

4. What is the exact position of each of the following inlets of the sea:—Loch Long, Kyles of Bute, Loch Fyne, Loch Linnhe? What are the branches of the Moray Firth?   12 marks.

5. Give the position and the geographical designation of the following:—Bangkok, Negrais, Perim, Labrador, Tangier, Susquehana.
    12 marks.

6. In what counties are the following towns, and what are they noted for:—Yarmouth, St. Albans, Chesterfield, Chatham, Helensburgh, Peterhead?   O marks.

7. The degrees of latitude are of unequal length, and so also are the degrees of longitude. Explain the reason in each case.   O marks.

8. In what parts of Ireland are the following minerals found:—Lead, iron pyrites, clayslate?   O marks.

9. On what rivers are the following towns:—Manchester, Warwick Guildford, Merthyr-Tydvil? What is the seaport of Merthyr-Tydvil?
    O marks.

10. Name the three largest of the British West Indian Islands, with their chief towns and productions.   O marks.

PENMANSHIP.—10 Marks.

Half an hour allowed for this exercise.

Your penmanship will be judged from the neatness and accuracy with which you copy the following passages:—

> Darkling I listen ; and for many a time
> I have been half in love with easeful Death,
> Called him soft names in many a mused rhyme,
> To take into the air my quiet breath ;
> Now more than ever it seems rich to die,
> To cease upon the midnight with no pain,
> While thou art pouring forth thy soul abroad
> In such an ecstasy !
> Still would'st thou sing, and I have ears in vain—
> To thy high requiem become a sod.

The clouds of his allegory may seem to spread into shapeless forms, but they are still the clouds of a glowing atmosphere. Though his story grows desultory, the sweetness and grace of his manner still abide by him. We always rise from perusing him with melody in the mind's ear and with pictures of romantic beauty impressed on the imagination.

Appendix I.
Examination Questions.
Female Teachers.
C Papers.

DICTATION AND SPELLING BOOK SUPERSEDED.
60 Marks (including 20 Marks for Dictation).
One hour and a half allowed for this paper.

N.B.—*Only five questions to be attempted.*

Mr. STRONGE, Head Inspector.
Mr. DALY, District Inspector.

The Dictation exercise is to be taken from the Sixth Book, page 346, from " And like snow did they descend " to "and behind them a desert."   20 marks.

1. What is accent ? Give examples of words having (a) a secondary accent ; (b) unsettled accentuation ; (c) different accentuation to denote difference of meaning. To what does Dr. Sullivan ascribe the occurrence of the weak accent in words of three syllables ?   6 marks.

2. Why are the following words considered as difficult or irregular in spelling or pronunciation :—*inveigle, soiree, tenet, surfeit, satyr, atrocity* ?   6 marks.

3. Give the derivations of the following words—*utter, lass, court, rifle, sheriff, mayor.*   6 marks.

4. How are the ordinary Lesson Books to be made use of in teaching children to spell ?   6 marks.

5. What words are liable to be confounded by incorrect speakers with *ingenious, lineament, elicit* ? Give the meanings of both words of each pair.   6 marks.

6. Explain the origin of the Italicised letter in each of the following words—*arrogate, occur, anticipate.*   3 marks.

7. Name, with examples, some terminations in which the position of the accent serves as a guide to the pronunciation of the final syllable.   3 marks.

8. What words are pronounced like or nearly like the following—*pencil, whilst, depositary* ? Give the meaning of both words in each pair.   3 marks.

9. Form frequentatives from *poss, roam, whine.*   3 marks.

10. Correct, where necessary, or justify the spelling of the following words, in each case referring to the rule—*paddock, bienous, tainess.*   3 marks.

GRAMMAR AND DERIVATIONS.—60 Marks.
Two hours allowed for this paper.

N.B.—*Only five questions, of which the parsing exercise must be one, are to be attempted.*

Mr. PURSER, Head Inspector.
Mr. MURPHY, District Inspector.

1.
" My *birthday* "—*what* a different *sound*
That word had in my youthful ears !
When first our *scanty* years are told
It means like pastime to grow old ;
And *as* youth counts the shining links
That time around him binds so fast,
Pleased with the task he little thinks
How *hard* that chain *will* press at last,
Vain *was* the man, and *false* as *vain,*
Who said, '*were* he ordained to run
His long career of life again,
He *would do all that he had done.'*

Parse fully the words in *Italics.*   20 marks

Appendix I.
Exami-
nation
Questions.

Female
Teachers.

C Papers.

2. Give a general analysis of the following:—

The whale possesses no gills through which it may respire and renew its blood through the agency of the water, but breathes atmospheric air in the same manner as the other mammalia.

10 marks.

3. Correct or justify each of the following sentences, giving your reason :—

(a) He played the worser part.

(b) O thou, my lips inspire,
Who touched Isaiah's hallowed lips with fire.

(c) I hoped to leave school in January.

(d) Some children can only read words of four letters.

(e) The bread that has been eat is soon forgotten.

10 marks.

4. Point out the exact difference of signification between the past tense, and the present perfect tense, and illustrate by examples.

10 marks.

5. Explain the force of the following prefixes, and state from what language each is derived :—

un, prae, apo, peri, subter.   10 marks.

6. Construct phrases to show *either* as (a) a pronoun, (b) a conjunction.   5 marks.

7. Give rules as to the ellipsis of the relative pronoun.

5 marks.

8. Write notes of a lesson on the formation of the plural of nouns, omitting words derived from foreign languages.

5 marks.

9. Explain the meaning of the terms—*finite* and *indefinite* moods.

5 marks.

10. Name four verbs that have both a transitive and an intransitive form.   5 marks.

LESSON BOOKS.—50 Marks.

An hour and a half allowed for this paper.

N.B.—Only five questions to be attempted.

Mr. SULLIVAN, Head Inspector.
Mr. W. J. BROWN, District Inspector.

1. As an exercise in composition write an essay on Old Irish Books, or give an account of the Giants' Causeway.   10 marks.

2. Mention the chief events which attended the third voyage of Columbus, and also those which occurred on his return from that voyage.   10 marks.

3. Mention the circumstances which are said to have caused King Alfred to study Latin. Name two of his translations from Latin authors. Were they mere translations? Explain.   10 marks.

4. In describing Westminster Abbey, Addison remarks, "I observed that the present war had filled the church with many of these uninhabited monuments."

(a) What do you understand by "the present war"?

(b) Explain the phrase "uninhabited monuments."   10 marks.

Appendix L.

Exami-
nation
Questions.

Sample
Papers.

O Papers.

5. In case of apparent death from drowning, what treatment should be adopted by a person endeavouring to restore life?
10 marks.

6. How is starch prepared for use? 5 marks.

7. How is lunar caustic prepared? Mention some of its uses.
5 marks.

8. In the lesson on Travellers' Wonders, Captain Compass describes the food eaten by the inhabitants of a country which he visited. Give the substance of his description, and after describing each food tell its name. 5 marks.

9. What were the circumstances under which Mahommed Reza Khan obtained the government of Bengal? 5 marks.

10. Give the date, the parties engaged, and the result of the Battle of Hohenlinden. 5 marks.

III.—MONITORS OF THIRD YEAR

Monitors.
D Papers.

METHODS OF TEACHING.—60 Marks.

Two hours allowed for this paper.

N.B.—Only four questions to be attempted.

Mr. Downing, Head Inspector.
Mr. M'Glade, District Inspector.

1. How may you detect if a First Class pupil is merely repeating a lesson by rote instead of actually reading it; and how may you ascertain whether the pupil has been allowed to pass through the previous lessons in this imperfect manner? 15 marks.

2. When should children be expected to divide by *factors*; and to what degree of difficulty should this process be taught to pupils still learning the Simple Rules? 15 marks.

3. What fact makes Spelling at first seem of very serious difficulty; and what circumstance greatly lessens the difficulty of learning to spell?
15 marks.

4. At a map lesson, you are directed to "teach features of the same kind together." Explain fully what you are to avoid doing, and what course you are to pursue, in order to comply with this direction.
15 marks.

5. How are the tables of weights and measures best taught, and how may a ready knowledge of these tables be kept up? 8 marks.

6. How should a pupil be made to comport himself when reading in class? 8 marks.

7. When is a child of Infant class fit to be advanced to a new lesson?
7 marks.

8. What faults needing correction are apt to occur at the ends of some of the lines of dictation exercises? 7 marks.

ARITHMETIC.—100 marks.

· Two hours and a half allowed for this paper.

N.B.—*Only four questions to be attempted.*

Mr. Strong, Head Inspector.
Mr. O'Riordan, District Inspector.

1 (a.) Define the terms—Concrete number, prime number, descending reduction, ratio. Give one example in each case.

(b.) Being given the value of a ratio, and the antecedent, how do you find the consequent?   35 marks.

2. I buy 56 lbs. of tea at 3s. 6d. a lb., and sell one-half of it at 3d. an oz.: at what price per oz. must I sell the other half, in order to gain, on the whole, 50 per cent.?   25 marks.

3. Taking gold as worth at the Mint £3 17s. 10½d. per oz., and silver at 2½d. per oz. How many sovereigns weigh as much as 100 half-crowns? The amount of alloy in the coins may be neglected.

25 marks.

4. Divide 6 gallons and 7 pints by

$$1\tfrac{1}{2} + \frac{3\tfrac{1}{4} - \tfrac{1}{3}}{3\tfrac{1}{3} + \tfrac{1}{3}} - (2\tfrac{3}{4} \text{ of } \tfrac{1}{13}) - \tfrac{3}{7}.$$

25 marks

5. If a 2d. loaf weighs 33 oz. when wheat is 54s. per quarter, what is the price of wheat per quarter when the 3d. loaf weighs 24 oz.?

15 marks.

6. Extract the square root of $514\tfrac{11}{16}$.   10 marks.

7. Find the rent of 40 acres 2 roods 20 perches, statute measure, at £1 8s. 9d. per Irish acre.   15 marks.

8. Find by Practice the price of 3 tons 11 cwt. 2 qrs. 8 oz. at £1 14s. 3d. per cwt.   10 marks.

GRAMMAR.—60 Marks.

Two hours allowed for this paper.

N.B.—*Only four questions, of which the parsing exercise must be one, are to be attempted.*

Mr. Power, Head Inspector,
Mr. Dickie, District Inspector.

1. Parse the words in *italics*:—

If the oak—the true British *oak*—*be* the *forest* king, *let us give him at least* a *partner* in his majesty ; and let the chestnut, *whose* noble *head is crowned* by the hand of spring with a regal diadem, *gemmed* with *myriads* of *pearly,* and *golden,* and *ruby flowers,* let her be *queen of* the woods.   24 marks.

2. Correct the following sentences, giving reasons for your changes:—

(a.) This picture of the king's does not resemble him.

(b.) None of my hands are empty.

(c.) I have been here this two hours.

(d.) If one went unto them from the dead, they will not repent.

12 marks.

3. Write out the first and second persons singular of the second future indicative, of the perfect potential, and of the present subjunctive of the verb *to be*.   12 marks.

4. Name the three kinds of pronouns, and their subdivisions. Give two examples of each.   12 marks.

5. Decline *lady, sheep, child,* in singular and plural.   6 marks.

6. In the following sentences change the verbs into the passive voice, if possible; if this cannot be done, state why :—

   (a.) The mother loves her child.
   (b.) I went to him every day.
   (c.) No man can serve two masters.
   (d.) Let him write a letter.   6 marks.

7. Illustrate by examples the fact that adjectives may be used as substantives, and substantives as adjectives.   6 marks.

8. Derive the following words, and state from what language each is drawn :—*Antagonist, malicious, contagious, irradiate.*   6 marks.

PENMANSHIP.—40 Marks.

Half an hour allowed for this exercise.

Your penmanship will be judged from the neatness and accuracy with which you copy the following passages :—

Forlorn ! the very word is like a bell
To toll me back from thee to my sole self !
Adieu ! the fancy cannot cheat so well
As she is famed to do, deceiving elf.
Adieu ! adieu ! thy plaintive anthem fades
Past the near meadows, over the still stream,
Up the hill-side ; and now 'tis buried deep
In the next valley glades :
Was it a vision, or a waking dream ?
Fled is that music : do I wake or sleep ?

When Paradise Lost first appeared, though it was not neglected, it attracted no crowd of imitators, and made no visible change in the poetical practice of the age. Milton stood alone and aloof above his times ; the bard of immortal subjects, and, as far as there is perpetuity in language, of immortal fame. The very choice of those subjects bespeaks a contempt for any species of excellence that was attainable by other men.

DICTATION AND SPELLING BOOK SUPERSEDED.

50 Marks (including 30 Marks for Dictation).

One hour and a half allowed for this paper.

N.B.—*Only four questions to be attempted.*

Mr. STRONGE, Head Inspector.
Mr. DALY, District Inspector.

The Dictation Exercise is to be taken from the Fifth Book, page 281, from "The disturbed state of Portugal," down to "superiority."   30 marks.

1. Form two adjectives from *pity* by adding the affixes *ful* and *ous*, a noun from *rob*, and a diminutive from *hill*, and quote the rule of spelling or exception to rule under which each falls.   8 marks.

Appendix L.
Exami-
nation
Questions.
Monitors.
D Papers.

2. Correct the spelling of the following words and give reasons for the changes you make :—*disunde, misconstrue, peacable, allurment.*
8 marks.

3. Quote or form sentences to illustrate the difference in meaning between—*mend* and *mead*; *principle* and *principal*; *effected* and *affected*; *stationery* and *stationary.*
8 marks.

4. Give the meanings of *site, fane, coarse*; and name in the case of each (giving the meanings) *two* other words similarly pronounced.
6 marks.

5. Correct the spelling of *awaful, trafficing, mischrif*, and *modeler*, and give reasons for your corrections.
4 marks.

6. Write out the fourth rule for spelling and give four examples, one for each of the following affixes, *able, ish, ance, ous.*
4 marks.

7. Give the different meanings of *dist, shaft, moor, bale.*   4 marks.

8. What words are frequently confounded by incorrect speakers with *salary, ordinance, eminent*? Write out the pairs of words in tabular form giving the meaning of every word.
3 marks.

— —

GEOMETRY AND MENSURATION.— 50 Marks.

Two hours and a half allowed for this paper.

N.B.—Only four questions to be attempted

Mr. SULLIVAN, Head Inspector.
Mr. M'NEILL, District Inspector.

1. Prove the second part of Euc. I. 28, independently of I. 27, and of the first part; and when proved, derive I. 27 and the first part of I. 28.
13 marks.

2. If the extremities of two unequal parallel straight lines be joined, the lines drawn will meet if sufficiently produced through the extremities of the shorter parallel.
12 marks.

3. The breadth of a rectangular garden is 115 links ; what should be its length so that it may contain one rood. Give the answer (1) in links ; (2) in feet.
13 marks.

4. In a right-angled triangle the square on the hypotenuse is equal to the sum of the squares on the other sides.
12 marks.

5. Show how to construct a triangle with sides equal to three given straight lines. What condition must be fulfilled by these three given lines in order to render the problem possible ?
6 marks.

6. Given the difference of the side and the diagonal of a square, to construct it.
7 marks.

7. Each side of an isosceles triangle is 20 feet 6 inches, and the perpendicular is 16 feet. Find the area of the triangle.   7 marks.

8. Give definitions of the following :—*A square*; *a right angle*; *a circle*; *a straight line*; *a triangle.*
5 marks

BOOK-KEEPING.—50 Marks.

Two hours allowed for this paper.

N.B.—*Only four questions to be attempted.*

Mr. CONNELLAN, Head Inspector.

Mr. M'MILLAN, District Inspector.

1.

	£.	s.	d.
1804, May 1—Cash in hand,	320	0	0
Tea, 1,350 lbs., at 1s. 6d.,	03	15	0
„ 2—Sold for cash, 120 lbs. tea, at 2s.,	12	0	0
„ 3—Sold to W. Blair, 500 lbs. at 2s.,	50	0	0
„ 4—Bought of J. Wilson, 360 lbs. at 1s. 6d.,	27	0	0
„ 4—Sold to J. Crawford, 200 lbs. at 2s.,	20	0	0
„ 4—Sold for cash, 160 lbs. at 2s.,	16	0	0
„ 5—W. Blair paid me	50	0	0
„ 5—Bought of J. Wilson, 200 lbs. at 1s. 6d.,	15	0	0
„ 6—Paid J. Wilson,	30	0	0

Journalize these transactions. 14 marks.

2. Open the necessary accounts, post the items, and close the books, valuing tea unsold at 1s. 6d. per lb. 14 marks.

3. Paid J. Ryan the balance of my
account by giving him J. Pigott's
acceptance for . . £40 0 0
And cash in full for remainder, . 18 0 0
————
£58 0 0

Journalize. 12 marks.

4. What is meant by balancing an account? On which side may the balance be found in the following accounts:—Cash, Tea, Balance? 10 marks.

5. What is meant by discounting a bill? I hold J. Williamson's acceptance for £200, due six months hence, and get it discounted at the National Bank for £190. Journalize. 9 marks.

6. It appears from the tea account I have gained £50, and from the tobacco account that I have lost £40. Write out the entry that shows the gain or loss. 6 marks.

7. Write down as a Journal entry the item in the Balance Account which shows that I am worth £5,000 when all the accounts are closed. 5 marks.

8. What account shows whether the accounts in the Ledger have been correctly kept or not? Explain your answer. 5 marks.

———

ALGEBRA.—50 Marks.

Two hours and a half allowed for this paper.

N.B.—*Only four questions to be attempted.*

Mr. STRONGE, Head Inspector.

Mr. GROGAN, District Inspector.

1. At what time after six o'clock are the hands of a watch—

(a) directly opposite;

(b) at right angles to each other? 14 marks.

Appendix L.
Exami-
nation
Questions.
Monitors.
D' Papers.

2. Simplify—

$$\frac{1}{(a-b)(b-c)} + \frac{1}{(c-a)(b-c)} + \frac{1}{(n-c)(b-a)}.$$

13 marks.

3. Solve—

$$\frac{x+y}{5} - \frac{x-y}{9} = 3;$$

$$\frac{x-y}{3} + \frac{x+y}{10} = 0$$

13 marks.

4. Extract the square root of—

$$x^4 - ax^3 + \frac{a^2b^2}{4}.$$

13 marks.

5. If $2x = 3$ and $y = -0.4$, find $x^2 y^3$. 7 marks.

6. Define factor, coefficient, trinomial, index. 6 marks.

7. Solve—

$$\frac{a}{bx} + \frac{b}{ax} = a^2 + b^2.$$

6 marks.

8. Divide $a^5 + a^4b - a^3 - a^2b^2 + 2ab^3 - b^4$ by $a^2 - a + b.$ 6 marks.

———

LESSON BOOKS.—50 Marks.

Two hours allowed for this paper.

N.B.—*Only four questions to be attempted.*

Mr. SULLIVAN, Head Inspector.
Dr. MORAN, District Inspector.

1. As an exercise in composition write in your own words the story of *Ali Beg.* 16 marks.

2. What was Captain Compass's chief object in the conversations which he had with his children as to "*travellers' wonders*"? Give an example showing how he carried out this object. 10 marks.

3. Write out the lines from *The Deserted Village*, from "*Vain transitory splendours*" to "*The mantling bliss goes round.*" 13 marks.

4. Explain the following extracts from the "*Elegy in a Country Churchyard*":—

    (a) "*The stubborn glebe.*"

    (b) "*The unlettered muse.*"

    (c) "*Melancholy marked him for her own.*"

    (d) "*Some village Hampden.*" 12 marks.

5. Explain the causes of rain. 7 marks.

6. Write out the ten lines commencing—

"*Teach me, sprite or bird.*" 8 marks.

7. What remedies should be used when lime gets on the front of the eye or under the eye-lids? 5 marks.

8. In what way are lighthouses useful? What are the duties of the man who has charge of a lighthouse? What are "*wreckers*"? 5 marks.

Appendix I.

Examination Questions.

Model Syllabus.

D Papers.

GEOGRAPHY.—60 Marks.

Two hours allowed for this paper.

N.B.—*Only four questions to be attempted.*

Mr. CONNELLAN, Head Inspector.
Mr. ALEXANDER, District Inspector

1. Draw an outline map of Ireland. Fill in the boundaries of your native county and of the counties bordering thereon. Mark your native county thus—N.C.   15 marks.
2. Explain why the orbit of the earth is an ellipse.   15 marks.
3. Name the three principal mountain ranges in Scotland, and give the name and height of the highest summit in each.   15 marks.
4. Describe the positions of the following :—Gulf of Tartary, Nova Zembla, Strait of Magellan, Lebnan, Lake Garda.   15 marks
5. Name the provinces of British India, with the capital of each.
                                                    8 marks
6. Name the extreme northern, southern, eastern, and western points of Ireland. Give the latitude of the northern and southern points, and the longitude of the eastern and western points.
                                                    8 marks.
7. Explain, and illustrate by diagrams, how summer and winter are caused.   8 marks
8. Name the largest lake in England, Ireland, Scotland and Wales, respectively, stating the precise position of each.   6 marks.

AGRICULTURE.—50 Marks.

Two hours and a half allowed for this paper.

N.B.—*Only four questions to be attempted.*

Mr. CONNELLAN, Head Inspector.
Mr. CRAIG, District Inspector.

1. Why should land intended for root crops be grubbed rather than cross-ploughed in spring?   14 marks.
2. State some of the precautions necessary to keep fowl in health.
                                                    12 marks.
3. At what age, and in what manner, should calves be accustomed to dry food?   12 marks.
4. What is the most profitable way of utilising liquid manure, and why?   12 marks.
5. Manures act in several ways; give four of these ways.
                                                    7 marks.
6. How is malt to be prepared for use in making butter?
                                                    6 marks.
7. State how the ground should be prepared before the planting of fruit trees.   6 marks.
8. At what stage of growth should the following crops be mown :—

    (a.) Italian ryegrass.
    (b.) Perennial ryegrass.
    (c.) Clover.
    (d.) Mixed meadows.   6 marks.

DRAWING.—50 Marks.

Three hours allowed for this subject.

N.B.—*The name of the Monitor and of his School to be written on each paper.*

Mr. NEWELL, Head Inspector.
Mr. CRAIG, District Inspector.

I.—FREEHAND DRAWING.—30 Marks.

Copy the example given, enlarged in breadth about one inch, and proportionately throughout.

II.—OBJECT DRAWING.—12 Marks.

The examiner will lay a book over the centre of a small square table, about three feet high. On the book he will place a flower pot, lying on its side. These objects are not to face the candidates directly. A drawing of the top of the table, with the objects upon it, is to be made, which should fairly fill the paper.

III.—PRACTICAL GEOMETRY.—18 Marks.

NOTE.—*Any three of the following questions may be attempted. Answers should be written on one side of the paper only, and where a construction is not obvious, an explanation should be given, the points being marked with letters.*

Full credit will not be allowed for a question, unless the construction is neatly drawn, and all lines are shown.

1. Construct any triangle A B C, and bisect it by a line parallel to A C.   6 marks.

2. Construct a regular pentagon of 2 inches side, and inscribe a square in it.   6 marks.

3. Construct a scale of two inches to the furlong, showing perches.   6 marks.

4. Inscribe four equal circles in a square of two inch side; each circle is to touch two others, and one side of the square.   3 marks.

5. Draw a tangent to a point P in a given arc of a circle without using the centre.   3 marks.

6. Show how to divide a line A B proportionally to the divisions C d, d e, e f, f D of another line C D.   3 marks.

MUSIC—(HULLAH).—50 Marks.

One hour and a half allowed for this paper.

Not more than four questions to be attempted.

Mr. P. GOODMAN, Examiner in Music.

1. Write out (1) the Major scale of which this is the "Leading Note":—

and (2) the Major scale of which the same note is the Dominant.
                                                                  14 marks.

Appendix L.

Examination Questions.

Matters

D Papers.

2. Write over the note

the following Intervals :—a Perfect Fifth ; Major Seventh ; Minor Second ; Perfect Fourth ; Perfect Octave ; Major Sixth.   13 marks.

3. Transpose the following into the scale of Fa (F). Prefix signature :—

75 marks.

4. Write three bars containing *notes and rests* in each of the following times :—C, 3/2, 3/4.   12 marks.

5. Name all the minor thirds in the Major scale of Re (D).   8 marks.

6. Write the following at the same pitch in the treble clef. Prefix time signature :—

6 marks.

7. State the Major scales represented by the following signatures :—

5 marks.

8. Name the following rests :—

6 marks.

MUSIC.—TONIC SOL-FA.—50 Marks.

One hour and a half allowed for this paper.

N.B.—*Only four questions to be attempted.*

Mr. P. GOODMAN, Examiner in Music.

1. Explain the different "steps" of the Tonic Sol-fa Method of teaching to sing.   14 marks.

2. Copy the following and write in figures (1, 1/2, 1/4, &c.) over each note and rest, its value in pulses or fractions of a pulse :—

||d   :— . r : m . f |s , l . s, f: m   : |

| : r | d ;   — |

13 marks.

2 A

Appendix L.
Exami-
nation
Questions.

Monitors.
D Papers.

3. Write a minor sixth over each of the following notes :—

$$s; \; m; \; l; \; fe.$$

13 marks.

4. Which is the highest and which the lowest of the following Keys :—

Ab, F♯, D, C, D♭, E.

12 marks.

5. Which are the Strong and which the Leaning Tones of the Scale ?

7 marks.

6. Write (a.) one octave lower.

(a) $\{ |\ d : m : l\ |\ s : - : f\ |\ m : r : t_1\ |\ d : - : - | \}$

(b.) two octaves lower.

(b) $|\ d' : t\ |\ d' : r'\ |\ m' : l'\ |\ s' : -\ |\ f' : r'\ |\ t : - |$

8 marks.

7. Write the Standard Scale of Pitch.

6 marks.

8. Between what tones of the Scale are the "little steps" of the Scale to be found ?

8 marks.

Monitresses.
D Papers.

IV.—MONITRESSES OF THIRD YEAR.

METHODS OF TEACHING.—60 Marks.

Two hours allowed for this paper.

N.B.—*Only four questions to be attempted.*

Mr. Dowsing, Head Inspector.
Mr. M'Glade, District Inspector.

1. What sections of First Book are printed on tablets ? At an early stage, how would you apportion the time between reading from tablets, and reading from books ?

15 marks.

2. Describe fully the proper position of a pupil when writing, the proper position of the copy-book, and the proper mode of holding and using the pen.

15 marks.

3. It is recommended that pupils of Fifth and Sixth Classes should keep note-books to aid them in learning to spell correctly. Explain how these note-books are to be used.

15 marks.

4. Describe the various steps towards teaching the notation required in First Class.

15 marks.

5. What consonants are often indistinctly pronounced by children ? What is the remedy in such cases ?

8 marks.

6. Give three reasons why signals are better than verbal orders.

8 marks.

7 What signs of supervision should appear in the copy-books ?

7 marks.

8. Describe how to use the ball-frame when commencing to teach the Multiplication Table.

7 marks.

ARITHMETIC.—100 Marks.

Two hours and a half allowed for this paper.

N.B.—*Only four questions to be attempted.*

Mr. Seymour, Head Inspector.
Mr. O'Riordan, District Inspector.

1. (a) "Multiply the Principal by the time and rate per cent., and divide the product by 100." Explain the reason of this rule.
   (b) Of what sum at 3½ per cent. for 9 months, is 2s. 6d. the interest?
   25 marks.

2. A grocer's profits are one-fourth of his receipts when he sells tea at 4s. 4d. a lb. How much per cent. would he gain by selling the tea at 5s. a lb.?
   25 marks.

3. If a rupee be worth 1s. 5d., and a dollar 4s. 2½d.; how many dollars must be given in exchange for 1,000 rupees?
   25 marks.

4. If 16 men, working 10 hours a day, complete a work in 25 days, how many men will do half as much in twice the time, working 8 hours a day?
   25 marks.

5. Divide the difference of ·3 and ·175 by the product of ·045 and ·125, and reduce your answer to a vulgar fraction.
   13 marks.

6. Find by Practice the cost of 19 yds., 3 qrs., 3 nails, at £1 4s. 8d. per yard.
   10 marks.

7. A bankrupt, whose assets were £70 10s., paid 3½d. in the £ to his creditors: of how much were they the losers?
   10 marks.

8. State the "short rule" for finding what any number of pence per day will amount to in a year (365 days). Show the application of this rule in finding how much 7 pence per day for 365 days will amount to.
   15 marks.

GEOGRAPHY.—60 marks.

Two hours allowed for this paper.

N.B.—*Only four questions to be attempted.*

Mr. Connellan, Head Inspector.
Mr. Woosley, District Inspector.

1. Draw an outline map of Ireland, as large as your paper will allow, and indicate on it the different mountain ranges, marking and naming the highest point of each range.
   15 marks.

2. Where and what are Portland Bill, Spithead, The Peak, Buchan Ness, Skiddaw?
   15 marks.

3. Why does any given time of day come earlier to the east of a continent than to the west? How does this fact help us to determine the position of places on the earth's surface?
   15 marks.

4. Refer each of the following towns to its proper county:—Kidderminster, Wrexham, Thurso, Dunkeld, Ripon.
   15 marks.

5. Describe precisely the position of the following places:—Amara, Booian, Outch, Neilgherry Hills.
   8 marks.

6. Where are the following found in Ireland:—Salt, copper, marble?
   6 marks.

7. Define the following terms:—"Antipodes," "Perihelion," "Spheroid," "Nadir."
   8 marks.

8. What do the following separate:—Menai Strait, Solent, Firth of Forth, Firth of Tay?
   8 marks.

2 A 2

PENMANSHIP.—40 Marks.

Half an hour allowed for this exercise.

Your penmanship will be judged from the neatness and accuracy with which you copy the following passage :—

Darkling I listen : and for many a time
I have been half in love with easeful Death,
Called him soft names in many a mused rhyme,
To take into the air my quiet breath ;
Now more than ever it seems rich to die,
To cease upon the midnight with no pain,
While thou art pouring forth thy soul abroad
In such an ecstasy !
Still would'st thou sing, and I have ears in vain—
To thy high requiem become a sod.

The clouds of his allegory may seem to spread into shapeless forms, but they are still the clouds of a glowing atmosphere. Though his story grows desultory, the sweetness and grace of his manner still abide by him. We always rise from perusing him with melody in the mind's ear and with pictures of romantic beauty impressed on the imagination.

SPELLING BOOK, &c.,—50 Marks (including 20 Marks for Dictation).

One hour and a half allowed for this paper.

N.B.—*Only four questions to be attempted.*

Mr. STRONGE, Head Inspector.
Mr. DALY, District Inspector.

The passage for Dictation is taken from the Fifth Book of Lessons, pages 165-166. "The various elements" to "different forms."
20 marks.

1. What obvious reason is there for Rule II. of Spelling so far as it relates to monosyllables? What are the exceptions to this Rule, and how far can they be justified ?
8 marks.

2. Re-write the following sentence correcting the misspelled words "A gristly hare disturbed the even tenure of my way by immerging from his layer and walking with gapeing mouth strait up to me."
8 marks.

3. Write out the past tense of *lay, stay, travel, frolic,* and state which rule each form exemplifies, or to which it is an exception.
8 marks.

4. Correct the spelling of the following words, assigning your reasons : *increcable, existance, attendent.*
6 marks.

5. What words are liable to be confounded with *alley, spacious, opposite, errand* ?
4 marks.

6. Of what rule for spelling is *almost* an example ? What are the exceptions to the rule ?
3 marks.

7. To what class of verbal distinctions do *steppe, cygnet, rye, char,* belong ? Give the other words of the pairs, and the meanings of all.
4 marks.

8. Write out adjectives formed from *umbrage* and *rebel,* and past participles formed from *combat* and *abut.* . . . . 4 marks.

GRAMMAR.—60 Marks.

Two hours allowed for this paper.

N.B.—*Only four of these questions, of which the parsing exercise must be one, are to be attempted.*

Mr. PURSER, Head Inspector.
Mr. MURPHY, District Inspector.

1. Parse the words in *italics* :—

Another citizen, very rich and *respected*, rose up and *said*, he *would be* the second to his companion *Eustace*. After him James Wismart, who was very rich in merchandise, *offered* himself *as companion* to his two cousins ; as did *Peter Wismart*, his brother. Two *others* then named *themselves*, which completed the number *demanded* by the king of England). 24 marks.

2. Correct the following sentences, if necessary, and give the reasons for your corrections :—

   (*a*) Mine is the best apple ; it is better than yours.
   (*b*) She is stronger than Mary, but not the wiser.
   (*c*) He said the remarks are on the second and third page.
   (*d*) It was neither of these three men. 12 marks.

3. Write out a table of defective verbs, showing what parts are still in use. 12 marks.

4. What is meant by the *government* of transitive verbs? Of what may the "object" consist? 12 marks.

5. Write out a list of the words in our language which begin with a silent *h*. 6 marks.

6. When are *w* and *y* consonants? Name the unnecessary letters of our alphabet. 6 marks.

7. Conjugate the following verbs :—*gild, dame, flee, sit, abide,* and 6 marks.

8. What is the meaning of each of the following prefixes? Illustrate by examples :—*mis, anti, intro, dis, hypo, retro.* 6 marks.

LESSON BOOKS.—50 Marks.

An hour and a half allowed for this paper.

N.B.—*Only four questions to be attempted.*

Mr. SULLIVAN, Head Inspector.
Dr. MORAN, District Inspector.

1. As an exercise in composition, write in your own words the story of the child who was lost on the Grampian Mountains, and saved by a shepherd's dog. 15 marks.

2. Describe the manner in which salt is manufactured from the water of salt springs. What is meant by rock-salt, what by bay-salt? Mention some of the chief uses of salt. 15 marks.

3. Write out the lines from the ode " *To a Skylark,*" beginning with

     " Like a poet hidden "

and ending with—

     " Which screen it from the view.' 10 marks.

Appendix I.
Examination
Questions.
Monitresses.
D Papers.

4. Explain the following extracts from "*The Vanity of Human Wishes*":—

    (a.) "Through him the rays of regal bounty shine."
    (b.) "On Moscow's walls till Gothic standards fly."
    (c.) "His fall was destined to a barren strand,
        A petty fortress, and a dubious hand."
    (d.) "Superfluous lags the veteran on the stage."   12 marks

5. How do bees prepare the substance called bee-bread?
        7 marks.

6. Write out eight lines commencing :—
    "All but yon widowed, solitary thing."
from Goldsmith's poem on *The Deserted Village*.   8 marks.

7. What is the main point to be looked to in drawing a barn? How may this end be attained?   5 marks.

8. Give in your own words a description of the objects which, according to the lesson on foreign countries, a traveller may expect to see in Switzerland.   5 marks.

—

DRAWING.—50 Marks.

Three hours allowed for this subject.

N.B.—*The name of the Monitress and of her School to be written on each paper.*

    Mr. NEWELL, Head Inspector.
    Mr. CASSO, District Inspector.

I.—FREEHAND DRAWING.—20 Marks.

A drawing of the example supplied is to be made on an enlarged scale ; the height to be increased about 1 inch, and the breadth in proportion.

II.—OBJECT DRAWING.—12 Marks.

The Examiner will place on a small table, about 2 feet 0 inches high, a plain kitchen candlestick with a candle in it. A drawing of these objects, table and candlestick, is to be made so as fairly to fill the paper.

III.—PRACTICAL GEOMETRY.—18 Marks.

NOTE.—*Any three of the following questions may be attempted. Answers should be written on one side of the paper only, and where a construction is not obvious, an explanation should be given, the points being marked with letters.*

Full credit will not be allowed for a question, unless the construction is neatly drawn, and all lines are shown.

1. Draw any irregular four-sided figure, and find a square equal to it in area.   6 marks.

2. Make a square of 2·5 inches side, and inscribe an equilateral triangle in it.   6 marks.

Appendix I.
Examination Questions.
Needlework.
D Paper.

3. Construct an octagon whose longest diagonal shall be 3 inches.
    6 marks.

4. Construct a scale of 3 inches to the mile, showing furlongs.
    3 marks.

5. In a circle of 1 inch radius inscribe a triangle with angles of 30°, 60°, and 90°.
    3 marks.

6. Given one side of a rectangle ½ an inch, and the diagonal 1¼ inch, construct the rectangle.
    3 marks.

MUSIC—(HULLAH).—50 Marks.

An hour and a half allowed for this paper.

Not more than four questions to be attempted.

Mr. P. Goodman, Examiner in Music.

1. Write out (1) the Major Scale which has for its Tonic the note a Major Third below,

and (2) the Major Scale which has for its Tonic the note a Minor Third below the same.
    14 marks.

2. In the Scale of Sol (G) find an example of each of the following Intervals:—Minor Third; Imperfect Fifth; Major Second; Minor Sixth; Pluperfect Fourth; and Major Third.
    12 marks.

3. Fill up the following bars with rests:—

    12 marks.

4. Transpose the following a minor third higher; prefix Key Signature:—

    12 marks.

5. Write in the treble clef the key signatures only of the Major Scales of Re flat (D♭) and Si natural (B).
    6 marks.

6. Write out in full the words of which the following are contractions and explain their meaning:—*f*, *p*, *mf*, *cres.*, *sf*, *dim.*   6 marks.

7. Write this an octave higher in the treble clef, and an octave lower in the bass clef.

    7 marks.

8. What are the Minor Seconds in the scale of Fa (F) major?
    6 marks.

TONIC SOL-FA.—50 marks.

One hour and a half allowed for this paper.

N.B.—*Only four questions to be attempted.*

— Mr. P. Goodman, Examiner in Music.

1. Explain the chordal structure of the scale.   14 marks.

2. Re-write the following in four pulse measure, doubling the value of each note and rest :—

$$\| d^{l} \,.\, t : - .\; l \,|s\quad .\quad : f \,.s.f | m \,.\,,\; r: d \qquad \|$$

12 marks.

3. Write a major third above and a major third below the following notes :—

$$|\; r \;|\; l \;|\; f \;|\; t_{1} \,\|$$

12 marks.

4. Write the following keys in their order of pitch—commencing with the lowest :— .

B♭, F♯, D, A, C♯, G, C.

12 marks.

5. How are the mental effects of the tones of the scale caused ?

7 marks.

6. What is ba ? In what "step" of the method is it introduced ?

6 marks.

7. Between what tones of the scale are the "greater steps" of the scale to be found ?

6 marks.

8. Write two octaves higher :—

$$| d :m|r : t_{1} \; l : s_{1}|s :-| d^{l} : t \;|d^{l}: f|m: r \;|d :-\|$$

6 marks.

V.—EXTRA SUBJECTS—MALES.

LATIN.—50 marks.

Two hours allowed for this paper.

Only five questions to be attempted—to include at least one from each group, A, B, C.

Mr. Newell, Head Inspector.
Dr. Beatty, District Inspector.

A.

1. Translate into English :—

Festinate, viri ; nam quae tam sera moratur
Segnities ? alii rapiunt incensa feruntque
Pergama : vos celsis nunc primum a navibus itis ?
Dixit : et extemplo (neque enim responsa dabantur
Fida satis) sequit medios delapsus in hostes.
Obstupuit, retroque pedem cum voce repressit.
Improvisum aspris veluti qui sentibus anguem
Pressit humi nitens, trepidusque repente refugit
Attollentem iras, et caerula colla tumentem.—Virgil.

10 marks.

2. Hodie quoque in legibus magistratibusque rogandis usurpatur idem
jus, vi adempta: priusquam populus suffragium ineat, in incertum
comitiorum eventum patres auctores fiunt. Tum interrex contione
advocata "quod bonum faustum felixque sit" inquit, "Quirites, regem
create: ita patribus visum est. Patres deinde, si dignum, qui secundus
ab Romulo numeretur, creavitis, auctores fient." Adeo id gratum plebi
fuit, ut, ne victi beneficio viderentur, id modo sciverunt iuberentque,
ut senatus decernerent, qui Romae regnaret.—LIVY.

10 marks.

3. Instructo exercitu magis ut loci natura dejectusque collis et
necessitas temporis, quam ut rei militaris ratio atque ordo, postulabat,
quum diversis locis legiones, aliae alia in parte hostibus resisterent,
saepibusque densissimis, ut ante demonstravimus, interjectis prospectus
impediretur; neque certa subsidia collocari, neque quid in quaque parte
opus esset provideri, neque ab uno omnia imperia administrari poterant.
Itaque, in tanta rerum iniquitate, fortunae quoque eventus varii
sequebantur.—CAESAR.   10 marks.

B.

4. Translate into Latin :—

But when experience taught me that the untameable barbarism of
the Goths would not suffer them to live beneath the sway of law, and
that the abolition of the institutions on which the State rested would
involve the ruin of the State itself, I chose the glory of renewing and
maintaining by Gothic strength the fame of Rome, desiring to go down
to posterity as the restorer of that Roman power which it was beyond
my power to replace.   10 marks.

5. Translate into Latin :—

(1.) *Who will deny that these things are for the interest of the
republic?*

(2.) *It is the part of a wise man, as long as he lives, to prefer
virtue to all things.*

(3.) *They say that the rule of expediency is not the same as that of
honour.*

(4.) *Almost from a boy he has devoted himself to literature.*

(5.) *He died at the age of thirty-three.*   5 marks.

C.

6. Give the perfects and supines of *amo, lavo, alo, indulgeo, repo,
tondeo, cedo, flecto, tendo, edo.*   10 marks.

7. Express in Latin :—

It is not doubtful

(b) *I am ashamed.*

(c) *Do you not think?*

(d) *I knew what you were doing.*

(e) *Hard to be spoken.*   5 marks.

8. What are the comparatives and superlatives of :—

nequam, frugi, maximus, maledicus, falsus?   5 marks.

9. State and illustrate the rules for the translation into Latin of the
word "any."   5 marks.

10. Write a short life of Pyrrhus.   5 marks.

LATIN.—50 Marks.

Two hours allowed for this paper.

N.B.—*Only five questions to be attempted—to include at least one from each group A, B, C.*

Mr. NEWELL, Head Inspector.
Dr. BEATTY, District Inspector.

A.

1. Translate into English—

> Fando aliquod, si forte tuas pervenit ad aures
> Belidæ nomen Palamedis, et inclyta famâ
> Gloria ; quem falsâ sub proditione Pelasgi
> Insontem, infando indicio, quia bella vetabat,
> Demisere neci—nunc casum lumine lugent—
> Illi me comitem, et consanguinitate propinquum,
> Pauper in arma pater primis huc misit ab annis.
> Dum stabat regno incolumis, regumque vigebat
> Consiliis, et nos aliquod nomenque decusque
> Gessimus.—VIRGIL.   10 marks.

2. Consertis deinde manibus cum iam non motus tantum corporum agitatioque anceps telorum armorumque sed vulnera quoque et sanguis spectaculo essent, duo Romani super alium alius vulnerati tribus Albanis exspirantes corruerant. Ad quorum casum cum conclamasset gaudio Albanus exercitus, Romanas legiones iam spes tota, nondum tamen cura deseruerat, exanimes vice unius, quem tres Curiatii circumsteterant. Forte is integer fuit, ut universis solus nequaquam par, sic adversus singulos ferox.—LIVY.   10 marks.

3. Castris munitis, vineas agere, quæque ad oppugnandum usui erant, comparare cœpit. Interim omnis ex fuga Suessionum multitudo in oppidum proximâ nocte convenit. Celeriter vineis ad oppidum actis, aggere jacto, turribusque constitutis, magnitudine operum, quæ neque viderant antè Galli neque audierant, et celeritate Romanorum permoti, legatos ad Cæsarem de deditione mittunt, et petentibus Remis ut conservarentur, impetrant.—CÆSAR.   10 marks.

B.

4. Translate into Latin :—

He threw neither garments nor odours upon the funeral pyre, but the arms and the war horse of the departed were burned and buried with him. The turf was his only sepulchre, the memory of his valour his only monument. Even tears were forbidden to the men. "It was esteemed honourable," says the historian, "for women to lament, for men to remember."   10 marks.

5. Translate into Latin :—

(1.) I doubt whether I ought to do this.
(2.) I have unwillingly offended Caius.
(3.) He promises to come to the assistance of the Helvetii.
(4.) Old age is by nature somewhat loquacious.
(5.) Tiberius died on the sixteenth of March.   5 marks.

C.

6. Give the perfects and supines of *flo, caveo, hereo, coquo, arulo, terro, sino, pello, ruo, lacesso.*   10 marks.

7. State anything you know in Roman history in connexion with the following cities :—*Tarentum, Syracuse, Numantia, Veii, Corinth.*
5 marks.

8. Give the idiomatic English translation of :—

> *operae pretium est ;*
> *e re mea est ;*
> *nolim factum ;*
> *nollem factum ;*
> *unquam sea adventum.*   5 marks.

9. Decline in full the pronouns : *is* and *idem.*   5 marks.

10. At Tarentum ; at Tibur ; at Gabii. Translate these expressions into Latin, and state in full the rules as to the proper cases in such instances.   5 marks.

FRENCH.—50 Marks.

An hour and a half allowed for this paper.

*Only five questions are to be attempted, one at least from each section
A, B, C.*

Mr. NEWELL, Head Inspector.
Mr. HYNES, District Inspector.

1. Translate into English :—

A.

Calypso ayant montré à Télémaque toutes ces beautés naturelles, lui dit : Reposez-vous ; vos habits sont mouillés, il est temps que vous en changiez ; ensuite nous nous reverrons, et je vous raconterai des histoires dont votre cœur sera touché. En même temps elle le fit entrer avec Mentor dans le lieu le plus secret et le plus reculé d'une grotte voisine de celle où la déesse demeurait.—*Télémaque.*   10 marks.

2.   Renvoyez, dit quelqu'un, les ânes qui sont lourds'
    Et les lièvres sujets à des terreurs paniques.
    Point du tout, dit le roi ; je les veux employer.
    Notre troupe sans eux ne serait pas complète.
    L'âne effraie les gens, nous servant de trompette,
    Et le lièvre pourra nous servir de courrier.

        Le monarque prudent et sage
    De ses moindres sujets sait tirer quelque usage,
        Et connaît les divers talents.
    Il n'est rien d'inutile aux personnes de sens.—LA FONTAINE.
10 marks.

3.   Jérusalem pleura de se voir profanée ;
    Des enfants de Lévi la troupe consternée
    En poussa vers le ciel des hurlements affreux.
    Moi seul donnant l'exemple aux timides Hébreux,
    Déserteur de leur loi, j'approuvai l'entreprise,
    Et par là de Baal méritai la prêtrise ;
    Par là je me rendis terrible à mon rival,
    Je ceignis la tiare, et marchai son égal.—*Athalie.*
10 marks.

B.

4. Translate into French :—

It was under the reign of Aurungzebe that this wild class of plunderers first descended from their mountains; and soon after his death, every corner of his wide empire learned to tremble at the mighty name of Mahrattas. Many fertile vice-royalties were entirely subdued by them. Their dominions stretched across the peninsula from sea to sea. Mahratta captains reigned at Poonah, at Gualior, in Guzerat, in Berar and in Tanjore. Nor did they, though they had become great sovereigns, therefore cease to be freebooters.

10 marks.

5. Express in French :—

 (a) *Have you heard from him?*
 (b) *It was not until then;*
 (c) *Such was the custom with the English;*
 (d) *The horse is in the stable;*
 (e) *There are two hundred cows in this field.*

5 marks.

C.

6. Correct, or justify the spelling of the past participle in the following sentences, giving your reason in each case :—

 (a) Les livres que j'ai *faits* relier ;
 (b) Les efforts que ce travail lui a *coûté* ;
 (c) Elle nous ont *répondues* ;
 (d) Elles se sont *arrogé* ce droit ;
 (e) Voici les lettres ; les as-tu *lu* ? 10 marks.

7. Write out the future tense of *valoir, seoir, naître*.

5 marks.

8. When does the past participle accompanied by the auxiliary "*avoir*" agree with the direct object, and when not? Give examples.

5 marks.

9. When is the second person singular used in French in addressing a person? 5 marks.

10. Distinguish between *un auteur pauvre*, and *un pauvre auteur* ; *un homme grand*, and *un grand homme* ; *l'air mourant*, and *le mourant air* ; *un habit nouveau*, and *un nouvel habit*. 5 marks.

FRENCH.—50 Marks.

One hour and a half allowed for this paper.

N.B.—Only five questions are to be attempted—one at least from each group, A, B, C.

Mr. Newell, Head Inspector.
Mr. Hynes, District Inspector.

A.

1. Translate into English :—

Jamais je n'en ai abusé; jamais il ne m'a échappé une seule parole qui pût découvrir le moindre secret. Souvent les prétendants tâchaient de me faire parler, espérant qu'un enfant, qui pourrait avoir vu ou entendu quelque chose d'important, ne saurait pas se retenir; mais je savais bien leur répondre sans mentir, et sans leur apprendre ce que je ne devais pas dire.—*Télémaque.*

10 marks

2. Tout tremble aux environs, et cette alarme est l'ouvrage d'un
Moucheron.   Il lui pique tantôt l'échine, tantôt la gorge : en vain le
Lion fait agir sa queue et s'en bat les flancs.   Enfin l'insecte lui entre
dans les narines, et le tourmente à un tel point, que le roi des animaux
tomble de douleur, et se déchire lui-même de ses propres griffes. L'insecte
triomphe, et le quitte tout glorieux ; et comme il se retirait, en publiant
par tout sa victoire, il rencontre une toile d'Araignée, où il s'embarrasse,
et devint la proie d'un autre insecte.—LA FONTAINE.

10 marks.

3   Mais où sont ces honneurs à David tant promis,
           Et prédits même encore à Salomon son fils ?
           Hélas ! nous espérions que de leur race heureuse
           Devait sortir de rois une suite nombreuse,
           Que sur toute tribu, sur toute nation,
           L'un d'eux établirait sa domination,
           Ferait cesser partout la discorde et la guerre,
           Et verrait à ses pieds tous les rois de la terre.

                                             Athalie.
                                             10 marks.

B.

4. Translate into French :—

It was to the lot of a prince three years old, called Sebastian, that
the crown of Portugal had fallen by this event.   Hardly was the young
prince of age when he announced a campaign against the Moors.   Muley-
Mahomet, who had been driven out by one of his relatives, had applied
to Sebastian for help.   In vain did his counsellors and even the king of
Spain represent to the young monarch that such an expedition was a
dangerous, nay, even a rash enterprise ; Sebastian was deaf to all
entreaties and warnings.   *10 marks.*

5. Express in French :—

       (a) *It is six by my watch*
       (b) *To judge by his appearance.*
       (c) *To sell by weight.*
       (d) *Older by ten years.*
       (e) *By the end of the week.*

                                             5 marks

C.

6. Correct or justify the spelling of the past participle in the following sentences, giving your reason in each case :—

       (a) Je les ai *vus* frapper le fer ;
       (b) Je n'ai pas encore *lu* la lettre ;
       (c) La grande sécheresse qu'il a *faite* ;
       (d) J'abandonnai toutes les espérances que j'avais *conçues* ;
       (e) *Effrayés* par cette tempête, ils se crurent perdus.

                                             10 marks.

7. Write down the present participle of—

                    Savoir,
                    Plaire,
                    Saire,
                    Coudre,
                    Faire.

                                             5 marks.

Appendix L.

Examination Questions.

Male Teachers.

A, B, or C Paper.

8. Translate the following adverbial phrases :—

      Tant soit-peu.
      En bas.
      A qui mieux mieux.
      Bon gré mal gré.
      A jamais.   5 marks.

9. Write down in French :—

     (a)   80.
     (b)   90.
     (c)   200.
     (d)   2000.
     (e)   170.   5 marks.

10   What is the feminine of *exprès, malin, franc, oblong, pécheur* ?
                                     5 marks.

A' Paper

BOTANY.—50 Marks.

One hour and a half allowed for this paper.

N.B.—*Only five questions to be attempted.*

Mr. CONNELLAN, Head Inspector.
Mr. DALTON, District Inspector.

1. Give an outline of a lesson on the field poppy, fumitory, and wall-flower, designed to illustrate the principles of classification and the relationship of natural orders.   10 marks.

2. Describe the wood of an exogenous tree, and illustrate by a drawing of a cross-section.   10 marks.

3. Flower, monopetalous ; ovary, inferior ; stamens, on corolla ; name two orders to which this description applies, and show how to distinguish between them.   10 marks.

4. Describe the common ivy as to its stem, leaves and flower.
                                 10 marks.

5. Describe and give examples of the following kinds of leaf formation :—*decurrent, sessile, stipulate, peltate, bi-pinnatifid.*   10 marks.

6. Describe the structure of the leaf (a) of the oak, (b) of grass.
                                 5 marks.

7. What is æstivation ? Describe the following forms of it :—*circinate, involute, imbricate.*   5 marks.

8. How is the ovule fertilised in angiospermous plants ? What is cross-fertilisation ?   5 marks.

9. Mention some of the carbonaceous compounds that enter into the composition of plants.   5 marks.

10. To what order does each of the following plants belong :—hawthorn, dandelion, shamrock ?   5 marks.

A, B, or C Paper.

BOTANY.—50 Marks.

One hour and a half allowed.

N.B.—*Only five questions to be attempted.*

Mr. CONNELLAN, Head Inspector.
Mr. DALTON, District Inspector.

1. Give the technical names and refer to their natural orders—oak, daffodil, forget-me-not, bindweed. Briefly describe the flower of any one of these plants.   10 marks.

2. Give the essential characters of the Cistaceæ or rock-roses, and say how they can be readily distinguished by their calyx.   10 marks.

3. From what plants, and from what parts of them, do we obtain chicory, chocolate, cotton, indign, turpentine?   10 marks.

4. Describe the common flax as to its flower and vegetable structure.   10 marks.

5. State how the Dipsaceæ differ from the Valerianaceæ, and give an example of each.   10 marks.

6. What is inflorescence? What parts of it are denoted by *peduncle, rachis, involucre, pedicel?*   5 marks.

7. Describe the stems of endogens.   5 marks.

8. Give an example of plants having the following form of leaf:— *lanceolate, palmate, pinnate, serrate, entire.*   5 marks.

9. Give examples of *monadelphous* and *diadelphous* arrangement of stamens.   5 marks.

10. Explain what is meant by the following forms of *inflorescence:*— the *spike,* the *cyme,* the *panicle.*   5 marks.

MUSIC—(HULLAH).—50 Marks

One hour and a half allowed for this paper.

N.B.—*Only five questions to be attempted.*

Mr. P. GOODMAN, Examiner in Music.

1. Write in treble and bass clefs—prefixing signatures—the relative minors of the following three Major scales: Mi flat (E♭): Si natural (B): Re (D).   12 marks.

2. Name the following Intervals, and state what each becomes on Inversion:—

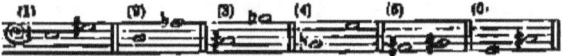

19 marks.

3. Copy the following and prefix proper Time signature to each bar:—

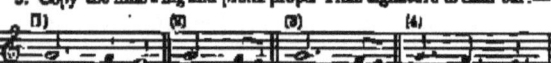

8 marks.

4. Transpose the following into the key of G. Prefix key and time signatures:—

12 marks.

Appendix L.

Examination
Questions.

Male
Teachers.

A. B, & C
Papers.

5. State the Dominant, Sub-dominant and Leading Note of each of the following Major scales :—Si natural (B) : Re flat (Db) : La flat (Ab) : Sol (G).
6 marks.

6. Add to the following (1) such accidentals as will make it a Minor scale, and (2) such notes and accidentals as will make it a chromatic scale :—

5 marks.

7. Write out correctly the first eight bars of any of the songs in the Manual, or of any Irish melody you know.   6 marks.

8. Write the following at the same pitch in the bass stave :—

5 marks.

9. How many pluperfect fourths are found in a Major scale ?
4 marks.

10. State what practices or habits you would regard as faulty in a singing class, and how you would propose to remedy them.
5 marks.

DRAWING.

Three hours allowed for this subject.

N.B.—The name of the Teacher and of his School to be written on each paper

Mr. NEWELL, Head Inspector.
Mr. CRAIG, District Inspector.

I.—FREEHAND DRAWING.—50 Marks.

The example given is to be copied on a slightly larger scale, so as to be about an inch higher, and the whole in proportion.

II.—OBJECT DRAWING.—50 Marks.

The examiner will place horizontally about 2 feet 6 inches from the floor, a small blackboard. On this he will put a set of weights and scales. The scales are not to face the candidates directly. The weights are to stand about six inches in front of the scales, and in a row. The blackboard, etc., to be drawn so as fairly to fill the paper.

Appendix L.
Examination Questions.
Male Teachers.
A, B, and C Papers.

III.—PRACTICAL GEOMETRY AND PERSPECTIVE.
50 Marks.

NOTE—*Only five of the following questions may be attempted. Answers should be written on one side of the paper only, and where the construction is not obvious, an explanation should be given, the points being marked with letters.*

Full credit will not be allowed for a question, unless the construction is neatly drawn, and all lines are shown.

N.B.— *In addition to an ordinary case of instruments, set squares and a 12-inch rule may be used.*

1. What are the traces of a line? When will a line have only one trace, and when none? A line has two traces 3 inches apart, It is inclined 40°, and its horizontal trace is 1 inch below the ground line. Find its vertical trace.   10 marks.

2. Place in perspective a cylinder 4 feet in diameter and 5 feet long. Its ends to be parallel to the picture plane, and the nearest end 3 feet to the right, and 2 feet in the picture. (Height of eye, 5 feet ; line of direction, 11 feet ; scale, ⅓ inch to the foot).   12 marks.

3. A line A B is 1·6 inches from the centre of a circle of ·8 inch radius. A point P, in the line, is 2 inches from the centre of the circle. Draw a second circle to touch the line A B in the point P, and also the given circle, (1) externally, (2) and to include it.   10 marks.

4. Two lines cross each other at equal angles. Draw four equal circles, each to touch both lines.   8 marks.

5. Draw a rectangle of 4-inch, and of 2½-inch sides. Within it inscribe an ellipse, which shall touch the centre of each side of the rectangle tangentially.   10 marks.

6. Assume any three points, A, B, and C, by their projections, and determine the oblique plane containing them.   5 marks.

7. Draw the plan and elevation of a cube of 5 feet, standing on one edge, its sloping faces making 45° with the horizontal plane, and its vertical faces parallel to the vertical plane.   5 marks.

8. Construct a square having a side of 3 inches, and also a scalene triangle of equal area, one of the angles at the base being 30°.   5 marks.

9. Circumscribe a circle of 2·25 inches diameter by a triangle whose sides are in the ratio of 3 : 4 : 6.   5 marks.

·10. Draw a circle of 1·5 inches radius, and divide it into four parts, equal to each other, both in area and perimeter.   5 marks.

MUSIC.—TONIC SOL-FA.—50 Marks.
An hour and a half allowed for this paper.

N.B.—*Only five questions to be attempted.*

Mr. P. GOODMAN, Examiner in Music.

1. Translate (a) into the Tonic Sol-fa notation.

    (b) Into the Staff notation, using the crotchet for the pulse

(a)

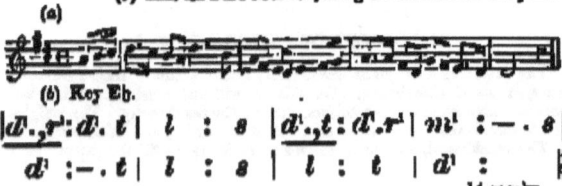

(b) Key E♭.

$$|\, d\,.,r^1 : d^1 .\, t \,|\, l \,:\, s \,|\, d^1 .,t : d^1 . r^1 \,|\, m^1 \,:-\,.\,s \,|$$

$$d^1 \,:-\,.\,t \,|\, l \,:\, s \,|\, l \,:\, t \,|\, d^1 \,:\, \|$$

14 marks.

2. The following are notes in the centre column of the Modulator—

$$l\ f\ ta\ s\ m\ d\ d^1\ r^1\ ta\ s\ l\ m\ f.$$

Write the notes which correspond to these in the first column to the left of the centre column on the Modulator.   12 marks.

3. Name the following Intervals: give number of Index degrees in each, and state what each becomes on Inversion.

(1)	(2)	(3)	(4)	(5)	(6)
m	f	d^1	ta	l	t
t_1	l_1	r	m	fe	f

12 marks.

4. Write the time names of the following :—

(a) $|\ m,r,d,m:\ s\ .\ s_1\ |\ l\ .\ t\ ,\ d:\ r\ .\ |$

(b) $|\ d_1t_1,d:\ m\ :-\ .\ r\ |\ m.,f:\ s\ :\ |$

(c) $|\ s\ ,\ -,m:\ l\ ,\ t\ .\ d^1\ |\ f\ .\ s\ ,\ f:\ m\ \}$

$\quad |\quad .\ r\ :\ l_1\ .,\ t_1\ |\ d\ :\ -\ ||$

6 marks.

5. Which of the following notes is highest in pitch and which lowest ?

(a) t_1 in Key F.   (c) s in Key E♭.   (e) l in Key B♭.

(b) m in Key D   (d) r in Key C.   (f) s_1 in Key A.

6 marks.

6. Explain the following terms :—

Fourth Step; Key tone; Measure; Bridge-note; Pulse; M.72.

6 marks.

7. Write the names for *Doh sharp*; *me flat*; *lah sharp*; *lah flat*; *soh sharp*; *ray flat.*   4 marks.

8. Describe the Mental Effects of the different tones of the scale when sung slowly. What modifies these effects ?   5 marks.

9. Transcribe the following into two-pulse measure—that is, write in one pulse what is here given in three pulses.

$$|\ d\ :-\ :r\ |m:r:d\ |s\ :-\ :\ l\ |s\ :-\ :-\ |d^1:\ t:l\ |s\ :r:f\ |$$

$$|m:-:-\ |-:-:-\ ||$$

5 marks

10. In teaching the Singing Class should the teacher sing *with* the pupils or *to* them ? Give reasons for your answer.   5 marks.

HANDICRAFT— 50 Marks.

One hour and a half allowed for this paper.

N.B. —Only five questions to be attempted.

Mr. Newell, Head Inspector.
Mr. Robinson, Assistant Surveyor, Board of Public Works.

1. Give a sketch of a carpenter's bench, and describe how you would make one.   10 marks.

2. Name the various kinds of timber which may be comprised in the classes of "hard wood" and "soft wood," and state the purposes for which each is best suited.   10 marks.

3. Describe fully the materials and tools required in soldering tin, lead, and zinc. How is the solder prepared, and the soldering iron tinned?   10 marks.

4. State how you would set and sharpen a saw, grind and sharpen planes, chisels, and moulding planes. What do you understand by the terms *cutting iron* and *counter iron* as applied to planes?   10 marks.

5. The circular vaulted roof of a hall measures 105 feet 6 inches in the arch, and 275 feet 5 inches in length; what will the painting come to at one shilling per square yard? The plaster has never been painted; describe how this roof should be prepared and painted.   10 marks.

6. Name the various tools required in carpenters' and joiners' work, and state approximately the cost of each.   5 marks.

7. State how you would prepare *lime-wash* of a good colour, and fit to resist the weather.   5 marks.

8. How would you proceed to put hinges and locks on doors of the following kinds:—ledged; framed and sheeted; framed, panelled and moulded? Name the description to be used in each case.   5 marks.

9. Describe how you would *sheet* the inside of the roof of a school-room with deal boards.   5 marks.

10. Give full instructions for staining a border to a floor; colour, dark oak or mahogany.   5 marks.

———

HYGIENE.—50 Marks.

One hour and a half allowed for this paper.

N.B.—Only five questions to be attempted.

Mr. Newell, Head Inspector.
Mr. Heaven, District Inspector.

1. Describe the most efficient mode of ventilating house drains.   10 marks.

2. What are the chief causes of broken sleep, and what is the danger of using sleeping draughts?   10 marks.

3. Describe the changes produced by different degrees of heat in the juices and solid parts of meat.   10 marks.

4. Account for the self-purifying power of rivers.   10 marks.

5. Mention the different systems adopted for the removal of excreta, and those for the purification of sewage matter.   10 marks.

6. Describe fully either *Sylvester's* or *Howard's* method for treating the apparently drowned.   5 marks.

2 a 2

7. State some means for correcting sluggish or irregular action of the bowels. 5 marks.

8. Describe briefly the air cells of the lungs as to their situation, number and use. 5 marks.

9. What are the physical qualities which might justify you in concluding that a sample of water was fit to drink? 5 marks.

10. Describe the circulation of the blood in mankind, supposing it to start from the left ventricle. 5 marks.

———

GREEK.—50 Marks.

Two hours allowed for this paper.

*Only five questions to be attempted, one at least from each section,
A, B, C.*

Mr. NEWELL, Head Inspector.
Dr. BEATTY, District Inspector.

A.

1. Translate into English :—

> τὸν δ' ἀμείβετ' ἔπειτα Θέτις κατὰ δάκρυ χέουσα·
> ὤμοι, τέκνον ἐμόν, τί νύ σ' ἔτρεφον αἰνὰ τεκοῦσα;
> αἴθ' ὄφελες παρὰ νηυσὶν ἀδάκρυτος καὶ ἀπήμων
> ἦσθαι, ἐπεί νύ τοι αἶσα μίνυνθά περ, οὔ τι μάλα δήν·
> νῦν δ' ἅμα τ' ὠκύμορος καὶ ὀιζυρὸς περὶ πάντων
> ἔπλεο· τῷ σε κακῇ αἴσῃ τέκον ἐν μεγάροισιν.
> τοῦτο δέ τοι ἐρέουσα ἔπος Διὶ τερπικεραύνῳ
> εἶμ' αὐτὴ πρὸς Ὄλυμπον ἀγάννιφον, αἴ κε πίθηται.

HOMER.

10 marks.

2. καὶ πρῶτον μὲν ἦν αὐτῷ πόλεμος πρὸς Πισίδας καὶ Μυσούς· στρατευόμενος οὖν καὶ αὐτὸς εἰς ταύτας τὰς χώρας, οὓς ἑώρα ἐθέλοντας κινδυνεύειν, τούτους καὶ ἄρχοντας ἐποίει, ἧς κατεστρέφετο χώρας, ἔπειτα δὲ καὶ ἄλλως ἑώρας ἐτίμα· ὥστε φαίνεσθαι τοὺς μὲν ἀγαθοὺς εὐδαιμονεστάτους, τοὺς δὲ κακοὺς δούλους τούτων, ἀξιοῦν εἶναι. τοιγαροῦν πολλὴ ἦν ἀφθονία αὐτῷ τῶν ἐθελόντων κινδυνεύειν, ὅπου τις οἴοιτο Κῦρον αἰσθήσεσθαι.

XENOPHON.

10 marks.

3. τί οὖν ποτ' αἴτιον, θαυμάζετ' ἴσως, τοῦ καὶ τοὺς Ὀλυνθίους καὶ τοὺς Ἐρετριεῖς καὶ τοὺς Ὠρείτας ἥδιον πρὸς τοὺς ὑπὲρ Φιλίππου λέγοντας ἔχειν, ἢ τοὺς ὑπὲρ ἑαυτῶν; ὥσπερ καὶ παρ' ὑμῖν, ὅτι τοῖς μὲν ὑπὲρ τοῦ βελτίστου λέγουσιν οὐδὲ βουλομένοις ἔνεστιν ἐνίοτε πρὸς χάριν οὐδὲν εἰπεῖν· τὰ γὰρ πράγματ' ἀνάγκη σκοπεῖν ὅπως σωθήσεται· οἱ δ' ἐν αὐτοῖς, οἷς χαρίζονται, Φιλίππῳ συμπράττουσιν·

DEMOSTHENES.

10 marks.

B.

4. Translate into Greek :—

But of this man's praises I will say nothing, not because I fear that small credence shall be given to the testimony that cometh out of a friend's mouth; but because his virtue and learning are greater and of more excellence than that I am able to praise them ; and also in all places so famous and so perfectly well known that they need not and ought not of me to be praised, unless I would seem to show and set forth the brightness of the sun with a candle, as the proverb saith.
10 marks.

5. Translate into Greek :—

I fear that we shall forget our road home.

I will go away on condition that you will yourselves set out at nightfall.

It is profitable to men to be pious.

If you have more than enough give some to your friends. 5 marks.

C.

6. Give the perfect of κιρνάντημι, the 1st aor. pass. of σκεδάννυμι, the 2nd aor. pass. of μίγνυμι, the future of ὁράω, the 2nd aor. of βαίνω.
10 marks.

7. Give the dates and results of the following battles—

Plataea, Leuctra, Issus, Ægos-potami, Ipsus. 5 marks.

8. Distinguish between the uses of οὐ and μή, and illustrate by examples. 5 marks.

9. Write out in full the persons of οἶδα (I know) and ᾖδη (I know)
5 marks.

10. Give an account of the Sicilian Expedition. 5 marks.

GREEK.—50 Marks.

Two hours and a half allowed for this paper.

Only five questions to be attempted—to include at least one from each group, A, B, C.

Mr. NEWELL, Head Inspector.
Dr. BEATTY, District Inspector.

A.

Translate into English :—

1.   Ὣς εἰπὼν πρόιει, κρατερὸν δ' ἐπὶ μῦθον ἔτελλεν.
τὼ δ' ἄκοντε βάτην παρὰ θῖν' ἁλὸς ἀτρυγέτοιο,
μυρμιδόνων δ' ἐπί τε κλισίας καὶ νῆας ἱκέσθην,
τὸν δ' εὗρον παρά τε κλισίῃ καὶ νηὶ μελαίνῃ
ἥμενον· οὐδ' ἄρα τώγε ἰδὼν γήθησεν Ἀχιλλεύς.
τὼ μὲν ταρβήσαντε καὶ αἰδομένω βασιλῆα
στήτην, οὐδέ τί μιν προσεφώνεον οὐδ' ἐρέοντο.
αὐτὰρ ὁ ἔγνω ᾗσιν ἐνὶ φρεσί, φώνησέν τε·

HOMER.
10 marks.

Appendix I

Examination
Questions

Male
Teachers.

4. B, or C
Paper.

2. εἴς γε μὲν δικαιοσύνην, εἰ τις αὐτῷ φανερὸς γένοιτο ἐπιδεῖν βουλόμενος, περὶ παντὸς ἐποιεῖτο τούτους πλουσιωτέρους ποιεῖν τῶν ἐκ τοῦ ἀδίκου φιλοκερδούντων. καὶ γὰρ οὖν ἄλλα τε πολλὰ δικαίως αὐτῷ διεχειρίζετο, καὶ στρατεύματι ἀληθινῷ ἐχρήσατο. καὶ γὰρ στρατηγοὶ καὶ λοχαγοὶ οὐ χρημάτων ἕνεκα πρὸς ἐκεῖνον ἔπλευσαν, ἀλλ' ἐπεὶ ἔγνωσαν κερδαλεώτερον εἶναι Κύρῳ καλῶς πειθαρχεῖν, ἢ τὸ κατὰ μῆνα κέρδος.

XENOPHON.

10 marks.

3. ὡς οὖν ὑπὲρ τῶν ἐσχάτων ἐσομένου τοῦ ἀγῶνος ὑμῖν, οὕτω προσήκει γιγνώσκειν, καὶ τοὺς πεπρακότας αὑτοὺς ἐκείνῳ φανερῶς μισεῖν καὶ ἀποτυμπανίσαι· οὐ γὰρ ἔστιν, οὐκ ἔστι τῶν ἔξω τῆς πόλεως ἐχθρῶν κρατῆσαι, πρὶν ἂν τοὺς ἐν αὐτῇ τῇ πόλει κολάσητε ἐχθρούς, ἀλλ' ἀνάγκη τούτοις ὥσπερ προβόλοις προσπταίοντας ὑστερίζειν ἐκείνων. πόθεν οἴεσθε νῦν αὐτὸν ὑβρίζειν ὑμᾶς, οὐδὲν γὰρ ἄλλο ἔμοιγε δοκεῖ ποιεῖν ἢ τοῦτο, καὶ τοὺς μὲν ἄλλους εὖ ποιοῦντα, εἰ μηδὲν ἄλλο, ἐξαπατᾶν, ὑμῖν δὲ ἀπειλεῖν ἤδη.

DEMOSTHENES.

10 marks.

B

4. Translate into Greek :—

Messengers were then sent through Persia and all the neighbouring kingdoms to announce that the great king required a tutor who could teach his son to govern aright. To him who would set forth the best plan of education was promised more wealth than he had beheld in his dreams of youth.   10 marks.

5. Translate into Greek :—

If I possessed a talent, I would not ask you for pay.

When you have managed the affairs of the State well, you shall manage mine also.

If you do this, you will become more powerful than ever.

Most men follow their neighbours.

Whilst you are still at leisure, speak.   5 marks.

C.

6. Write out in full the present indicative active of :—
τιμάω, δουλόω, ποιέω, ἵστημι, and δίδωμι.   10 marks.

7. State what you know about the Achaean League.   5 marks.
8. What moods and tenses are joined to μή to express prohibition? Distinguish the respective meanings.   5 marks.
9. Name the case or cases which are used with each of the following :—
πλήν, διά, πρός, ἀντί, σύν.   5 marks.

10. Write out the genitive singular of :—
Ζεύς, ἕδρα, ὄρνις, Ἄρης, γόνυ.   5 marks.

IRISH.—50 Marks.

Time—Two hours.

Only FIVE *questions are to be attempted, viz. :—One in Section A, two in Section B, and two in Section C.*

Mr. LEHANE, District Inspector.

SECTION A.

1. Translate into Irish :—

Just then the king happened to raise his eyes to the roof, and he saw, hanging from one of the rafters, by a thread of its own spinning, a spider which was trying to swing from one beam of the roof to another. The first attempt the spider made was a failure. A second time it tried, but did not succeed in reaching the beam.   10 marks.

2. Translate into Irish :—

All the rain that falls does not lie on the surface of the earth ; some of it sinks into the soil and makes it rich and fertile, nourishing the roots of plants, and feeding their stems with juice or sap.   5 marks.

SECTION B.

3. Translate into English :—

Do réir Prateatac Corpl ar trí bliadhna tearta no tá céo fro placair Teart Dé Danann an Grunn.   Tá an rannro lair rin :—

      Seate m-bliadhna nóeat ir céo—
      An t-arrort rin noca brég,
      Do Thuat Dé Danann go n-gur
      An Grunn a n-ara-placair.   10 marks.

4. Translate into English :—

"Do bár rin víb" ar Fionn "act go tagad ríb áine bam ma atar." "Ní ful ór, ná airgeo, ná ronnter, ná iolrhanne buan, ná bótámne againn no bearrranaor veir a Fhinn" ar rue. "Ná h-iarr áine orrta a Fhinn" ar Oirín.   10 marks.

5. Translate into English :—

An beagán v'Fheararb bolg tearba ar an g-cat ro no tuavon an ertíob ra Tuatal Dé Danann gan h-ártgoo rau Aramn íte, Reaëramn, Innre Gall agur iomao oilén ar áeana, agur no toahnartórtoo tonnta go b-amrrn na g-córeavat no beit a b-placair Grunonn.   5 marks.

6. Translate into English :—

Do bí bean ann rao ó fom, agur ní pá anet. Do rug an gé ro ub Grada gat morón. Ba mian leir an innaot an eirro óir an rao a bert aet : agur mon rin vé, no marb rí an gé—agur ruair rí nat ramb órt rin bró annr an rgé, agur go ramb rí mar gat gé ele.   5 marks.

Appendix I.
Examination Questions.
Male Teachers.
A⁴ Paper.

SECTION C.

7. Write short notes on the syntactical construction of sentences containing the numeral *dá, two.*   10 marks.

8. Illustrate by reference to English words, the sounds of the vowels in Irish (*a*) when the vowel is long and (*b*) when the vowel is short.   10 marks.

9. Give the infinitive mood and the future tense of the verb *gaḃaim, I find.*   5 marks.

10. Where are the places mentioned in Question 5? Give the modern name of each.   5 marks.

A, B, or C Papers.

IRISH.—50 Marks.

Time—two hours.

Only FIVE *questions are to be attempted, viz. :—One in Section A, two in Section B, and two in Section C.*

Mr. LEAHY, District Inspector.

SECTION A.

1. Translate into Irish :—

Bruce started to his feet. "Six times," he exclaimed, "I also failed in my efforts. I will try once more. Perhaps, like the spider, I shall be successful this time." Filled with fresh hope, he crossed over to Scotland, gathered another army together, attacked the enemy, and gained a decisive victory.   10 marks.

2. Translate into Irish :—

"Thou old fool," replied the fox, "hadst thou but half as much sense as thou hast beard, thou wouldst never have believed that I would hazard my own life to save thine."   5 marks.

SECTION B.

3. Translate into English :—

Dála Thuaté Dé Danann, mar do conncadar lucht na Srua ag buadṁgad ar lucht na críce, triallaid for a n-agla d'aonḃaróm ar an g-cric sin, agur ní ḋearnadar comnaṁde go rángadar go ciúl Laélonn orton, Cronnladtonnart, mar mác Láir na Norwegia, mar a ḃ-fearrḟaror páilre ó lucht na críce ar iomad a n-oaluroan agur a n-áiteonra.   10 marks.

4. Translate into English :—

"Masreat" ar Gránne "fágra na h-aé ar an táṁan ro, agur do ḃḟyra coṁconrṁcatc vant fearrda." Do tárplang Diarmano an Sruad an áta, agur do nig eat leir tarr an át anonn agur d'fágaiḃ ar gat taoḃ don orrat iao, agur do ḟaḋ fém agur Gránne mile fur an orrat rian, agur do teaḋoar a ṁéip do laoḃ taoiḃ oirgro Chonnaic.   10 marks.

5. Translate into English :—

" Oíc an buinean atá ann," ap Diapmuid, "a luct na bréige, aguɪ
na longaincaíze, aguɪ na leictpóize ; aguɪ ní h-é eagla bap láihe
atá opm, att le nenhicon oppaib nat ngeobamn tugab amat."
                                                              5 marks.

6. Translate into English :—

Mapg peallaɪ ap a tapaɪo. Ní cantleatt gin ríbáilen. Copat
piáince acolat. Uathan Dé top eagna é.   5 marks.

Juvenile L.
Examination
Question.
Male
Teachers.
A, B, or C
Paper.

SECTION C.

7. Write short notes on the construction of sentences containing
collective nouns.   10 marks.

8. Write a note on the verb in the sentence :— Lact bem5 anna
lın.   10 marks.

9. Name the long diphthongs in Irish. Illustrate their regular
sounds by reference to suitable Irish and English words.   5 marks.

10. Who was Nudha Airgiodlamh ? Why was he so named ?
                                                              5 marks.

FRENCH.—50 Marks.

An hour and a half allowed for this paper.

N.B.—*Only five questions to be attempted—one at least from each
group A, B, C.*

Mr. Newell, Head Inspector.
Mr. Hynes, District Inspector.

French
Teachers.
A, B, or C
Paper.

A.

1. Translate into English :—

Oh qu'un est malheureux, disait-il, quand on est au-dessus du reste des
hommes ! souvent on ne peut voir la vérité par ses propres yeux : on est
environné de gens qui l'empêchent d'arriver jusqu'à celui qui commande ;
chacun est intéressé à le tromper ; chacun, sous une apparence de zèle,
cache son ambition. On fait semblant d'aimer le roi, et on n'aime que
les richesses qu'il donne : on l'aime si peu que, pour obtenir ses faveurs,
on le flatte et on le trahit.—*Télémaque.*   10 marks.

2.   Les Levantins en leur légende
            Disent qu'un certain rat, las des soins d'ici-bas,
                  Dans un fromage de Hollande
                  Se retira loin du tracas.
                  La solitude était profonde,
                  S'étendant partout à la ronde.
            Notre hermite nouveau subsistait là-dedans.
                  Il fit tant, des pieds et des dents,
            Qu'en peu de jours il eut au fond de l'ermitage,
                  Le vivre et le couvert.—*La Fontaine.*   10 marks.

3. Leurs enfants ont déjà leur audace hautaine.
Mais que veut Athalie en cette occasion ?
D'où naît dans son conseils cette confusion ?
Par l'insolent Joad ce matin offensée,
Et d'un enfant fatal en songe menacée,
Elle allait immoler Joad en son courroux,
Et dans ce temple enfin placer Baal et vous.
Vous m'en aviez déjà coulé votre joie ;
Et j'espérais ma part d'une si riche proie.
Qui fait changer ainsi ses vœux irrésolus ?—*Athalie.*

10 marks.

B.

4. Translate into French—

Here, when the weather was fine and our labour soon finished, we usually sat together to enjoy an extensive landscape in the calm of the evening. Here, too, we drank tea, which now was become an occasional banquet; and as we had it but seldom, it diffused a new joy, the preparations for it being made with no small share of bustle and ceremony. On these occasions, our two little ones always read for us, and they were regularly served after we had done.

10 marks.

5. Express in French—

(a.) *He has broken his arm ;*

(b.) *A cannon ball carried off his leg ;*

(c.) *Give me your hand ;*

(d.) *His feet are cold ;*

(e.) *She has lost her sight.*

5 marks.

C.

6. Write out all the persons of the present indicative of *acquérir, jeter, pouvoir, espérer, cueillir.*

10 marks.

7. Distinguish between *Second* and *Deuxième*, *Vers* and *Envers.* Illustrate by examples.

5 marks.

8. Give the meanings of *le mousse,* and *la mousse ; le souris,* and *la souris ; le voile,* and *la voile ; le somme,* and *la somme ; le manche,* and *la manche.*

5 marks.

9. What are the past participles of *croître, boire, mettre, suivre,* and *joindre ?*

5 marks.

10. Express in French—

(a.) *His son and thine ;*

(b.) *Thy flower and his ;*

(c.) *My rose and yours ;*

(d.) *Your aunt and theirs ;*

(e.) *My wood and yours.*

5 marks.

BOTANY.—50 Marks.

One hour and a half allowed for this paper.

N.B.—*Only five questions to be attempted.*

Mr. CONNELLAN, Head Inspector.
Mr. DALTON, District Inspector.

1. What are the two classes of *phanerogams*? Distinguish between them in respect of *seed, woody structure, leaf venation, flower.*
10 marks.

2. Describe common wheat as to its *leaves and glumes.* How is this plant classed?
10 marks.

3. Give the numbers which express the arrangements of the leaves on the stem in the cases of any four plants.
10 marks.

4. Explain fully the terms used in the following description:—*Stamens, hypogynous; ovaries, superior; stigmas, simple; carpels,* indehiscent.
10 marks.

5. Give the common names of *taraxacum officinale, conium maculatum, trifolium pratense, nymphæa alba;* state their orders, and give a short description of any one of them.
10 marks.

6. What are the chief characters of the natural order *primulaceæ*? Name four plants belonging to this order.
5 marks.

7. Distinguish the following forms of inflorescence and give an example of each—*umbel, raceme, spadix, catkin.*
5 marks.

8. Explain clearly the principal functions of the leaves of plants.
5 marks.

9. Describe the reproductive organs of *Filices.*
5 marks.

10. Name plants whose root is an example of the following:—*Corm, rhizome, bulb.*
5 marks.

MUSIC—(HULLAH).—50 Marks.

An hour and a half allowed for this paper.

N.B.—*Only five questions to be attempted.*

Mr. P. GOODMAN, Examiner in Music.

1. Explain the terms *Major, Minor, Diatonic, Chromatic,* as applied to a Scale; and write, commencing on the note Fa (F), an example of each of those scales ascending and descending.
10 marks.

2. Write in treble and bass clefs—prefixing key signature—the Major scales of Mi natural (E), and La flat (A♭); and the minor scales commencing on Fa♯ (F♯) and Si flat (B♭).
10 marks.

3. Name the following Intervals, and state what each becomes on Inversion.

. . 12 marks.

Appendix L.
Exam.
tation
Questions.

Female
Teachers.

A, B, or C
Papers.

4. Write one bar with each of the following Time Signatures, and say in what kind of Time each bar is written.

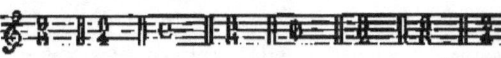

8 marks.

5. Transpose the following into the key of La♭. Prefix key and time signatures :—

10 marks.

6. Correct what you consider wrong in the following :—

8 marks.

7. Write in treble and bass clefs the signatures of the following major and minor scales:—Mi flat (E♭), Re (D) and La (A).

8 marks.

8. Write the five principal Italian words used to indicate the pace at which a piece of music is to be performed.   6 marks.

9. Explain the difference between the following :—

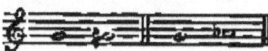

4 marks.

10. Name the Major Sevenths in the scale of Si flat (B♭).

5 marks.

DRAWING.

Three hours allowed for this subject.

N B.—The name of the Teacher and of her School to be written on each paper.

Mr. NEWELL, Head Inspector.
Mr. CRAIG, District Inspector.

I.—FREEHAND DRAWING.—50 Marks.

Copy the example supplied on a slightly larger scale—say about an inch higher—the rest in proportion.

II.—OBJECT DRAWING.—50 Marks.

The Examiner will place on an ordinary chair, not directly facing the Candidates, a small open wicker hand-basket. Hanging over the side nearest the Candidates let there be a few ivy or other large leaves, so that the light may fall upon them. A drawing of these objects is to be made, which should fairly fill the paper.

III.—PRACTICAL GEOMETRY AND PERSPECTIVE.
50 Marks.

NOTE.—Only five of the following questions may be attempted. Answers should be written on one side of the paper only, and where the construction is not obvious, an explanation should be given, the points being marked with letters.

Full credit will not be allowed for a question, unless the construction is neatly drawn, and all lines are shown.

N.B.—In addition to an ordinary case of instruments, set squares and a 12-inch rule may be used

1. A regular hexagonal prism has its axis inclined 45° to the paper and one face parallel to the vertical plane; draw its plan and elevation. Height of prism, 3 inches, side of base, 1·5 inches.　　10 marks.

2. Place in perspective an octagonal pyramid 8 feet high, having sides of base 2 feet each. The nearest side of base is to be parallel to, and on the picture line 4 feet to the right.
(Scale—¼ inch to 1 foot. Length of Line of Direction—11 feet. Distance between Horizontal and Base Line—9 feet).　　12 marks.

3. Within a regular octagon of ½ inch sides inscribe 4 equal circles, each touching two others and two sides of the octagon.　　10 marks.

4. Show the plans and elevations of the following points, using the same ground line for all :—

A, 3 inches above the horizontal plane, 1·8 inches before the vertical plane.

B, 2 inches above the horizontal plane, 3·5 inches behind the vertical plane.

C, 2·5 inches below the horizontal plane, ·4 inches before the vertical plane.

D, in the horizontal plane, 2·5 inches before the vertical plane.
　　10 marks.

5. Show how to construct a triangle similar to one triangle, and equal to another.　　8 marks.

6. Construct an equilateral triangle of 2·5 inches side. In it inscribe three equal semicircles, having their diameters adjacent, and each semicircle to touch only one side of the triangle.　　5 marks.

7. Construct a triangle whose sides are as 4 : 5 : 7, the longest side to be 3 inches long.　　5 marks.

8. Given 3 lines, 1 inch, 1½ inch, and 2 inches long, you are required to find a fourth proportional greater than any of them.　　5 marks.

9. About a regular hexagon of ½ inch sides describe six equal circles, each touching one side of the hexagon and two other circles.
　　5 marks.

10. Given the lengths of the axes, show how to draw an ellipse with pins and a thread.　　5 marks.

———

HYGIENE.—50 Marks.

One hour and a half allowed for this paper.

Only five questions to be attempted.

Mr. NEWELL, Head Inspector.
Mr. HEARNE, District Inspector.

1. What impurities are removed from foul water (a) by agitation with air, (b) by filtration, (c) by distillation?　　10 marks.

Appendix L.
Exami-
nation
Questions.

Female
Teachers.

2. What is a warm bath? Describe its uses, and distinguish between its direct and its indirect effects.   10 marks.

3. What chemical change does milk undergo in the process of digestion in the stomach? What advantage arises therefrom?   10 marks.

4. State some of the means which are adopted to test the soundness of the joints of house drains.   10 marks.

5. Mention special precautions which should be taken to prevent the spread of *diphtheria*, *measles*, *scarlatina*, *typhoid fever*, and *cholera*.
   10 marks.

6. What are fogs? Why are they unhealthy?   5 marks.

7. How many teeth are found in the adult? Describe the classes into which the teeth are divided, and explain the structure of a single tooth.   5 marks.

8. What are the most effectual means of preventing a cold?
   5 marks.

9. What is a balanced food? What is the cheapest well-balanced food on which to maintain, in full health, a strong man employed in daily hard work?   5 marks.

10. Enumerate the evil effects which arise from deficiency of water for drinking and general domestic purposes.   5 marks.

ELEMENTARY PHYSICS.—50 Marks.

One hour and a half allowed for this paper.

N.B.—*Only five questions to be attempted.*

Mr. PURSER, Head Inspector.
Mr. HEADEN, District Inspector.

1. Describe the construction and use of the mercurial barometer.
   10 marks.

2. What is sound? What is required for its production, and what causes the difference in sounds, as, for instance, in the case of two musical notes?   10 marks.

3. "It is easier to stand on our feet than on stilts." "It is impossible to stand on one foot if we keep the side of that foot close to a high vertical wall." Explain the reason in each case.   10 marks.

4. Why is (a) steel *tempered* and (b) glass *annealed*? Explain the process in each case.   10 marks.

5. Describe the different kinds of levers, and give two familiar examples of each kind.   10 marks.

6. For scientific experiments why are metal mirrors preferable to glass mirrors?   5 marks.

7. What are the conditions required in a perfect balance?
   5 marks.

8. What is a parachute? Explain its action.   5 marks.

9. By what two means besides pumping additional air into it may a partially filled air-bladder be made to distend?   5 marks.

10. Why is it that water boils more rapidly in a metallic vessel than in one of porcelain of equal thickness?   5 marks.

AGRICULTURE.—50 Marks.

Two hours allowed for this paper.

N.B.—Only five questions to be attempted.

Mr. CONNELLAN, Head Inspector.
Mr. CRAIG, District Inspector.

1. Give in detail the various points to be attended to in the treatment of milk by the person in charge of the dairy (a) where the cream only is churned, (b) where the whole milk is churned. 10 marks.

2. Name three varieties of white wheat and two of red. To what kind of soil is each sort, red and white, adapted? How is wheat sown after a clover crop? 10 marks.

3. How should elevated land or mountain sheep-pastures be drained? 10 marks.

4. What is the difference required in the treatment of store pigs according as they are intended for pork or intended for bacon? 10 marks.

5. What are the prevailing faults in the present management of the greater number of small farms? Sketch briefly the system recommended as an improvement preparatory to the establishment of a suitable rotation on such holdings. 10 marks.

6. Give a description of the Devon Cow. For what kind of soils is it suitable? 5 marks.

7. State why red clover is so extensively grown in the eastern and south-eastern counties of England in preference to rye grasses. 5 marks.

8. Describe the cultivation of the Cauliflower. 5 marks.

9. What is the use of woody fibre as a food? 5 marks.

10. Describe the espalier mode of training fruit trees, and mention its advantages. 5 marks.

DOMESTIC ECONOMY.—50 Marks.

One hour and a half allowed for this paper.

N.B.—Only five questions to be attempted.

Mr. STRONGE, Head Inspector.
Mr. MORGAN, District Inspector.

1. From what sources do we obtain the mineral or bone-making food necessary to build up and maintain the human body? Describe fully. 10 marks.

2. Describe the process of extracting sugar from the sugar-cane. From what other sources is sugar obtained? 10 marks.

3. Name the constituents of which milk is composed. Give their proportions, and describe an instrument used for testing the purity of milk. 10 marks.

4. What meats contain the greatest proportion of nourishment; and what meats are most easy of digestion? 10 marks.

5. State the best immediate remedies to be applied in the following cases:—a sprain; a cut of large vein or artery; a gathering or whitlow; a scald. 10 marks.

Appendix L.
Exami-
nation
Questions,
Female
Teachers.

6. What is charcoal, and what is its special advantage as a fuel? What danger may arise from its use, and how is this to be guarded against?
5 marks.

7. What quantity of food of various kinds does a full-grown man require every twenty-four hours?
5 marks.

8. What percentage of fat is found in cocoa, in cheese, in oatmeal; and what percentage of albumen in eggs and in fish?
5 marks.

9. What should determine the intervals between meals? Give five good rules as to eating.
5 marks.

10. Give a brief account of the working of the Post Office Savings Bank, and explain how it is connected with the National Schools.
5 marks.

— —

MUSIC.—TONIC SOL-FA.—50 Marks.

An hour and a half allowed for this paper.

N.B.—*Only five questions to be attempted.*

Mr. P. Goodman, Examiner in Music.

1. Translate (a) into the Tonic Sol-fa notation,

       (b) into the Staff notation, using the crotchet for the pulse.

(a)

(b) Key F—

$$[: d., r \mid m : m : m., f \mid m : r]$$
$$\{: m.s \mid l : r : r., m \mid r : - \}$$
$$[: d., r \mid m : f.m : r.d \mid s_t :- .l_t]$$
$$\{: d.r \mid m : d : d.r \mid d :- \|$$

14 marks.

2. If the first note of the following becomes r, how will the other notes be named:—$l \ m \ fe \ s \ r \ fe \ s \ r^1 \ d^1 \ t \ d^1 \ d \ m \ fe \ s$?
12 marks.

3. Write two measures each, of four pulse, six pulse, and three pulse measure. Use the note d throughout, and introduce halves and quarters of pulses in each example.
6 marks.

4. Name the following Intervals, state number of index degrees in each, and what each becomes on Inversion:—

l	s	m^1	d^1	ma	s
t_1	r	s	m	r	do

10 marks.

5. Describe the Hand Signs used in teaching Tune in the Tonic Sol-fa Method.
8 marks.

Appendix I.

Exam-
ining
Questions.

Female
Teachers.

A, B, or C
Papers,

6. Re-arrange the following in ascending order as regards pitch, beginning with the lowest note and ending with the highest :—

(1) m l fe r s d ta l_1 r s_1 f t_1.

(2) r s m l_1 d^1 ta d f_1 r^1 fe m^1 l.

6 marks.

7. How do the Accents of the Measure differ from the Accents within the Pulse?

5 marks.

8. Re-write the following, doubling the value of each note and rest :—

$$|| s \cdot f : m \cdot , f | s \quad : - \quad | f \quad : - \cdot s | l , s \cdot f : m \cdot r |$$
$$| m \cdot r , d : t , \cdot r | d \quad :$$

5 marks.

9. When sung slowly what is the mental effect of r, s, m, l?

4 marks.

10. On what system would you proceed to divide your class into Trebles and Altos for part singing?

5 marks.

———

KINDERGARTEN.—50 Marks.

Two hours allowed for this subject.

N.B.—*Only five questions to be attempted.*

Mr. Purser, Head Inspector.
Mr. Headen, District Inspector.

1. Give full directions for three games with First Gift, and explain what educational advantages you would expect from them.

10 marks.

2. Draw up a time table for an Infant school of 65 children, in which each division shall receive daily half-an-hour's separate instruction, and half an hour's simultaneous instruction in Kindergarten. (Staff—Teacher and two monitors).

10 marks.

3. " All mental development begins with concrete beings." Explain this principle, and show how it is applied in the Kindergarten system.

10 marks.

4. Whether should drawing or writing be taught first, and why? Discuss the importance of drawing in Kindergarten, and in practical life.

10 marks.

5. Name ten objects you would select as suitable for "Object lessons"; and write out notes of a lesson on any one of these objects. 10 marks.

6. Draw five " forms of life " suitable for Fifth Gift.   5 marks.

7. Give a complete list of essential Kindergarten materials, and the quantity of each required for a school of 60 children—classes represented—Infants, I. and II.

5 marks.

8. Describe the principal characteristics of a suitable school-song.

5 marks.

9. Explain clearly the distinction between the "gifts" and the " occupations " in Kindergarten.

5 marks.

10. " To develop the hand is one of the most important tasks of education." What does this mean and how is it effected in Kindergarten?

5 marks.

2 C

Appendix L.
Examination Questions.
Female Teachers.
A, B, or C.
Papers.

IRISH.—50 Marks.

Time—3 hours.

Only FIVE questions are to be attempted, viz. :—one in Section A, two in Section B, and two in Section C.

Mr. LEHANE, District Inspector.

SECTION A.

1. Translate into Irish :—

Long afterwards the simple people believed that Red Hugh was not dead at all; he was a fairy king, and lived in a bright and glorious palace under the hill, with a splendid fairy retinue. And they called the hill Mullaghshee, or Mullinashee, which means the hill of the fairy palace.   10 marks.

2. Translate into Irish :—

One piercing shriek from a woman's voice was heard, and then the cries of the villagers exclaiming, " Hannah Lamond's child, Hannah Lamond's child. The eagle has carried it off."   5 marks.

SECTION B.

3. Translate into English—

Ġroeaḋ ní roinn creaċaḋ vo ḃí raxonna, aċc realeiḋeaċ Flaiṫir, eaḋon, ṡaḋ ro m-bliaḋain aṡ ṡaḋ aon vloḃ aṁ vaṁuḃ aniaḋ a vaḃramon tuar a n-aṁṁannaiḋ na cṁiṁṁ. Ar ṁine vo ṡorṁiov na h-aṁṁanṁa ro von cruan ruoṡ rom, vo ḃriṡ ṡon aḃ Coll Céit aṡar ṡruan ra véé aṁaṁta véiṁ.   10 marks.

4. Translate into English—

" Caran Ṁiarmava Uí Oḃarḃṁe an ceann ṫo ṁerrrar Fiann orruṁḃra, aṡar vá m-biaṁ riḃra Uon riḃe caro roam mṁarṁṁa ní léiṡraṁ Viarmṁo O Uṁḋṁe an ceann rerrar Fiann orruṁḃra lé ṫ a ceann rein." " Crevo ṁo na ceoṁa ṫo rerrar Fiann orruṁen " ar ṁaṁ.   10 marks.

5. Translate into English—

Vo ḃiory Viarrṁero ar a ḃvla on car ra, aṡar vo ṫéirṡ Ṡ ṁánna rṁa ṁo ṡceora, aṡ ṁ a vaḃanṁa ra " Aṡ ra Ḃran .ı. aḃ rṁinn aḃ Cḃeanḃall aṡ cano lo raṁaḃ ṫaṁaṁṁe roṁ Ṁinonn rein."   5 marks.

6. Translate into English—

Ḃí an laoṫ-ṁaṁa vonn. Ḃí an raṁṁ-raṁa ṡlic. Oḃaṁn cano aṡur oḃan virṡa. Ruaṁ an ceol ḃinn. Dier virṡa aṁṁir. Clear aṁrell bám.   5 marks.

SECTION C.

7. What two meanings may the pronoun *sé* do have ? Give examples with a view to illustrate your answer.   10 marks.

8. Give the nominative plural of the following nouns :—múr a wall, fear a man, cúir a cause, obair work, rpealaróir a mower, and móin a bog. What declension does each noun belong to ? 10 marks.

9. Decline the nouns ceó a fog, and mí a month.   5 marks.

10. Where are Brugh na Boinne and Garbh-abha na bh-Fiann ?   5 marks.

ALGEBRA.—50 Marks.

Two hours allowed for this paper.

N.B.—Only five questions to be attempted.

Mr. STRONGE, Head Inspector.
Mr. CROMIE, District Inspector.

1. There are two numbers in the ratio 4 : 7 ; if 21 be added to the first and subtracted from the second, the proportion is reversed : find the numbers.   10 marks.

2. What value must be substituted for x in order that the expressions—

$$\frac{x-\frac{1}{2}}{2}-\frac{x-\frac{1}{3}}{3} \text{ and } \frac{x-\frac{1}{4}}{4}-\frac{x-\frac{1}{5}}{5}$$

may be equal. Prove the correctness of your work.   10 marks.

3. Solve the equation—

$$\frac{x^2-4x}{x-2}+\frac{x^2-1}{x+1}=39.$$

10 marks.

4. If $a=\frac{1}{2}, b=-1, x=0, y=-\frac{1}{3}$, find the value of

$$\frac{(b-y)^2}{ax-b^2}-\frac{(y-a)^2}{by-abx}+\frac{(a-b)^2}{b^2-xy}.$$

10 marks.

5. Show that—

$$\frac{a}{2na-2nx}+\frac{b}{2nb-2nx} \text{ becomes } \frac{1}{n} \text{ when } x=\frac{1}{2}(a+b).$$

10 marks.

6. The difference of the squares of two consecutive numbers is 35 : find the numbers.   5 marks.

7. Find the simple value of—

$$(a^2-b^2-c^2-2bc)\div\frac{a+b+c}{a+b-c}.$$

5 marks.

8. Solve the equation—

$$\sqrt{x+9}=1+\sqrt{x}.$$

5 marks.

9. Reduce to its lowest terms—

$$\frac{x^2+3x+2}{x^2+2x+1}\times\frac{x^2+5x+6}{x^2+7x+12}$$

5 marks.

10. Simplify—

$$3a-[b+\{2a-(b-c)\}]+\frac{1}{4}+\frac{2c^2-\frac{1}{4}}{2c+1}.$$

5 marks.

Appendix L.
Examination Questions.
French Teachers.

GEOMETRY AND MENSURATION.—50 Marks.

[Two hours and a half allowed for this paper.

N.B.—*Only five questions to be attempted.*

Mr. SULLIVAN, Head Inspector.
Mr. KELLY, District Inspector.

1. The sum of the squares on the sides of a parallelogram is equal to the sum of the squares on its diagonals.   10 marks.

2. The line joining the middle points of the sides of any triangle is equal to half the base.   10 marks.

3. The area of a circle is 50 feet; find the side of the inscribed square.   10 marks.

4. Prove Euc., Book II., Prop. 12, by describing squares on the sides of the triangle.   10 marks.

5. Construct a right-angled triangle, being given the hypotenuse and the difference of the sides.   10 marks.

6. If a right line be divided into any two parts, the sum of the squares on the whole line and either segment is equal to twice the rectangle contained by the whole line and that segment, together with the square on the other segment.   5 marks.

7. The bisectors of the three internal angles of a triangle are concurrent.   5 marks.

8. Find the surface of a cone whose slant height is 40, the circumference of its base being 18.   5 marks.

9. Construct a square equal to a given rectilineal figure.   5 marks.

10. The perimeter of a quadrilateral is greater than the sum of its diagonals.   5 marks.

ANNUAL EXAMINATIONS of TEACHERS and MONITORS, JULY, 1894.

Annual Examinations of Teachers and Monitors.

SYNOPSIS of SPECIAL REPORTS furnished by EXAMINERS with reference to the fulness or otherwise of the knowledge of the different subjects exhibited by Teachers and Monitors at the Annual Examinations of 1894.

Methods of Teaching candidates for First Class, and First of First Class.

The Examiners in *Methods of Teaching* report that in case of candidates for promotion to First Class the answering on the whole was good, showing earnest preparation on the part of the candidates, as out of the large number examined there was not a single failure. The questions on the Time Table arrangements were very fairly answered, while that on the appropriate exercises for Infants was generally missed. The knowledge displayed of the Commissioners' Rules was wanting in accuracy, very few of the answers deserving full marks, while questions bearing on the school accounts were for the most part fully and accurately answered.

Candidates for Second Class.

The knowledge of Methods of Teaching displayed by the candidates examined on Second Class papers was on the whole of a satisfactory character; and the manner as to neatness in which the exercises were executed was fair. Those of the candidates in Training Colleges were, as in previous years, much superior to the exercises from the ordinary districts both as to fulness of knowledge and composition.

One remarkable feature in the exercises of all candidates was the deficiency in the answers to the questions on the Board's Regulations and Programmes, e.g., but few attempted the questions as to the Forms of Agreement, and of these scarcely one was correct.

As regards the answering in this subject of candidates examined on Third Class papers, the Examiner reports that in the case of the Queen's Scholars the answering showed a full knowledge of the subject, as tested by the examination papers, and the exercises were neatly executed; on the part of the candidates for classification and for admission to the Training Colleges the answering showed a marked improvement on that of previous years. In a few instances out of those competing for the Colleges, the writing was bad and the spelling indifferent.

The Fifth Year Monitors showed a very full knowledge of the subject-matter of the *Hand book of Methods of Teaching.* The Commissioners' Rules and Methods of keeping the school accounts were seldom accurately given. The Examiner complains of the want of neatness and arrangement observable in most of the exercises, and of the entire absence of punctuation in many of them, particularly those of the female candidates.

The answering of the Third Year Monitors in *Methods of Teaching* showed an intimate acquaintance with the portion of the text-book prescribed. The knowledge displayed by the Female Monitors, with very few exceptions, was slightly superior to that of the males. The writing and general neatness of the exercises were highly satisfactory and compare very favourably with those of more highly classed teachers.

The Examiner in Arithmetic reports that the questions set to candidates First of First and First Class were of the usual high standard, and embraced the most difficult problems treated of in the most advanced works on the subject. In general the answers were methodically and neatly arranged, and the operations were correctly worked out. Upon the whole, the answering was not so high as in 1893, but there were few, not more than two or three, who answered below 20 per cent. There were also very few who answered up to 100 per cent. The answering ranged in the case of most of the candidates from 40 to 70 per cent.

The answering of the Teachers and Queen's Scholars who were examined on Second Class Papers in *Arithmetic* was fair. The males showed a more satisfactory knowledge than the females, especially in the solution of questions necessitating an acquaintance with the theory of the subject, but in many cases the introduction of the methods and symbols of Algebra was not regarded as irregular. In several instances calculations, which could hardly be performed by a mental process, did not appear in the written exercises, and more results were entered. Inaccuracy and untidiness were exceptional.

The style of the work in *Arithmetic* was superior in the case of the Queen's Scholars. There was a good deal of untidy, ill-arranged work from the ordinary candidates who, in many instances, gave evidence of their very indifferent preparation. In general the male candidates scored better than the females. Only twenty-five did less than five questions, of whom three attempted only two, very few attempted more than five. The Arithmetical exercises of the male monitors of Fifth Year were good, high percentage of answering was obtained, accuracy and neatness of work were on the whole creditable. The exercises of the Fifth Year Female Monitors were on the whole mediocre, the percentage gained was

Appendix.
Annual
Examinations of
Teachers
and
Monitors.

Third Year
Monitors,
Geography,
Candidates
for First and
First and
First Class.

Candidates
for Second
Class.

Candidates
for Third
Class and
for training.

Fifth Year
Monitors.

Third Year
Monitors.

Handwriting (all
candidates).

low; the work was very inaccurate, even neatness of execution fell in very many cases to a low ebb.

The answering in Arithmetic of Third Year Monitors, both male and female, was of a satisfactory character. The rules were correctly applied, but in comparatively few cases were the reasons for the rules thoughtfully discussed. In general the exercises were neatly worked out.

The Examiner reports that the general answering in Geography of male candidates for First of First and First Class was very fair, in some instances excellent: in these latter an extremely accurate acquaintance with the contents of the recognized text book, Geography Generalised, was shown. Generally speaking, the exercises were neatly written, and the matter methodically arranged.

The Examiner reports in reference to the extent and character of the knowledge of Geography shown by the female Teachers examined, also in regard to the neatness of the exercises sent in :—Map drawing does not appear to be growing in popularity ; very few attempts were made either by the Queen's Scholars or by candidates at the district centres ; on the whole, the specimens sent in were at least equal to those of former years.

The answering on Astronomy showed an effort had been made to make up this branch as treated in the Geography Generalised, and a tolerably intelligent grasp of the subject was displayed in most instances. The mistakes most frequently made occurred in connexion with the question in regard to the phases of the moon. The local Geography had, as a rule, been carefully made up, and with creditable attention to details, the study of atlases is gaining ground.

The Examiner reports that the answering in Geography of candidates for promotion to Second Class was on the whole good, and gave evidence of careful study and instruction. The only branch decidedly weak was map drawing. In the districts few attempted to draw a map, and in the Training Colleges the number who could draw one well was small. The exercises were neatly and carefully written, and the answering usually well expressed, and free from grammatical or orthographical errors.

The Examiners report that the examination papers in Geography written by the First Year Queen's Scholars (Mistresses) and the candidates for Training Colleges were in general of a satisfactory character in point of knowledge and style of penmanship and arrangement. The candidates for admission to the Colleges showed appreciably more preparation than in previous years, and displayed a remarkable recollection of places and facts connected with them, but the answering in some cases disclosed an exclusive exercise of memory, unaccompanied by reflection. Map drawing was seldom attempted, owing, perhaps, to the formidable character of the exercises proposed.

The Examiner reports that the answering in Geography of Monitors of Fifth Year may be considered as fairly satisfactory. Map drawing does not appear to have been carefully or skilfully taught, but, except in a comparatively few instances, a close acquaintance with the text books on the subject was exhibited by the candidates.

The Examiner reports that Third Year Monitors showed in general sound knowledge of the text books in Geography. There were many excellently worked papers submitted by them, and very few absolute failures occurred. Map drawing continues to be only passable.

The Examiner in Handwriting reports that the general character of the exercises of Male and Female Teachers and Monitors, of all ranks, was excellent. The writing throughout was uniformly bold and well formed, and the similarity of style that characterised the specimens from all parts of the country was striking.

The Examiner reports that the exercises in *Spelling* of candidates for
Second Class were, as in previous years, of a satisfactory degree of
merit. The great majority of the candidates, and particularly those from
the Training Colleges, showed a minute acquaintance with the text book
in *spelling*. Failures to secure any marks in *Dictation* were not
uncommon, but in many cases this was compensated by the candidates
obtaining marks in the text book paper, consequently absolute failures
were rare.

The Examiner reports that the exercises of the male candidates showed
very fair proficiency in *Dictation* and *Spelling*, and in many cases,
especially in connection with those pupils examined in the Training
Colleges, satisfactory proficiency. The answering of quite a number of
the candidates, showed that the Spelling Book superseded had been
little studied. With reference to the exercise of the female Teachers
fair merit has been exhibited as a rule. The dictation exercises
generally were satisfactory, and except in the case of the manifestly
weak candidates a tolerably close acquaintance with the Spelling Book
was displayed—these backward candidates were less in number than in
previous years.

The Examiner reports that the average percentage obtained by the
male candidates in *Dictation* and *Spelling* was 54. The exercises were
executed with neatness, and showed fair knowledge of the subject. The
average percentage obtained by the female candidates was 62. The
exercises were neatly executed and showed a very fair knowledge of the
subject by the candidates.

The Examiner reports that of the Third Year Monitors under examination the errors in *Dictation* were more numerous than usual, especially
among the female candidates, but that a satisfactory acquaintance with the
rules of *Spelling*, as given in the text book, was exhibited by nearly all
the candidates.

The Examiner reports that the papers examined by him in *Grammar*,
as ought to be expected from candidates for any division of First Class,
were, with very few exceptions, of a high character as to the fulness and
accuracy of the answering.

The Examiner reports that the working of the parsing exercise,
generally speaking, showed little intelligence, although the passages
given presented few difficulties that a good Sixth Class pupil could not
overcome. This remark does not apply, however, to the Training
Colleges. Increased attention has been given to the analysis of
sentences, and this exercise was, as a rule, well done by the Queen's
Scholars—comparatively few of the candidates at the district centres
attempted this part of the paper. With regard to the questions based
on the Grammar text-books they were generally answered correctly,
fully, and word for word from the book. The Examiner reports that
the exercises in *Grammar* were neatly executed and showed a very fair
acquaintance on the part of the candidates with the matter of the
Board's text books. The majority of the candidates were satisfactorily
proficient in parsing—occasional signs of negligence were to be found,
but failures were very few.

The Examiner reports that the parsing exercise was much better
done in the case of the male candidates than in previous years. Quite
a large proportion of the candidates obtained full marks. Very few, on
the other hand, did the question in analysis correctly. The other
questions proposed were answered correctly, as a rule, and, generally
too, with intelligent appreciation of the force of the terms used.
A lower standard of knowledge was shown by the female monitors,
both of parsing and formal grammar. Examiner noted often rules and

Appendix L.
Annual
Examination of
Teachers
and
Monitors.
explanations introduced which were quite inapplicable to the point under review. The general knowledge of the female candidates considered absolutely, is satisfactory and an advance on previous years. The Examiner reports that the male Monitors did the parsing exercise fairly. The correction of erroneous was very often not satisfactorily done—and an exceedingly small proportion attempted derivations.

Third Year Monitors. The answering of the female monitors generally gave evidence of a satisfactory knowledge of the subject. Penmanship and orthography, moreover, were as a rule of a very creditable character.

Lesson Books, candidates for Second Class. The Examiner in *Lesson Books* reports that on the whole the exercises were written out with a fair amount of neatness, and a creditable acquaintance with the subject was exhibited by the candidates. The papers from the several Training Colleges were very good, and there was nothing approaching a failure from any of them. The proportion of failures amongst the candidates from the districts was also much smaller than on previous occasions.

Candidates for Third Class. The Examiner in *Lesson Books* reports that the answers presented few distinguishing features, no candidate obtained full marks in the subject. The Queen's Scholars, as might be expected, acquitted themselves fairly well.

Fifth Year Monitors. The Examiner in *Lesson Books* on the whole can speak in favourable terms of the results of the examination. The candidates appeared in general to have a better acquaintance with the subject than in previous years, while the standard of answering was not high—in the great majority of cases it ranged between 30 and 60 per cent.—yet there was a smaller number of absolute failures, and there was also an almost complete absence of nonsensical answers. The candidates displayed, in many cases, the power of expressing themselves in clear and sensible language, and did not often stray into irrelevancies.

Third Year Monitors. The Examiner in *Lesson Books* reports, as regards the answering of Third Year Monitors, that the proportion of failures was equivalent to about one per cent., a considerable improvement, especially in regard to the girls, over last year. This, so far as it goes, is satisfactory, and yet it is difficult to find any excuse for failure on a paper of so elementary a character. The questions, as a rule, were taken from lessons which should be thoroughly familiar to all the candidates; and were, especially on the girls' paper, extremely simple and direct. Where any reflection was necessary, when the answer demanded anything more than verbal knowledge, the questions were either left untried or tried unsuccessfully. This remark applies however more to the papers of the girls. The boys generally exhibited more intelligence and more grasp of the substance, and in their answers absurdities occur more rarely. Two other points deserve attention. The first is the glaring neglect of punctuation in the composition exercises of the girls. The second is in the transcription of poetry, the neglect of the division into lines and stanzas.

Agriculture. Candidates for Second Class. The Examiner in *Agriculture* reports that the answering of the Training College candidates was, as a rule full, though in several cases verbose, and was executed with considerable neatness. The exercises of the other candidates, though otherwise very fair, were not executed with as much neatness as those of the Training candidates, and contained a higher percentage of misspelled words, chiefly technical terms.

Candidates for Third Class. The Examiner in *Agriculture* reports the answering of candidates for Third Class and for admission to Training as being, on the whole, of a fair character. Many of the Queen's Scholars, in particular, showed a very full acquaintance with the subject, and gave answers at once concise, complete, and well arranged.

The Examiner in *Agriculture* reports that the majority of the monitors of Fifth Year candidates for classification had a satisfactory knowledge of the prescribed course; very few obtained a high percentage of marks, but the average merit was satisfactory.

The Examiner in *Agriculture* of exercises of Monitors of Third Year report that the average percentage of marks obtained was fairly high. Very few of those examined failed, and the great majority showed by their answering that they possessed a satisfactory knowledge of the subject.

The Examiner of the exercises of the female teachers on a special paper in *Agriculture* reports that 14 candidates presented themselves for examination in this subject, 2 of whom were Queen's Scholars. Of the 14, 6 obtained the necessary percentage which entitles to a certificate of competency to teach the subject with a view to earning Results fees. The exercises of the candidates were, as a rule, carefully and neatly executed.

The Examiner in *Book-keeping* reports that in case of candidates for promotion to Second Class the answering of the mistresses was not so good as that of the masters, but that year by year the answering in this subject of teachers examined at the district compares less and less unfavourably with that of the students in training.

The Examiner in *Book-keeping* reports that the answering of the Queen's Scholars examined in Third Class papers was, in general, very satisfactory. An intimate acquaintance with the Programme was shown, and the work was neatly written out. The majority of those examined as candidates for training possessed but a superficial knowledge of the subject.

The Examiner in *Book-keeping* reports that the exercises of the Fifth Year Monitors were, on the whole, fair. Very few candidates obtained full marks on the paper, but, on the other hand, the failures were not numerous. A number of candidates do not seem to have yet acquired a grasp of the mode of dealing with bill transactions.

The Examiner of the exercises in *Book-keeping* of the Third Year Monitors reports that, generally throughout the country, the candidates obtained a very high percentage of marks. This is well shown by the fact that, though 36 out of the 840 examined obtained full marks, only 7 failed to obtain the qualifying minimum. With a few exceptions the handwriting was neat, and the figures carefully made.

The Examiner in *Geometry and Mensuration*, of the candidates for First of First Class or First Class report that the prescribed course had been carefully read and was well known, but the candidates had not been trained to write out the solutions and hence a defective arrangement of the proof was often presented and much unnecessary verbiage introduced into the answers. As in former years the questions in Mensuration were not often attempted. These questions were comparatively easy, yet candidates seemed to prefer the difficult questions set from the prepared or Geometry portion of the programme.

The Examiner of the exercises in *Geometry and Mensuration* of candidates for Second Class, reports that he considers the answering this year more satisfactory than on any previous occasion since he began to mark the subject. The questions were very easy, and presented no difficulty to a fairly prepared candidate—even making allowance for this fact, however, there was a distinct improvement. There were fewer bad papers, the diagrams were more neatly drawn and lettered, fewer symbols were used, and new fangled terms were more sparingly introduced.

The Examiner of the exercises of Third Class candidates in *Geometry and Mensuration* reports that the answering of the Queen's Scholars and unclassed Teachers, shows that in general they were well prepared in this subject for the examination, but the exercises of the candidates for

Appendix L.
training indicated that they possessed only a moderate knowledge of this subject.

Annual Examinations of Teachers and Monitors.
The Examiner reports that the answering of the Pupil Teachers and Monitors of Fifth Year in Geometry and Mensuration was very fair, and on the whole showed careful preparation on the programme.

Geometry and Mensuration. Fifth Year Monitors.
The Examiner in *Geometry and Mensuration* reports that the Third Year Monitors displayed in general a satisfactory knowledge of the prescribed course; there were few absolute failures. In the style of answering, however, especially in the use of recognised abbreviations and signs, there is still room for very considerable improvement. In the exercises coming from certain districts the constant recurrence of the same mistake, based on a wrong assumption, would appear due to ignorance or carelessness on the part of those responsible for the instruction of the Monitors.

Geometry and Mensuration. Third Year Monitors.

Algebra. Candidates for First of First and First Class.
The Examiner in *Algebra* reports that the answering of candidates for First Class was generally of a fair character, and testified that careful and diligent preparation had been made for this examination. In a few instances the answering was exceptionally good, and principles were employed in the solution of questions which denoted extensive reading and a knowledge of the higher branches of algebra. Candidates, however, did not show sufficient readiness and dexterity in factorizing algebraic expressions, and their want of expertness in this respect necessitated long, cumbersome solutions being given to several questions. The solutions were, on the whole, neatly and skilfully arranged.

Candidates for Second Class.
The Examiner in *Algebra* is unable to report on the part of candidates for Second Class any distinct advance in the acquaintance with algebraic processes being displayed in the work of this year as compared with the previous year. Candidates still require to give increased attention to factorizing—facility in this process being of incalculable advantage in all algebraic work. The Queen's scholars displayed, as might be expected, a better acquaintance with the method and greater facility in most of the processes of solution than the average candidate at the district centres.

Candidates for Third Class.
The Examiner reports that the exercises in *Algebra* of the candidates for Third Class were good, but those of the candidates for Training were by no means satisfactory, and often displayed a meagre acquaintance with the subject and inadequate tuition.

Fifth Year Monitors.
The Examiner in *Algebra* reports that the general character of the answering of the Fifth Year Monitors was moderately satisfactory. The number of good papers written by the candidates was very limited; whilst there was a very considerable number of cases of failure, or on the borderland. Neatness is still very much neglected in the working of the questions.

Third Year Monitors.
The Examiner reports that the answering of the Third Year Monitors in *Algebra* was of a very fair description. The most striking defect was that the shortest methods of solution were often not adopted.

Trigonometry.
The Examiner in *Trigonometry* reports that the general answering in Plane Trigonometry was fair. The majority of the candidates had carefully studied the greater part of the prescribed course, and the solutions they submitted were clearly stated and neatly worked out. The portion of the subject which deals with the inscribed and circumscribed circles of a triangle and with polygons had received insufficient attention. Only one of the few papers in Spherical Trigonometry possessed special merit.

Mechanics.
The Examiner in *Mechanics* reports that the general proficiency of the candidates for First Class was moderate. The candidates had evidently paid more attention to the text of books on the prescribed course than to the working of the exercises. They consequently in many

cases attempted, without success, those questions on the papers the solution of which do not follow directly from the more well known formulæ; work generally neat. The candidates for Second Class from the Training Colleges were well prepared, and their work showed that they had a good grasp of the elementary principles of Mechanics. The work done by the remaining candidates was not nearly so good; the elementary parts of the text-book had not been mastered, and the solutions given to several questions were not based on mechanical principles. These candidates seem to be self-taught, and have not succeeded in gaining clear ideas of the first principles of this subject. The exercises were neatly and carefully executed.

The Examiner in *Hydrostatics* and *Hydraulics* reports that the answering showed a very fair knowledge of the subject on the part of the candidates. Comparatively few of the Teachers failed, and a considerable proportion of them obtained respectable marks.

The Examiner in *Magnetism* and *Electricity* reports that the answering in those subjects was generally below mediocrity; for the most part it appeared to be the result of abstract reading, rather than of practical acquaintance with the subject itself. In no branch of physical science, perhaps, can it be seen more readily who has and who has not familiarised and strengthened his knowledge by experiment and actual handling of instruments than in this. It is to be regretted that it was largely evident that no such practical knowledge of the subject was shown by the bulk of the Teachers examined, with the exception of the students of one Training College, who appeared to write of apparatus they had seen and handled, experiments they had performed, and principles they had tested and applied with much confidence and ability.

The Examiner in *Heat and Steam Engine* reports that the answering, though somewhat better than in the last named, was still below mediocrity.

The Examiner in *Light and Sound* reports that the candidates for First Division of First Class showed a very satisfactory acquaintance with both these branches—there was only 1 failure out of 33 examined; on the other hand, the candidates for Second Division of First Class answered poorly, 9 failing out of 53.

The Examiner in *Chemistry* reports that no candidates presented themselves either in Organic or Inorganic Chemistry. In Agricultural Chemistry, of the papers of candidates for First Division of First Class, the majority were very fair, several were good, and there were none bad. Of the papers of the candidates for Second Division of First Class, there were 5 failures on very poor papers, and several other papers were very weak, showing great lack of acquaintance with *Chemistry*, and so making several ludicrous and absurd mistakes.

The Examiner in *English Literature* reports that the answering was remarkably good, the knowledge of the vast majority of the candidates was both comprehensive and accurate, notwithstanding the length of the course prescribed. Besides *Hamlet*, the candidates were examined in three cantos of the "Lay of the Last Minstrel." English Literature seems to be a favourite study, especially with female candidates.

The Examiner reports that the answering in *History* was, as usual, very meagre.

The Examiner in *English Composition* reports that the essays were, on the whole, well written; it was gratifying to observe a marked improvement.

The Examiner in *Vocal Music* reports that whether it was that the papers set this year were somewhat easier than those of the previous year, or that the Music Teachers of the Training Colleges were better prepared, the answering was much better. In the Male Training Colleges the Tonic

Appendix L. Sol-Fa paper was particularly well done. The answering of the female
Annual Queen's Scholars was scarcely so good. From the districts some very
Examina- good Tonic Sol-Fa papers were returned.
tions of
Teachers   The Hullah papers for Female Teachers were, on the whole, well
and answered. In the Hullah paper set for male candidates *intervals* were
Monitors. strong and *scales* weak.

Drawing.   The Examiner in *Drawing* reports that the exercises were, as a rule,
very neatly executed. The proficiency in *Freehand* was pretty good on
the whole. *Object Drawing*, however, has evidently been little practised;
comparatively few attempted it, and the attempts, with very few exceptions, were poor. The number of those who took up *Practical Geometry*
and *Perspective* was likewise small, but they displayed a fair knowledge
of the subject.

Kindergar-   The Examiner in *Kindergarten* reports the results as fairly satis-
ten. factory. Two important questions requiring, for a full answer, a sound
knowledge of principles were not successfully treated, though attempted
by nearly all the candidates; probably the fact that no text-book is
prescribed accounts, in some measure, for the meagre answers to these
two questions, whose difficulty was not appreciated by the candidate.

Elementary   The Examiner in *Elementary Physics* reports that 16 candidates
Physics. were examined; their answering was creditable, and considerably better
than last year. They appear to have been taught with much care and
skill, and to have studied the subject carefully.

Hygiene.   The Examiner in *Hygiene* reports that 101 Female Teachers were
examined in this branch, and 45 qualified to receive a certificate of
competency. The general answering may, therefore, be described as
middling, and much inferior to the previous year. Of the males the
knowledge of this subject was satisfactory in case of candidates who
were not students in training.

Domestic   The Examiner in *Domestic Economy* reports that the exercises in this
Economy. branch were highly satisfactory. Of 71 examined, 64 qualified to receive
a certificate of competency.

Botany.   The Examiner in *Botany* reports that the candidates' knowledge of
this subject was very slight. No candidate had a satisfactory knowledge,
although the tests were not difficult.

French.   The Examiner in *French* reports that the majority of the candidates
succeeded in obtaining very good marks. The translation of the passages
from the prescribed authors, by which sixty per cent. of the total marks
can be obtained, was generally good. The rendering of English into
French was inferior; the knowledge of grammar fair.

Latin and   The Examiner in *Latin* and *Greek* reports that he found the exercises
Greek. in these subjects, as a rule, executed neatly and legibly. In Greek
only four papers were worked, of which 1 showed a considerable
acquaintance with the subject; 2, a fair and useful knowledge. The
number of those who presented themselves in Latin was much larger—
about 4 showed a very considerable and superior proficiency, and
several others translated some of the prescribed passages into English
with fair accuracy. Few attempted the translation into Latin of continuous English prose.

Irish.   The Examiner in *Irish* reports that the number of Teachers examined
was far greater than in any previous year. Candidates were examined
in the counties of Donegal, Dublin, Mayo, Galway, Cork, and
Kerry. Nearly all those examined speak Irish fluently. The candidates examined in Dublin were not natives of Dublin: they came from
Cork and Clare. Some of those examined are good Irish scholars, and
possess a literary and critical knowledge of the language far beyond what
is required in the course prescribed for Teachers' Examination.

ANALYSIS OF ANSWERING.

The following is an analysis of the answering at the July Examinations of 1894 :—

ORDINARY NATIONAL SCHOOLS.

		Examined.	Successful.	Percentage.
A' Papers (Candidates for Fixed Divisions of First Class),		107	86	87·0
A² Second,		126	80	64·7
B Second Class,		234	152	65·1
C Total,		45	26	47·8
(Monitors of Fifth Year),		807	694	86·2
D Third,		843	583	69·6

MODEL SCHOOLS.

Teachers,		13	10	79·9
Pupil Teachers,		187	135	85·3
Monitors,		19	20	105·0

TRAINING COLLEGES.

Total (including Marlborough-street),		672	640	95·1

TOTAL,		3,557	3,193	87·9

* There were 383 young persons examined for admission to the different Colleges a considerable proportion of whom were also undergoing examination in their capacity as monitors or pupil teachers, and there were 2,621 distinct examinations in the different extra branches.

EXTRA SUBJECTS.

Total Number Examined (including those Examined from the Training Colleges) for registration as being competent to teach :—

Subject.	Number Examined.			Number passed.			Percentage of Passes.		
	Males.	Females.	Total.	Males.	Females.	Total.	Males.	Females.	Total.
Agriculture (Females),	–	14	14	–	8	8	–	57·1	57·1
Algebra,	–	8	8	–	1	1	–	52·0	50·0
Botany,	1	–	1	0	–	0	60·0	–	60·0
Chemistry (Agricultural),	1	–	1	1	–	1	100·0	–	100·0
Cookery,	–	167	167	–	163	163	–	97·7	97·7
Domestic Economy,	–	75	75	–	62	62	–	81·2	81·2
Drawing,	267	555	712	150	145	295	58·2	57·9	58·7
French,	69	61	130	47	20	67	45·7	73·1	67·8
Greek,	4	–	4	2	–	2	50·0	–	50·0
Handicraft,	67	–	67	47	–	47	79·1	–	79·1
Heat and Steam Engine,	1	–	1	1	–	1	57·2	–	57·2
Hydrostatics,	67	–	67	27	–	27	51·8	–	51·0
Hygiene,	46	100	146	4	41	60	11·9	44·0	54·3
Irish,	25	2	27	20	2	22	57·2	66·0	51·3
Kindergarten,	–	124	124	–	86	86	–	57·1	57·2
Latin,	29	–	29	11	–	11	57·9	–	57·9
Light and Sound,	1	–	1	1	–	1	100·0	–	100·0
Magnetism and Electricity,	34	–	34	22	–	22	52·9	–	51·9
Mechanics,	67	–	67	25	–	25	57·1	–	57·4
Music—									
Singing (Staff),	30	110	140	24	57	139	54·4	54·4	54·0
" (Tonic Sol-Fa),	170	75	245	130	259	359	76·4	57·4	57·5
Harmonium,	69	102	171	41	79	98	57·2	70·5	57·7
Organ,	–	8	8	–	6	6	–	57·5	57·5
Piano,	1	71	72	1	17	18	100·0	57·0	57·5
Physics (Elementary),	–	14	14	–	14	14	–	57·1	57·1
Trigonometry (Spherical),	1	–	1	0	–	0	50·0	–	50·0

* Subject to further test as to practical knowledge, except in the case of Training College Candidates.

APPENDIX M.

I.—TABLE showing the Number of POOR LAW UNIONS which became contributory each year from the passing of the Act 38 & 39 Vict., cap. 96 (An Act to provide for additional Payments to Teachers of National Schools in Ireland).

Year.	Number of Unions.	Year.	Number of Unions.
1876-7,	70	1886-7,	30
1877-8,	30	1887-8,	61
1878-9,	39	1888-9,	14
1879-80,	11	1889-90,	13
1880-81,	18	1890-91,	8
1881-2,	16	1891-2,	22
1882-3,	20	1892-3,	75
1883-4,	29	1893-4,	24
1884-5,	77	1894-5,	65
1885-6,	21		

II.—LIST of Twenty-five POOR LAW UNIONS which became contributory, for the year 1894-5, under the Act 38 & 39 Vict., cap. 96 (An Act to provide for additional Payments to Teachers of National Schools in Ireland); and the respective amounts paid out of the Rates.

Names of Poor Law Unions.	Rates.	Names of Poor Law Unions.	Rates.
	£ s. d.		£ s. d.
Ballymahon,	329 1 9	Kells,	489 11 9
Ballyvaghan,	109 15 7	Kilmallock,	738 12 2
Balrothery,	412 13 6	Milford,	216 16 2
Belfast,	4,039 1 7	Mullingar,	824 14 1
Castlecomer,	248 19 10	Navan,	449 8 8
Cloghcen,	462 16 9	Newry,	1,904 6 1
Cloghan,	127 7 6	Oldcastle,	449 16 1
Cork,	3,116 0 2	Rathdrum,	638 8 8
Croom,	276 13 11	Siralmon,	727 1 6
Delvin,	534 6 2	Trim,	849 1 8
Downpatrick,	1,054 3 0	Tullamore,	538 16 2
Dunguanon,	691 13 2	Kilfbberwan,*	8 8 8
Edenderry,	860 15 1		
Drumstown,	987 6 7	Total,†	22,373 23 5

APPENDIX N.

SPECIAL TABULATION of RESULTS EXAMINATIONS of PUPILS of

(1.) MODEL SCHOOLS.

The total number of Model Schools examined for results within the twelve months ended 31st December, 1894, was 84.

Number of pupils on school rolls on last day of month preceding inspection :—

Males, 6,095 ; Females, 4,371 ; Total, 10,466.

Number who had made 100 attendances or over within the results year, and were present and examined on day of inspection for results was :—

Males, 4,392 ; Females, 2,738 ; Total, 7,080.

Per-centage to number on Rolls, 67·2.

The average daily attendance for twelve months ending last day of month immediately preceding the Results Examination in the respective schools was :—

Males, 4,539 ; Females, 3,108 ; Total, 7,647.

Percentage of number examined to the average daily attendance was 91·9.

The following figures show the number of pupils examined, and the number who passed at the Results Examinations :—

GRADES.	Number examined.	Number passed.	Per-centage passed.
Infants,	969	945	97·5
First Class,	621	612	99·6
Second Class,	783	637	67·7
Third Class,	965	848	87·8
Fourth Class,	981	862	87·9
Fifth Class (First Stage),	923	762	84·5
Fifth Class (Second Stage),	840	701	83·4
Sixth Class,	889	752	84·7
Total,	7,080	6,307	88·3

Percentage of pupils examined in each class to the total number examined in all the classes :—

Per-centage in Infants' Grade,	.	15·2
„ Class I.,	.	10·2
„ Class II.,	.	11·1
„ Class III.,	.	13·6
„ Class IV.,	.	13·9
„ Class V¹.,	.	12·6
„ Class V².,	.	11·3
„ Class VI.,	.	12·1
Total,	.	100·0

Model Schools.

LITERARY CLASSIFICATION of the PUPILS who attended once or oftener within the last fourteen days of the month immediately preceding Results Examination in each Model School in 1894.

Schools.	Infants.	Class I.	Class II.	Class III.	Class IV.	Class V.	Class VI.	Class VI.	Total.
Central Model,	196	131	193	234	229	298	144	171	1,587
West Dublin,	163	64	79	70	79	53	31	19	548
Inchicore,	108	63	68	76	48	40	36	69	458
Glasnevin,	31	9	8	11	5	3	3	4	34
Athy,	16	14	14	11	5	9	4	11	64
Ballisodare,	21	8	10	6	10	9	9	23	33
Ballymena,	49	26	32	45	48	68	46	69	360
Belfast,	70	63	83	155	158	168	194	218	1,238
Clonmel,	35	14	23	23	15	23	10	25	171
Coleraine,	28	13	19	18	30	31	28	75	231
Cork,	100	58	56	65	44	56	45	71	450
Dungannon,	19	8	17	15	15	11	11	5	100
Enniskerry,	28	14	11	15	10	18	18	10	102
Enniskillen,	25	22	19	25	29	34	23	40	228
Galway,	11	21	18	18	13	13	8	11	105
Kilkenny,	11	8	7	9	18	12	15	18	82
Limerick,	45	31	31	30	38	64	17	41	318
Londonderry,	80	68	87	53	66	63	35	79	483
Newry,	78	27	33	62	41	37	33	41	372
Newtownards,	69	31	23	33	29	25	34	41	287
Sligo,	44	14	26	46	34	31	29	43	268
Trim,	26	22	19	22	17	18	18	19	161
Waterford,	20	17	8	14	18	15	8	21	127
Ballymoney,	78	33	39	78	84	39	29	73	440
Carrickfergus,	40	34	22	27	30	67	60	83	283
Larne,	69	33	34	43	47	51	26	57	337
Monaghan,	72	30	23	28	29	34	19	28	243
Newtownstewart,	29	22	21	20	21	18	14	18	164
Omagh,	64	50	43	45	60	31	30	64	616
Portrush,	28	17	16	13	22	16	19	23	145
Total,	1,529	915	1,034	1,229	1,189	1,122	957	1,546	8,700
Per-centage,	17·5	9·4	10·7	12·7	12·2	11·2	9·9	15·9	
Per-centage,	17·5	39·6			40·7				

MODEL SCHOOLS,
GENERAL ABSTRACT of ANSWERING.

Classes.	No. of Pupils examined from Registers	No. of Pupils reported satisfactory by Inspectors	Percentage of the Number of Pupils examined	Classes.	No. of Pupils examined from Registers	No. of Pupils reported satisfactory by Inspectors	Percentage of the Number of Pupils examined
READING.				**GRAMMAR.**			
Class I.,	891	860	96·9	Class III.,	963	612	81·3
„ II.,	783	718	94·2	„ IV.,	931	748	79·0
„ III.,	943	835	87·2	„ V.,	925	653	71·2
„ IV.,	991	865	87·3	„ V.,	840	582	69·3
„ V.,	925	910	88·4	„ VI.,	808	573	64·5
„ V.,	846	839	96·7	Total,	4,597	3,373	73·4
„ VI.,	838	843	84·9				
Total,	6,061	5,871	86·9	**GEOGRAPHY.**			
				Class III.,	963	829	86·1
WRITING.				„ IV.,	991	807	87·3
Class I.,	691	678	98·0	„ V.,	925	708	76·6
„ II.,	783	763	97·4	„ V.,	840	834	75·5
„ III.,	943	838	88·6	„ VI.,	688	573	64·6
„ IV.,	991	878	88·5	Total,	4,597	3,553	73·4
„ V.,	925	873	94·4				
„ V.,	840	672	97·8	**AGRICULTURE.**			
„ VI.,	688	729	93·4	Class IV.,	307	197	64·2
Total,	6,061	5,893	97·3	„ V.,	281	216	73·2
				„ V.,	268	200	74·9
ARITHMETIC.				„ VI.,	371	183	67·5
Class I.,	691	640	84·0	Total,	1,187	796	86·6
„ II.,	783	787	89·2				
„ III.,	943	874	90·7				
„ IV.,	991	854	88·1	**BOOK-KEEPING.**			
„ V.,	925	820	88·7	Class V.,	508	414	81·4
„ V.,	846	712	84·7	„ V.,	482	390	81·4
„ VI.,	688	721	83·4	„ VI.,	568	433	77·6
Total,	6,061	5,575	89·4	Total,	1,558	1,237	79·0
SPELLING.				**NEEDLEWORK.**			
Class I.,	691	651	85·6	Class II.,	318	277	87·9
„ II.,	783	668	88·1	„ III.,	492	375	89·3
„ III.,	943	637	85·9	„ IV.,	424	405	81·8
„ IV.,	991	780	81·4	„ V.,	368	317	81·3
„ V.,	925	804	86·3	„ V.,	313	291	93·0
„ V.,	846	794	81·4	„ VI.,	185	163	90·4
„ VI.,	868	780	88·9	Total,	3,008	1,875	85·4
Total,	6,061	5,861	87·9				

2 D

Printed for Her Majesty's Stationery Office...

(2) WORKHOUSE SCHOOLS.

The total number of Workhouse Schools examined for results within the twelve months ended 31st December, 1894, was 155.

Number of pupils on school rolls on last day of month preceding inspection :—

  Males, 3,283; Females, 2,469; Total, 5,752.

Number who made 100 attendances, or over, within the results year and were present and examined on day of inspection :—

  Males, 2,172; Females, 1,594; Total, 3,766.

  Per-centage to number on Rolls, 65·5.

The average daily attendance for 12 months ending last day of month immediately preceding the Results Examinations in the respective schools was :—

  Males, 2,876; Females, 2,168; Total, 5,044.

Percentage of number examined to the average daily attendance was 74·5.

The following figures show the number of pupils examined, and the number who passed at the Results Examinations :—

CLASSES.	Number examined.	Number passed.	Per-centage passed.
Infants, ...	1,159	1,086	93·7
First Class, . . .	720	594	82·5
Second Class, . . .	661	577	87·2
Third Class, . . .	525	446	85·0
Fourth Class, . . .	524	350	78·2
Fifth Class (First Stage), .	238	181	76·0
Fifth Class (Second Stage), .	107	86	80·2
Sixth Class, . . .	32	24	75·0
Total, . . .	3,766	3,253	86·4

Per-centage of pupils examined in each class to the total number examined in all the classes :—

 Per-centage in Infants' Grade, . 30·8
   „ Class L, . . 19·1
   „ Class II., . . 17·5
   „ Class III., . . 13·9
   „ Class IV., . . 8·5
   „ Class V¹., . . 6·3
   „ Class V²., . . 2·9
   „ Class VI., . . ·9

    Total, . . . 100·0

WORKHOUSE SCHOOLS,

GENERAL ABSTRACT OF ANSWERING.

CLASSES.	No. of Pupils examined in each subject.	No. of Pupils answered in each subject.	Percentage of Pupils examined.	CLASSES.	No. of Pupils examined in each subject.	No. of Pupils answered in each subject.	Percentage of Pupils examined.
READING.				**GRAMMAR.**			
Class I.,	730	689	93·6	Class III.,	525	406	77·3
„ II.,	691	630	96·3	„ IV.,	321	243	75·0
„ III.,	325	317	90·5	„ V.,	230	118	73·9
„ IV.,	624	231	90·7	„ V.,	107	70	83·4
„ VI.,	238	234	90·3	„ VI.,	33	20	83·5
„ V₆,	192	192	100·0	Total,	1,238	211	74·3
„ VI.,	23	22	100·0	**GEOGRAPHY.**			
Total,	2,807	2,337	97·3	Class III.,	428	437	83·2
WRITING.				„ IV.,	324	377	83·4
Class I.,	730	513	56·9	„ V₆,	230	216	83·2
„ II.,	691	636	89·5	„ V₆,	107	90	84·1
„ III.,	325	321	90·2	„ VL,	32	91	45·6
„ IV.,	324	221	69·8	Total,	1,226	1,615	84·4
„ V.,	218	230	96·5	**AGRICULTURE.**			
„ V.,	107	103	98·3	Class IV.,	148	60	60·3
„ VL,	33	63	100·0	„ V.,	91	61	67·6
Total,	2,807	2,472	88·5	„ V.,	65	57	69·6
ARITHMETIC.				„ VL,	23	15	65·2
Class I.,	730	619	84·7	Total,	315	202	64·5
„ II.,	691	591	89·4	**BOOK-KEEPING.**			
„ III.,	325	459	99·8	Class VI.,	28	21	75·0
„ IV.,	324	247	78·3	„ V.,	71	19	90·4
„ V.,	228	184	81·5	„ VI.,	5	2	100·0
„ V.,	107	83	80·7	Total,	51	62	83·2
„ VL,	33	23	71·9	**NEEDLEWORK.**			
Total,	2,807	2,217	85·0	Class II.,	324	271	86·4
SPELLING.				„ III.,	316	289	86·8
Class I.,	730	680	91·7	„ IV.,	145	143	59·6
„ II.,	691	577	87·3	„ V.,	57	57	89·6
„ III.,	325	442	84·3	„ V.,	86	65	87·3
„ IV.,	324	278	65·6	„ VI.,	11	11	100·0
„ V.,	228	204	54·1	Total,	704	789	53·5
„ V.,	167	88	97·9				
„ VL,	83	29	88·6				
Total,	2,807	2,888	88·6				

(3.) EVENING SCHOOLS.

The total number of Evening Schools examined for results within the twelve months ended 31st December, 1894, was 39.

Number of pupils on school rolls on last day of month preceding inspection:—

Males, 2,067; Females, 754; Total, 2,821.

Number who had made 50 attendances, or over, within the results year, and were present and examined on day of inspection for results fees:—

Males, 700; Females, 400; Total, 1,100.
Percentage to number on Rolls, 39·0.

The average daily attendance for twelve months ended last day of month immediately preceding the Results Examinations in the respective schools was:—

Males, 1,086; Females, 468; Total, 1,554.

Per-centage of number examined to the average daily attendance was 70·8.

The following figures show the number of pupils examined and the number who passed at the Results Examinations:—

CLASS.	Number examined.	Number passed.	Percentage passed.
First Class, ...	105	72	68·8
Second Class, . . .	163	115	70·5
Third Class, ...	173	109	63·3
Fourth Class, ...	202	89	44·0
Fifth Class (First Stage), . .	178	94	52·8
Fifth Class (Second Stage), .	120	54	45·0
Sixth Class, ...	157	71	45·2
Total, . . .	1,100	604	54·9

Percentage of pupils examined in each class to the total number examined in all the classes:—

Percentage in Class I.. . . . . 9·5
      „   Class II., ... 14·8
      „   Class III., ... 15·9
      „   Class IV., ... 18·4
      „   Class V¹., ... 16·2
      „   Class V²., ... 10·9
      „   Class VI., ... 14·3

                    Total, . . . 100·0

Appendix V

EVENING SCHOOLS.

GENERAL ABSTRACT of ANSWERING.

Classes.	No. of Pupils Examined in subject	No. of those that answered in subject	Percentage of those that answered in subject	Classes.	No. of Pupils Examined in subject	No. of those that answered in subject	Percentage of those that answered in subject
READING.				**ARITHMETIC.**			
Class I.,	105	87	82·8	Class I.,	165	98	54·8
„ II.,	163	130	79·8	„ II.,	163	125	62·8
„ III.,	175	150	86·8	„ III.,	175	114	65·1
„ IV.,	203	178	88·1	„ IV.,	202	91	45·0
„ V.,	178	171	88·1	„ V.,	178	80	50·6
„ VI.,	180	118	85·6	„ VI.,	123	54	45·0
„ VII.,	157	154	98·6	„ VII.,	157	71	43·2
Total,	1,100	989	89·8	Total,	1,180	643	52·4
				SPELLING.			
WRITING.				Class I.,	165	84	68·9
Class I.,	105	101	89·2	„ II.,	163	93	52·1
„ II.,	163	156	84·7	„ III.,	175	108	61·9
„ III.,	175	171	87·7	„ IV.,	203	122	60·8
„ IV.,	203	183	91·5	„ V.,	178	118	66·1
„ V.,	178	168	89·3	„ VI.,	123	86	70·2
„ VI.,	180	118	88·6	„ VII.,	157	144	91·7
„ VII.,	157	157	100·0	Total,	1,180	743	67·0
Total,	1,120	1,045	88·0	**BOOK-KEEPING.**			
				Class V.,	6	1	63·4
				„ VI.,	6	6	102·6
				„ VII.,	9	2	129·6
				Total,	11	9	51·6

(4.) CONVENT AND MONASTERY SCHOOLS.

The total number of Convent and Monastery Schools examined for results within the twelve months ended 31st December, 1894, was 308.

Number of pupils on school rolls on last day of month preceding inspection :—

Males, 20,449; Females, 76,865; Total, 103,314.

Number who made 100 attendances or over within the results year and were present and examined on day of inspection :—

Males, 16,264; Females, 49,623; Total, 65,887.
Percentage to number on Rolls, 62·8.

The average daily attendance for twelve months ending last day of month immediately preceding the Results Examinations in the respective schools was :—

Males, 16,998; Females, 50,654; Total, 67,652.

Percentage of number examined to the average daily attendance was 97·4.

The following figures show the number of pupils examined, and the number who passed at the Results Examinations :—

Grades.	Number examined.	Number passed.	Percentage passed.
Infants, ...	22,016	21,231	96·7
First Class, . . .	9,495	8,863	93·4
Second Class, . . .	8,811	8,009	90·8
Third Class, . . .	7,323	6,415	87·6
Fourth Class, . . .	6,086	5,199	85·3
Fifth Class (First Stage), .	4,872	4,134	84·9
Fifth Class (Second Stage), .	3,425	2,845	83·1
Sixth Class, . . .	3,929	3,502	89·1
Total, . . .	65,887	60,175	91·3

Percentage of pupils examined in each class to the total number examined in all the classes:—

Percentage in Infants' Grade,	.	.	. 33·4
„ Class I.,	.	.	14·3
„ Class II.,	.	.	13·4
„ Class III.,	.	.	11·1
„ Class IV.,	.	.	9·8
„ Class V¹.,	.	.	7·4
„ Class V².,	.	.	5·2
„ Class VI.,	.	.	6·0
	Total,	.	. 100·0

CONVENT AND MONASTERY SCHOOLS.

GENERAL ABSTRACT of ANSWERING.

Appendix S.

CLASSES	No. of Pupils examined in each Subject	No. of Pupils who passed	Percentage of Pupils in No. of Pupils examined	CLASSES	No. of Pupils examined in each Subject	No. of Pupils who passed	Percentage of Pupils passed
READING.				**GRAMMAR.**			
Class I.,	8,425	8,211	97·6	Class III.,	7,328	5,830	80·0
„ II.	8,811	8,533	96·7	„ IV.,	6,903	4,425	72·0
„ III.,	7,225	7,040	96·1	„ V.,	4,872	3,474	71·2
„ IV.,	5,790	5,534	97·3	„ VI.,	5,425	2,509	76·9
„ V.,	4,873	4,768	95·9	„ VI.,	3,957	3,043	77·4
„ VI.,	3,425	3,381	90·0	Total,	24,423	19,101	73·7
„ VI.,	3,929	3,783	94·9				
Total,	43,671	42,639	97·3	**GEOGRAPHY.**			
				Class III.,	7,329	5,091	83·2
WRITING.				„ IV.,	8,580	4,775	78·4
Class I.,	8,625	8,373	96·9	„ V.,	4,571	3,621	78·7
„ II.,	8,811	8,718	90·9	„ V.,	3,431	2,468	77·9
„ III.,	7,823	7,277	99·4	„ VI.,	3,93	6,563	78·0
„ IV.,	6,600	6,040	90·2	Total,	25,425	20,433	79·7
„ V.,	1,973	4,098	95·9				
„ V.,	3,125	3,280	94·1	**AGRICULTURE.**			
„ VI.,	3,929	3,749	94·2	Class IV.,	928	114	47·9
Total,	44,671	43,197	96·3	„ VI.,	851	116	57·7
				„ V.,	361	63	64·4
ARITHMETIC.				„ VI.,	134	82	61·2
Class I.,	8,425	8,023	93·7	Total,	671	377	55·6
„ II.,	8,811	8,151	93·0				
„ III.,	7,323	6,927	90·5				
„ IV.,	6,600	6,265	93·4	**BOOK-KEEPING.**			
„ V.,	4,873	4,270	87·6	Class VI.,	1,350	1,532	76·1
„ V.,	8,625	2,870	92·9	„ VI.,	1,168	856	73·9
„ VI.,	3,929	3,441	97·9	„ VI.,	903	673	73·6
Total,	43,671	80,716	94·5	Total,	3,611	2,861	78·2
SPELLING.				**NEEDLEWORK.**			
Class I.,	8,125	8,780	93·3	Class II.,	6,918	6,234	91·3
„ II.,	8,811	7,984	93·4	„ III.,	6,811	5,900	83·0
„ III.,	7,373	6,633	76·9	„ IV.,	5,638	5,150	86·1
„ IV.,	8,634	4,344	73·0	„ V.,	4,271	3,501	85·8
„ V.,	4,873	4,118	84·3	„ V.,	3,068	2,861	86·8
„ V.,	3,645	3,039	96·1	„ VI.,	3,384	3,906	87·7
„ VI.,	3,928	3,671	96·9	Total,	29,257	27,863	91·2
Total,	44,671	37,918	84·6				

APPENDIX O.

The "REID" BEQUEST.

REID BEQUEST.

The Trustees of the Will of the late R. T. Reid, Esq., LL.D., of Bombay, who munificently bequeathed £9,435 towards the advancement of Education in the County Kerry (his native county), have authorised the following Scheme of Prizes to be awarded out of the proceeds of the Bequest, by the Commissioners of National Education.

PART I.

During the Five years' service of a Monitor, there are two Principal Examinations, viz., one at the end of his Third year, and the other at the end of his Fifth year. After each of these Principal Examinations, the Reid Prizes will be awarded to the Six best answerers of each degree of service amongst the Male Monitors of the National Schools of the County Kerry, provided that the answering in every case shall be of a satisfactory character. The following is the scale of Prizes :—

(a.) At end of Monitors' Third Year of Service :—

First Prize,	...	—	...	...	...	£20
Second „	...	...	...	...	...	18
Third „	...	...	...	...	...	16
Fourth „	...	—	...	...	...	14
Fifth „	...	—	...	...	...	12
Sixth „	...	...	...	...	—	10
						£90

(b.) At end of Monitors' Fifth Year of Service :—

First Prize,	...	...	—	...	...	£25
Second „	...	...	...	...	...	22
Third „	...	...	...	...	...	20
Fourth „	...	...	...	...	...	18
Fifth „	...	...	...	...	...	16
Sixth „	...	...	—	...	...	14
						£115

This portion of the Scheme came into operation at the Examination of July, 1886.

PART II.

The Trustees, also, in pursuance of the express stipulations of the Testator, propose to apply £80 a year to the maintenance of Two Reid Exhibitions in Trinity College, Dublin, of the value of £40 each, to enable Students of the County Kerry, who have successfully passed the final examination at the close of their Course of Training in the Marlborough-street Training College, to matriculate in Trinity College, and to pass on, without dropping a year, to the Degree in Arts.

The recommendation of Candidates for the Reid Exhibitions, Trinity College, will be made by the Professors of the Marlborough-street Training College.

Part I.—Result of the July Examinations, 1894.

In accordance with the Reid Request Scheme (Part I.) for the advancement of Education in the County Kerry, immediately after the results of the July, 1894, Examinations of Monitors employed in the National Schools of Kerry had been ascertained, the Commissioners of National Education selected the Six best answerers amongst Monitors in the Third year of service, and the Six best answerers amongst Monitors of Fifth year, and made the following awards :—

Prize Monitors of Third Year.

Dist.	Roll No.	School.		Monitor.		Prize.
						£
28	1,683	Ballyduff,	. m.	John Fay,	. .	20
,,	13,916	Reen,	. m.	John Leahan,	.	18
54	10,194	Kilmurry,	. m.	Patrick P. Kenney,	.	16
54	12,673	Strand Street,	. (2)	Daniel Sheivery,	.	14
,,	1,722	Farranakilla,	.	Patrick Morris,	.	12
28	2,120	Gortnakaki,	.	Robert Seanley,	. .	10

Prize Monitors of Fifth Year.

Dist.	Roll No.	School.		Monitor.		Prize.
						£
30	542	Kilmury,	. m.	William Lawlor,	. .	25
,,	1,889	Ballyduff,	. m.	Andrew Grogan,	.	23
54	12,856	Strand Street,	. (1)	Thomas Mariary,	.	20
57	9,539	Macnagrun,	. m.	Patrick Cahill,	.	18
28	5,883	Kilflynn,	.	Edmund Fuller,	.	15
57	10,228	Caherdaniel,	. m.	Thos. F. Maughan,	.	14

Part II.—Exhibitions in Trinity College, Dublin.

Under the conditions of Part II. of this Scheme, an Exhibition of £40 per annum was awarded in February, 1894, to Mr. Patrick Buckley, Principal Teacher of Shandrum National School, County Cork, and in January, 1895, an Exhibition of a similar amount was awarded to Mr. John Kennelly, of Moyola Park National School, County Londonderry—both these teachers are natives of the County Kerry.

APPENDIX P.

CARLISLE AND BLAKE PREMIUMS.

Extract from Appendix to Commissioners' Rules—Edition of 1890.

THE CARLISLE AND BLAKE PREMIUM FUND.

1. The Commissioners of National Education are empowered to allocate to the teachers of ordinary National Schools[*] the interest accruing from the Private Bequests' Fund in Premiums, to be called "The Carlisle and Blake Premiums."

2. The interest from the accumulated funds available for premiums now amounts to £80 a year, and this sum will be distributed in premiums of £5 each—one for the most deserving Principal Teacher in each of the Districts every fourth year, upon the following conditions:—

    (a.) That the average attendance and the regularity of the attendance of the pupils are satisfactory.

    (b.) That a fair proportion of the pupils have passed in the higher classes.

    (c.) That, if a boys' or mixed school, taught by a master in a rural district, agriculture is fairly taught to the boys of the senior classes; and, if a girls' school (rural or town), needlework is carefully attended to.

    (d.) That the state of the school has been reported, during the previous two years as satisfactory in respect to efficiency, moral tone, order, cleanliness, discipline, school accounts, supply of requisites, and observance of the Board's rules.

3. No teacher will be eligible for a premium twice in succession.

4. The names of the teachers to whom premiums are awarded will be published in the annual report of the Board.

[*] Teachers of Model Schools, Convent Schools, or other special schools, are not eligible for this premium.

The "The Carlisle and Blake" Premiums are awarded at the rate of *Appendix I*
£5 to one successful candidate in each school district in every fourth
year.   The Teachers who secured the Prizes for 1894 were :—

Names.	School.	District.
Eliza Hill, . . .	Merryville National School .	County Antrim.
Sarah Hagryven, . .	Cromlin-road	, " "
Ellen M'Keen, . .	Ballyeure ,	, " "
Mary J. Cushine, .	Clandrummond ,	, Armagh.
Mary Gildea, . .	Glenties ,	, Donegal.
James Rowan, .	Killymakight ,	, Londonderry.
Miss Sharkey, . .	Sion Mills ,	, Tyrone.
Ossie Burke, . .	St. Mary's ,	, Cork.
Thomas Molyneux, .	Lyracrompane ,	, Kerry.
William B. Joyce, .	St. Vincent de Paul's ,	, Limerick.
John Sankey, .	Terryglass ,	, Tipperary.
James Robertson, .	Howth-road, ,	, Dublin.
John Mulligan, .	Arklow N. ,	, Wicklow.
Bridget O'Keane, .	Killasser ,	, Mayo.
Wm. M'Cormick, .	Rasharw ,	, Roscommon.
Bartholomew Hanlon, .	Ballinacarrow ,	, Sligo.

www.ingramcontent.com/pod-product-compliance
Lightning Source LLC
Chambersburg PA
CBHW022018110726
47901CB00006B/1571